THE
MELROSE
EDITION

ALICE BRIDGNORTH

W. MULREADY. R.A.

Peveril of the Peak

By

Sir Walter Scott, Bart.

London

The Caxton Publishing Co.

PEVERIL OF THE PEAK

CHAPTER I

When civil dudgeon first grew high,
And men fell out, they knew not why ;
When foul words, jealousies, and fears,
Set folk together by the ears—
—BUTLER.

WILLIAM, the Conqueror of England, was, or supposed himself to be, the father of a certain William Peveril, who attended him to the battle of Hastings, and there distinguished himself. The liberal-minded monarch, who assumed in his charters the veritable title of Gulielmus Bastardus, was not likely to let his son's illegitimacy be any bar to the course of his royal favour, when the laws of England were issued from the mouth of the Norman victor, and the lands of the Saxons were at his unlimited disposal. William Peveril obtained a liberal grant of property and lordships in Derbyshire, and became the erecter of that Gothic fortress, which, hanging over the mouth of the Devil's Cavern, so well known to tourists, gives the name of Castleton to the adjacent village.

From this feudal Baron, who chose his nest upon the principles on which an eagle selects her eyry, and built it in such a fashion as if he had intended it, as an Irishman said of the Martello towers, for the sole purpose of puzzling posterity, there was, or conceived themselves to be, descended (for their pedigree was rather hypothetical) an opulent family of knightly rank, in the same county of Derby. The great fief of Castleton, with its adjacent wastes and forests, and all the wonders which they contain, had been forfeited in King John's stormy days, by one William Peveril, and had been granted anew to the Lord Ferrers of that day. Yet this William's descendants, though no longer possessed of what they alleged to have been their original property, were long distinguished by the proud title of Peverils of the Peak, which served to mark their high descent and lofty pretensions.

In Charles the Second's time, the representative of this

A

ancient family was Sir Geoffrey Peveril, a man who had many
of the ordinary attributes of an old-fashioned country gentleman, and very few individual traits to distinguish him from
the general portrait of that worthy class of mankind. He was
proud of small advantages, angry at small disappointments,
incapable of forming any resolution or opinion abstracted from
his own prejudices—he was proud of his birth, lavish in his
housekeeping, convivial with those kindred and acquaintances,
who would allow his superiority in rank—contentious and
quarrelsome with all that crossed his pretensions—kind to the
poor, except when they plundered his game—a Royalist in his
political opinions, and one who detested alike a Roundhead,
a poacher, and a Presbyterian. In religion Sir Geoffrey was a
high-churchman, of so exalted a strain that many thought he
still nourished in private the Roman Catholic tenets, which his
family had only renounced in his father's time, and that he had
a dispensation for conforming in outward observances to the
Protestant faith. There was at least such a scandal amongst
the Puritans, and the influence which Sir Geoffrey Peveril
certainly appeared to possess amongst the Catholic gentlemen
of Derbyshire and Cheshire, seemed to give countenance to the
rumour.

Such was Sir Geoffrey, who might have passed to his grave
without further distinction than a brass-plate in the chancel,
had he not lived in times which forced the most inactive spirits
into exertion, as a tempest influences the sluggish waters of the
deadest mere. When the Civil Wars broke out, Peveril of the
Peak, proud from pedigree, and brave by constitution, raised a
regiment for the King, and showed upon several occasions more
capacity for command than men had heretofore given him
credit for.

Even in the midst of the civil turmoil, he fell in love with,
and married, a beautiful and amiable young lady of the noble
house of Stanley ; and from that time had the more merit in
his loyalty, as it divorced him from her society, unless at very
brief intervals, when his duty permitted an occasional visit to
his home. Scorning to be allured from his military duty by
domestic inducements, Peveril of the Peak fought on for several
rough years of civil war, and performed his part with sufficient
gallantry, until his regiment was surprised and cut to pieces
by Poyntz, Cromwell's enterprising and successful general of
cavalry. The defeated Cavalier escaped from the field of battle,
and, like a true descendant of William the Conqueror, disdaining
submission, threw himself into his own castellated mansion,
which was attacked and defended in a siege of that irregular
kind which caused the destruction of so many baronial residences
during the course of those unhappy wars. Martindale Castle

after having suffered severely from the cannon which Cromwell himself brought against it, was at length surrendered when in the last extremity. Sir Geoffrey himself became a prisoner, and while his liberty was only restored upon a promise of remaining a peaceful subject to the Commonwealth in future, his former delinquencies, as they were termed by the ruling party, were severely punished by fine and sequestration.

But neither his forced promise, nor the fear of farther unpleasant consequences to his person or property, could prevent Peveril of the Peak from joining the gallant Earl of Derby the night before the fatal engagement in Wiggan Lane, where the Earl's forces were dispersed. Sir Geoffrey having had his share in that action, escaped with the relics of the Royalists after the defeat, to join Charles II. He witnessed also the final defeat of Worcester, where he was a second time made prisoner ; and as, in the opinion of Cromwell and the language of the times, he was regarded as an obstinate malignant, he was in great danger of having shared with the Earl of Derby his execution at Bolton-le-Moor, having partaken with him the dangers of two actions. But Sir Geoffrey's life was preserved by the interest of a friend, who possessed influence in the councils of Oliver.—This was a Mr. Bridgenorth, a gentleman of middling quality, whose father had been successful in some commercial adventure during the peaceful reign of James I. ; and who had bequeathed his son a considerable sum of money, in addition to the moderate patrimony which he inherited from his father.

The substantial, though small-sized, brick building of Moultrassie Hall, was but two miles distant from Martindale Castle, and the young Bridgenorth attended the same school with the heir of the Peverils. A sort of companionship, if not intimacy, took place betwixt them, which continued during their youthful sports—the rather that Bridgenorth, though he did not at heart admit Sir Geoffrey's claims of superiority to the extent which the other's vanity would have exacted, paid deference in a reasonable degree to the representative of a family so much more ancient and important than his own, without conceiving that he in any respect degraded himself by doing so.

Mr. Bridgenorth did not, however, carry his complaisance so far as to embrace Sir Geoffrey's side during the Civil War. On the contrary, as an active Justice of the Peace, he rendered much assistance in arraying the militia in the cause of the Parliament, and for some time held a military commission in that service. This was partly owing to his religious principles, for he was a zealous Presbyterian, partly to his political ideas, which, without being absolutely democratical, favoured the popular side of the great national question. Besides, he was a moneyed man, and to a certain extent had a shrewd eye to his

worldly interest. He understood how to improve the opportunities which civil war afforded, of advancing his fortune, by
a dexterous use of his capital; and he was not at a loss to
perceive that these were likely to be obtained in joining the
Parliament; while the King's cause, as it was managed, held
out nothing to the wealthy but a course of exaction and com-
pulsory loans. For these reasons, Bridgenorth became a decided
Roundhead, and all friendly communication betwixt his neighbour and him was abruptly broken asunder. This was done
with the less acrimony, that, during the Civil War, Sir Geoffrey
was almost constantly in the field, following the vacillating and
unhappy fortunes of his master; while Major Bridgenorth, who
soon renounced active military service, resided chiefly in London,
and only occasionally visited the Hall.

Upon these visits, it was with great pleasure he received the
intelligence, that Lady Peveril had shown much kindness to
Mrs. Bridgenorth, and had actually given her and her family
shelter in Martindale Castle, when Moultrassie Hall was
threatened with pillage by a body of Prince Rupert's ill-
disciplined Cavaliers. This acquaintance had been matured
by frequent walks together, which the vicinity of their places
of residence suffered the Lady Peveril to have with Mrs. Bridgenorth, who deemed herself much honoured in being thus
admitted into the society of so distinguished a lady. Major
Bridgenorth heard of this growing intimacy with great pleasure,
and he determined to repay the obligation, as far as he could
without much hurt to himself, by interfering with all his
influence, in behalf of her unfortunate husband. It was chiefly
owing to Major Bridgenorth's mediation, that Sir Geoffrey's
life was saved after the battle of Worcester. He obtained him
permission to compound for his estate on easier terms than
many who had been less obstinate in malignancy; and, finally,
when, in order to raise the money to the composition, the
Knight was obliged to sell a considerable portion of his patrimony, Major Bridgenorth became the purchaser, and that at a
larger price than had been paid to any Cavalier under such
circumstances, by a member of the Committee for Sequestrations.
It is true, the prudent committeeman did not, by any means,
lose sight of his own interest in the transaction, for the price
was, after all, very moderate, and the property lay adjacent to
Moultrassie Hall, the value of which was at least trebled by
the acquisition. But then it was also true, that the unfortunate
owner must have submitted to much worse conditions, had the
committeeman used, as others did, the full advantages which
his situation gave him; and Bridgenorth took credit to himself,
and received it from others, for having, on this occasion, fairly
sacrificed his interest to his liberality.

Sir Geoffrey Peveril was of the same opinion, and the rather that Mr. Bridgenorth seemed to bear his exaltation with great moderation, and was disposed to show him personally the same deference in his present sunshine of prosperity, which he had exhibited formerly in their early acquaintance. It is but justice to Major Bridgenorth to observe, that in this conduct he paid respect as much to the misfortunes as to the pretensions of his far-descended neighbour, and that, with the frank generosity of a blunt Englishman, he conceded points of ceremony, about which he himself was indifferent, merely because he saw that his doing so gave pleasure to Sir Geoffrey.

Peveril of the Peak did justice to his neighbour's delicacy, in consideration of which he forgot many things. He forgot that Major Bridgenorth was already in possession of a fair third of his estate, and had various pecuniary claims affecting the remainder, to the extent of one-third more. He endeavoured even to forget, what it was still more difficult not to remember, the altered situation in which they and their mansions now stood to each other.

Before the Civil War, the superb battlements and turrets of Martindale Castle looked down on the red brick-built Hall, as it stole out from the green plantations, just as an oak in Martindale Chase would have looked beside one of the stunted and formal young beech-trees with which Bridgenorth had graced his avenue; but after the siege which we have commemorated, the enlarged and augmented Hall was as much predominant in the landscape over the shattered and blackened ruins of the Castle, of which only one wing was left habitable, as the youthful beech, in all its vigour of shoot and bud, would appear to the same aged oak stripped of its boughs, and rifted by lightning, one-half laid in shivers on the ground, and the other remaining a blackened and ungraceful trunk, rent and splintered, and without either life or leaves. Sir Geoffrey could not but feel, that the situation and prospects were exchanged as disadvantageously for himself as the appearance of their mansions; and that though the authority of the man in office under the Parliament, the sequestrator, and the committeeman, had been only exerted for the protection of the Cavalier and the malignant, they would have been as effectual if applied to procure his utter ruin; and that he was become a client, while his neighbour was elevated into a patron.

There were two considerations, besides the necessity of the case and the constant advice of his lady, which enabled Peveril of the Peak to endure, with some patience, this state of degradation. The first was, that the politics of Major Bridgenorth began, on many points, to assimilate themselves to his own. As a Presbyterian, he was not an utter enemy to monarchy, and had been considerably shocked at the unexpected trial and execution of the King; as a civilian and a man of property, he feared the domination of the military; and though he wished not to see Charles restored by force of arms, yet he arrived at the conclusion, that to bring back the heir of the royal family on such terms of composition as might ensure the protection of those popular immunities and privileges for which the Long Parliament had at first contended, would be the surest and most desirable termination to the mutations in state affairs which had agitated Britain. Indeed, the Major's ideas on this point approached so nearly those of his neighbour, that he had well-nigh suffered Sir Geoffrey, who had a finger in almost all the conspiracies of the Royalists, to involve him in the unfortunate rising of Penruddock and Groves, in the west, in which many of the Presbyterian interest, as well as the Cavalier party, were engaged. And though his habitual prudence eventually kept him out of this and other dangers, Major Bridgenorth was considered during the last years of Cromwell's domination, and the interregnum which succeeded, as a disaffected person to the Commonwealth, and a favourer of Charles Stewart.

But besides this approximation to the same political opinions, another bond of intimacy united the families of the Castle and the Hall. Major Bridgenorth, fortunate, and eminently so, in all his worldly transactions, was visited by severe and reiterated misfortunes in his family, and became, in this particular, an object of compassion to his poorer and more decayed neighbour. Betwixt the breaking out of the Civil War and the Restoration, he lost successively a family of no less than six children, apparently through a delicacy of constitution, which cut off the little prattlers at the early age when they most wind themselves round the heart of the parents.

In the beginning of the year 1658, Major Bridgenorth was childless; ere it ended, he had a daughter, indeed, but her birth was purchased by the death of an affectionate wife, whose constitution had been exhausted by maternal grief, and by the anxious and harrowing reflection, that from her the children they had lost derived that delicacy of health, which proved unable to undergo the tear and wear of existence. The same voice which told Bridgenorth that he was father of a living child (it was the friendly voice of Lady Peveril), communicated to him the melancholy intelligence that he was no longer a husband. The feelings of Major Bridgenorth were strong and deep, rather than hasty and vehement; and his grief assumed the form of a sullen stupor, from which neither the friendly remonstrances of Sir Geoffrey, who did not fail to be with his neighbour at this distressing conjuncture, even though he knew he must meet the Presbyterian pastor, nor the ghostly exhortations of this latter person, were able to rouse the unfortunate widower.

At length Lady Peveril, with the ready invention of a female sharpened by the sight of distress and the feelings of sympathy, tried on the sufferer one of those experiments by which grief is often awakened from despondency into tears. She placed in Bridgenorth's arms the infant whose birth had cost him so dear, and conjured him to remember that his Alice was not yet dead, since she survived in the helpless child she had left to his paternal care.

"Take her away—take her away!" said the unhappy man, and they were the first words he had spoken; "let me not look on her—it is but another blossom that has bloomed to fade, and the tree that bore it will never flourish more!"

He almost threw the child into Lady Peveril's arms, placed his hands before his face, and wept aloud. Lady Peveril did not say "be comforted," but she ventured to promise that the blossom should ripen to fruit.

"Never, never!" said Bridgenorth; "take the unhappy child away, and let me only know when I shall wear black for her—Wear black!" he exclaimed, interrupting himself, "what other colour shall I wear during the remainder of my life?"

"I will take the child for a season," said Lady Peveril, "since the sight of her is so painful to you; and the little Alice shall share the nursery of our Julian, until it shall be pleasure and not pain for you to look on her."

"That hour will never come," said the unhappy father; "her doom is written—she will follow the rest—God's will be done.—Lady, I thank you—I trust her to your care; and I thank God that my eye shall not see her dying agonies."

Without detaining the reader's attention longer on this painful theme, it is enough to say that the Lady Peveril did undertake the duties of a mother to the little orphan; and perhaps it was owing, in a great measure, to her judicious treatment of the infant, that its feeble hold of life was preserved, since the glimmering spark might probably have been altogether smothered, had it, like the Major's former children, undergone the over-care and over-nursing of a mother rendered nervously cautious and anxious by so many successive losses. The lady was the more ready to undertake this charge, that she herself had lost two infant children; and that she attributed the preservation of the third, now a fine healthy child of three years old, to Julian's being subjected to rather a different course of diet and treatment than was then generally practised. She resolved to follow the same regimen with the little orphan which she had observed in the case of her own boy; and it was

equally successful. By a more sparing use of medicine, by a
bolder admission of fresh air, by a firm, yet cautious attention
to encourage rather than to supersede the exertions of nature,
the puny infant, under the care of an excellent nurse, gradually
improved in strength and in liveliness.

Sir Geoffrey, like most men of his frank and good-natured
disposition, was naturally fond of children, and so much compassionated the sorrows of his neighbour, that he entirely forgot
his being a Presbyterian, until it became necessary that the
infant should be christened by a teacher of that persuasion.

This was a trying case—the father seemed incapable of giving
direction; and that the threshold of Martindale Castle should
be violated by the heretical step of a dissenting clergyman, was
matter of horror to its orthodox owner. He had seen the
famous Hugh Peters, with a Bible in one hand and a pistol in
the other, ride in triumph through the court-door when Martindale was surrendered; and the bitterness of that hour had
entered like iron into his soul. Yet such was Lady Peveril's
influence over the prejudices of her husband, that he was
induced to connive at the ceremony taking place in a remote
garden house, which was not properly within the precincts of
the Castle-wall. The lady even dared to be present while the
ceremony was performed by the Reverend Master Solsgrace,
who had once preached a sermon of three hours' length before
the House of Commons, upon a thanksgiving occasion after the
relief of Exeter. Sir Geoffrey Peveril took care to be absent
the whole day from the Castle, and it was only from the great
interest which he took in the washing, perfuming, and as it
were purification of the summer-house, that it could have been
guessed he knew anything of what had taken place in it.

But, whatever prejudices the good Knight might entertain
against his neighbour's form of religion, they did not in any
way influence his feelings towards him as a sufferer under
severe affliction. The mode in which he showed his sympathy
was rather singular, but exactly suited the character of both,
and the terms on which they stood with each other.

Morning after morning the good Baronet made Moultrassie
Hall the termination of his walk or ride, and said a single word
of kindness as he passed. Sometimes he entered the old parlour
where the proprietor sat in solitary wretchedness and despondency; but more frequently (for Sir Geoffrey did not pretend
to great talents of conversation), he paused on the terrace, and
stopping or halting his horse by the latticed window, said
aloud to the melancholy inmate, " How is it with you, Master
Bridgenorth?" (the Knight would never acknowledge his
neighbour's military rank of Major); " I just looked in to
bid you keep a good heart, man, and to tell you that Julian

is well, and little Alice is well, and all are well at Martindale
Castle."

A deep sigh, sometimes coupled with "I thank you, Sir
Geoffrey; my grateful duty waits on Lady Peveril," was generally Bridgenorth's only answer. But the news was received
on the one part with the kindness which was designed upon
the other; it gradually became less painful and more interesting; the lattice window was never closed, nor was the leathern
easy-chair which stood next to it ever empty, when the usual
hour of the Baronet's momentary visit approached. At length
the expectation of that passing minute became the pivot upon
which the thoughts of poor Bridgenorth turned during all the
rest of the day. Most men have known the influence of such
brief but ruling moments at some period of their lives. The
moment when a lover passes the window of his mistress—the
moment when the epicure hears the dinner-bell,—is that into
which is crowded the whole interest of the day; the hours
which precede it are spent in anticipation; the hours which
follow, in reflection on what has passed; and fancy dwelling
on each brief circumstance, gives to seconds the duration of
minutes, to minutes that of hours. Thus seated in his lonely
chair, Bridgenorth could catch at a distance the stately step of
Sir Geoffrey, or the heavy tramp of his war-horse, Black Hastings, which had borne him in many an action; he could hear
the hum of "The King shall enjoy his own again," or the
habitual whistle of "Cuckolds and Roundheads," die into reverential silence, as the Knight approached the mansion of
affliction; and then came the strong hale voice of the huntsman
soldier with its usual greeting.

By degrees the communication became something more pro-
tracted, as Major Bridgenorth's grief, like all human feelings,
lost its overwhelming violence, and permitted him to attend, in
some degree, to what passed around him, to discharge various
duties which pressed upon him, and to give a share of attention to the situation of the country, distracted as it was by
the contending factions, whose strife only terminated in the
Restoration. Still, however, though slowly recovering from the
effects of the shock which he had sustained, Major Bridgenorth
felt himself as yet unable to make up his mind to the effort
necessary to see his infant; and though separated by so short
a distance from the being in whose existence he was more
interested than in anything the world afforded, he only made
himself acquainted with the windows of the apartment where
little Alice was lodged, and was often observed to watch them
from the terrace, as they brightened in the evening under the
influence of the setting sun. In truth, though a strong-minded
man in most respects, he was unable to lay aside the gloomy

impression that this remaining pledge of affection was soon to be conveyed to that grave which had already devoured all besides that was dear to him ; and he awaited in miserable suspense the moment when he should hear that symptoms of the fatal malady had begun to show themselves.

The voice of Peveril continued to be that of a comforter until the month of April 1660, when it suddenly assumed a new and different tone. "The King shall enjoy his own again," far from ceasing, as the hasty tread of Black Hastings came up the avenue, bore burden to the clatter of his hoofs on the paved courtyard, as Sir Geoffrey sprang from his great war-saddle, now once more garnished with pistols of two feet in length, and, armed with steel-cap, back and breast, and a truncheon in his hand, he rushed into the apartment of the astonished Major, with his eyes sparkling, and his cheek inflamed, while he called out, "Up! up, neighbour! No time now to mope in the chimney-corner! Where is your buff-coat and broadsword, man ? Take the true side once in your life, and mend past mistakes. The King is all lenity, man—all royal nature and mercy. I will get your full pardon."

"What means all this ?" said Bridgenorth—"Is all well with you—all well at Martindale Castle, Sir Geoffrey ?"

"Well as you could wish them, Alice, and Julian, and all. But I have news worth twenty of that—Monk has declared at London against those stinking scoundrels the Rump. Fairfax is up in Yorkshire—for the King—for the King, man ! Churchmen, Presbyterians, and all, are in buff and bandoleer for King Charles. I have a letter from Fairfax to secure Derby and Chesterfield with all the men I can make. D—n him, fine that I should take orders from him ! But never mind that—all are friends now, and you and I, good neighbour, will charge abreast, as good neighbours should. See there ! read—read— read—and then boot and saddle in an instant.

> 'Hey for cavaliers—ho for cavaliers,
>   Pray for cavaliers,
>   Dub-a-dub, dub-a-dub,
>   Have at old Beelzebub,
>   Oliver shakes in his bier !' "

After thundering forth this elegant effusion of loyal enthusiasm, the sturdy Cavalier's heart became too full. He threw himself on a seat, and exclaiming, " Did ever I think to live to see this happy day !" he wept, to his own surprise, as much as to that of Bridgenorth.

Upon considering the crisis in which the country was placed, it appeared to Major Bridgenorth, as it had done to Fairfax, and other leaders of the Presbyterian party, that their frank embracing of the royal interest was the wisest and most patriotic measure which they could adopt in the circumstances, when all ranks and classes of men were seeking refuge from the uncertainty and varied oppression attending the repeated contests between the factions of Westminster Hall and of Wallingford House. Accordingly he joined with Sir Geoffrey, with less enthusiasm indeed, but with equal sincerity, taking such measures as seemed proper to secure their part of the country on the King's behalf, which was done as effectually and peaceably as in other parts of England. The neighbours were both at Chesterfield, when news arrived that the King had landed in England; and Sir Geoffrey instantly announced his purpose of waiting upon his Majesty, even before his return to the Castle of Martindale.

"Who knows, neighbour," he said, "whether Sir Geoffrey Peveril will ever return to Martindale? Titles must be going amongst them yonder, and I have deserved something among the rest.—Lord Peveril would sound well—or stay, Earl of Martindale—no, not of Martindale—Earl of the Peak.—Meanwhile, trust your affairs to me—I will see you secured—I would you had been no Presbyterian, neighbour—a knighthood,—I mean a knight-bachelor, not a knight-baronet,—would have served your turn well."

"I leave these things to my betters, Sir Geoffrey," said the Major, "and desire nothing so earnestly as to find all well at Martindale when I return."

"You will—you will find them all well," said the Baronet; "Julian, Alice, Lady Peveril, and all of them—Bear my commendations to them, and kiss them all, neighbour, Lady Peveril and all—you may kiss a Countess when I come back; all will go well with you now you are turned honest man."

"I always meant to be so, Sir Geoffrey," said Bridgenorth calmly.

"Well, well, well—no offence meant," said the Knight, "all is well now—so you to Moultrassie Hall, and I to Whitehall. Said I well, aha! So ho, mine host, a stoup of Canary to the King's health ere we get to horse—I forgot, neighbour—you drink no healths."

"I wish the King's health as sincerely as if I drank a gallon to it," replied the Major; "and I wish you, Sir Geoffrey, all success on your journey, and a safe return."

CHAPTER II

Why, then, we will have bellowing of beeves,
Broaching of barrels, brandishing of spigots ;
Blood shall flow freely, but it shall be gore
Of herds and flocks, and venison and poultry,
Join'd to the brave heart's-blood of John-a-Barleycorn !
—OLD PLAY.

WHATEVER rewards Charles might have condescended to bestow
in acknowledgment of the sufferings and loyalty of Peveril of
the Peak, he had none in his disposal equal to the pleasure
which Providence had reserved for Bridgenorth on his return to
Derbyshire. The exertion to which he had been summoned,
had had the usual effect of restoring to a certain extent the
activity and energy of his character, and he felt it would be
unbecoming to relapse into the state of lethargic melancholy
from which it had roused him. Time also had its usual effect
in mitigating the subjects of his regret ; and when he had passed
one day at the Hall in regretting that he could not expect the
indirect news of his daughter's health, which Sir Geoffrey used
to communicate in his almost daily call, he reflected that it
would be in every respect becoming that he should pay a personal visit at Martindale Castle, carry thither the remembrances
of the Knight to his lady, assure her of his health, and satisfy
himself respecting that of his daughter. He armed himself
for the worst—he called to recollection the thin cheeks, faded
eye, wasted hand, pallid lip, which had marked the decaying
health of all his former infants.

"I shall see," he said, "these signs of mortality once more—
I shall once more see a beloved being to whom I have given
birth, gliding to the grave which ought to enclose me long
before her. No matter—it is unmanly so long to shrink from
that which must be—God's will be done !"

He went accordingly, on the subsequent morning, to Martindale Castle, and gave the lady the welcome assurances of her
husband's safety, and of his hopes of preferment.

"For the first, may Almighty God be praised !" said the
Lady Peveril ; "and be the other as our gracious and restored
Sovereign may will it. We are great enough for our means,
and have means sufficient for contentment, though not for
splendour. And now I see, good Master Bridgenorth, the folly
of putting faith in idle presentiments of evil. So often had Sir
Geoffrey's repeated attempts in favour of the Stewarts led him
into new misfortunes, that when, the other morning, I saw him
once more dressed in his fatal armour, and heard the sound of

his trumpet, which had been so long silent, it seemed to me as if I saw his shroud, and heard his death-knell. I say this to you, good neighbour, the rather because I fear your own mind has been harassed with anticipations of impending calamity, which it may please God to avert in your case as it has done in mine; and here comes a sight which bears good assurance of it."

The door of the apartment opened as she spoke, and two lovely children entered. The eldest, Julian Peveril, a fine boy betwixt four and five years old, led in his hand, with an air of dignified support and attention, a little girl of eighteen months, who rolled and tottered along, keeping herself with difficulty upright by the assistance of her elder, stronger, and masculine companion.

Bridgenorth cast a hasty and fearful glance upon the countenance of his daughter, and, even in that glimpse, perceived, with exquisite delight, that his fears were unfounded. He caught her in his arms, pressed her to his heart, and the child, though at first alarmed at the vehemence of his caresses, presently, as if prompted by Nature, smiled in reply to them. Again he held her at some distance from him, and examined her more attentively; he satisfied himself that the complexion of the young cherub he had in his arms was not the hectic tinge of disease, but the clear hue of ruddy health; and that though her little frame was slight, it was firm and springy.

" I did not think that it could have been thus," he said, looking to Lady Peveril, who had sat observing the scene with great pleasure ; " but praise be to God in the first instance, and next, thanks to you, madam, who have been His instrument."

" Julian must lose his playfellow now, I suppose ? " said the lady ; " but the Hall is not distant, and I will see my little charge often. Dame Martha, the housekeeper at Moultrassie, has sense, and is careful. I will tell her the rules I have observed with little Alice, and——"

" God forbid my girl should ever come to Moultrassie," said Major Bridgenorth hastily ; " it has been the grave of her race. The air of the low grounds suited them not—or there is perhaps a fate connected with the mansion. I will seek for her some other place of abode."

" That you shall not, under your favour be it spoken, Major Bridgenorth," answered the lady. " If you do so, we must suppose that you are undervaluing my qualities as a nurse. If she goes not to her father's house, she shall not quit mine. I will keep the little lady as a pledge of her safety and my own skill ; and since you are afraid of the damp of the low grounds, I hope you will come here frequently to visit her."

This was a proposal which went to the heart of Major Bridge-

north. It was precisely the point which he would have given
worlds to arrive at, but which he saw no chance of attaining.

It is too well known, that those whose families are long
pursued by such a fatal disease as existed in his, become, it
may be said, superstitious respecting its fatal effects, and ascribe
to place, circumstance, and individual care, much more perhaps
than these can in any case contribute to avert the fatality of
constitutional distemper. Lady Peveril was aware that this was
peculiarly the impression of her neighbour; that the depression
of his spirits, the excess of his care, the feverishness of his
apprehensions, the restraint and gloom of the solitude in which
he dwelt, were really calculated to produce the evil which most
of all he dreaded. She pitied him, she felt for him, she was
grateful for former protection received at his hands—she had
become interested in the child itself. What female fails to
feel such interest in the helpless creature she has tended? And
to sum the whole up, the dame had a share of human vanity;
and being a sort of Lady Bountiful in her way (for the character was not then confined to the old and the foolish), she was
proud of the skill by which she had averted the probable attacks
of hereditary malady, so inveterate in the family of Bridgenorth.
It needed not, perhaps, in other cases, that so many reasons
should be assigned for an act of neighbourly humanity; but
civil war had so lately torn the country asunder, and broken
all the usual ties of vicinage and good neighbourhood, that it
was unusual to see them preserved among persons of different
political opinions.

Major Bridgenorth himself felt this; and while the tear
of joy in his eye showed how gladly he would accept Lady
Peveril's proposal, he could not help stating the obvious inconveniences attendant upon her scheme, though it was in the
tone of one who would gladly hear them overruled. "Madam,"
he said, "your kindness makes me the happiest and most
thankful of men; but can it be consistent with your own convenience? Sir Geoffrey has his opinions on many points, which
have differed, and probably do still differ, from mine. He is
high-born, and I of middling parentage only. He uses the
Church Service, and I the Catechism of the Assembly of
Divines at Westminster——"

"I hope you will find prescribed in neither of them," said
the Lady Peveril, "that I may not be a mother to your
motherless child. I trust, Master Bridgenorth, the joyful
Restoration of his Majesty, a work wrought by the direct
hand of Providence, may be the means of closing and healing
all civil and religious dissensions among us, and that, instead of
showing the superior purity of our faith, by persecuting those
who think otherwise from ourselves on doctrinal points, we shall

endeavour to show its real Christian tendency, by emulating each other in actions of good-will towards man, as the best way of showing our love to God."

"Your ladyship speaks what your own kind heart dictates," answered Bridgenorth, who had his own share of the narrow-mindedness of the time; "and sure am I, that if all who call themselves loyalists and Cavaliers, thought like you—and like my friend Sir Geoffrey"—(this he added after a moment's pause, being perhaps rather complimentary than sincere)—"we, who thought it our duty in time past to take arms for freedom of conscience, and against arbitrary power, might now sit down in peace and contentment. But I wot not how it may fall. You have sharp and hot spirits amongst you; I will not say our power was always moderately used, and revenge is sweet to the race of fallen Adam."

"Come, Master Bridgenorth," said the Lady Peveril gaily, "those evil omenings do but point out conclusions, which, unless they were so anticipated, are most unlikely to come to pass. You know what Shakspeare says—

'To fly the boar before the boar pursues,
    Were to incense the boar to follow us,
    And make pursuit when he did mean no chase.'

But I crave your pardon—it is so long since we have met, that I forgot you love no play-books."

"With reverence to your ladyship," said Bridgenorth, "I were much to blame did I need the idle words of a Warwick-shire stroller, to teach me my grateful duty to your ladyship on this occasion, which appoints me to be directed by you in all things which my conscience will permit."

"Since you permit me such influence, then," replied the Lady Peveril, "I shall be moderate in exercising it, in order that I may, in my domination at least, give you a favourable impression of the new order of things. So, if you will be a subject of mine for one day, neighbour, I am going, at my lord and husband's command, to issue out my warrants to invite the whole neighbourhood to a solemn feast at the Castle, on Thursday next; and I not only pray you to be personally present, but to prevail on your worthy pastor, and such neighbours and friends, high and low, as may think in your own way, to meet with the rest of the neighbourhood, to rejoice on this joyful occasion of the King's Restoration, and thereby to show that we are to be henceforward a united people."

The parliamentarian Major was considerably embarrassed by this proposal. He looked upward, and downward, and around, cast his eye first to the oak-carved ceiling, and anon fixed it upon the floor; then threw it around the room till it lighted on his child, the sight of whom suggested another and a better train of reflections than ceiling and floor had been able to supply.

" Madam," he said, " I have long been a stranger to festivity, perhaps from constitutional melancholy, perhaps from the depression which is natural to a desolate and deprived man, in whose ear mirth is marred, like a pleasant air when performed on a mistuned instrument. But though neither my thoughts nor temperament are Jovial or Mercurial, it becomes me to be grateful to Heaven for the good He has sent me by the means of your ladyship. David, the man after God's own heart, did wash and eat bread when his beloved child was removed— mine is restored to me, and shall I not show gratitude under a blessing, when he showed resignation under an affliction? Madam, I will wait on your gracious invitation with acceptance ; and such of my friends with whom I may possess influence, and whose presence your ladyship may desire, shall accompany me to the festivity, that our Israel may be as one people."

Having spoken these words with an aspect which belonged more to a martyr than to a guest bidden to a festival, and having kissed, and solemnly blessed his little girl, Major Bridgenorth took his departure for Moultrassie Hall.

CHAPTER III

Here's neither want of appetite nor mouths ;
Pray Heaven we be not scant of meat or mirth !
—Old Play.

Even upon ordinary occasions, and where means were ample, a great entertainment in those days was not such a sinecure as in modern times, when the lady who presides has but to intimate to her menials the day and hour when she wills it to take place. At that simple period, the lady was expected to enter deeply into the arrangement and provision of the whole affair ; and from a little gallery, which communicated with her own private apartment, and looked down upon the kitchen, her shrill voice was to be heard, from time to time, like that of the warning spirit in a tempest, rising above the clash of pots and stewpans—the creaking of spits—the clattering of marrow-bones and cleavers—the scolding of cooks—and all the other various kinds of din which form an accompaniment to dressing a large dinner.

But all this toil and anxiety was more than doubled in the

MAJOR BRIDGNORTH'S VISIT TO HIS CHILD AT
MARTINDALE CASTLE

PAINTING BY ALFRED JOHANNOT

case of the approaching feast at Martindale Castle, where the presiding Genius of the festivity was scarce provided with adequate means to carry her hospitable purpose into effect. The tyrannical conduct of husbands, in such cases, is universal; and I scarce know one householder of my acquaintance who has not, on some ill-omened and most inconvenient season, announced suddenly to his innocent helpmate, that he had invited

> " Some odious Major Rock,
> To drop in at six o'clock,"

to the great discomposure of the lady, and the discredit, perhaps, of her domestic arrangements.

Peveril of the Peak was still more thoughtless; for he had directed his lady to invite the whole honest men of the neigh-bourhood to make good cheer at Martindale Castle, in honour of the blessed Restoration of his most sacred Majesty, without precisely explaining where the provisions were to come from. The deer-park had lain waste ever since the siege; the dovecot could do little to furnish forth such an entertainment; the fish-ponds, it is true, were well provided (which the neighbouring Presbyterians noted as a suspicious circumstance); and game was to be had for the shooting, upon the extensive heaths and hills of Derbyshire. But these were but the secondary parts of a banquet; and the house-steward and bailiff, Lady Peveril's only coadjutors and counsellors, could not agree how the butcher-meat—the most substantial part, or, as it were, the main body of the entertainment—was to be supplied. The house-steward threatened the sacrifice of a fine yoke of young bullocks, which the bailiff, who pleaded the necessity of their agricultural services, tenaciously resisted; and Lady Peveril's good and dutiful nature did not prevent her from making some impatient reflections on the want of consideration of her absent Knight, who had thus thoughtlessly placed her in so embarrassing a situation.

These reflections were scarcely just, if a man is only respon-sible for such resolutions as he adopts when he is fully master of himself. Sir Geoffrey's loyalty, like that of many persons in his situation, had, by dint of hopes and fears, victories and defeats, struggles and sufferings, all arising out of the same moving cause, and turning, as it were, on the same pivot, acquired the character of an intense and enthusiastic passion; and the singular and surprising change of fortune, by which his highest wishes were not only gratified, but far exceeded, occasioned for some time a kind of intoxication of loyal rapture which seemed to pervade the whole kingdom. Sir Geoffrey had seen Charles and his brothers, and had been received by

B

the merry monarch with that graceful, and at the same time frank urbanity, by which he conciliated all who approached him; the Knight's services and merits had been fully acknowledged, and recompense had been hinted at, if not expressly promised. Was it for Peveril of the Peak, in the jubilee of his spirits, to consider how his wife was to find beef and mutton to feast his neighbours?

Luckily, however, for the embarrassed lady, there existed some one who had composure of mind sufficient to foresee this difficulty. Just as she had made up her mind, very reluctantly, to become debtor to Major Bridgenorth for the sum necessary to carry her husband's commands into effect, and whilst she was bitterly regretting this departure from the strictness of her usual economy, the steward, who, by-the-bye, had not been absolutely sober since the news of the King's landing at Dover, burst into the apartment, snapping his fingers, and showing more marks of delight than was quite consistent with the dignity of my lady's large parlour.

"What means this, Whitaker?" said the lady, somewhat peevishly; for she was interrupted in the commencement of a letter to her neighbour on the unpleasant business of the proposed loan,—"Is it to be always thus with you?—Are you dreaming?"

"A vision of good omen, I trust," said the steward, with a triumphant flourish of the hand; "far better than Pharaoh's, though, like his, it be of fat kine."

"I prithee be plain, man," said the lady, "or fetch some one who can speak to purpose."

"Why, odds-my-life, madam," said the steward, "mine errand can speak for itself. Do you not hear them low? Do you not hear them bleat? A yoke of fat oxen, and half a score prime wethers. The Castle is victualled for this bout, let them storm when they will; and Gatherill may have his d—d mains ploughed to the boot."

The lady, without farther questioning her elated domestic, rose and went to the window, where she certainly beheld the oxen and sheep which had given rise to Whitaker's exultation. "Whence come they?" said she, in some surprise.

"Let them construe that who can," answered Whitaker; "the fellow who drove them was a west-country man, and only said they came from a friend to help to furnish out your ladyship's entertainment; the man would not stay to drink—I am sorry he would not stay to drink—I crave your ladyship's pardon for not keeping him by the ears to drink—it was not my fault."

"That I'll be sworn it was not," said the lady.

"Nay, madam, by G—, I assure you it was not," said the zealous steward; "for, rather than the Castle should lose credit,

I drank his health myself in double ale, though I had had my morning draught already. I tell you the naked truth, my lady, by G—!"

"It was no great compulsion, I suppose," said the lady; "but, Whitaker, suppose you should show your joy on such occasions, by drinking and swearing a little less, rather than a little more, would it not be as well, think you?"

"I crave your ladyship's pardon," said Whitaker, with much reverence; "I hope I know my place. I am your ladyship's poor servant; and I know it does not become me to drink and swear like your ladyship—that is, like his honour, Sir Geoffrey, I would say. But I pray you, if I am not to drink and swear after my degree, how are men to know Peveril of the Peak's steward,—and I may say butler too, since I have had the keys of the cellar ever since old Spigots was shot dead on the north-west turret, with a black jack in his hand,—I say, how is an old Cavalier like me to be known from those cuckoldy Round-heads that do nothing but fast and pray, if we are not to drink and swear according to our degree?"

The lady was silent, for she well knew speech availed nothing; and, after a moment's pause, proceeded to intimate to the steward that she would have the persons, whose names were marked in a written paper, which she delivered to him, invited to the approaching banquet.

Whitaker, instead of receiving the list with the mute ac-quiescence of a modern Major Domo, carried it into the recess of one of the windows, and, adjusting his spectacles, began to read it to himself. The first names, being those of distin-guished Cavalier families in the neighbourhood, he muttered over in a tone of approbation—paused and pshawed at that of Bridgenorth—yet acquiesced, with the observation, "But he is a good neighbour, so it may pass for once." But when he read the name and surname of Nehemiah Solsgrace, the Presbyterian parson, Whitaker's patience altogether forsook him; and he declared he would as soon throw himself into Eldon-hole,* as consent that the intrusive old puritan howlet, who had usurped the pulpit of a sound orthodox divine, should ever darken the gates of Martindale Castle by any message or mediation of his. "The false crop-eared hypocrites," cried he, with a hearty oath, "have had their turn of the good weather. The sun is on our side of the hedge now, and we will pay off old scores, as sure as my name is Richard Whitaker."

"You presume on your long services, Whitaker, and on your master's absence, or you had not dared to use me thus," said the lady.

---

* A chasm in the earth supposed to be unfathomable, one of the wonders of the Peak.

The unwonted agitation of her voice attracted the attention of the refractory steward, notwithstanding his present state of elevation; but he no sooner saw that her eye glistened, and her cheek reddened, than his obstinacy was at once subdued.

"A murrain on me," he said, "but I have made my lady angry in good earnest! and that is an unwonted sight for to see.—I crave your pardon, my lady! It was not poor Dick Whitaker disputed your honourable commands, but only that second draught of double ale. We have put a double stroke of malt to it, as your ladyship well knows, ever since the happy Restoration. To be sure I hate a fanatic as I do the cloven foot of Satan; but then your honourable ladyship hath a right to invite Satan himself, cloven foot and all, to Martindale Castle; and to send me to hell's gate with a billet of invitation—and so your will shall be done."

The invitations were sent round accordingly, in all due form; and one of the bullocks was sent down to be roasted whole at the market-place of a little village called Martindale-Moultrassie, which stood considerably to the eastward both of the Castle and Hall, from which it took its double name, at about an equal distance from both; so that, suppose a line drawn from the one manor-house to the other, to be the base of a triangle, the village would have occupied the salient angle. As the said village, since the late transference of a part of Peveril's property, belonged to Sir Geoffrey and to Bridgenorth in nearly equal portions, the lady judged it not proper to dispute the right of the latter to add some hogsheads of beer to the popular festivity.

In the meanwhile, she could not but suspect the Major of being the unknown friend who had relieved her from the dilemma arising from the want of provisions; and she esteemed herself happy when a visit from him, on the day preceding the proposed entertainment, gave her, as she thought, an opportunity of expressing her gratitude.

CHAPTER IV

No, sir—I will not pledge—I'm one of those
Who think good wine needs neither bush nor preface
To make it welcome. If you doubt my word,
Fill the quart-cup, and see if I will choke on't.
—OLD PLAY.

THERE was a serious gravity of expression in the disclamation with which Major Bridgenorth replied to the thanks tendered to him by Lady Peveril, for the supply of provisions which had reached her Castle so opportunely. He seemed first not to be aware what she alluded to; and, when she explained the circumstance, he protested so seriously that he had no share in the benefit conferred, that Lady Peveril was compelled to believe him, the rather that, being a man of plain downright character, affecting no refined delicacy of sentiment, and practising almost a quaker-like sincerity of expression, it would have been much contrary to his general character to have made such a disavowal, unless it were founded in truth.

"My present visit to you, madam," said he, "had indeed some reference to the festivity of to-morrow." Lady Peveril listened, but as her visitor seemed to find some difficulty in expressing himself, she was compelled to ask an explanation. "Madam," said the Major, "you are not perhaps entirely ignorant that the more tender-conscienced among us have scruples at certain practices, so general amongst your people at times of rejoicing, that you may be said to insist upon them as articles of faith, or at least greatly to resent their omission."

"I trust, Master Bridgenorth," said the Lady Peveril, not fully comprehending the drift of his discourse, "that we shall, as your entertainers, carefully avoid all allusions or reproaches founded on past misunderstanding."

"We would expect no less, madam, from your candour and courtesy," said Bridgenorth; "but I perceive you do not fully understand me. To be plain, then, I allude to the fashion of drinking healths, and pledging each other in draughts of strong liquor, which most among us consider as a superfluous and sinful provoking of each other to debauchery, and the excessive use of strong drink; and which, besides, if derived, as learned divines have supposed, from the custom of the blinded Pagans, who made libations and invoked idols when they drank, may be justly said to have something in it heathenish, and allied to demon-worship."

The lady had already hastily considered all the topics which were likely to introduce discord into the proposed festivity; but this very ridiculous, yet fatal discrepancy, betwixt the manners of the parties on convivial occasions, had entirely escaped her. She endeavoured to soothe the objecting party, whose brows were knit like one who had fixed an opinion by which he was determined to abide.

"I grant," she said, "my good neighbour, that this custom is at least idle, and may be prejudicial if it leads to excess in the use of liquor, which is apt enough to take place without such conversation. But I think, when it hath not this consequence, it is a thing indifferent, affords a unanimous mode of expressing our good wishes to our friends, and our loyal duty to our sovereign; and, without meaning to put any force upon the inclination of those who believe otherwise, I cannot see how I can deny my guests and friends the privilege of drinking a health to the King, or to my husband, after the old English fashion."

"My lady," said the Major, "if the age of fashion were to command it, Popery is one of the oldest English fashions that I have heard of; but it is our happiness that we are not benighted like our fathers, and therefore we must act according to the light that is in us, and not after their darkness. I had myself the honour to attend the Lord-Keeper Whitelocke, when, at the table of the Chamberlain of the kingdom of Sweden, he did positively refuse to pledge the health of his Queen, Christina, thereby giving great offence, and putting in peril the whole purpose of that voyage; which it is not to be thought so wise a man would have done, but that he held such compliance a thing not merely indifferent, but rather sinful and damnable."

"With all respect to Whitelocke," said the Lady Peveril, "I continue of my own opinion, though, Heaven knows, I am no friend to riot or wassail. I would fain accommodate myself to your scruples, and will discourage all other pledges; but surely those of the King and of Peveril of the Peak may be permitted?"

"I dare not," answered Bridgenorth, "lay even the ninety-ninth part of a grain of incense upon an altar erected to Satan."

"How, sir!" said the lady; "do you bring Satan into comparison with our master King Charles, and with my noble lord and husband?"

"Pardon me, madam," answered Bridgenorth, "I have no such thoughts—indeed they would ill become me. I do wish the King's health and Sir Geoffrey's devoutly, and I will pray for both. But I see not what good it should do their health if I should prejudice my own by quaffing pledges out of quart flagons."

"Since we cannot agree upon this matter," said Lady Peveril, "we must find some resource by which to offend those of neither party. Suppose you winked at our friends drinking these pledges, and we should connive at your sitting still?"

But neither would this composition satisfy Bridgenorth, who was of opinion, as he expressed himself, that it would be holding a candle to Beelzebub. In fact, his temper, naturally stubborn, was at present rendered much more so by a previous conference with his preacher, who, though a very good man in the main, was particularly and illiberally tenacious of the petty distinctions which his sect adopted; and while he thought with considerable apprehension on the accession of power which Popery, Prelacy, and Peveril of the Peak, were like to acquire by the late Revolution, became naturally anxious to put his flock on their guard, and prevent their being kidnapped by the wolf. He disliked extremely that Major Bridgenorth, indisputably the head of the Presbyterian interest in that neighbourhood, should have given his only daughter to be, as he termed it, nursed by a Canaanitish woman; and he told him plainly that he liked not this going to feast in the high places with the uncircumcised in heart, and looked on the whole conviviality only as a making-merry in the house of Tirzah.

Upon receiving this rebuke from his pastor, Bridgenorth began to suspect he might have been partly wrong in the readiness which, in his first ardour of gratitude, he had shown to enter into intimate intercourse with the Castle of Martindale; but he was too proud to avow this to the preacher, and it was not till after a considerable debate betwixt them, that it was mutually agreed their presence at the entertainment should depend upon the condition, that no healths or pledges should be given in their presence. Bridgenorth, therefore, as the delegate and representative of his party, was bound to stand firm against all entreaty, and the lady became greatly embarrassed. She now regretted sincerely that her well-intended invitation had ever been given, for she foresaw that its rejection was to awaken all former subjects of quarrel, and perhaps to lead to new violences amongst people who had not many years since been engaged in civil war. To yield up the disputed point to the Presbyterians, would have been to offend the Cavalier party, and Sir Geoffrey in particular, in the most mortal degree; for they made it as firm a point of honour to give healths, and compel others to pledge them, as the Puritans made it a deep article of religion to refuse both. At length the lady changed the discourse, introduced that of Major Bridgenorth's child, caused it to be sent for, and put into his arms. The mother's stratagem took effect; for, though the parliamentary major stood firm, the father, as in the case of the Governor of Tilbury, was softened, and he agreed that his friends should accept a compromise. This was, that the major himself, the reverend divine, and such of their friends as held strict Puritan tenets, should form a separate party in the Large Parlour, while the Hall should be occupied by the jovial Cavaliers; and that each party should regulate their potations after their own conscience, or after their own fashion.

Major Bridgenorth himself seemed greatly relieved after this important matter had been settled. He had held it matter of conscience to be stubborn in maintaining his own opinion, but was heartily glad when he escaped from the apparently inevitable necessity of affronting Lady Peveril by the refusal

of her invitation. He remained longer than usual, and spoke
and smiled more than was his custom. His first care on his
return was to announce to the clergyman and his congregation
the compromise which he had made, and this not as a matter
for deliberation, but one upon which he had already resolved;
and such was his authority among them, that though the
preacher longed to pronounce a separation of the parties, and
to exclaim—"To your tents, O Israel!" he did not see the
chance of being seconded by so many, as would make it worth
while to disturb the unanimous acquiescence in their delegate's
proposal.

Nevertheless, each party being put upon the alert by the
consequences of Major Bridgenorth's embassy, so many points
of doubt and delicate discussion were started in succession, that
the Lady Peveril, the only person, perhaps, who was desirous
of achieving an effectual reconciliation between them, incurred,
in reward for her good intentions, the censure of both factions,
and had much reason to regret her well-meant project of bringing the Capulets and Montagues of Derbyshire together on the
same occasion of public festivity.

As it was now settled that the guests were to form two
different parties, it became not only a subject of dispute betwixt
themselves, which should be first admitted within the Castle
of Martindale, but matter of serious apprehension to Lady
Peveril and Major Bridgenorth, lest, if they were to approach
by the same avenue and entrance, a quarrel might take place
betwixt them, and proceed to extremities, even before they
reached the place of entertainment. The lady believed she
had discovered an admirable expedient for preventing the possibility of such interference, by directing that the Cavaliers
should be admitted by the principal entrance, while the Roundheads should enter the Castle through a great breach which
had been made in the course of the siege, and across which
there had been since made a sort of by-path to drive the cattle
down to their pasture in the wood. By this contrivance the
Lady Peveril imagined she had altogether avoided the various
risks which might occur from two such parties encountering
each other, and disputing for precedence. Several other circumstances of less importance were adjusted at the same time,
and apparently so much to the satisfaction of the Presbyterian
teacher, that, in a long lecture on the subject of the Marriage
Garment, he was at the pains to explain to his hearers, that
outward apparel was not alone meant by that scriptural expression, but also a suitable frame of mind for enjoyment of peaceful
festivity; and therefore he exhorted the brethren, that whatever might be the errors of the poor blinded malignants, with
whom they were in some sort to eat and drink upon the morrow,

they ought not on this occasion to show any evil will against
them, lest they should therein become troublers of the peace of
Israel.

Honest Doctor Dummerar, the ejected Episcopal Vicar of
Martindale *cum* Moultrassie, preached to the Cavaliers on the
same subject. He had served the cure before the breaking out
of the rebellion, and was in high favour with Sir Geoffrey, not
merely on account of his sound orthodoxy and deep learning,
but his exquisite skill in playing at bowls, and his facetious
conversation over a pipe and tankard of October. For these
latter accomplishments, the Doctor had the honour to be
recorded by old Century White amongst the roll of lewd,
incompetent, profligate clergymen of the Church of England,
whom he denounced to God and man, on account chiefly of the
heinous sin of playing at games of skill and chance, and of
occasionally joining in the social meetings of their parishioners.
When the King's party began to lose ground, Doctor Dummerar
left his vicarage, and, betaking himself to the camp, showed
upon several occasions, when acting as chaplain to Sir Geoffrey
Peveril's regiment, that his portly bodily presence included a
stout and masculine heart. When all was lost, and he himself,
with most other loyal divines, was deprived of his living, he
made such shift as he could ; now lurking in the garrets of old
friends in the University, who shared with him, and such as
him, the slender means of livelihood which the evil times had
left them ; and now lying hid in the houses of the oppressed
and sequestrated gentry, who respected at once his character and
sufferings. When the Restoration took place, Doctor Dummerar
emerged from some one of his hiding-places, and hied him to
Martindale Castle, to enjoy the triumph inseparable from this
happy change.

His appearance at the Castle in his full clerical dress, and
the warm reception which he received from the neighbouring
gentry, added not a little to the alarm which was gradually
extending itself through the party which were so lately the
uppermost. It is true, Doctor Dummerar framed (honest worthy
man) no extravagant views of elevation or preferment; but the
probability of his being replaced in the living, from which he
had been expelled under very flimsy pretences, inferred a severe
blow to the Presbyterian divine, who could not be considered
otherwise than as an intruder. The interest of the two preachers,
therefore, as well as the sentiments of their flocks, were at
direct variance ; and here was another fatal objection in the
way of Lady Peveril's scheme of a general and comprehensive
healing ordinance.

Nevertheless, as we have already hinted, Doctor Dummerar
behaved as handsomely upon the occasion as the Presbyterian

incumbent had done. It is true, that in a sermon which he preached in the Castle hall to several of the most distinguished Cavalier families, besides a world of boys from the village, who went to see the novel circumstance of a parson in a cassock and surplice, he went at great length into the foulness of the various crimes committed by the rebellious party during the late evil times, and greatly magnified the merciful and peaceful nature of the honourable Lady of the Manor, who condescended to look upon, or receive into her house in the way of friendship and hospitality, men holding the principles which had led to the murder of the King—the slaying and despoiling his loyal subjects—and the plundering and breaking down of the Church of God. But then he wiped all this handsomely up again, with the observation, that since it was the will of their gracious and newly-restored Sovereign, and the pleasure of the worshipful Lady Peveril, that this contumacious and rebellious race should be, for a time, forborne by their faithful subjects, it would be highly proper that all the loyal liegemen should, for the present, eschew subjects of dissension or quarrel with these sons of Shimei; which lesson of patience he enforced by the comfortable assurance, that they could not long abstain from their old rebellious practices; in which case, the Royalists would stand exculpated before God and man, in extirpating them from the face of the earth.

The close observers of the remarkable passages of the times from which we draw the events of our history, have left it upon record, that these two several sermons, much contrary, doubtless, to the intention of the worthy divines by whom they were delivered, had a greater effect in exasperating, than in composing, the disputes betwixt the two factions. Under such evil auspices, and with corresponding forebodings on the mind of Lady Peveril, the day of festivity at length arrived.

By different routes, and forming each a sort of procession, as if the adherents of each party were desirous of exhibiting its strength and numbers, the two several factions approached Martindale Castle; and so distinct did they appear in dress, aspect, and manners, that it seemed as if the revellers of a bridal party, and the sad attendants upon a funeral solemnity, were moving towards the same point from different quarters.

The puritanical party was by far the fewer in numbers, for which two excellent reasons might be given. In the first place, they had enjoyed power for several years, and, of course, became unpopular among the common people, never at any time attached to those, who, being in the immediate possession of authority, are often obliged to employ it in controlling their humours. Besides, the country people of England had, and still have, an animated attachment to field sports, and a natural unrestrained joviality of disposition, which rendered them impatient under the severe discipline of the fanatical preachers; while they were not less naturally discontented with the military despotism of Cromwell's Major-Generals. Secondly, the people were fickle as usual, and the return of the King had novelty in it, and was therefore popular. The side of the Puritans was also deserted at this period by a numerous class of more thinking and prudential persons, who never forsook them till they became unfortunate. These sagacious personages were called in that age the Waiters upon Providence, and deemed it a high delinquency towards Heaven if they afforded countenance to any cause longer than it was favoured by fortune.

But, though thus forsaken by the fickle and the selfish, a solemn enthusiasm, a stern and determined depth of principle, a confidence in the sincerity of their own motives, and the manly English pride which inclined them to cling to their former opinions, like the traveller in the fable to his cloak, the more strongly that the tempest blew around them, detained in the ranks of the Puritans many, who, if no longer formidable from numbers, were still so from their character. They consisted chiefly of the middling gentry, with others whom industry or successful speculations in commerce or in mining had raised into eminence—the persons who feel most umbrage from the overshadowing aristocracy, and are usually the most vehement in defence of what they hold to be their rights. Their dress was in general studiously simple and unostentatious, or only remarkable by the contradictory affectation of extreme simplicity or carelessness. The dark colour of their cloaks, varying from absolute black to what was called sad-coloured — their steeple-crowned hats, with their broad shadowy brims—their long swords, suspended by a simple strap around the loins, without shoulder-belt, sword-knot, plate, buckles, or any of the other decorations with which the Cavaliers loved to adorn their trusty rapiers,—the shortness of their hair, which made their ears appear of disproportioned size,—above all, the stern and gloomy gravity of their looks, announced their belonging to that class of enthusiasts, who, resolute and undismayed, had cast down the former fabric of government, and who now regarded with somewhat more than suspicion, that which had been so unexpectedly substituted in its stead. There was gloom in their countenances; but it was not that of dejection, far less of despair. They looked like veterans after a defeat, which may have checked their career and wounded their pride, but has left their courage undiminished.

The melancholy, now become habitual, which overcast Major Bridgenorth's countenance, well qualified him to act as the chief of the group who now advanced from the village. When they reached the point by which they were first to turn aside into the wood which surrounded the Castle, they felt a momentary impression of degradation, as if they were yielding the high road to their old and oft-defeated enemies the Cavaliers. When they began to ascend the winding path, which had been the daily passage of the cattle, the opening of the wooded glade gave them a view of the Castle ditch, half choked with the rubbish of the breach, and of the breach itself, which was made at the angle of a large square flanking-tower, one-half of which had been battered into ruins, while the other fragment remained in a state strangely shattered and precarious, and seemed to be tottering above the huge aperture in the wall. A stern still smile was exchanged among the Puritans, as the sight reminded them of the victories of former days. Holdfast Clegg, a millwright of Derby, who had been himself active at the siege, pointed to the breach, and said, with a grim smile to Mr. Solsgrace, "I little thought, that when my own hand helped to level the cannon which Oliver pointed against yon tower, we should have been obliged to climb like foxes up the very walls which we won by our bow and by our spear. Methought these malignants had then enough of shutting their gates and making high their horn against us."

"Be patient, my brother," said Solsgrace; "be patient, and let not thy soul be disquieted. We enter not this high place dishonourably, seeing we ascend by the gate which the Lord opened to the godly."

The words of the pastor were like a spark to gunpowder. The countenances of the mournful retinue suddenly expanded, and, accepting what had fallen from him as an omen and a light from heaven how they were to interpret their present situation, they uplifted, with one consent, one of the triumphant songs in which the Israelites celebrated the victories which had been vouchsafed to them over the heathen inhabitants of the Promised Land :—

" Let God arise, and then His foes
    Shall turn themselves to flight,
His enemies for fear shall run,
    And scatter out of sight ;

And as wax melts before the fire,
    And wind blows smoke away,
So in the presence of the Lord,
    The wicked shall decay.

God's army twenty thousand is,
    Of angels bright and strong,
The Lord also in Sinai
    Is present them among.

Thou didst, O Lord, ascend on high,
And captive led'st them all,
Who, in times past, Thy chosen flock
In bondage did enthral."

These sounds of devotional triumph reached the joyous band of the Cavaliers, who, decked in whatever pomp their repeated misfortunes and impoverishment had left them, were moving towards the same point, though by a different road, and were filling the principal avenue to the Castle, with tiptoe mirth and revelry. The two parties were strongly contrasted; for, during that period of civil dissension, the manners of the different factions distinguished them as completely as separate uniforms might have done. If the Puritan was affectedly plain in his dress, and ridiculously precise in his manners, the Cavalier often carried his love of ornament into tawdry finery, and his contempt of hypocrisy into licentious profligacy. Gay gallant fellows, young and old, thronged together towards the ancient Castle, with general and joyous manifestation of those spirits, which, as they had been buoyant enough to support their owners during the worst of times, as they termed Oliver's usurpation, were now so inflated as to transport them nearly beyond the reach of sober reason. Feathers waved, lace glittered, spears jingled, steeds caracoled; and here and there a petronel, or pistol, was fired off by some one, who found his own natural talents for making a noise inadequate to the dignity of the occasion. Boys—for, as we said before, the rabble were with the uppermost party, as usual—halloo'd and whooped, "Down with the Rump," and "Fie upon Oliver!" Musical instruments, of as many different fashions as were then in use, played all at once, and without any regard to each other's tune; and the glee of the occasion, while it reconciled the pride of the high-born of the party to fraternise with the general rout, derived an additional zest from the conscious triumph, that their exultation was heard by their neighbours, the crestfallen Roundheads.

When the loud and sonorous swell of the psalm-tune, multiplied by all the echoes of the cliffs and ruinous halls, came full upon their ear, as if to warn them how little they were to reckon upon the depression of their adversaries, at first it was answered with a scornful laugh, raised to as much height as the scoffers' lungs would permit, in order that it might carry to the psalmodists the contempt of their auditors; but this was a forced exertion of party spleen. There is something in melancholy feelings more natural to an imperfect and suffering state than in those of gaiety, and when they are brought into collision, the former seldom fail to triumph. If a funeral-train and wedding-procession were to meet unexpectedly, it will readily be allowed that the mirth of the last would be speedily merged in the gloom of the others. But the Cavaliers, moreover, had sympathies of a different kind. The psalm-tune, which now came rolling on their ear, had been heard too often, and upon too many occasions had preceded victory gained over the malignants, to permit them, even in their triumph, to hear it without emotion. There was a sort of pause, of which the party themselves seemed rather ashamed, until the silence was broken by the stout old knight, Sir Jasper Cranbourne, whose gallantry was so universally acknowledged, that he could afford, if we may use such an expression, to confess emotions, which men whose courage was in any respect liable to suspicion, would have thought it imprudent to acknowledge.

"Adad," said the old Knight, "may I never taste claret again, if that is not the very tune with which the prick-eared villains began their onset at Wiggan Lane, where they trowled us down like so many ninepins! Faith, neighbours, to say truth, and shame the devil, I did not like the sound of it above half."

"If I thought the round-headed rogues did it in scorn of us," said Dick Wildblood of the Dale, "I would cudgel their psalmody out of their peasantly throats with this very truncheon;" a motion which, being seconded by old Roger Raine, the drunken tapster of the Peveril Arms in the village, might have brought on a general battle, but that Sir Jasper forbade the feud.

"We'll have no ranting, Dick," said the old Knight to the young Franklin; "adad, man, we'll have none, for three reasons: first, because it would be ungentle to Lady Peveril; then, because it is against the King's peace; and, lastly, Dick, because if we did set on the psalm-singing knaves, thou mightest come by the worst, my boy, as has chanced to thee before."

"Who, I! Sir Jasper?" answered Dick—"I come by the worst!—I'll be d—d if it ever happened but in that accursed lane, where we had no more flank, front, or rear, than if we had been so many herrings in a barrel."

"That was the reason, I fancy," answered Sir Jasper, "that you, to mend the matter, scrambled into the hedge, and stuck there, horse and man, till I beat thee through it with my leading-staff; and then, instead of charging to the front, you went right-about, and away as fast as your feet would carry you."

This reminiscence produced a laugh at Dick's expense, who was known, or at least suspected, to have more tongue in his head than mettle in his bosom. And this sort of rallying on the part of the Knight having fortunately abated the resentment which had begun to awaken in the breasts of the royalist cavalcade, farther cause for offence was removed, by the sudden ceasing of the sounds which they had been disposed to interpret into those of premeditated insult.

This was owing to the arrival of the Puritans at the bottom of the large and wide breach, which had been formerly made in the wall of the Castle by their victorious cannon. The sight of its gaping heaps of rubbish, and disjointed masses of building, up which slowly winded a narrow and steep path, such as is made amongst ancient ruins by the rare passage of those who occasionally visit them, was calculated, when contrasted with the grey and solid massiveness of the towers and curtains which yet stood uninjured, to remind them of their victory over the stronghold of their enemies, and how they had bound nobles and princes with fetters of iron.

But feelings more suitable to the purpose of their visit to Martindale Castle, were awakened in the bosoms even of these stern sectaries, when the Lady of the Castle, still in the very prime of beauty and of womanhood, appeared at the top of the breach with her principal female attendants, to receive her guests with the honour and courtesy becoming her invitation. She had laid aside the black dress which had been her sole attire for several years, and was arrayed with a splendour not unbecoming her high descent and quality. Jewels, indeed, she had none; but her long and dark hair was surmounted with a chaplet made of oak leaves, interspersed with lilies; the former being the emblem of the King's preservation in the Royal Oak, and the latter of his happy Restoration. What rendered her presence still more interesting to those who looked on her, was the presence of the two children whom she held in either hand; one of whom was well known to them all to be the child of their leader, Major Bridgenorth, who had been restored to life and health by the almost maternal care of the Lady Peveril.

If even the inferior persons of the party felt the healing influence of her presence, thus accompanied, poor Bridgenorth was almost overwhelmed with it. The strictness of his cast and manners permitted him not to sink on his knee, and kiss the hand which held his little orphan; but the deepness of his obeisance—the faltering tremor of his voice—and the glistening of his eye, showed a grateful respect for the lady whom he addressed, deeper and more reverential than could have been expressed even by Persian prostration. A few courteous and mild words, expressive of the pleasure she found in once more seeing her neighbours as her friends—a few kind inquiries, addressed to the principal individuals among her guests, concerning their families and connections, completed her triumph over angry thoughts and dangerous recollections,

and disposed men's bosoms to sympathise with the purposes
of the meeting.

Even Solsgrace himself, although imagining himself bound
by his office and duty to watch over and counteract the wiles
of the "Amalekitish woman," did not escape the sympathetic
infection; being so much struck with the marks of peace and
good-will exhibited by Lady Peveril, that he immediately
raised the psalm—

> " O what a happy thing it is,
> And joyful, for to see
> Brethren to dwell together in
> Friendship and unity ! "

Accepting this salutation as a mark of courtesy repaid, the
Lady Peveril marshalled in person this party of her guests
to the apartment, where ample good cheer was provided for
them; and had even the patience to remain while Master
Nehemiah Solsgrace pronounced a benediction of portentous
length, as an introduction to the banquet. Her presence
was in some measure a restraint on the worthy divine, whose
prolusion lasted the longer, and was the more intricate and
embarrassed, that he felt himself debarred from rounding it
off by his usual alliterative petition for deliverance from Popery,
Prelacy, and Peveril of the Peak, which had become so habitual
to him, that, after various attempts to conclude with some
other form of words, he found himself at last obliged to pronounce the first words of his usual *formula* aloud, and mutter
the rest in such a manner as not to be intelligible even by
those who stood nearest to him.

The minister's silence was followed by all the various sounds
which announce the onset of a hungry company on a well-
furnished table ; and at the same time gave the lady an opportunity to leave the apartment, and look to the accommodation
of her other company. She felt, indeed, that it was high time
to do so ; and that the royalist guests might be disposed to
misapprehend, or even to resent, the prior attentions which
she had thought it prudent to offer to the Puritans.

These apprehensions were not altogether ill-founded. It was
in vain that the steward had displayed the royal standard, with
its proud motto of *Tandem Triumphans,* on one of the great
towers which flanked the main entrance of the Castle ; while,
from the other, floated the banner of Peveril of the Peak, under
which many of those who now approached had fought during
all the vicissitudes of civil war. It was in vain he repeated
his clamorous "Welcome, noble Cavaliers ! welcome, generous
gentlemen !" There was a slight murmur amongst them, that
their welcome ought to have come from the mouth of the

Colonel's lady—not from that of a menial. Sir Jasper Cranbourne, who had sense as well as spirit and courage, and who
was aware of his fair cousin's motives, having been indeed
consulted by her upon all the arrangements which she had
adopted, saw matters were in such a state that no time ought
to be lost in conducting the guests to the banqueting apartment, where a fortunate diversion from all these topics of rising
discontent might be made, at the expense of the good cheer of
all sorts, which the lady's care had so liberally provided.

The stratagem of the old soldier succeeded in its utmost
extent. He assumed the great oaken-chair usually occupied
by the steward at his audits ; and Dr. Dummerar having pronounced a brief Latin benediction (which was not the less
esteemed by the hearers that none of them understood it), Sir
Jasper exhorted the company to wet their appetites to the
dinner by a brimming cup to his Majesty's health, filled as
high and as deep as their goblets would permit. In a moment
all was bustle, with the clang of wine-cups and of flagons. In
another moment the guests were on their feet like so many
statues, all hushed as death, but with eyes glancing with expectation, and hands outstretched, which displayed their loyal
brimmers. The voice of Sir Jasper, clear, sonorous, and emphatic, as the sound of his war-trumpet, announced the health
of the restored Monarch, hastily echoed back by the assemblage,
impatient to render it due homage. Another brief pause was
filled by the draining of their cups, and the mustering breath
to join in a shout so loud, that not only the rafters of the old
hall trembled while they echoed it back, but the garlands of
oaken boughs and flowers with which they were decorated,
waved wildly, and rustled as if agitated by a sudden whirlwind.
This rite observed, the company proceeded to assail the good
cheer with which the table groaned, animated as they were to
the attack both by mirth and melody, for they were attended
by all the minstrels of the district, who, like the Episcopal
clergy, had been put to silence during the reign of the self-
entitled saints of the Commonwealth. The social occupation
of good eating and drinking, the exchange of pledges betwixt
old neighbours who had been fellow-soldiers in the moment of
resistance—fellow-sufferers in the time of depression and sub-
jugation, and were now partners in the same general subject of
congratulation, soon wiped from their memory the trifling cause
of complaint, which in the minds of some had darkened the
festivity of the day ; so that when the Lady Peveril walked
into the hall, accompanied as before with the children and her
female attendants, she was welcomed with the acclamations
due to the mistress of the banquet and of the Castle—the dame
of the noble Knight, who had led most of them to battle with

c

an undaunted and persevering valour, which was worthy of better success.

Her address to them was brief and matronly, yet spoken with so much feeling as found its way to every bosom. She apologised for the lateness of her personal welcome, by reminding them that there were then present in Martindale Castle that day, persons whom recent happy events had converted from enemies into friends, but on whom the latter character was so recently imposed, that she dared not neglect with them any point of ceremonial. But those whom she now addressed, were the best, the dearest, the most faithful friends of her husband's house, to whom and to their valour Peveril had not only owed those successes, which had given them and him fame during the late unhappy times, but to whose courage she in particular had owed the preservation of their leader's life, even when it could not avert defeat. A word or two of heartfelt congratulation on the happy restoration of the royal line and authority, completed all which she had boldness to add, and, bowing gracefully round her, she lifted a cup to her lips as if to welcome her guests.

There still remained, and especially amongst the old Cavaliers of the period, some glimmering of that spirit which inspired Froissart, when he declares that a knight hath double courage at need, when animated by the looks and words of a beautiful and virtuous woman. It was not until the reign which was commencing at the moment we are treating of, that the unbounded licence of the age, introducing a general course of profligacy, degraded the female sex into mere servants of pleasure, and, in so doing, deprived society of that noble tone of feeling towards the sex, which, considered as a spur to "raise the clear spirit," is superior to every other impulse, save those of religion and of patriotism. The beams of the ancient hall of Martindale Castle instantly rang with a shout louder and shriller than that at which they had so lately trembled, and the names of the Knight of the Peak and his lady were proclaimed amid waving of caps and hats, and universal wishes for their health and happiness.

Under these auspices the Lady Peveril glided from the hall, and left free space for the revelry of the evening.

That of the Cavaliers may be easily conceived, since it had the usual accompaniments of singing, jesting, quaffing of healths, and playing of tunes, which have in almost every age and quarter of the world been the accompaniments of festive cheer. The enjoyments of the Puritans were of a different and less noisy character. They neither sung, jested, heard music, nor drank healths; and yet they seemed not the less, in their own phrase, to enjoy the creature-comforts, which the frailty of humanity rendered grateful to their outward man. Old Whitaker even protested, that, though much the smaller party in point of numbers, they discussed nearly as much sack and claret as his own more jovial associates. But those who considered the steward's prejudices, were inclined to think, that, in order to produce such a result, he must have thrown in his own by-drinkings—no inconsiderable item—to the sum total of the Presbyterian potations.

Without adopting such a partial and scandalous report, we shall only say, that on this occasion, as on most others, the rareness of indulgence promoted the sense of enjoyment, and that those who made abstinence, or at least moderation, a point of religious principle, enjoyed their social meeting the better that such opportunities rarely presented themselves. If they did not actually drink each other's healths, they at least showed, by looking and nodding to each other as they raised their glasses, that they all were sharing the same festive gratification of the appetite, and felt it enhanced, because it was at the same time enjoyed by their friends and neighbours. Religion, as it was the principal topic of their thoughts, became also the chief subject of their conversation, and as they sat together in small separate knots, they discussed doctrinal and metaphysical points of belief, balanced the merits of various preachers, compared the creeds of contending sects, and fortified by scriptural quotations those which they favoured. Some contests arose in the course of these debates, which might have proceeded farther than was seemly, but for the cautious interference of Major Bridgenorth. He suppressed also, in the very bud, a dispute betwixt Gaffer Hodgeson of Charnelycot and the Reverend Mr. Solsgrace, upon the tender subject of lay-preaching and lay-ministering; nor did he think it altogether prudent or decent to indulge the wishes of some of the warmer enthusiasts of the party, who felt disposed to make the rest partakers of their gifts in extemporaneous prayer and exposition. These were absurdities that belonged to the time, which, however, the Major had sense enough to perceive were unfitted, whether the offspring of hypocrisy or enthusiasm, for the present time and place.

The Major was also instrumental in breaking up the party at an early and decorous hour, so that they left the Castle long before their rivals, the Cavaliers, had reached the springtide of their merriment; an arrangement which afforded the greatest satisfaction to the lady, who dreaded the consequences which might not improbably have taken place, had both parties met at the same period and point of retreat.

It was near midnight ere the greater part of the Cavaliers, meaning such as were able to effect their departure without assistance, withdrew to the village of Martindale Moultrassie, with the benefit of the broad moon to prevent the chance of accidents. Their shouts, and the burden of their roaring chorus of—

" The King shall enjoy his own again ! "

were heard with no small pleasure by the lady, heartily glad that the riot of the day was over without the occurrence of any unpleasing accident. The rejoicing was not, however, entirely ended ; for the elevated Cavaliers, finding some of the villagers still on foot around a bonfire on the street, struck merrily in with them—sent to Roger Raine of the Peveril Arms, the loyal publican whom we have already mentioned, for two tubs of merry stingo (as it was termed), and lent their own powerful assistance at the *dusting* it off to the health of the King and the loyal General Monk. Their shouts for a long time disturbed, and even alarmed, the little village ; but no enthusiasm is able to withstand for ever the natural consequences of late hours, and potations pottle-deep. The tumult of the exulting Royalists at last sunk into silence, and the moon and the owl were left in undisturbed sovereignty over the old tower of the village church, which, rising white above a circle of knotty oaks, was tenanted by the bird, and silvered by the planet.

CHAPTER V

'Twas when they raised, 'mid sap and siege,
The banners of their rightful liege,
    At their she-captain's call,
Who, miracle of womankind !
Lent mettle to the meanest hind
    That mann'd her castle wall.
                        —WILLIAM S. ROSE.

ON the morning succeeding the feast, the Lady Peveril, fatigued with the exertions and the apprehensions of the former day, kept her apartment for two or three hours later than her own active habits, and the matutinal custom of the time, rendered usual. Meanwhile, Mistress Ellesmere, a person of great trust in the family, and who assumed much authority in her mistress's absence, laid her orders upon Deborah, the governante, immediately to carry the children to their airing in the park, and not to let any one enter the gilded chamber, which was usually their sporting-place. Deborah, who often rebelled, and sometimes successfully, against the deputed authority of Ellesmere, privately resolved that it was about to rain, and that the gilded chamber was a more suitable place for the children's exercise than the wet grass of the park on a raw morning.

But a woman's brain is sometimes as inconstant as a popular assembly; and presently after she had voted the morning was like to be rainy, and that the gilded chamber was the fittest play-room for the children, Mistress Deborah came to the somewhat inconsistent resolution, that the park was the fittest place for her own morning walk. It is certain, that during the unrestrained jovialty of the preceding evening, she had danced till midnight with Lance Outram the park-keeper; but how far the seeing him just pass the window in his woodland trim, with a feather in his hat, and a crossbow under his arm, influenced the discrepancy of the opinions Mistress Deborah formed concerning the weather, we are far from presuming to guess. It is enough for us, that, so soon as Mistress Ellesmere's back was turned, Mistress Deborah carried the children into the gilded chamber, not without a strict charge (for we must do her justice) to Master Julian to take care of his little wife, Mistress Alice; and then, having taken so satisfactory a precaution, she herself glided into the park by the glass-door of the still-room, which was nearly opposite to the great breach.

The gilded chamber in which the children were, by this arrangement, left to amuse themselves, without better guardianship than what Julian's manhood afforded, was a large apartment, hung with stamped Spanish leather, curiously gilded, representing, in a manner now obsolete, but far from unpleasing, a series of tilts and combats betwixt the Saracens of Grenada, and the Spaniards under the command of King Ferdinand and Queen Isabella, during that memorable siege, which was terminated by the overthrow of the last fragments of the Moorish empire in Spain.

The little Julian was careering about the room for the amusement of his infant friend, as well as his own, mimicking with a reed the menacing attitude of the Abencerrages and Zegris engaged in the Eastern sport of hurling the JERID, or javelin; and at times sitting down beside her, and caressing her into silence and good humour, when the petulant or timid child chose to become tired of remaining an inactive spectator of his boisterous sport; when, on a sudden, he observed one of the panelled compartments of the leather hangings slide apart, so as to show a fair hand, with its fingers resting upon its edge, prepared, it would seem, to push it still farther back. Julian was much surprised, and somewhat frightened, at what he witnessed, for the tales of the nursery had strongly impressed on his mind the terrors of the invisible world. Yet, naturally bold and high-spirited, the little champion placed himself beside his defenceless sister, continuing to brandish his weapon in her defence, as boldly as he had himself been an Abencerrage of Grenada.

The panel, on which his eye was fixed, gradually continued to slide back, and display more and more the form to which the hand appertained, until, in the dark aperture which was disclosed, the children saw the figure of a lady in a mourning dress, past the meridian of life, but whose countenance still retained traces of great beauty, although the predominant character both of her features and person was an air of almost royal dignity. After pausing a moment on the threshold of the portal which she had thus unexpectedly disclosed, and looking with some surprise at the children, whom she had not probably observed while engaged with the management of the panel, the stranger stepped into the apartment, and the panel, upon a touch of a spring, closed behind her so suddenly, that Julian almost doubted it had ever been open, and began to apprehend that the whole apparition had been a delusion.

The stately lady, however, advanced to him, and said, " Are not you the little Peveril ? "

" Yes," said the boy, reddening, not altogether without a juvenile feeling of that rule of chivalry which forbade any one to disown his name, whatever danger might be annexed to the avowal of it.

" Then," said the stately stranger, " go to your mother's room, and tell her to come instantly to speak with me."

" I wo'not," said the little Julian.

" How ? " said the lady,—" so young and so disobedient ?— but you do but follow the fashion of the time. Why will you not go, my pretty boy, when I ask it of you as a favour ? "

" I would go, madam," said the boy, " but "—and he stopped short, still drawing back as the lady advanced on him, but still holding by the hand Alice Bridgenorth, who, too young to understand the nature of the dialogue, clung, trembling, to her companion.

The stranger saw his embarrassment, smiled, and remained standing fast, while she asked the child once more, " What are you afraid of, my brave boy—and why should you not go to your mother on my errand ? "

" Because," answered Julian firmly, " if I go, little Alice must stay alone with you."

" You are a gallant fellow," said the lady, " and will not disgrace your blood. which never left the weak without pro- tection."

The boy understood her not, and still gazed with anxious apprehension, first on her who addressed him, and then upon his little companion, whose eyes, with the vacant glance of

infancy, wandered from the figure of the lady to that of her
companion and protector, and at length, infected by a portion
of the fear which the latter's magnanimous efforts could not
entirely conceal, she flew into Julian's arms, and, clinging to
him, greatly augmented his alarm, and by screaming aloud,
rendered it very difficult for him to avoid the sympathetic fear
which impelled him to do the same.

There was something in the manner and bearing of this unexpected inmate which might justify awe at least, if not fear,
when joined to the singular and mysterious mode in which she
had made her appearance. Her dress was not remarkable, being
the hood and female riding attire of the time, such as was worn
by the inferior class of gentlewomen; but her black hair was
very long, and, several locks having escaped from under her
hood, hung down dishevelled on her neck and shoulders. Her
eyes were deep black, keen, and piercing, and her features had
something of a foreign expression. When she spoke, her language was marked by a slight foreign accent, although, in construction, it was pure English. Her slightest tone and gesture
had the air of one accustomed to command and to be obeyed;
the recollection of which probably suggested to Julian the
apology he afterwards made for being frightened, that he took
the stranger for an "enchanted queen."

While the stranger lady and the children thus confronted
each other, two persons entered almost at the same instant,
but from different doors, whose haste showed that they had
been alarmed by the screams of the latter.

The first was Major Bridgenorth, whose ears had been
alarmed with the cries of his child, as he entered the hall,
which corresponded with what was called the gilded chamber.
His intention had been to remain in the more public apartment,
until the Lady Peveril should make her appearance, with the
good-natured purpose of assuring her that the preceding day of
tumult had passed in every respect agreeably to his friends, and
without any of those alarming consequences which might have
been apprehended from a collision betwixt the parties. But
when it is considered how severely he had been agitated by
apprehensions for his child's safety and health, too well justified
by the fate of those who had preceded her, it will not be
thought surprising that the infantine screams of Alice induced
him to break through the barriers of form, and intrude farther
into the interior of the house than a sense of strict propriety
might have warranted.

He burst into the gilded chamber, therefore, by a side-door
and narrow passage, which communicated betwixt that apartment and the hall, and, snatching the child up in his arms,
endeavoured, by a thousand caresses, to stifle the screams which

burst yet more violently from the little girl, on beholding herself in the arms of one to whose voice and manner she was,
but for one brief interview, an entire stranger.

Of course, Alice's shrieks were redoubled, and seconded by
those of Julian Peveril, who, on the appearance of this second
intruder, was frightened into resignation of every more manly
idea of rescue than that which consisted in invoking assistance
at the very top of his lungs.

Alarmed by this noise, which in half a minute became very
clamorous, Lady Peveril, with whose apartment the gilded
chamber was connected by a private door of communication
opening into her wardrobe, entered on the scene. The instant
she appeared, the little Alice, extricating herself from the grasp
of her father, ran towards *her* protectress, and when she had
once taken hold of her skirts, not only became silent, but turned
her large blue eyes, in which the tears were still glistening, with
a look of wonder rather than alarm, towards the strange lady.
Julian manfully brandished his reed, a weapon which he had
never parted with during the whole alarm, and stood prepared
to assist his mother if there should be danger in the encounter
betwixt her and the stranger.

In fact, it might have puzzled an older person to account for
the sudden and confused pause which the Lady Peveril made,
as she gazed on her unexpected guest, as if dubious whether she
did, or did not recognise, in her still beautiful though wasted
and emaciated features, a countenance which she had known
well under far different circumstances.

The stranger seemed to understand her cause of hesitation,
for she said in that heart-thrilling voice which was peculiarly
her own—

"Time and misfortune have changed me much, Margaret—
that every mirror tells me—yet methinks, Margaret Stanley
might still have known Charlotte de la Tremouille."

The Lady Peveril was little in the custom of giving way to
sudden emotion, but in the present case she threw herself on her
knees in a rapture of mingled joy and grief, and, half embracing
those of the stranger, exclaimed, in broken language—

"My kind, my noble benefactress—the princely Countess of
Derby—the royal Queen in Man—could I doubt your voice,
your features, for a moment—Oh, forgive, forgive me!"

The Countess raised the suppliant kinswoman of her husband's
house, with all the grace of one accustomed from early birth to
receive homage and to grant protection. She kissed the Lady
Peveril's forehead, and passed her hand in a caressing manner
over her face as she said—

"You too are changed, my fair cousin, but it is a change
becomes you, from a pretty and timid maiden to a sage and

comely matron. But my own memory, which I once held a good one, has failed me strangely, if this gentleman be Sir Geoffrey Peveril."

"A kind and good neighbour only, madam," said Lady Peveril; "Sir Geoffrey is at Court."

"I understood so much," said the Countess of Derby, "when I arrived here last night."

"How, madam!" said Lady Peveril—"Did you arrive at Martindale Castle—at the house of Margaret Stanley, where you have such right to command, and did not announce your presence to her?"

"Oh, I know you are a dutiful subject, Margaret," answered the Countess, "though it be in these days a rare character—but it was our pleasure," she added, with a smile, "to travel incognito—and finding you engaged in general hospitality, we desired not to disturb you with our royal presence."

"But how and where were you lodged, madam?" said Lady Peveril; "or why should you have kept secret a visit which would, if made, have augmented tenfold the happiness of every true heart that rejoiced here yesterday?"

"My lodging was well cared for by Ellesmere—your Ellesmere now, as she was formerly mine—she has acted as quartermaster ere now, you know, and on a broader scale; you must excuse her—she had my positive order to lodge me in the most secret part of your Castle"—(here she pointed to the sliding panel)—"she obeyed orders in that, and I suppose also in sending you now hither."

"Indeed I have not yet seen her," said the lady, "and therefore was totally ignorant of a visit so joyful, so surprising."

"And I," said the Countess, "was equally surprised to find none but these beautiful children in the apartment where I thought I heard you moving. Our Ellesmere has become silly—your good-nature has spoiled her—she has forgotten the discipline she learned under me."

"I saw her run through the wood," said the Lady Peveril, after a moment's recollection, "undoubtedly to seek the person who has charge of the children, in order to remove them."

"Your own darlings, I doubt not," said the Countess, looking at the children. "Margaret, Providence has blessed you."

"That is my son," said Lady Peveril, pointing to Julian, who stood devouring their discourse with greedy ear; "the little girl—I may call mine too." Major Bridgenorth, who had in the meantime again taken up his infant, and was engaged in caressing it, set it down as the Countess of Derby spoke, sighed deeply, and walked towards the oriel window. He was well aware that the ordinary rules of courtesy would have rendered it proper that he should withdraw entirely, or at least offer to do so; but he was not a man of ceremonious politeness, and he had a particular interest in the subjects on which the Countess's discourse was likely to turn, which induced him to dispense with ceremony. The ladies seemed indeed scarce to notice his presence. The Countess had now assumed a chair, and motioned to the Lady Peveril to sit upon a stool which was placed by her side. "We will have old times once more, though there are here no roaring of rebel guns to drive you to take refuge at my side, and almost in my pocket."

"I have a gun, madam," said little Julian, "and the park-keeper is to teach me how to fire it next year."

"I will list you for my soldier, then," said the Countess.

"Ladies have no soldiers," said the boy, looking wistfully at her.

"He has the true masculine contempt of our frail sex, I see," said the Countess; "it is born with the insolent varlets of mankind, and shows itself so soon as they are out of their long clothes.—Did Ellesmere never tell you of Latham House and Charlotte of Derby, my little master?"

"A thousand thousand times," said the boy, colouring; "and how the Queen of Man defended it six weeks against three thousand Roundheads, under Rogue Harrison the butcher."

"It was your mother defended Latham House," said the Countess, "not I, my little soldier—Hadst thou been there, thou hadst been the best captain of the three."

"Do not say so, madam," said the boy, "for mamma would not touch a gun for all the universe."

"Not I, indeed, Julian," said his mother; "there I was for certain, but as useless a part of the garrison——"

"You forget," said the Countess, "you nursed our hospital, and made lint for the soldiers' wounds."

"But did not papa come to help you?" said Julian.

"Papa came at last," said the Countess, "and so did Prince Rupert—but not, I think, till they were both heartily wished for.—Do you remember that morning, Margaret, when the round-headed knaves, that kept us pent up so long, retreated without bag or baggage, at the first glance of the Prince's standards appearing on the hill—and how you took every high-crested captain you saw for Peveril of the Peak, that had been your partner three months before at the Queen's mask? Nay, never blush for the thought of it—it was an honest affection—and though it was the music of trumpets that accompanied you both to the old chapel, which was almost entirely ruined by the enemy's bullets; and though Prince Rupert, when he gave you away at the altar, was clad in buff and bandoleer, with pistols in his belt, yet I trust these warlike signs were no type of future discord?"

"Heaven has been kind to me," said Lady Peveril, "in blessing me with an affectionate husband."

"And in preserving him to you," said the Countess, with a deep sigh; "while mine, alas! sealed with his blood his devotion to his king *—Oh, had he lived to see this day!"

"Alas! alas! that he was not permitted!" answered Lady Peveril; "how had that brave and noble Earl rejoiced in the unhoped-for redemption of our captivity!"

The Countess looked on Lady Peveril with an air of surprise.

"Thou hast not then heard, cousin, how it stands with our house?—How indeed had my noble lord wondered, had he been told that the very monarch for whom he had laid down his noble life on the scaffold at Bolton-le-Moor, should make it his first act of restored monarchy to complete the destruction of our property, already well-nigh ruined in the royal cause, and to persecute me his widow!"

"You astonish me, madam!" said the Lady Peveril. "It cannot be, that you—that you, the wife of the gallant, the faithful, the murdered Earl — you, Countess of Derby, and Queen in Man—you, who took on you even the character of a soldier, and seemed a man when so many men proved women —that you should sustain evil from the event which has fulfilled—exceeded — the hopes of every faithful subject — it cannot be!"

"Thou art as simple, I see, in this world's knowledge as ever, my fair cousin," answered the Countess. "This restoration, which has given others security, has placed me in danger—this change which relieved other Royalists, scarce less zealous, I presume to think, than I—has sent me here a fugitive, and in concealment, to beg shelter and assistance from you, fair cousin."

"From me," answered the Lady Peveril—"from me, whose youth your kindness sheltered—from the wife of Peveril, your gallant Lord's companion in arms—you have a right to command everything; but, alas! that you should need such assistance as I can render—forgive me, but it seems like some ill-omened vision of the night—I listen to your words as if I hoped to be relieved from their painful import by awaking."

"It is indeed a dream—a vision," said the Countess of Derby; "but it needs no seer to read it—the explanation hath been long since given—Put not your faith in princes. I can soon remove your surprise.—This gentleman, your friend, is doubtless *honest?*"

The Lady Peveril well knew that the Cavaliers, like other factions, usurped to themselves the exclusive denomination of

---

* The Earl of Derby and King in Man was beheaded at Bolton-on-the-Moors, after having been made prisoner in a previous skirmish in Wiggan Lane.

the *honest* party, and she felt some difficulty in explaining that her visitor was not honest in that sense of the word.

"Had we not better retire, madam?" she said to the Countess, rising, as if in order to attend her. But the Countess retained her seat.

"It was but a question of habit," she said; "the gentleman's principles are nothing to me, for what I have to tell you is widely blazed, and I care not who hears my share of it. You remember—you must have heard, for I think Margaret Stanley would not be indifferent to my fate—that after my husband's murder at Bolton, I took up the standard which he never dropped until his death, and displayed it with my own hand in our Sovereignty of Man."

"I did indeed hear so, madam," said the Lady Peveril; "and that you had bidden a bold defiance to the rebel government, even after all other parts of Britain had submitted to them. My husband, Sir Geoffrey, designed at one time to have gone to your assistance with some few followers; but we learned that the island was rendered to the Parliament party, and that you, dearest lady, were thrown into prison."

"But you heard not," said the Countess, "how that disaster befell me.—Margaret, I would have held out that island against the knaves as long as the sea continued to flow around it. Till the shoals which surround it had become safe anchorage—till its precipices had melted beneath the sunshine—till of all its strong abodes and castles not one stone remained upon another, —would I have defended against these villainous hypocritical rebels, my dear husband's hereditary dominion. The little kingdom of Man should have been yielded only when not an arm was left to wield a sword, not a finger to draw a trigger in its defence. But treachery did what force could never have done. When we had foiled various attempts upon the island by open force—treason accomplished what Blake and Lawson, with their floating castles, had found too hazardous an enterprise— a base rebel, whom we had nursed in our own bosoms, betrayed us to the enemy. This wretch was named Christian——"

Major Bridgenorth started and turned towards the speaker, but instantly seemed to recollect himself, and again averted his face. The Countess proceeded, without noticing the interruption, which, however, rather surprised Lady Peveril, who was acquainted with her neighbour's general habits of indifference and apathy, and therefore the more surprised at his testifying such sudden symptoms of interest. She would once again have moved the Countess to retire to another apartment, but Lady Derby proceeded with too much vehemence to endure interruption.

"This Christian," she said, "had eat of my lord his sovereign's bread, and drunk of his cup, even from childhood—for his fathers had been faithful servants to the House of Man and Derby. He himself had fought bravely by my husband's side, and enjoyed all his confidence; and when my princely Earl was martyred by the rebels, he recommended to me, amongst other instructions communicated in the last message I received from him, to continue my confidence in Christian's fidelity. I obeyed, although I never loved the man. He was cold and phlegmatic, and utterly devoid of that sacred fire which is the incentive to noble deeds, suspected, too, of leaning to the cold metaphysics of Calvinistic sublety. But he was brave, wise, and experienced, and, as the event proved, possessed but too much interest with the islanders. When these rude people saw themselves without hope of relief, and pressed by a blockade, which brought want and disease into their island, they began to fall off from the faith which they had hitherto shown."

"What!" said the Lady Peveril, "could they forget what was due to the widow of their benefactor—she who had shared with the generous Derby the task of bettering their condition?"

"Do not blame them," said the Countess; "the rude herd acted but according to their kind—in present distress they forgot former benefits, and, nursed in their earthen hovels, with spirits suited to their dwellings, they were incapable of feeling the glory which is attached to constancy in suffering. But that Christian should have headed their revolt—that he, born a gentleman, and bred under my murdered Derby's own care in all that was chivalrous and noble—that *he* should have forgot a hundred benefits — why do I talk of benefits?—that he should have forgotten that kindly intercourse which binds man to man far more than the reciprocity of obligation—that he should have headed the ruffians who broke suddenly into my apartment—immured me with my infants in one of my own castles, and assumed or usurped the tyranny of the island —that this should have been done by William Christian, my vassal, my servant, my friend, was a deed of ungrateful treachery, which even this age of treason will scarcely parallel!"

"And you were then imprisoned," said the Lady Peveril, "and in your own sovereignty?"

"For more than seven years I have endured strict captivity," said the Countess. "I was indeed offered my liberty, and even some means of support, if I would have consented to leave the island, and pledge my word that I would not endeavour to repossess my son in his father's rights. But they little knew the princely house from which I spring—and as little the royal house of Stanley which I uphold, who hoped to humble Charlotte of Tremouille into so base a composition. I would rather have starved in the darkest and lowest vault of Rushin Castle, than have consented to aught which might diminish in one hair's-breadth the right of my son over his father's sovereignty!"

"And could not your firmness, in a case where hope seemed lost, induce them to be generous and dismiss you without conditions?"

"They knew me better than thou dost, wench," answered the Countess; "once at liberty, I had not been long without the means of disturbing their usurpation, and Christian would have as soon uncaged a lioness to combat with, as have given me the slightest power of returning to the struggle with him. But time had liberty and revenge in store—I had still friends and partisans in the island, though they were compelled to give way to the storm. Even among the islanders at large, most had been disappointed in the effects which they expected from the change of power. They were loaded with exactions by their new masters, their privileges were abridged, and their immunities abolished, under the pretext of reducing them to the same condition with the other subjects of the pretended republic. When the news arrived of the changes which were current in Britain, these sentiments were privately communicated to me. Calcott and others acted with great zeal and fidelity; and a rising, effected as suddenly and effectually as that which had made me a captive, placed me at liberty and in possession of the sovereignty of Man, as Regent for my son, the youthful Earl of Derby. Do you think I enjoyed that sovereignty long without doing justice on that traitor Christian?"

"How, madam," said Lady Peveril, who, though she knew the high and ambitious spirit of the Countess, scarce anticipated the extremities to which it was capable of hurrying her —"Have you imprisoned Christian?"

"Ay, wench—in that sure prison which felon never breaks from," answered the Countess.

Bridgenorth, who had insensibly approached them, and was listening with an agony of interest which he was unable any longer to suppress, broke in with the stern exclamation—

"Lady, I trust you have not dared——"

The Countess interrupted him in her turn.

"I know not who you are who question—and you know not me when you speak to me of that which I dare, or dare not do. But you seem interested in the fate of this Christian, and you shall hear it.—I was no sooner placed in possession of my rightful power, than I ordered the Dempster of the island to hold upon the traitor a High Court of Justice, with all the formalities of the isle, as prescribed in its oldest records. The Court was held in the open air, before the Dempster and the Keys of the island, assembled under the vaulted cope of heaven, and seated on the terrace of the Zonwald Hill, where of old

Druid and Scald held their courts of judgment. The criminal was heard at length in his own defence, which amounted to little more than those specious allegations of public considera- tion, which are ever used to colour the ugly front of treason. He was fully convicted of his crime, and he received the doom of a traitor."

" But which, I trust, is not yet executed ? " said Lady Peveril, not without an involuntary shudder.

" You are a fool, Margaret," said the Countess sharply; "think you I delayed such an act of justice, until some wretched intrigues of the new English Court might have prompted their interference ? No, wench—he passed from the judgment-seat to the place of execution, with no farther delay than might be necessary for his soul's sake. He was shot to death by a file of musketeers in the common place of execution called Hango Hill."

Bridgenorth clasped his hands together, wrung them, and groaned bitterly.

" As you seem interested for this criminal," added the Countess, addressing Bridgenorth, " I do him but justice in repeating to you, that his death was firm and manly, becoming the general tenor of his life, which, but for that gross act of traitorous ingratitude, had been fair and honourable. But what of that ? The hypocrite is a saint, and the false traitor a man of honour, till opportunity, that faithful touchstone, proves their metal to be base."

" It is false, woman—it is false ! " said Bridgenorth, no longer suppressing his indignation.

" What means this bearing, Master Bridgenorth ? " said Lady Peveril, much surprised. " What is this Christian to you, that you should insult the Countess of Derby under my roof ? "

" Speak not to me of countesses and of ceremonies," said Bridgenorth ; " grief and anger leave me no leisure for idle observances to humour the vanity of overgrown children.—O Christian—worthy, well worthy, of the name thou didst bear ! My friend—my brother—the brother of my blessed Alice— the only friend of my desolate estate ! art thou then cruelly murdered by a female fury, who, but for thee, had deservedly paid with her own blood that of God's saints, which she, as well as her tyrant husband, had spilled like water !—Yes, cruel murderess ! " he continued, addressing the Countess, " he whom thou hast butchered in thy insane vengeance, sacrificed for many a year the dictates of his own conscience to the interest of thy family, and did not desert it till thy frantic zeal for royalty had well-nigh brought to utter perdition the little community in which he was born. Even in confining thee, he acted but as the friends of the madman, who bind him with iron for his own preservation; and for thee, as I can bear witness, he was the only barrier between thee and the wrath of the Commons of England; and but for his earnest remonstrances, thou hadst suffered the penalty of thy malignancy, even like the wicked wife of Ahab."

"Master Bridgenorth," said Lady Peveril, "I will allow for your impatience upon hearing these unpleasing tidings; but there is neither use nor propriety in farther urging this question. If in your grief you forget other restraints, I pray you to remember that the Countess is my guest and kinswoman, and is under such protection as I can afford her. I beseech you, in simple courtesy, to withdraw, as what must needs be the best and most becoming course in these trying circumstances."

"Nay, let him remain," said the Countess, regarding him with composure, not unmingled with triumph; "I would not have it otherwise; I would not that my revenge should be summed up in the stinted gratification which Christian's death hath afforded. This man's rude and clamorous grief only proves that the retribution I have dealt has been more widely felt than by the wretched sufferer himself. I would I knew that it had but made sore as many rebel hearts, as there were loyal breasts afflicted by the death of my princely Derby!"

"So please you, madam," said Lady Peveril, "since Master Bridgenorth hath not the manners to leave us upon my request, we will, if your ladyship lists, leave him, and retire to my apartment.—Farewell, Master Bridgenorth; we will meet hereafter on better terms."

"Pardon me, madam," said the Major, who had been striding hastily through the room, but now stood fast, and drew himself up, as one who has taken a resolution;—"to yourself I have nothing to say but what is respectful; but to this woman I must speak as a magistrate. She has confessed a murder in my presence—the murder too of my brother-in-law—as a man, and as a magistrate, I cannot permit her to pass from hence, excepting under such custody as may prevent her farther flight. She has already confessed that she is a fugitive, and in search of a place of concealment, until she should be able to escape into foreign parts.—Charlotte, Countess of Derby, I attach thee of the crime of which thou hast but now made thy boast."

"I shall not obey your arrest," said the Countess composedly; "I was born to give, but not to receive such orders. What have your English laws to do with my acts of justice and of government, within my son's hereditary kingdom? Am I not Queen in Man, as well as Countess of Derby? A feudatory Sovereign indeed; but yet independent so long as my dues of homage are duly discharged. What right can you assert over me?"

"That given by the precepts of Scripture," answered Bridge-north—"'Whoso spilleth man's blood, by man shall his blood be spilled.' Think not the barbarous privileges of ancient feudal customs will avail to screen you from the punishment due for an Englishman murdered upon pretexts inconsistent with the act of indemnity."

"Master Bridgenorth," said Lady Peveril, "if by fair terms you desist not from your present purpose, I tell you that I neither dare, nor will, permit any violence against this honourable lady within the walls of my husband's castle."

"You will find yourself unable to prevent me from executing my duty, madam," said Bridgenorth, whose native obstinacy now came in aid of his grief and desire of revenge; "I am a magistrate, and act by authority."

"I know not that," said Lady Peveril. "That you *were* a magistrate, Master Bridgenorth, under the late usurping powers, I know well; but till I hear of your having a commission in the name of the King, I now hesitate to obey you as such."

"I shall stand on small ceremony," said Bridgenorth. "Were I no magistrate, every man has title to arrest for murder against the terms of the indemnities held out by the King's proclamations, and I will make my point good."

"What indemnities? What proclamations?" said the Countess of Derby indignantly. "Charles Stuart may, if he pleases (and it doth seem to please him), consort with those whose hands have been red with the blood, and blackened with the plunder, of his father and of his loyal subjects. He may forgive them if he will, and count their deeds good service. What has that to do with this Christian's offence against me and mine? Born a Mankesman—bred and nursed in the island—he broke the laws under which he lived, and died for the breach of them, after the fair trial which they allowed.—Methinks, Margaret, we have enough of this peevish and foolish magistrate—I attend you to your apartment."

Major Bridgenorth placed himself betwixt them and the door, in a manner which showed him determined to interrupt their passage; when the Lady Peveril, who thought she had already showed more deference to him in this matter than her husband was likely to approve of, raised her voice, and called loudly on her steward, Whitaker. That alert person, who had heard high talking, and a female voice with which he was unacquainted, had remained for several minutes stationed in the anteroom, much afflicted with the anxiety of his own curiosity. Of course he entered in an instant.

"Let three of the men instantly take arms," said his lady; "bring them into the anteroom, and wait my farther orders."

CHAPTER VI

You shall have no worse prison than my chamber,
Nor jailer than myself.
                                —THE CAPTAIN.

THE command which Lady Peveril laid on her domestics to arm themselves, was so unlike the usual gentle acquiescence of her manners, that Major Bridgenorth was astonished. "How mean you, madam?" said he; "I thought myself under a friendly roof."

"And you are so, Master Bridgenorth," said the Lady Peveril, without departing from the natural calmness of her voice and manner; "but it is a roof which must not be violated by the outrage of one friend against another."

"It is well, madam," said Bridgenorth, turning to the door of the apartment. "The worthy Master Solsgrace has already foretold, that the time was returned when high houses and proud names should be once more an excuse for the crimes of those who inhabit the one and bear the other. I believed him not, but now see he is wiser than I. Yet think not I will endure this tamely. The blood of my brother—of the friend of my bosom—shall not long call from the altar, 'How long, O Lord, how long!' If there is one spark of justice left in this unhappy England, that proud woman and I shall meet where she can have no partial friend to protect her."

So saying, he was about to leave the apartment, when Lady Peveril said, "You depart not from this place, Master Bridgenorth, unless you give me your word to renounce all purpose against the noble Countess's liberty upon the present occasion."

"I would sooner," answered he, "subscribe to my own dishonour, madam, written down in express words, than to any such composition. If any man offers to interrupt me, his blood be on his own head!" As Major Bridgenorth spoke, Whitaker threw open the door, and showed that, with the alertness of an old soldier, who was not displeased to see things tend once more towards a state of warfare, he had got with him four stout fellows in the Knight of the Peak's livery, well armed with swords and carabines, buff-coats, and pistols at their girdles.

"I will see," said Major Bridgenorth, "if any of these men be so desperate as to stop me, a freeborn Englishman, and a magistrate in the discharge of my duty."

So saying, he advanced upon Whitaker and his armed assistants, with his hand on the hilt of his sword.

"Do not be so desperate, Master Bridgenorth," exclaimed

Lady Peveril ; and added, in the same moment, " Lay hold upon, and disarm him, Whitaker; but do him no injury."

Her commands were obeyed. Bridgenorth, though a man of moral resolution, was not one of those who undertook to cope in person with odds of a description so formidable. He half drew his sword, and offered such show of resistance as made it necessary to secure him by actual force ; but then yielded up his weapon, and declared that, submitting to force which one man was unable to resist, he made those who commanded, and who employed it, responsible for assailing his liberty without a legal warrant.

"Never mind a warrant on a pinch, Master Bridgenorth," said old Whitaker ; "sure enough you have often acted upon a worse yourself. My lady's word is as good a warrant, sure, as Old Noll's commission ; and you bore that many a day, Master Bridgenorth, and, moreover, you laid me in the stocks for drinking the King's health, Master Bridgenorth, and never cared a farthing about the laws of England."

"Hold your saucy tongue, Whitaker," said the Lady Peveril ; "and do you, Master Bridgenorth, not take it to heart that you are detained prisoner for a few hours, until the Countess of Derby can have nothing to fear from your pursuit. I could easily send an escort with her that might bid defiance to any force you could muster; but I wish, Heaven knows, to bury the remembrance of old civil dissensions, not to awaken new. Once more, will you think better on it—assume your sword again, and forget whom you have now seen at Martindale Castle ? "

" Never," said Bridgenorth. " The crime of this cruel woman will be the last of human injuries which I can forget. The last thought of earthly kind which will leave me, will be the desire that justice shall be done on her."

" If such be your sentiments," said Lady Peveril, " though they are more allied to revenge than to justice, I must provide for my friend's safety, by putting restraint upon your person. In this room you will be supplied with every necessary of life, and every convenience; and a message shall relieve your domestics of the anxiety which your absence from the Hall is not unlikely to occasion. When a few hours, at most two days, are over, I will myself relieve you from confinement, and demand your pardon for now acting as your obstinacy compels me to do."

The Major made no answer, but that he was in her hands, and must submit to her pleasure ; and then turned sullenly to the window, as if desirous to be rid of their presence.

The Countess and the Lady Peveril left the apartment arm in arm ; and the lady issued forth her directions to Whitaker concerning the mode in which she was desirous that Bridgenorth should be guarded and treated during his temporary confinement; at the same time explaining to him, that the safety of the Countess of Derby required that he should be closely watched.

In all proposals for the prisoner's security, such as the regular relief of guards, and the like, Whitaker joyfully acquiesced, and undertook, body for body, that he should be detained in captivity for the necessary period. But the old steward was not half so docile when it came to be considered how the captive's bedding and table should be supplied; and he thought Lady Peveril displayed a very undue degree of attention to her prisoner's comforts. "I warrant," he said, "that the cuckoldy Roundhead ate enough of our fat beef yesterday to serve him for a month; and a little fasting will do his health good. Marry, for drink, he shall have plenty of cold water to cool his hot liver, which I will be bound is still hissing with the strong liquors of yesterday. And as for bedding, there are the fine dry boards—more wholesome than the wet straw I lay upon when I was in the stocks, I trow."

"Whitaker," said the lady peremptorily, "I desire you to provide Master Bridgenorth's bedding and food in the way I have signified to you; and to behave yourself towards him in all civility."

"Lack-a-day! yes, my lady," said Whitaker; "you shall have all your directions punctually obeyed; but as an old servant, I cannot but speak my mind."

The ladies retired after this conference with the steward in the antechamber, and were soon seated in another apartment, which was peculiarly dedicated to the use of the mistress of the mansion—having, on the one side, access to the family bedroom; and, on the other, to the still-room which communicated with the garden. There was also a small door which, ascending a few steps, led to that balcony, already mentioned, that overhung the kitchen; and the same passage, by a separate door, admitted to the principal gallery in the chapel; so that the spiritual and temporal affairs of the Castle were placed almost at once within the reach of the same regulating and directing eye.*

In the tapestried room, from which issued these various sally-

---

* This peculiar collocation of apartments may be seen at Haddon Hall, Derbyshire, once a seat of the Vernons, where, in the lady's pew in the chapel, there is a sort of scuttle, which opens into the kitchen, so that the good lady could ever and anon, without much interruption of her religious duties, give an eye that the roast-meat was not permitted to burn, and that the turn-broche did his duty.

ports, the Countess and Lady Peveril were speedily seated;
and the former, smiling upon the latter, said, as she took her
hand, "Two things have happened to-day, which might have
surprised me, if anything ought to surprise me in such times:
—the first is, that yonder roundheaded fellow should have
dared to use such insolence in the house of Peveril of the Peak.
If your husband is yet the same honest and downright Cavalier
whom I once knew, and had chanced to be at home, he would
have thrown the knave out of window. But what I wonder at
still more, Margaret, is your generalship. I hardly thought you
had courage sufficient to have taken such decided measures,
after keeping on terms with the man so long. When he spoke
of justices and warrants, you looked so overawed that I thought
I felt the clutch of the parish-beadles on my shoulder, to drag
me to prison as a vagrant."

"We owe Master Bridgenorth some deference, my dearest
lady," answered the Lady Peveril; "he has served us often
and kindly, in these late times; but neither he, nor any one
else, shall insult the Countess of Derby in the house of Margaret
Stanley."

"Thou art become a perfect heroine, Margaret," replied the
Countess.

"Two sieges, and alarms innumerable," said Lady Peveril,
"may have taught me presence of mind. My courage is, I
believe, as slender as ever."

"Presence of mind *is* courage," answered the Countess.
"Real valour consists not in being insensible to danger, but in
being prompt to confront and disarm it;—and we may have
present occasion for all that we possess," she added, with some
slight emotion, "for I hear the trampling of horses' steps on the
pavement of the court."

In one moment, the boy Julian, breathless with joy, came
flying into the room, to say that papa was returned, with
Lamington and Sam Brewer; and that he was himself to ride
Black Hastings to the stable. In the second, the tramp of the
honest Knight's heavy jack-boots was heard, as, in his haste to
see his lady, he ascended the staircase by two steps at a time.
He burst into the room; his manly countenance and disordered
dress showing marks that he had been riding fast; and without
looking to any one else, caught his good lady in his arms, and
kissed her a dozen of times.—Blushing, and with some difficulty,
Lady Peveril extricated herself from Sir Geoffrey's arms; and
in a voice of bashful and gentle rebuke, bid him, for shame,
observe who was in the room.

"One," said the Countess, advancing to him, "who is right
glad to see that Sir Geoffrey Peveril, though turned courtier
and favourite, still values the treasure which she had some

share in bestowing upon him. You cannot have forgot the
raising of the leaguer of Latham House!"

"The noble Countess of Derby!" said Sir Geoffrey, doffing
his plumed hat with an air of deep deference, and kissing with
much reverence the hand which she held out to him; "I am
as glad to see your ladyship in my poor house, as I would be
to hear that they had found a vein of lead in the Brown Tor.
I rode hard, in the hope of being your escort through the
country. I feared you might have fallen into bad hands, hearing
there was a knave sent out with a warrant from the Council."

"When heard you so? and from whom?"

"It was from Cholmondley of Vale Royal," said Sir Geoffrey;
"he is come down to make provision for your safety through
Cheshire; and I promised to bring you there in safety. Prince
Rupert, Ormond, and other friends, do not doubt the matter
will be driven to a fine; but they say the Chancellor, and
Harry Bennet, and some others of the over-sea counsellors, are
furious at what they call a breach of the King's proclamation.
Hang them, say I !—They left us to bear all the beating; and
now they are incensed that we should wish to clear scores with
those who rode us like nightmares!"

"What did they talk of for my chastisement?" said the
Countess.

"I wot not," said Sir Geoffrey; "some friends, as I said,
from our kind Cheshire, and others, tried to bring it to a fine;
but some, again, spoke of nothing but the Tower, and a long
imprisonment."

"I have suffered imprisonment long enough for King Charles's
sake," said the Countess; "and have no mind to undergo it at
his hand. Besides, if I am removed from the personal superintendence of my son's dominions in Man, I know not what
new usurpation may be attempted there. I must be obliged
to you, cousin, to contrive that I may get in security to Vale
Royal, and from thence I know I shall be guarded safely to
Liverpool."

"You may rely on my guidance and protection, noble lady,"
answered her host, "though you had come here at midnight,
and with the rogue's head in your apron, like Judith in the
Holy Apocrypha, which I joy to hear once more aloud in
churches."

"Do the gentry resort much to the Court?" said the lady.

"Ay, madam," replied Sir Geoffrey; "and according to our
saying, when miners do begin to bore in these parts, it is *for
the grace of God, and what they there may find.*"

"Meet the old Cavaliers with much countenance?" continued the Countess.

"Faith, madam, to speak truth," replied the Knight, "the

King hath so gracious a manner, that it makes every man's hopes blossom, though we have seen but few that have ripened into fruit."

"You have not, yourself, my cousin," answered the Countess, "had room to complain of ingratitude, I trust? Few have less deserved it at the King's hand."

Sir Geoffrey was unwilling, like most prudent persons, to own the existence of expectations which had proved fallacious, yet had too little art in his character to conceal his disappointment entirely. "Who, I, madam?" he said; "Alas! what should a poor country knight expect from the King, besides the pleasure of seeing him in Whitehall once more, and enjoying his own again? And his Majesty was very gracious when I was presented, and spoke to me of Worcester, and of my horse, Black Hastings—he had forgot his name, though—faith, and mine, too, I believe, had not Prince Rupert whispered it to him. And I saw some old friends, such as his Grace of Ormond, Sir Marmaduke Langdale, Sir Philip Musgrave, and so forth; and had a jolly rouse or two, to the tune of old times."

"I should have thought so many wounds received—so many dangers risked—such considerable losses—merited something more than a few smooth words," said the Countess.

"Nay, my lady, there were other friends of mine who had the same thought," answered Peveril. "Some were of opinion that the loss of so many hundred acres of fair land was worth some reward of honour at least; and there were who thought my descent from William the Conqueror—craving your ladyship's pardon for boasting it in your presence—would not have become a higher rank or title worse than the pedigree of some who have been promoted. But what said the witty Duke of Buckingham, forsooth? (whose grandsire was a Lei'stershire Knight—rather poorer, and scarcely so well-born as myself—Why, he said, that if all of my degree who deserved well of the King in the late times were to be made peers, the House of Lords must meet upon Salisbury Plain!"

"And that bad jest passed for a good argument!" said the Countess; "and well it might, where good arguments pass for bad jests. But here comes one I must be acquainted with."

This was little Julian, who now re-entered the hall, leading his little sister, as if he had brought her to bear witness to the boastful tale which he told his father, of his having manfully ridden Black Hastings to the stable-yard, alone in the saddle; and that Saunders, though he walked by the horse's head, did not once put his hand upon the rein, and Brewer, though he stood beside him, scarce held him by the knee. The father kissed the boy heartily; and the Countess, calling him to her so soon as Sir Geoffrey had set him down, kissed his forehead

also, and then surveyed all his features with a keen and penetrating eye.

"He is a true Peveril," said she, "mixed as he should be
with some touch of the Stanley. Cousin, you must grant me
my boon, and when I am safely established, and have my
present affair arranged, you must let me have this little Julian
of yours some time hence, to be nurtured in my house, held as
my page, and the playfellow of the little Derby. I trust in
Heaven, they will be such friends as their fathers have been,
and may God send them more fortunate times!"

"Marry, and I thank you for the proposal with all my heart,
madam," said the Knight. "There are so many noble houses
decayed, and so many more in which the exercise and discipline
for the training of noble youths is given up and neglected, that
I have often feared I must have kept Gil to be young master
at home; and I have had too little nurture myself to teach
him much, and so he would have been a mere hunting hawking
knight of Derbyshire. But in your ladyship's household, and
with the noble young Earl, he will have all, and more than all,
the education which I could desire."

"There shall be no distinction betwixt them, cousin," said
the Countess; "Margaret Stanley's son shall be as much the
object of care to me as my own, since you are kindly disposed
to entrust him to my charge.—You look pale, Margaret," she
continued, "and the tear stands in your eye? Do not be so
foolish, my love—what I ask is better than you can desire for
your boy; for the house of my father, the Duke de la Tremouille,
was the most famous school of chivalry in France; nor have I
degenerated from him, or suffered any relaxation in that noble
discipline which trained young gentlemen to do honour to their
race. You can promise your Julian no such advantages, if you
train him up a mere home-bred youth."

"I acknowledge the importance of the favour, madam," said
Lady Peveril, "and must acquiesce in what your ladyship
honours us by proposing, and Sir Geoffrey approves of; but
Julian is an only child, and——"

"An only son," said the Countess, "but surely not an only
child. You pay too high deference to our masters, the male
sex, if you allow Julian to engross all your affection, and spare
none for this beautiful girl."

So saying, she set down Julian, and, taking Alice Bridgenorth
on her lap, began to caress her; and there was, notwithstanding
her masculine character, something so sweet in the tone of her
voice and in the cast of her features, that the child immediately
smiled, and replied to her marks of fondness. This mistake
embarrassed Lady Peveril exceedingly. Knowing the blunt
impetuosity of her husband's character, his devotion to the

memory of the deceased Earl of Derby, and his corresponding veneration for his widow, she was alarmed for the consequences of his hearing the conduct of Bridgenorth that morning, and was particularly desirous that he should not learn it save from herself in private, and after due preparation. But the Countess's error led to a more precipitate disclosure.

"That pretty girl, madam," answered Sir Geoffrey, "is none of ours—I wish she were. She belongs to a neighbour hard by—a good man, and, to say truth, a good neighbour—though he was carried off from his allegiance in the late times by a d—d Presbyterian scoundrel, who calls himself a parson, and whom I hope to fetch down from his perch presently, with a wannion to him! He has been cock of the roost long enough.— There are rods in pickle to switch the Geneva cloak with, I can tell the sour-faced rogues that much. But this child is the daughter of Bridgenorth — neighbour Bridgenorth, of Moultrassie Hall."

"Bridgenorth?" said the Countess; "I thought I had known all the honourable names in Derbyshire—I remember nothing of Bridgenorth.—But stay—was there not a sequestrator and committeeman of that name? Sure, it cannot be he?"

Peveril took some shame to himself, as he replied, "It is the very man whom your ladyship means, and you may conceive the reluctance with which I submitted to receive good offices from one of his kidney; but had I not done so, I should have scarce known how to find a roof to cover Dame Margaret's head."

The Countess, as he spoke, raised the child gently from her lap, and placed it upon the carpet, though little Alice showed a disinclination to the change of place, which the lady of Derby and Man would certainly have indulged in a child of patrician descent and loyal parentage.

"I blame you not," she said; "no one knows what temptation will bring us down to. Yet I *did* think Peveril of the Peak would have resided in its deepest cavern, sooner than owed an obligation to a regicide."

"Nay, madam," answered the Knight, "my neighbour is bad enough, but not so bad as you would make him; he is but a Presbyterian—that I must confess—but not an Independent."

"A variety of the same monster," said the Countess, "who hallooed while the others hunted, and bound the victim whom the Independents massacred. Betwixt such sects I prefer the Independents. They are at least bold, bare-faced, merciless villains, have more of the tiger in them, and less of the crocodile. I have no doubt it was that worthy gentleman who took it upon him this morning——"

She stopped short, for she saw Lady Peveril was vexed and embarrassed.

"I am," she said, "the most luckless of beings. I have said something, I know not what, to distress you, Margaret—Mystery is a bad thing, and betwixt us there should be none."

"There is none, madam," said Lady Peveril, something impatiently; "I waited but an opportunity to tell my husband what had happened—Sir Geoffrey, Master Bridgenorth was unfortunately here when the Lady Derby and I met; and he thought it part of his duty to speak of——"

"To speak of what?" said the Knight, bending his brows. "You were ever something too fond, dame, of giving way to the usurpation of such people."

"I only mean," said Lady Peveril, "that as the person—he to whom Lord Derby's story related—was the brother of his late lady, he threatened—but I cannot think that he was serious."

"Threaten?—threaten the Lady of Derby and Man in my house!—the widow of my friend—the noble Charlotte of Latham House!—by Heaven, the prick-eared slave shall answer it! How comes it that my knaves threw him not out of the window?"

"Alas! Sir Geoffrey, you forget how much we owe him," said the lady.

"Owe him!" said the Knight, still more indignant; for in his singleness of apprehension he conceived that his wife alluded to pecuniary obligations,—"if I do owe him some money, hath he not security for it? and must he have the right, over and above, to domineer and play the magistrate in Martindale Castle?—Where is he?—what have you made of him? I will —I must speak with him."

"Be patient, Sir Geoffrey," said the Countess, who now discerned the cause of her kinswoman's apprehension; "and be assured I did not need your chivalry to defend me against this discourteous faitour, as *Morte d'Arthur* would have called him. I promise you my kinswoman hath fully righted my wrong; and I am so pleased to owe my deliverance entirely to her gallantry, that I charge and command you, as a true Knight, not to mingle in the adventure of another."

Lady Peveril, who knew her husband's blunt and impatient temper, and perceived that he was becoming angry, now took up the story, and plainly and simply pointed out the cause of Master Bridgenorth's interference.

"I am sorry for it," said the Knight; "I thought he had more sense; and that this happy change might have done some good upon him. But you should have told me this instantly— It consists not with my honour that he should be kept prisoner in this house, as if I feared anything he could do to annoy the noble Countess, while she is under my roof, or within twenty miles of this Castle."

So saying, and bowing to the Countess, he went straight to the gilded chamber, leaving Lady Peveril in great anxiety for the event of an angry meeting between a temper hasty as that of her husband, and stubborn like that of Bridgenorth. Her apprehensions were, however, unnecessary; for the meeting was not fated to take place.

When Sir Geoffrey Peveril, having dismissed Whitaker and his sentinels, entered the gilded chamber, in which he expected to find his captive, the prisoner had escaped, and it was easy to see in what manner. The sliding panel had, in the hurry of the moment, escaped the memory of Lady Peveril, and of Whitaker, the only persons who knew anything of it. It was probable that a chink had remained open, sufficient to indicate its existence to Bridgenorth; who withdrawing it altogether, had found his way into the secret apartment with which it communicated, and from thence to the postern of the Castle by another secret passage, which had been formed in the thickness of the wall, as is not uncommon in ancient mansions; the lords of which were liable to so many mutations of fortune, that they usually contrived to secure some lurking place and secret mode of retreat from their fortresses. That Bridgenorth had discovered and availed himself of this secret mode of retreat was evident; because the private doors communicating with the postern and the sliding panel in the gilded chamber were both left open.

Sir Geoffrey returned to the ladies with looks of perplexity. While he deemed Bridgenorth within his reach, he was apprehensive of nothing he could do; for he felt himself his superior in personal strength, and in that species of courage which induces a man to rush, without hesitation, upon personal danger. But when at a distance, he had been for many years accustomed to consider Bridgenorth's power and influence as something formidable; and notwithstanding the late change of affairs, his ideas so naturally reverted to his neighbour as a powerful friend or dangerous enemy, that he felt more apprehension on the Countess's score, than he was willing to acknowledge even to himself. The Countess observed his downcast and anxious brow, and requested to know if her stay there was likely to involve him in any trouble, or in any danger.

"The trouble should be welcome," said Sir Geoffrey, "and more welcome the danger, which should come on such an account. My plan was, that your ladyship should have honoured Martindale with a few days' residence, which might have been kept private until the search after you was ended. Had I seen this fellow Bridgenorth, I have no doubt I could have compelled him to act discreetly; but he is now at liberty, and will keep out of my reach; and, what is worse, he has the secret of the priest's chamber."

Here the Knight paused, and seemed much embarrassed.

"You can, then, neither conceal nor protect me?" said the Countess.

"Pardon, my honoured lady," answered the Knight, "and let me say out my say. The plain truth is, that this man hath many friends among the Presbyterians here, who are more numerous than I would wish them; and if he falls in with the pursuivant fellow who carries the warrant of the Privy Council, it is likely he will back him with force sufficient to try to execute it. And I doubt whether any of our friends can be summoned together in haste, sufficient to resist such a power as they are like to bring together."

"Nor would I wish any friends to take arms, in my name, against the King's warrant, Sir Geoffrey," said the Countess.

"Nay, for that matter," replied the Knight, "an his Majesty will grant warrants against his best friends, he must look to have them resisted. But the best I can think of in this emergence is—though the proposal be something inhospitable—that your ladyship should take presently to horse, if your fatigue will permit. I will mount also, with some brisk fellows, who will lodge you safe at Vale Royal, though the Sheriff stopped the way with a whole *posse comitatus.*"

The Countess of Derby willingly acquiesced in this proposal. She had enjoyed a night's sound repose in the private chamber, to which Ellesmere had guided her on the preceding evening, and was quite ready to resume her route, or flight—"she scarce knew," she said, "which of the two she should term it."

Lady Peveril wept at the necessity which seemed to hurry her earliest friend and protectress from under her roof, at the instant when the clouds of adversity were gathering around her; but she saw no alternative equally safe. Nay, however strong her attachment to Lady Derby, she could not but be more readily reconciled to her hasty departure, when she considered the inconvenience, and even danger, in which her presence, at such a time, and in such circumstances, was likely to involve a man so bold and hot-tempered as her husband Sir Geoffrey.

While Lady Peveril, therefore, made every arrangement which time permitted and circumstances required, for the Countess prosecuting her journey, her husband, whose spirits always rose with the prospect of action, issued his orders to Whitaker to get together a few stout fellows, with back and breast pieces, and steel-caps. "There are the two lackeys, and Outram and Saunders, besides the other groom fellow, and Roger Raine, and his son; but bid Roger not come drunk

again;—thyself, young Dick of the Dale and his servant, and a
file or two of the tenants,—we shall be enough for any force
they can make. All these are fellows that will strike hard, and
ask no question why—their hands are ever readier than their
tongues, and their mouths are more made for drinking than
speaking."

Whitaker, apprised of the necessity of the case, asked if he
should not warn Sir Jasper Cranbourne.

"Not a word to him, as you live," said the Knight; "this
may be an outlawry, as they call it, for what I know; and
therefore I will bring no lands or tenements into peril, saving
mine own. Sir Jasper hath had a troublesome time of it for
many a year. By my will, he shall sit quiet for the rest of's
days."

CHAPTER VII

Fang.—A rescue ! a rescue !
Mrs. Quickly.—Good people, bring a rescue or two.
—HENRY IV. *Part I.*

THE followers of Peveril were so well accustomed to the sound
of "Boot and Saddle," that they were soon mounted and in
order; and in all the form, and with some of the dignity of
danger, proceeded to escort the Countess of Derby through the
hilly and desert tract of country which connects the frontier
of the shire with the neighbouring county of Cheshire. The
cavalcade moved with considerable precaution, which they had
been taught by the discipline of the Civil Wars. One wary
and well-mounted trooper rode about two hundred yards in
advance; followed, at about half that distance, by two more,
with their carabines advanced, as if ready for action. About
one hundred yards behind the advance, came the main body;
where the Countess of Derby, mounted on Lady Peveril's
ambling palfrey (for her own had been exhausted by the
journey from London to Martindale Castle), accompanied by
one groom, of approved fidelity, and one waiting-maid, was
attended and guarded by the Knight of the Peak, and three files
of good and practised horsemen. In the rear came Whitaker,
with Lance Outram, as men of especial trust, to whom the
covering the retreat was confided. They rode, as the Spanish
proverb expresses it, "with the beard on the shoulder," looking
around, that is, from time to time, and using every precaution
to have the speediest knowledge of any pursuit which might
take place.

But, however wise in discipline, Peveril and his followers

were somewhat remiss in civil policy. The Knight had communicated to Whitaker, though without any apparent necessity,
the precise nature of their present expedition; and Whitaker
was equally communicative to his comrade Lance, the keeper.
" It is strange enough, Master Whitaker," said the latter, when
he had heard the case, " and I wish you, being a wise man,
would expound it;—why, when we have been wishing for the
King—and praying for the King—and fighting for the King—
and dying for the King, for these twenty years, the first thing
we find to do on his return, is to get into harness to resist his
warrant ? "

" Pooh! you silly fellow," said Whitaker, " that is all you
know of the true bottom of our quarrel! Why, man, we
fought for the King's person against his warrant, all along from
the very beginning; for I remember the rogues' proclamations, and so forth, always ran in the name of the King and
Parliament."

" Ay! was it even so ? " replied Lance. " Nay, then, if they
begin the old game so soon again, and send out warrants in
the King's name against his loyal subjects, well fare our stout
Knight, say I, who is ready to take them down in their stocking-
soles. And if Bridgenorth takes the chase after us, I shall not
be sorry to have a knock at him for one."

" Why, the man, bating he is a pestilent Roundhead and
Puritan," said Whitaker, " is no bad neighbour. What has he
done to thee, man ? "

" He has poached on the manor," answered the keeper.

" The devil he has! " replied Whitaker. " Thou must be
jesting, Lance. Bridgenorth is neither hunter nor hawker; he
hath not so much of honesty in him."

" Ay, but he runs after game you little think of, with his
sour, melancholy face, that would scare babes and curdle milk,"
answered Lance.

" Thou canst not mean the wenches ? " said Whitaker; " why,
he hath been melancholy mad with moping for the death of his
wife. Thou knowest our lady took the child, for fear he should
strangle it for putting him in mind of its mother, in some of his
tantrums. Under her favour, and among friends, there are
many poor Cavaliers' children, that care would be better bestowed upon—But to thy tale."

" Why, thus it runs," said Lance. " I think you may have
noticed, Master Whitaker, that a certain Mistress Deborah hath
manifested a certain favour for a certain person in a certain
household."

" For thyself, to wit," answered Whitaker; " Lance Outram,
thou art the vainest coxcomb——"

" Coxcomb ? " said Lance; " why, 'twas but last night the

whole family saw her, as one would say, fling herself at my head."

"I would she had been a brickbat then, to have broken it, for thy impertinence and conceit," said the steward.

"Well, but do but hearken. The next morning—that is, this very blessed morning—I thought of going to lodge a buck in the park, judging a bit of venison might be wanted in the larder, after yesterday's wassail; and, as I passed under the nursery window, I did but just look up to see what madam governante was about; and so I saw her, through the casement, whip on her hood and scarf as soon as she had a glimpse of me. Immediately after I saw the still-room door open, and made sure she was coming through the garden, and so over the breach and down to the park; and so, thought I, 'Aha, Mistress Deb, if you are so ready to dance after my pipe and tabor, I will give you a couranto before you shall come up with me.' And so I went down Ivy-tod Dingle, where the copse is tangled, and the ground swampy, and round by Haxley-bottom, thinking all the while she was following, and laughing in my sleeve at the round I was giving her."

"You deserved to be ducked for it," said Whitaker, "for a weather-headed puppy; but what is all this Jack-a-lantern story to Bridgenorth?"

"Why, it was all along of he, man," continued Lance, "that is, of Bridgenorth, that she did not follow me—Gad, I first walked slow, and then stopped, and then turned back a little, and then began to wonder what she had made of herself, and to think I had borne myself something like a jackass in the matter."

"That I deny," said Whitaker, "never jackass but would have borne him better—but go on."

"Why, turning my face towards the Castle, I went back as if I had my nose bleeding, when just by the Copely thorn, which stands, you know, a flight-shot from the postern-gate, I saw Madam Deb in close conference with the enemy."

"What enemy?" said the steward.

"What enemy! why, who but Bridgenorth? They kept out of sight, and among the copse; but, thought I, it is hard if I cannot stalk you, that have stalked so many bucks. If so, I had better give my shafts to be pudding pins. So I cast round the thicket, to watch their waters; and may I never bend crossbow again, if I did not see him give her gold, and squeeze her by the hand!"

"And was that all you saw pass between them?" said the steward.

"Faith, and it was enough to dismount me from my hobby," said Lance. "What! when I thought I had the prettiest girl

in the Castle dancing after my whistle, to find that she gave
me the bag to hold, and was smuggling in a corner with a rich
old Puritan!"

"Credit me, Lance, it is not as thou thinkest," said Whitaker.
"Bridgenorth cares not for these amorous toys, and thou
thinkest of nothing else. But it is fitting our Knight should
know that he has met with Deborah in secret, and given her
gold; for never Puritan gave gold yet, but it was earnest for
some devil's work done, or to be done."

"Nay, but," said Lance, "I would not be such a dog-bolt
as to go and betray the girl to our master. She hath a right
to follow her fancy, as the dame said who kissed her cow—
only I do not much approve her choice, that is all. He cannot
be six years short of fifty; and a verjuice countenance, under
the penthouse of a slouched beaver, and bag of meagre dried
bones, swaddled up in a black cloak, is no such temptation,
methinks."

"I tell you once more," said Whitaker, "you are mistaken;
and that there neither is, nor can be, any matter of love
between them, but only some intrigue, concerning, perhaps,
this same noble Countess of Derby. I tell thee, it behoves my
master to know it, and I will presently tell it to him."

So saying, and in spite of all the remonstrances which Lance
continued to make on behalf of Mistress Deborah, the steward
rode up to the main body of their little party, and mentioned to
the Knight, and the Countess of Derby, what he had just heard
from the keeper, adding at the same time his own suspicions,
that Master Bridgenorth of Moultrassie Hall was desirous to
keep up some system of espial in the Castle of Martindale,
either in order to secure his menaced vengeance on the Countess
of Derby, as authoress of his brother-in-law's death, or for some
unknown, but probably sinister purpose.

The Knight of the Peak was filled with high resentment at
Whitaker's communication. According to his prejudices, those
of the opposite faction were supposed to make up by wit and
intrigue what they wanted in open force; and he now hastily
conceived that his neighbour, whose prudence he always respected, and sometimes even dreaded, was maintaining, for his
private purposes, a clandestine correspondence with a member
of his family. If this was for the betrayal of his noble guest,
it argued at once treachery and presumption; or, viewing the
whole as Lance had done, a criminal intrigue with a woman so
near the person of Lady Peveril, was in itself, he deemed, a
piece of sovereign impertinence and disrespect on the part of
such a person as Bridgenorth, against whom Sir Geoffrey's anger
was kindled accordingly.

Whitaker had scarce regained his post in the rear, when he

THE COUNTESS OF DERBY QUITTING PEVERIL CASTLE

PAINTING BY H. MELVILLE

again quitted it, and galloped to the main body with more speed than before, with the unpleasing tidings that they were pursued by half a score of horsemen, and better.

"Ride on briskly to Hartley-nick," said the Knight, "and there, with God to help, we will bide the knaves.—Countess of Derby—one word and a short one—Farewell!—you must ride forward with Whitaker and another careful fellow, and let me alone to see that no one treads on your skirts."

"I will abide with you and stand them," said the Countess; "you know of old, I fear not to look on man's work."

"You *must* ride on, madam," said the Knight, "for the sake of the young Earl, and the rest of my noble friend's family. There is no manly work which can be worth your looking upon; it is but child's play that these fellows bring with them."

As she yielded a reluctant consent to continue her flight, they reached the bottom of Hartley-nick, a pass very steep and craggy, and where the road, or rather path, which had hitherto passed over more open ground, became pent up and confined, betwixt copsewood on the one side, and, on the other, the precipitous bank of a mountain stream.

The Countess of Derby, after an affectionate adieu to Sir Geoffrey, and having requested him to convey her kind commendations to her little page-elect and his mother, proceeded up the pass at a round pace, and with her attendants and escort, was soon out of sight. Immediately after she had disappeared, the pursuers came up with Sir Geoffrey Peveril, who had divided and drawn up his party so as completely to occupy the road at three different points.

The opposite party was led, as Sir Geoffrey had expected, by Major Bridgenorth. At his side was a person in black, with a silver greyhound on his arm; and he was followed by about eight or ten inhabitants of the village of Martindale Moultrassie, two or three of whom were officers of the peace, and others were personally known to Sir Geoffrey as favourers of the subverted government.

As the party rode briskly up, Sir Geoffrey called to them to halt; and as they continued advancing, he ordered his own people to present their pistols and carabines; and after assuming that menacing attitude, he repeated, with a voice of thunder, "Halt, or we fire!"

The other party halted accordingly, and Major Bridgenorth advanced, as if to parley.

"Why, how now, neighbour," said Sir Geoffrey, as if he had at that moment recognised him for the first time,—"what makes you ride so sharp this morning? Are you not afraid to harm your horse, or spoil your spurs?"

E

"Sir Geoffrey," said the Major, "I have no time for jesting —I'm on the King's affairs."

"Are you sure it is not upon Old Noll's, neighbour? You used to hold his the better errand," said the Knight, with a smile which gave occasion to a horse-laugh among his followers.

"Show him your warrant," said Bridgenorth to the man in black formerly mentioned, who was a pursuivant. Then taking the warrant from the officer, he gave it to Sir Geoffrey—"To this, at least, you will pay regard."

"The same regard which you would have paid to it a month back or so," said the Knight, tearing the warrant to shreds.— "What a plague do you stare at? Do you think you have a monopoly of rebellion, and that we have not a right to show a trick of disobedience in our turn?"

"Make way, Sir Geoffrey Peveril," said Bridgenorth, "or you will compel me to do that I may be sorry for. I am in this matter the avenger of the blood of one of the Lord's saints, and I will follow the chase while Heaven grants me an arm to make my way."

"You shall make no way here but at your peril," said Sir Geoffrey; "this is my ground—I have been harassed enough for these twenty years by saints, as you call yourselves. I tell you, master, you shall neither violate the security of my house, nor pursue my friends over the grounds, nor tamper, as you have done, amongst my servants, with impunity. I have had you in respect for certain kind doings, which I will not either forget or deny, and you will find it difficult to make me draw a sword or bend a pistol against you; but offer any hostile move- ment, or presume to advance a foot, and I will make sure of you presently. And for these rascals, who come hither to annoy a noble lady on my bounds, unless you draw them off, I will presently send some of them to the devil before their time."

"Make room at your proper peril," said Major Bridgenorth; and he put his right hand on his holster-pistol. Sir Geoffrey closed with him instantly, seized him by the collar, and spurred Black Hastings, checking him at the same time, so that the horse made a courbette, and brought the full weight of his chest against the counter of the other. A ready soldier might, in Bridgenorth's situation, have rid himself of his adversary with a bullet. But Bridgenorth's courage, notwithstanding his having served some time with the Parliament army, was rather of a civil than a military character; and he was inferior to his adver- sary, not only in strength and horsemanship, but also and especially in the daring and decisive resolution which made Sir Geoffrey thrust himself readily into personal contest. While, therefore, they tugged and grappled together upon terms which bore such little accordance with their long acquaintance and close neighbourhood, it was no wonder that Bridgenorth should be unhorsed with much violence. While Sir Geoffrey sprung from the saddle, the party of Bridgenorth advanced to rescue their leader, and that of the Knight to oppose them. Swords were unsheathed, and pistols presented; but Sir Geoffrey, with the voice of a herald, commanded both parties to stand back, and to keep the peace.

The pursuivant took the hint, and easily found a reason for not prosecuting a dangerous duty. "The warrant," he said, "was destroyed. They that did it must be answerable to the Council; for his part, he could proceed no farther without his commission."

"Well said, and like a peaceable fellow!" said Sir Geoffrey. —Let him have refreshment at the Castle—his nag is sorely out of condition.—Come, neighbour Bridgenorth, get up, man— I trust you have had no hurt in this mad affray? I was loath to lay hand on you, man, till you plucked out your petronel."

As he spoke thus, he aided the Major to rise. The pursuivant, meanwhile, drew aside; and with him the constable and head-borough, who were not without some tacit suspicion, that though Peveril was interrupting the direct course of law in this matter, yet he was likely to have his offence considered by favourable judges; and therefore it might be as much for their interest and safety to give way as to oppose him. But the rest of the party, friends of Bridgenorth, and of his principles, kept their ground notwithstanding this defection, and seemed, from their looks, sternly determined to rule their conduct by that of their leader, whatever it might be.

But it was evident that Bridgenorth did not intend to renew the struggle. He shook himself rather roughly free from the hands of Sir Geoffrey Peveril; but it was not to draw his sword. On the contrary, he mounted his horse with a sullen and de-jected air; and, making a sign to his followers, turned back the same road which he had come. Sir Geoffrey looked after him for some minutes. "Now, there goes a man," said he, "who would have been a right honest fellow had he not been a Pres-byterian. But there is no heartiness about them—they can never forgive a fair fall upon the sod—they bear malice, and that I hate as I do a black cloak, or a Geneva skull-cap, and a pair of long ears rising on each side on't, like two chimneys at the gable ends of a thatched cottage. They are as sly as the devil to boot; and, therefore, Lance Outram, take two with you, and keep after them, that they may not turn our flank, and get on the track of the Countess again after all."

"I had as soon they should course my lady's white tame doe," answered Lance, in the spirit of his calling. He proceeded to execute his master's orders by dogging Major Bridgenorth at a distance, and observing his course from such heights as commanded the country. But it was soon evident that no manœuvre was intended, and that the Major was taking the direct road homeward. When this was ascertained, Sir Geoffrey dismissed most of his followers; and retaining only his own domestics, rode hastily forward to overtake the Countess.

It is only necessary to say farther, that he completed his purpose of escorting the Countess of Derby to Vale Royal, without meeting any further hindrance by the way. The lord of the mansion readily undertook to conduct the high-minded lady to Liverpool, and the task of seeing her safely embarked for her son's hereditary dominions, where there was no doubt of her remaining in personal safety until the accusation against her for breach of the Royal Indemnity, by the execution of Christian, could be brought to some compromise.

For a length of time this was no easy matter. Clarendon, then at the head of Charles's administration, considered her rash action, though dictated by motives which the human breast must, in some respects, sympathise with, as calculated to shake the restored tranquillity of England, by exciting the doubts and jealousies of those who had to apprehend the consequences of what is called, in our own time, a *reaction*. At the same time, the high services of this distinguished family—the merits of the Countess herself—the memory of her gallant husband—and the very peculiar circumstances of jurisdiction which took the case out of all common rules, pleaded strongly in her favour; and the death of Christian was at length only punished by the imposition of a heavy fine, amounting, we believe, to many thousand pounds; which was levied, with great difficulty, out of the shattered estates of the young Earl of Derby.

CHAPTER VIII

My native land, good night!
—BYRON.

LADY PEVERIL remained in no small anxiety for several hours after her husband and the Countess had departed from Martindale Castle; more especially when she learned that Major Bridgenorth, concerning whose motions she made private inquiry, had taken horse with a party, and was gone to the westward in the same direction with Sir Geoffrey.

At length her immediate uneasiness in regard to the safety of her husband and the Countess was removed, by the arrival of Whitaker, with her husband's commendations, and an account of the scuffle betwixt himself and Major Bridgenorth.

Lady Peveril shuddered to see how nearly they had approached to renewal of the scenes of civil discord; and while she was thankful to Heaven for her husband's immediate preservation, she could not help feeling both regret and apprehension for the consequences of his quarrel with Major Bridgenorth. They had now lost an old friend, who had showed himself such under those circumstances of adversity by which friendship is most severely tried; and she could not disguise from herself that Bridgenorth, thus irritated, might be a troublesome, if not a dangerous enemy. His rights as a creditor, he had hitherto used with gentleness; but if he should employ rigour, Lady Peveril, whose attention to domestic economy had made her much better acquainted with her husband's affairs than he was himself, foresaw considerable inconvenience from the measures which the law put in his power. She comforted herself with the recollection, however, that she had still a strong hold on Bridgenorth, through his paternal affection, and from the fixed opinion which he had hitherto manifested, that his daughter's health could only flourish while under her charge. But any expectations of reconciliation which Lady Peveril might probably have founded on this circumstance, were frustrated by an incident which took place in the course of the following morning.

The governante, Mistress Deborah, who has been already mentioned, went forth, as usual, with the children, to take their morning exercise in the Park, attended by Rachael, a girl who acted occasionally as her assistant in attending upon them. But not as usual did she return. It was near the hour of breakfast, when Ellesmere, with an unwonted degree of primness in her mouth and manner, came to acquaint her lady that Mistress Deborah had not thought proper to come back from the Park, though the breakfast hour approached so near.

"She will come, then, presently," said Lady Peveril with indifference.

Ellesmere gave a short and doubtful cough, and then proceeded to say, that Rachael had been sent home with little Master Julian, and that Mistress Deborah had been pleased to say, she would walk on with Miss Bridgenorth as far as Moultrassie Holt; which was a point at which the property of the Major, as matters now stood, bounded that of Sir Geoffrey Peveril.

"Is the wench turned silly," exclaimed the lady, something angrily, "that she does not obey my orders, and return at regular hours?"

"She may be turning silly," said Ellesmere mysteriously;

"or she may be turning too sly; and I think it were as well your ladyship looked to it."

"Looked to what, Ellesmere?" said the lady impatiently. "You are strangely oracular this morning. If you know anything to the prejudice of this young woman, I pray you speak it out."

"I prejudice!" said Ellesmere; "I scorn to prejudice man, woman, or child, in the way of a fellow-servant; only I wish your ladyship to look about you, and use your own eyes—that is all."

"You bid me use my own eyes, Ellesmere; but I suspect," answered the lady, "you would be better pleased were I contented to see through your spectacles. I charge you—and you know I will be obeyed—I charge you to tell me what you know or suspect about this girl, Deborah Debbitch."

"I see through spectacles!" exclaimed the indignant Abigail; "your ladyship will pardon me in that, for I never use them, unless a pair that belonged to my poor mother, which I put on when your ladyship wants your pinners curiously wrought. No woman above sixteen ever did white-seam without barnacles. And then as to suspecting, I suspect nothing; for as your ladyship hath taken Mistress Deborah Debbitch from under my hand, to be sure it is neither bread nor butter of mine. Only" (here she began to speak with her lips shut, so as scarce to permit a sound to issue, and mincing her words as if she pinched off the ends of them before she suffered them to escape),—"only, madam, if Mistress Deborah goes so often of a morning to Moultrassie Holt, why, I should not be surprised if she should never find the way back again."

"Once more, what do you mean, Ellesmere? You were wont to have some sense—let me know distinctly what the matter is."

"Only, madam," pursued the Abigail, "that since Bridgenorth came back from Chesterfield, and saw you at the Castle Hall, Mistress Deborah has been pleased to carry the children every morning to that place; and it has so happened that she has often met the Major, as they call him, there in his walks; for he can walk about now like other folks; and I warrant you she hath not been the worse of the meeting—one way at least, for she hath bought a new hood might serve yourself, madam; but whether she hath had anything in hand besides a piece of money, no doubt your ladyship is best judge."

Lady Peveril, who readily adopted the more good-natured construction of the governante's motives, could not help laughing at the idea of a man of Bridgenorth's precise appearance, strict principles, and reserved habits, being suspected of a design of gallantry; and readily concluded, that Mistress Deborah had found her advantage in gratifying his parental affection by a frequent sight of his daughter during the few days which intervened betwixt his first seeing little Alice at the Castle, and the events which had followed. But she was somewhat surprised, when, an hour after the usual breakfast hour, during which neither the child nor Mistress Deborah appeared, Major Bridgenorth's only man-servant arrived at the Castle on horseback, dressed as for a journey; and having delivered a letter addressed to herself, and another to Mistress Ellesmere, rode away without waiting any answer.

There would have been nothing remarkable in this, had any other person been concerned; but Major Bridgenorth was so very quiet and orderly in all his proceedings—so little liable to act hastily or by impulse, that the least appearance of bustle where he was concerned, excited surprise and curiosity.

Lady Peveril broke her letter hastily open, and found that it contained the following lines :—

> "*For the Hands of the Honourable and Honoured Lady*
> *Peveril—These :*

"Madam—Please it your Ladyship,—I write more to excuse myself to your ladyship, than to accuse either you or others, in respect that I am sensible it becomes our frail nature better to confess our own imperfections, than to complain of those of others. Neither do I mean to speak of past times, particularly in respect of your worthy ladyship, being sensible that if I have served you in that period when our Israel might be called triumphant, you have more than requited me, in giving to my arms a child, redeemed, as it were, from the vale of the shadow of death. And therefore, as I heartily forgive to your ladyship the unkind and violent measure which you dealt to me at our last meeting (seeing that the woman who was the cause of strife is accounted one of your kindred people), I do entreat you, in like manner, to pardon my enticing away from your service the young woman called Deborah Debbitch, whose nurture, instructed as she hath been under your ladyship's direction, is, it may be, indispensable to the health of my dearest child. I had purposed, madam, with your gracious permission, that Alice should have remained at Martindale Castle, under your kind charge, until she could so far discern betwixt good and evil, that it should be matter of conscience to teach her the way in which she should go. For it is not unknown to your ladyship, and in no way do I speak it reproachfully, but rather sorrowfully, that a person so excellently gifted as yourself—I mean touching natural qualities—has not yet received that true light, which is a lamp to the paths, but are contented to stumble in darkness, and among the graves of dead men. It has been my prayer in the watches of the night, that your ladyship should cease from the doctrine which causeth to err; but I grieve to say, that our candlestick being about to be removed, the land will most likely be involved in deeper darkness than ever; and the return of the King, to which I and many looked forward as a manifestation of divine favour, seems to prove little else than a permitted triumph of the Prince of the Air, who setteth about to restore his Vanity-fair of bishops, deans, and such like, extruding the peaceful ministers of the word, whose labours have proved faithful to many hungry souls. So, hearing from a sure hand, that commission has gone forth to restore these dumb dogs, the followers of Laud and of Williams, who were cast forth by the late Parliament, and that an Act of Conformity, or rather of deformity, of worship, was to be expected, it is my purpose to flee from the wrath to come, and to seek some corner where I may dwell in peace, and enjoy liberty of conscience. For who would abide in the Sanctuary, after the carved work thereof is broken down, and when it hath been made a place for owls, and satyrs of the wilderness?—And herein I blame myself, madam, that I went in the singleness of my heart too readily into that carousing in the house of feasting, wherein my love of union, and my desire to show respect to your ladyship, were made a snare to me. But I trust it will be an atonement, that I am now about to absent myself from the place of my birth, and the house of my fathers, as well as from the place which holdeth the dust of those pledges of my affection. I have also to remember, that in this land my honour (after the worldly estimation) hath been abated, and my utility circumscribed, by your husband, Sir Geoffrey Peveril; and that without any chance of my obtaining reparation at his hand, whereby I may say the hand of a kinsman was lifted up against my credit and my life. These things are bitter to the taste of the old Adam; wherefore to prevent farther bickerings, and, it may be, bloodshed, it is better that I leave this land for a time. The affairs which remain to be settled between Sir Geoffrey and myself, I shall place in the hand of the righteous Master Joachim Win-the-Fight, an attorney in Chester, who will arrange them with such attention to Sir Geoffrey's convenience, as justice, and the due exercise of the law, will permit; for, as I trust I shall have grace to resist the temptation to make the weapons of carnal warfare the instruments of my revenge, so I scorn to effect it through the means of Mammon. Wishing, madam, that the Lord may grant you every blessing, and, in especial, that which is over all others, namely, the true knowledge of His way, I remain, your devoted servant to command,   RALPH BRIDGENORTH.

"*Written at Moultrassie Hall, this tenth
  day of July*, 1660."

So soon as Lady Peveril had perused this long and singular homily, in which it seemed to her that her neighbour showed more spirit of religious fanaticism than she could have supposed him possessed of, she looked up and beheld Ellesmere,—with a countenance in which mortification, and an affected air of contempt, seemed to struggle together,—who, tired with watching the expression of her mistress's countenance, applied for confirmation of her suspicions in plain terms.

"I suppose, madam," said the waiting-woman, "the fanatic fool intends to marry the wench? They say he goes to shift the country. Truly it's time, indeed; for, besides that the whole neighbourhood would laugh him to scorn, I should not be surprised if Lance Outram, the keeper, gave him a buck's head to bear; for that is all in the way of his office."

"There is no great occasion for your spite at present, Ellesmere," replied her lady. "My letter says nothing of marriage; but it would appear that Master Bridgenorth, being to leave this country, has engaged Deborah to take care of his child; and I am sure I am heartily glad of it, for the infant's sake."

"And I am glad of it for my own," said Ellesmere; "and, indeed, for the sake of the whole house.—And your ladyship thinks she is not like to be married to him? Troth, I could never see how he should be such an idiot; but perhaps she is going to do worse; for she speaks here of coming to high preferment, and that scarce comes by honest servitude nowadays; then she writes me about sending her things, as if I were mistress of the wardrobe to her ladyship—ay, and recommends Master Julian to the care of my age and experience, forsooth, as if she needed to recommend the dear little jewel to me; and then, to speak of my age—But I will bundle away her rags to the Hall, with a witness!"

"Do it with all civility," said the lady, "and let Whitaker send her the wages for which she has served, and a broad-piece over and above; for though a light-headed young woman, she was kind to the children."

"I know who is kind to their servants, madam, and would spoil the best ever pinned a gown."

"I spoiled a good one, Ellesmere, when I spoiled thee," said the lady; "but tell Mistress Deborah to kiss the little Alice for me, and to offer my good wishes to Major Bridgenorth, for his temporal and future happiness."

She permitted no observation or reply, but dismissed her attendant, without entering into farther particulars.

When Ellesmere had withdrawn, Lady Peveril began to reflect, with much feeling of compassion, on the letter of Major Bridgenorth; a person in whom there were certainly many excellent qualities, but whom a series of domestic misfortunes, and the increasing gloom of a sincere, yet stern feeling of devotion, rendered lonely and unhappy; and she had more than one anxious thought for the happiness of the little Alice, brought up, as she was likely to be, under such a father. Still the removal of Bridgenorth was, on the whole, a desirable event; for while he remained at the Hall, it was but too likely that some accidental collision with Sir Geoffrey might give rise to a rencontre betwixt them, more fatal than the last had been.

In the meanwhile, she could not help expressing to Doctor Dummerar her surprise and sorrow, that all which she had done and attempted, to establish peace and unanimity betwixt the contending factions, had been perversely fated to turn out the very reverse of what she had aimed at.

"But for my unhappy invitation," she said, "Bridgenorth would not have been at the Castle on the morning which succeeded the feast, would not have seen the Countess, and would not have incurred the resentment and opposition of my husband. And but for the King's return, an event which was so anxiously expected as the termination of all our calamities, neither the noble lady nor ourselves had been engaged in this new path of difficulty and danger."

"Honoured madam," said Doctor Dummerar, "were the affairs of this world to be guided implicitly by human wisdom, or were they uniformly to fall out according to the conjectures of human foresight, events would no longer be under the domination of that time and chance, which happen unto all men, since we should, in the one case, work out our own purposes to a certainty, by our own skill, and in the other, regulate our conduct according to the views of unerring prescience. But man is, while in this vale of tears, like an uninstructed bowler, so to speak, who thinks to attain the jack, by delivering his bowl straight forward upon it, being ignorant that there is a concealed bias within the spheroid, which will make it, in all probability, swerve away, and lose the cast."

Having spoken this with a sententious air, the Doctor took his shovel-shaped hat, and went down to the Castle green, to conclude a match of bowls with Whitaker, which had probably suggested this notable illustration of the uncertain course of human events.

Two days afterwards, Sir Geoffrey arrived. He had waited at Vale Royal till he heard of the Countess's being safely embarked for Man, and then had posted homeward to his Castle and Dame Margaret. On his way, he learned from some of his attendants, the mode in which his lady had conducted the entertainment which she had given to the neighbourhood at his order; and notwithstanding the great deference he usually showed in cases where Lady Peveril was concerned, he heard of her liberality towards the Presbyterian party with great indignation.

"I could have admitted Bridgenorth," he said, "for he always bore him in neighbourly and kindly fashion till this last career—I could have endured him, so he would have drunk the King's health, like a true man—but to bring that snuffling scoundrel Solsgrace, with all his beggarly, long-eared congregation, to hold a conventicle in my father's house—to let them domineer it as they listed—why, I would not have permitted them such liberty, when they held their head the highest! They never, in the worst of times, found any way into Martindale Castle but what Noll's cannon made for them; and that they should come and cant there, when good King Charles is returned—By my hand, Dame Margaret shall hear of it!"

But, notwithstanding these ireful resolutions, resentment altogether subsided in the honest Knight's breast, when he saw the fair features of his lady lightened with affectionate joy at his return in safety. As he took her in his arms and kissed her, he forgave her ere he mentioned her offence.

"Thou hast played the knave with me, Meg," he said, shaking his head, and smiling at the same time, "and thou knowest in what manner; but I think thou art true church-woman, and didst only act from some silly womanish fancy of keeping fair with these roguish Roundheads. But let me have no more of this. I had rather Martindale Castle were again rent by their bullets, than receive any of the knaves in the way of friendship—I always except Ralph Bridgenorth of the Hall, if he should come to his senses again."

Lady Peveril was here under the necessity of explaining what she had heard of Master Bridgenorth—the disappearance of the governante with his daughter, and placed Bridgenorth's letter in his hand. Sir Geoffrey shook his head at first, and then laughed extremely, at the idea that there was some little love-intrigue between Bridgenorth and Mistress Deborah.

"It is the true end of a dissenter," he said, "to marry his own maid-servant, or some other person's. Deborah is a good likely wench, and on the merrier side of thirty, as I should think."

"Nay, nay," said the Lady Peveril, "you are as uncharitable as Ellesmere—I believe it but to be affection to his child."

"Pshaw! pshaw!" answered the Knight, "women are eternally thinking of children; but among men, dame, many one caresses the infant that he may kiss the child's maid; and where's the wonder or the harm either, if Bridgenorth should marry the wench? Her father is a substantial yeoman; his family has had the same farm since Bosworthfield—as good a pedigree as that of the great-grandson of a Chesterfield brewer, I trow. But let us hear what he says for himself—I shall spell it out if there is any roguery in the letter about love and liking, though it might escape your innocence, Dame Margaret."

The Knight of the Peak began to peruse the letter accordingly, but was much embarrassed by the peculiar language in which it was couched. "What he means by moving of candlesticks, and breaking down of carved work in the church, I cannot guess; unless he means to bring back the large silver candlesticks which my grandsire gave to be placed on the altar at Martindale Moultrassie; and which his crop-eared friends, like sacrilegious villains as they are, stole and melted down. And in like manner, the only breaking I know of, was when they pulled down the rails of the communion table (for which some of their fingers are hot enough by this time), and when the brass ornaments were torn down from the Peveril monuments; and that was breaking and removing with a vengeance. However, dame, the upshot is, that poor Bridgenorth is going to leave the neighbourhood. I am truly sorry for it, though I never saw him oftener than once a day, and never spoke to him above two words. But I see how it is—that little shake by the shoulder sticks in his stomach; and yet, Meg, I did but lift him out of the saddle as I might have lifted thee into it, Margaret —I was careful not to hurt him; and I did not think him so tender in point of honour as to mind such a thing much; but I see plainly where his sore lies; and I warrant you I will manage that he stays at the Hall, and that you get back Julian's little companion. Faith, I am sorry myself at the thought of losing the baby, and of having to choose another ride when it is not hunting weather, than round by the Hall, with a word at the window."

"I should be very glad, Sir Geoffrey," said Lady Peveril, "that you could come to a reconciliation with this worthy man, for such I must hold Master Bridgenorth to be."

"But for his dissenting principles, as good a neighbour as ever lived," said Sir Geoffrey.

"But I scarce see," continued the lady, "any possibility of bringing about a conclusion so desirable."

"Tush, dame," answered the Knight, "thou knowest little of such matters. I know the foot he halts upon, and you shall see him go as sound as ever."

Lady Peveril had, from her sincere affection and sound sense, as good a right to claim the full confidence of her husband, as any woman in Derbyshire; and, upon this occasion, to confess the truth, she had more anxiety to know his purpose than her sense of their mutual and separate duties permitted her in general to entertain. She could not imagine what mode of reconciliation with his neighbour, Sir Geoffrey (no very acute judge of mankind or their peculiarities) could have devised, which might not be disclosed to her; and she felt some secret anxiety lest the means resorted to might be so ill chosen as to render the breach rather wider. But Sir Geoffrey would give no opening for farther inquiry. He had been long enough colonel of a regiment abroad, to value himself on the right of absolute command at home; and to all the hints which his lady's ingenuity could devise and throw out, he only answered, "Patience, Dame Margaret, patience. This is no case for thy handling. Thou shalt know enough on't by-and-by, dame.— Go, look to Julian. Will the boy never have done crying for lack of that little sprout of a Roundhead? But we will have little Alice back with us in two or three days, and all will be well again."

As the good Knight spoke these words, a post winded his horn in the court, and a large packet was brought in, addressed to the worshipful Sir Geoffrey Peveril, Justice of the Peace, and so forth; for he had been placed in authority as soon as the King's Restoration was put upon a settled basis. Upon opening the packet, which he did with no small feeling of importance, he found that it contained the warrant which he had solicited for replacing Doctor Dummerar in the parish, from which he had been forcibly ejected during the usurpation.

Few incidents could have given more delight to Sir Geoffrey. He could forgive a stout able-bodied sectary or nonconformist, who enforced his doctrines in the field by downright blows on the casques and cuirasses of himself and other Cavaliers. But he remembered with most vindictive accuracy, the triumphant entrance of Hugh Peters through the breach of his Castle; and for his sake, without nicely distinguishing betwixt sects or their teachers, he held all who mounted a pulpit without warrant from the Church of England—perhaps he might also in private except that of Rome—to be disturbers of the public tranquillity—seducers of the congregation from their lawful preachers—instigators of the late Civil War—and men well disposed to risk the fate of a new one.

Then, on the other hand, besides gratifying his dislike to Solsgrace, he saw much satisfaction in the task of replacing his old friend and associate in sport and in danger, the worthy Doctor Dummerar, in his legitimate rights, and in the ease and comforts of his vicarage. He communicated the contents of the packet, with great triumph, to the lady, who now perceived the sense of the mysterious paragraph in Major Bridgenorth's letter, concerning the removal of the candlestick, and the extinction of light and doctrine in the land. She pointed this out to Sir Geoffrey, and endeavoured to persuade him that a door was now opened to reconciliation with his neighbour, by executing the commission which he had received in an easy and moderate manner, after due delay, and with all respect to the feelings both of Solsgrace and his congregation, which circumstances admitted of. This, the lady argued, would be doing no injury whatever to Doctor Dummerar;—nay, might be the means of reconciling many to his ministry, who might otherwise be disgusted with it for ever, by the premature expulsion of a favourite preacher.

There was much wisdom, as well as moderation, in this advice; and, at another time, Sir Geoffrey would have had sense enough to have adopted it. But who can act composedly or prudently in the hour of triumph? The ejection of Mr. Solsgrace was so hastily executed, as to give it some appearance of persecution; though, more justly considered, it was the restoring of his predecessor to his legal rights. Solsgrace himself seemed to be desirous to make his sufferings as manifest as possible. He held out to the last; and on the Sabbath after he had received intimation of his ejection, attempted to make his way to the pulpit, as usual, supported by Master Bridgenorth's attorney, Win-the-Fight, and a few zealous followers.

Just as their party came into the churchyard on the one side, Doctor Dummerar, dressed in full pontificals, in a sort of triumphal procession, accompanied by Peveril of the Peak, Sir Jasper Cranbourne, and other Cavaliers of distinction, entered at the other.

To prevent an actual struggle in the church, the parish officers were sent to prevent the farther approach of the Presbyterian minister; which was effected without farther damage than a broken head, inflicted by Roger Raine, the drunken innkeeper of the Peveril Arms, upon the Presbyterian attorney of Chesterfield.

Unsubdued in spirit, though compelled to retreat by superior force, the undaunted Mr. Solsgrace retired to the vicarage; where under some legal pretext which had been started by Mr. Win-the-Fight (in that day unaptly named), he attempted to maintain himself—bolted gates—barred windows—and, as report said (though falsely), made provision of fire-arms to resist the officers. A scene of clamour and scandal accordingly took place, which being reported to Sir Geoffrey, he came in person, with some of his attendants carrying arms—forced the outer-gate and inner-doors of the house; and proceeding to the study, found no other garrison save the Presbyterian parson, with the attorney, who gave up possession of the premises, after making protestation against the violence that had been used.

The rabble of the village being by this time all in motion,

Sir Geoffrey, both in prudence and good-nature, saw the propriety of escorting his prisoners, for so they might be termed, safely through the tumult; and accordingly conveyed them in person, through much noise and clamour, as far as the avenue of Moultrassie Hall, which they chose for the place of their retreat.

But the absence of Sir Geoffrey gave the rein to some disorders, which, if present, he would assuredly have restrained. Some of the minister's books were torn and flung about as treasonable and seditious trash, by the zealous parish-officers or their assistants. A quantity of his ale was drunk up in healths to the King and Peveril of the Peak. And, finally, the boys, who bore the ex-parson no good-will for his tyrannical interference with their games at skittles, foot-ball, and so forth, and, moreover, remembered the unmerciful length of his sermons, dressed up an effigy with his Geneva gown and band, and his steeple-crowned hat, which they paraded through the village, and burned on the spot whilom occupied by a stately Maypole, which Solsgrace had formerly hewed down with his own reverend hands.

Sir Geoffrey was vexed at all this, and sent to Mr. Solsgrace, offering satisfaction for the goods which he had lost; but the Calvinistical divine replied, "From a thread to a shoe-latchet, I will not take anything that is thine. Let the shame of the work of thy hands abide with thee."

Considerable scandal, indeed, arose against Sir Geoffrey Peveril as having proceeded with indecent severity and haste upon this occasion; and rumour took care to make the usual additions to the reality. It was currently reported, that the desperate Cavalier, Peveril of the Peak, had fallen on a Presbyterian congregation, while engaged in the peaceable exercise of religion, with a band of armed men—had slain some, desperately wounded many more, and finally pursued the preacher to his vicarage, which he burned to the ground. Some alleged the clergyman had perished in the flames; and the most mitigated report bore, that he had only been able to escape by disposing his gown, cap, and band, near a window, in such a manner as to deceive them with the idea of his person being still surrounded by flames, while he himself fled by the back part of the house. And although few people believed in the extent of the atrocities thus imputed to our honest Cavalier, yet still enough of obloquy attached to him to infer very serious consequences, as the reader will learn at a future period of our history.

CHAPTER IX

Bessus.—'Tis a challenge, sir, is it not?
Gentleman.—'Tis an inviting to the field.
—KING AND NO KING.

FOR a day or two after this forcible expulsion from the vicarage, Mr. Solsgrace continued his residence at Moultrassie Hall, where the natural melancholy attendant on his situation added to the gloom of the owner of the mansion. In the morning, the ejected divine made excursions to different families in the neighbourhood, to whom his ministry had been acceptable in the days of his prosperity, and from whose grateful recollections of that period he now found sympathy and consolation. He did not require to be condoled with, because he was deprived of an easy and competent maintenance, and thrust out upon the common of life, after he had reason to suppose he would be no longer liable to such mutations of fortune. The piety of Mr. Solsgrace was sincere; and if he had many of the uncharitable prejudices against other sects, which polemical controversy had generated, and the Civil War brought to a head, he had also that deep sense of duty, by which enthusiasm is so often dignified, and held his very life little, if called upon to lay it down in attestation of the doctrines in which he believed. But he was soon to prepare for leaving the district which Heaven, he conceived, had assigned to him as his corner of the vineyard; he was to abandon his flock to the wolf—was to forsake those with whom he had held sweet counsel in religious communion —was to leave the recently converted to relapse into false doctrines, and forsake the wavering, whom his continued cares might have directed into the right path,—these were of themselves deep causes of sorrow, and were aggravated, doubtless, by those natural feelings with which all men, especially those whose duties or habits have confined them to a limited circle, regard the separation from wonted scenes, and their accustomed haunts of solitary musing, or social intercourse.

There was, indeed, a plan of placing Mr. Solsgrace at the head of a nonconforming congregation in his present parish, which his followers would have readily consented to endow with a sufficient revenue. But although the act for universal conformity was not yet passed, such a measure was understood to be impending, and there existed a general opinion among the Presbyterians, that in no hands was it likely to be more strictly enforced, than in those of Peveril of the Peak. Solsgrace himself considered not only his personal danger as being considerable,—for, assuming perhaps more consequence than was actually attached to him or his productions, he conceived the honest Knight to be his mortal and determined enemy,—but he also conceived that he should serve the cause of his Church by absenting himself from Derbyshire.

"Less known pastors," he said, "though perhaps more worthy of the name, may be permitted to assemble the scattered flocks in caverns or in secret wilds, and to them shall the gleaning of the grapes of Ephraim be better than the vintage of Abiezer. But I, that have so often carried the banner forth against the mighty—I, whose tongue hath testified, morning and evening, like the watchman upon the tower, against Popery, Prelacy, and the tyrant of the Peak—for me to abide here, were but to bring the sword of bloody vengeance amongst you, that the shepherd might be smitten, and the sheep scattered. The shedders of blood have already assailed me, even within that ground which they themselves call consecrated; and yourselves have seen the scalp of the righteous broken, as he defended my cause. Therefore, I will put on my sandals, and gird my loins, and depart to a far country, and there do as my duty shall call upon me, whether it be to act or to suffer—to bear testimony at the stake or in the pulpit."

Such were the sentiments which Mr. Solsgrace expressed to his desponding friends, and which he expatiated upon at more length with Major Bridgenorth; not failing, with friendly zeal, to rebuke the haste which the latter had shown to thrust out the hand of fellowship to the Amalekite woman, whereby he reminded him, "He had been rendered her slave and bondsman for a season, like Samson, betrayed by Delilah, and might have remained longer in the house of Dagon, had not Heaven pointed to him a way out of the snare. Also, it sprung originally from the Major's going up to feast in the high place of Baal, that he who was the champion of the truth was stricken down, and put to shame by the enemy, even in the presence of the host."

These objurgations seeming to give some offence to Major Bridgenorth, who liked, no better than any other man, to hear of his own mishaps, and at the same time to have them imputed to his own misconduct, the worthy divine proceeded to take shame to himself for his own sinful compliance in that matter; for to the vengeance justly due for that unhappy dinner at Martindale Castle (which was, he said, a crying of peace when there was no peace, and a dwelling in the tents of sin), he imputed his ejection from his living, with the destruction of some of his most pithy and highly prized volumes of divinity, with the loss of his cap, gown, and band, and a double hogshead of choice Derby ale.

F

The mind of Major Bridgenorth was strongly tinged with devotional feeling, which his late misfortunes had rendered more deep and solemn; and it is therefore no wonder, that, when he heard these arguments urged again and again, by a pastor whom he so much respected, and who was now a confessor in the cause of their joint faith, he began to look back with disapproval on his own conduct, and to suspect that he had permitted himself to be seduced by gratitude towards Lady Peveril, and by her special arguments in favour of a mutual and tolerating liberality of sentiments, into an action which had a tendency to compromise his religious and political principles.

One morning, as Major Bridgenorth had wearied himself with several details respecting the arrangement of his affairs, he was reposing in the leathern easy chair, beside the latticed window, a posture which, by natural association, recalled to him the memory of former times, and the feelings with which he was wont to expect the recurring visit of Sir Geoffrey, who brought him news of his child's welfare,—" Surely," he said, thinking, as it were, aloud, " there was no sin in the kindness with which I then regarded that man."

Solsgrace, who was in the apartment, and guessed what passed through his friend's mind, acquainted as he was with every point of his history, replied—" When God caused Elijah to be fed by ravens, while hiding at the brook Cherith, we hear not of his fondling the unclean birds, whom, contrary to their ravening nature, a miracle compelled to minister to him."

" It may be so," answered Bridgenorth, " yet the flap of their wings must have been gracious in the ear of the famished prophet, like the tread of his horse in mine. The ravens, doubtless, resumed their nature when the season was passed, and even so it has fared with him.—Hark!" he exclaimed, starting, " I hear his horse's hoof tramp even now."

It was seldom that the echoes of that silent house and courtyard were awakened by the trampling of horses, but such was now the case.

Both Bridgenorth and Solsgrace were surprised at the sound, and even disposed to anticipate some farther oppression on the part of government, when the Major's old servant introduced, with little ceremony (for his manners were nearly as plain as his master's), a tall gentleman on the farther side of middle life, whose vest and cloak, long hair, slouched hat and drooping feather, announced him as a Cavalier. He bowed formally, but courteously, to both gentlemen, and said, that he was " Sir Jasper Cranbourne, charged with an especial message to Master Ralph Bridgenorth of Moultrassie Hall, by his honourable friend Sir Geoffrey Peveril of the Peak, and that he requested to know whether Master Bridgenorth would be pleased to receive his acquittal of commission here or elsewhere."

"Anything which Sir Geoffrey Peveril can have to say to me," said Major Bridgenorth, " may be told instantly, and before my friend, from whom I have no secrets."

"The presence of any other friend were, instead of being objectionable, the thing in the world most to be desired," said Sir Jasper, after a moment's hesitation, and looking at Mr. Solgrace ; " but this gentleman seems to be a sort of clergyman."

" I am not conscious of any secrets," answered Bridgenorth, "nor do I desire to have any, in which a clergyman is an unfitting confidant."

" At your pleasure," replied Sir Jasper. " The confidence, for aught I know, may be well enough chosen, for your divines (always under your favour) have proved no enemies to such matters as I am to treat with you upon."

"Proceed, sir," answered Mr. Bridgenorth gravely; "and I pray you to be seated, unless it is rather your pleasure to stand."

" I must, in the first place, deliver myself of my small commission," answered Sir Jasper, drawing himself up ; " and it will be after I have seen the reception thereof, that I shall know whether I am, or am not, to sit down at Moultrassie Hall. —Sir Geoffrey Peveril, Master Bridgenorth, hath carefully considered with himself the unhappy circumstances which at present separate you as neighbours. And he remembers many passages in former times—I speak his very words—which incline him to do all that can possibly consist with his honour, to wipe out unkindness between you ; and for this desirable object, he is willing to condescend in a degree, which, as you could not have expected, it will no doubt give you great pleasure to learn."

" Allow me to say, Sir Jasper," said Bridgenorth, " that this is unnecessary. I have made no complaints of Sir Geoffrey—I have required no submission from him—I am about to leave this country ; and what affairs we may have together, can be as well settled by others as by ourselves."

" In a word," said the divine, " the worthy Major Bridgenorth hath had enough of trafficking with the ungodly, and will no longer, on any terms, consort with them."

" Gentlemen both," said Sir Jasper, with imperturbable politeness, bowing, " you greatly mistake the tenor of my commission, which you will do as well to hear out, before making any reply to it.—I think, Master Bridgenorth, you cannot but remember your letter to the Lady Peveril, of which I have here a rough copy, in which you complain of the hard measure which you have received at Sir Geoffrey's hand, and, in particular, when he pulled you from your horse at or near Hartley-nick. Now, Sir Geoffrey thinks so well of you, as to believe, that, were it not for the wide difference betwixt his descent and rank and your own, you would have sought to bring this matter to a gentleman-like arbitrament, as the only mode whereby your stain may be honourably wiped away. Wherefore, in this slight note, he gives you, in his generosity, the offer of what you, in your modesty (for to nothing else does he impute your acquiescence), have declined to demand of him. And withal, I bring you the measure of his weapon; and when you have accepted the cartel which I now offer you, I shall be ready to settle the time, place, and other circumstances of your meeting."

"And I," said Solsgrace, with a solemn voice, "should the Author of Evil tempt my friend to accept of so bloodthirsty a proposal, would be the first to pronounce against him sentence of the greater excommunication."

"It is not you whom I address, reverend sir," replied the envoy; "your interest, not unnaturally, may determine you to be more anxious about your patron's life than about his honour. I must know, from himself, to which *he* is disposed to give the preference."

So saying, and with a graceful bow, he again tendered the challenge to Major Bridgenorth. There was obviously a struggle in that gentleman's bosom, between the suggestions of human honour and those of religious principle; but the latter prevailed. He calmly waived receiving the paper which Sir Jasper offered to him, and spoke to the following purpose:—"It may not be known to you, Sir Jasper, that since the general pouring out of Christian light upon this kingdom, many solid men have been led to doubt whether the shedding human blood by the hand of a fellow-creature be in *any* respect justifiable. And although this rule appears to me to be scarcely applicable to our state in this stage of trial, seeing that such non-resistance, if general, would surrender our civil and religious rights into the hands of whatsoever daring tyrants might usurp the same; yet I am, and have been, inclined to limit the use of carnal arms to the case of necessary self-defence, whether such regards our own person, or the protection of our country against invasion; or of our rights of property, and the freedom of our laws and of our conscience, against usurping power. And as I have never shown myself unwilling to draw my sword in any of the latter causes, so you shall excuse my suffering it now to remain in the scabbard, when, having sustained a grievous injury, the man who inflicted it summons me to combat, either upon an idle punctilio, or, as is more likely, in mere bravado."

"I have heard you with patience," said Sir Jasper; "and now, Master Bridgenorth, take it not amiss, if I beseech you to bethink yourself better on this matter. I vow to Heaven, sir, that your honour lies a-bleeding; and that in condescending to afford you this fair meeting, and thereby giving you some chance to stop its wounds, Sir Geoffrey has been moved by a tender sense of your condition, and an earnest wish to redeem your dishonour. And it will be but the crossing of your blade with his honoured sword for the space of some few minutes, and you will either live or die a noble and honoured gentleman. Besides, that the Knight's exquisite skill of fence may enable him, as his good-nature will incline him, to disarm you with some flesh wound, little to the damage of your person, and greatly to the benefit of your reputation."

"The tender mercies of the wicked," said Master Solsgrace emphatically, by way of commenting on this speech, which Sir Jasper had uttered very pathetically, "are cruel."

"I pray to have no farther interruption from your reverence," said Sir Jasper; "especially as I think this affair very little concerns you; and I entreat that you permit me to discharge myself regularly of my commission from my worthy friend."

So saying, he took his sheathed rapier from his belt, and passing the point through the silk thread which secured the letter, he once more, and literally at sword point, gracefully tendered it to Major Bridgenorth, who again waved it aside, though colouring deeply at the same time, as if he was putting a marked constraint upon himself—drew back, and made Sir Jasper Cranbourne a deep bow.

"Since it is to be thus," said Sir Jasper, "I must myself do violence to the seal of Sir Geoffrey's letter, and read it to you, that I may fully acquit myself of the charge entrusted to me, and make you, Master Bridgenorth, equally aware of the generous intentions of Sir Geoffrey on your behalf."

"If," said Major Bridgenorth, "the contents of the letter be to no other purpose than you have intimated, methinks farther ceremony is unnecessary on this occasion, as I have already taken my course."

"Nevertheless," said Sir Jasper, breaking open the letter, "it is fitting that I read to you the letter of my worshipful friend." And he read accordingly as follows:—

"For the worthy hands of Ralph Bridgenorth, Esquire, of Moultrassie Hall—These:

"By the honoured conveyance of the Worshipful Sir Jasper Cranbourne, Knight, of Long-Mallington.

"MASTER BRIDGENORTH,—We have been given to understand by your letter to our loving wife, Dame Margaret Peveril, that you hold hard construction of certain passages betwixt you and I, of a late date, as if your honour should have been, in some sort, prejudiced by what then took place. And although you have not thought it fit to have direct recourse to me, to request such satisfaction as is due from one gentleman of condition to another, yet I am fully minded that this proceeds only from modesty, arising out of the distinction of our degree, and from no lack of that courage which you have heretofore displayed, I would I could say in a good cause. Wherefore I am purposed to give you, by my friend, Sir Jasper Cranbourne, a meeting, for the sake of doing that which doubtless you entirely long for. Sir Jasper will deliver you the length of my weapon, and appoint circumstances and an hour for our meeting; which, whether early or late—on foot or horseback—with rapier or backsword— I refer to yourself, with all the other privileges of a challenged person; only desiring, that if you decline to match my weapon, you will send me forthwith the length and breadth of your own. And nothing doubting that the issue of this meeting must needs be to end, in one way or other, all unkindness betwixt two near neighbours,—I remain, your humble servant to command,

"GEOFFREY PEVERIL OF THE PEAK.

"Given from my poor house of Martindale Castle, this same —— of ——, sixteen hundred and sixty."

"Bear back my respects to Sir Geoffrey Peveril," said Major Bridgenorth. "According to his light, his meaning may be fair towards me; but tell him that our quarrel had its rise in his own wilful aggression towards me; and that though I wish to be in charity with all mankind, I am not so wedded to his friendship as to break the laws of God, and run the risk of suffering or committing murder, in order to regain it. And for you, sir, methinks your advanced years and past misfortunes might teach you the folly of coming on such idle errands."

"I shall do your message, Master Ralph Bridgenorth," said Sir Jasper; "and shall then endeavour to forget your name, as a sound unfit to be pronounced, or even remembered, by a man of honour. In the meanwhile, in return for your uncivil advice, be pleased to accept of mine; namely, that as your religion prevents your giving a gentleman satisfaction, it ought to make you very cautious of offering him provocation."

So saying, and with a look of haughty scorn, first at the Major, and then at the divine, the envoy of Sir Geoffrey put his hat on his head, replaced his rapier in its belt, and left the apartment. In a few minutes afterwards, the tread of his horse died away at a considerable distance.

Bridgenorth had held his hand upon his brow ever since his departure, and a tear of anger and shame was on his face as he raised it when the sound was heard no more. "He carries this answer to Martindale Castle," he said. "Men will hereafter think of me as a whipped, beaten, dishonourable fellow, whom every one may baffle and insult at their pleasure. It is well I am leaving the house of my father."

Master Solsgrace approached his friend with much sympathy, and grasped him by the hand. "Noble brother," he said, with unwonted kindness of manner, "though a man of peace, I can judge what this sacrifice hath cost to thy manly spirit. But God will not have from us an imperfect obedience. We must not, like Ananias and Sapphira, reserve behind some darling lust, some favourite sin, while we pretend to make sacrifice of our worldly affections. What avails it to say that we have but secreted a little matter, if the slightest remnant of the accursed thing remain hidden in our tent? Would it be a defence in thy prayers to say, I have not murdered this man for the lucre of gain, like a robber—nor for the acquisition of power, like a tyrant,—nor for the gratification of revenge, like a darkened savage; but because the imperious voice of worldly honour said, 'Go forth—kill or be killed—is it not I that have sent thee?' Bethink thee, my worthy friend, how thou couldst frame such a vindication in thy prayers; and if thou art forced to tremble at the blasphemy of such an excuse, remember in thy prayers the thanks due to Heaven, which enabled thee to resist the strong temptation."

"Reverend and dear friend," answered Bridgenorth, "I feel that you speak the truth. Bitterer, indeed, and harder, to the old Adam, is the text which ordains him to suffer shame, than that which bids him to do valiantly for the truth. But happy am I that my path through the wilderness of this world will, for some space at least, be along with one, whose zeal and friendship are so active to support me when I am fainting in the way."

While the inhabitants of Moultrassie Hall thus communicated together upon the purport of Sir Jasper Cranbourne's visit, that worthy knight greatly excited the surprise of Sir Geoffrey Peveril, by reporting the manner in which his embassy had been received.

"I took him for a man of other metal," said Sir Geoffrey ;— "nay, I would have sworn it, had any one asked my testimony. But there is no making a silken purse out of a sow's ear. I have done a folly for him that I will never do for another: and that is, to think a Presbyterian would fight without his preacher's permission. Give them a two hours' sermon, and let them howl a psalm to a tune that is worse than the cries of a flogged hound, and the villains will lay on like threshers; but for a calm, cool, gentleman-like turn upon the sod, hand to hand, in a neighbourly way, they have not honour enough to undertake it. But enough of our crop-eared cur of a neighbour.

—Sir Jasper, you will tarry with us to dine, and see how Dame Margaret's kitchen smokes; and after dinner I will show you a long-winged falcon fly. She is not mine, but the Countess's, who brought her from London on her fist almost the whole way, for all the haste she was in, and left her with me to keep the perch for a season."

This match was soon arranged, and Dame Margaret overheard the good Knight's resentment mutter itself off, with those feelings with which we listen to the last growling of the thunderstorm; which, as the black cloud sinks beneath the hill, at once assures us that there has been danger, and that the peril is over. She could not, indeed, but marvel in her own mind at the singular path of reconciliation with his neighbour which her husband had, with so much confidence, and in the actual sincerity of his goodwill to Mr. Bridgenorth, attempted to open; and she blessed God internally that it had not terminated in bloodshed. But these reflections she locked carefully within her own bosom, well knowing that they referred to subjects in which the Knight of the Peak would neither permit his sagacity to be called in question, nor his will to be controlled.

The progress of the history hath hitherto been slow; but after this period so little matter worthy of mark occurred at Martindale, that we must hurry over hastily the transactions of several years.

CHAPTER X

Cleopatra.—Give me to drink mandragora,
That I may sleep away this gap of time.
—Antony and Cleopatra.

THERE passed, as we hinted at the conclusion of the last chapter, four or five years after the period we have dilated upon; the events of which scarcely require to be discussed, so far as our present purpose is concerned, in as many lines. The Knight and his Lady continued to reside at their Castle—she, with prudence and with patience, endeavouring to repair the damages which the Civil Wars had inflicted upon their fortune; and murmuring a little when her plans of economy were interrupted by the liberal hospitality, which was her husband's principal expense, and to which he was attached, not only from his own English heartiness of disposition, but from ideas of maintaining the dignity of his ancestry—no less remarkable, according to the tradition of their buttery, kitchen, and cellar, for the fat beeves which they roasted, and the mighty ale which they brewed, than for their extensive estates, and the number of their retainers.

The world, however, upon the whole, went happily and easily with the worthy couple. Sir Geoffrey's debt to his neighbour Bridgenorth continued, it is true, unabated; but he was the only creditor upon the Martindale estate—all others being paid off. It would have been most desirable that this encumbrance also should be cleared, and it was the great object of Dame Margaret's economy to effect the discharge; for although interest was regularly settled with Master Win-the-Fight, the Chesterfield attorney, yet the principal sum, which was a large one, might be called for at an inconvenient time. The man, too, was gloomy, important, and mysterious, and always seemed as if he was thinking upon his broken head in the churchyard of Martindale-cum-Moultrassie.

Dame Margaret sometimes transacted the necessary business with him in person; and when he came to the Castle on these occasions, she thought she saw a malicious and disobliging expression in his manner and countenance. Yet his actual conduct was not only fair, but liberal; for indulgence was given, in the way of delay of payment, whenever circumstances rendered it necessary to the debtor to require it. It seemed to Lady Peveril that the agent, in such cases, was acting under the strict orders of his absent employer, concerning whose welfare she could not help feeling a certain anxiety.

Shortly after the failure of the singular negotiation for attaining peace by combat, which Peveril had attempted to open with Major Bridgenorth, that gentleman left his seat of Moultrassie Hall in the care of his old housekeeper, and departed, no one knew whither, having in company with him his daughter Alice and Mrs. Deborah Debbitch, now formally installed in all the duties of a governante; to these was added the Reverend Master Solsgrace. For some time public rumour persisted in asserting, that Major Bridgenorth had only retreated to a distant part of the country for a season, to achieve his supposed purpose of marrying Mrs. Deborah, and of letting the news be cold, and the laugh of the neighbourhood be ended, ere he brought her down as mistress of Moultrassie Hall. This rumour died away; and it was then affirmed, that he had removed to foreign parts, to ensure the continuance of health in so delicate a constitution as that of little Alice. But when the Major's dread of Popery was remembered, together with the still deeper antipathies of worthy Master Nehemiah Solsgrace, it was resolved unanimously, that nothing less than what they might deem a fair chance of converting the Pope would have induced the parties to trust themselves within Catholic dominions. The most prevailing opinion was, that they had gone to New England, the refuge then of many whom too intimate concern with the affairs of the late times, or the desire of enjoying uncontrolled freedom of conscience, had induced to emigrate from Britain.

Lady Peveril could not help entertaining a vague idea, that Bridgenorth was not so distant. The extreme order in which everything was maintained at Moultrassie Hall, seemed — no disparagement to the care of Dame Dickens the housekeeper, and the other persons engaged—to argue, that the master's eye was not so very far off, but that its occasional inspection might be apprehended. It is true, that neither the domestics nor the attorney answered any questions respecting the residence of Master Bridgenorth; but there was an air of mystery about them when interrogated, that seemed to argue more than met the ear.

About five years after Master Bridgenorth had left the country, a singular incident took place. Sir Geoffrey was absent at the Chesterfield races, and Lady Peveril, who was in the habit of walking around every part of the neighbourhood unattended, or only accompanied by Ellesmere, or her little boy, had gone down one evening upon a charitable errand to a solitary hut, whose inhabitant lay sick of a fever, which was supposed to be infectious. Lady Peveril never allowed apprehensions of this kind to stop "devoted charitable deeds;" but she did not choose to expose either her son or her attendant to the risk which she herself, in some confidence that she knew precautions for escaping the danger, did not hesitate to incur.

Lady Peveril had set out at a late hour in the evening, and the way proved longer than she expected — several circumstances also occurred to detain her at the hut of her patient. It was a broad autumn moonlight, when she prepared to return homeward through the broken glades and upland which divided her from the Castle. This she considered as a matter of very little importance, in so quiet and sequestered a country, where the road lay chiefly through her own domains, especially as she had a lad about fifteen years old, the son of her patient, to escort her on the way. The distance was better than two miles, but might be considerably abridged by passing through an avenue belonging to the estate of Moultrassie Hall, which she had avoided as she came, not from the ridiculous rumours which pronounced it to be haunted, but because her husband was much displeased when any attempt was made to render the walks of the Castle and Hall common to the inhabitants of both. The good lady, in consideration, perhaps, of extensive latitude allowed to her in the more important concerns of the family, made a point of never interfering with her husband's whims or prejudices; and it is a compromise which we would heartily recommend to all managing matrons of our acquaintance; for it is surprising how much real power will be cheerfully resigned to the fair sex, for the pleasure of being allowed to ride one's hobby in peace and quiet.

Upon the present occasion, however, although the Dobby's Walk* was within the inhabited domains of the Hall, the Lady Peveril determined to avail herself of it, for the purpose of shortening her road home, and she directed her steps accordingly. But when the peasant-boy, her companion, who had hitherto followed her, whistling cheerily, with a hedge-bill in his hand, and his hat on one side, perceived that she turned to the stile which entered to the Dobby's Walk, he showed symptoms of great fear, and at length coming to the lady's side, petitioned her, in a whimpering tone,—" Don't ye now— don't ye now, my lady, don't ye go yonder."

Lady Peveril, observing that his teeth chattered in his head, and that his whole person exhibited great signs of terror, began to recollect the report, that the first Squire of Moultrassie, the brewer of Chesterfield, who had bought the estate, and then died of melancholy for lack of something to do (and, as was said, not without suspicions of suicide), was supposed to walk in this sequestered avenue, accompanied by a large headless mastiff, which, when he was alive, was a particular favourite of the ex-brewer. To have expected any protection from her escort, in the condition to which superstitious fear had reduced him, would have been truly a hopeless trust; and Lady Peveril, who was not apprehensive of any danger, thought there would be great cruelty in dragging the cowardly boy into a scene which he regarded with so much apprehension. She gave him, therefore, a silver piece, and permitted him to return. The latter boon seemed even more acceptable than the first; for ere she could return the purse into her pocket, she heard the wooden clogs of her bold convoy in full retreat, by the way from whence they came.

Smiling within herself at the fear she esteemed so ludicrous, Lady Peveril ascended the stile, and was soon hidden from the broad light of the moonbeams, by the numerous and entangled boughs of the huge elms, which, meeting from either side, totally overarched the old avenue. The scene was calculated to excite solemn thoughts; and the distant glimmer of a light from one of the numerous casements in the front of Moultrassie Hall, which lay at some distance, was calculated to make them even melancholy. She thought of the fate of that family—of the deceased Mrs. Bridgenorth, with whom she had often walked in this very avenue, and who, though a woman of no high parts or accomplishments, had always testified the deepest

* Dobby, an old English name for goblin.

respect, and the most earnest gratitude, for such notice as she had shown to her. She thought of her blighted hopes—her premature death—the despair of her self-banished husband—the uncertain fate of their orphan child, for whom she felt, even at this distance of time, some touch of a mother's affection.

Upon such sad subjects her thoughts were turned, when, just as she attained the middle of the avenue, the imperfect and checkered light which found its way through the silvan archway, showed her something which resembled the figure of a man. Lady Peveril paused a moment, but instantly advanced;—her bosom, perhaps, gave one startled throb, as a debt to the superstitious belief of the times, but she instantly repelled the thought of supernatural appearances. From those that were merely mortal, she had nothing to fear. A marauder on the game was the worst character whom she was likely to encounter; and he would be sure to hide himself from her observation. She advanced, accordingly, steadily; and, as she did so, had the satisfaction to observe that the figure, as she expected, gave place to her, and glided away amongst the trees on the left-hand side of the avenue. As she passed the spot on which the form had been so lately visible, and bethought herself that this wanderer of the night might, nay must, be in her vicinity, her resolution could not prevent her mending her pace, and that with so little precaution, that, stumbling over the limb of a tree, which, twisted off by a late tempest, still lay in the avenue, she fell, and, as she fell, screamed aloud. A strong hand in a moment afterwards added to her fears by assisting her to rise, and a voice, to whose accents she was not a stranger, though they had been long unheard, said, "Is it not you, Lady Peveril?"

"It is I," said she, commanding her astonishment and fear; "and if my ear deceive me not, I speak to Master Bridgenorth."

"I was that man," said he, "while oppression left me a name."

He spoke nothing more, but continued to walk beside her for a minute or two in silence. She felt her situation embarrassing; and to divest it of that feeling, as well as out of real interest in the question, she asked him, "How her god-daughter Alice now was?"

"Of god-daughter, madam," answered Major Bridgenorth, "I know nothing; that being one of the names which have been introduced, to the corruption and pollution of God's ordinances. The infant who owed to your ladyship (so called) her escape from disease and death, is a healthy and thriving girl, as I am given to understand by those in whose charge she is lodged, for I have not lately seen her. And it is even the recollection of these passages, which in a manner impelled me, alarmed also by your fall, to offer myself to you at this time and mode, which in other respects is no way consistent with my present safety."

"With your safety, Master Bridgenorth?" said the Lady Peveril; "surely, I could never have thought that it was in danger!"

"You have some news, then, yet to learn, madam," said Major Bridgenorth; "but you will hear in the course of to-morrow, reasons why I dare not appear openly in the neighbourhood of my own property, and wherefore there is small judgment in committing the knowledge of my present residence to any one connected with Martindale Castle."

"Master Bridgenorth," said the lady, "you were in former times prudent and cautious—I hope you have been misled by no hasty impression—by no rash scheme—I hope——"

"Pardon my interrupting you, madam," said Bridgenorth. "I have indeed been changed—ay, my very heart within me hath been changed. In the times to which your ladyship (so called) thinks proper to refer, I was a man of this world—bestowing on it all my thoughts—all my actions, save formal observances—little deeming what was the duty of a Christian man, and how far his self-denial ought to extend—even unto his giving all as if he gave nothing. Hence I thought chiefly on carnal things—on the adding of field to field, and wealth to wealth—of balancing between party and party—securing a friend here, without losing a friend there—But Heaven smote me for my apostasy, the rather that I abused the name of religion, as a self-seeker, and a most blinded and carnal will-worshipper—But I thank Him who hath at length brought me out of Egypt."

In our day—although we have many instances of enthusiasm among us—we might still suspect one who avowed it thus suddenly and broadly of hypocrisy, or of insanity; but according to the fashion of the times, such opinions as those which Bridgenorth expressed were openly pleaded, as the ruling motives of men's actions. The sagacious Vane—the brave and skilful Harrison—were men who acted avowedly under the influence of such. Lady Peveril, therefore, was more grieved than surprised at the language she heard Major Bridgenorth use, and reasonably concluded that the society and circumstances in which he might lately have been engaged, had blown into a flame the spark of eccentricity which always smouldered in his bosom. This was the more probable, considering that he was melancholy by constitution and descent—that he had been unfortunate in several particulars—and that no passion is more

easily nursed by indulgence, than the species of enthusiasm of
which he now showed tokens. She therefore answered him by
calmly hoping, "That the expression of his sentiments had not
involved him in suspicion or in danger."

"In suspicion, madam?" answered the Major;—"for I cannot
forbear giving to you, such is the strength of habit, one of those
idle titles by which we poor potsherds are wont, in our pride,
to denominate each other—I walk not only in suspicion, but
in that degree of danger, that, were your husband to meet me
at this instant—me, a native Englishman, treading on my own
lands—I have no doubt he would do his best to offer me to
the Moloch of Roman superstition, who now rages abroad for
victims among God's people."

"You surprise me by your language, Major Bridgenorth,"
said the lady, who now felt rather anxious to be relieved from
his company, and with that purpose walked on somewhat
hastily. He mended his pace, however, and kept close by
her side.

"Know you not," said he, "that Satan hath come down upon
earth with great wrath, because his time is short? The next
heir to the crown is an avowed Papist; and who dare assert,
save sycophants and time-servers, that he who wears it is not
equally ready to stoop to Rome, were he not kept in awe by a
few noble spirits in the Commons' House? You believe not
this—yet in my solitary and midnight walks, when I thought
on your kindness to the dead and to the living, it was my
prayer that I might have the means granted to warn you—
and lo! Heaven hath heard me."

"Major Bridgenorth," said Lady Peveril, "you were wont to
be moderate in these sentiments—comparatively moderate, at
least, and to love your own religion without hating that of
others."

"What I was while in the gall of bitterness and in the bond
of iniquity, it signifies not to recall," answered he. "I was
then like to Gallio, who cared for none of these things. I
doted on creature comforts—I clung to worldly honour and
repute—my thoughts were earthward—or those I turned to
Heaven were cold, formal, pharisaical meditations—I brought
nothing to the altar save straw and stubble. Heaven saw need
to chastise me in love—I was stript of all that I clung to on
earth—my worldly honour was torn from me—I went forth an
exile from the home of my fathers, a deprived and desolate man
—a baffled, and beaten, and dishonoured man. But who shall
find out the ways of Providence? Such were the means by
which I was chosen forth as a champion for the truth—holding
my life as nothing, if thereby that may be advanced. But this
was not what I wished to speak of. Thou hast saved the

earthly life of my child—let me save the eternal welfare of yours."

Lady Peveril was silent. They were now approaching the point where the avenue terminated in a communication with a public road, or rather pathway, running through an unenclosed common field; this the lady had to prosecute for a little way, until a turn of the path gave her admittance into the Park of Martindale. She now felt sincerely anxious to be in the open moonshine, and avoided reply to Bridgenorth that she might make the more haste. But as they reached the junction of the avenue and the public road, he laid his hand on her arm, and commanded rather than requested her to stop. She obeyed. He pointed to a huge oak, of the largest size, which grew on the summit of a knoll in the open ground which terminated the avenue, and was exactly so placed as to serve for a termination to the vista. The moonshine without the avenue was so strong, that, amidst the flood of light which it poured on the venerable tree, they could easily discover, from the shattered state of the boughs on one side, that it had suffered damage from lightning. "Remember you," he said, "when we last looked together on that tree? I had ridden from London, and brought with me a protection from the committee for your husband; and as I passed the spot—here on this spot where we now stand, you stood with my lost Alice—two—the last two of my beloved infants gambolled before you. I leaped from my horse—to her I was a husband—to those a father—to you a welcome and revered protector—What am I now to any one?" He pressed his hand on his brow, and groaned in agony of spirit.

It was not in the Lady Peveril's nature to hear sorrow without an attempt at consolation. "Master Bridgenorth," she said, "I blame no man's creed, while I believe and follow my own; and I rejoice that in yours you have sought consolation for temporal afflictions. But does not every Christian creed teach us alike, that affliction should soften our heart?"

"Ay, woman," said Bridgenorth sternly, "as the lightning which shattered yonder oak hath softened its trunk. No; the seared wood is the fitter for the use of the workmen—the hardened and the dried-up heart is that which can best bear the task imposed by these dismal times. God and man will no longer endure the unbridled profligacy of the dissolute—the scoffing of the profane—the contempt of the divine laws—the infraction of human rights. The times demand righters and avengers, and there will be no want of them."

"I deny not the existence of much evil," said Lady Peveril, compelling herself to answer, and beginning at the same time to walk forward; "and from hearsay, though not, I thank Heaven, from observation, I am convinced of the wild debauchery of the times. But let us trust it may be corrected without such violent remedies as you hint at. Surely the ruin of a second civil war—though I trust your thoughts go not that dreadful length—were at best a desperate alternative."

"Sharp, but sure," replied Bridgenorth. "The blood of the Paschal lamb chased away the destroying angel—the sacrifices offered on the threshing-floor of Araunah, stayed the pestilence. Fire and sword are severe remedies, but they purge and purify."

"Alas! Major Bridgenorth," said the lady, "wise and moderate in your youth, can you have adopted in your advanced life the thoughts and language of those whom you yourself beheld drive themselves and the nation to the brink of ruin?"

"I know not what I then was—you know not what I now am," he replied, and suddenly broke off; for they even then came forth into the open light, and it seemed as if, feeling himself under the lady's eye, he was disposed to soften his tone and his language.

At the first distinct view which she had of his person, she was aware that he was armed with a short sword, a poniard, and pistols at his belt—precautions very unusual for a man who formerly had seldom, and only on days of ceremony, carried a walking rapier, though such was the habitual and constant practice of gentlemen of his station in life. There seemed also something of more stern determination than usual in his air, which indeed had always been rather sullen than affable; and ere she could repress the sentiment, she could not help saying, "Master Bridgenorth, you are indeed changed."

"You see but the outward man," he replied; "the change within is yet deeper. But it was not of myself that I desired to talk—I have already said, that as you have preserved my child from the darkness of the grave, I would willingly preserve yours from that more utter darkness, which, I fear, hath involved the path and walks of his father."

"I must not hear this of Sir Geoffrey," said the Lady Peveril; "I must bid you farewell for the present; and when we again meet at a more suitable time, I will at least listen to your advice concerning Julian, although I should not perhaps incline to it."

"That more suitable time may never come," replied Bridgenorth. "Time wanes, eternity draws nigh. Hearken! it is said to be your purpose to send the young Julian to be bred up in yonder bloody island, under the hand of your kinswoman, that cruel murderess, by whom was done to death a man more worthy of vital existence than any that she can boast among her vaunted ancestry. These are current tidings—Are they true?"

"I do not blame you, Master Bridgenorth, for thinking

harshly of my cousin of Derby," said Lady Peveril; "nor do I altogether vindicate the rash action of which she hath been guilty. Nevertheless, in her habitation, it is my husband's opinion and my own, that Julian may be trained in the studies and accomplishments becoming his rank, along with the young Earl of Derby."

"Under the curse of God, and the blessing of the Pope of Rome," said Bridgenorth. "You, lady, so quick-sighted in matters of earthly prudence, are you blind to the gigantic pace at which Rome is moving to regain this country, once the richest gem in her usurped tiara? The old are seduced by gold—the youth by pleasure—the weak by flattery—cowards by fear—and the courageous by ambition. A thousand baits for each taste, and each bait concealing the same deadly hook."

"I am well aware, Master Bridgenorth," said Lady Peveril, "that my kinswoman is a Catholic;* but her son is educated in the Church of England's principles, agreeably to the command of her deceased husband."

"Is it likely," answered Bridgenorth, "that she, who fears not shedding the blood of the righteous, whether on the field or scaffold, will regard the sanction of her promise when her religion bids her break it? Or, if she does, what shall your son be the better, if he remain in the mire of his father? What are your Episcopal tenets but mere Popery? save that ye have chosen a temporal tyrant for your Pope, and substitute a mangled mass in English for that which your predecessors pronounced in Latin.—But why speak I of these things to one who hath ears, indeed, and eyes, yet cannot see, listen to, or understand what is alone worthy to be heard, seen, and known? Pity that what hath been wrought so fair and exquisite in form and disposition, should be yet blind, deaf, and ignorant, like the things which perish!"

"We shall not agree on these subjects, Master Bridgenorth," said the lady, anxious still to escape from this strange conference, though scarce knowing what to apprehend; "once more, I must bid you farewell."

"Stay yet an instant," he said, again laying his hand on her arm; "I would stop you if I saw you rushing on the brink of an actual precipice—let me prevent you from a danger still greater. How shall I work upon your unbelieving mind? Shall I tell you that the debt of bloodshed yet remains a debt to be paid by the bloody house of Derby? And wilt thou send thy son to be among those from whom it shall be exacted?"

"You wish to alarm me in vain, Master Bridgenorth," answered

* I have elsewhere noticed that this is a deviation from the truth— Charlotte, Countess of Derby, was a Huguenot.

the lady; "what penalty can be exacted from the Countess, for an action, which I have already called a rash one, has been long since levied."

"You deceive yourself," retorted he sternly. "Think you a paltry sum of money, given to be wasted on the debaucheries of Charles, can atone for the death of such a man as Christian —a man precious alike to heaven and to earth? Not on such terms is the blood of the righteous to be poured forth! Every hour's delay is numbered down as adding interest to the grievous debt, which will one day be required from that blood-thirsty woman."

At this moment the distant tread of horses was heard on the road on which they held this singular dialogue. Bridgenorth listened a moment, and then said, "Forget that you have seen me —name not my name to your nearest or dearest—lock my counsel in your breast—profit by it, and it shall be well with you."

So saying, he turned from her, and plunging through a gap in the fence, regained the cover of his own wood, along which the path still led.

The noise of horses advancing at full trot now came nearer; and Lady Peveril was aware of several riders, whose forms rose indistinctly on the summit of the rising ground behind her. She became also visible to them; and one or two of the foremost made towards her at increased speed, challenging her as they advanced with the cry of "Stand! Who goes there?" The foremost who came up, however, exclaimed, "Mercy on us, if it be not my lady!" and Lady Peveril, at the same moment, recognised one of her own servants. Her husband rode up immediately afterwards, with, "How now, Dame Margaret? What makes you abroad so far from home and at an hour so late?"

Lady Peveril mentioned her visit at the cottage, but did not think it necessary to say aught of having seen Major Bridgenorth; afraid, it may be, that her husband might be displeased with that incident.

"Charity is a fine thing and a fair," answered Sir Geoffrey; "but I must tell you, you do ill, dame, to wander about the country like a quacksalver, at the call of every old woman who has a colic-fit; and at this time of night especially, and when the land is so unsettled besides."

"I am sorry to hear that it is so," said the lady. "I had heard no such news."

"News?" repeated Sir Geoffrey, "why, here has a new plot broken out among the Roundheads, worse than Venner's by a butt's length; * and who should be so deep in it as our old

* The celebrated insurrection of the Anabaptists and Fifth Monarchy men in London, in the year 1661.

neighbour Bridgenorth? There is search for him everywhere; and I promise you if he is found, he is like to pay old
scores."

"Then I am sure, I trust he will not be found," said Lady
Peveril.

"Do you so?" replied Sir Geoffrey. "Now I, on my part,
hope that he will; and it shall not be my fault if he be not;
for which effect I will presently ride down to Moultrassie, and
make strict search, according to my duty; there shall neither
rebel nor traitor earth so near Martindale Castle, that I will
assure them. And you, my lady, be pleased for once to dispense with a pillion, and get up, as you have done before,
behind Saunders, who shall convey you safe home."

The Lady obeyed in silence; indeed she did not dare to trust
her voice in an attempt to reply, so much was she disconcerted
with the intelligence she had just heard.

She rode behind the groom to the Castle, where she awaited
in great anxiety the return of her husband. He came back at
length; but to her great relief, without any prisoner. He then
explained more fully than his haste had before permitted, that
an express had come down to Chesterfield, with news from
Court of a proposed insurrection amongst the old Commonwealth men, especially those who had served in the army; and
that Bridgenorth, said to be lurking in Derbyshire, was one of
the principal conspirators.

After some time, this report of a conspiracy seemed to die
away like many others of that period. The warrants were
recalled, but nothing more was seen or heard of Major Bridgenorth; although it is probable he might safely enough have
shown himself as openly as many did who lay under the same
circumstances of suspicion.

About this time also, Lady Peveril, with many tears, took a
temporary leave of her son Julian, who was sent, as had long
been intended, for the purpose of sharing the education of the
young Earl of Derby. Although the boding words of Bridgenorth sometimes occurred to Lady Peveril's mind, she did not
suffer them to weigh with her in opposition to the advantages which the patronage of the Countess of Derby secured to
her son.

The plan seemed to be in every respect successful; and when,
from time to time, Julian visited the house of his father, Lady
Peveril had the satisfaction to see him, on every occasion,
improved in person and in manner, as well as ardent in the
pursuit of more solid acquirements. In process of time he
became a gallant and accomplished youth, and travelled for
some time upon the continent with the young Earl. This
was the more especially necessary for the enlarging of their

acquaintance with the world; because the Countess had never appeared in London, or at the Court of King Charles, since her flight to the Isle of Man in 1660; but had resided in solitary and aristocratic state, alternately on her estates in England and in that island.

This had given to the education of both the young men, otherwise as excellent as the best teachers could render it, something of a narrow and restricted character; but though the disposition of the young Earl was lighter and more volatile than that of Julian, both the one and the other had profited, in a considerable degree, by the opportunities afforded them. It was Lady Derby's strict injunction to her son, now returning from the continent, that he should not appear at the Court of Charles. But having been for some time of age, he did not think it absolutely necessary to obey her in this particular; and had remained for some time in London, partaking the pleasures of the gay Court there, with all the ardour of a young man bred up in comparative seclusion.

In order to reconcile the Countess to this transgression of her authority (for he continued to entertain for her the profound respect in which he had been educated), Lord Derby agreed to make a long sojourn with her in her favourite island, which he abandoned almost entirely to her management.

Julian Peveril had spent at Martindale Castle a good deal of the time which his friend had bestowed in London; and at the period to which, passing over many years, our story has arrived, as it were, *per saltum*, they were both living as the Countess's guests, in the Castle of Rushin, in the venerable kingdom of Man.

CHAPTER XI

Mona—long hid from those who roam the main.
—COLLINS.

THE Isle of Man, in the middle of the seventeenth century, was very different, as a place of residence, from what it is now. Men had not then discovered its merit as a place of occasional refuge from the storms of life, and the society to be there met with was of a very uniform tenor. There were no smart fellows, whom fortune had tumbled from the seat of their barouches— no plucked pigeons or winged rooks—no disappointed speculators—no ruined miners—in short, no one worth talking to. The society of the island was limited to the natives themselves, and a few merchants, who lived by contraband trade. The amusements were rare and monotonous, and the mercurial young Earl was soon heartily tired of his dominions. The islanders, also, become too wise for happiness, had lost relish for the harmless and somewhat childish sports in which their simple ancestors had indulged themselves. May was no longer ushered in by the imaginary contest between the Queen of returning winter and advancing spring; the listeners no longer sympathised with the lively music of the followers of the one, or the discordant sounds with which the other asserted a more noisy claim to attention. Christmas, too, closed, and the steeples no longer jangled forth a dissonant peal. The wren, to seek for which used to be the sport dedicated to the holytide, was left unpursued and unslain. Party spirit had come among these simple people, and destroyed their good humour, while it left them their ignorance. Even the races, a sport generally interesting to people of all ranks, were no longer performed, because they were no longer interesting. The gentlemen were divided by feuds hitherto unknown, and each seemed to hold it scorn to be pleased with the same diversions that amused those of the opposite faction. The hearts of both parties revolted from the recollection of former days, when all was peace among them, when the Earl of Derby, now slaughtered, used to bestow the prize, and Christian, since so vindictively executed, started horses to add to the amusement.

Julian was seated in the deep recess which led to a latticed window of the old Castle; and, with his arms crossed, and an air of profound contemplation, was surveying the long perspective of ocean, which rolled its successive waves up to the foot of the rock on which the ancient pile is founded. The Earl was suffering under the infliction of ennui—now looking into a volume of Homer—now whistling—now swinging on his chair—now traversing the room—till, at length, his attention became swallowed up in admiration of the tranquillity of his companion.

"King of Men!" he said, repeating the favourite epithet by which Homer describes Agamemnon,—"I trust, for the old Greek's sake, he had a merrier office than being King of Man—Most philosophical Julian, will nothing rouse thee—not even a bad pun on my own royal dignity?"

"I wish you would be a little more the King in Man," said Julian, starting from his reverie, "and then you would find more amusement in your dominions."

"What! dethrone that royal Semiramis my mother," said the young lord, "who has as much pleasure in playing Queen as if she were a real Sovereign?—I wonder you can give me such counsel."

"Your mother, as you well know, my dear Derby, would be delighted, did you take any interest in the affairs of the island."

"Ay, truly, she would permit me to be King; but she would choose to remain Viceroy over me. Why, she would only gain a subject the more, by my converting my spare time, which is so very valuable to me, to the cares of royalty. No, no, Julian, she thinks it power, to direct all the affairs of these poor Manxmen; and, thinking it power, she finds it pleasure. I shall not interfere, unless she hold a high court of justice again. I cannot afford to pay another fine to my brother, King Charles—But I forget—this is a sore point with you."

"With the Countess, at least," replied Julian; "and I wonder you will speak of it."

"Why, I bear no malice against the poor man's memory any more than yourself, though I have not the same reasons for holding it in veneration," replied the Earl of Derby; "and yet I have some respect for it too. I remember their bringing him out to die—It was the first holiday I ever had in my life, and I heartily wish it had been on some other account."

"I would rather hear you speak of anything else, my lord," said Julian.

"Why, there it goes," answered the Earl; "whenever I talk of anything that puts you on your mettle, and warms your blood, that runs as cold as a merman's—to use a simile of this happy island—hey pass! you press me to change the subject.— Well, what shall we talk of?—O Julian, if you had not gone down to earth yourself among the castles and caverns of Derbyshire, we should have had enough of delicious topics—the playhouses, Julian—Both the King's house and the Duke's—Louis's establishment is a jest to them;—and the Ring in the Park, which beats the Corso at Naples—and the beauties, who beat the whole world!"

"I am very willing to hear you speak on the subject, my lord," answered Julian; "the less I have seen of the London world myself, the more I am likely to be amused by your account of it."

"Ay, my friend—but where to begin?—with the wit of Buckingham, and Sedley, and Etherege, or with the grace of Harry Jermyn—the courtesy of the Duke of Monmouth, or with the loveliness of La Belle Hamilton—of the Duchess of Richmond—of Lady ——, the person of Roxalana, the smart humour of Mrs. Nelly——"

"Or what say you to the bewitching sorceries of Lady Cynthia?" demanded his companion.

"Faith, I would have kept these to myself," said the Earl, "to follow your prudent example. But since you ask me, I fairly own I cannot tell what to say of them; only I think of them twenty times as often as all the beauties I have spoken of. And yet she is neither the twentieth part so beautiful as the plainest of these Court beauties, nor so witty as the dullest I have named, nor so modish—that is the great matter—as the most obscure. I cannot tell what makes me dote on her, except that she is as capricious as her whole sex put together."

"That I should think a small recommendation," answered his companion.

"Small, do you term it," replied the Earl, "and write yourself a brother of the angle? Why, which like you best? to pull a dead strain on a miserable gudgeon, which you draw ashore by main force, as the fellows here tow in their fishing-boats—or a lively salmon, that makes your rod crack, and your line whistle—plays you ten thousand mischievous pranks—wearies your heart out with hopes and fears—and is only laid panting on the bank, after you have shown the most unmatchable display of skill, patience, and dexterity?—But I see you have a mind to go on angling after your own old fashion. Off laced coat, and on brown jerkin;—lively colours scare fish in the sober waters of the Isle of Man;—faith, in London you will catch few, unless the bait glistens a little. But you *are* going?—Well, good luck to you. I will take to the barge;—the sea and wind are less inconstant than the tide you have embarked on."

"You have learned to say all these smart things in London, my lord," answered Julian; "but we shall have you a penitent for them, if Lady Cynthia be of my mind. Adieu, and pleasure till we meet."

The young men parted accordingly; and while the Earl betook him to his pleasure voyage, Julian, as his friend had prophesied, assumed the dress of one who means to amuse himself with angling. The hat and feather were exchanged for a cap of grey cloth; the deeply-laced cloak and doublet for a simple jacket of the same colour, with hose conforming; and finally, with rod in hand, and pannier at his back, mounted upon a handsome Manx pony, young Peveril rode briskly over the country which divided him from one of those beautiful streams that descend to the sea from the Kirk-Merlagh mountains.

Having reached the spot where he meant to commence his day's sport, Julian let his little steed graze, which, accustomed to the situation, followed him like a dog; and now and then, when tired of picking herbage in the valley through which the stream winded, came near her master's side, and, as if she had been a curious amateur of the sport, gazed on the trouts as Julian brought them struggling to the shore. But Fairy's master showed, on that day, little of the patience of a real angler, and took no heed to old Isaac Walton's recommendation, to fish the streams inch by inch.   He chose, indeed, with an angler's eye, the most promising casts, where the stream broke sparkling over a stone, affording the wonted shelter to a trout; or where, gliding away from a rippling current to a still eddy, it streamed under the projecting bank, or dashed from the pool of some low cascade.   By this judicious selection of spots whereon to employ his art, the sportsman's basket was soon sufficiently heavy, to show that his occupation was not a mere pretext; and so soon as this was the case, he walked briskly up the glen, only making a cast from time to time, in case of his being observed from any of the neighbouring heights.

It was a little green and rocky valley through which the brook strayed, very lonely, although the slight track of an unformed road showed that it was occasionally traversed, and that it was not altogether void of inhabitants.   As Peveril advanced still farther, the right bank reached to some distance from the stream, leaving a piece of meadow ground, the lower part of which, being close to the brook, was entirely covered with rich herbage, being possibly occasionally irrigated by its overflow.   The higher part of the level ground afforded a stance for an old house, of a singular structure, with a terraced garden, and a cultivated field or two beside it.   In former times, a Danish or Norwegian fastness had stood here, called the Black Fort, from the colour of a huge heathy hill, which, rising behind the building, appeared to be the boundary of the valley, and to afford the source of the brook.   But the original structure had been long demolished, as, indeed, it probably only consisted of dry stones, and its materials had been applied to the construction of the present mansion—the work of some churchman during the sixteenth century, as was evident from the huge stone-work of its windows, which scarce left room for light to pass through, as well as from two or three heavy buttresses, which projected from the front of the house, and exhibited on their surface little niches for images.   These had been carefully destroyed, and pots of flowers were placed in the niches in their stead, besides their being ornamented by creeping plants of various kinds, fancifully twined around them. The garden was also in good order; and though the spot was extremely solitary, there was about it altogether an air of comfort, accommodation, and even elegance, by no means generally characteristic of the habitations of the island at the time.

With much circumspection, Julian Peveril approached the low Gothic porch, which defended the entrance of the mansion from the tempests incident to its situation, and was, like the buttresses, overrun with ivy and other creeping plants.   An iron ring, contrived so as when drawn up and down to rattle against the bar of notched iron through which it was suspended, served the purpose of a knocker; and to this he applied himself, though with the greatest precaution.

He received no answer for some time, and indeed it seemed as if the house was totally uninhabited; when, at length, his impatience getting the upper hand, he tried to open the door, and, as it was only upon the latch, very easily succeeded. He passed through a little low-arched hall, the upper end of which was occupied by a staircase, and turning to the left, opened the door of a summer parlour, wainscoted with black oak, and very simply furnished with chairs and tables of the same materials; the former cushioned with leather. The apartment was gloomy —one of those stone-shafted windows which we have mentioned, with its small latticed panes, and thick garland of foliage, admitting but an imperfect light.

Over the chimneypiece (which was of the same massive materials with the panelling of the apartment) was the only ornament of the room; a painting, namely, representing an officer in the military dress of the Civil Wars. It was a green jerkin, then the national and peculiar wear of the Manxmen; his short band which hung down on the cuirass—the orange-coloured scarf, but, above all, the shortness of his close-cut hair, showing evidently to which of the great parties he had belonged. His right hand rested on the hilt of his sword; and in the left he held a small Bible, bearing the inscription, "*In hoc signo.*" The countenance was of a light complexion, with fair and almost effeminate blue eyes, and an oval form of face —one of those physiognomies, to which, though not otherwise unpleasing, we naturally attach the idea of melancholy and of misfortune.* Apparently it was well known to Julian Peveril; for after having looked at it for a long time, he could not forbear muttering aloud, "What would I give that that man had never been born, or that he still lived!"

"How now—how is this?" said a female, who entered the room as he uttered this reflection. "*You* here, Master Peveril, in spite of all the warnings you have had! You here in the possession of folk's house when they are abroad, and talking to yourself, as I shall warrant!"

"Yes, Mistress Deborah," said Peveril, "I am here once

---

* I am told that a portrait of the unfortunate William Christian is still preserved in the family of Waterson of Ballnahow of Kirk Church, Rushin. William Dhône is dressed in a green coat without collar or cape, after the fashion of those puritanic times, with the head in a close cropt wig, resembling the bishop's peruke of the present day. The countenance is youthful and well-looking, very unlike the expression of foreboding melancholy. I have so far taken advantage of this criticism, as to bring my ideal portrait in the present edition, nearer to the complexion at least of the fair-haired William Dhône.

more, as you see, against every prohibition, and in defiance of all danger.—Where is Alice ? "

"Where you will never see her, Master Julian—you may satisfy yourself of that," answered Mistress Deborah, for it was that respectable governante; and sinking down at the same time upon one of the large leathern chairs, she began to fan herself with her handkerchief, and complain of the heat in a most ladylike fashion.

In fact, Mistress Debbitch, while her exterior intimated a considerable change of condition for the better, and her countenance showed the less favourable effects of the twenty years which had passed over her head, was in mind and manners very much what she had been when she battled the opinions of Madam Ellesmere at Martindale Castle. In a word, she was self-willed, obstinate, and coquettish as ever, otherwise no ill-disposed person. Her present appearance was that of a woman of the better rank. From the sobriety of the fashion of her dress, and the uniformity of its colours, it was plain she belonged to some sect which condemned superfluous gaiety in attire ; but no rules, not those of a nunnery or of a quaker's society, can prevent a little coquetry in that particular, where a woman is desirous of being supposed to retain some claim to personal attention. All Mistress Deborah's garments were so arranged as might best set off a good-looking woman, whose countenance indicated ease and good cheer—who called herself five-and-thirty, and was well entitled, if she had a mind, to call herself twelve or fifteen years older.

Julian was under the necessity of enduring all her tiresome and fantastic airs, and awaiting with patience till she had "prinked herself and pinned herself"—flung her hoods back, and drawn them forward—snuffed at a little bottle of essences —closed her eyes like a dying fowl—turned them up like a duck in a thunderstorm ; when at length, having exhausted her round of *minauderies,* she condescended to open the conversation.

"These walks will be the death of me," she said, "and all on your account, Master Julian Peveril ; for if Dame Christian should learn that you have chosen to make your visits to her niece, I promise you Mistress Alice would be soon obliged to find other quarters, and so should I."

"Come now, Mistress Deborah, be good-humoured," said Julian ; "consider, was not all this intimacy of ours of your own making ? Did you not make yourself known to me the very first time I strolled up this glen with my fishing-rod, and tell me that you were my former keeper, and that Alice had been my little playfellow ? And what could there be more natural, than that I should come back and see two such agreeable persons as often as I could ? "

"Yes," said Dame Deborah; "but I did not bid you fall in love with us, though, or propose such a matter as marriage either to Alice or myself."

"To do you justice, you never did, Deborah," answered the youth; "but what of that? Such things will come out before one is aware. I am sure you must have heard such proposals fifty times when you least expected them."

"Fie, fie, fie, Master Julian Peveril," said the governante; "I would have you to know that I have always so behaved myself, that the best of the land would have thought twice of it, and have very well considered both what he was going to say, and how he was going to say it, before he came out with such proposals to me."

"True, true, Mistress Deborah," continued Julian; "but all the world hath not your discretion. Then Alice Bridgenorth is a child—a mere child; and one always asks a baby to be one's little wife, you know. Come, I know you will forgive me. Thou wert ever the best-natured, kindest woman in the world; and you know you have said twenty times we were made for each other."

"Oh no, Master Julian Peveril; no, no, no!" ejaculated Deborah. "I may indeed have said your estates were born to be united; and to be sure it is natural for me, that come of the old stock of the yeomanry of Peveril of the Peak's estate, to wish that it was all within the ring fence again; which sure enough it might be, were you to marry Alice Bridgenorth. But then there is the knight your father, and my lady your mother; and there is her father, that is half crazy with his religion; and her aunt that wears eternal black grogram for that unlucky Colonel Christian; and there is the Countess of Derby, that would serve us all with the same sauce if we were thinking of anything that would displease her. And besides all that, you have broke your word with Mistress Alice, and everything is over between you; and I am of opinion it is quite right it should be all over. And perhaps it may be, Master Julian, that I should have thought so a long time ago, before a child like Alice put it into my head; but I am so good-natured."

No flatterer like a lover, who wishes to carry his point.

"You are the best-natured, kindest creature in the world, Deborah.—But you have never seen the ring I bought for you at Paris. Nay, I will put it on your finger myself;—what! your foster-son, whom you loved so well, and took such care of?"

He easily succeeded in putting a pretty ring of gold, with a humorous affectation of gallantry, on the fat finger of Mistress Deborah Debbitch. Hers was a soul of a kind often to be met with, both among the lower and higher vulgar, who, without being, on a broad scale, accessible to bribes or corruption, are nevertheless much attached to perquisites, and considerably biassed in their line of duty, though perhaps insensibly, by the love of petty observances, petty presents, and trivial compliments. Mistress Debbitch turned the ring round, and round, and round, and at length said, in a whisper, "Well, Master Julian Peveril, it signifies nothing denying anything to such a young gentleman as you, for young gentlemen are always so obstinate! and so I may as well tell you, that Mistress Alice walked back from Kirk-Truagh along with me, just now, and entered the house at the same time with myself."

"Why did you not tell me so before?" said Julian, starting up; "where—where is she?"

"You had better ask why I tell you so *now*, Master Julian," said Dame Deborah; "for, I promise you, it is against her express commands; and I would not have told you, had you not looked so pitiful;—but as for seeing you, that she will not —and she is in her own bedroom, with a good oak door shut and bolted upon her—that is one comfort.—And so, as for any breach of trust on my part—I promise you the little saucy minx gives it no less name—it is quite impossible."

"Do not say so, Deborah—only go—only try—tell her to hear me—tell her I have a hundred excuses for disobeying her commands—tell her I have no doubt to get over all obstacles at Martindale Castle."

"Nay, I tell you it is all in vain," replied the Dame. "When I saw your cap and rod lying in the hall, I did but say, 'There he is again,' and she ran up the stairs like a young deer; and I heard key turned, and bolt shot, ere I could say a single word to stop her—I marvel you heard her not."

"It was because I am, as I ever was, an owl—a dreaming fool, who let all those golden minutes pass, which my luckless life holds out to me so rarely.—Well—tell her I go—go for ever—go where she will hear no more of me—where no one shall hear more of me!"

"Oh, the Father!" said the dame, "hear how he talks!— What will become of Sir Geoffrey, and your mother, and of me, and of the Countess, if you were to go so far as you talk of? And what would become of poor Alice too? for I will be sworn she likes you better than she says, and I know she used to sit and look the way that you used to come up the stream, and now and then ask me if the morning were good for fishing. And all the while you were on the continent, as they call it, she scarcely smiled once, unless it was when she got two beautiful long letters about foreign parts."

"Friendship, Dame Deborah — only friendship — cold and calm remembrance of one who, by your kind permission, stole in on your solitude now and then, with news from the living world without—Once, indeed, I thought—but it is all over— farewell."

So saying, he covered his face with one hand, and extended the other, in the act of bidding adieu to Dame Debbitch, whose kind heart became unable to withstand the sight of his affliction.

" Now, do not be in such haste," she said ; " I will go up again, and tell her how it stands with you, and bring her down, if it is in woman's power to do it."

And so saying, she left the apartment, and ran upstairs.

Julian Peveril, meanwhile, paced the apartment in great agitation, waiting the success of Deborah's intercession ; and she remained long enough absent to give us time to explain, in a short retrospect, the circumstances which had led to his present situation.

CHAPTER XII

> Ah me ! for aught that ever I could read,
> Could ever hear by tale or history,
> The course of true love never did run smooth !
> —MIDSUMMER NIGHT'S DREAM.

THE celebrated passage which we have prefixed to this chapter has, like most observations of the same author, its foundation in real experience. The period at which love is formed for the first time, and felt most strongly, is seldom that at which there is much prospect of its being brought to a happy issue. The state of artificial society opposes many complicated obstructions to early marriages; and the chance is very great, that such obstacles prove insurmountable. In fine, there are few men who do not look back in secret to some period of their youth, at which a sincere and early affection was repulsed, or betrayed, or became abortive from opposing circumstances. It is these little passages of secret history, which leave a tinge of romance in every bosom, scarce permitting us, even in the most busy or the most advanced period of life, to listen with total indifference to a tale of true love.

Julian Peveril had so fixed his affections, as to insure the fullest share of that opposition which early attachments are so apt to encounter. Yet nothing so natural as that he should have done so. In early youth, Dame Debbitch had accidentally met with the son of her first patroness, and who had himself been her earliest charge, fishing in the little brook already noticed, which watered the valley in which she resided with

Alice Bridgenorth. The dame's curiosity easily discovered who he was; and besides the interest which persons in her condition usually take in the young people who have been under their charge, she was delighted with the opportunity to talk about former times—about Martindale Castle, and friends there— about Sir Geoffrey and his good lady—and, now and then, about Lance Outram the park-keeper.

The mere pleasure of gratifying her inquiries, would scarce have had power enough to induce Julian to repeat his visits to the lonely glen; but Deborah had a companion—a lovely girl —bred in solitude, and in the quiet and unpretending tastes which solitude encourages—spirited, also, and inquisitive, and listening, with laughing cheek, and an eager eye, to every tale which the young angler brought from the town and castle.

The visits of Julian to the Black Fort were only occasional— so far Dame Deborah showed common-sense—which was, per- haps, inspired by the apprehension of losing her place, in case of discovery. She had, indeed, great confidence in the strong and rooted belief—amounting almost to superstition—which Major Bridgenorth entertained, that his daughter's continued health could only be insured by her continuing under the charge of one who had acquired Lady Peveril's supposed skill in treating those subject to such ailments. This belief Dame Deborah had improved to the utmost of her simple cunning,— always speaking in something of an oracular tone, upon the subject of her charge's health, and hinting at certain mysterious rules necessary to maintain it in the present favourable state. She had availed herself of this artifice, to procure for herself and Alice a separate establishment at the Black Fort; for it was originally Major Bridgenorth's resolution, that his daughter and her governante should remain under the same roof with the sister-in-law of his deceased wife, the widow of the unfor- tunate Colonel Christian. But this lady was broken down with premature age, brought on by sorrow; and, in a short visit which Major Bridgenorth made to the island, he was easily prevailed on to consider her house at Kirk-Truagh, as a very cheerless residence for his daughter. Dame Deborah, who longed for domestic independence, was careful to increase this impression by alarming her patron's fears on account of Alice's health. The mansion of Kirk-Truagh stood, she said, much exposed to the Scottish winds, which could not but be cold, as they came from a country where, as she was assured, there was ice and snow at midsummer. In short, she prevailed, and was put into full possession of the Black Fort, a house which, as well as Kirk-Truagh, belonged formerly to Christian, and now to his widow.

Still, however, it was enjoined on the governante and her

charge, to visit Kirk-Truagh from time to time, and to consider themselves as under the management and guardianship of Mistress Christian—a state of subjection, the sense of which Deborah endeavoured to lessen, by assuming as much freedom of conduct as she possibly dared, under the influence, doubtless, of the same feelings of independence, which induced her, at Martindale Hall, to spurn the advice of Mistress Ellesmere.

It was this generous disposition to defy control which induced her to procure for Alice, secretly, some means of education, which the stern genius of puritanism would have proscribed. She ventured to have her charge taught music—nay, even dancing; and the picture of the stern Colonel Christian trembled on the wainscot where it was suspended, while the sylph-like form of Alice, and the substantial person of Dame Deborah, executed French *chaussées* and *borées,* to the sound of a small kit, which screamed under the bow of Monsieur De Pigal, half smuggler, half dancing-master. This abomination reached the ears of the Colonel's widow, and by her was communicated to Bridgenorth, whose sudden appearance in the island showed the importance he attached to the communication. Had she been faithless to her own cause, that had been the latest hour of Mrs. Deborah's administration. But she retreated into her stronghold.

"Dancing," she said, "was exercise, regulated and timed by music; and it stood to reason, that it must be the best of all exercise for a delicate person, especially as it could be taken within doors, and in all states of the weather."

Bridgenorth listened, with a clouded and thoughtful brow, when, in exemplification of her doctrine, Mistress Deborah, who was no contemptible performer on the viol, began to jangle Sellenger's Round, and desired Alice to dance an old English measure to the tune. As the half-bashful, half-smiling girl, about fourteen—for such was her age—moved gracefully to the music, the father's eye unavoidably followed the light spring of her step, and marked with joy the rising colour in her cheek. When the dance was over, he folded her in his arms, smoothed her somewhat disordered locks with a father's affectionate hand, smiled, kissed her brow, and took his leave, without one single word farther interdicting the exercise of dancing. He did not himself communicate the result of his visit at the Black Fort to Mrs. Christian, but she was not long of learning it, by the triumph of Dame Deborah on her next visit.

"It is well," said the stern old lady; "my brother Bridgenorth hath permitted you to make a Herodias of Alice, and teach her dancing. You have only now to find her a partner for life—I shall neither meddle nor make more in their affairs."

In fact, the triumph of Dame Deborah, or rather of Dame

Nature, on this occasion, had more important effects than the former had ventured to anticipate; for Mrs. Christian, though she received with all formality the formal visits of the gover- nante and her charge, seemed thenceforth so pettish with the issue of her remonstrance, upon the enormity of her niece dancing to a little fiddle, that she appeared to give up inter- ference in her affairs, and left Dame Debbitch and Alice to manage both education and housekeeping—in which she had hitherto greatly concerned herself — much after their own pleasure.

It was in this independent state that they lived, when Julian first visited their habitation; and he was the rather encouraged to do so by Dame Deborah, that she believed him to be one of the last persons in the world with whom Mistress Christian would have desired her niece to be acquainted—the happy spirit of contradiction superseding, with Dame Deborah, on this, as on other occasions, all consideration of the fitness of things. She did not act altogether without precaution neither. She was aware she had to guard not only against any reviving interest or curiosity on the part of Mistress Christian, but against the sudden arrival of Major Bridgenorth, who never failed once in the year to make his appearance at the Black Fort when least expected, and to remain there for a few days. Dame Debbitch, therefore, exacted of Julian, that his visits should be few and far between; that he should condescend to pass for a relation of her own, in the eyes of two ignorant Manx girls and a lad, who formed her establishment; and that he should always appear in his angler's dress made of the simple *Loughtan,* or buff-coloured wool of the island, which is not subjected to dyeing. By these cautions, she thought his intimacy at the Black Fort would be entirely unnoticed, or considered as immaterial, while, in the meantime, it furnished much amuse- ment to her charge and herself.

This was accordingly the case during the earlier part of their intercourse, while Julian was a lad, and Alice a girl two or three years younger. But as the lad shot up to youth, and the girl to womanhood, even Dame Deborah Debbitch's judgment saw danger in their continued intimacy. She took an oppor- tunity to communicate to Julian who Miss Bridgenorth actually was, and the peculiar circumstances which placed discord between their fathers. He heard the story of their quarrel with interest and surprise, for he had only resided occasionally at Martindale Castle, and the subject of Bridgenorth's quarrel with his father had never been mentioned in his presence. His imagination caught fire at the sparks afforded by this singular story; and, far from complying with the prudent re- monstrance of Dame Deborah, and gradually estranging himself from the Black Fort and its fair inmate, he frankly declared, he considered his intimacy there, so casually commenced, as intimating the will of Heaven, that Alice and he were designed for each other, in spite of every obstacle which passion or prejudice could raise up betwixt them. They had been companions in infancy; and a little exertion of memory enabled him to recall his childish grief for the unexpected and sudden disappearance of his little companion, whom he was destined again to meet with in the early bloom of opening beauty, in a country which was foreign to them both.

Dame Deborah was confounded at the consequences of her communication, which had thus blown into a flame the passion which she hoped it would have either prevented or extinguished. She had not the sort of head which resists the masculine and energetic remonstrances of passionate attachment, whether addressed to her on her own account, or on behalf of another. She lamented, and wondered, and ended her feeble opposition, by weeping, and sympathising, and consenting to allow the continuance of Julian's visits, provided he should only address himself to Alice as a friend; to gain the world, she would consent to nothing more. She was not, however, so simple, but that she also had her forebodings of the designs of Providence on this youthful couple; for certainly they could not be more formed to be united than the good estates of Martindale and Moultrassie.

Then came a long sequence of reflections. Martindale Castle wanted but some repairs to be almost equal to Chatsworth. The Hall might be allowed to go to ruin; or, what would be better, when Sir Geoffrey's time came (for the good knight had seen service, and must be breaking now), the Hall would be a good dowery-house, to which my lady and Ellesmere might retreat; while (empress of the still-room, and queen of the pantry) Mistress Deborah Debbitch should reign housekeeper at the Castle, and extend, perhaps, the crown-matrimonial to Lance Outram, provided he was not become too old, too fat, or too fond of ale.

Such were the soothing visions under the influence of which the dame connived at an attachment, which lulled also to pleasing dreams, though of a character so different, her charge and her visitant.

The visits of the young angler became more and more frequent; and the embarrassed Deborah, though foreseeing all the dangers of discovery, and the additional risk of an explanation betwixt Alice and Julian, which must necessarily render their relative situation so much more delicate, felt completely overborne by the enthusiasm of the young lover, and was compelled to let matters take their course.

H

The departure of Julian for the continent interrupted the course of his intimacy at the Black Fort, and while it relieved the elder of its inmates from much internal apprehension, spread an air of languor and dejection over the countenance of the younger, which, at Bridgenorth's next visit to the Isle of Man, renewed all his terrors for his daughter's constitutional malady.

Deborah promised faithfully she should look better the next morning, and she kept her word. She had retained in her possession for some time a letter which Julian had, by some private conveyance, sent to her charge, for his youthful friend. Deborah had dreaded the consequences of delivering it as a billet-doux, but, as in the case of the dance, she thought there could be no harm in administering it as a remedy.

It had complete effect; and next day the cheeks of the maiden had a tinge of the rose, which so much delighted her father, that, as he mounted his horse, he flung his purse into Deborah's hand, with the desire she should spare nothing that could make herself and his daughter happy, and the assurance that she had his full confidence.

This expression of liberality and confidence from a man of Major Bridgenorth's reserved and cautious disposition, gave full plumage to Mistress Deborah's hopes; and emboldened her not only to deliver another letter of Julian's to the young lady, but to encourage more boldly and freely than formerly the intercourse of the lovers when Peveril returned from abroad.

At length, in spite of all Julian's precaution, the young Earl became suspicious of his frequent solitary fishing parties; and he himself, now better acquainted with the world than formerly, became aware that his repeated visits and solitary walks with a person so young and beautiful as Alice, might not only betray prematurely the secret of his attachment, but be of essential prejudice to her who was its object.

Under the influence of this conviction, he abstained, for an unusual period, from visiting the Black Fort. But when he next indulged himself with spending an hour in the place where he would gladly have abode for ever, the altered manner of Alice—the tone in which she seemed to upbraid his neglect, penetrated his heart, and deprived him of that power of self-command, which he had hitherto exercised in their interviews. It required but a few energetic words to explain to Alice at once his feelings, and to make her sensible of the real nature of her own. She wept plentifully, but her tears were not all of bitterness. She sat passively still, and without reply, while he explained to her, with many an interjection, the circumstances which had placed discord between their families; for hitherto, all that she had known was, that Master Peveril, belonging to the household of the great Countess or Lady of Man, must observe some precautions in visiting a relative of the unhappy Colonel Christian. But, when Julian concluded his tale with the warmest protestations of eternal love, "My poor father!" she burst forth, "and was this to be the end of all thy precautions?—This, that the son of him that disgraced and banished thee, should hold such language to your daughter?"

"You err, Alice, you err," cried Julian eagerly. "That I hold this language—that the son of Peveril addresses thus the daughter of your father—that he thus kneels to you for forgiveness of injuries which passed when we were both infants, shows the will of Heaven, that in our affection should be quenched the discord of our parents. What else could lead those who parted infants on the hills of Derbyshire, to meet thus in the valleys of Man?"

Alice, however new such a scene, and, above all, her own emotions, might be, was highly endowed with that exquisite delicacy which is imprinted in the female heart, to give warning of the slightest approach to impropriety in a situation like hers.

"Rise, rise, Master Peveril," she said; "do not do yourself and me this injustice—we have done both wrong—very wrong; but my fault was done in ignorance. O God! my poor father, who needs comfort so much—is it for me to add to his misfortunes? Rise!" she added more firmly; "if you retain this unbecoming posture any longer, I will leave the room, and you shall never see me more."

The commanding tone of Alice overawed the impetuosity of her lover, who took in silence a seat removed to some distance from hers, and was again about to speak. "Julian," said she in a milder tone, "you have spoken enough, and more than enough. Would you had left me in the pleasing dream in which I could have listened to you for ever! but the hour of wakening is arrived." Peveril waited the prosecution of her speech as a criminal while he waits his doom; for he was sufficiently sensible that an answer, delivered not certainly without emotion, but with firmness and resolution, was not to be interrupted. "We have done wrong," she repeated, "very wrong; and if we now separate for ever, the pain we may feel will be but a just penalty for our error. We should never have met: meeting, we should part as soon as possible. Our farther intercourse can but double our pain at parting. Farewell, Julian; and forget we ever have seen each other!"

"Forget!" said Julian; "never, never. To _you_, it is easy to speak the word—to think the thought. To _me_, an approach to either can only be by utter destruction. Why should you doubt that the feud of our fathers, like so many of which we have heard, might be appeased by our friendship? You are my only friend. I am the only one whom Heaven has assigned to you. Why should we separate for the fault of others, which befell when we were but children?"

"You speak in vain, Julian," said Alice; "I pity you—perhaps I pity myself—indeed, I should pity myself, perhaps, the most of the two; for you will go forth to new scenes and new faces, and will soon forget me; but, I, remaining in this solitude, how shall I forget?—that, however, is not now the question—I can bear my lot, and it commands us to part."

"Hear me yet a moment," said Peveril; "this evil is not, cannot be remediless. I will go to my father,—I will use the intercession of my mother, to whom he can refuse nothing—I will gain their consent—they have no other child—and they must consent, or lose him for ever. Say, Alice, if I come to you with my parents' consent to my suit, will you again say, with that tone so touching and so sad, yet so incredibly determined—Julian, we must part?" Alice was silent. "Cruel girl, will you not even deign to answer me?" said her lover.

"We answer not those who speak in their dreams," said Alice. "You ask me what I would do were impossibilities performed. What right have you to make such suppositions, and ask such a question?"

"Hope, Alice, Hope," answered Julian, "the last support of the wretched, which even you surely would not be cruel enough to deprive me of. In every difficulty, in every doubt, in every danger, Hope will fight even if he cannot conquer. Tell me once more, if I come to you in the name of my father—in the name of that mother, to whom you partly owe your life, what would you answer to me?"

"I would refer you to my own father," said Alice, blushing, and casting her eyes down; but instantly raising them again, she repeated, in a firmer and a sadder tone, "Yes, Julian, I would refer you to my father; and you would find that your pilot, Hope, had deceived you; and that you had but escaped the quicksands to fall upon the rocks."

"I would that could be tried!" said Julian. "Methinks I could persuade your father that in ordinary eyes our alliance is not undesirable. My family have fortune, rank, long descent —all that fathers look for when they bestow a daughter's hand."

"All this would avail you nothing," said Alice. "The spirit of my father is bent upon the things of another world; and if he listened to hear you out, it would be but to tell you that he spurned your offers."

"You know not—you know not, Alice," said Julian. "Fire can soften iron—thy father's heart cannot be so hard, or his prejudices so strong, but I shall find some means to melt him. Forbid me not—Oh, forbid me not at least the experiment!"

"I can but advise," said Alice; "I can forbid you nothing; for, to forbid, implies power to command obedience. But if you will be wise, and listen to me—Here, and on this spot, we part for ever!"

"Not so, by Heaven!" said Julian, whose bold and sanguine temper scarce saw difficulty in attaining aught which he desired. "We now part, indeed, but it is that I may return armed with my parents' consent. They desire that I should marry— in their last letters they pressed it more openly—they shall have their desire; and such a bride as I will present to them has not graced their house since the Conqueror gave it origin. Farewell, Alice! Farewell, for a brief space!"

She replied, "Farewell, Julian! Farewell for ever!"

Julian, within a week of this interview, was at Martindale Castle, with the view of communicating his purpose. But the task which seems easy at a distance, proves as difficult, upon a nearer approach, as the fording of a river, which from afar appeared only a brook. There lacked not opportunities of entering upon the subject; for in the first ride which he took with his father, the Knight resumed the subject of his son's marriage, and liberally left the lady to his choice; but under the strict proviso, that she was of a loyal and an honourable family;—if she had fortune, it was good and well, or rather, it was better than well; but if she was poor, why, "there is still some picking," said Sir Geoffrey, "on the bones of the old estate; and Dame Margaret and I will be content with the less, that you young folks may have your share of it. I am turned frugal already, Julian. You see what a north-country shambling bit of a Galloway nag I ride upon—a different beast, I wot, from my own old Black Hastings, who had but one fault, and that was his wish to turn down Moultrassie avenue."

"Was that so great a fault?" said Julian, affecting indifference, while his heart was trembling, as it seemed to him, almost in his very throat.

"It used to remind me of that base, dishonourable Presbyterian fellow, Bridgenorth," said Sir Geoffrey; "and I would as lief think of a toad:—they say he has turned Independent, to accomplish the full degree of rascality.—I tell you, Gill, I turned off the cow-boy, for gathering nuts in his woods—I would hang a dog that would so much as kill a hare there.— But what is the matter with you? You look pale."

Julian made some indifferent answer, but too well understood, from the language and tone which his father used, that his prejudices against Alice's father were both deep and envenomed, as those of country gentlemen often become, who, having little to do or think of, are but too apt to spend their time in nursing and cherishing petty causes of wrath against their next neighbours.

In the course of the same day, he mentioned the Bridgenorths to his mother, as if in a casual manner. But the Lady Peveril instantly conjured him never to mention the name, especially in his father's presence.

"Was that Major Bridgenorth, of whom I have heard the name mentioned," said Julian, "so very bad a neighbour?"

"I do not say so," said Lady Peveril; "nay, we were more than once obliged to him, in the former unhappy times; but your father and he took some passages so ill at each other's hands, that the least allusion to him disturbs Sir Geoffrey's temper, in a manner quite unusual, and which, now that his health is somewhat impaired, is sometimes alarming to me. For Heaven's sake, then, my dear Julian, avoid upon all occasions the slightest allusion to Moultrassie, or any of its inhabitants."

This warning was so seriously given, that Julian himself saw that mentioning his secret purpose would be the sure way to render it abortive, and therefore he returned disconsolate to the Isle.

Peveril had the boldness, however, to make the best he could of what had happened, by requesting an interview with Alice, in order to inform her what had passed betwixt his parents and him on her account. It was with great difficulty that this boon was obtained; and Alice Bridgenorth showed no slight degree of displeasure, when she discovered, after much circum- locution, and many efforts to give an air of importance to what he had to communicate, that all amounted but to this, that Lady Peveril continued to retain a favourable opinion of her father, Major Bridgenorth, which Julian would fain have repre- sented as an omen of their future more perfect reconciliation."

"I did not think you would thus have trifled with me, Master Peveril," said Alice, assuming an air of dignity; "but I will take care to avoid such intrusion in future—I request you will not again visit the Black Fort; and I entreat of you, good Mistress Debbitch, that you will no longer either encourage or permit this gentleman's visits, as the result of such persecution will be to compel me to appeal to my aunt and father for another place of residence, and perhaps also for another and more prudent companion."

This last hint struck Mistress Deborah with so much terror, that she joined her ward in requiring and demanding Julian's instant absence, and he was obliged to comply with their request. But the courage of a youthful lover is not easily sub- dued; and Julian, after having gone through the usual round of trying to forget his ungrateful mistress, and again entertaining his passion with augmented violence, ended by the visit to the Black Fort, the beginning of which we narrated in the last chapter.

We then left him anxious for, yet almost fearful of, an interview with Alice, which he had prevailed upon Deborah to solicit; and such was the tumult of his mind, that, while he traversed the parlour, it seemed to him that the dark melancholy eyes of the slaughtered Christian's portrait followed him wherever he went, with the fixed, chill, and ominous glance, which announced to the enemy of his race mishap and misfortune.

The door of the apartment opened at length, and these visions were dissipated.

CHAPTER XIII

Parents have flinty hearts! No tears can move them.
—OTWAY.

WHEN Alice Bridgenorth at length entered the parlour where her anxious lover had so long expected her, it was with a slow step, and a composed manner. Her dress was arranged with an accurate attention to form, which at once enhanced the appearance of its puritanic simplicity, and struck Julian as a bad omen; for although the time bestowed upon the toilet may, in many cases, intimate the wish to appear advantageously at such an interview, yet a ceremonious arrangement of attire is very much allied with formality, and a preconceived determination to treat a lover with cold politeness.

The sad-coloured gown—the pinched and plaited cap, which carefully obscured the profusion of long dark-brown hair—the small ruff, and the long sleeves, would have appeared to great disadvantage on a shape less graceful than Alice Bridgenorth's; but an exquisite form, though not, as yet, sufficiently rounded in the outlines to produce the perfection of female beauty, was able to sustain and give grace even to this unbecoming dress. Her countenance, fair and delicate, with eyes of hazel, and a brow of alabaster, had, notwithstanding, less regular beauty than her form, and might have been justly subjected to criticism. There was, however, a life and spirit in her gaiety, and a depth of sentiment in her gravity, which made Alice, in conversation with the very few persons with whom she associated, so fascinating in her manners and expression, whether of language or countenance—so touching, also, in her simplicity and purity of thought, that brighter beauties might have been overlooked in her company. It was no wonder, therefore, that an ardent character like Julian, influenced by these charms, as well as by the secrecy and mystery attending his intercourse with Alice, should prefer the recluse of the Black Fort to all others with whom he had become acquainted in general society.

His heart beat high as she came into the apartment, and it was almost without an attempt to speak that his profound obeisance acknowledged her entrance.

"This is a mockery, Master Peveril," said Alice, with an effort to speak firmly, which yet was disconcerted by a slightly tremulous inflection of voice—"a mockery, and a cruel one. You come to this lone place, inhabited only by two women, too simple to command your absence—too weak to enforce it—you come, in spite of my earnest request—to the neglect of your own time—to the prejudice, I may fear, of my character—you abuse the influence you possess over the simple person to whom I am entrusted—All this you do, and think to make it up by low reverences and constrained courtesy! Is this honourable, or is it fair?—Is it," she added, after a moment's hesitation— "is it kind?"

The tremulous accent fell especially on the last word she uttered, and it was spoken in a low tone of gentle reproach, which went to Julian's heart.

"If," said he, "there was a mode by which, at the peril of my life, Alice, I could show my regard—my respect—my devoted tenderness—the danger would be dearer to me than ever was pleasure."

"You have said such things often," said Alice, "and they are such as I ought not to hear, and do not desire to hear. I have no tasks to impose on you—no enemies to be destroyed— no need or desire of protection—no wish, Heaven knows, to expose you to danger—It is your visits here alone to which danger attaches. You have but to rule your own wilful temper—to turn your thoughts and your cares elsewhere, and I can have nothing to ask—nothing to wish for. Use your own reason—consider the injury you do yourself—the injustice you do us—and let me, once more, in fair terms, entreat you to absent yourself from this place—till—till——"

She paused, and Julian eagerly interrupted her.—"Till when, Alice?—till when?—impose on me any length of absence which your severity can inflict, short of a final separation—Say, Begone for years, but return when these years are over; and, slow and wearily as they must pass away, still the thought that they must at length have their period, will enable me to live through them. Let me, then, conjure thee, Alice, to name a date—to fix a term—to say till *when!*"

"Till you can bear to think of me only as a friend and sister."

"That is a sentence of eternal banishment indeed!" said Julian; "it is seeming, no doubt, to fix a term of exile, but attaching to it an impossible condition."

"And why impossible, Julian?" said Alice, in a tone of persuasion; "were we not happier ere you threw the mask from your own countenance, and tore the veil from my foolish eyes? Did we not meet with joy, spend our time happily, and part cheerily, because we transgressed no duty, and incurred no self-reproach? Bring back that state of happy ignorance, and you shall have no reason to call me unkind. But while you form schemes which I know to be visionary, and use language of such violence and passion, you shall excuse me if I now, and once for all, declare, that since Deborah shows herself unfit for the trust reposed in her, and must needs expose me to persecutions of this nature, I will write to my father, that he may fix me another place of residence; and in the meanwhile I will take shelter with my aunt at Kirk-Truagh."

"Hear me, unpitying girl," said Peveril, "hear me, and you shall see how devoted I am to obedience, in all that I can do to oblige you! You say you were happy when we spoke not on such topics—well—at all expense of my own suppressed feelings, that happy period shall return. I will meet you—walk with you—read with you—but only as a brother would with his sister, or a friend with his friend; the thoughts I may nourish, be they of hope or of despair, my tongue shall not give birth to, and therefore I cannot offend; Deborah shall be ever by your side, and her presence shall prevent my even hinting at what might displease you—only do not make a crime to me of those thoughts which are the dearest part of my existence; for believe me it were better and kinder to rob me of existence itself."

"This is the mere ecstasy of passion, Julian," answered Alice Bridgenorth; "that which is unpleasant, our selfish and stubborn will represents as impossible. I have no confidence in the plan you propose—no confidence in your resolution, and less than none in the protection of Deborah. Till you can renounce, honestly and explicitly, the wishes you have lately expressed, we must be strangers;—and could you renounce them even at this moment, it were better that we should part for a long time; and, for Heaven's sake, let it be as soon as possible—perhaps it is even now too late to prevent some unpleasant accident—I thought I heard a noise."

"It was Deborah," answered Julian. "Be not afraid, Alice; we are secure against surprise."

"I know not," said Alice, "what you mean by such security

—I have nothing to hide. I sought not this interview; on the contrary, averted it as long as I could—and am now most desirous to break it off."

"And wherefore, Alice, since you say it must be our last? Why should you shake the sand which is passing so fast? the very executioner hurries not the prayers of the wretches upon the scaffold.—And see you not—I will argue as coldly as you can desire—see you not that you are breaking your own word, and recalling the hope which yourself held out to me?"

"What hope have I suggested? What word have I given, Julian?" answered Alice. "You yourself build wild hopes in the air, and accuse me of destroying what had never any earthly foundation. Spare yourself, Julian—spare me—and in mercy to us both depart, and return not again till you can be more reasonable."

"Reasonable?" replied Julian; "it is you, Alice, who will deprive me altogether of reason. Did you not say, that if our parents could be brought to consent to our union, you would no longer oppose my suit?"

"No—no—no," said Alice eagerly, and blushing deeply,—"I did not say so, Julian—it was your own wild imagination which put construction on my silence and my confusion."

"You do *not* say so, then?" answered Julian; "and if all other obstacles were removed, I should find one in the cold flinty bosom of her who repays the most devoted and sincere affection with contempt and dislike?—Is that," he added, in a deep tone of feeling—"is that what Alice Bridgenorth says to Julian Peveril?"

"Indeed—indeed, Julian," said the almost weeping girl, "I do not say so—I say nothing, and I ought not to say anything concerning what I might do, in a state of things which can never take place. Indeed, Julian, you ought not thus to press me. Unprotected as I am—wishing you well—very well—why should you urge me to say or do what would lessen me in my own eyes? to own affection for one from whom fate has separated me for ever? It is ungenerous—it is cruel—it is seeking a momentary and selfish gratification to yourself, at the expense of every feeling which I ought to entertain."

"You have said enough, Alice," said Julian, with sparkling eyes; "you have said enough in deprecating my urgency, and I will press you no farther. But you overrate the impediments which lie betwixt us—they must and shall give way."

"So you said before," answered Alice, "and with what probability, your own account may show. You dared not to mention the subject to your own father—how should you venture to mention it to mine?"

"That I will soon enable you to decide upon. Major Bridgenorth, by my mother's account, is a worthy and an estimable man. I will remind him, that to my mother's care he owes the dearest treasure and comfort of his life; and I will ask him if it is a just retribution to make that mother childless. Let me but know where to find him, Alice, and you shall soon hear if I have feared to plead my cause with him."

"Alas!" answered Alice, "you well know my uncertainty as to my dear father's residence. How often has it been my earnest request to him that he would let me share his solitary abode, or his obscure wanderings! But the short and infrequent visits which he makes to this house are all that he permits me of his society. Something I might surely do, however little, to alleviate the melancholy by which he is oppressed."

"Something we might both do," said Peveril. "How willingly would I aid you in so pleasing a task! All old griefs should be forgotten—all old friendships revived. My father's prejudices are those of an Englishman—strong, indeed, but not insurmountable by reason. Tell me, then, where Major Bridgenorth is, and leave the rest to me; or let me but know by what address your letters reach him, and I will forthwith essay to discover his dwelling."

"Do not attempt it, I charge you," said Alice. "He is already a man of sorrows; and what would he think were I capable of entertaining a suit so likely to add to them? Besides, I could not tell you, if I would, where he is now to be found. My letters reach him from time to time, by means of my aunt Christian; but of his address I am entirely ignorant."

"Then, by Heaven," answered Julian, "I will watch his arrival in this island, and in this house; and ere he has locked thee in his arms, he shall answer to me on the subject of my suit."

"Then demand that answer now," said a voice from without the door, which was at the same time slowly opened—"Demand that answer now, for here stands Ralph Bridgenorth."

As he spoke, he entered the apartment with his usual slow and sedate step—raised his flapp'd and steeple-crowned hat from his brows, and, standing in the midst of the room, eyed alternately his daughter and Julian Peveril with a fixed and penetrating glance.

"Father!" said Alice, utterly astonished, and terrified besides, by his sudden appearance at such a conjuncture,—"Father, I am not to blame."

"Of that anon, Alice," said Bridgenorth; "meantime retire to your apartment—I have that to say to this youth which will not endure your presence."

"Indeed—indeed, father," said Alice, alarmed at what she

supposed these words indicated, "Julian is as little to be blamed as I! It was chance, it was fortune, which caused our meeting together." Then suddenly rushing forward, she threw her arms around her father, saying, "Oh, do him no injury—he meant no wrong! Father, you were wont to be a man of reason and of religious peace."

"And wherefore should I not be so now, Alice?" said Bridgenorth, raising his daughter from the ground, on which she had almost sunk in the earnestness of her supplication. "Dost thou know aught, maiden, which should inflame my anger against this young man, more than reason or religion may bridle? Go—go to thy chamber. Compose thine own passions—learn to rule these—and leave it to me to deal with this stubborn young man."

Alice arose, and, with her eyes fixed on the ground, retired slowly from the apartment. Julian followed her steps with his eyes till the last wave of her garment was visible at the closing door; then turned his looks to Major Bridgenorth, and then sunk them on the ground. The Major continued to regard him in profound silence; his looks were melancholy and even austere; but there was nothing which indicated either agitation or keen resentment. He motioned to Julian to take a seat, and assumed one himself. After which he opened the conversation in the following manner :—

"You seemed but now, young gentleman, anxious to learn where I was to be found. Such I at least conjectured, from the few expressions which I chanced to overhear; for I made bold, though it may be contrary to the code of modern courtesy, to listen a moment or two, in order to gather upon what subject so young a man as you entertained so young a woman as Alice, in a private interview."

"I trust, sir," said Julian, rallying spirits in what he felt to be a case of extremity, "you have heard nothing on my part which has given offence to a gentleman, whom, though unknown, I am bound to respect so highly."

"On the contrary," said Bridgenorth, with the same formal gravity, "I am pleased to find that your business is, or appears to be, with me, rather than with my daughter. I only think you had done better to have entrusted it to me in the first instance, as my sole concern."

The utmost sharpness of attention which Julian applied, could not discover if Bridgenorth spoke seriously or ironically to the above purpose. He was, however, quick-witted beyond his experience, and was internally determined to endeavour to discover something of the character and the temper of him with whom he spoke. For that purpose, regulating his reply in the same tone with Bridgenorth's observation, he said, that not having the advantage to know his place of residence, he had applied for information to his daughter.

"Who is now known to you for the first time?" said Bridgenorth. "Am I so to understand you?"

"By no means," answered Julian, looking down; "I have been known to your daughter for many years; and what I wished to say, respects both her happiness and my own."

"I must understand you," said Bridgenorth, "even as carnal men understand each other on the matters of this world. You are attached to my daughter by the cords of love; I have long known this."

"You, Master Bridgenorth?" exclaimed Peveril—"*You* have long known it?"

"Yes, young man. Think you, that as the father of an only child, I could have suffered Alice Bridgenorth—the only living pledge of her who is now an angel in heaven—to have remained in this seclusion without the surest knowledge of all her material actions? I have, in person, seen more, both of her and of you, than you could be aware of; and when absent in the body, I had the means of maintaining the same superintendence. Young man, they say that such love as you entertain for my daughter teaches much subtilty; but believe not that it can overreach the affection which a widowed father bears to an only child."

"If," said Julian, his heart beating thick and joyfully, "if you have known this intercourse so long, may I not hope that it has not met your disapprobation?"

The Major paused for an instant, and then answered, "In some respects, certainly not. Had it done so — had there seemed aught on your side, or on my daughter's, to have rendered your visits here dangerous to her, or displeasing to me, she had not been long the inhabitant of this solitude, or of this island. But be not so hasty as to presume, that all which you may desire in this matter can be either easily or speedily accomplished."

"I foresee, indeed, difficulties," answered Julian; "but with your kind acquiescence, they are such as I trust to remove. My father is generous—my mother is candid and liberal. They loved you once; I trust they will love you again. I will be the mediator betwixt you—peace and harmony shall once more inhabit our neighbourhood, and——"

Bridgenorth interrupted him with a grim smile; for such it seemed, as it passed over a face of deep melancholy. "My daughter well said, but short while past, that you were a dreamer of dreams—an architect of plans and hopes fantastic as the visions of the night. It is a great thing you ask of me; —the hand of my only child—the sum of my worldly substance, though that is but dross in comparison. You ask the key of the only fountain from which I may yet hope to drink one pleasant draught; you ask to be the sole and absolute keeper of my earthly happiness—and what have you offered, or what have you to offer in return, for the surrender you require of me?"

"I am but too sensible," said Peveril, abashed at his own hasty conclusions, "how difficult it may be."

"Nay, but interrupt me not," replied Bridgenorth, "till I show you the amount of what you offer me in exchange for a boon, which, whatever may be its intrinsic value, is earnestly desired by you, and comprehends all that is valuable on earth which I have it in my power to bestow. You may have heard, that in the late times I was the antagonist of your father's principles and his profane faction, but not the enemy of his person."

"I have ever heard," replied Julian, "much the contrary; and it was but now that I reminded you that you had been his friend."

"Ay. When he was in affliction and I in prosperity, I was neither unwilling, nor altogether unable, to show myself such. Well, the tables are turned—the times are changed. A peaceful and unoffending man might have expected from a neighbour, now powerful in his turn, such protection, when walking in the paths of the law, as all men, subjects of the same realm, have a right to expect even from perfect strangers. What chances? I pursue, with the warrant of the King and law, a murderess, bearing on her hand the blood of my near connection, and I had, in such a case, a right to call on every liege subject to render assistance to the execution. My late friendly neighbour, bound, as a man and a magistrate, to give ready assistance to a legal action—bound, as a grateful and obliged friend, to respect my rights and my person—thrusts himself betwixt me—me, the avenger of blood—and my lawful captive; beats me to the earth, at once endangering my life, and, in mere human eyes, sullying mine honour; and under his protection, the Midianitish woman reaches, like a sea-eagle, the nest which she hath made in the wave-surrounded rocks, and remains there till gold, duly administered at Court, wipes out all memory of her crime, and baffles the vengeance due to the memory of the best and bravest of men.—But," he added, apostrophising the portrait of Christian, "thou art not yet forgotten, my fair-haired William! The vengeance which dogs thy murderess is slow, —but it is sure!"

There was a pause of some moments, which Julian Peveril, willing to hear to what conclusion Major Bridgenorth was finally to arrive, did not care to interrupt. Accordingly, in a few minutes, the latter proceeded.—"These things," he said, "I recall not in bitterness, so far as they are personal to me—I recall them not in spite of heart, though they have been the means of banishing me from my place of residence, where my fathers dwelt, and where my earthly comforts lie interred. But the public cause sets farther strife betwixt your father and me. Who so active as he to execute the fatal edict of black St. Bartholomew's day, when so many hundreds of gospel-preachers were expelled from house and home—from hearth and altar—from church and parish, to make room for belly-gods and thieves? Who, when a devoted few of the Lord's people were united to lift the fallen standard, and once more advance the good cause, was the readiest to break their purpose—to search for, persecute, and apprehend them? Whose breath did I feel warm on my neck—whose naked sword was thrust within a foot of my body, whilst I lurked darkling, like a thief in concealment, in the house of my fathers?—It was Geoffrey Peveril's—it was your father's!—What can you answer to all this, or how can you reconcile it with your present wishes?"

Julian, in reply, could only remark, "That these injuries had been of long standing—that they had been done in heat of times, and heat of temper, and that Master Bridgenorth, in Christian kindness, should not entertain a keen resentment of them, when a door was opened for reconciliation."

"Peace, young man," said Bridgenorth, "thou speakest of thou knowest not what. To forgive our human wrongs is Christian-like and commendable; but we have no commission to forgive those which have been done to the cause of religion and of liberty; we have no right to grant immunity, or to shake hands with those who have poured forth the blood of our brethren." He looked at the picture of Christian, and was silent for a few minutes, as if he feared to give too violent way to his own impetuosity, and resumed the discourse in a milder tone.

"These things I point out to you, Julian, that I may show you how impossible, in the eyes of a merely worldly man, would be the union which you are desirous of. But Heaven hath at times opened a door, where man beholds no means of issue. Julian, your mother, for one to whom the truth is unknown, is, after the fashion of the world, one of the best, and one of the wisest of women; and Providence, which gave her so fair a form, and tenanted that form with a mind as pure as the original frailty of our vile nature will permit, means not, I trust, that she shall continue to the end to be a vessel of wrath and perdition. Of your father I say nothing—he is what the times and example of others, and the counsels of his lordly priest, have made him; and of him, once more, I say nothing, save that I have power over him, which ere now he might have felt, but that there is one within his chambers, who might have suffered in his suffering. Nor do I wish to root up your ancient family. If I prize not your boast of family honours and pedigree, I would not willingly destroy them; more than I would pull down a moss-grown tower, or hew to the ground an ancient oak, save for the straightening of the common path, and the advantage of the public. I have, therefore, no resentment against the humbled House of Peveril—nay, I have regard to it in its depression."

He here made a second pause, as if he expected Julian to say something. But notwithstanding the ardour with which the young man had pressed his suit, he was too much trained in ideas of the importance of his family, and in the better habit of respect for his parents, to hear, without displeasure, some part of Bridgenorth's discourse.

"The House of Peveril," he replied, "was never humbled."

"Had you said the sons of that House had never been *humble*," answered Bridgenorth, "you would have come nearer the truth.—Are *you* not humbled? Live you not here, the lackey of a haughty woman, the play-companion of an empty youth? If you leave this Isle, and go to the Court of England, see what regard will there be paid to the old pedigree that deduces your descent from kings and conquerors. A scurril or obscene jest, an impudent carriage, a laced cloak, a handful of gold, and the readiness to wager it on a card, or a die, will better advance you at the Court of Charles, than your father's ancient name, and slavish devotion of blood and fortune to the cause of *his* father."

"That is, indeed, but too probable," said Peveril; "but the Court shall be no element of mine. I will live like my fathers, among my people, care for their comforts, decide their differences——"

"Build Maypoles, and dance around them," said Bridgenorth, with another of those grim smiles which passed over his features like the light of a sexton's torch, as it glares and is reflected by the window of the church, when he comes from locking a funeral vault. "No, Julian, these are not times in which, by the dreaming drudgery of a country magistrate, and the petty cares of a country proprietor, a man can serve his unhappy country. There are mighty designs afloat, and men are called to make their choice betwixt God and Baal. The ancient superstition—the abomination of our fathers—is raising its head, and flinging abroad its snares, under the protection of the princes of the earth; but she raises not her head unmarked or unwatched; the true English hearts are as thousands, which wait but a signal to arise as one man, and show the kings of the earth that they have combined in vain! We will cast their cords from us—the cup of their abominations we will not taste."

"You speak in darkness, Master Bridgenorth," said Peveril. "Knowing so much of me, you may, perhaps, also be aware, that I at least have seen too much of the delusions of Rome, to desire that they should be propagated at home."

"Else, wherefore do I speak to thee friendly and so free?" said Bridgenorth. "Do I not know, with what readiness of early wit you baffled the wily attempts of the woman's priest, to seduce thee from the Protestant faith? Do I not know, how thou wast beset when abroad, and that thou didst both hold thine own faith, and secure the wavering belief of thy friend? Said I not, this was done like the son of Margaret Peveril? Said I not, he holdeth, as yet, but the dead letter—but the seed which is sown shall one day sprout and quicken?—Enough, however, of this. For to-day this is thy habitation. I will see in thee neither the servant of that daughter of Eshbaal, nor the son of him who pursued my life, and blemished my honours; but thou shalt be to me, for this day, as the child of her, without whom my house had been extinct."

So saying, he stretched out his thin, bony hand, and grasped that of Julian Peveril; but there was such a look of mourning in his welcome, that whatever delight the youth anticipated, spending so long a time in the neighbourhood of Alice Bridgenorth, perhaps in her society, or however strongly he felt the prudence of conciliating her father's good-will, he could not help feeling as if his heart was chilled in his company.

CHAPTER XIV

This day at least is friendship's—on the morrow
Let strife come an she will.
                              —OTWAY.

DEBORAH DEBBITCH, summoned by her master, now made her appearance, with her handkerchief at her eyes, and an appearance of great mental trouble. "It was not my fault, Major Bridgenorth," she said; "how could I help it? like will to like—the boy would come—the girl would see him."

"Peace, foolish woman," said Bridgenorth, "and hear what I have got to say."

"I know what your honour has to say well enough," said Deborah. "Service, I wot, is no inheritance nowadays—some are wiser than other some—if I had not been wheedled away from Martindale, I might have had a house of mine own by this time."

I

"Peace, idiot!" said Bridgenorth; but so intent was Deborah on her vindication, that he could but thrust the interjection, as it were edgewise, between her exclamations, which followed as thick as is usual in cases, where folks endeavour to avert deserved censure by a clamorous justification ere the charge be brought.

"No wonder she was cheated," she said, "out of sight of her own interest, when it was to wait on pretty Miss Alice. All your honour's gold should never have tempted me, but that I knew she was but a dead castaway, poor innocent, if she were taken away from my lady or me.—And so this is the end on't!—up early, and down late—and this is all my thanks!—But your honour had better take care what you do—she has the short cough yet sometimes—and should take physic, spring and fall."

"Peace, chattering fool!" said her master, so soon as her failing breath gave him an opportunity to strike in, "thinkest thou I knew not of this young gentleman's visits to the Black Fort, and that, if they had displeased me, I would not have known how to stop them?"

"Did I know that your honour knew of his visits!" exclaimed Deborah, in a triumphant tone,—for, like most of her condition, she never sought farther for her defence than a lie, however inconsistent and improbable—"Did I know that your honour knew of it!—Why, how should I have permitted his visits else? I wonder what your honour takes me for! Had I not been sure it was the thing in this world that your honour most desired, would I have presumed to lend it a hand forward? I trust I know my duty better. Hear if I ever asked another youngster into the house, save himself—for I knew your honour was wise, and quarrels cannot last for ever, and love begins where hatred ends; and, to be sure, they love as if they were born one for the other—and then, the estates of Moultrassie and Martindale suit each other like sheath and knife."

"Parrot of a woman, hold your tongue!" said Bridgenorth, his patience almost completely exhausted; "or, if you will prate, let it be to your playfellows in the kitchen, and bid them get ready some dinner presently, for Master Peveril is far from home."

"That I will, and with all my heart," said Deborah; "and if there are a pair of fatter fowls in Man than shall clap their wings on the table presently, your honour shall call me goose as well as parrot." She then left the apartment.

"It is to such a woman as that," said Bridgenorth, looking after her significantly, "that you conceived me to have abandoned the charge of my only child! But enough of this subject—we will walk abroad, if you will, while she is engaged in a province fitter for her understanding."

So saying, he left the house, accompanied by Julian Peveril, and they were soon walking side by side, as if they had been old acquaintances.

It may have happened to many of our readers, as it has done to ourselves, to be thrown by accident into society with some individual whose claims to what is called a *serious* character stand considerably higher than our own, and with whom, therefore, we have conceived ourselves likely to spend our time in a very stiff and constrained manner; while, on the other hand, our destined companion may have apprehended some disgust from the supposed levity and thoughtless gaiety of a disposition so different from his own. Now it has frequently happened, that when we, with that urbanity and good-humour which is our principal characteristic, have accommodated ourself to our companion, by throwing as much seriousness into our conversation as our habits will admit, he, on the other hand, moved by our liberal example, hath divested his manners of a part of their austerity; and our conversation has, in consequence, been of that pleasant texture, betwixt the useful and agreeable, which best resembles " the fairy-web of night and day," usually called in prose the twilight. It is probable both parties may, on such occasions, have been the better for their encounter, even if it went no farther than to establish for the time a community of feeling between men, who, separated more perhaps by temper than by principle, are too apt to charge each other with profane frivolity on the one hand, or fanaticism on the other.

It fared thus in Peveril's walk with Bridgenorth, and in the conversation which he held with him.

Carefully avoiding the subject on which he had already spoken, Major Bridgenorth turned his conversation chiefly on foreign travel, and on the wonders he had seen in distant countries, and which he appeared to have marked with a curious and observant eye. This discourse made the time fly light away; for although the anecdotes and observations thus communicated were all tinged with the serious and almost gloomy spirit of the narrator, they yet contained traits of interest and of wonder, such as are usually interesting to a youthful ear, and were particularly so to Julian, who had, in his disposition, some cast of the romantic and adventurous.

It appeared that Bridgenorth knew the south of France, and could tell many stories of the French Huguenots, who already began to sustain those vexations which a few years afterwards were summed up by the revocation of the Edict of Nantz. He had even been in Hungary, for he spoke as from personal knowledge of the character of several of the heads of the great Protestant insurrection, which at this time had taken place under the celebrated Tekeli; and laid down solid reasons why they were entitled to make common cause with the Great Turk, rather than submit to the Pope of Rome. He talked also of Savoy, where those of the reformed religion still suffered a cruel persecution; and he mentioned with a swelling spirit, the protection which Oliver had afforded to the oppressed Protestant Churches; "therein showing himself," he added, "more fit to wield the supreme power, than those who, claiming it by right of inheritance, use it only for their own vain and voluptuous pursuits."

"I did not expect," said Peveril modestly, "to have heard Oliver's panegyric from you, Master Bridgenorth."

"I do not panegyrise him," answered Bridgenorth; "I speak but truth of that extraordinary man, now being dead, whom, when alive, I feared not to withstand to his face. It is the fault of the present unhappy King, if he make us look back with regret to the days when the nation was respected abroad, and when devotion and sobriety were practised at home.—But I mean not to vex your spirit by controversy. You have lived amongst those who find it more easy and more pleasant to be the pensioners of France than her controllers—to spend the money which she doles out to themselves, than to check the tyranny with which she oppresses our poor brethren of the religion. When the scales shall fall from thine eyes, all this thou shalt see; and seeing, shalt learn to detest and despise it."

By this time they had completed their walk, and were returned to the Black Fort, by a different path from that which had led them up the valley. The exercise and the general tone of conversation had removed, in some degree, the shyness and embarrassment which Peveril originally felt in Bridgenorth's presence, and which the tenor of his first remarks had rather increased than diminished. Deborah's promised banquet was soon on the board; and in simplicity as well as neatness and good order, answered the character she had claimed for it. In one respect alone, there seemed some inconsistency, perhaps a little affectation. Most of the dishes were of silver, and the plates were of the same metal; instead of the trenchers and pewter which Peveril had usually seen employed on similar occasions at the Black Fort.

Presently, with the feeling of one who walks in a pleasant dream from which he fears to awake, and whose delight is mingled with wonder and with uncertainty, Julian Peveril found himself seated between Alice Bridgenorth and her father —the being he most loved on earth, and the person whom he had ever considered as the great obstacle to their intercourse. The confusion of his mind was such, that he could scarcely reply to the importunate civilities of Dame Deborah; who, seated with them at table in her quality of governante, now dispensed the good things which had been prepared under her own eye.

As for Alice she seemed to have formed a resolution to play the mute; for she answered not, excepting briefly, to the questions of Dame Debbitch; nay, even when her father, which happened once or twice, attempted to bring her forward in the conversation, she made no farther reply than respect for him rendered absolutely necessary.

Upon Bridgenorth himself, then, devolved the task of entertaining the company; and contrary to his ordinary habits, he did not seem to shrink from it. His discourse was not only easy, but almost cheerful, though ever and anon crossed by some expressions indicative of natural and habitual melancholy, or prophetic of future misfortune and woe. Flashes of enthusiasm, too, shot along his conversation, gleaming like the sheet-lightning of an autumn eve, which throws a strong, though momentary illumination, across the sober twilight, and all the surrounding objects, which, touched by it, assume a wilder and more striking character. In general, however, Bridgenorth's remarks were plain and sensible; and as he aimed at no graces of language, any ornament which they received arose out of the interest with which they were impressed on his hearers. For example, when Deborah, in the pride and vulgarity of her heart, called Julian's attention to the plate from which they had been eating, Bridgenorth seemed to think an apology necessary for such superfluous expense.

"It was a symptom," he said, "of approaching danger, when such men, as were not usually influenced by the vanities of life, employed much money in ornaments composed of the precious metals. It was a sign that the merchant could not obtain a profit for the capital, which, for the sake of security, he invested in this inert form. It was a proof that the noblemen or gentlemen feared the rapacity of power, when they put their wealth into forms the most portable and the most capable of being hidden; and it showed the uncertainty of credit, when a man of judgment preferred the actual possession of a mass of silver to the convenience of a goldsmith's or a banker's receipt. While a shadow of liberty remained," he said, "domestic rights were last invaded; and, therefore, men disposed upon their cupboards and tables the wealth which in these places would remain longest, though not perhaps finally, sacred from the grasp of a tyrannical government. But let there be a demand for capital to support a profitable commerce, and the mass is at once consigned to the furnace, and, ceasing to be a vain and cumbrous ornament of the banquet, becomes a potent and active agent for furthering the prosperity of the country."

"In war, too," said Peveril, "plate has been found a ready resource."

"But too much so," answered Bridgenorth. "In the late times, the plate of the nobles and gentry, with that of the colleges, and the sale of the crown-jewels, enabled the King to make his unhappy stand, which prevented matters returning to a state of peace and good order, until the sword had attained an undue superiority both over King and Parliament."

He looked at Julian as he spoke, much as he who proves a horse offers some object suddenly to his eyes, then watches to see if he starts or blenches from it. But Julian's thoughts were too much bent on other topics to manifest any alarm. His answer referred to a previous part of Bridgenorth's discourse, and was not returned till after a brief pause. "War, then," he said, "war, the grand impoverisher, is also a creator of the wealth which it wastes and devours?"

"Yes," replied Bridgenorth, "even as the sluice brings into action the sleeping waters of the lake, which it finally drains. Necessity invents arts and discovers means; and what necessity is sterner than that of civil war? Therefore, even war is not in itself unmixed evil, being the creator of impulses and energies which could not otherwise have existed in society."

"Men should go to war, then," said Peveril, "that they may send their silver plate to the mint, and eat from pewter dishes and wooden platters?"

"Not so, my son," said Bridgenorth. Then checking himself as he observed the deep crimson in Julian's cheek and brow, he added, "I crave your pardon for such familiarity; but I meant not to limit what I said even now to such trifling consequences, although it may be something salutary to tear men from their pomps and luxuries, and teach those to be Romans who would otherwise be Sybarites. But I would say, that times of public danger, as they call into circulation the miser's hoard and the proud man's bullion, and so add to the circulating wealth of the country, do also call into action many a brave and noble spirit, which would otherwise lie torpid, give no example to the living, and bequeath no name to future ages. Society knows not, and cannot know, the mental treasures which slumber in her bosom, till necessity and opportunity call forth the statesman and the soldier from the shades of lowly life to the parts they are designed by Providence to perform, and the stations which nature had qualified them to hold. So rose Oliver—so rose Milton—so rose many another name which cannot be forgotten —even as the tempest summons forth and displays the address of the mariner."

"You speak," said Peveril, "as if national calamity might be, in some sort, an advantage."

"And if it were not so," replied Bridgenorth, "it had not existed in this state of trial, where all temporal evil is alleviated by something good in its progress or result, and where all that is good is close coupled with that which is in itself evil."

"It must be a noble sight," said Julian, "to behold the slumbering energies of a great mind awakened into energy, and to see it assume the authority which is its due over spirits more meanly endowed."

"I once witnessed," said Bridgenorth, "something to the same effect; and as the tale is brief, I will tell it you, if you will :—

"Amongst my wanderings, the Transatlantic settlements have not escaped me ; more especially the country of New England, into which our native land has shaken from her lap, as a drunkard flings from him his treasures, so much that is precious in the eyes of God and of His children. There thousands of our best and most godly men—such whose righteousness might come between the Almighty and His wrath, and prevent the ruin of cities—are content to be the inhabitants of the desert, rather encountering the unenlightened savages, than stooping to extinguish, under the oppression practised in Britain, the light that is within their own minds. There I remained for a time, during the wars which the colony maintained with Philip, a great Indian Chief, or Sachem, as they were called, who seemed a messenger sent from Satan to buffet them. His cruelty was great—his dissimulation profound ; and the skill and promptitude with which he maintained a destructive and desultory warfare, inflicted many dreadful calamities on the settlement. I was, by chance, at a small village in the woods, more than thirty miles from Boston, and in its situation exceedingly lonely, and surrounded with thickets. Nevertheless, there was no idea of any danger from the Indians at that time, for men trusted to the protection of a considerable body of troops who had taken the field for protection of the frontiers, and who lay, or were supposed to lie, betwixt the hamlet and the enemy's country. But they had to do with a foe, whom the devil himself had inspired at once with cunning and cruelty. It was on a Sabbath morning, when we had assembled to take sweet counsel together in the Lord's house. Our temple was but constructed of wooden logs ; but when shall the chant of trained hirelings, or the sounding of tin and brass tubes amid the aisles of a minster, arise so sweetly to Heaven, as did the psalm in which we united at once our voices and our hearts ! An excellent worthy, who now sleeps in the Lord, Nehemiah Solsgrace, long the companion of my pilgrimage, had just begun to wrestle in prayer, when a woman, with disordered looks and dishevelled hair, entered our chapel in a distracted manner, screaming incessantly, 'The Indians ! The Indians !'—In that land no man dares separate himself from his means of defence; and whether in the city or in the field, in the ploughed land or the forest, men keep beside them their weapons, as did the Jews at the rebuilding of the Temple. So we sallied forth with our guns and pikes, and heard the whoop of these incarnate devils, already in possession of a part of the town, and exercising their cruelty on the few whom weighty causes or indisposition had withheld from public worship; and it was remarked as a judgment, that, upon that bloody Sabbath, Adrian Hanson, a Dutchman, a man well enough disposed towards man, but whose mind was altogether given to worldly gain, was shot and scalped as he was summing his weekly gains in his warehouse. In fine, there was much damage done; and although our arrival and entrance into combat did in some sort put them back, yet being surprised and confused, and having no appointed leader of our band, the devilish enemy shot hard at us, and had some advantage. It was pitiful to hear the screams of women and children amid the report of guns and the whistling of bullets, mixed with the ferocious yells of these savages, which they term their war-whoop. Several houses in the upper part of the village were soon on fire; and the roaring of the flames, and crackling of the great beams as they blazed, added to the horrible confusion; while the smoke which the wind drove against us gave farther advantage to the enemy, who fought, as it were, invisible, and under cover, whilst we fell fast by their unerring fire. In this state of confusion, and while we were about to adopt the desperate project of evacuating the village, and, placing the women and children in the centre, of attempting a retreat to the nearest settlement, it pleased Heaven to send us unexpected assistance. A tall man, of a reverend appearance, whom no one of us had ever seen before, suddenly was in the midst of us, as we hastily agitated the resolution of retreating. His garments were of the skin of the elk, and he wore sword and carried gun; I never saw anything more august than his features, overshadowed by locks of grey hair, which mingled with a long beard of the same colour. 'Men and brethren,' he said, in a voice like that which turns back the flight, 'why sink your hearts? and why are you thus disquieted? Fear ye that the God we serve will give you up to yonder heathen dogs? Follow me, and you shall see this day that there is a captain in Israel!' He uttered a few brief but distinct orders, in the tone of one who was accustomed to command; and such was the influence of his appearance, his mien, his language, and his presence of mind, that he was implicitly obeyed by men who had never seen him until that moment. We were hastily divided, by his orders, into two bodies; one of which maintained the defence of the village with more courage than ever, convinced that the Unknown was sent by God to our rescue. At his command they assumed the best and most sheltered positions for exchanging their deadly fire with the Indians; while, under cover of the smoke, the stranger sallied from the town, at the head of the other division of the New England men, and, fetching a circuit, attacked the Red Warriors in the rear. The surprise, as is usual amongst savages, had complete effect; for they doubted not that they were assailed in their turn, and placed betwixt two hostile parties by the return of a detachment from the provincial army. The heathens fled in confusion, abandoning the half-won village, and leaving behind them such a number of their warriors, that the tribe hath never recovered its loss. Never shall I forget the figure of our venerable leader, when our men, and not they only, but the women and children of the village, rescued from the tomahawk and scalping-knife, stood crowded around him, yet scarce venturing to approach his person, and more minded, perhaps, to worship him as a descended angel, than to thank him as a fellow-mortal. 'Not unto me be the glory,' he said; 'I am but an implement, frail as yourselves, in the hand of Him who is strong to deliver. Bring me a cup of water, that I may allay my parched throat, ere I essay the task of offering thanks where they are most due.' I was nearest to him as he spoke, and I gave into his hand the water he requested. At that moment we exchanged glances, and it seemed to me that I recognised a noble friend whom I had long since deemed in glory; but he gave me no time to speak, had speech been prudent. Sinking on his knees, and signing us to obey him, he poured forth a strong and energetic thanksgiving for the turning back of the battle, which, pronounced with a voice loud and clear as a war-trumpet, thrilled through the joints and marrow of the hearers. I have heard many an act of devotion in my life, had Heaven vouchsafed me grace to profit by them; but such a prayer as this, uttered amid the dead and the dying, with a rich tone of mingled triumph and adoration, was beyond them all—it was like the song of the inspired prophetess who dwelt beneath the palm-tree between Ramah and Bethel. He was silent; and for a brief space we remained with our faces bent to the earth—no man daring to lift his head. At length we looked up, but our deliverer was no longer amongst us; nor was he ever again seen in the land which he had rescued."

Here Bridgenorth, who had told this singular story with an eloquence and vivacity of detail very contrary to the usual dryness of his conversation, paused for an instant, and then resumed—"Thou seest, young man, that men of valour and of discretion are called forth to command in circumstances of national exigence, though their very existence is unknown in the land which they are predestined to deliver."

"But what thought the people of the mysterious stranger?" said Julian, who had listened with eagerness, for the story was of a kind interesting to the youthful and the brave.

"Many things," answered Bridgenorth, "and, as usual, little to the purpose. The prevailing opinion was, notwithstanding his own disclamation, that the stranger was really a super-natural being; others believed him an inspired champion, transported in the body from some distant climate, to show us the way to safety; others, again, concluded that he was a recluse, who, either from motives of piety, or other cogent reasons, had become a dweller in the wilderness, and shunned the face of man."

"And, if I may presume to ask," said Julian, "to which of these opinions were you disposed to adhere?"

"The last suited best with the transient though close view with which I had perused the stranger's features," replied Bridgenorth; "for although I dispute not that it may please Heaven, on high occasions, even to raise one from the dead in defence of his country, yet I doubted not then, as I doubt not now, that I looked on the living form of one, who had indeed powerful reasons to conceal him in the cleft of the rock."

"Are these reasons a secret?" asked Julian Peveril.

"Not properly a secret," replied Bridgenorth; "for I fear not thy betraying what I might tell thee in private discourse; and besides, wert thou so base, the prey lies too distant for any hunters to whom thou couldst point out its traces. But the name of this worthy will sound harsh in thy ear, on account of one action of his life—being his accession to a great measure, which made the extreme isles of the earth to tremble. Have you never heard of Richard Whalley?"

"Of the regicide?" exclaimed Peveril, starting.

"Call his act what thou wilt," said Bridgenorth; "he was not less the rescuer of that devoted village, that, with other leading spirits of the age, he sat in the judgment-seat when Charles Stewart was arraigned at the bar, and subscribed the sentence that went forth upon him."

"I have ever heard," said Julian, in an altered voice, and colouring deeply, "that you, Master Bridgenorth, with other Presbyterians, were totally averse to that detestable crime, and were ready to have made joint-cause with the Cavaliers in pre-venting so horrible a parricide."

"If it were so," replied Bridgenorth, "we have been richly rewarded by his successor."

"Rewarded!" exclaimed Julian; "does the distinction of good and evil, and our obligation to do the one and forbear the other, depend on the reward which may attach to our actions?"

"God forbid," answered Bridgenorth; "yet those who view the havoc which this house of Stewart have made in the Church and State—the tyranny which they exercise over men's persons and consciences—may well doubt whether it be lawful to use weapons in their defence. Yet you hear me not praise, or even vindicate the death of the King, though so far deserved, as he was false to his oath as a Prince and Magistrate. I only tell you what you desired to know, that Richard Whalley, one of the late King's judges, was he of whom I have just been speaking. I knew his lofty brow, though time had made it balder and higher; his grey eye retained all its lustre; and though the grizzled beard covered the lower part of his face, it prevented me not from recognising him. The scent was hot after him for his blood; but by the assistance of those friends whom Heaven had raised up for his preservation, he was concealed carefully, and emerged only to do the will of Providence in the matter of that battle. Perhaps his voice may be heard in the field once more, should England need one of her noblest hearts."

"Now, God forbid!" said Julian.

"Amen," returned Bridgenorth. "May God avert civil war, and pardon those whose madness would bring it on us!"

There was a long pause, during which Julian, who had scarce lifted his eyes towards Alice, stole a glance in that direction, and was struck by the deep cast of melancholy which had stolen over features, to which a cheerful, if not gay expression, was most natural. So soon as she caught his eye, she remarked, and, as Julian thought, with significance, that the shadows were lengthening, and evening coming on.

He heard; and although satisfied that she hinted at his departure, he could not, upon the instant, find resolution to break the spell which detained him. The language which Bridgenorth held was not only new and alarming, but so contrary to the maxims in which he was brought up, that, as a son of Sir Geoffrey Peveril of the Peak, he would, in another case, have thought himself called upon to dispute its conclusions, even at the sword's point. But Bridgenorth's opinions were delivered with so much calmness—seemed so much the result of conviction—that they excited in Julian rather a spirit of wonder, than of angry controversy. There was a character of sober decision, and sedate melancholy, in all that he said, which, even had he not been the father of Alice (and perhaps Julian was not himself aware how much he was influenced by that circumstance), would have rendered it difficult to take personal offence. His language and sentiments were of that quiet, yet decided kind, upon which it is difficult either to fix controversy, or quarrel, although it be impossible to acquiesce in the conclusions to which they lead.

While Julian remained, as if spell-bound to his chair, scarce more surprised at the company in which he found himself, than at the opinions to which he was listening, another circumstance reminded him that the proper time of his stay at Black Fort had been expended. Little Fairy, the Manx pony, which, well accustomed to the vicinity of Black Fort, used to feed near the house while her master made his visits there, began to find his present stay rather too long. She had been the gift of the Countess to Julian, whilst a youth, and came of a high-spirited mountain breed, remarkable alike for hardiness, for longevity, and for a degree of sagacity approaching to that of the dog. Fairy showed the latter quality, by the way in which she chose to express her impatience to be moving homewards. At least such seemed the purpose of the shrill neigh with which she startled the female inmates of the parlour, who, the moment afterwards, could not forbear smiling to see the nose of the pony advanced through the opened casement.

"Fairy reminds me," said Julian, looking to Alice, and rising, "that the term of my stay here is exhausted."

"Speak with me yet one moment," said Bridgenorth, with-drawing him into a Gothic recess of the old-fashioned apart-ment, and speaking so low that he could not be overheard by Alice and her governante, who, in the meantime, caressed, and fed with fragments of bread the intruder Fairy.

"You have not, after all," said Bridgenorth, "told me the cause of your coming hither." He stopped, as if to enjoy his embarrassment, and then added, "And indeed it were most unnecessary that you should do so. I have not so far forgotten the days of my youth, or those affections which bind poor frail humanity but too much to the things of this world. Will you find no words to ask of me the great boon which you seek, and which, peradventure, you would not have hesitated to have made your own, without my knowledge, and against my con-sent?—Nay, never vindicate thyself, but mark me farther. The patriarch bought his beloved by fourteen years' hard service to her father Laban, and they seemed to him but as a few days. But he that would wed my daughter must serve, in comparison, but a few days; though in matters of such mighty import, that they shall seem as the service of many years. Reply not to me now, but go, and peace be with you."

He retired so quickly, after speaking, that Peveril had literally not an instant to reply. He cast his eyes around the apartment, but Deborah and her charge had also disappeared. His gaze rested for a moment on the portrait of Christian, and his imagination suggested that his dark features were illuminated by a smile of haughty triumph. He stared, and looked more attentively—it was but the effect of the evening beam, which touched the picture at the instant. The effect was gone, and there remained but the fixed, grave, inflexible features of the republican soldier.

Julian left the apartment as one who walks in a dream; he mounted Fairy, and, agitated by a variety of thoughts, which he was unable to reduce to order, he returned to Castle Rushin before the night sat down.

Here he found all in movement. The Countess, with her son, had, upon some news received, or resolution formed, during his absence, removed, with a principal part of their family, to the yet stronger Castle of Holm-Peel, about eight miles' distance across the island; and which had been suffered to fall into a much more dilapidated condition than that of Castletown, so far as it could be considered as a place of residence. But as a fortress, Holm-Peel was stronger than Castletown; nay, unless assailed regularly, was almost impregnable; and was always held by a garrison belonging to the Lords of Man. Here Peveril arrived at nightfall. He was told in the fishing-village, that the night-bell of the Castle had been rung earlier than usual, and the watch set with circumstances of unusual and jealous precaution.

Resolving, therefore, not to disturb the garrison by entering at that late hour, he obtained an indifferent lodging in the town for the night, and determined to go to the Castle early on the succeeding morning. He was not sorry thus to gain a few hours of solitude, to think over the agitating events of the preceding day.

CHAPTER XV

——What seem'd its head,
The likeness of a kingly crown had on.
—PARADISE LOST.

SODOR, or Holm-Peel, so is named the castle to which our Julian directed his course early on the following morning, is one of those extraordinary monuments of antiquity with which this singular and interesting island abounds. It occupies the whole of a high rocky peninsula, or rather an island, for it is surrounded by the sea at high-water, and scarcely accessible even when the tide is out, although a stone causeway, of great solidity, erected for the express purpose, connects the island with the mainland. The whole space is surrounded by double walls of great strength and thickness; and the access to the interior, at the time which we treat of, was only by two flights of steep and narrow steps, divided from each other by a strong tower and guard-house; under the former of which, there is an entrance-arch.   The open space within the walls extends to two acres, and contains many objects worthy of antiquarian curiosity.   There were, besides the castle itself, two cathedral churches, dedicated, the earlier to St. Patrick, the latter to St. Germain; besides two smaller churches; all of which had become, even in that day, more or less ruinous.   Their decayed walls, exhibiting the rude and massive architecture of the most remote period, were composed of a ragged grey-stone, which formed a singular contrast with the bright red freestone of which the window-cases, corner-stones, arches, and other ornamental parts of the building, were composed.

Besides these four ruinous churches, the space of ground enclosed by the massive exterior walls of Holm-Peel exhibited many other vestiges of the olden time.   There was a square mound of earth, facing, with its angles to the points of the compass, one of those motes, as they were called, on which, in ancient times, the northern tribes elected or recognised their chiefs, and held their solemn popular assemblies, or *comitia*. There was also one of those singular towers, so common in Ireland as to have proved the favourite theme of her antiquaries; but of which the real use and meaning seems yet to be hidden in the mist of ages.   This of Holm-Peel had been converted to the purpose of a watch-tower.   There were, besides, Runic monuments, of which the legends could not be deciphered; and later inscriptions to the memory of champions, of whom the names only were preserved from oblivion.   But tradition and superstitious eld, still most busy where real history is silent, had filled up the long blank of accurate information with tales of Sea-kings and Pirates, Hebridean Chiefs and Norwegian Resolutes, who had formerly warred against, and in defence of, this famous castle.   Superstition, too, had her tales of fairies, ghosts, and spectres—her legions of saints and demons, of fairies and of familiar spirits, which in no corner of the British empire are told and received with more absolute credulity than in the Isle of Man.

Amidst all these ruins of an older time arose the Castle itself,—now ruinous—but in Charles II.'s reign well garrisoned, and, in a military point of view, kept in complete order.   It was a venerable and very ancient building, containing several apartments of sufficient size and height to be termed noble. But in the s rrender of the island by Christian, the furniture had been, in a great measure, plundered or destroyed by the republican soldiers; so that, as we have before hinted, its present state was ill adapted for the residence of the noble proprietor. Yet it had been often the abode, not only of the Lords of Man, but of those state prisoners whom the Kings of Britain sometimes committed to their charge.

In this Castle of Holm-Peel the great king-maker, Richard, Earl of Warwick, was confined, during one period of his eventful life, to ruminate at leisure on his farther schemes of ambition. And here, too, Eleanor, the haughty wife of the good Duke of Gloucester, pined out in seclusion the last days of her banishment. The sentinels pretended that her discontented spectre was often visible at night, traversing the battlements of the external walls, or standing motionless beside a particular solitary turret of one of the watch-towers with which they are flanked; but dissolving into air at cock-crow, or when the bell tolled from the yet remaining tower of St. Germain's church.

Such was Holm-Peel, as records inform us, till towards the end of the seventeenth century.

It was in one of the lofty but almost unfurnished apartments of this ancient Castle that Julian Peveril found his friend the Earl of Derby, who had that moment sat down to a breakfast composed of various sorts of fish. "Welcome, most imperial Julian," he said; "welcome to our royal fortress; in which, as yet, we are not like to be starved with hunger, though wellnigh dead for cold."

Julian answered by inquiring the meaning of this sudden movement.

"Upon my word," replied the Earl, "you know nearly as much of it as I do. My mother has told me nothing about it; supposing, I believe, that I shall at length be tempted to inquire; but she will find herself much mistaken. I shall give her credit for full wisdom in her proceedings, rather than put her to the trouble to render a reason, though no woman can render one better."

"Come, come; this is affectation, my good friend," said Julian. "You should inquire into these matters a little more curiously."

"To what purpose?" said the Earl. "To hear old stories about the Tinwald laws, and the contending rights of the lords and the clergy, and all the rest of that Celtic barbarism, which, like Burgesse's thorough-paced doctrine, enters at one ear, paces through, and goes out at the other?"

"Come, my lord," said Julian, "you are not so indifferent as you would represent yourself—you are dying of curiosity to know what this hurry is about; only you think it the courtly humour to appear careless about your own affairs."

"Why, what should it be about," said the young Earl

"unless some factious dispute between our Majesty's minister, Governor Nowel, and our vassals? or perhaps some dispute betwixt our Majesty and the ecclesiastical jurisdictions? for all which our Majesty cares as little as any king in Christendom."

"I rather suppose there is intelligence from England," said Julian. "I heard last night in Peel-town, that Greenhalgh is come over with unpleasant news."

"He brought me nothing that was pleasant, I wot well," said the Earl. "I expected something from St. Evremond or Hamilton—some new plays by Dryden or Lee, and some waggery or lampoons from the Rose Coffee-house; and the fellow has brought me nothing but a parcel of tracts about Protestants and Papists, and a folio play-book, one of the conceptions, as she calls them, of that old mad-woman the Duchess of Newcastle."

"Hush, my lord, for Heaven's sake," said Peveril; "here comes the Countess; and you know she takes fire at the least slight to her ancient friend."

"Let her read her ancient friend's works herself, then," said the Earl, "and think her as wise as she can; but I would not give one of Waller's songs, or Denham's satires, for a whole cart-load of her Grace's trash.—But here comes our mother with care on her brow."

The Countess of Derby entered the apartment accordingly, holding in her hand a number of papers. Her dress was a mourning habit, with a deep train of black velvet, which was borne by a little favourite attendant, a deaf and dumb girl, whom, in compassion to her misfortune, the Countess had educated about her person for some years. Upon this unfortunate being, with the touch of romance which marked many of her proceedings, Lady Derby had conferred the name of Fenella, after some ancient princess of the island. The Countess herself was not much changed since we last presented her to our readers. Age had rendered her step more slow, but not less majestic; and while it traced some wrinkles on her brow, had failed to quench the sedate fire of her dark eye. The young men rose to receive her with the formal reverence which they knew she loved, and were greeted by her with equal kindness.

"Cousin Peveril," she said (for so she always called Julian, in respect of his mother being a kinswoman of her husband), "you were ill abroad last night, when we much needed your counsel."

Julian answered with a blush which he could not prevent, "That he had followed his sport among the mountains too far—had returned late—and finding her ladyship was removed from Castletown, had instantly followed the family hither; but as the night-bell was rung, and the watch set, he had deemed it more respectful to lodge for the night in the town."

"It is well," said the Countess; "and, to do you justice, Julian, you are seldom a truant neglecter of appointed hours, though, like the rest of the youth of this age, you sometimes suffer your sports to consume too much of time that should be spent otherwise. But for your friend Philip, he is an avowed contemner of good order, and seems to find pleasure in wasting time, even when he does not enjoy it."

"I have been enjoying my time just now at least," said the Earl, rising from table, and picking his teeth carelessly. "These fresh mullets are delicious, and so is the Lachrymæ Christi. I pray you to sit down to breakfast, Julian, and partake the goods my royal foresight has provided. Never was King of Man nearer being left to the mercy of the execrable brandy of his dominions. Old Griffiths would never, in the midst of our speedy retreat of last night, have had sense enough to secure a few flasks, had I not given him a hint on that important subject. But presence of mind amid danger and tumult, is a jewel I have always possessed."

"I wish, then, Philip, you would exert it to better purpose," said the Countess, half smiling, half displeased; for she doated upon her son with all a mother's fondness, even when she was most angry with him for being deficient in the peculiar and chivalrous disposition which had distinguished his father, and which was so analogous to her own romantic and high-minded character. "Lend me your signet," she added with a sigh; "for it were, I fear, vain to ask you to read over these despatches from England, and execute the warrants which I have thought necessary to prepare in consequence."

"My signet you shall command with all my heart, madam," said Earl Philip; "but spare me the revision of what you are much more capable to decide upon. I am, you know, a most complete *Roi fainéant*, and never once interfered with my *Maire de palais* in her proceedings."

The Countess made signs to her little train-bearer, who immediately went to seek for wax and a light, with which she presently returned.

In the meanwhile the Countess continued, addressing Peveril. "Philip does himself less than justice. When you were absent, Julian (for if you had been here I would have given you the credit of prompting your friend), he had a spirited controversy with the Bishop, for an attempt to enforce spiritual censures against a poor wretch, by confining her in the vault under the chapel." *

* Beneath the only one of the four churches in Castle Rushin, which is or was kept a little in repair, is a prison or dungeon, for ecclesiastical offenders. "This," says Waldron, "is certainly one of the most dreadful places that imagination can form; the sea runs under it through the hollows of the rock with such a continual roar, that you would think it

"Do not think better of me than I deserve," said the Earl to Peveril; "my mother has omitted to tell you the culprit was pretty Peggy of Ramsey, and her crime what in Cupid's courts would have been called a peccadillo."

"Do not make yourself worse than you are," replied Peveril, who observed the Countess's cheek redden,—"you know you would have done as much for the oldest and poorest cripple in the island. Why, the vault is under the burial-ground of the chapel, and, for aught I know, under the ocean itself, such a roaring do the waves make in its vicinity. I think no one could remain there long, and retain his reason."

"It is an infernal hole," answered the Earl, "and I will have it built up one day—that is full certain.—But hold—hold—for God's sake, madam—what are you going to do?—Look at the seal before you put it to the warrant—you will see it is a choice antique cameo Cupid, riding on a flying fish—I had it for twenty zechins, from Signor Furabosco at Rome—a most curious matter for an antiquary, but which will add little faith to a Manx warrant."

"How can you trifle thus, you simple boy?" said the Countess, with vexation in her tone and look. "Let me have your signet, or rather, take these warrants, and sign them yourself."

"My signet—my signet—Oh! you mean that with the three monstrous legs, which I supposed was devised as the most preposterous device, to represent our most absurd Majesty of Man.—The signet—I have not seen it since I gave it to Gibbon, my monkey, to play with.—He did whine for it most piteously—I hope he has not gemmed the green breast of ocean with my symbol of sovereignty!"

"Now, by Heaven," said the Countess, trembling, and colouring deeply with anger, "it was your father's signet! the last pledge which he sent, with his love to me, and his blessing to thee, the night before they murdered him at Bolton!"

"Mother, dearest mother," said the Earl, startled out of his apathy, and taking her hand, which he kissed tenderly, "I did but jest—the signet is safe.—Peveril knows that it is so.—Go fetch it, Julian, for Heaven's sake—here are my keys—it is in the left-hand drawer of my travelling cabinet—Nay, mother, forgive me—it was but a *mauvaise plaisanterie*; only an ill-imagined jest, ungracious, and in bad taste, I allow—but only one of Philip's follies. Look at me, dearest mother, and forgive me."

were every moment breaking in upon you, and over it are the vaults for burying the dead. The stairs descending to this place of terrors are not above thirty, but so steep and narrow, that they are very difficult to go down, a child of eight or nine years not being able to pass them but sideways."—WALDRON'S *Description of the Isle of Man, in his Works*, p. 105, folio.

The Countess turned her eyes towards him, from which the tears were fast falling.

"Philip," she said, "you try me too unkindly, and too severely. If times are changed, as I have heard you allege—if the dignity of rank, and the high feelings of honour and duty, are now drowned in giddy jests and trifling pursuits, let *me* at least, who live secluded from all others, die without perceiving the change which has happened, and, above all, without perceiving it in mine own son. Let me not learn the general prevalence of this levity, which laughs at every sense of dignity or duty, through your personal disrespect—Let me not think that when I die——"

"Speak nothing of it, mother," said the Earl, interrupting her affectionately. "It is true, I cannot promise to be all my father and his fathers were; for we wear silk vests for their steel coats, and feathered beavers for their crested helmets. But believe me, though to be an absolute Palmerin of England is not in my nature, no son ever loved a mother more dearly, or would do more to oblige her. And that you may own this, I will forthwith not only seal the warrants, to the great endangerment of my precious fingers, but also read the same from end to end, as well as the despatches thereunto appertaining."

A mother is easily appeased, even when most offended; and it was with an expanding heart that the Countess saw her son's very handsome features, while reading these papers, settle into an expression of deep seriousness, such as they seldom wore. It seemed to her as if the family likeness to his gallant but unfortunate father increased, when the expression of their countenances became similar in gravity. The Earl had no sooner perused the despatches, which he did with great attention, than he rose and said, "Julian, come with me."

The Countess looked surprised. "I was wont to share your father's counsels, my son," she said; "but do not think that I wish to intrude myself upon yours. I am too well pleased to see you assume the power and the duty of thinking for yourself, which is what I have so long urged you to do. Nevertheless, my experience, who have been so long administrator of your authority in Man, might not, I think, be superfluous to the matter in hand."

"Hold me excused, dearest mother," said the Earl gravely. "The interference was none of my seeking; had you taken your own course, without consulting me, it had been well; but since I have entered on the affair—and it appears sufficiently important—I must transact it to the best of my own ability."

"Go, then, my son," said the Countess, "and may Heaven enlighten thee with its counsel, since thou wilt have none of mine.—I trust that you, Master Peveril, will remind him of what is fit for his own honour; and that only a coward abandons his rights, and only a fool trusts his enemies."

The Earl answered not, but, taking Peveril by the arm, led him up a winding stair to his own apartment, and from thence into a projecting turret, where, amidst the roar of waves and sea-mews' clang, he held with him the following conversation :—

"Peveril, it is well I looked into these warrants. My mother queens it at such a rate as may cost me not only my crown, which I care little for, but perhaps my head, which, though others may think little of, I would feel it an inconvenience to be deprived of."

"What on earth is the matter?" said Peveril, with considerable anxiety.

"It seems," said the Earl of Derby, "that old England, who takes a frolicsome brain-fever once every two or three years, for the benefit of her doctors, and the purification of the torpid lethargy brought on by peace and prosperity, is now gone stark staring mad on the subject of a real or supposed Popish plot. I read one programme on the subject, by a fellow called Oates, and thought it the most absurd foolery I ever perused. But that cunning fellow Shaftesbury, and some others amongst the great ones, having taken it up, and are driving on at such a rate as makes harness crack, and horses smoke for it. The King, who has sworn never to kiss the pillow his father went to sleep on, temporises, and gives way to the current; the Duke of York, suspected and hated on account of his religion, is about to be driven to the continent; several principal Catholic nobles are in the Tower already; and the nation, like a bull at Tutbury-running, is persecuted with so many inflammatory rumours and pestilent pamphlets, that she has cocked her tail, flung up her heels, taken the bit betwixt her teeth, and is as furiously unmanageable as in the year 1642."

"All this you must have known already," said Peveril; "I wonder you told me not of news so important."

"It would have taken long to tell," said the Earl; "moreover, I desired to have you *solus*; thirdly, I was about to speak when my mother entered; and, to conclude, it was no business of mine. But these despatches of my politic mother's private correspondent put a new face on the whole matter; for it seems some of the informers—a trade which, having become a thriving one, is now pursued by many—have dared to glance at the Countess herself as an agent in this same plot—ay, and have found those that are willing enough to believe their report."

"On mine honour," said Peveril, "you both take it with

great coolness. I think the Countess the more composed of
the two; for, except her movement hither, she exhibited no
mark of alarm, and, moreover, seemed no way more anxious to
communicate the matter to your lordship than decency rendered
necessary."

"My good mother," said the Earl, "loves power, though
it has cost her dear. I wish I could truly say that my neglect
of business is entirely assumed in order to leave it in her hands,
but that better motive combines with natural indolence. But
she seems to have feared I should not think exactly like her in
this emergency, and she was right in supposing so."

"How comes the emergency upon you?" said Julian; "and
what form does the danger assume?"

"Marry, thus it is," said the Earl: "I need not bid you
remember the affair of Colonel Christian. That man, besides
his widow, who is possessed of large property—Dame Christian
of Kirk Truagh, whom you have often heard of, and perhaps
seen—left a brother called Edward Christian, whom you never
saw at all. Now this brother—but I dare say you know all
about it."

"Not I, on my honour," said Peveril; "you know the
Countess seldom or never alludes to the subject."

"Why," replied the Earl, "I believe in her heart she is
something ashamed of that gallant act of royalty and supreme
jurisdiction, the consequences of which maimed my estate so
cruelly.—Well, cousin, this same Edward Christian was one
of the dempsters at the time, and, naturally enough, was
unwilling to concur in the sentence which adjudged his *ainé*
to be shot like a dog. My mother, who was then in high
force, and not to be controlled by any one, would have served
the dempster with the same sauce with which she dressed his
brother, had he not been wise enough to fly from the island.
Since that time, the thing has slept on all hands; and though
we knew that Dempster Christian made occasionally secret
visits to his friends in the island, along with two or three other
Puritans of the same stamp, and particularly a prick-eared
rogue, called Bridgenorth, brother-in-law to the deceased, yet
my mother, thank Heaven, has hitherto had the sense to
connive at them, though, for some reason or other, she holds
this Bridgenorth in especial disfavour."

"And why," said Peveril, forcing himself to speak, in order
to conceal the very unpleasant surprise which he felt, "why
does the Countess now depart from so prudent a line of
conduct?"

"You must know the case is now different. The rogues are
not satisfied with toleration—they would have supremacy.
They have found friends in the present heat of the popular

mind. My mother's name, and especially that of her confessor, Aldrick the Jesuit, have been mentioned in this beautiful maze of a plot, which, if any such at all exists, she knows as little of as you or I. However, she is a Catholic, and that is enough; and I have little doubt, that if the fellows could seize on our scrap of a kingdom here, and cut all our throats, they would have the thanks of the present House of Commons, as willingly as old Christian had those of the Rump, for a similar service."

"From whence did you receive all this information?" said Peveril, again speaking, though by the same effort which a man makes who talks in his sleep.

"Aldrick has seen the Duke of York in secret, and his Royal Highness, who wept while he confessed his want of power to protect his friends—and it is no trifle will wring tears from him—told him to send us information that we should look to our safety, for that Dempster Christian and Bridgenorth were in the island, with secret and severe orders; that they had formed a considerable party there, and were likely to be owned and protected in anything they might undertake against us. The people of Ramsey and Castletown are unluckily discontented about some new regulation of the imposts; and to tell you the truth, though I thought yesterday's sudden remove a whim of my mother's, I am almost satisfied they would have blockaded us in Rushin Castle, where we could not have held out for lack of provisions. Here we are better supplied, and, as we are on our guard, it is likely the intended rising will not take place."

"And what is to be done in this emergency?" said Peveril.

"That is the very question, my gentle coz," answered the Earl. "My mother sees but one way of going to work, and that is by royal authority. Here are the warrants she had prepared, to search for, take, and apprehend the bodies of Edward Christian and Robert—no, Ralph Bridgenorth, and bring them to instant trial. No doubt, she would soon have had them in the Castle court, with a dozen of the old matchlocks levelled against them—that is her way of solving all sudden difficulties."

"But in which, I trust, you do not acquiesce, my lord," answered Peveril, whose thoughts instantly reverted to Alice, if they could ever be said to be absent from her.

"Truly I acquiesce in no such matter," said the Earl. "William Christian's death cost me a fair half of my inheritance. I have no fancy to fall under the displeasure of my royal brother, King Charles, for a new escapade of the same kind. But how to pacify my mother, I know not. I wish the insurrection would take place, and then, as we are better provided than they can be, we might knock the knaves on the head; and yet, since they began the fray, we should keep the law on our side."

"Were it not better," said Peveril, "if by any means these men could be induced to quit the island?"

"Surely," replied the Earl; "but that will be no easy matter —they are stubborn on principle, and empty threats will not move them. This stormblast in London is wind in their sails, and they will run their length, you may depend on it. I have sent orders, however, to clap up the Manxmen upon whose assistance they depended, and if I can find the two worthies themselves, here are sloops enough in the harbour—I will take the freedom to send them on a pretty distant voyage, and I hope matters will be settled before they return to give an account of it."

At this moment a soldier belonging to the garrison approached the two young men, with many bows and tokens of respect. "How now, friend?" said the Earl to him. "Leave off thy courtesies, and tell thy business."

The man, who was a native islander, answered in Manx, that he had a letter for his honour, Master Julian Peveril. Julian snatched the billet hastily, and asked whence it came.

"It was delivered to him by a young woman," the soldier replied, "who had given him a piece of money to deliver it into Master Peveril's own hand."

"Thou art a lucky fellow, Julian," said the Earl. "With that grave brow of thine, and thy character for sobriety and early wisdom, you set the girls a-wooing, without waiting till they are asked; whilst I, their drudge and vassal, waste both language and leisure, without getting a kind word or look, far less a billet-doux."

This the young Earl said with a smile of conscious triumph, as in fact he valued himself not a little upon the interest which he supposed himself to possess with the fair sex.

Meanwhile the letter impressed on Peveril a different train of thoughts from what his companion apprehended. It was in Alice's hand, and contained these few words :—

"I fear what I am going to do is wrong; but I must see you. Meet me at noon at Goddard Crovan's Stone, with as much secrecy as you may."

The letter was signed only with the initials A. B.; but Julian had no difficulty in recognising the handwriting, which he had often seen, and which was remarkably beautiful. He stood suspended, for he saw the difficulty and impropriety of withdrawing himself from the Countess and his friend at this moment of impending danger; and yet, to neglect this invitation was not to be thought of. He paused in the utmost perplexity.

"Shall I read your riddle?" said the Earl. "Go where love calls you—I will make an excuse to my mother—only, most grave anchorite, be hereafter more indulgent to the failings of others than you have been hitherto, and blaspheme not the power of the little deity."

"Nay, but, Cousin Derby—" said Peveril, and stopped short, for he really knew not what to say. Secured himself by a virtuous passion from the contagious influence of the time, he had seen with regret his noble kinsman mingle more in its irregularities than he approved of, and had sometimes played the part of a monitor. Circumstances seemed at present to give the Earl a right of retaliation. He kept his eye fixed on his friend, as if he waited till he should complete his sentence, and at length exclaimed, "What! cousin, quite *à-la-mort*! Oh, most judicious Julian! Oh, most precise Peveril! have you bestowed so much wisdom on me that you have none left for yourself? Come, be frank—tell me name and place—or say but the colour of the eyes of the most emphatic she—or do but let me have the pleasure to hear thee say, 'I love!'—confess one touch of human frailty—conjugate the verb *amo*, and I will be a gentle schoolmaster, and you shall have, as father Richards used to say, when we were under his ferule, '*licentia exeundi*.'"

"Enjoy your pleasant humour at my expense, my lord," said Peveril; "I fairly will confess thus much, that I would fain, if it consisted with my honour and your safety, have two hours at my own disposal; the more especially as the manner in which I shall employ them may much concern the safety of the island."

"Very likely, I dare say," answered the Earl, still laughing. "No doubt you are summoned out by some Lady Politic Wouldbe of the isle, to talk over some of the breast-laws: but never mind—go, and go speedily, that you may return as quick as possible. I expect no immediate explosion of this grand conspiracy. When the rogues see us on our guard, they will be cautious how they break out. Only, once more, make haste."

Peveril thought this last advice was not to be neglected; and, glad to extricate himself from the raillery of his cousin, walked down towards the gate of the Castle, meaning to cross over to the village, and there take horse at the Earl's stables, for the place of rendezvous.

FENELLA

H. HOWARD. R.A

CHAPTER XVI

Acasto.—Can she not speak?
Oswald.—If speech be only in accented sounds,
Framed by the tongue and lips, the maiden's dumb;
But if by quick and approhonsivo look,
By motion, sign, and glance, to give each meaning,
Express as clothed in language, be term'd speech,
She hath that wondrous faculty; for her eyes,
Like the bright stars of heaven, can hold discourse,
Though it be mute and soundless.
                            —OLD PLAY.

AT the head of the first flight of steps which descended towards the difficult and well-defended entrance of the Castle of Holm-Peel, Peveril was met and stopped by the Countess's train-bearer. This little creature—for she was of the least and slightest size of womankind—was exquisitely well formed in all her limbs, which the dress she usually wore (a green silk tunic, of a peculiar form) set off to the best advantage. Her face was darker than the usual hue of Europeans; and the profusion of long and silken hair, which, when she undid the braids in which she commonly wore it, fell down almost to her ankles, was also rather a foreign attribute. Her countenance resembled a most beautiful minia-ture; and there was a quickness, decision, and fire, in Fenella's look, and especially in her eyes, which was probably rendered yet more alert and acute, because, through the imperfection of her other organs, it was only by sight that she could obtain information of what passed around her.

The pretty mute was mistress of many little accomplish-ments, which the Countess had caused to be taught to her in compassion for her forlorn situation, and which she learned with the most surprising quickness. Thus, for example, she was exquisite in the use of the needle, and so ready and in-genious a draughtswoman, that, like the ancient Mexicans, she sometimes made a hasty sketch with her pencil the means of conveying her ideas, either by direct or emblematical represen-tation. Above all, in the art of ornamental writing, much studied at that period, Fenella was so great a proficient, as to rival the fame of Messrs. Snow, Shelley, and other masters of the pen, whose copybooks, preserved in the libraries of the curious, still show the artists smiling on the frontispiece in all the honours of flowing gowns and full-bottomed wigs, to the eternal glory of caligraphy.

The little maiden had, besides these accomplishments, much ready wit and acuteness of intellect. With Lady Derby, and with the two young gentlemen, she was a great favourite, and used much freedom in conversing with them, by means of a system of signs which had been gradually established amongst them, and which served all ordinary purposes of communication.

But, though happy in the indulgence and favour of her mistress, from whom indeed she was seldom separate, Fenella was by no means a favourite with the rest of the household. In fact, it seemed that her temper, exasperated perhaps by a sense of her misfortune, was by no means equal to her abilities. She was very haughty in her demeanour, even towards the upper domestics, who in that establishment were of a much higher rank and better birth than in the families of the nobility in general. These often complained, not only of her pride and reserve, but of her high and irascible temper and vindictive disposition. Her passionate propensity had been indeed idly encouraged by the young men, and particularly by the Earl, who sometimes amused himself with teasing her, that he might enjoy the various singular motions and murmurs by which she expressed her resentment. Towards him, these were of course only petulant and whimsical indications of pettish anger. But when she was angry with others of inferior degree —before whom she did not control herself—the expression of her passion, unable to display itself in language, had something even frightful, so singular were the tones, contortions, and gestures, to which she had recourse. The lower domestics, to whom she was liberal almost beyond her apparent means, observed her with much deference and respect, but much more from fear than from any real attachment; for the caprices of her temper displayed themselves even in her gifts; and those who most frequently shared her bounty, seemed by no means assured of the benevolence of the motives which dictated her liberality.

All these peculiarities led to a conclusion consonant with Manx superstition. Devout believers in all the legends of fairies so dear to the Celtic tribes, the Manx people held it for certainty that the elves were in the habit of carrying off mortal children before baptism, and leaving in the cradle of the new-born babe one of their own brood, which was almost always imperfect in some one or other of the organs proper to humanity. Such a being they conceived Fenella to be; and the smallness of her size, her dark complexion, her long locks of silken hair, the singularity of her manners and tones, as well as the caprices of her temper, were to their thinking all attributes of the irritable, fickle, and dangerous race from which they supposed her to be sprung. And it seemed, that although no jest appeared to offend her more than when Lord Derby called her in sport the Elfin Queen, or otherwise alluded to her supposed connection with "the pigmy folk," yet still her perpetually affecting to wear the colour of green, proper to the fairies, as well as some other peculiarities, seemed voluntarily assumed by her, in order to countenance the superstition, perhaps because it gave her more authority among the lower orders.

Many were the tales circulated respecting the Countess's *Elf*, as Fenella was currently called in the island; and the malcontents of the stricter persuasion were convinced, that no one but a Papist and a malignant would have kept near her person a creature of such doubtful origin. They conceived that Fenella's deafness and dumbness were only towards those of this world, and that she had been heard talking, and singing, and laughing most elvishly, with the invisibles of her own race. They alleged, also, that she had a *Double*, a sort of apparition resembling her, which slept in the Countess's ante-room, or bore her train, or wrought in her cabinet, while the real Fenella joined the song of the mermaids on the moonlight sands, or the dance of the fairies in the haunted valley of Glenmoy, or on the heights of Snawfell and Barool. The sentinels, too, would have sworn they had seen the little maiden trip past them in their solitary night walks, without their having it in their power to challenge her, any more than if they had been as mute as herself. To all this mass of absurdities the better informed paid no more attention than to the usual idle exaggerations of the vulgar, which so frequently connect that which is unusual with what is supernatural.

Such, in form and habits, was the little female, who, holding in her hand a small old-fashioned ebony rod, which might have passed for a divining wand, confronted Julian on the top of the flight of steps which led down the rock from the Castle court. We ought to observe, that as Julian's manner to the unfortunate girl had been always gentle, and free from those teasing jests in which his gay friend indulged, with less regard to the peculiarity of her situation and feelings; so Fenella, on her part, had usually shown much greater deference to him than to any of the household, her mistress, the Countess, always excepted.

On the present occasion, planting herself in the very midst of the narrow descent, so as to make it impossible for Peveril to pass by her, she proceeded to put him to the question by a series of gestures, which we will endeavour to describe. She commenced by extending her hand slightly, accompanied with the sharp inquisitive look which served her as a note of interrogation. This was meant as an inquiry whether he was going to a distance. Julian, in reply, extended his arm more than half, to intimate that the distance was considerable. Fenella looked grave, shook her head, and pointed to the Countess's window, which was visible from the spot where they stood. Peveril smiled, and nodded, to intimate there was no danger in quitting her mistress for a short space. The little maiden next touched an eagle's feather which she wore in her hair, a sign which she usually employed to designate the Earl, and then looked inquisitively at Julian once more, as if to say, " Goes he with you ? " Peveril shook his head, and, somewhat wearied by these interrogatories, smiled, and made an effort to pass. Fenella frowned, struck the end of her ebony rod perpendicularly on the ground, and again shook her head, as if opposing his departure. But finding that Julian persevered in his purpose, she suddenly assumed another and a milder mood, held him by the skirt of his cloak with one hand, and raised the other in an imploring attitude, whilst every feature of her lively countenance was composed into the like expression of supplication; and the fire of the large dark eyes, which seemed in general so keen and piercing as almost to over-animate the little sphere to which they belonged, seemed quenched, for the moment, in the large drops which hung on her long eyelashes, but without falling.

Julian Peveril was far from being void of sympathy towards the poor girl, whose motives in opposing his departure appeared to be her affectionate apprehension for her mistress's safety. He endeavoured to reassure her by smiles, and, at the same time, by such signs as he could devise, to intimate that there was no danger, and that he would return presently ; and having succeeded in extricating his cloak from her grasp, and in passing her on the stair, he began to descend the steps as speedily as he could, in order to avoid farther importunity.

But with activity much greater than his, the dumb maiden hastened to intercept him, and succeeded by throwing herself, at the imminent risk of life and limb, a second time into the pass which he was descending, so as to interrupt his purpose. In order to achieve this, she was obliged to let herself drop a considerable height from the wall of a small flanking battery, where two patereroes were placed to scour the pass, in case any enemy could have mounted so high. Julian had scarce time to shudder at her purpose, as he beheld her about to spring from the parapet, ere, like a thing of gossamer, she stood light and uninjured on the rocky platform below. He endeavoured, by the gravity of his look and gesture, to make her understand how much he blamed her rashness; but the reproof, though obviously quite intelligible, was entirely thrown away. A hasty wave of her hand intimated how she contemned the danger and the remonstrance; while, at the same time, she instantly resumed, with more eagerness than before, the earnest and impressive gestures by which she endeavoured to detain him in the fortress.

Julian was somewhat staggered by her pertinacity. "Is it possible," he thought, "that any danger can approach the Countess, of which this poor maiden has, by the extreme acuteness of her observation, obtained knowledge which has escaped others?"

He signed to Fenella hastily to give him the tablets and the pencil which she usually carried with her, and wrote on them the question, "Is there danger near to your mistress, that you thus stop me?"

"There is danger around the Countess," was the answer instantly written down; "but there is much more in your own purpose."

"How?—what?—what know you of my purpose?" said Julian, forgetting, in his surprise, that the party he addressed had neither ear to comprehend, nor voice to reply to uttered language. She had regained her book in the meantime, and sketched, with a rapid pencil, on one of the leaves, a scene which she showed to Julian. To his infinite surprise he recognised Goddard Crovan's Stone, a remarkable monument, of which she had given the outline with sufficient accuracy; together with a male and female figure, which, though only indicated by a few slight touches of the pencil, bore yet, he thought, some resemblance to himself and Alice Bridgenorth.

When he had gazed on the sketch for an instant with surprise, Fenella took the book from his hand, laid her finger upon the drawing, and slowly and sternly shook her head, with a frown which seemed to prohibit the meeting which was there represented. Julian, however, though disconcerted, was in no shape disposed to submit to the authority of his monitress. By whatever means she, who so seldom stirred from the Countess's apartment, had become acquainted with a secret which he thought entirely his own, he esteemed it the more necessary to keep the appointed rendezvous, that he might learn from Alice, if possible, how the secret had transpired. He had also formed the intention of seeking out Bridgenorth; entertaining an idea that a person so reasonable and calm as he had shown himself in their late conference, might be persuaded, when he understood that the Countess was aware of his intrigues, to put an end to her danger and his own, by withdrawing from the island. And could he succeed in this point, he should at once, he thought, render a material benefit to the father of his beloved Alice—remove the Earl from his state of anxiety—save the Countess from a second time putting her feudal jurisdiction in opposition to that of the Crown of England—and secure quiet possession of the island to her and her family.

With this scheme of mediation in his mind, Peveril determined to rid himself of the opposition of Fenella to his departure, with less ceremony than he had hitherto observed towards her; and suddenly lifting up the damsel in his arms before she was aware of his purpose, he turned about, set her down on the steps above him, and began to descend the pass himself as speedily as possible. It was then that the dumb maiden gave full course to the vehemence of her disposition; and clapping her hands repeatedly, expressed her displeasure in a sound, or rather a shriek, so extremely dissonant, that it resembled more the cry of a wild creature, than anything which could have been uttered by female organs. Peveril was so astounded at the scream as it rung through the living rocks, that he could not help stopping and looking back in alarm, to satisfy himself that she had not sustained some injury. He saw her, however, perfectly safe, though her face seemed inflamed and distorted with passion. She stamped at him with her foot, shook her clenched hand, and turning her back upon him, without farther adieu, ran up the rude steps as lightly as a kid could have tripped up that rugged ascent, and paused for a moment at the summit of the first flight.

Julian could feel nothing but wonder and compassion for the impotent passion of a being so unfortunately circumstanced, cut off, as it were, from the rest of mankind, and incapable of receiving in childhood that moral discipline which teaches us mastery of our wayward passions, ere yet they have attained their meridian strength and violence. He waved his hand to her, in token of amicable farewell; but she only replied by once more menacing him with her little hand clenched; and then ascending the rocky staircase with almost preternatural speed, was soon out of sight.

Julian, on his part, gave no farther consideration to her conduct or its motives, but hastening to the village on the mainland, where the stables of the Castle were situated, he again took his palfrey from the stall, and was soon mounted and on his way to the appointed place of rendezvous, much marvelling, as he ambled forward with speed far greater than was promised by the diminutive size of the animal he was mounted on, what could have happened to produce so great a change in Alice's conduct towards him, that in place of enjoining his absence as usual, or recommending his departure from the island, she should now voluntarily invite him to a meeting. Under impression of the various doubts which succeeded each other in his imagination, he sometimes pressed Fairy's sides with his legs; sometimes laid his holly rod lightly on her neck; sometimes incited her by his voice, for the mettled animal needed neither whip nor spur, and achieved the distance betwixt the Castle of Holm-Peel and the stone at Goddard Crovan, at the rate of twelve miles within the hour.

The monumental stone, designed to commemorate some feat of an ancient King of Man, which had been long forgotten, was erected on the side of a narrow lonely valley, or rather glen, secluded from observation by the steepness of its banks, upon a projection of which stood the tall, shapeless, solitary rock, frowning, like a shrouded giant, over the brawling of the small rivulet which watered the ravine.

CHAPTER XVII

This a love-meeting? See the maiden mourns,
And the sad suitor bends his looks on earth.
There's more hath pass'd between them than belongs
To Love's sweet sorrows.
—OLD PLAY.

As he approached the monument of Goddard Crovan, Julian cast many an anxious glance to see whether any object visible beside the huge grey stone should apprise him, whether he was anticipated, at the appointed place of rendezvous, by her who had named it. Nor was it long before the flutter of a mantle, which the breeze slightly waved, and the motion necessary to replace it upon the wearer's shoulders, made him aware that Alice had already reached their place of meeting. One instant set the palfrey at liberty, with slackened girths and loosened reins, to pick its own way through the dell at will; another placed Julian Peveril by the side of Alice Bridgenorth.

That Alice should extend her hand to her lover, as with the ardour of a young greyhound he bounded over the obstacles of the rugged path, was as natural as that Julian, seizing on the hand so kindly stretched out, should devour it with kisses, and, for a moment or two, without reprehension; while the other hand, which should have aided in the liberation of its fellow, served to hide the blushes of the fair owner. But Alice, young as she was, and attached to Julian by such long habits of kindly intimacy, still knew well how to subdue the tendency of her own treacherous affections.

"This is not right," she said, extricating her hand from Julian's grasp, "this is not right, Julian. If I have been too rash in admitting such a meeting as the present, it is not you that should make me sensible of my folly."

Julian Peveril's mind had been early illuminated with that touch of romantic fire which deprives passion of selfishness, and confers on it the high and refined tone of generous and disinterested devotion. He let go the hand of Alice with as much respect as he could have paid to that of a princess; and when she seated herself upon a rocky fragment, over which nature had stretched a cushion of moss and lichen, interspersed with wild flowers, backed with a bush of copsewood, he took his place beside her, indeed, but at such distance as to intimate the duty of an attendant, who was there only to hear and to obey. Alice Bridgenorth became more assured as she observed the power which she possessed over her lover; and the self-command which Peveril exhibited, which other damsels in her situation might have judged inconsistent with intensity of passion, she appreciated more justly, as a proof of his respectful and disinterested sincerity. She recovered, in addressing him, the tone of confidence which rather belonged to the scenes of their early acquaintance, than to those which had passed betwixt them since Peveril had disclosed his affection, and thereby had brought restraint upon their intercourse.

"Julian," she said, "your visit of yesterday—your most ill-timed visit, has distressed me much. It has misled my father —it has endangered you. At all risks, I resolved that you should know this, and blame me not if I have taken a bold and imprudent step in desiring this solitary interview, since you are aware how little poor Deborah is to be trusted."

"Can you fear misconstruction from me, Alice?" replied Peveril warmly; "from me, whom you have thus highly favoured—thus deeply obliged?"

"Cease your protestations, Julian," answered the maiden; "they do but make me the more sensible that I have acted over boldly. But I did for the best.—I could not see you whom I have known so long—you, who say you regard me with partiality——"

"Say that I regard you with partiality!" interrupted Peveril in his turn. "Ah, Alice, with a cold and doubtful phrase you have used to express the most devoted, the most sincere affection!"

"Well, then," said Alice sadly, "we will not quarrel about words; but do not again interrupt me.—I could not, I say, see you, who, I believe, regard me with sincere though vain and fruitless attachment, rush blindfold into a snare, deceived and seduced by those very feelings towards me."

"I understand you not, Alice," said Peveril; "nor can I see any danger to which I am at present exposed. The sentiments which your father has expressed towards me, are of a nature irreconcilable with hostile purposes. If he is not offended with the bold wishes I may have formed,—and his whole behaviour shows the contrary,—I know not a man on earth from whom I have less cause to apprehend any danger or ill-will."

"My father," said Alice, "means well by his country, and well by you; yet I sometimes fear he may rather injure than serve his good cause ; and still more do I dread, that in attempting to engage you as an auxiliary, he may forget those ties which ought to bind you, and I am sure which will bind you, to a different line of conduct from his own."

"You lead me into still deeper darkness, Alice," answered Peveril. "That your father's especial line of politics differs widely from mine, I know well; but how many instances have occurred, even during the bloody scenes of civil warfare, of good and worthy men laying the prejudice of party affections aside, and regarding each other with respect, and even with friendly attachment, without being false to principle on either side ?"

"It may be so," said Alice; "but such is not the league which my father desires to form with you, and that to which he hopes your misplaced partiality towards his daughter may afford a motive for your forming with him."

"And what is it," said Peveril, "which I would refuse, with such a prospect before me ?"

"Treachery and dishonour !" replied Alice ; "whatever would render you unworthy of the poor boon at which you aim—ay, were it more worthless than I confess it to be."

"Would your father," said Peveril, as he unwillingly received the impression which Alice designed to convey,—"would he, whose views of duty are so strict and severe—would he wish to involve me in aught, to which such harsh epithets as treachery and dishonour can be applied with the slightest shadow of truth ?"

"Do not mistake me, Julian," replied the maiden; "my father is incapable of requesting aught of you that is not to his thinking just and honourable ; nay, he conceives that he only claims from you a debt, which is due as a creature to the Creator, and as a man to your fellow-men."

"So guarded, where can be the danger of our intercourse ?" replied Julian. "If he be resolved to require, and I determined to accede to, nothing save what flows from conviction, what have I to fear, Alice ? And how is my intercourse with your father dangerous ? Believe not so ; his speech has already made impression on me in some particulars, and he listened with candour and patience to the objections which I made occasionally. You do Master Bridgenorth less than justice in confounding him with the unreasonable bigots in policy and religion, who can listen to no argument but what favours their own prepossessions."

"Julian," replied Alice ; "it is you who misjudge my father's powers, and his purpose with respect to you, and who overrate your own powers of resistance. I am but a girl, but I have been taught by circumstances to think for myself, and to con-

L

sider the character of those around me. My father's views in ecclesiastical and civil policy are as dear to him as the life which he cherishes only to advance them. They have been, with little alteration, his companions through life. They brought him at one period into prosperity, and when they suited not the times, he suffered for having held them. They have become not only a part, but the very dearest part, of his existence. If he shows them not to you at first, in the flexible strength which they have acquired over his mind, do not believe that they are the less powerful. He who desires to make converts, must begin by degrees. But that he should sacrifice to an inexperienced young man, whose ruling motive he will term a childish passion, any part of those treasured principles which he has maintained through good repute and bad repute—Oh, do not dream of such an impossibility! If you meet at all, you must be the wax, he the seal—you must receive, he must bestow, an absolute impression."

"That," said Peveril, "were unreasonable. I will frankly avow to you, Alice, that I am not a sworn bigot to the opinions entertained by my father, much as I respect his person. I could wish that our Cavaliers, or whatsoever they are pleased to call themselves, would have some more charity towards those who differ from them in Church and State. But to hope that I would surrender the principles in which I have lived, were to suppose me capable of deserting my benefactress, and breaking the hearts of my parents."

"Even so I judged of you," answered Alice; "and therefore I asked this interview, to conjure that you will break off all intercourse with our family—return to your parents—or, what will be much safer, visit the continent once more, and abide till God sends better days to England, for these are black with many a storm."

"And can you bid me go, Alice?" said the young man, taking her unresisting hand; "can you bid me go, and yet own an interest in my fate?—Can you bid me, for fear of dangers, which, as a man, as a gentleman, and a loyal one, I am bound to show my face to, meanly abandon my parents, my friends, my country—suffer the existence of evils which I might aid to prevent—forego the prospect of doing such little good as might be in my power—fall from an active and honourable station, into the condition of a fugitive and time-server—Can you bid me do all this, Alice? Can you bid me do all this, and, in the same breath, bid farewell for ever to you and happiness?—It is impossible—I cannot surrender at once my love and my honour."

"There is no remedy," said Alice, but she could not suppress a sigh while she said so—"there is no remedy—none whatever.

What we might have been to each other, placed in more favourable circumstances, it avails not to think of now; and, circumstanced as we are, with open war about to break out betwixt our parents and friends, we can be but well-wishers—cold and distant well-wishers, who must part on this spot, and at this hour, never to meet again."

"No, by Heaven!" said Peveril, animated at the same time by his own feelings, and by the sight of the emotions which his companion in vain endeavoured to suppress,—"No, by Heaven!" he exclaimed, "we part not—Alice, we part not. If I am to leave my native land, you shall be my companion in my exile. What have you to lose?—Whom have you to abandon?—Your father?—The good old cause, as it is termed, is dearer to him than a thousand daughters; and setting him aside, what tie is there between you and this barren isle—between my Alice and any spot of the British dominions, where her Julian does not sit by her?"

"O Julian," answered the maiden, "why make my duty more painful by visionary projects, which you ought not to name, or I to listen to? Your parents—my father—it cannot be!"

"Fear not for my parents, Alice," replied Julian, and pressing close to his companion's side, he ventured to throw his arm around her; "they love me, and they will soon learn to love, in Alice, the only being on earth who could have rendered their son happy. And for your own father, when State and Church intrigues allow him to bestow a thought upon you, will he not think that your happiness, your security, is better cared for when you are my wife, than were you to continue under the mercenary charge of yonder foolish woman? What could his pride desire better for you, than the establishment which will one day be mine? Come then, Alice, and since you condemn me to banishment—since you deny me a share in those stirring achievements which are about to agitate England—come! do you—for you only can—do you reconcile me to exile and inaction, and give happiness to one, who, for your sake, is willing to resign honour."

"It cannot—it cannot be," said Alice, faltering as she uttered her negative. "And yet," she said, "how many in my place—left alone and unprotected, as I am—But I must not—I must not—for your sake, Julian, I must not."

"Say not for my sake you must not, Alice," said Peveril eagerly; "this is adding insult to cruelty. If you will do aught for my sake, you will say yes; or you will suffer this dear head to drop on my shoulder—the slightest sign—the moving of an eyelid, shall signify consent. All shall be prepared within an hour; within another the priest shall unite us; and within a third, we leave the isle behind us, and seek our fortunes on the continent." But while he spoke, in joyful anticipation of the consent which he implored, Alice found means to collect together her resolution, which, staggered by the eagerness of her lover, the impulse of her own affections, and the singularity of her situation,—seeming, in her case, to justify what would have been most blamable in another,—had more than half abandoned her.

The result of a moment's deliberation was fatal to Julian's proposal. She extricated herself from the arm which had pressed her to his side—arose, and repelling his attempts to approach or detain her, said, with a simplicity not unmingled with dignity, "Julian, I always knew I risked much in inviting you to this meeting; but I did not guess that I could have been so cruel both to you and to myself, as to suffer you to discover what you have to-day seen too plainly—that I love you better than you love me. But since you do know it, I will show you that Alice's love is disinterested—She will not bring an ignoble name into your ancient house. If hereafter, in your line, there should arise some who may think the claims of the hierarchy too exorbitant, the powers of the crown too extensive, men shall not say these ideas were derived from Alice Bridgenorth, their whig granddame."

"Can you speak thus, Alice?" said her lover. "Can you use such expressions? and are you not sensible that they show plainly it is your own pride, not regard for me, that makes you resist the happiness of both?"

"Not so, Julian; not so," answered Alice, with tears in her eyes; "it is the command of duty to us both—of duty, which we cannot transgress, without risking our happiness here and hereafter. Think what I, the cause of all, should feel, when your father frowns, your mother weeps, your noble friends stand aloof, and you, even you yourself, shall have made the painful discovery, that you have incurred the contempt and resentment of all to satisfy a boyish passion; and that the poor beauty, once sufficient to mislead you, is gradually declining under the influence of grief and vexation. This I will not risk. I see distinctly it is best we should here break off and part; and I thank God, who gives me light enough to perceive, and strength enough to withstand, your folly as well as my own. Farewell, then, Julian; but first take the solemn advice which I called you hither to impart to you:—Shun my father—you cannot walk in his paths, and be true to gratitude and to honour. What he doth from pure and honourable motives, you cannot aid him in, except upon the suggestion of a silly and interested passion, at variance with all the engagements you have formed at coming into life."

"Once more, Alice," answered Julian, "I understand you

not. If a course of action is good, it needs no vindication from the actor's motives—if bad, it can derive none."

"You cannot blind me with your sophistry, Julian," replied Alice Bridgenorth, "any more than you can overpower me with your passion. Had the patriarch destined his son to death upon any less ground than faith and humble obedience to a divine commandment, he had meditated a murder and not a sacrifice. In our late bloody and lamentable wars, how many drew swords on either side, from the purest and most honourable motives? How many from the culpable suggestions of ambition, self-seeking, and love of plunder? Yet while they marched in the same ranks, and spurred their horses at the same trumpet-sound, the memory of the former is dear to us as patriots or loyalists—that of those who acted on mean or unworthy promptings, is either execrated or forgotten. Once more, I warn you, avoid my father—leave this island, which will be soon agitated by strange incidents—while you stay, be on your guard—distrust everything—be jealous of every one, even of those to whom it may seem almost impossible, from circumstances, to attach a shadow of suspicion—trust not the very stones of the most secret apartment in Holm-Peel, for that which hath wings shall carry the matter."

Here Alice broke off suddenly, and with a faint shriek; for, stepping from behind the stunted copse which had concealed him, her father stood unexpectedly before them.

The reader cannot have forgotten that this was the second time in which the stolen interviews of the lovers had been interrupted by the unexpected apparition of Major Bridgenorth. On this second occasion his countenance exhibited anger mixed with solemnity, like that of the spirit to a ghost-seer, whom he upbraids with having neglected a charge imposed at their first meeting. Even his anger, however, produced no more violent emotion than a cold sternness of manner in his speech and action. "I thank you, Alice," he said to his daughter, "for the pains you have taken to traverse my designs towards this young man, and towards yourself. I thank you for the hints you have thrown out before my appearance, the suddenness of which alone has prevented you from carrying your confidence to a pitch which would have placed my life and that of others at the discretion of a boy, who, when the cause of God and his country is laid before him, has not leisure to think of them, so much is he occupied with such a baby-face as thine." Alice, pale as death, continued motionless, with her eyes fixed on the ground, without attempting the slightest reply to the ironical reproaches of her father.

"And you," continued Major Bridgenorth, turning from his daughter to her lover,—"you, sir, have well repaid the liberal confidence which I placed in you with so little reserve. You I have to thank also for some lessons, which may teach me to rest satisfied with the churl's blood which nature has poured into my veins, and with the rude nurture which my father allotted to me."

"I understand you not, sir," replied Julian Peveril, who, feeling the necessity of saying something, could not, at the moment, find anything more fitting to say.

"Yes, sir, I thank you," said Major Bridgenorth, in the same cold sarcastic tone, "for having shown me that breach of hospitality, infringement of good faith, and such like peccadilloes, are not utterly foreign to the mind and conduct of the heir of a knightly house of twenty descents. It is a great lesson to me, sir: for hitherto I had thought with the vulgar, that gentle manners went with gentle blood. But perhaps courtesy is too chivalrous a quality to be wasted in intercourse with a round-headed fanatic like myself."

"Major Bridgenorth," said Julian, "whatever has happened in this interview which may have displeased you, has been the result of feelings suddenly and strongly animated by the crisis of the moment—nothing was premeditated."

"Not even your meeting, I suppose?" replied Bridgenorth, in the same cold tone. "You, sir, wandered hither from Home-Peel—my daughter strolled forth from the Black Fort; and chance, doubtless, assigned you a meeting by the stone of Goddard Crovan?—Young man, disgrace yourself by no more apologies—they are worse than useless.—And you, maiden, who, in your fear of losing your lover, could verge on betraying what might have cost a father his life—begone to your home. I will talk with you at more leisure, and teach you practically those duties which you seem to have forgotten."

"On my honour, sir," said Julian, "your daughter is guiltless of all that can offend you; she resisted every offer which the headstrong violence of my passion urged me to press upon her."

"And, in brief," said Bridgenorth, "I am not to believe that you met in this remote place of rendezvous by Alice's special appointment?"

Peveril knew not what to reply, and Bridgenorth again signed with his hand to his daughter to withdraw.

"I obey you, father," said Alice, who had by this time recovered from the extremity of her surprise,—"I obey you; but Heaven is my witness that you do me more than injustice in suspecting me capable of betraying your secrets, even had it been necessary to save my own life or that of Julian. That you are walking in a dangerous path I well know; but you do it with your eyes open, and are actuated by motives of which you can estimate the worth and value. My sole wish was, that this young man should not enter blindfold on the same perils; and I had a right to warn him, since the feelings by which he is hoodwinked had a direct reference to me."

"'Tis well, minion," said Bridgenorth, "you have spoken your say. Retire, and let me complete the conference which you have so considerately commenced."

"I go, sir," said Alice.—"Julian, to you my last words are, and I would speak them with my last breath—Farewell, and caution!"

She turned from them, disappeared among the underwood, and was seen no more.

"A true specimen of womankind," said her father, looking after her, "who would give the cause of nations up, rather than endanger a hair of her lover's head. — You, Master Peveril, doubtless, hold her opinion, that the best love is a safe love!"

"Were danger alone in my way," said Peveril, much surprised at the softened tone in which Bridgenorth made this observation, "there are few things which I would not face to—to—deserve your good opinion."

"Or rather to win my daughter's hand," said Bridgenorth. "Well, young man, one thing has pleased me in your conduct, though of much I have my reasons to complain—one thing *has* pleased me. You have surmounted that bounding wall of aristocratical pride, in which your father, and, I suppose, his fathers, remained imprisoned, as in the precincts of a feudal fortress—you have leaped over this barrier, and shown yourself not unwilling to ally yourself with a family whom your father spurns as low-born and ignoble."

However favourable this speech sounded towards success in his suit, it so broadly stated the consequences of that success so far as his parents were concerned, that Julian felt it in the last degree difficult to reply. At length, perceiving that Major Bridgenorth seemed resolved quietly to await his answer, he mustered up courage to say, "The feelings which I entertain towards your daughter, Master Bridgenorth, are of a nature to supersede many other considerations, to which in any other case, I should feel it my duty to give the most reverential attention. I will not disguise from you, that my father's prejudices against such a match would be very strong; but I devoutly believe they would disappear when he came to know the merit of Alice Bridgenorth, and to be sensible that she only could make his son happy."

"In the meanwhile, you are desirous to complete the union which you propose without the knowledge of your parents, and take the chance of their being hereafter reconciled to it? So

I understand, from the proposal which you made but lately to my daughter."

The turns of human nature, and of human passion, are so irregular and uncertain, that although Julian had but a few minutes before urged to Alice a private marriage, and an elopement to the continent, as a measure upon which the whole happiness of his life depended, the proposal seemed not to him half so delightful when stated by the calm, cold, dictatorial accents of her father. It sounded no longer like the dictates of ardent passion, throwing all other considerations aside, but as a distinct surrender of the dignity of his house to one who seemed to consider their relative situation as the triumph of Bridgenorth over Peveril. He was mute for a moment, in the vain attempt to shape his answer so as at once to intimate acquiescence in what Bridgenorth stated, and a vindication of his own regard for his parents, and for the honour of his house.

This delay gave rise to suspicion, and Bridgenorth's eye gleamed, and his lip quivered while he gave vent to it. "Hark ye, young man—deal openly with me in this matter, if you would not have me think you the execrable villain who would have seduced an unhappy girl, under promises which he never designed to fulfil. Let me but suspect this, and you shall see, on the spot, how far your pride and your pedigree will preserve you against the just vengeance of a father."

"You do me wrong," said Peveril—"you do me infinite wrong, Major Bridgenorth, I am incapable of the infamy which you allude to. The proposal I made to your daughter was as sincere as ever was offered by man to woman. I only hesitated, because you think it necessary to examine me so very closely; and to possess yourself of all my purposes and sentiments, in their fullest extent, without explaining to me the tendency of your own."

"Your proposal, then, shapes itself thus," said Bridgenorth: —"You are willing to lead my only child into exile from her native country, to give her a claim to kindness and protection from your family, which you know will be disregarded, on condition I consent to bestow her hand on you, with a fortune sufficient to have matched that of your ancestors, when they had most reason to boast of their wealth. This, young man, seems no equal bargain. And yet," he continued, after a momentary pause, "so little do I value the goods of this world, that it might not be utterly beyond thy power to reconcile me to the match which you have proposed to me, however unequal it may appear."

"Show me but the means which can propitiate your favour, Major Bridgenorth," said Peveril,—"for I will not doubt that they will be consistent with my honour and duty—and you shall soon see how eagerly I will obey your directions, or submit to your conditions."

"They are summed in few words," answered Bridgenorth. "Be an honest man, and the friend of your country."

"No one has ever doubted," replied Peveril, "that I am both."

"Pardon me," replied the Major; "no one has, as yet, seen you show yourself either. Interrupt me not—I question not your will to be both; but you have hitherto neither had the light nor the opportunity necessary for the display of your principles, or the service of your country. You have lived when an apathy of mind, succeeding to the agitations of the Civil War, had made men indifferent to state affairs, and more willing to cultivate their own ease, than to stand in the gap when the Lord was pleading with Israel. But we are Englishmen; and with us such unnatural lethargy cannot continue long. Already, many of those who most desired the return of Charles Stewart, regard him as a King whom Heaven, importuned by our entreaties, gave to us in His anger. His unlimited licence—an example so readily followed by the young and the gay around him—has disgusted the minds of all sober and thinking men. I had not now held conference with you in this intimate fashion, were I not aware that you, Master Julian, were free from such stain of the times. Heaven, that rendered the King's course of licence fruitful, had denied issue to his bed of wedlock; and in the gloomy and stern character of his bigoted successor, we already see what sort of monarch shall succeed to the crown of England. This is a critical period, at which it necessarily becomes the duty of all men to step forward, each in his degree, and aid in rescuing the country which gave us birth." Peveril remembered the warning which he had received from Alice, and bent his eyes on the ground, without returning any reply. "How is it, young man," continued Bridgenorth, after a pause—"so young as thou art, and bound by no ties of kindred profligacy with the enemies of your country, you can be already hardened to the claims she may form on you at this crisis?"

"It were easy to answer you generally, Major Bridgenorth," replied Peveril—"It were easy to say that my country cannot make a claim on me which I will not promptly answer at the risk of lands and life. But in dealing thus generally, we should but deceive each other. What is the nature of this call? By whom is it to be sounded? And what are to be the results? for I think you have already seen enough of the evils of civil war, to be wary of again awakening its terrors in a peaceful and happy country."

"They that are drenched with poisonous narcotics," said the Major, "must be awakened by their physicians, though it were with the sound of the trumpet. Better that men should die bravely, with their arms in their hands, like free-born Englishmen, than that they should slide into the bloodless but dishonoured grave which slavery opens for its vassals—But it is not of war that I was about to speak," he added, assuming a milder tone. "The evils of which England now complains, are such as can be remedied by the wholesome administration of her own laws, even in the state in which they are still suffered to exist. Have these laws not a right to the support of every individual who lives under them? Have they not a right to yours?"

As he seemed to pause for an answer, Peveril replied, "I have to learn, Major Bridgenorth, how the laws of England have become so far weakened as to require such support as mine. When that is made plain to me, no man will more willingly discharge the duty of a faithful liegeman to the law as well as the King. But the laws of England are under the guardianship of upright and learned judges, and of a gracious monarch."

"And of a House of Commons," interrupted Bridgenorth, "no longer doting upon restored monarchy, but awakened, as with a peal of thunder, to the perilous state of our religion, and of our freedom. I appeal to your own conscience, Julian Peveril, whether this awakening hath not been in time, since you yourself know, and none better than you, the secret but rapid strides which Rome has made to erect her Dagon of idolatry within our Protestant land."

Here Julian seeing, or thinking he saw, the drift of Bridgenorth's suspicions, hastened to exculpate himself from the thought of favouring the Roman Catholic religion. "It is true," he said, "I have been educated in a family where that faith is professed by one honoured individual, and that I have since travelled in Popish countries; but even for these very reasons I have seen Popery too closely to be friendly to its tenets. The bigotry of the laymen—the persevering arts of the priesthood—the perpetual intrigue for the extension of the forms without the spirit of religion—the usurpation of that Church over the consciences of men—and her impious pretensions to infallibility, are as inconsistent to my mind as they can seem to yours, with common-sense, rational liberty, freedom of conscience, and pure religion."

"Spoken like the son of your excellent mother," said Bridgenorth, grasping his hand; "for whose sake I have consented to endure so much from your house unrequited, even when the means of requital were in my own hand."

"It was indeed from the instructions of that excellent parent," said Peveril, "that I was enabled, in my early youth, to resist and repel the insidious attacks made upon my religious faith by the Catholic priests into whose company I was necessarily thrown. Like her, I trust to live and die in the faith of the reformed Church of England."

"The Church of England!" said Bridgenorth, dropping his young friend's hand, but presently resuming it—"Alas! that Church, as now constituted, usurps scarcely less than Rome herself upon men's consciences and liberties; yet, out of the weakness of this half-reformed Church, may God be pleased to work out deliverance to England, and praise to Himself. I must not forget, that one whose services have been in the cause incalculable, wears the garb of an English priest, and hath had Episcopal ordination. It is not for us to challenge the instrument, so that our escape is achieved from the net of the fowler. Enough, that I find thee not as yet enlightened with the purer doctrine, but prepared to profit by it when the spark shall reach thee. Enough, in especial, that I find thee willing to uplift thy testimony to cry aloud and spare not, against the errors and arts of the Church of Rome. But remember, what thou hast now said, thou wilt soon be called upon to justify, in a manner the most solemn—the most awful."

"What I have said," replied Julian Peveril, "being the unbiassed sentiments of my heart, shall, upon no proper occasion, want the support of my open avowal; and I think it strange you should doubt me so far."

"I doubt thee not, my young friend," said Bridgenorth; "and I trust to see that name rank high amongst those by whom the prey shall be rent from the mighty. At present, thy prejudices occupy thy mind like the strong keeper of the house mentioned in Scripture. But there shall come a stronger than he, and make forcible entry, displaying on the battlements that sign of faith in which alone there is found salvation.—Watch, hope, and pray, that the hour may come."

There was a pause in the conversation, which was first broken by Peveril. "You have spoken to me in riddles, Major Bridgenorth; and I have asked you for no explanation. Listen to a caution on my part, given with the most sincere good-will. Take a hint from me, and believe it, though it is darkly expressed. You are here—at least are believed to be here—on an errand dangerous to the Lord of the island. That danger will be retorted on yourself, if you make Man long your place of residence. Be warned, and depart in time."

"And leave my daughter to the guardianship of Julian

Peveril! Runs not your counsel so, young man?" answered
Bridgenorth. "Trust my safety, Julian, to my own prudence. I have been accustomed to guide myself through
worse dangers than now environ me. But I thank you for
your caution, which I am willing to believe was at least partly
disinterested."

"We do not, then, part in anger?" said Peveril.

"Not in anger, my son," said Bridgenorth, "but in love and
strong affection. For my daughter, thou must forbear every
thought of seeing her, save through me. I accept not thy
suit, neither do I reject it; only this I intimate to you, that
he who would be my son, must first show himself the true
and loving child of his oppressed and deluded country. Farewell; do not answer me now, thou art yet in the gall of
bitterness, and it may be that strife (which I desire not) should
fall between us. Thou shalt hear of me sooner than thou
thinkest for."

He shook Peveril heartily by the hand, and again bid him
farewell, leaving him under the confused and mingled impression of pleasure, doubt, and wonder. Not a little surprised to
find himself so far in the good graces of Alice's father, that his
suit was even favoured with a sort of negative encouragement,
he could not help suspecting, as well from the language of the
daughter as of the father, that Bridgenorth was desirous, as the
price of his favour, that he should adopt some line of conduct
inconsistent with the principles in which he had been educated.

"You need not fear, Alice," he said in his heart; "not
even your hand would I purchase by aught which resembled
unworthy or truckling compliance with tenets which my heart
disowns; and well I know, were I mean enough to do so, even
the authority of thy father were insufficient to compel thee to
the ratification of so mean a bargain. But let me hope better
things. Bridgenorth, though strong-minded and sagacious, is
haunted by the fears of Popery, which are the bugbears of his
sect. My residence in the family of the Countess of Derby is
more than enough to inspire him with suspicions of my faith,
from which, thank Heaven, I can vindicate myself with truth
and a good conscience."

So thinking, he again adjusted the girths of his palfrey,
replaced the bit which he had slipped out of its mouth, that
it might feed at liberty, and mounting, pursued his way back
to the Castle of Holm-Peel, where he could not help fearing
that something extraordinary might have happened in his
absence.

But the old pile soon rose before him, serene, and sternly
still, amid the sleeping ocean. The banner, which indicated
that the Lord of Man held residence within its ruinous precincts,

hung motionless by the ensign-staff. The sentinels walked to and fro on their posts, and hummed or whistled their Manx airs. Leaving his faithful companion, Fairy, in the village as before, Julian entered the Castle, and found all within in the same state of quietness and good order which external appearances had announced.

CHAPTER XVIII

Now rede me, rede me, brother dear,
    Throughout Merry England,
Where will I find a messenger,
    Betwixt us two to send.
        —BALLAD OF KING ESTMERE.

JULIAN's first rencounter, after re-entering the Castle, was with its young Lord, who received him with his usual kindness and lightness of humour.

"Thrice welcome, Sir Knight of Dames," said the Earl; "here you rove gallantly, and at free will, through our dominions, fulfilling of appointments, and achieving amorous adventures; while we are condemned to sit in our royal halls, as dull and as immovable as if our Majesty was carved on the stern of some Manx smuggling dogger, and christened the King Arthur of Ramsey."

"Nay, in that case you would take the sea," said Julian, "and so enjoy travel and adventure enough."

"Oh, but suppose me wind-bound, or detained in harbour by a revenue pink, or ashore, if you like it, and lying high and dry upon the sand. Imagine the royal image in the dullest of all predicaments, and you have not equalled mine."

"I am happy to hear, at least, that you have had no disagreeable employment," said Julian; "the morning's alarm has blown over, I suppose?"

"In faith it has, Julian; and our close inquiries cannot find any cause for the apprehended insurrection. That Bridgenorth is in the island seems certain; but private affairs of consequence are alleged as the cause of his visit; and I am not desirous to have him arrested unless I could prove some malpractices against him and his companions. In fact, it would seem we had taken the alarm too soon. My mother speaks of consulting you on the subject, Julian; and I will not anticipate her solemn communication. It will be partly apological, I suppose; for we begin to think our retreat rather unroyal, and that, like the wicked, we have fled when no man pursued. This idea afflicts my mother, who, as a Queen-Dowager, a

Queen-Regent, a heroine, and a woman in general, would be extremely mortified to think that her precipitate retreat hither had exposed her to the ridicule of the islanders; and she is disconcerted and out of humour accordingly. In the meanwhile, my sole amusement has been the grimaces and fantastic gestures of that ape Fenella, who is more out of humour, and more absurd, in consequence, than you ever saw her. Morris says, it is because you pushed her downstairs, Julian—how is that?"

"Nay, Morris has misreported me," answered Julian; "I did but lift her *up* stairs to be rid of her importunity; for she chose, in her way, to contest my going abroad in such an obstinate manner, that I had no other mode of getting rid of her."

"She must have supposed your departure, at a moment so critical, was dangerous to the state of our garrison," answered the Earl; "it shows how dearly she esteems my mother's safety, how highly she rates your prowess. But, thank Heaven, there sounds the dinner-bell. I would the philosophers, who find a sin and waste of time in good cheer, could devise us any pastime half so agreeable."

The meal which the young Earl had thus longed for, as a means of consuming a portion of the time which hung heavy on his hands, was soon over; as soon, at least, as the habitual and stately formality of the Countess's household permitted. She herself, accompanied by her gentlewomen and attendants, retired early after the tables were drawn; and the young gentlemen were left to their own company. Wine had, for the moment, no charms for either; for the Earl was out of spirits from ennui, and impatience of his monotonous and solitary course of life; and the events of the day had given Peveril too much matter for reflection, to permit his starting amusing or interesting topics of conversation. After having passed the flask in silence betwixt them once or twice, they withdrew each to a separate embrasure of the windows of the dining apartment, which, such was the extreme thickness of the wall, were deep enough to afford a solitary recess, separated, as it were, from the chamber itself. In one of these sat the Earl of Derby, busied in looking over some of the new publications which had been forwarded from London; and at intervals confessing how little power or interest these had for him, by yawning fearfully as he looked out on the solitary expanse of waters, which, save from the flight of a flock of sea-gulls, or of a solitary cormorant, offered so little of variety to engage his attention.

Peveril, on his part, held a pamphlet also in his hand, without giving, or affecting to give it, even his occasional attention. His whole soul turned upon the interview which he had had that day with Alice Bridgenorth, and with her father; while he

in vain endeavoured to form any hypothesis which could explain
to him why the daughter, to whom he had no reason to think
himself indifferent, should have been so suddenly desirous of
their eternal separation, while her father, whose opposition he
so much dreaded, seemed to be at least tolerant of his addresses.
He could only suppose, in explanation, that Major Bridgenorth
had some plan in prospect, which it was in his own power to
farther or to impede; while, from the demeanour, and indeed
the language, of Alice, he had but too much reason to apprehend
that her father's favour could only be conciliated by something,
on his own part, approaching to dereliction of principle. But
by no conjecture which he could form, could he make the least
guess concerning the nature of that compliance, of which Bridgenorth seemed desirous. He could not imagine, notwithstanding
Alice had spoken of treachery, that her father would dare to
propose to him uniting in any plan by which the safety of the
Countess, or the security of her little kingdom of Man, was to be
endangered. This carried such indelible disgrace in the front,
that he could not suppose the scheme proposed to him by any
who was not prepared to defend with his sword, upon the spot,
so flagrant an insult offered to his honour. And such a proceeding was totally inconsistent with the conduct of Major
Bridgenorth in every other respect, besides his being too calm
and cold-blooded to permit of his putting a mortal affront upon
the son of his old neighbour, to whose mother he confessed so
much of obligation.

While Peveril in vain endeavoured to extract something like
a probable theory out of the hints thrown out by the father and
by the daughter—not without the additional and lover-like
labour of endeavouring to reconcile his passion to his honour
and conscience—he felt something gently pull him by the cloak.
He unclasped his arms, which, in meditation, had been folded
on his bosom; and withdrawing his eyes from the vacant prospect
of sea-coast and sea which they perused, without much consciousness upon what they rested, he beheld beside him the little
dumb maiden, the elfin Fenella. She was seated on a low
cushion or stool, with which she had nestled close to Peveril's
side, and had remained there for a short space of time, expecting,
no doubt, he would become conscious of her presence; until, tired
of remaining unnoticed, she at length solicited his attention in
the manner which we have described. Startled out of his reverie
by this intimation of her presence, he looked down, and could
not, without interest, behold this singular and helpless being.

Her hair was unloosened, and streamed over her shoulders in
such length, that much of it lay upon the ground, and in such
quantity, that it formed a dark veil, or shadow, not only around
her face, but over her whole slender and minute form. From

the profusion of her tresses looked forth her small and dark, but well-formed features, together with the large and brilliant black eyes; and her whole countenance was composed into the imploring look of one who is doubtful of the reception she is about to meet with from a valued friend, while she confesses a fault, pleads an apology, or solicits a reconciliation. In short, the whole face was so much alive with expression, that Julian, though her aspect was so familiar to him, could hardly persuade himself but that her countenance was entirely new. The wild, fantastic, elvish vivacity of the features, seemed totally vanished, and had given place to a sorrowful, tender, and pathetic cast of countenance, aided by the expression of the large dark eyes, which, as they were turned up towards Julian, glistened with moisture, that, nevertheless, did not overflow the eyelids.

Conceiving that her unwonted manner arose from a recollection of the dispute which had taken place betwixt them in the morning, Peveril was anxious to restore the little maiden's gaiety, by making her sensible that there dwelt on his mind no unpleasing recollection of their quarrel. He smiled kindly, and shook her hand in one of his; while, with the familiarity of one who had known her from childhood, he stroked down her long dark tresses with the other. She stooped her head, as if ashamed, and, at the same time, gratified with his caresses—and he was thus induced to continue them, until, under the veil of her rich and abundant locks, he suddenly felt his other hand, which she still held fast in hers, slightly touched with her lips, and, at the same time, moistened with a tear.

At once, and for the first time in his life, the danger of being misinterpreted in his familiarity with a creature to whom the usual modes of explanation were a blank, occurred to Julian's mind; and, hastily withdrawing his hand, and changing his posture, he asked of her, by a sign which custom had rendered familiar, whether she brought any message to him from the Countess. In an instant Fenella's whole deportment was changed. She started up, and arranged herself in her seat with the rapidity of lightning; and, at the same moment, with one turn of her hand, braided her length of locks into a natural head-dress of the most beautiful kind. There was, indeed, when she looked up, a blush still visible on her dark features; but their melancholy and languid expression had given place to that of wild and restless vivacity, which was most common to them. Her eyes gleamed with more than their wonted fire, and her glances were more piercingly wild and unsettled than usual. To Julian's inquiry, she answered, by laying her hand on her heart—a motion by which she always indicated the Countess—and rising, and taking the direction of her apartment, she made a sign to Julian to follow her.

The distance was not great betwixt the dining apartment and that to which Peveril now followed his mute guide; yet, in going thither, he had time enough to suffer cruelly from the sudden suspicion, that this unhappy girl had misinterpreted the uniform kindness with which he had treated her, and hence come to regard him with feelings more tender than those which belong to friendship. The misery which such a passion was likely to occasion to a creature in her helpless situation, and actuated by such lively feelings, was great enough to make him refuse credit to the suspicion which pressed itself upon his mind; while, at the same time, he formed the internal resolution so to conduct himself towards Fenella, as to check such misplaced sentiments, if indeed she unhappily entertained them towards him.

When they reached the Countess's apartment, they found her with writing implements, and many sealed letters before her. She received Julian with her usual kindness; and having caused him to be seated, beckoned to the mute to resume her needle. In an instant Fenella was seated at an embroidering-frame; where, but for the movement of her dexterous fingers, she might have seemed a statue, so little did she move from her work either head or eye. As her infirmity rendered her presence no bar to the most confidential conversation, the Countess proceeded to address Peveril as if they had been literally alone together.

"Julian," she said, " I am not now about to complain to you of the sentiments and conduct of Derby. He is your friend— he is my son. He has kindness of heart and vivacity of talent; and yet——"

"Dearest lady," said Peveril, " why will you distress yourself with fixing your eye on deficiencies which arise rather from a change of times and manners, than any degeneracy of my noble friend? Let him be once engaged in his duty, whether in peace or war, and let me pay the penalty if he acquits not himself becoming his high station."

"Ay," replied the Countess; "but when will the call of duty prove superior to that of the most idle or trivial indulgence which can serve to drive over the lazy hour? His father was of another mould; and how often was it my lot to entreat that he would spare, from the rigid discharge of those duties which his high station imposed, the relaxation absolutely necessary to recruit his health and his spirits!"

"Still, my dearest lady," said Peveril, " you must allow, that the duties to which the times summoned your late honoured lord, were of a more stirring, as well as a more peremptory cast, than those which await your son."

"I know not that," said the Countess. " The wheel appears

M

to be again revolving; and the present period is not unlikely to bring back such scenes as my younger years witnessed.—Well, be it so; they will not find Charlotte de la Tremouille broken in spirit, though depressed by years. It was even on this subject I would speak with you, my young friend. Since our first early acquaintance—when I saw your gallant behaviour as I issued forth to your childish eye, like an apparition, from my place of concealment in your father's castle—it has pleased me to think you a true son of Stanley and Peveril. I trust your nurture in this family has been ever suited to the esteem in which I hold you.—Nay, I desire no thanks.—I have to require of you, in return, a piece of service, not perhaps entirely safe to yourself, but which, as times are circumstanced, no person is so well able to render to my house."

"You have been ever my good and noble lady," answered Peveril, "as well as my kind, and I may say maternal, protectress. You have a right to command the blood of Stanley in the veins of every one—You have a thousand rights to command it in mine." *

"My advices from England," said the Countess, "resemble more the dreams of a sick man, than the regular information which I might have expected from such correspondents as mine;—their expressions are like those of men who walk in their sleep, and speak by snatches of what passes in their dreams. It is said, a plot, real or fictitious, has been detected among the Catholics, which has spread far wider and more uncontrollable terror than that of the fifth of November. Its outlines seem utterly incredible, and are only supported by the evidence of wretches, the meanest and most worthless in the creation; yet it is received by the credulous people of England with the most undoubting belief."

"This is a singular delusion, to rise without some real ground," answered Julian.

"I am no bigot, cousin, though a Catholic," replied the Countess. "I have long feared that the well-meant zeal of our priests for increasing converts, would draw on them the suspicion of the English nation. These efforts have been renewed with double energy since the Duke of York conformed to the Catholic faith; and the same event has doubled the hate and jealousy of the Protestants. So far, I fear, there may be just cause for suspicion, that the Duke is a better Catholic than an Englishman, and that bigotry has involved him, as avarice, or the needy greed of a prodigal, has engaged his brother, in relations with France, whereof England may have too much reason to complain. But the gross, thick, and palpable fabrica-

* The reader cannot have forgotten that the Earl of Derby was head of the great house of Stanley.

tions of conspiracy and murder, blood and fire—the imaginary armies—the intended massacres—form a collection of falsehoods, that one would have thought indigestible, even by the coarse appetite of the vulgar for the marvellous and horrible; but which are, nevertheless, received as truth by both Houses of Parliament, and questioned by no one who is desirous to escape the odious appellation of friend to the bloody Papists, and favourer of their infernal schemes of cruelty."

"But what say those who are most likely to be affected by these wild reports?" said Julian. "What say the English Catholics themselves?—a numerous and wealthy body, comprising so many noble names?"

"Their hearts are dead within them," said the Countess. "They are like sheep penned up in the shambles, that the butcher may take his choice among them. In the obscure and brief communications which I have had by a secure hand, they do but anticipate their own utter ruin, and ours—so general is the depression, so universal the despair."

"But the King," said Peveril,—"the King and the Protestant Royalists—what say they to this growing tempest?"

"Charles," replied the Countess, "with his usual selfish prudence, truckles to the storm; and will let cord and axe do their work on the most innocent men in his dominions, rather than lose an hour of pleasure in attempting their rescue. And, for the Royalists, either they have caught the general delirium which has seized on Protestants in general, or they stand aloof and neutral, afraid to show any interest in the unhappy Catholics, lest they be judged altogether such as themselves, and abettors of the fearful conspiracy in which they are alleged to be engaged. In fact, I cannot blame them. It is hard to expect that mere compassion for a persecuted sect—or, what is yet more rare, an abstract love of justice—should be powerful enough to engage men to expose themselves to the awakened fury of a whole people; for, in the present state of general agitation, whoever disbelieves the least tittle of the enormous improbabilities which have been accumulated by these wretched reformers, is instantly hunted down, as one who would smother the discovery of the Plot. It is indeed an awful tempest; and, remote as we lie from its sphere, we must expect soon to feel its effects."

"Lord Derby already told me something of this," said Julian; "and that there were agents in this island whose object was to excite insurrection."

"Yes," answered the Countess, and her eye flashed fire as she spoke; "and had my advice been listened to, they had been apprehended in the very fact; and so dealt with, as to be a warning to all others how they sought this independent principality on such an errand. But my son, who is generally so culpably negligent of his own affairs, was pleased to assume the management of them upon this crisis."

"I am happy to learn, madam," answered Peveril, "that the measures of precaution which my kinsman has adopted, have had the complete effect of disconcerting the conspiracy."

"For the present, Julian; but they should have been such as would have made the boldest tremble to think of such infringement of our rights in future. But Derby's present plan is fraught with greater danger; and yet there is something in it of gallantry, which has my sympathy."

"What is it, madam?" inquired Julian anxiously; "and in what can I aid it, or avert its dangers?"

"He purposes," said the Countess, "instantly to set forth for London. He is, he says, not merely the feudal chief of a small island, but one of the noble Peers of England, who must not remain in the security of an obscure and distant castle, when his name, or that of his mother, is slandered before his Prince and people. He will take his place, he says, in the House of Lords, and publicly demand justice for the insult thrown on his house, by perjured and interested witnesses."

"It is a generous resolution, and worthy of my friend," said Julian Peveril. "I will go with him and share his fate, be it what it may."

"Alas, foolish boy!" answered the Countess, "as well may you ask a hungry lion to feel compassion, as a prejudiced and furious people to do justice. They are like the madman at the height of frenzy, who murders without compunction his best and dearest friend; and only wonders and wails over his own cruelty, when he is recovered from his delirium."

"Pardon me, dearest lady," said Julian, "this cannot be. The noble and generous people of England cannot be thus strangely misled. Whatever prepossessions may be current among the more vulgar, the House of Legislature cannot be deeply infected by them—they will remember their own dignity."

"Alas! cousin," answered the Countess, "when did Englishmen, even of the highest degree, remember anything, when hurried away by the violence of party feeling? Even those who have too much sense to believe in the incredible fictions which gull the multitude, will beware how they expose them, if their own political party can gain a momentary advantage by their being accredited. It is amongst such, too, that your kinsman has found friends and associates. Neglecting the old friends of his house, as too grave and formal companions for the humour of the times, his intercourse has been with the versatile Shaftesbury—the mercurial Buckingham—men who would not hesitate to sacrifice to the popular Moloch of the day, whatsoever or whomsoever, whose ruin could propitiate the deity.—Forgive a mother's tears, kinsman; but I see the scaffold at Bolton again erected. If Derby goes to London while these bloodhounds are in full cry, obnoxious as he is, and I have made him by my religious faith, and my conduct in this island, he dies his father's death. And yet upon what other course to resolve!——"

"Let me go to London, madam," said Peveril, much moved by the distress of his patroness; "your ladyship was wont to rely something on my judgment. I will act for the best—will communicate with those whom you point out to me, and only with them; and I trust soon to send you information that this delusion, however strong it may now be, is in the course of passing away; at the worst, I can apprise you of the danger, should it menace the Earl or yourself; and may be able also to point out the means by which it may be eluded."

The Countess listened with a countenance in which the anxiety of maternal affection, which prompted her to embrace Peveril's generous offer, struggled with her native disinterested and generous disposition. "Think what you ask of me, Julian," she replied with a sigh. "Would you have me expose the life of my friend's son to those perils to which I refuse my own? —No, never!"

"Nay, but, madam," replied Julian, "I do not run the same risk—my person is not known in London—my situation, though not obscure in my own country, is too little known to be noticed in that huge assemblage of all that is noble and wealthy. No whisper, I presume, however indirect, has connected my name with the alleged conspiracy. I am a Protestant, above all; and can be accused of no intercourse, direct or indirect, with the Church of Rome. My connections also lie amongst those, who, if they do not, or cannot, befriend me, cannot, at least, be dangerous to me. In a word, I run no danger where the Earl might incur great peril."

"Alas!" said the Countess of Derby, "all this generous reasoning may be true; but it could only be listened to by a widowed mother. Selfish as I am, I cannot but reflect that my kinswoman has, in all events, the support of an affectionate husband—such is the interested reasoning to which we are not ashamed to subject our better feelings."

"Do not call it so, madam," answered Peveril; "think of me as the younger brother of my kinsman. You have ever done by me the duties of a mother; and have a right to my filial service, were it at a risk ten times greater than a journey to London, to inquire into the temper of the times. I will instantly go and announce my departure to the Earl."

"Stay, Julian," said the Countess; "if you must make this journey in our behalf,—and, alas! I have not generosity enough to refuse your noble proffer,—you must go alone, and without communication with Derby. I know him well; his lightness of mind is free from selfish baseness; and for the world, would he not suffer you to leave Man without his company. And if he went with you, your noble and disinterested kindness would be of no avail—you would but share his ruin, as the swimmer who attempts to save a drowning man is involved in his fate, if he permit the sufferer to grapple with him."

"It shall be as you please, madam," said Peveril. "I am ready to depart upon half-an-hour's notice."

"This night, then," said the Countess, after a moment's pause—"this night I will arrange the most secret means of carrying your generous project into effect; for I would not excite that prejudice against you, which will instantly arise, were it known you had so lately left this island, and its Popish lady. You will do well, perhaps, to use a feigned name in London."

"Pardon me, madam," said Julian; "I will do nothing that can draw on me unnecessary attention; but to bear a feigned name, or affect any disguise beyond living with extreme privacy, would, I think, be unwise as well as unworthy; and what, if challenged, I might find some difficulty in assigning a reason for, consistent with perfect fairness of intentions."

"I believe you are right," answered the Countess, after a moment's consideration; and then added, "You propose, doubtless, to pass through Derbyshire, and visit Martindale Castle?"

"I should wish it, madam, certainly," replied Peveril, "did time permit, and circumstances render it advisable."

"Of that," said the Countess, "you must yourself judge. Despatch is, doubtless, desirable; on the other hand, arriving from your own family-seat, you will be less an object of doubt and suspicion, than if you posted up from hence, without even visiting your parents. You must be guided in this,—in all,—by your own prudence. Go, my dearest son—for to me you should be dear as a son—go, and prepare for your journey. I will get ready some despatches, and a supply of money—Nay, do not object. Am I not your mother; and are you not discharging a son's duty? Dispute not my right of defraying your expenses. Nor is this all; for, as I must trust your zeal and prudence to act in our behalf when occasion shall demand, I will furnish you with effectual recommendations to our friends and kindred, entreating and enjoining them to render whatever aid you may require, either for your own protection, or the advancement of what you may propose in our favour."

Peveril made no farther opposition to an arrangement, which in truth the moderate state of his own finances rendered almost indispensable, unless with his father's assistance; and the Countess put into his hand bills of exchange to the amount of two hundred pounds, upon a merchant in the city. She then dismissed Julian for the space of an hour; after which, she said, she must again require his presence.

The preparations for his journey were not of a nature to divert the thoughts which speedily pressed on him. He found that half-an-hour's conversation had once more completely changed his immediate prospects and plans for the future. He had offered to the Countess of Derby a service, which her uniform kindness had well deserved at his hand; but, by her accepting it, he was upon the point of being separated from Alice Bridgenorth, at a time when she was become dearer to him than ever, by her avowal of mutual passion. Her image rose before him, such as he had that day pressed her to his bosom—her voice was in his ear, and seemed to ask whether he could desert her in the crisis which everything seemed to announce as impending. But Julian Peveril, his youth considered, was strict in judging his duty, and severely resolved in executing it. He trusted not his imagination to pursue the vision which presented itself; but resolutely seizing his pen, wrote to Alice the following letter, explaining his situation, as far as justice to the Countess permitted him to do so :—

"I leave you, dearest Alice," thus ran the letter.—"I leave you; and though, in doing so, I but obey the command you have laid on me, yet I can claim little merit for my compliance, since, without additional and most forcible reasons in aid of your orders, I fear I should have been unable to comply with them. But family affairs of importance compel me to absent myself from this island, for, I fear, more than one week. My thoughts, hopes, and wishes will be on the moment that shall restore me to the Black Fort, and its lovely valley. Let me hope that yours will sometimes rest on the lonely exile, whom nothing could render such, but the command of honour and duty. Do not fear that I mean to involve you in a private correspondence, and let not your father fear it. I could not love you so much, but for the openness and candour of your nature; and I would not that you concealed from Major Bridgenorth one syllable of what I now avow. Respecting other matters, he himself cannot desire the welfare of our common country with more zeal than I do. Differences may occur concerning the mode in which that is to be obtained; but, in the principle, I am convinced there can be only one mind between us; nor can I refuse to listen to his experience and wisdom, even where they may ultimately fail to convince me.

Farewell—Alice, farewell! Much might be added to that melancholy word, but nothing that could express the bitterness with which it is written. Yet I could transcribe it again and again, rather than conclude the last communication which I can have with you for some time. My sole comfort is, that my stay will scarce be so long as to permit you to forget one who never can forget you."

He held the paper in his hand for a minute after he had folded, but before he had sealed it, while he hurriedly debated in his own mind whether he had not expressed himself towards Major Bridgenorth in so conciliating a manner as might excite hopes of proselytism, which his conscience told him he could not realise with honour. Yet, on the other hand, he had no right, from what Bridgenorth had said, to conclude that their principles were diametrically irreconcilable; for though the son of a high Cavalier, and educated in the family of the Countess of Derby, he was himself, upon principle, an enemy of prerogative, and a friend to the liberty of the subject. And with such considerations, he silenced all internal objections on the point of honour; although his conscience secretly whispered that these conciliatory expressions towards the father were chiefly dictated by the fear, that during his absence Major Bridgenorth might be tempted to change the residence of his daughter, and perhaps to convey her altogether out of his reach.

Having sealed his letter, Julian called his servant, and directed him to carry it under cover of one addressed to Mrs. Debbitch, to a house in the town of Rushin, where packets and messages intended for the family at Black Fort were usually deposited; and for that purpose to take horse immediately. He thus got rid of an attendant, who might have been in some degree a spy on his motions. He then exchanged the dress he usually wore for one more suited to travelling; and, having put a change or two of linen into a small cloak-bag, selected as arms a strong doubled-edged sword and an excellent pair of pistols, which last he carefully loaded with double bullets. Thus appointed, and with twenty pieces in his purse, and the bills we have mentioned secured in a private pocket-book, he was in readiness to depart as soon as he should receive the Countess's commands.

The buoyant spirit of youth and hope, which had, for a moment, been chilled by the painful and dubious circumstances in which he was placed, as well as the deprivation which he was about to undergo, now revived in full vigour. Fancy, turning from more painful anticipations, suggested to him that he was now entering upon life, at a crisis when resolution and talents were almost certain to make the fortune of their possessor. How could he make a more honourable entry on the bustling scene, than sent by, and acting in behalf of, one of the noblest houses in England; and should he perform what his charge might render incumbent with the resolution and the prudence necessary to secure success, how many occurrences might take place to render his mediation necessary to Bridgenorth; and thus enable him, on the most equal and honourable terms, to establish a claim to his gratitude and to his daughter's hand.

Whilst he was dwelling on such pleasing, though imaginary prospects, he could not help exclaiming aloud—"Yes, Alice, I will win thee nobly!" The words had scarce escaped his lips, when he heard at the door of his apartment, which the servant had left ajar, a sound like a deep sigh, which was instantly succeeded by a gentle tap—"Come in," replied Julian, somewhat ashamed of his exclamation, and not a little afraid that it had been caught up by some eavesdropper—"Come in," he again repeated; but his command was not obeyed; on the contrary, the knock was repeated somewhat louder. He opened the door, and Fenella stood before him.

With eyes that seemed red with recent tears, and with a look of the deepest dejection, the little mute, first touching her bosom, and beckoning with her finger, made to him the usual sign that the Countess desired to see him—then turned, as if to usher him to her apartment. As he followed her through the long gloomy vaulted passages which afforded communication betwixt the various apartments of the castle, he could not but observe that her usual light trip was exchanged for a tardy and mournful step, which she accompanied with low inarticulate moaning (which she was probably the less able to suppress, because she could not judge how far it was audible), and also with wringing of the hands, and other marks of extreme affliction.

At this moment a thought came across Peveril's mind, which, in spite of his better reason, made him shudder involuntarily. As a Peaksman, and a long resident in the Isle of Man, he was well acquainted with many a superstitious legend, and particularly with a belief, which attached to the powerful family of the Stanleys, for their peculiar demon, a Banshie, or female spirit, who was wont to shriek "foreboding evil times;" and who was generally seen weeping and bemoaning herself before the death of any person of distinction belonging to the family. For an instant, Julian could scarcely divest himself of the belief that the wailing, jibbering form, which glided before him, with a lamp in her hand, was a genius of his mother's race, come to announce to him his predestined doom. It instantly occurred to him as an analogous reflection, that if the suspicion which had crossed his mind concerning Fenella was a just one, her ill-fated attachment to him, like that of the prophetic spirit to his family, could bode nothing but disaster, and lamentation, and woe.

CHAPTER XIX

Now, hoist the anchor, mates—and let the sails
Give their broad bosom to the buxom wind,
Like lass that woos a lover.
—ANONYMOUS.

THE presence of the Countess dispelled the superstitious feeling, which, for an instant, had encroached on Julian's imagination, and compelled him to give attention to the matters of ordinary life. "Here are your credentials," she said, giving him a small packet, carefully packed up in a sealskin cover; "you had better not open them till you come to London. You must not be surprised to find that there are one or two addressed to men of my own persuasion. These, for all our sakes, you will observe caution in delivering."

"I go your messenger, madam," said Peveril; "and whatever you desire me to charge myself with, of that I undertake the care. Yet allow me to doubt whether an intercourse with Catholics will at this moment forward the purposes of my mission."

"You have caught the general suspicion of this wicked sect already," said the Countess, smiling, "and are the fitter to go amongst Englishmen in their present mood. But, my cautious friend, these letters are so addressed, and the persons to whom they are addressed so disguised, that you will run no danger in conversing with them. Without their aid, indeed, you will not be able to obtain the accurate information you go in search of. None can tell so exactly how the wind sets, as the pilot whose vessel is exposed to the storm. Besides, though you Protestants deny our priesthood the harmlessness of the dove, you are ready enough to allow us a full share of the wisdom of the serpent; in plain terms, their means of information are extensive, and they are not deficient in the power of applying it. I therefore wish you to have the benefit of their intelligence and advice, if possible."

"Whatever you impose upon me as a part of my duty, madam, rely on its being discharged punctually," answered Peveril. "And, now, as there is little use in deferring the execution of a purpose when once fixed, let me know your ladyship's wishes concerning my departure."

"It must be sudden and secret," said the Countess; "the island is full of spies; and I would not wish that any of them should have notice that an envoy of mine was about to leave Man for London. Can you be ready to go on board to-morrow?"

"To-night—this instant if you will," said Julian,—"my little preparations are complete."

"Be ready, then, in your chamber, at two hours after midnight. I will send one to summon you, for our secret must be communicated, for the present, to as few as possible. A foreign sloop is engaged to carry you over; then make the best of your way to London, by Martindale Castle, or otherwise, as you find most advisable. When it is necessary to announce your absence, I will say you are gone to see your parents. But stay—your journey will be on horseback, of course, from Whitehaven. You have bills of exchange, it is true; but are you provided with ready money to furnish yourself with a good horse?"

"I am sufficiently rich, madam," answered Julian; "and good nags are plenty in Cumberland. There are those among them who know how to come by them good and cheap."

"Trust not to that," said the Countess. "Here is what will purchase for you the best horse on the Borders.—Can you be simple enough to refuse it?" she added, as she pressed on him a heavy purse, which he saw himself obliged to accept.

"A good horse, Julian," continued the Countess, "and a good sword, next to a good heart and head, are the accomplishments of a cavalier."

"I kiss your hands, then, madam," said Peveril, "and humbly beg you to believe, that whatever may fail in my present undertaking, my purpose to serve you, my noble kinswoman and benefactress, can at least never swerve or falter."

"I know it, my son, I know it; and may God forgive me if my anxiety for your friend has sent you on dangers which should have been his! Go—go—May saints and angels bless you! Fenella shall acquaint him that you sup in your own apartment. So indeed will I; for to-night I should be unable to face my son's looks. Little will he thank me for sending you on his errand; and there will be many to ask, whether it was like the Lady of Latham to trust her friend's son on the danger which should have been braved by her own. But oh! Julian, I am now a forlorn widow, whom sorrow has made selfish!"

"Tush, madam," answered Peveril; "it is more unlike the Lady of Latham to anticipate dangers which may not exist at all, and to which, if they do indeed occur, I am less obnoxious than my noble kinsman. Farewell!—All blessings attend you, madam. Commend me to Derby, and make him my excuses. I shall expect a summons at two hours after midnight."

They took an affectionate leave of each other; the more affectionate, indeed, on the part of the Countess, that she could not entirely reconcile her generous mind to exposing Peveril to danger on her son's behalf; and Julian betook himself to his solitary apartment.

His servant soon afterwards brought him wine and refreshments; to which, notwithstanding the various matters he had to occupy his mind, he contrived to do reasonable justice. But when this needful occupation was finished, his thoughts began to stream in upon him like a troubled tide—at once recalling the past, and anticipating the future. It was in vain that he wrapped himself in his riding cloak, and, lying down on his bed, endeavoured to compose himself to sleep. The uncertainty of the prospect before him—the doubt how Bridgenorth might dispose of his daughter during his absence—the fear that the Major himself might fall into the power of the vindictive Countess, besides a numerous train of vague and half-formed apprehensions, agitated his blood, and rendered slumber impossible. Alternately to recline in the old oaken easy-chair, and listen to the dashing of the waves under the windows, mingled, as the sound was, with the scream of the sea-birds; or to traverse the apartment with long and slow steps, pausing occasionally to look out on the sea, slumbering under the influence of a full moon, which tipped each wave with silver—such were the only pastimes he could invent, until midnight had passed for one hour; the next was wasted in anxious expectation of the summons of departure.

At length it arrived—a tap at his door was followed by a low murmur, which made him suspect that the Countess had again employed her mute attendant as the most secure minister of her pleasure on this occasion. He felt something like impropriety in this selection; and it was with a feeling of impatience alien to the natural generosity of his temper, that, when he opened the door, he beheld the dumb maiden standing before him. The lamp which he held in his hand showed his features distinctly, and probably made Fenella aware of the expression which animated them. She cast her large dark eyes mournfully on the ground; and, without again looking him in the face, made him a signal to follow her. He delayed no longer than was necessary to secure his pistols in his belt, wrap his cloak closer around him, and take his small portmanteau under his arm. Thus accoutred, he followed her out of the Keep, or inhabited part of the Castle, by a series of obscure passages leading to a postern gate, which she unlocked with a key, selected from a bundle which she carried at her girdle.

They now stood in the castle-yard, in the open moonlight, which glimmered white and ghastly on the variety of strange and ruinous objects to which we have formerly alluded, and which gave the scene rather the appearance of some ancient cemetery, than of the interior of a fortification. The round and elevated tower—the ancient mount, with its quadrangular sides facing the ruinous edifices which once boasted the name of Cathedral—seemed of yet more antique and anomalous form, when seen by the pale light which now displayed them. To one of these churches Fenella took the direct course, and was followed by Julian; although he at once divined, and was superstitious enough to dislike, the path which she was about to adopt. It was by a secret passage through this church that in former times the guard-room of the garrison, situated at the lower and external defences, communicated with the Keep of the Castle; and through this passage were the keys of the Castle every night carried to the Governor's apartment, so soon as the gates were locked, and the watch set. The custom was given up in James the First's time, and the passage abandoned, on account of the well-known legend of the *Mauthe Dog*—a fiend, or demon, in the shape of a large, shaggy, black mastiff, by which the church was said to be haunted. It was devoutly believed, that in former times this spectre became so familiar with mankind, as to appear almost nightly in the guard-room, issuing from the passage which we have mentioned at night, and retiring to it at daybreak. The soldiers became partly familiarised to its presence; yet not so much so as to use any licence of language while the apparition was visible; until one fellow, rendered daring by intoxication, swore he would know whether it was dog or devil, and, with his drawn sword, followed the spectre when it retreated by the usual passage. The man returned in a few minutes, sobered by terror, his mouth gaping, and his hair standing on end, under which horror he died; but, unhappily for the lovers of the marvellous, altogether unable to disclose the horrors which he had seen. Under the evil repute arising from this tale of wonder, the guard-room was abandoned, and a new one constructed. In like manner, the guards after that period held another and more circuitous communication with the Governor or Seneschal of the Castle; and that which lay through the ruinous church was entirely abandoned.

In defiance of the legendary terrors which tradition had attached to the original communication, Fenella, followed by Peveril, now boldly traversed the ruinous vaults through which it lay—sometimes only guided over heaps of ruins by the precarious light of the lamp borne by the dumb maiden—sometimes having the advantage of a gleam of moonlight, darting into the dreary abyss through the shafted windows, or through breaches made by time. As the path was by no means a straight one, Peveril could not but admire the intimate acquaintance with the mazes which his singular companion displayed, as well as the boldness with which she traversed them. He himself was not so utterly void of the prejudices of the times, but that he contemplated, with some apprehension, the possibility of their intruding on the lair of the phantom hound, of which he had heard so often; and in every remote sigh of the breeze among the ruins, he thought he heard him baying at the mortal footsteps which disturbed his gloomy realm. No such terrors, however, interrupted their journey; and in the course of a few minutes, they attained the deserted and now ruinous guard-house. The broken walls of the little edifice served to conceal them from the sentinels, one of whom was keeping a drowsy watch at the lower gate of the Castle; whilst another, seated on the stone steps which communicated with the parapet of the bounding and exterior wall, was slumbering, in full security, with his musket peacefully grounded by his side. Fenella made a sign to Peveril to move with silence and caution, and then showed him, to his surprise, from the window of the deserted guard-room, a boat, for it was now high water, with four rowers, lurking under the cliff on which the Castle was built; and made him farther sensible that he was to have access to it by a ladder of considerable height placed at the window of the ruin.

Julian was both displeased and alarmed by the security and carelessness of the sentinels, who had suffered such preparations to be made without observation or alarm given; and he hesitated whether he should not call the officer of the guard, upbraid him with negligence, and show him how easily Holm-Peel, in spite of its natural strength, and although reported impregnable, might be surprised by a few resolute men. Fenella seemed to guess his thoughts with that extreme acuteness of observation which her deprivations had occasioned her acquiring. She laid one hand on his arm, and a finger of the other on her own lips, as if to enjoin forbearance; and Julian, knowing that she acted by the direct authority of the Countess, obeyed her accordingly; but with the internal resolution to lose no time in communicating his sentiments to the Earl, concerning the danger to which the Castle was exposed on this point.

In the meantime, he descended the ladder with some precaution, for the steps were unequal, broken, wet, and slippery; and having placed himself in the stern of the boat, made a signal to the men to push off, and turned to take farewell of his guide. To his utter astonishment, Fenella rather slid down, than descended regularly, the perilous ladder, and, the boat being already pushed off, made a spring from the last step of it with incredible agility, and seated herself beside Peveril, ere he could express either remonstrance or surprise. He commanded the men once more to pull in to the precarious landing-place; and throwing into his countenance a part of the displeasure which he really felt, endeavoured to make her comprehend the necessity of returning to her mistress. Fenella folded her arms, and looked at him with a haughty smile, which completely expressed the determination of her purpose. Peveril was extremely embarrassed; he was afraid of offending the Countess, and interfering with her plan, by giving alarm, which otherwise he was much tempted to have done. On Fenella, it was evident, no species of argument which he could employ was likely to make the least impression; and the question remained, how, if she went on with him, he was to rid himself of so singular and inconvenient a companion, and provide, at the same time, sufficiently for her personal security.

The boatmen brought the matter to a decision; for, after lying on their oars for a minute, and whispering among themselves in Low Dutch or German, they began to pull stoutly, and were soon at some distance from the Castle. The possibility of the sentinels sending a musket-ball, or even a cannon-shot, after them, was one of the contingencies which gave Peveril momentary anxiety; but they left the fortress, as they must have approached it, unnoticed, or at least unchallenged —a carelessness on the part of the garrison, which, notwithstanding that the oars were muffled, and that the men spoke little, and in whispers, argued, in Peveril's opinion, great negligence on the part of the sentinels. When they were a little way from the Castle, the men began to row briskly towards a small vessel which lay at some distance. Peveril had, in the meantime, leisure to remark, that the boatmen spoke to each other doubtfully, and bent anxious looks on Fenella, as if uncertain whether they had acted properly in bringing her off.

After about a quarter of an hour's rowing, they reached the little sloop, where Peveril was received by the skipper, or captain, on the quarter-deck, with an offer of spirits or refreshments. A word or two among the seamen withdrew the captain from his hospitable cares, and he flew to the ship's side, apparently to prevent Fenella from entering the vessel. The men and he talked eagerly in Dutch, looking anxiously at Fenella as they spoke together; and Peveril hoped the result would be, that the poor young woman should be sent ashore again. But she baffled whatever opposition could be offered to her; and when the accommodation-ladder, as it is called, was withdrawn, she snatched the end of a rope, and climbed on board with the dexterity of a sailor, leaving them no means of preventing her entrance, save by actual violence, to which apparently they did not choose to have recourse. Once on deck, she took the captain by the sleeve, and led him to the head of the vessel, where they seemed to hold intercourse in a manner intelligible to both.

Peveril soon forgot the presence of the mute, as he began to muse upon his own situation, and the probability that he was separated for some considerable time from the object of his affections. "Constancy," he repeated to himself,—"Constancy." And, as if in coincidence with the theme of his reflections, he fixed his eyes on the polar star, which that night twinkled with more than ordinary brilliancy. Emblem of pure passion and steady purpose—the thoughts which arose as he viewed its clear and unchanging light, were disinterested and noble. To seek his country's welfare, and secure the blessings of domestic peace—to discharge a bold and perilous duty to his friend and patron—to regard his passion for Alice Bridgenorth, as the loadstar which was to guide him to noble deeds—were the resolutions which thronged upon his mind, and which exalted his spirits to that state of romantic melancholy, which perhaps is ill exchanged even for feelings of joyful rapture.

He was recalled from those contemplations by something which nestled itself softly and closely to his side—a woman's sigh sounded so near him, as to disturb his reverie; and as he turned his head, he saw Fenella seated beside him, with her eyes fixed on the same star which had just occupied his own. His first emotion was that of displeasure; but it was impossible to persevere in it towards a being so helpless in many respects, so interesting in others; whose large dark eyes were filled with dew, which glistened in the moonlight; and the source of whose emotions seemed to be in a partiality which might well claim indulgence, at least from him who was the object of it. At the same time, Julian resolved to seize the present opportunity, for such expostulations with Fenella on the strangeness of her conduct, as the poor maiden might be able to comprehend. He took her hand with great kindness, but at the same time with much gravity, pointed to the boat, and to the Castle, whose towers and extended walls were now scarce visible in the distance; and thus intimated to her the necessity of her return to Holm-Peel. She looked down, and shook her head, as if negativing his proposal with obstinate decision. Julian renewed his expostulation by look and gesture—pointed to his own heart, to intimate the Countess —and bent his brows, to show the displeasure which she must entertain. To all which the maiden only answered by her tears.

At length, as if driven to explanation by his continued remonstrances, she suddenly seized him by the arm, to arrest

HOLM PEEL CASTLE—FENELLA AND JULIAN PEVERIL

PAINTING BY F. W. TOPHAM

his attention—cast her eye hastily around, as if to see whether she was watched by any one—then drew the other hand, edgewise, across her slender throat—pointed to the boat, and to the Castle, and nodded.

On this series of signs, Peveril could put no interpretation, excepting that he was menaced with some personal danger, from which Fenella seemed to conceive that her presence was a protection. Whatever was her meaning, her purpose seemed unalterably adopted; at least it was plain he had no power to shake it. He must therefore wait till the end of their short voyage, to disembarrass himself of his companion; and, in the meanwhile, acting on the idea of her having harboured a misplaced attachment to him, he thought he should best consult her interest, and his own character, in keeping at as great a distance from her as circumstances admitted. With this purpose, he made the sign she used for going to sleep, by leaning his head on his palm; and having thus recommended to her to go to rest, he himself desired to be conducted to his berth.

The captain readily showed him a hammock, in the aftercabin, into which he threw himself, to seek that repose which the exercise and agitation of the preceding day, as well as the lateness of the hour, made him now feel desirable. Sleep, deep and heavy, sunk down on him in a few minutes, but it did not endure long. In his sleep he was disturbed by female cries; and at length, as he thought, distinctly heard the voice of Alice Bridgenorth call on his name.

He awoke, and starting up to quit his bed, became sensible, from the motion of the vessel, and the swinging of the hammock, that his dream had deceived him. He was still startled by its extreme vivacity and liveliness. "Julian Peveril, help! Julian Peveril!" The sounds still rung in his ears — the accents were those of Alice — and he could scarce persuade himself that his imagination had deceived him. Could she be in the same vessel? The thought was not altogether inconsistent with her father's character, and the intrigues in which he was engaged; but then, if so, to what peril was she exposed, that she invoked his name so loudly?

Determined to make instant inquiry, he jumped out of his hammock, half-dressed as he was, and stumbling about the little cabin, which was as dark as pitch, at length, with considerable difficulty, reached the door. The door, however, he was altogether unable to open; and was obliged to call loudly to the watch upon deck. The skipper, or captain, as he was called, being the only person aboard who could speak English, answered to the summons, and replied to Peveril's demand, what noise that was?—that a boat was going off with the young

N

woman—that she whimpered a little as she left the vessel—and "dat vaas all."

This explanation satisfied Julian, who thought it probable that some degree of violence might have been absolutely necessary to remove Fenella; and although he rejoiced at not having witnessed it, he could not feel sorrow that such had been employed. Her pertinacious desire to continue on board, and the difficulty of freeing himself, when he should come ashore, from so singular a companion, had given him a good deal of anxiety on the preceding night, which he now saw removed by this bold stroke of the captain.

His dream was thus fully explained. Fancy had caught up the inarticulate and vehement cries with which Fenella was wont to express resistance or displeasure — had coined them into language, and given them the accents of Alice Bridgenorth. Our imagination plays wilder tricks with us almost every night.

The captain now undid the door, and appeared with a lantern; without the aid of which Peveril could scarce have regained his couch, where he now slumbered secure and sound, until day was far advanced, and the invitation of the captain called him up to breakfast.

CHAPTER XX

Now, what is this that haunts me like my shadow,
Frisking and mumming like an elf in moonlight?
—BEN JONSON.

PEVERIL found the master of the vessel rather less rude than those in his station of life usually are, and received from him full satisfaction concerning the fate of Fenella, upon whom the captain bestowed a hearty curse, for obliging him to lay-to until he had sent his boat ashore, and had her back again.

"I hope," said Peveril, "no violence was necessary to reconcile her to go ashore? I trust she offered no foolish resistance?"

"Resist! mein Gott," said the captain, "she did resist like a troop of horse—she did cry, you might hear her at Whitehaven —she did go up the rigging like a cat up a chimney; but dat vas ein trick of her old trade."

"What trade do you mean?" said Peveril.

"Oh," said the seaman, "I vas know more about her than you, Meinheer. I vas know that she vas a little, very little girl, and prentice to one seiltanzer, when my lady yonder had the good luck to buy her."

" A seiltanzer ! " said Peveril ; " what do you mean by that ? "

" I mean a rope-danzer, a mountebank, a Hans pickel-harring. I vas know Adrian Brackel vell—he sell de powders dat empty men's stomach, and fill him's own purse. Not know Adrian Brackel, mein Gott ! I have smoked many a pound of tabak with him."

Peveril now remembered that Fenella had been brought into the family when he and the young Earl were in England, and while the Countess was absent on an expedition to the continent. Where the Countess found her, she never communicated to the young men ; but only intimated, that she had received her out of compassion, in order to relieve her from a situation of extreme distress.

He hinted so much to the communicative seaman, who replied, " that for distress he knew nocht's on't ; only, that Adrian Brackel beat her when she would not dance on the rope, and starved her when she did, to prevent her growth." The bargain between the Countess and the mountebank, he said, he had made himself ; because the Countess had hired his brig upon her expedition to the continent. None else knew where she came from. The Countess had seen her on a public stage at Ostend—compassionated her helpless situation, and the severe treatment she received—and had employed him to purchase the poor creature from her master, and charged him with silence towards all her retinue.—" And so I do keep silence," continued the faithful confidant, " van I am in the havens of Man ; but when I am on the broad seas, den my tongue is mine own, you know. Die foolish beoples in the island, they say she is a wechsel-balg—what you call a fairy-elf changeling. My faith, they do not never have seen ein wechsel-balg ; for I saw one myself at Cologne, and it was twice as big as yonder girl, and did break the poor people, with eating them up, like de great big cuckoo in the sparrow's nest ; but this Venella eat no more than other girls—it was no wechsel-balg in the world."

By a different train of reasoning, Julian had arrived at the same conclusion ; in which, therefore, he heartily acquiesced. During the seaman's prosing, he was reflecting within himself, how much of the singular flexibility of her limbs and movements the unfortunate girl must have derived from the discipline and instructions of Adrian Brackel ; and also how far the germs of her wilful and capricious passions might have been sown during her wandering and adventurous childhood. Aristocratic, also, as his education had been, these anecdotes respecting Fenella's original situation and education, rather increased his pleasure at having shaken off her company ; and yet he still felt desirous to know any farther particulars which the seaman could communicate on the same subject. But he had already told all he knew. Of her parents he knew nothing, except that "her father must have been a damned hundsfoot, and a schelm, for selling his own flesh and blood to Adrian Brackel;" for by such a transaction had the mountebank became possessed of his pupil.

This conversation tended to remove any passing doubts which might have crept on Peveril's mind concerning the fidelity of the master of the vessel, who appeared from thence to have been a former acquaintance of the Countess, and to have enjoyed some share of her confidence. The threatening motion used by Fenella, he no longer considered as worthy of any notice, excepting as a new mark of the irritability of her temper.

He amused himself with walking the deck, and musing on his past and future prospects, until his attention was forcibly arrested by the wind, which began to rise in gusts from the north-west, in a manner so unfavourable to the course they intended to hold, that the master, after many efforts to beat against it, declared his bark, which was by no means an excellent sea-boat, was unequal to making Whitehaven; and that he was compelled to make a fair wind of it, and run for Liverpool. To this course Peveril did not object. It saved him some land journey, in case he visited his father's castle; and the Countess's commission would be discharged as effectually the one way as the other.

The vessel was put, accordingly, before the wind, and ran with great steadiness and velocity. The captain, notwithstanding, pleading some nautical hazards, chose to lie off, and did not attempt the mouth of the Mersey until morning, when Peveril had at length the satisfaction of being landed upon the quay of Liverpool, which even then showed symptoms of the commercial prosperity that has since been carried to such a height.

The master, who was well acquainted with the port, pointed out to Julian a decent place of entertainment, chiefly frequented by seafaring people; for, although he had been in the town formerly, he did not think it proper to go anywhere at present where he might have been unnecessarily recognised. Here he took leave of the seaman, after pressing upon him with difficulty a small present for his crew. As for his passage, the captain declined any recompense whatever; and they parted upon the most civil terms.

The inn to which he was recommended was full of strangers, seamen, and mercantile people, all intent upon their own affairs, and discussing them with noise and eagerness, peculiar to the business of a thriving seaport. But although the general clamour of the public room, in which the guests mixed with each other, related chiefly to their own commercial dealings, there was a general theme mingling with them, which was alike common and interesting to all; so that, amidst disputes about freight, tonnage, demurrage, and such like, were heard the emphatic sounds of "Deep, damnable, accursed plot,"— "Bloody Papist villains,"—"The King in danger—the gallows too good for them," and so forth.

The fermentation excited in London had plainly reached even this remote seaport, and was received by the inhabitants with the peculiar stormy energy which invests men in their situation with the character of the winds and waves with which they are chiefly conversant. The commercial and nautical interests of England were indeed particularly anti-Catholic; although it is not, perhaps, easy to give any distinct reason why they should be so, since theological disputes in general could scarce be considered as interesting to them. But zeal, amongst the lower orders at least, is often in an inverse ratio to knowledge; and sailors were not probably the less earnest and devoted Protestants, that they did not understand the controversy between the Churches. As for the merchants, they were almost necessarily inimical to the gentry of Lancashire and Cheshire; many of whom still retained the faith of Rome, which was rendered ten times more odious to the men of commerce, as the badge of their haughty aristocratic neighbours.

From the little which Peveril heard of the sentiments of the people of Liverpool, he imagined he should act most prudently in leaving the place as soon as possible, and before any suspicion should arise of his having any connection with the party which appeared to have become so obnoxious.

In order to accomplish his journey, it was first necessary that he should purchase a horse; and for this purpose he resolved to have recourse to the stables of a dealer well known at the time, and who dwelt in the outskirts of the place; and having obtained directions to his dwelling, he went thither to provide himself.

Joe Bridlesley's stables exhibited a large choice of good horses; for that trade was in former days more active than at present. It was an ordinary thing for a stranger to buy a horse for the purpose of a single journey, and to sell him, as well as he could, when he had reached the point of his destination; and hence there was a constant demand, and a corresponding supply; upon both of which, Bridlesley, and those of his trade, contrived, doubtless, to make handsome profits.

Julian, who was no despicable horse-jockey, selected for his purpose a strong well-made horse, about sixteen hands high, and had him led into the yard, to see whether his paces corresponded with his appearance. As these also gave perfect satisfaction to the customer, it remained only to settle the price with Bridlesley; who of course swore his customer had pitched upon the best horse ever darkened the stable-door, since he had dealt that way; that no such horses were to be had nowadays, for that the mares were dead that foaled them; and having named a corresponding price, the usual haggling commenced betwixt the seller and purchaser, for adjustment of what the French dealers call *le prix juste*.

The reader, if he be at all acquainted with this sort of traffic, well knows it is generally a keen encounter of wits, and attracts the notice of all the idlers within hearing, who are usually very ready to offer their opinions, or their evidence. Amongst these, upon the present occasion, was a thin man, rather less than the ordinary size, and meanly dressed; but whose interference was in a confident tone, and such as showed himself master of the subject on which he spoke. The price of the horse being settled to about fifteen pounds, which was very high for the period, that of the saddle and bridle had next to be adjusted, and the thin mean-looking person before-mentioned, found nearly as much to say on this subject as on the other. As his remarks had a conciliating and obliging tendency towards the stranger, Peveril concluded he was one of those idle persons, who, unable or unwilling to supply themselves with the means of indulgence at their own cost, do not scruple to deserve them at the hands of others, by a little officious complaisance; and considering that he might acquire some useful information from such a person, was just about to offer him the courtesy of a morning draught, when he observed he had suddenly left the yard. He had scarce remarked this circumstance, before a party of customers entered the place, whose haughty assumption of importance claimed the instant attention of Bridlesley, and all his militia of grooms and stable-boys.

"Three good horses," said the leader of the party, a tall bulky man, whose breath was drawn full and high, under a consciousness of fat, and of importance—"three good and able-bodied horses, for the service of the Commons of England."

Bridlesley said he had some horses which might serve the Speaker himself at need; but that, to speak Christian truth, he had just sold the best in his stable to that gentleman present, who, doubtless, would give up the bargain if the horse was needed for the service of the State.

"You speak well, friend," said the important personage; and advancing to Julian, demanded, in a very haughty tone, the surrender of the purchase which he had just made.

Peveril, with some difficulty, subdued the strong desire which he felt to return a round refusal to so unreasonable a request, but fortunately, recollecting that the situation in which he at present stood, required, on his part, much circumspection, he replied simply, that upon showing him any warrant to seize upon horses for the public service, he must of course submit to resign his purchase.

The man, with an air of extreme dignity, pulled from his pocket, and thrust into Peveril's hand, a warrant, subscribed by the Speaker of the House of Commons, empowering Charles Topham, their officer of the Black Rod, to pursue and seize upon the persons of certain individuals named in the warrant; and of all other persons who are, or should be, accused by competent witnesses, of being accessory to, or favourers of, the hellish and damnable Popish Plot, at present carried on within the bowels of the kingdom; and charging all men, as they loved their allegiance, to render the said Charles Topham their readiest and most effective assistance, in execution of the duty entrusted to his care.

On perusing a document of such weighty import, Julian had no hesitation to give up his horse to this formidable functionary; whom somebody compared to a lion, which, as the House of Commons was pleased to maintain such an animal, they were under the necessity of providing for by frequent commitments; until "Take him, Topham," became a proverb, and a formidable one, in the mouth of the public.

The acquiescence of Peveril procured him some grace in the sight of the emissary; who, before selecting two horses for his attendants, gave permission to the stranger to purchase a grey horse, much inferior, indeed, to that which he had resigned, both in form and in action, but very little lower in price, as Mr. Bridlesley, immediately on learning the demand for horses upon the part of the Commons of England, had passed a private resolution in his own mind, augmenting the price of his whole stud, by an imposition of at least twenty per cent., *ad valorem*.

Peveril adjusted and paid the price with much less argument than on the former occasion; for, to be plain with the reader, he had noticed in the warrant of Mr. Topham, the name of his father, Sir Geoffrey Peveril of Martindale Castle, engrossed at full length, as one of those subjected to arrest by that officer.

When aware of this material fact, it became Julian's business to leave Liverpool directly, and carry the alarm to Derbyshire, if, indeed, Mr. Topham had not already executed his charge in that county, which he thought unlikely, as it was probable they would commence by securing those who lived nearest to the seaports. A word or two which he overheard strengthened his hopes.

"And hark ye, friend," said Mr. Topham; "you will have the horses at the door of Mr. Shortell, the mercer, in two hours, as we shall refresh ourselves there with a cool tankard, and learn what folks live in the neighbourhood that may be concerned in my way. And you will please to have that saddle padded, for I am told the Derbyshire roads are rough.—And you, Captain Dangerfield, and Master Everett, you must put on your Protestant spectacles, and show me where there is the shadow of a priest, or of a priest's favourer; for I am come down with a broom in my cap to sweep this north country of such like cattle."

One of the persons he thus addressed, who wore the garb of a broken-down citizen, only answered, "Ay, truly, Master Topham, it is time to purge the garner."

The other, who had a formidable pair of whiskers, a red nose, and a tarnished laced coat, together with a hat of Pistol's dimensions, was more loquacious. "I take it on my damnation," said this zealous Protestant witness, "that I will discover the marks of the beast on every one of them betwixt sixteen and seventy, as plainly as if they had crossed themselves with ink, instead of holy water. Since we have a King willing to do justice, and a House of Commons to uphold prosecutions, why, damn me, the cause must not stand still for lack of evidence."

"Stick to that, noble captain," answered the officer; "but, prithee, reserve thy oaths for the court of justice; it is but sheer waste to throw them away, as you do in your ordinary conversation."

"Fear you nothing, Master Topham," answered Dangerfield; "it is right to keep a man's gifts in use; and were I altogether to renounce oaths in my private discourse, how should I know how to use one when I needed it? But you hear me use none of your Papist abjurations. I swear not by the mass, or before George, or by anything that belongs to idolatry; but such downright oaths as may serve a poor Protestant gentleman, who would fain serve Heaven and the King."

"Bravely spoken, most noble Festus," said his yoke-fellow. "But do not suppose, that although I am not in the habit of garnishing my words with oaths out of season, I shall be wanting, when called upon, to declare the height and the depth, the width and the length, of this hellish plot against the King and the Protestant faith."

Dizzy, and almost sick, with listening to the undisguised brutality of these fellows, Peveril, having with difficulty prevailed on Bridlesley to settle his purchase, at length led forth his grey steed; but was scarce out of the yard, when he heard the following alarming conversation pass, of which he seemed himself the object.

"Who is that youth?" said the slow soft voice of the more

precise of the two witnesses. "Methinks I have seen him somewhere before. Is he from these parts?"

"Not that I know of," said Bridlesley; who, like all the other inhabitants of England at the time, answered the inter-rogatories of these fellows with the deference which is paid in Spain to the questions of an inquisitor. "A stranger—entirely a stranger—never saw him before—a wild young colt, I warrant him; and knows a horse's mouth as well as I do."

"I begin to bethink me I saw such a face as his at the Jesuits' consult, in the White Horse Tavern," answered Everett.

"And I think I recollect," said Captain Dangerfield——

"Come, come, master and captain," said the authoritative voice of Topham, "we will have none of your recollections at present. We all know what these are likely to end in. But I will have you know, you are not to run till the leash is slipped. The young man is a well-looking lad, and gave up his horse handsomely for the service of the House of Commons. He knows how to behave himself to his betters, I warrant you; and I scarce think he has enough in his purse to pay the fees."

This speech concluded the dialogue, which Peveril, finding himself so much concerned in the issue, thought it best to hear to an end. Now, when it ceased, to get out of the town unob-served, and take the nearest way to his father's castle, seemed his wisest plan. He had settled his reckoning at the inn, and brought with him to Bridlesley's the small portmanteau which contained his few necessaries, so that he had no occasion to return thither. He resolved, therefore, to ride some miles before he stopped, even for the purpose of feeding his horse; and being pretty well acquainted with the country, he hoped to be able to push forward to Martindale Castle sooner than the worshipful Master Topham; whose saddle was, in the first place, to be padded, and who, when mounted, would, in all probability, ride with the precaution of those who require such security against the effects of a hard trot.

Under the influence of these feelings, Julian pushed for Warrington, a place with which he was well acquainted; but, without halting in the town, he crossed the Mersey, by the bridge built by an ancestor of his friend the Earl of Derby, and continued his route towards Dishley, on the borders of Derbyshire. He might have reached this latter village easily, had his horse been fitter for a forced march; but in the course of the journey, he had occasion, more than once, to curse the official dignity of the person who had robbed him of his better steed, while taking the best direction he could through a country with which he was only generally acquainted.

At length, near Altringham, a halt became unavoidable; and Peveril had only to look for some quiet and sequestered place of refreshment. This presented itself, in the form of a small cluster of cottages; the best of which united the characters of an alehouse and a mill, where the sign of the Cat (the landlord's faithful ally in defence of his meal-sacks), booted as high as Grimalkin in the fairy tale, and playing on the fiddle for the more grace, announced that John Whitecraft united the two honest occupations of landlord and miller; and, doubtless, took toll from the public in both capacities.

Such a place promised a traveller, who journeyed incognito, safer, if not better accommodation, than he was like to meet with in more frequented inns; and at the door of the Cat and Fiddle, Julian halted accordingly.

CHAPTER XXI

In these distracted times, when each man dreads
The bloody stratagems of busy heads.
                                        —OTWAY.

AT the door of the Cat and Fiddle, Julian received the usual attention paid to the customers of an inferior house of entertainment. His horse was carried by a ragged lad, who acted as hostler, into a paltry stable; where, however, the nag was tolerably supplied with food and litter.

Having seen the animal on which his comfort, perhaps his safety, depended, properly provided for, Peveril entered the kitchen, which indeed was also the parlour and hall of the little hostelry, to try what refreshment he could obtain for himself. Much to his satisfaction, he found there was only one guest in the house besides himself; but he was less pleased when he found that he must either go without dinner, or share with that single guest the only provisions which chanced to be in the house, namely, a dish of trouts and eels, which their host, the miller, had brought in from his mill-stream.

At the particular request of Julian, the landlady undertook to add a substantial dish of eggs and bacon, which perhaps she would not have undertaken for, had not the sharp eye of Peveril discovered the flitch hanging in its smoky retreat, when, as its presence could not be denied, the hostess was compelled to bring it forward as a part of her supplies.

She was a buxom dame about thirty, whose comely and cheerful countenance did honour to the choice of the jolly miller, her loving mate; and was now stationed under the shade of an old-fashioned huge projecting chimney, within which it was her province to "work i' the fire," and provide for the wearied wayfaring man, the good things which were to send him rejoicing on his course. Although, at first, the honest woman seemed little disposed to give herself much additional trouble on Julian's account, yet the good looks, handsome figure, and easy civility of her new guest, soon bespoke the principal part of her attention; and while busy in his service, she regarded him, from time to time, with looks, where something like pity mingled with complacency. The rich smoke of the rasher, and the eggs with which it was flanked, already spread itself through the apartment; and the hissing of these savoury viands bore chorus to the simmering of the pan, in which the fish were undergoing a slower decoction. The table was covered with a clean huckaback napkin, and all was in preparation for the meal, which Julian began to expect with a good deal of impatience, when the companion, who was destined to share it with him, entered the apartment.

At the first glance Julian recognised, to his surprise, the same indifferently dressed, thin-looking person, who, during the first bargain which he had made with Bridlesley, had officiously interfered with his advice and opinion. Displeased at having the company of any stranger forced upon him, Peveril was still less satisfied to find one who might make some claim of acquaintance with him, however slender, since the circumstances in which he stood compelled him to be as reserved as possible. He therefore turned his back upon his destined messmate, and pretended to amuse himself by looking out of the window, determined to avoid all intercourse until it should be inevitably forced upon him.

In the meanwhile, the other stranger went straight up to the landlady, where she toiled on household cares intent, and demanded of her, what she meant by preparing bacon and eggs, when he had positively charged her to get nothing ready but the fish.

The good woman, important as every cook in the discharge of her duty, deigned not for some time so much as to acknowledge that she heard the reproof of her guest; and when she did so, it was only to repel it in a magisterial and authoritative tone.—"If he did not like bacon—(bacon from their own hutch, well fed on pease and bran)—if he did not like bacon and eggs —(new-laid eggs, which she had brought in from the hen-roost with her own hands)—why so put case—it was the worse for his honour, and the better for those who did."

"The better for those who like them?" answered the guest; "that is as much as to say I am to have a companion, good woman."

"Do not good woman me, sir," replied the miller's wife, "till I call you good man; and, I promise you, many would scruple to do that to one who does not love eggs and bacon of a Friday."

"Nay, my good lady," said her guest, "do not fix any misconstruction upon me—I dare say the eggs and the bacon are excellent; only they are rather a dish too heavy for my stomach."

"Ay, or your conscience perhaps, sir," answered the hostess. "And now, I bethink me, you must needs have your fish fried with oil, instead of the good drippings I was going to put to them. I would I could spell the meaning of all this now; but I warrant John Bigstaff, the constable, could conjure something out of it."

There was a pause here; but Julian, somewhat alarmed at the tone which the conversation assumed, became interested in watching the dumb show which succeeded. By bringing his head a little towards the left, but without turning round, or quitting the projecting latticed window where he had taken his station, he could observe that the stranger, secured, as he seemed to think himself, from observation, had sidled close up to the landlady, and, as he conceived, had put a piece of money into her hand. The altered tone of the miller's moiety corresponded very much with this supposition.

"Nay, indeed, and forsooth," she said, "her house was Liberty Hall; and so should every publican's be. What was it to her what gentlefolks ate or drank, providing they paid for it honestly? There were many honest gentlemen, whose stomachs could not abide bacon, grease, or dripping, especially on a Friday; and what was that to her, or any one in her line, so gentlefolks paid honestly for the trouble? Only, she would say, that her bacon and eggs could not be mended betwixt this and Liverpool, and that she would live and die upon."

"I shall hardly dispute it," said the stranger; and turning towards Julian, he added, "I wish this gentleman, who I suppose is my trencher-companion, much joy of the dainties which I cannot assist him in consuming."

"I assure you, sir," answered Peveril, who now felt himself compelled to turn about, and reply with civility, "that it was with difficulty I could prevail on my landlady to add my cover to yours, though she seems now such a zealot for the consumption of eggs and bacon."

"I am zealous for nothing," said the landlady, "save that men would eat their victuals, and pay their score; and if there be enough in one dish to serve two guests, I see little purpose in dressing them two; however, they are ready now, and done to a nicety.—Here, Alice! Alice!"

The sound of that well-known name made Julian start; but the Alice who replied to the call ill resembled the vision which his imagination connected with the accents, being a dowdy slipshod wench, the drudge of the low inn which afforded him shelter. She assisted her mistress in putting on the table the dishes which the latter had prepared; and a foaming jug of home-brewed ale being placed betwixt them, was warranted by Dame Whitecraft as excellent; "for," said she, "we know by practice that too much water drowns the miller, and we spare it on our malt as we would in our mill-dam."

"I drink to your health in it, dame," said the elder stranger; "and a cup of thanks for these excellent fish; and to the drowning of all unkindness between us."

"I thank you, sir," said the dame, "and wish you the like; but I dare not pledge you, for our Gaffer says the ale is brewed too strong for women; so I only drink a glass of canary at a time with a gossip, or any gentleman guest that is so minded."

"You shall drink one with me, then, dame," said Peveril, "so you will let me have a flagon."

"That you shall, sir, and as good as ever was broached; but I must to the mill, to get the key from the goodman."

So saying, and tucking her clean gown through the pocket-holes, that her steps might be the more alert, and her dress escape dust, off she tripped to the mill, which lay close adjoining.

"A dainty dame, and dangerous, is the miller's wife," said the stranger, looking at Peveril. "Is not that old Chaucer's phrase?"

"I—I believe so," said Peveril, not much read in Chaucer, who was then even more neglected than at present; and much surprised at a literary quotation from one of the mean appearance exhibited by the person before him.

"Yes," answered the stranger, "I see that you, like other young gentlemen of the time, are better acquainted with Cowley and Waller, than with the 'well of English undefiled.' I cannot help differing. There are touches of nature about the old bard of Woodstock, that, to me, are worth all the turns of laborious wit in Cowley, and all the ornate and artificial simplicity of his courtly competitor. The description, for instance, of his country coquette—

> 'Wincing she was, as is a wanton colt,
> Sweet as a flower, and upright as a bolt.'

Then, again, for pathos, where will you mend the dying scene of Arcite?

> 'Alas, my heartis queen! alas, my wife!
> Giver at once, and ender of my life.
> What is this world?—What axen men to have?
> Now with his love—now in his cold grave
> Alone, withouten other company.'

But I tire you, sir; and do injustice to the poet, whom I remember but by halves."

"On the contrary, sir," replied Peveril, "you make him more intelligible to me in your recitation, than I have found him when I have tried to peruse him myself."

"You were only frightened by the antiquated spelling, and 'the letters black,'" said his companion. "It is many a scholar's case, who mistakes a nut, which he could crack with a little exertion, for a bullet, which he must needs break his teeth on; but yours are better employed.—Shall I offer you some of this fish?"

"Not so, sir," replied Julian, willing to show himself a man of reading in his turn; "I hold with old Caius, and profess to fear judgment, to fight where I cannot choose, and to eat no fish."

The stranger cast a startled look around him at this observation, which Julian had thrown out, on purpose to ascertain, if possible, the quality of his companion, whose present language was so different from the character he had assumed at Bridlesley's. His countenance, too, although the features were of an ordinary, not to say mean cast, had that character of intelligence which education gives to the most homely face; and his manners were so easy and disembarrassed, as plainly showed a complete acquaintance with society, as well as the habit of mingling with it in the higher stages. The alarm which he had evidently shown at Peveril's answer, was but momentary; for he almost instantly replied, with a smile, "I promise you, sir, that you are in no dangerous company; for notwithstanding my fish dinner, I am much disposed to trifle with some of your savoury mess, if you will indulge me so far."

Peveril accordingly reinforced the stranger's trencher with what remained of the bacon and eggs, and saw him swallow a mouthful or two with apparent relish; but presently after he began to dally with his knife and fork, like one whose appetite was satiated; and then took a long draught of the black jack, and handed his platter to the large mastiff dog, who, attracted by the smell of the dinner, had sat down before him for some time, licking his chops, and following with his eye every morsel which the guest raised to his head.

"Here, my poor fellow," said he, "thou hast had no fish, and needest this supernumerary trencher-load more than I do. I cannot withstand thy mute supplication any longer."

The dog answered these courtesies by a civil shake of the tail, while he gobbled up what was assigned him by the stranger's benevolence, in the greater haste, that he heard his mistress's voice at the door.

"Here is the canary, gentlemen," said the landlady; "and

the goodman has set off the mill, to come to wait on you himself. He always does so, when company drink wine."

"That he may come in for the host's, that is, for the lion's share," said the stranger, looking at Peveril.

"The shot is mine," said Julian; "and if mine host will share it, I will willingly bestow another quart on him, and on you, sir. I never break old customs."

These sounds caught the ear of Gaffer Whitecraft, who had entered the room, a strapping specimen of his robust trade, prepared to play the civil, or the surly host, as his company should be acceptable or otherwise. At Julian's invitation, he doffed his dusty bonnet—brushed from his sleeve the looser particles of his professional dust—and sitting down on the end of a bench, about a yard from the table, filled a glass of canary, and drank to his guests, and "especially to this noble gentleman," indicating Peveril, who had ordered the canary.

Julian returned the courtesy by drinking his health, and asking what news were about in the country?

"Nought, sir, I hears on nought, except this Plot, as they call it, that they are pursuing the Papishers about; but it brings water to my mill, as the saying is. Between expresses hurrying hither and thither, and guards and prisoners riding to and again, and the custom of the neighbours, that come to speak over the news of an evening, nightly, I may say, instead of once a week, why, the spigot is in use, gentlemen, and your land thrives; and then I, serving as constable, and being a known Protestant, I have tapped, I may venture to say, it may be ten stands of ale extraordinary, besides a reasonable sale of wine for a country corner. Heaven make us thankful, and keep all good Protestants from Plot and Popery."

"I can easily conceive, my friend," said Julian, "that curiosity is a passion which runs naturally to the alehouse; and that anger, and jealousy, and fear, are all of them thirsty passions, and great consumers of home-brewed. But I am a perfect stranger in these parts; and I would willingly learn, from a sensible man like you, a little of this same Plot, of which men speak so much, and appear to know so little."

"Learn a little of it?—Why, it is the most horrible—the most damnable, bloodthirsty beast of a Plot—But hold, hold, my good master; I hope, in the first place, you believe there is a Plot; for, otherwise, the Justice must have a word with you, as sure as my name is John Whitecraft."

"It shall not need," said Peveril; "for I assure you, mine host, I believe in the Plot as freely and fully as a man can believe in anything he cannot understand."

"God forbid that anybody should pretend to understand it," said the implicit constable; "for his worship the Justice says it is a mile beyond him; and he be as deep as most of them. But men may believe, though they do not understand; and that is what the Romanists say themselves. But this I am sure of, it makes a rare stirring time for justices, and witnesses, and constables.—So here's to your health again, gentlemen, in a cup of neat canary."

"Come, come, John Whitecraft," said his wife, "do not you demean yourself by naming witnesses along with justices and constables. All the world knows how they come by their money."

"Ay, but all the world knows that they *do* come by it, dame; and that is a great comfort. They rustle in their canonical silks, and swagger in their buff and scarlet, who but they?—Ay, ay, the cursed fox thrives—and not so cursed neither. Is there not Doctor Titus Oates, the saviour of the nation—does he not live at Whitehall, and eat off plate, and have a pension of thousands a year, for what I know? and is he not to be Bishop of Litchfield, so soon as Dr. Doddrum dies?"

"Then I hope Dr. Doddrum's reverence will live these twenty years; and I dare say I am the first that ever wished such a wish," said the hostess. "I do not understand these doings, not I; and if a hundred Jesuits came to hold a consult at my house, as they did at the White Horse Tavern, I should think it quite out of the line of business to bear witness against them, provided they drank well, and paid their score."

"Very true, dame," said her elder guest; "that is what I call keeping a good publican conscience; and so I will pay my score presently, and be jogging on my way."

Peveril, on his part, also demanded a reckoning, and discharged it so liberally, that the miller flourished his hat as he bowed, and the hostess courtesied down to the ground.

The horses of both guests were brought forth; and they mounted, in order to depart in company. The host and hostess stood in the doorway, to see them depart. The landlord proffered a stirrup-cup to the elder guest, while the landlady offered Peveril a glass from her own peculiar bottle. For this purpose, she mounted on the horse-block, with flask and glass in hand; so that it was easy for the departing guest, although on horseback, to return the courtesy in the most approved manner, namely, by throwing his arm over his landlady's shoulder, and saluting her at parting.

Dame Whitecraft did not decline this familiarity; for there is no room for traversing upon a horse-block, and the hands which might have served her for resistance, were occupied with glass and bottle—matters too precious to be thrown away in such a struggle. Apparently, however, she had something else in her head; for as, after a brief affectation of reluctance, she permitted Peveril's face to approach hers, she whispered in his ear, "Beware of trepans!"—an awful intimation, which, in those days of distrust, suspicion, and treachery, was as effectual in interdicting free and social intercourse, as the advertisement of "man-traps and spring-guns," to protect an orchard. Pressing her hand, in intimation that he comprehended her hint, she shook his warmly in return, and bade God speed him. There was a cloud on John Whitecraft's brow; nor did his final farewell sound half so cordial as that which had been spoken within doors. But then Peveril reflected, that the same guest is not always equally acceptable to landlord and landlady; and unconscious of having done anything to excite the miller's displeasure, he pursued his journey without thinking farther of the matter.

Julian was a little surprised, and not altogether pleased, to find that his new acquaintance held the same road with him. He had many reasons for wishing to travel alone; and the hostess's caution still rung in his ears. If this man, possessed of so much shrewdness as his countenance and conversation intimated, versatile, as he had occasion to remark, and disguised beneath his condition, should prove, as was likely, to be a concealed Jesuit or seminary-priest, travelling upon their great task of the conversion of England, and rooting out of the Northern heresy,—a more dangerous companion, for a person in his own circumstances, could hardly be imagined; since keeping society with him might seem to authorise whatever reports had been spread concerning the attachment of his family to the Catholic cause. At the same time, it was very difficult, without actual rudeness, to shake off the company of one who seemed determined, whether spoken to or not, to remain alongside of him.

Peveril tried the experiment of riding slow; but his companion, determined not to drop him, slackened his pace, so as to keep close by him. Julian then spurred his horse to a full trot; and was soon satisfied, that the stranger, notwithstanding the meanness of his appearance, was so much better mounted than himself, as to render vain any thoughts of outriding him. He pulled up his horse to a more reasonable pace, therefore, in a sort of despair. Upon his doing so, his companion, who had been hitherto silent, observed, that Peveril was not so well qualified to try speed upon the road, as he would have been had he abode by his first bargain of horse-flesh that morning.

Peveril assented dryly, but observed, that the animal would serve his immediate purpose, though he feared it would render him indifferent company for a person better mounted.

"By no means," answered his civil companion; "I am one

of those who have travelled so much, as to be accustomed to make my journey at any rate of motion which may be most agreeable to my company."

Peveril made no reply to this polite intimation, being too sincere to tender the thanks which, in courtesy, were the proper answer.—A second pause ensued, which was broken by Julian asking the stranger whether their roads were likely to lie long together in the same direction.

"I cannot tell," said the stranger, smiling, "unless I knew which way you were travelling."

"I am uncertain how far I shall go to-night," said Julian, willingly misunderstanding the purport of the reply.

"And so am I," replied the stranger; "but though my horse goes better than yours, I think it will be wise to spare him; and in case our road continues to lie the same way, we are likely to sup, as we have dined together."

Julian made no answer whatever to this round intimation, but continued to ride on, turning, in his own mind, whether it would not be wisest to come to a distinct understanding with his pertinacious attendant, and to explain, in so many words, that it was his pleasure to travel alone. But, besides that the sort of acquaintance which they had formed during dinner, rendered him unwilling to be directly uncivil towards a person of gentleman-like manners, he had also to consider that he might very possibly be mistaken in this man's character and purpose; in which case, the cynically refusing the society of a sound Protestant, would afford as pregnant matter of suspicion, as travelling in company with a disguised Jesuit.

After brief reflection, therefore, he resolved to endure the encumbrance of the stranger's society, until a fair opportunity should occur to rid himself of it; and, in the meantime, to act with as much caution as he possibly could, in any communication that might take place between them; for Dame Whitecraft's parting caution still rang anxiously in his ears, and the consequences of his own arrest upon suspicion, must deprive him of every opportunity of serving his father, or the Countess, or Major Bridgenorth, upon whose interest, also, he had promised himself to keep an eye.

While he revolved these things in his mind, they had journeyed several miles without speaking; and now entered upon a more waste country, and worse roads, than they had hitherto found, being, in fact, approaching the more hilly district of Derbyshire. In travelling on a very stony and uneven lane, Julian's horse repeatedly stumbled; and, had he not been supported by the rider's judicious use of the bridle, must at length certainly have fallen under him.

"These are times which crave wary riding, sir," said his

companion; "and by your seat in the saddle, and your hand on the rein, you seem to understand it to be so."

"I have been long a horseman, sir," answered Peveril.

"And long a traveller, too, sir, I should suppose; since by the great caution you observe, you seem to think the human tongue requires a curb, as well as the horse's jaws."

"Wiser men than I have been of opinion," answered Peveril, "that it were a part of prudence to be silent, when men have little or nothing to say."

"I cannot approve of their opinion," answered the stranger. "All knowledge is gained by communication, either with the dead, through books, or, more pleasingly, through the conversation of the living. The *deaf and dumb*, alone, are excluded from improvement; and surely their situation is not so enviable that we should imitate them."

At this illustration, which awakened a startling echo in Peveril's bosom, the young man looked hard at his companion; but in the composed countenance, and calm blue eye, he read no consciousness of a farther meaning than the words immediately and directly implied. He paused a moment, and then answered, "You seem to be a person, sir, of shrewd apprehension; and I should have thought it might have occurred to you, that in the present suspicious times, men may, without censure, avoid communication with strangers. You know not me; and to me you are totally unknown. There is not room for much discourse between us, without trespassing on the general topics of the day, which carry in them seeds of quarrel between friends, much more betwixt strangers. At any other time, the society of an intelligent companion would have been most acceptable upon my solitary ride; but at present——"

"At present!" said the other, interrupting him. "You are like the old Romans, who held that *hostis* meant both a stranger and an enemy. I will therefore be no longer a stranger. My name is Ganlesse—by profession I am a Roman Catholic priest—I am travelling here in dread of my life—and I am very glad to have you for a companion."

"I thank you for the information with all my heart," said Peveril; "and to avail myself of it to the uttermost, I must beg of you to ride forward, or lag behind, or take a side-path, at your own pleasure; for as I am no Catholic, and travel upon business of high concernment, I am exposed both to risk and delay, and even to danger, by keeping such suspicious company. And so, Master Ganlesse, keep your own pace, and I will keep the contrary; for I beg leave to forbear your company."

As Peveril spoke thus, he pulled up his horse, and made a full stop.

The stranger burst out a-laughing. "What!" he said, "you forbear my company for a trifle of danger? Saint Anthony! How the warm blood of the Cavaliers is chilled in the young men of the present day! This young gallant, now, has a father, I warrant, who has endured as many adventures for hunting priests, as a knight-errant for distressed damsels."

"This raillery avails nothing, sir," said Peveril. "I must request you will keep your own way."

"My way is yours," said the pertinacious Master Ganlesse, as he called himself; "and we will both travel the safer, that we journey in company. I have the receipt of fern-seed, man, and walk invisible. Besides, you would not have me quit you in this lane, where there is no turn to right or left?"

Peveril moved on, desirous to avoid open violence—for which the indifferent tone of the traveller, indeed, afforded no apt pretext—yet highly disliking his company, and determined to take the first opportunity to rid himself of it.

The stranger proceeded at the same pace with him, keeping cautiously on his bridle hand, as if to secure that advantage in case of a struggle. But his language did not intimate the least apprehension. "You do me wrong," he said to Peveril, "and you equally wrong yourself. You are uncertain where to lodge to-night—trust to my guidance. Here is an ancient hall, within four miles, with an old knightly Pantaloon for its lord—an all-be-ruffed Dame Barbara for the lady gay—a Jesuit, in a butler's habit, to say grace—an old tale of Edgehill and Worster fights to relish a cold venison pasty, and a flask of claret mantled with cobwebs—a bed for you in the priest's hiding-hole—and, for aught I know, pretty Mistress Betty, the dairy-maid, to make it ready."

"This has no charms for me, sir," said Peveril, who, in spite of himself, could not but be amused with the ready sketch which the stranger gave of many an old mansion in Cheshire and Derbyshire, where the owners retained the ancient faith of Rome.

"Well, I see I cannot charm you in this way," continued his companion; "I must strike another key. I am no longer Ganlesse, the seminary priest, but (changing his tone, and snuffling in the nose) Simon Canter, a poor preacher of the Word, who travels this way to call sinners to repentance; and to strengthen, and to edify, and to fructify among the scattered remnant who hold fast the truth.—What say you to this, sir?"

"I admire your versatility, sir, and could be entertained with it at another time. At present sincerity is more in request."

"Sincerity!" said the stranger;—"a child's whistle, with but two notes in it—yea, yea, and nay, nay. Why, man, the very Quakers have renounced it, and have got in its stead a

gallant recorder, called Hypocrisy, that is somewhat like Sincerity in form, but of much greater compass, and combines the
whole gamut.   Come, be ruled—be a disciple of Simon Canter
for the evening, and we will leave the old tumble-down castle
of the knight aforesaid, on the left hand, for a new brick-built
mansion, erected by an eminent salt-boiler from Namptwich,
who expects the said Simon to make a strong spiritual pickle
for the preservation of a soul somewhat corrupted by the evil
communications of this wicked world.   What say you ?   He has
two daughters—brighter eyes never beamed under a pinched
hood ; and for myself, I think there is more fire in those who
live only to love and to devotion, than in your court beauties,
whose hearts are running on twenty follies besides.   You know
not the pleasure of being conscience-keeper to a pretty precisian,
who in one breath repeats her foibles, and in the next confesses
her passion.   Perhaps, though, you may have known such in
your day ?   Come, sir, it grows too dark to see your blushes ;
but I am sure they are burning on your cheek."

"You take great freedom, sir," said Peveril, as they now
approached the end of the lane, where it opened on a broad
common ;   "and you seem rather to count more on my forbearance, than you have room to do with safety.   We are now nearly
free of the lane which has made us companions for this last half
hour.   To avoid your farther company, I will take the turn to
the left, upon that common ; and if you follow me, it shall be
at your peril.   Observe, I am well armed ; and you will fight
at odds."

"Not at odds," returned the provoking stranger, "while I
have my brown jennet, with which I can ride round and round
you at pleasure ; and this text, of a handful in length (showing
a pistol which he drew from his bosom), which discharges
very convincing doctrine on the pressure of a forefinger, and is
apt to equalise all odds, as you call them, of youth and strength.
Let there be no strife between us, however—the moor lies
before us—choose your path on it—I take the other."

"I wish you good night, sir," said Peveril to the stranger.
"I ask your forgiveness, if I have misconstrued you in anything ;
but the times are perilous, and a man's life may depend on the
society in which he travels."

"True," said the stranger ; "but in your case, the danger is
already undergone, and you should seek to counteract it.   You
have travelled in my company long enough to devise a handsome branch of the Popish Plot.   How will you look, when you
see come forth, in comely folio form, The Narrative of Simon
Canter, otherwise called Richard Ganlesse, concerning the
horrid Popish Conspiracy for the Murder of the King, and
Massacre of all Protestants, as given on oath to the Honourable

House of Commons; setting forth, how far Julian Peveril, younger of Martindale Castle, is concerned in carrying on the same——"

"How, sir? What mean you?" said Peveril, much startled.

"Nay, sir," replied his companion, "do not interrupt my title-page. Now that Oates and Bedloe have drawn the great prizes, the subordinate discoverers get little but by the sale of their Narrative; and Janeway, Newman, Simmons, and every bookseller of them, will tell you that the title is half the narrative. Mine shall therefore set forth the various schemes you have communicated to me, of landing ten thousand soldiers from the Isle of Man upon the coast of Lancashire; and marching into Wales, to join the ten thousand pilgrims who are to be shipped from Spain; and so completing the destruction of the Protestant religion, and of the devoted city of London. Truly, I think such a Narrative, well spiced with a few horrors, and published *cum privilegio parliamenti*, might, though the market be somewhat overstocked, be still worth some twenty or thirty pieces."

"You seem to know me, sir," said Peveril; "and if so, I think I may fairly ask you your purpose in thus bearing me company, and the meaning of all this rhapsody. If it be mere banter, I can endure it within proper limit; although it is uncivil on the part of a stranger. If you have any farther purpose, speak it out; I am not to be trifled with."

"Good, now," said the stranger, laughing, "into what an unprofitable chafe you have put yourself! An Italian *fuoruscito*, when he desires a parley with you, takes aim from behind a wall, with his long gun, and prefaces his conference with *Posso tirare*. So does your man-of-war fire a gun across the bows of a Hansmogan Indiaman, just to bring her to; and so do I show Master Julian Peveril, that, if I were one of the honour-able society of witnesses and informers, with whom his imagi-nation has associated me for these two hours past, he is as much within my danger now, as what he is ever likely to be." Then, suddenly changing his tone to serious, which was in general ironical, he added, "Young man, when the pestilence is diffused through the air of a city, it is in vain men would avoid the disease, by seeking solitude, and shunning the company of their fellow-sufferers."

"In what, then, consists their safety?" said Peveril, willing to ascertain, if possible, the drift of his companion's purpose.

"In following the counsels of wise physicians;" such was the stranger's answer.

"And as such," said Peveril, "you offer me your advice?"

"Pardon me, young man," said the stranger haughtily, "I see no reason I should do so.—I am not," he added, in his former tone, "your fee'd physician—I offer no advice—I only say it would be wise that you sought it."

"And from whom, or where, can I obtain it?" said Peveril. "I wander in this country like one in a dream; so much a few months have changed it. Men who formerly occupied themselves with their own affairs, are now swallowed up in matters of state policy; and those tremble under the apprehension of some strange and sudden convulsion of empire, who were formerly only occupied by the fear of going to bed supperless. And to sum up the matter, I meet a stranger apparently well acquainted with my name and concerns, who first attaches himself to me, whether I will or no; and then refuses me an explanation of his business, while he menaces me with the strangest accusations."

"Had I meant such infamy," said the stranger, "believe me, I had not given you the thread of my intrigue. But be wise, and come on with me. There is, hard by, a small inn, where, if you can take a stranger's warrant for it, we shall sleep in perfect security."

"Yet you yourself," said Peveril, "but now were anxious to avoid observation; and in that case, how can you protect me?"

"Pshaw! I did but silence that tattling landlady, in the way in which such people are most readily hushed; and for Topham, and his brace of night owls, they must hawk at other and lesser game than I should prove."

Peveril could not help admiring the easy and confident indifference with which the stranger seemed to assume a superiority to all the circumstances of danger around him; and after hastily considering the matter with himself, came to the resolution to keep company with him for this night, at least; and to learn, if possible, who he really was, and to what party in the estate he was attached. The boldness and freedom of his talk seemed almost inconsistent with his following the perilous, though at that time the gainful trade of an informer. No doubt, such persons assumed every appearance which could insinuate them into the confidence of their destined victims; but Julian thought he discovered in this man's manner, a wild and reckless frankness, which he could not but connect with the idea of sincerity in the present case. He therefore answered, after a moment's recollection, "I embrace your proposal, sir; although, by doing so, I am reposing a sudden, and perhaps an unwary, confidence."

"And what am I, then, reposing in you?" said the stranger. "Is not our confidence mutual?"

"No; much the contrary. I know nothing of you whatever —you have named me; and, knowing me to be Julian Peveril, know you may travel with me in perfect security."

"The devil I do!" answered his companion. "I travel in

the same security as with a lighted petard, which I may expect to explode every moment. Are you not the son of Peveril of the Peak, with whose name Prelacy and Popery are so closely allied, that no old woman of either sex in Derbyshire concludes her prayer without a petition to be freed from all three? And do you not come from the Popish Countess of Derby, bringing, for aught I know, a whole army of Manxmen in your pocket, with full complement of arms, ammunition, baggage, and a train of field artillery?"

"It is not very likely I should be so poorly mounted," said Julian, laughing, "if I had such a weight to carry. But lead on, sir. I see I must wait for your confidence, till you think proper to confer it; for you are already so well acquainted with my affairs, that I have nothing to offer you in exchange for it."

"*Allons*, then," said his companion; "give your horse the spur, and raise the curb rein, lest he measure the ground with his nose instead of his paces. We are not now more than a furlong or two from the place of entertainment."

They mended their pace accordingly, and soon arrived at the small solitary inn which the traveller had mentioned. When its light began to twinkle before them, the stranger, as if recollecting something he had forgotten, "By the way, you must have a name to pass by; for it may be ill travelling under your own, as the fellow who keeps this house is an old Cromwellian. What will you call yourself?—My name is—for the present—Ganlesse."

"There is no occasion to assume a name at all," answered Julian. "I do not incline to use a borrowed one, especially as I may meet with some one who knows my own."

"I will call you Julian, then," said Master Ganlesse; "for Peveril will smell, in the nostrils of mine host, of idolatry, conspiracy, Smithfield faggots, fish on Fridays, the murder of Sir Edmondsbury Godfrey, and the fire of purgatory."

As he spoke thus, they alighted under the great broad-branched oak tree, that served to canopy the ale-bench, which, at an earlier hour, had groaned under the weight of a frequent conclave of rustic politicians. Ganlesse, as he dismounted, whistled in a particularly shrill note, and was answered from within the house.

CHAPTER XXII

He was a fellow in a peasant's garb;
Yet one could censure you a woodcock's carving,
Like any courtier at the ordinary.
                                    —THE ORDINARY.

THE person who appeared at the door of the little inn to receive Ganlesse, as we mentioned in our last chapter, sung, as he came forward, this scrap of an old ballad,—

> " Good even to you, Diccon ;
> And how have you sped ;
> Bring you the bonny bride
> To banquet and bed ? "

To which Ganlesse answered, in the same tone and tune,—

> " Content thee, kind Robin ;
> He need little care,
> Who brings home a fat buck
> Instead of a hare."

" You have missed your blow, then ? " said the other, in reply.

" I tell you I have not," answered Ganlesse ; " but you will think of nought but your own thriving occupation—May the plague that belongs to it stick to it ! though it hath been the making of thee."

" A man must live, Diccon Ganlesse," said the other.

" Well, well," said Ganlesse, " bid my friend welcome, for my sake. Hast thou got any supper ? "

" Reeking like a sacrifice—Chaubert has done his best. That fellow is a treasure ! give him a farthing candle, and he will cook a good supper out of it.—Come in, sir. My friend's friend is welcome, as we say in my country."

" We must have our horses looked to first," said Peveril, who began to be considerably uncertain about the character of his companions—" that done, I am for you."

Ganlesse gave a second whistle ; a groom appeared, who took charge of both their horses, and they themselves entered the inn.

The ordinary room of a poor inn seemed to have undergone some alterations, to render it fit for company of a higher description. There were a beaufet, a couch, and one or two other pieces of furniture, of a style inconsistent with the appearance of the place. The tablecloth, which was already laid, was of the finest damask; and the spoons, forks, &c., were of silver. Peveril looked at this apparatus with some surprise; and again turning his eyes attentively upon his travelling companion, Ganlesse, he could not help discovering (by the aid of imagination, perhaps), that though insignificant in person, plain in features, and dressed like one in indigence, there lurked still about his person and manners, that indefinable ease of manner which belongs only to men of birth and quality, or to those who are in the constant habit of frequenting the best company. His companion, whom he called Will Smith, although tall and rather good-looking, besides being much better dressed, had not, nevertheless, exactly the same ease of demeanour; and was obliged to make up for the want, by an additional proportion of assurance. Who these two persons could be, Peveril could not attempt even to form a guess. There was nothing for it but to watch their manner and conversation.

After speaking a moment in whispers, Smith said to his companion, "We must go look after our nags for ten minutes, and allow Chaubert to do his office."

"Will not he appear, and minister before us, then?" said Ganlesse.

"What! he?—he shift a trencher—he hand a cup?—No, you forget whom you speak of. Such an order were enough to make him fall on his own sword—he is already on the borders of despair, because no craw-fish are to be had."

"Alack-a-day!" replied Ganlesse. "Heaven forbid I should add to such a calamity! To stable, then, and see we how our steeds eat their provender, while ours is getting ready."

They adjourned to the stable accordingly, which, though a poor one, had been hastily supplied with whatever was necessary for the accommodation of four excellent horses; one of which, that from which Ganlesse was just dismounted, the groom we have mentioned was cleaning and dressing by the light of a huge wax-candle.

"I am still so far Catholic," said Ganlesse, laughing, as he saw that Peveril noticed this piece of extravagance. "My horse is my saint, and I dedicate a candle to him."

"Without asking so great a favour for mine, which I see standing behind yonder old hen-coop," replied Peveril, "I will at least relieve him of his saddle and bridle."

"Leave him to the lad of the inn," said Smith; "he is not worthy of any other person's handling; and I promise you, if you slip a single buckle, you will so flavour of that stable duty, that you might as well eat roast-beef as ragouts, for any relish you will have of them."

"I love roast-beef as well as ragouts, at any time," said

Peveril, adjusting himself to a task which every young man should know how to perform when need is; "and my horse, though it be but a sorry jade, will champ better on hay and corn, than on an iron bit."

While he was unsaddling his horse, and shaking down some litter for the poor wearied animal, he heard Smith observe to Ganlesse,—"By my faith, Dick, thou hast fallen into poor Slender's blunder; missed Anne Page, and brought us a great lubberly post-master's boy."

"Hush, he will hear thee," answered Ganlesse; "there are reasons for all things—it is well as it is. But, prithee, tell thy fellow to help the youngster."

"What!" replied Smith, "d'ye think I am mad?—Ask Tom Beacon—Tom of Newmarket—Tom of ten thousand, to touch such a four-legged brute as that?—Why, he would turn me away on the spot—discard me, i'faith. It was all he would do to take in hand your own, my good friend; and if you consider him not the better, you are like to stand groom to him yourself to-morrow."

"Well, Will," answered Ganlesse, "I will say that for thee, thou hast a set of the most useless, scoundrelly, insolent vermin about thee, that ever ate up a poor gentleman's revenues."

"Useless? I deny it," replied Smith. "Every one of my fellows does something or other so exquisitely, that it were sin to make him do anything else—it is your jacks-of-all-trades who are masters of none.—But hark to Chaubert's signal. The coxcomb is twangling it on the lute, to the tune of *Eveillez-vous, belle endormie.*—Come, Master What d'ye call (addressing Peveril), — get ye some water, and wash this filthy witness from your hand, as Betterton says in the play; for Chaubert's cookery is like Friar Bacon's Head—time is—time was—time will soon be no more."

So saying, and scarce allowing Julian time to dip his hands in a bucket, and dry them on a horse-cloth, he hurried him from the stable back to the supper-chamber.

Here all was prepared for their meal, with an epicurean delicacy, which rather belonged to the saloon of a palace, than the cabin in which it was displayed. Four dishes of silver, with covers of the same metal, smoked on the table; and three seats were placed for the company. Beside the lower end of the board, was a small side-table, to answer the purpose of what is now called a dumb waiter; on which several flasks reared their tall, stately, and swan-like crests, above glasses and rummers. Clean covers were also placed within reach; and a small travelling-case of morocco, hooped with silver, displayed a number of bottles, containing the most approved sauces that culinary ingenuity had then invented.

Smith, who occupied the lower seat, and seemed to act as president of the feast, motioned the two travellers to take their places and begin. "I would not stay a grace-time," he said, "to save a whole nation from perdition. We could bring no chauffettes with any convenience; and even Chaubert is nothing, unless his dishes are tasted in the very moment of projection. Come, uncover, and let us see what he has done for us.—Hum!—ha!—ay—squab-pigeons—wildfowl—young chickens—venison cutlets—and a space in the centre, wet, alas! by a gentle tear from Chaubert's eye, where should have been the *soupe aux écrevisses*. The zeal of that poor fellow is ill repaid by his paltry ten louis per month."

"A mere trifle," said Ganlesse; "but, like yourself, Will, he serves a generous master."

The repast now commenced; and Julian, though he had seen his young friend the Earl of Derby, and other gallants, affect a considerable degree of interest and skill in the science of the kitchen, and was not himself either an enemy or a stranger to the pleasures of a good table, found that, on the present occasion, he was a mere novice. Both his companions, but Smith in especial, seemed to consider that they were now engaged in the only true and real business of life; and weighed all its minutiæ with a proportional degree of accuracy. To carve the morsel in the most delicate manner—and to apportion the proper seasoning with the accuracy of the chemist,—to be aware, exactly, of the order in which one dish should succeed another, and [to do plentiful justice to all—was a minuteness of science to which Julian had hitherto been a stranger. Smith accordingly treated him as a mere novice in epicurism, cautioning him to eat his soup before the bouilli, and to forget the Manx custom of bolting the boiled meat before the broth, as if Cutlar MacCulloch and all his whingers were at the door. Peveril took the hint in good part, and the entertainment proceeded with animation.

At length Ganlesse paused, and declared the supper exquisite. "But, my friend Smith," he added, "are your wines curious? When you brought all that trash of plates and trumpery into Derbyshire, I hope you did not leave us at the mercy of the strong ale of the shire, as thick and muddy as the squires who drink it?"

"Did I not know that *you* were to meet me, Dick Ganlesse?" answered their host. "And can you suspect me of such an omission? It is true, you must make champagne and claret serve, for my burgundy would not bear travelling. But if you have a fancy for sherry, or Vin de Cahors, I have a notion Chaubert and Tom Beacon have brought some for their own drinking."

"Perhaps the gentlemen would not care to impart," said Ganlesse.

"Oh, fie!—anything in the way of civility," replied Smith. "They are, in truth, the best-natured lads alive, when treated respectfully; so that if you would prefer——"

"By no means," said Ganlesse—"a glass of champagne will serve in a scarcity of better."

"The cork shall start obsequious to my thumb,"

said Smith; and as he spoke, he untwisted the wire, and the cork struck the roof of the cabin. Each guest took a large rummer glass of the sparkling beverage, which Peveril had judgment and experience enough to pronounce exquisite.

"Give me your hand, sir," said Smith; "it is the first word of sense you have spoken this evening."

"Wisdom, sir," replied Peveril, "is like the best ware in the pedlar's pack, which he never produces till he knows his customer."

"Sharp as mustard," returned the *bon vivant*; "but be wise, most noble pedlar, and take another rummer of this same flask, which you see I have held in an oblique position for your service—not permitting it to retrograde to the perpendicular. Nay, take it off before the bubble bursts on the rim, and the zest is gone."

"You do me honour, sir," said Peveril, taking the second glass. "I wish you a better office than that of my cup-bearer."

"You cannot wish Will Smith one more congenial to his nature," said Ganlesse. "Others have a selfish delight in the objects of sense, Will thrives, and is happy by imparting them to his friends."

"Better help men to pleasures than to pains, Master Ganlesse," answered Smith, somewhat angrily.

"Nay, wrath thee not, Will," said Ganlesse; "and speak no words in haste, lest you may have cause to repent at leisure. Do I blame thy social concern for the pleasures of others? Why, man, thou dost therein most philosophically multiply thine own. A man has but one throat, and can but eat, with his best efforts, some five or six times a day; but thou dinest with every friend that cuts up a capon, and art quaffing wine in other men's gullets, from morning to night—*et sic de cæteris.*"

"Friend Ganlesse," returned Smith, "I prithee beware—thou knowest I can cut gullets as well as tickle them."

"Ay, Will," answered Ganlesse carelessly; "I think I have seen thee wave thy whinyard at the throat of a Hogan-Mogan—a Netherlandish weasand, which expanded only on thy natural and mortal objects of aversion,—Dutch cheese, rye-bread, pickled herring, onions, and Geneva."

"For pity's sake, forbear the description!" said Smith; "thy words overpower the perfumes, and flavour the apartment like a dish of salmagundi!"

"But for an epiglottis like mine," continued Ganlesse, "down which the most delicate morsels are washed by such claret as thou art now pouring out, thou couldst not, in thy bitterest mood, wish a worse fate than to be necklaced somewhat tight by a pair of white arms."

"By a tenpenny cord," answered Smith; "but not till you were dead; that thereafter you be presently embowelled, you being yet alive; that your head be then severed from your body, and your body divided into quarters, to be disposed of at his Majesty's pleasure.—How like you that, Master Richard Ganlesse?"

"E'en as you like the thoughts of dining on bran-bread and milk-porridge—an extremity which you trust never to be reduced to. But all this shall not prevent me from pledging you in a cup of sound claret."

As the claret circulated, the glee of the company increased; and Smith placing the dishes which had been made use of upon the side-table, stamped with his foot on the floor, and the table sinking down a trap, again rose, loaded with olives, sliced neat's tongue, caviare, and other provocatives for the circulation of the bottle.

"Why, Will," said Ganlesse, "thou art a more complete mechanist than I suspected; thou hast brought thy scene-shifting inventions to Derbyshire in marvellously short time."

"A rope and pullies can be easily come by," answered Will; "and with a saw and a plane, I can manage that business in half a day. I love that knack of clean and secret conveyance—thou knowest it was the foundation of my fortunes."

"It may be the wreck of them too, Will," replied his friend.

"True, Diccon," answered Will; "but, *dum vivimus, vivamus,* —that is my motto; and therewith I present you a brimmer to the health of the fair lady you wot of."

"Let it come, Will," replied his friend; and the flask circulated briskly from hand to hand.

Julian did not think it prudent to seem a check on their festivity, as he hoped in its progress something might occur to enable him to judge of the character and purposes of his companions. But he watched them in vain. Their conversation was animated and lively, and often bore reference to the literature of the period, in which the elder seemed particularly well skilled. They also talked freely of the Court, and of that numerous class of gallants who were then described as "men of wit and pleasure about town;" and to which it seemed probable they themselves appertained.

At length the universal topic of the Popish Plot was started; upon which Ganlesse and Smith seemed to entertain the most opposite opinions. Ganlesse, if he did not maintain the authority of Oates in its utmost extent, contended, that at least it was confirmed in a great measure by the murder of Sir Edmondsbury Godfrey, and the letters written by Coleman to the confessor of the French King.

With much more noise, and less power of reasoning, Will Smith hesitated not to ridicule and run down the whole discovery, as one of the wildest and most causeless alarms which had ever been sounded in the ears of a credulous public. "I shall never forget," he said, "Sir Godfrey's most original funeral. Two bouncing parsons, well armed with sword and pistol, mounted the pulpit, to secure the third fellow who preached from being murdered in the face of the congregation. Three parsons in one pulpit—three suns in one hemisphere—no wonder men stood aghast at such a prodigy."

"What then, Will," answered his companion, "you are one of those who think the good knight murdered himself, in order to give credit to the Plot?"

"By my faith, not I," said the other; "but some true blue Protestant might do the job for him, in order to give the thing a better colour.—I will be judged by our silent friend, whether that be not the most feasible solution of the whole."

"I pray you, pardon me, gentlemen," said Julian; "I am but just landed in England, and am a stranger to the particular circumstances which have thrown the nation into such a ferment. It would be the highest degree of assurance in me to give my opinion betwixt gentlemen who argue the matter so ably; besides, to say truth, I confess weariness—your wine is more potent than I expected, or I have drunk more of it than I meant to do."

"Nay, if an hour's nap will refresh you," said the elder of the strangers, "make no ceremony with us. Your bed—all we can offer as such—is that old-fashioned Dutch-built sofa, as the last new phrase calls it. We shall be early stirrers to-morrow morning."

"And that we may be so," said Smith, "I propose that we do sit up all this night—I hate lying rough, and detest a pallet-bed. So have at another flask, and the newest lampoon to help it out—

'Now a plague of their votes
Upon Papists and Plots,
And be d—d Doctor Oates.
Tol de rol.'"

"Nay, but our Puritanic host," said Ganlesse.

"I have him in my pocket, man—his eyes, ears, nose, and

tongue," answered his boon companion, "are all in my possession."

"In that case, when you give him back his eyes and nose, I pray you keep his ears and tongue," answered Ganlesse. "Seeing and smelling are organs sufficient for such a knave—to hear and tell are things he should have no manner of pretensions to."

"I grant you it were well done," answered Smith; "but it were a robbing of the hangman and the pillory; and I am an honest fellow, who would give Dun* and the devil his due. So,

> ' All joy to great Cæsar,
> Long life, love, and pleasure;
> May the King live for ever,
> 'Tis no matter for us, boys.' "

While this Bacchanalian scene proceeded, Julian had wrapt himself closely in his cloak, and stretched himself on the couch which they had shown to him. He looked towards the table he had left—the tapers seemed to become hazy and dim as he gazed—he heard the sound of voices, but they ceased to convey any impression to his understanding; and in a few minutes, he was faster asleep than he had ever been in the whole course of his life.

CHAPTER XXIII

> The Gordon then his bugle blew,
> And said, awa, awa;
> The House of Rhodes is all on flame,
> I hauld it time to ga'.
> —OLD BALLAD.

WHEN Julian awaked the next morning, all was still and vacant in the apartment. The rising sun, which shone through the half-closed shutters, showed some relics of the last night's banquet, which his confused and throbbing head assured him had been carried into a debauch.

Without being much of a boon companion, Julian, like other young men of the time, was not in the habit of shunning wine, which was then used in considerable quantities; and he could not help being surprised, that the few cups he had drunk over night had produced on his frame the effects of excess. He rose

* Dun was the hangman of the day at Tyburn. He was successor of Gregory Brunden, who was by many believed to be the same who dropped the axe upon Charles I., though others were suspected of being the actual regicide.

up, adjusted his dress, and sought in the apartment for water to perform his morning ablutions, but without success. Wine there was on the table; and beside it one stool stood, and another lay, as if thrown down in the heedless riot of the evening. "Surely," he thought to himself, "the wine must have been very powerful, which rendered me insensible to the noise my companions must have made ere they finished their carouse."

With momentary suspicion he examined his weapons, and the packet which he had received from the Countess, and kept in a secret pocket of his upper coat, bound close about his person. All was safe; and the very operation reminded him of the duties which lay before him. He left the apartment where they had supped, and went into another, wretched enough, where, in a truckle-bed, were stretched two bodies, covered with a rug, the heads belonging to which were amicably deposited upon the same truss of hay. The one was the black shock-head of the groom; the other, graced with a long thrum nightcap, showed a grizzled pate, and a grave caricatured countenance, which the hook-nose and lantern-jaws proclaimed to belong to the Gallic minister of good cheer, whose praises he had heard sung forth on the preceding evening. These worthies seemed to have slumbered in the arms of Bacchus as well as of Morpheus, for there were broken flasks on the floor; and their deep snoring alone showed that they were alive.

Bent upon resuming his journey, as duty and expedience alike dictated, Julian next descended the trap-stair, and essayed a door at the bottom of the steps. It was fastened within. He called—no answer was returned. It must be, he thought, the apartment of the revellers, now probably sleeping as soundly as their dependants still slumbered, and as he himself had done a few minutes before. Should he awake them?—To what purpose? They were men with whom accident had involved him against his own will; and situated as he was, he thought it wise to take the earliest opportunity of breaking off from society which was suspicious, and might be perilous. Ruminating thus, he essayed another door, which admitted him to a bedroom, where lay another harmonious slumberer. The mean utensils, pewter measures, empty cans and casks, with which this room was lumbered, proclaimed it that of the host, who slept surrounded by his professional implements of hospitality and stock-in-trade.

This discovery relieved Peveril from some delicate embarrassment which he had formerly entertained. He put upon the table a piece of money, sufficient, as he judged, to pay his share of the preceding night's reckoning; not caring to be indebted for his entertainment to the strangers, whom he was leaving without the formality of an adieu.

P

His conscience cleared of this gentleman-like scruple, Peveril proceeded with a light heart, though somewhat a dizzy head, to the stable, which he easily recognised among a few other paltry outhouses. His horse, refreshed with rest, and perhaps not unmindful of his services the evening before, neighed as his master entered the stable; and Peveril accepted the sound as an omen of a prosperous journey. He paid the augury with a sieveful of corn; and, while his palfrey profited by his attention, walked into the fresh air to cool his heated blood, and consider what course he should pursue in order to reach the Castle of Martindale before sunset. His acquaintance with the country in general gave him confidence that he could not have greatly deviated from the nearest road; and with his horse in good condition, he conceived he might easily reach Martindale before nightfall.

Having adjusted his route in his mind, he returned into the stable to prepare his steed for the journey, and soon led him into the ruinous courtyard of the inn, bridled, saddled, and ready to be mounted. But as Peveril's hand was upon the mane, and his left foot in the stirrup, a hand touched his cloak, and the voice of Ganlesse said, " What, Master Peveril, is this your foreign breeding? or have you learned in France to take French leave of your friends?"

Julian started like a guilty thing, although a moment's reflection assured him that he was neither wrong nor in danger. "I cared not to disturb you," he said, "although I did come as far as the door of your chamber. I supposed your friend and you might require, after our last night's revel, rather sleep than ceremony. I left my own bed, though a rough one, with more reluctance than usual; and as my occasions oblige me to be an early traveller, I thought it best to depart without leave-taking. I have left a token for mine host on the table of his apartment."

" It was unnecessary," said Ganlesse; "the rascal is already overpaid.—But are you not rather premature in your purpose of departing? My mind tells me that Master Julian Peveril had better proceed with me to London, than turn aside for any purpose whatever. You may see already that I am no ordinary person, but a master-spirit of the time. For the cuckoo I travel with, and whom I indulge in his prodigal follies, he also has his uses. But you are of a different cast; and I not only would serve you, but even wish you, to be my own."

Julian gazed on this singular person when he spoke. We have already said his figure was mean and slight, with very ordinary and unmarked features, unless we were to distinguish the lightnings of a keen grey eye, which corresponded in its careless and prideful glance, with the haughty superiority which the stranger assumed in his conversation. It was not till after a momentary pause that Julian replied, "Can you wonder, sir, that in my circumstances—if they are indeed known to you so well as they seem—I should decline unnecessary confidence on the affairs of moment which have called me hither, or refuse the company of a stranger, who assigns no reason for desiring mine?"

"Be it as you list, young man," answered Ganlesse; "only remember hereafter, you had a fair offer—it is not every one to whom I would have made it. If we should meet hereafter, on other, and on worse terms, impute it to yourself and not to me."

"I understand not your threat," answered Peveril, "if a threat be indeed implied. I have done no evil—I feel no apprehension—and I cannot, in common sense, conceive why I should suffer for refusing my confidence to a stranger, who seems to require that I should submit me blindfold to his guidance."

"Farewell, then, Sir Julian of the Peak,—that may soon be," said the stranger, removing the hand which he had as yet left carelessly on the horse's bridle.

"How mean you by that phrase?" said Julian; "and why apply such a title to me?"

The stranger smiled, and only answered, "Here our conference ends. The way is before you. You will find it longer and rougher than that by which I would have guided you."

So saying, Ganlesse turned his back and walked toward the house. On the threshold he turned about once more, and seeing that Peveril had not yet moved from the spot, he again smiled and beckoned to him; but Julian, recalled by that sign to recollection, spurred his horse and set forward on his journey.

It was not long ere his local acquaintance with the country enabled him to regain the road to Martindale, from which he had diverged on the preceding evening for about two miles. But the roads, or rather the paths, of this wild country, so much satirised by their native poet, Cotton, were so complicated in some places, so difficult to be traced in others, and so unfit for hasty travelling in almost all, that in spite of Julian's utmost exertions, and though he made no longer delay upon the journey than was necessary to bait his horse at a small hamlet through which he passed at noon, it was nightfall ere he reached an eminence, from which, an hour sooner, the battlements of Martindale Castle would have been visible; and where, when they were hid in night, their situation was indicated by a light constantly maintained in a lofty tower, called the Warder's Turret; and which domestic beacon had acquired, through all the neighbourhood, the name of Peveril's Pole-star.

This was regularly kindled at curfew toll, and supplied with as much wood and charcoal as maintained the light till sunrise ; and at no period was the ceremonial omitted, saving during the space intervening between the death of a Lord of the Castle and his interment. When this last event had taken place, the nightly beacon was rekindled with some ceremony, and con-tinued till fate called the successor to sleep with his fathers. It is not known from what circumstance the practice of maintaining this light originally sprung. Tradition spoke of it doubtfully. Some thought it was the signal of general hospitality, which, in ancient times, guided the wandering knight, or the weary pilgrim, to rest and refreshment. Others spoke of it as a "love-lighted watchfire," by which the provi-dent anxiety of a former lady of Martindale guided her husband homeward through the terrors of a midnight storm. The less favourable construction of unfriendly neighbours of the dissent-ing persuasion, ascribed the origin and continuance of this practice to the assuming pride of the family of Peveril, who thereby chose to intimate their ancient *suzeraineté* over the whole country, in the manner of the admiral who carries the lantern in the poop, for the guidance of the fleet. And in the former times, our old friend, Master Solsgrace, dealt from the pulpit many a hard hit against Sir Geoffrey, as he that had raised his horn, and set up his candlestick on high. Certain it is, that all the Peverils, from father to son, had been especially attentive to the maintenance of this custom, as something intimately connected with the dignity of their family ; and in the hands of Sir Geoffrey, the observance was not likely to be omitted.

Accordingly, the polar-star of Peveril had continued to beam more or less brightly during all the vicissitudes of the Civil War ; and glimmered, however faintly, during the subsequent period of Sir Geoffrey's depression. But he was often heard to say, and sometimes to swear, that while there was a perch of woodland left to the estate, the old beacon-grate should not lack replenishing. All this his son Julian well knew ; and therefore it was with no ordinary feelings of surprise and anxiety, that, looking in the direction of the Castle, he per-ceived that the light was not visible. He halted—rubbed his eyes—shifted his position—and endeavoured, in vain, to per-suade himself that he had mistaken the point from which the polar-star of his house was visible, or that some newly inter-vening obstacle, the growth of a plantation, perhaps, or the erection of some building, intercepted the light of the beacon. But a moment's reflection assured him, that from the high and free situation which Martindale Castle bore in reference to the surrounding country, this could not have taken place; and the inference necessarily forced itself upon his mind, that Sir Geoffrey, his father, was either deceased, or that the family must have been disturbed by some strange calamity, under the pressure of which, their wonted custom and solemn usage had been neglected.

Under the influence of undefinable apprehension, young Peveril now struck the spurs into his jaded steed, and forcing him down the broken and steep path, at a pace which set safety at defiance, he arrived at the village of Martindale-Moultrassie, eagerly desirous to ascertain the cause of this ominous eclipse. The street, through which his tired horse paced slow and reluctantly, was now deserted and empty; and scarcely a candle twinkled from a casement, except from the latticed window of the little inn, called the Peveril Arms, from which a broad light shone, and several voices were heard in rude festivity.

Before the door of this inn, the jaded palfrey, guided by the instinct or experience which makes a hackney well acquainted with the outside of a house of entertainment, made so sudden and determined a pause, that, notwithstanding his haste, the rider thought it best to dismount, expecting to be readily supplied with a fresh horse by Roger Raine, the landlord, the ancient dependant of his family. He also wished to relieve his anxiety, by inquiring concerning the state of things at the Castle, when he was surprised to hear, bursting from the tap-room of the loyal old host, a well-known song of the Commonwealth time, which some puritanical wag had written in reprehension of the Cavaliers, and their dissolute courses, and in which his father came in for a lash of the satirist.

" Ye thought in the world there was no power to tame ye,
    So you tippled and drabb'd till the saints overcame ye ;
    ' Forsooth,' and ' Ne'er stir,' sir, have vanquish'd ' G— d—n me,'
            Which nobody can deny.

There was bluff old Sir Geoffrey loved brandy and mum well,
    And to see a beer-glass turned over the thumb well ;
    But he fled like the wind, before Fairfax and Cromwell,
            Which nobody can deny."

Some strange revolution, Julian was aware, must have taken place, both in the village and in the Castle, ere these sounds of unseemly insult could have been poured forth in the very inn which was decorated with the armorial bearings of his family ; and not knowing how far it might be advisable to intrude on these unfriendly revellers, without the power of repelling or chastising their insolence, he led his horse to a back-door, which, as he recollected, communicated with the landlord's apartment, having determined to make private inquiry of him concerning the state of matters at the Castle. He knocked repeatedly, and as often called on Roger Raine with an earnest but stifled voice. At length a female voice replied by the usual inquiry, "Who is there?"

"It is I, Dame Raine—I, Julian Peveril—tell your husband to come to me presently."

"Alack, and a well-a-day, Master Julian, if it be really you —you are to know my poor goodman has gone where he can come to no one; but, doubtless, we shall all go to him, as Matthew Chamberlain says."

"He is dead, then?" said Julian. "I am extremely sorry——"

"Dead six months and more, Master Julian; and let me tell you, it is a long time for a lone woman, as Matt Chamberlain says."

"Well, do you or your chamberlain undo the door. I want a fresh horse; and I want to know how things are at the Castle."

"The Castle—lack-a-day!—Chamberlain—Matthew Chamberlain—I say, Matt!"

Matt Chamberlain apparently was at no great distance, for he presently answered her call; and Peveril, as he stood close to the door, could hear them whispering to each other, and distinguish in a great measure what they said. And here it may be noticed, that Dame Raine, accustomed to submit to the authority of old Roger, who vindicated as well the husband's domestic prerogative, as that of the monarch in the state, had, when left a buxom widow, been so far incommoded by the exercise of her newly acquired independence, that she had recourse, upon all occasions, to the advice of Matt Chamberlain; and as Matt began no longer to go slipshod, and in a red nightcap, but wore Spanish shoes, and a high-crowned beaver (at least of a Sunday), and moreover was called Master Matthew by his fellow-servants, the neighbours in the village argued a speedy change of the name on the sign-post; nay, perhaps, of the very sign itself, for Matthew was a bit of a Puritan, and no friend to Peveril of the Peak.

"Now counsel me, an you be a man, Matt Chamberlain," said Widow Raine; "for never stir, if here be not Master Julian's own self, and he wants a horse, and what not, and all as if things were as they wont to be."

"Why, dame, an ye will walk by my counsel," said the Chamberlain, "e'en shake him off—let him be jogging while his boots are green. This is no world for folks to scald their fingers in other folks' broth."

"And that is well spoken, truly," answered Dame Raine; "but then look you, Matt, we have eaten their bread, and, as my poor goodman used to say——"

"Nay, nay, dame, they that walk by the counsel of the dead, shall have none of the living; and so you may do as you list; but if you will walk by mine, drop latch, and draw bolt, and bid him seek quarters farther—that is my counsel."

"I desire nothing of you, sirrah," said Peveril, "save but to know how Sir Geoffrey and his lady do?"

"Lack-a-day!—lack-a-day!" in a tone of sympathy, was the only answer he received from the landlady; and the conversation betwixt her and her chamberlain was resumed, but in a tone too low to be overheard.

At length Matt Chamberlain spoke aloud, and with a tone of authority: "We undo no doors at this time of night, for it is against the Justices' orders, and might cost us our licence; and for the Castle, the road up to it lies before you, and I think you know it as well as we do."

"And I know you," said Peveril, remounting his wearied horse, "for an ungrateful churl, whom, on the first opportunity, I will assuredly cudgel to a mummy."

To this menace Matthew made no reply, and Peveril presently heard him leave the apartment, after a few earnest words betwixt him and his mistress.

Impatient at this delay, and at the evil omen implied in these people's conversation and deportment, Peveril, after some vain spurring of his horse, which positively refused to move a step farther, dismounted once more, and was about to pursue his journey on foot, notwithstanding the extreme disadvantage under which the high riding-boots of the period laid those who attempted to walk with such encumbrances, when he was stopped by a gentle call from the window.

Her counsellor was no sooner gone, than the good-nature and habitual veneration of the dame for the house of Peveril, and perhaps some fear for her counsellor's bones, induced her to open the casement, and cry, but in a low and timid tone, "Hist! hist! Master Julian—be you gone?"

"Not yet, dame," said Julian; "though it seems my stay is unwelcome."

"Nay, but good young master, it is because men counsel so differently; for here was my poor old Roger Raine would have thought the chimney corner too cold for you; and here is Matt Chamberlain thinks the cold courtyard is warm enough."

"Never mind that, dame," said Julian; "do but only tell me what has happened at Martindale Castle? I see the beacon is extinguished."

"Is it in troth?—ay, like enough—then good Sir Geoffrey has gone to heaven with my old Roger Raine!"

"Sacred Heaven!" exclaimed Peveril; "when was my father taken ill?"

"Never as I knows of," said the dame; "but, about three hours since, arrived a party at the Castle, with buff-coats and bandoleers, and one of the Parliament's folks, like in Oliver's time. My old Roger Raine would have shut the gates of the inn against them, but he is in the churchyard, and Matt says it is against law; and so they came in and refreshed men and horses, and sent for Master Bridgenorth, that is at Moultrassie Hall even now; and so they went up to the Castle, and there was a fray, it is like, as the old Knight was no man to take napping, as poor Roger Raine used to say. Always the officers had the best on't; and reason there is, since they had the law of their side, as our Matthew says. But since the pole-star of the Castle is out, as your honour says, why, doubtless, the old gentleman is dead."

"Gracious Heaven!—Dear dame, for love or gold, let me have a horse to make for the Castle!"

"The Castle?" said the dame; "the Roundheads, as my poor Roger called them, will kill you as they have killed your father! Better creep into the woodhouse, and I will send Bett with a blanket and some supper—Or stay—my old Dobbin stands in the little stable beside the hencoop—e'en take him, and make the best of your way out of the country, for there is no safety here for you. Hear what songs some of them are singing at the tap!—so take Dobbin, and do not forget to leave your own horse instead."

Peveril waited to hear no farther, only, that just as he turned to go off to the stable, the compassionate female was heard to exclaim—"O Lord! what will Matthew Chamberlain say?" but instantly added, "Let him say what he will, I may dispose of what's my own."

With the haste of a double-fee'd hostler did Julian exchange the equipments of his jaded brute with poor Dobbin, who stood quietly tugging at his rackful of hay, without dreaming of the business which was that night destined for him. Notwithstanding the darkness of the place, Julian succeeded marvellous quickly in preparing for his journey; and leaving his own horse to find its way to Dobbin's rack by instinct, he leaped upon his new acquisition, and spurred him sharply against the hill, which rises steeply from the village to the Castle. Dobbin, little accustomed to such exertions, snorted, panted, and trotted as briskly as he could, until at length he brought his rider before the entrance-gate of his father's ancient seat.

The moon was now rising, but the portal was hidden from its

beams, being situated, as we have mentioned elsewhere, in a deep recess betwixt two large flanking towers. Peveril dismounted, turned his horse loose, and advanced to the gate, which, contrary to his expectation, he found open. He entered the large courtyard; and could then perceive that lights yet twinkled in the lower part of the building, although he had not before observed them, owing to the height of the outward walls. The main door, or great hall-gate, as it was called, was, since the partially decayed state of the family, seldom opened, save on occasions of particular ceremony. A smaller postern door served the purpose of ordinary entrance; and to that Julian now repaired. This also was open—a circumstance which would of itself have alarmed him, had he not already had so many causes for apprehension. His heart sunk within him as he turned to the left, through a small outward hall, towards the great parlour, which the family usually occupied as a sitting apartment; and his alarm became still greater, when, on a nearer approach, he heard proceeding from thence the murmur of several voices. He threw the door of the apartment wide; and the sight which was thus displayed, warranted all the evil bodings which he had entertained.

In front of him stood the old Knight, whose arms were strongly secured, over the elbows, by a leathern belt drawn tight round them, and made fast behind; two ruffianly-looking men, apparently his guards, had hold of his doublet. The scabbardless sword which lay on the floor, and the empty sheath which hung by Sir Geoffrey's side, showed the stout old Cavalier had not been reduced to this state of bondage without an attempt at resistance. Two or three persons, having their backs turned towards Julian, sat round a table, and appeared engaged in writing—the voices which he had heard were theirs, as they murmured to each other. Lady Peveril—the emblem of death, so pallid was her countenance—stood at the distance of a yard or two from her husband, upon whom her eyes were fixed with an intenseness of gaze, like that of one who looks her last on the object which she loves the best. She was the first to perceive Julian; and she exclaimed, "Merciful Heaven!—my son!—the misery of our house is complete!"

"My son!" echoed Sir Geoffrey, starting from the sullen state of dejection, and swearing a deep oath—"thou art come in the right time, Julian. Strike me one good blow—cleave me that traitorous thief from the crown to the brisket! and that done, I care not what comes next."

The sight of his father's situation made the son forget the inequality of the contest which he was about to provoke.

"Villains," he said, "unhand him!" and rushing on the

guards with his drawn sword, compelled them to let go Sir Geoffrey, and stand on their own defence.

Sir Geoffrey, thus far liberated, shouted to his lady. "Undo the belt, dame, and we will have three good blows for it yet—they must fight well that beat both father and son."

But one of those men who had started up from the writing-table when the fray commenced, prevented Lady Peveril from rendering her husband this assistance; while another easily mastered the hampered Knight, though not without receiving several severe kicks from his heavy boots—his condition permitting him no other mode of defence. A third, who saw that Julian, young, active, and animated with the fury of a son who fights for his parents, was compelling the two guards to give ground, seized on his collar, and attempted to master his sword. Suddenly dropping that weapon, and snatching one of his pistols, Julian fired it at the head of the person by whom he was thus assailed. He did not drop, but, staggering back as if he had received a severe blow, showed Peveril, as he sunk into a chair, the features of old Bridgenorth, blackened with the explosion, which had even set fire to a part of his grey hair. A cry of astonishment escaped from Julian; and in the alarm and horror of the moment, he was easily secured and disarmed by those with whom he had been at first engaged.

"Heed it not, Julian," said Sir Geoffrey; "heed it not, my brave boy—that shot has balanced all accompts!—but how—what the devil—he lives!—Was your pistol loaded with chaff? or has the foul fiend given him proof against lead?"

There was some reason for Sir Geoffrey's surprise, since, as he spoke, Major Bridgenorth collected himself—sat up in the chair as one who recovers from a stunning blow—then rose, and wiping with his handkerchief the marks of the explosion from his face, he approached Julian, and said, in the same cold unaltered tone in which he usually expressed himself, "Young man, you have reason to bless God, who has this day saved you from the commission of a great crime."

"Bless the devil, ye crop-eared knave!" exclaimed Sir Geoffrey; "for nothing less than the father of all fanatics saved your brains from being blown about like the rinsings of Beelzebub's porridge pot!"

"Sir Geoffrey," said Major Bridgenorth, "I have already told you, that with you I will hold no argument; for to you I am not accountable for any of my actions."

"Master Bridgenorth," said the lady, making a strong effort to speak, and to speak with calmness, "whatever revenge your Christian state of conscience may permit you to take on my husband—I—I, who have some right to experience compassion at your hand, for most sincerely did I compassionate you when the hand of Heaven was heavy on you—I implore you not to involve my son in our common ruin !—Let the destruction of the father and mother, with the ruin of our ancient house, satisfy your resentment for any wrong which you have ever received at my husband's hand."

"Hold your peace, housewife," said the Knight, "you speak like a fool, and meddle with what concerns you not.—Wrong at *my* hand ? The cowardly knave has ever had but even too much right. Had I cudgelled the cur soundly when he first bayed at me, the cowardly mongrel had been now crouching at my feet, instead of flying at my throat. But if I get through this action, as I have got through worse weather, I will pay off old scores, as far as tough crab-tree and cold iron will bear me out."

"Sir Geoffrey," replied Bridgenorth, "if the birth you boast of has made you blind to better principles, it might have at least taught you civility. What do you complain of ? I am a magistrate ; and I execute a warrant, addressed to me by the first authority in the state. I am a creditor also of yours ; and law arms me with powers to recover my own property from the hands of an improvident debtor."

"You a magistrate !" said the Knight ; "much such a magistrate as Noll was a monarch. Your heart is up, I warrant, because you have the King's pardon ; and are replaced on the bench, forsooth, to persecute the poor Papist. There was never turmoil in the state, but knaves had their vantage by it—never pot boiled, but the scum was cast uppermost."

"For God's sake, my dearest husband," said Lady Peveril, "cease this wild talk ! It can but incense Master Bridgenorth, who might otherwise consider, that in common charity——"

"Incense him !" said Sir Geoffrey, impatiently interrupting her ; "God's-death, madam, you will drive me mad ! Have you lived so long in this world, and yet expect consideration and charity from an old starved wolf like that ? And if he had it, do you think that I, or you, madam, as my wife, are subjects for his charity ?—Julian, my poor fellow, I am sorry thou hast come so unluckily, since thy petronel was not better loaded—but thy credit is lost for ever as a marksman."

This angry colloquy passed so rapidly on all sides, that Julian, scarce recovered from the extremity of astonishment with which he was overwhelmed at finding himself suddenly plunged into a situation of such extremity, had no time to consider in what way he could most effectually act for the succour of his parents. To speak Bridgenorth fair seemed the more prudent course ; but to this his pride could hardly stoop ; yet he forced himself to say, with as much calmness as he could assume, "Master Bridgenorth, since you act as a magistrate, I desire to be treated according to the laws of England; and demand to know of what we are accused, and by whose authority we are arrested?"

"Here is another howlet for ye!" exclaimed the impetuous old Knight; "his mother speaks to a Puritan of charity; and thou must talk of law to a round-headed rebel, with a wannion to you'! What warrant hath he, think ye, beyond the Parliament's or the devil's?"

"Who speaks of the Parliament?" said a person entering, whom Peveril recognised as the official person whom he had before seen at the horse-dealer's, and who now bustled in with all the conscious dignity of plenary authority,—"Who talks of the Parliament?" he exclaimed. "I promise you, enough has been found in this house to convict twenty plotters—Here be arms, and that good store. Bring them in, Captain."

"The very same," exclaimed the Captain, approaching, "which I mention in my printed Narrative of Information, lodged before the Honourable House of Commons; they were commissioned from old Vander Huys of Rotterdam, by orders of Don John of Austria, for the service of the Jesuits."

"Now, by this light," said Sir Geoffrey, "they are the pikes, musketoons, and pistols, that have been hidden in the garret ever since Naseby fight!"

"And here," said the Captain's yoke-fellow, Everett, "are proper priest's trappings—antiphoners, and missals, and copes, I warrant you—ay, and proper pictures, too, for Papists to mutter and bow over."

"Now plague on thy snuffling whine," said Sir Geoffrey; "here is a rascal will swear my grandmother's old farthingale to be priest's vestments, and the story book of Owlenspiegel a Popish missal!"

"But how's this, Master Bridgenorth?" said Topham, addressing the magistrate; "your honour has been as busy as we have; and you have caught another knave while we recovered these toys."

"I think, sir," said Julian, "if you look into your warrant, which, if I mistake not, names the persons whom you are directed to arrest, you will find you have no title to apprehend me."

"Sir," said the officer, puffing with importance, "I do not know who you are; but I would you were the best man in England, that I might teach you the respect due to the warrant of the House. Sir, there steps not the man within the British seas, but I will arrest him on authority of this bit of parchment; and I do arrest you accordingly.—What do you accuse him of, gentlemen?"

Dangerfield swaggered forward, and peeping under Julian's hat, "Stop my vital breath," he exclaimed, "but I have seen

you before, my friend, an I could but think where; but my
memory is not worth a bean, since I have been obliged to use
it so much of late, in the behalf of the poor state. But I do
know the fellow; and I have seen him amongst the Papists—
I'll take that on my assured damnation."

"Why, Captain Dangerfield," said the Captain's smoother,
but more dangerous associate,—"verily, it is the same youth
whom we saw at the horse-merchant's yesterday; and we had
matter against him then, only Master Topham did not desire us
to bring it out."

"Ye may bring out what ye will against him now," said
Topham, "for he hath blasphemed the warrant of the House.
I think ye said ye saw him somewhere."

"Ay, verily," said Everett, "I have seen him amongst the
seminary pupils at Saint Omer's—he was who but he with the
regents there."

"Nay, Master Everett, collect yourself," said Topham; "for,
as I think, you said you saw him at a consult of the Jesuits in
London."

"It was I said so, Master Topham," said the undaunted
Dangerfield; "and mine is the tongue that will swear it."

"Good Master Topham," said Bridgenorth, "you may sus-
pend farther inquiry at present, as it doth but fatigue and
perplex the memory of the King's witnesses."

"You are wrong, Master Bridgenorth—clearly wrong. It
doth but keep them in wind—only breathes them like grey-
hounds before a coursing match."

"Be it so," said Bridgenorth, with his usual indifference of
manner; "but at present this youth must stand committed
upon a warrant, which I will presently sign, of having assaulted
me while in discharge of my duty as a magistrate, for the rescue
of a person legally attached. Did you not hear the report of a
pistol?"

"I will swear to it," said Everett.

"And I," said Dangerfield. "While we were making search
in the cellar, I heard something very like a pistol-shot; but I
conceived it to be the drawing of a long-corked bottle of sack,
to see whether there were any Popish relics in the inside on't."

"A pistol-shot!" exclaimed Topham; "here might have
been a second Sir Edmondsbury Godfrey's matter.—Oh, thou
real spawn of the red old dragon! for he too would have resisted
the House's warrant, had we not taken him something at un-
awares.—Master Bridgenorth, you are a judicious magistrate, and
a worthy servant of the state—I would we had many such sound
Protestant justices. Shall I have this young fellow away with
his parents—what think you?—or will you keep him for re-
examination?"

"Master Bridgenorth," said Lady Peveril, in spite of her husband's efforts to interrupt her, "for God's sake, if ever you knew what it was to love one of the many children you have lost, or her who is now left to you, do not pursue your vengeance to the blood of my poor boy! I will forgive you all the rest—all the distress you have wrought—all the yet greater misery with which you threaten us; but do not be extreme with one who never can have offended you! Believe, that if your ears are shut against the cry of a despairing mother, those which are open to the complaint of all who sorrow, will hear my petition and your answer!"

The agony of mind and of voice with which Lady Peveril uttered these words, seemed to thrill through all present, though most of them were but too much inured to such scenes. Every one was silent, when, ceasing to speak, she fixed on Bridgenorth her eyes, glistening with tears, with the eager anxiety of one whose life or death seemed to depend upon the answer to be returned. Even Bridgenorth's inflexibility seemed to be shaken; and his voice was tremulous, as he answered, "Madam, I would to God I had the present means of relieving your great distress, otherwise than by recommending to you a reliance upon Providence; and that you take heed to your spirit, that it murmur not under this crook in your lot. For me, I am but as a rod in the hand of the strong man, which smites not of itself, but because it is wielded by the arm of him who holds the same."

"Even as I and my black rod are guided by the Commons of England," said Master Topham, who seemed marvellously pleased with the illustration.

Julian now thought it time to say something in his own behalf; and he endeavoured to temper it with as much composure as it was possible for him to assume. "Master Bridgenorth," he said, "I neither dispute your authority, nor this gentleman's warrant——"

"You do not?" said Topham. "Oh, ho, master youngster, I thought we should bring you to your senses presently!"

"Then, if you so will it, Master Topham," said Bridgenorth, "thus it shall be. You shall set out with early day, taking with you, towards London, the persons of Sir Geoffrey and Lady Peveril; and that they may travel according to their quality, you will allow them their coach, sufficiently guarded."

"I will travel with them myself," said Topham; "for these rough Derbyshire roads are no easy riding; and my very eyes are weary with looking on these bleak hills. In the coach I can sleep as sound as if I were in the House, and Master Bodderbrains on his legs."

"It will become you so to take your ease, Master Topham,"

answered Bridgenorth. "For this youth, I will take him under my charge, and bring him up myself."

"I may not be answerable for that, worthy Master Bridgenorth," said Topham, "since he comes within the warrant of the House."

"Nay, but," said Bridgenorth, "he is only under custody for an assault, with the purpose of a rescue; and I counsel you against meddling with him, unless you have stronger guard. Sir Geoffrey is now old and broken, but this young fellow is in the flower of his youth, and hath at his beck all the debauched young Cavaliers of the neighbourhood—You will scarce cross the country without a rescue."

Topham eyed Julian wistfully, as a spider may be supposed to look upon a stray wasp which has got into his web, and which he longs to secure, though he fears the consequences of attempting him.

Julian himself replied, "I know not if this separation be well or ill meant on your part, Master Bridgenorth; but on mine, I am only desirous to share the fate of my parents; and therefore I will give my word of honour to attempt neither rescue nor escape, on condition you do not separate me from them."

"Do not say so, Julian," said his mother; "abide with Master Bridgenorth—my mind tells me he cannot mean so ill by us as his rough conduct would now lead us to infer."

"And I," said Sir Geoffrey, "know, that between the doors of my father's house and the gates of hell, there steps not such a villain on the ground! And if I wish my hands ever to be unbound again, it is because I hope for one downright blow at a grey head, that has hatched more treason than the whole Long Parliament."

"Away with thee," said the zealous officer; "is Parliament a word for so foul a mouth as thine?—Gentlemen," he added, turning to Everett and Dangerfield, "you will bear witness to this."

"To his having reviled the House of Commons—by G—d, that I will!" said Dangerfield; "I will take it on my damnation."

"And verily," said Everett, "as he spoke of Parliament generally, he hath contemned the House of Lords also."

"Why, ye poor insignificant wretches," said Sir Geoffrey, "whose very life is a lie—and whose bread is perjury—would you pervert my innocent words almost as soon as they have quitted my lips? I tell you the country is well weary of you; and should Englishmen come to their senses, the jail, the pillory, the whipping-post, and the gibbet, will be too good preferment for such base blood-suckers.—And now, Master Bridgenorth, you and they may do your worst; for I will not open my mouth to utter a single word while I am in the company of such knaves."

"Perhaps, Sir Geoffrey," answered Bridgenorth, "you would better have consulted your own safety in adopting that resolution a little sooner—the tongue is a little member, but it causes much strife.—You, Master Julian, will please to follow me, and without remonstrance or resistance; for you must be aware that I have the means of compelling."

Julian was, indeed, but too sensible, that he had no other course but that of submission to superior force; but ere he left the apartment, he kneeled down to receive his father's blessing, which the old man bestowed not without a tear in his eye, and in the emphatic words, "God bless thee, my boy; and keep thee good and true to Church and King, whatever wind shall bring foul weather!"

His mother was only able to pass her hand over his head, and to implore him, in a low tone of voice, not to be rash or violent in any attempt to render them assistance. "We are innocent," she said, "my son—we are innocent—and we are in God's hands. Be the thought our best comfort and protection."

Bridgenorth now signed to Julian to follow him, which he did, accompanied, or rather conducted, by the two guards who had first disarmed him. When they had passed from the apartment, and were at the door of the outward hall, Bridgenorth asked Julian whether he should consider him as under parole; in which case, he said, he would dispense with all other security but his own promise.

Peveril, who could not help hoping somewhat from the favourable and unresentful manner in which he was treated by one whose life he had so recently attempted, replied, without hesitation, that he would give his parole for twenty-four hours, neither to attempt to escape by force nor by flight.

"It is wisely said," replied Bridgenorth; "for though you might cause bloodshed, be assured that your utmost efforts could do no service to your parents.—Horses there—horses to the courtyard!"

The trampling of horses was soon heard; and in obedience to Bridgenorth's signal, and in compliance with his promise, Julian mounted one which was presented to him, and prepared to leave the house of his fathers, in which his parents were now prisoners, and to go, he knew not whither, under the custody of one known to be the ancient enemy of his family. He was rather surprised at observing, that Bridgenorth and he were about to travel without any other attendants.

When they were mounted, and as they rode slowly towards the outer gate of the courtyard, Bridgenorth said to him, "It is not every one who would thus unreservedly commit his safety, by travelling at night, and unaided, with the hot-brained youth who so lately attempted his life."

"Master Bridgenorth," said Julian, "I might tell you truly, that I knew you not at the time when I directed my weapon against you; but I must also add, that the cause in which I used it, might have rendered me, even had I known you, a slight respecter of your person. At present, I do know you; and have neither malice against your person, nor the liberty of a parent to fight for. Besides, you have my word; and when was a Peveril known to break it?"

"Ay," replied his companion, "a Peveril—a Peveril of the Peak!—a name which has long sounded like a war-trumpet in the land; but which has now perhaps sounded its last loud note. Look back, young man, on the darksome turrets of your father's house, which uplift themselves as proudly on the brow of the hill, as their owners raised themselves above the sons of their people. Think upon your father, a captive—yourself in some sort a fugitive—your light quenched—your glory abased—your estate wrecked and impoverished. Think that Providence has subjected the destinies of the race of Peveril to one, whom, in their aristocratic pride, they held as a plebeian upstart. Think of this; and when you again boast of your ancestry, remember, that he who raiseth the lowly can also abase the high in heart."

Julian did indeed gaze for an instant, with a swelling heart, upon the dimly seen turrets of his paternal mansion, on which poured the moonlight, mixed with long shadows of the towers and trees. But while he sadly acknowledged the truth of Bridgenorth's observation, he felt indignant at his ill-timed triumph. "If fortune had followed worth," he said, "the Castle of Martindale, and the name of Peveril, had afforded no room for their enemy's vainglorious boast. But those who have stood high on Fortune's wheel, must abide by the consequence of its revolutions. This much I will at least say for my father's house, that it has not stood unhonoured; nor will it fall—if it is to fall —unlamented. Forbear, then, if you are indeed the Christian you call yourself, to exult in the misfortunes of others, or to confide in your own prosperity. If the light of our house be now quenched, God can rekindle it in His own good time."

Peveril broke off in extreme surprise; for as he spake the last words, the bright red beams of the family beacon began again to glimmer from its wonted watch-tower, checkering the pale moonbeam with a ruddier glow. Bridgenorth also gazed on this unexpected illumination with surprise, and not, as it seemed, without disquietude. "Young man," he resumed, "it can scarcely be but that Heaven intends to work great things by your hand, so singularly has that augury followed on your words."

So saying, he put his horse once more in motion; and looking back, from time to time, as if to assure himself that the beacon of the Castle was actually rekindled, he led the way through the well-known paths and alleys, to his own house of Moultrassie, followed by Peveril, who although sensible that the light might be altogether accidental, could not but receive as a good omen an event so intimately connected with the traditions and usages of his family.

They alighted at the hall-door, which was hastily opened by a female; and while the deep tone of Bridgenorth called on the groom to take their horses, the well-known voice of his daughter Alice was heard to exclaim in thanksgiving to God, who had restored her father in safety.

CHAPTER XXIV

We meet, as men see phantoms in a dream,
Which glide, and sigh, and sign, and move their lips,
But make no sound; or, if they utter voice,
'Tis but a low and undistinguish'd moaning,
Which has nor word nor sense of utter'd sound.
—THE CHIEFTAIN.

WE said, at the conclusion of the last chapter, that a female form appeared at the door of Moultrassie Hall; and that the well-known accents of Alice Bridgenorth were heard to hail the return of her father, from what she naturally dreaded as a perilous visit to the Castle of Martindale.

Julian, who followed his conductor with a throbbing heart into the lighted hall, was therefore prepared to see her whom he best loved, with her arms thrown around her father. The instant she had quitted his paternal embrace, she was aware of the unexpected guest who had returned in his company. A deep blush, rapidly succeeded by a deadly paleness, and again by a slighter suffusion, showed plainly to her lover that his sudden appearance was anything but indifferent to her. He bowed profoundly—a courtesy which she returned with equal formality, but did not venture to approach more nearly, feeling at once the delicacy of his own situation and of hers.

Major Bridgenorth turned his cold, fixed, grey, melancholy glance, first on the one of them and then on the other. "Some," he said gravely, " would, in my case, have avoided this meeting; but I have confidence in you both, although you are young, and beset with the snares incidental to your age. There are those within who should not know that ye have been acquainted. Wherefore, be wise, and be as strangers to each other."

Julian and Alice exchanged glances as her father turned from them, and lifting a lamp which stood in the entrance-hall, led the way to the interior apartment. There was little of consolation in this exchange of looks; for the sadness of Alice's glance was mingled with fear, and that of Julian clouded by an anxious sense of doubt. The look also was but momentary; for Alice, springing to her father, took the light out of his hand, and stepping before him, acted as the usher of both into the large oaken parlour, which has been already mentioned as the apartment in which Bridgenorth had spent the hours of dejection which followed the death of his consort and family. It was now lighted up as for the reception of company; and five or six persons sat in it, in the plain, black, stiff dress, which was affected by the formal Puritans of the time, in evidence of their contempt of the manners of the luxurious Court of Charles the Second; amongst whom, excess of extravagance in apparel, like excess of every other kind, was highly fashionable.

Julian at first glanced his eyes but slightly along the range of grave and severe faces which composed this society—men sincere, perhaps, in their pretensions to a superior purity of conduct and morals, but in whom that high praise was somewhat chastened by an affected austerity in dress and manners, allied to those Pharisees of old, who made broad their phylacteries, and would be seen of man to fast, and to discharge with rigid punctuality the observances of the law. Their dress was almost uniformly a black cloak and doublet, cut straight and close, and undecorated with lace or embroidery of any kind, black Flemish breeches and hose, square-toed shoes, with large roses made of serge ribbon. Two or three had large loose boots of calf-leather, and almost every one was begirt with a long rapier, which was suspended by leathern thongs, to a plain belt of buff, or of black leather. One or two of the elder guests, whose hair had been thinned by time, had their heads covered with a skull-cap of black silk or velvet, which, being drawn down betwixt the ears and the skull, and permitting no hair to escape, occasioned the former to project in the ungraceful manner which may be remarked in old pictures, and which procured for the Puritans the term of "prickeared Roundheads," so unceremoniously applied to them by their contemporaries.

These worthies were ranged against the wall, each in his ancient high-backed, long-legged chair; neither looking towards, nor apparently discoursing with each other; but plunged in their own reflections, or awaiting, like an assembly of Quakers, the quickening power of divine inspiration.

Major Bridgenorth glided along this formal society with noiseless step, and a composed severity of manner, resembling their own. He paused before each in succession, and apparently communicated, as he passed, the transactions of the evening, and the circumstances under which the heir of Martindale Castle was now a guest at Moultrassie Hall. Each seemed to stir at his brief detail, like a range of statues in an enchanted hall, starting into something like life, as a talisman is applied to them successively. Most of them, as they heard the narrative of their host, cast upon Julian a look of curiosity, blended with haughty scorn and the consciousness of spiritual superiority; though, in one or two instances, the milder influences of compassion were sufficiently visible. — Peveril would have undergone this gantlet of eyes with more impatience, had not his own been for the time engaged in following the motions of Alice, who glided through the apartment; and only speaking very briefly, and in whispers, to one or two of the company who addressed her, took her place beside a treble-hooded old lady, the only female of the party, and addressed herself to her in such earnest conversation, as might dispense with her raising her head, or looking at any others in the company.

Her father put a question, to which she was obliged to return an answer—" Where was Mistress Debbitch ? ".

" She had gone out," Alice replied, " early after sunset, to visit some old acquaintances in the neighbourhood, and she was not yet returned."

Major Bridgenorth made a gesture indicative of displeasure ; and, not content with that, expressed his determined resolution that Dame Deborah should no longer remain a member of his family. " I will have those," he said aloud, and without regarding the presence of his guests, " and those only, around me, who know to keep within the sober and modest bounds of a Christian family. Who pretends to more freedom, must go out from among us, as not being of us."

A deep and emphatic humming noise, which was at that time the mode in which the Puritans signified their applause, as well of the doctrines expressed by a favourite divine in the pulpit, as of those delivered in private society, ratified the approbation of the assessors, and seemed to secure the dismission of the unfortunate governante, who stood thus detected of having strayed out of bounds. Even Peveril, although he had reaped considerable advantages, in his early acquaintance with Alice, from the mercenary and gossiping disposition of her governess, could not hear of her dismissal without approbation, so much was he desirous, that, in the hour of difficulty which might soon approach, Alice might have the benefit of countenance and advice from one of her own sex of better manners, and less suspicious probity, than Mistress Debbitch.

Almost immediately after this communication had taken place, a servant in mourning showed his thin, pinched, and wrinkled visage in the apartment, announcing, with a voice more like a passing bell than the herald of a banquet, that refreshments were provided in an adjoining apartment. Gravely leading the way, with his daughter on one side, and the puritanical female whom we have distinguished on the other, Bridgenorth himself ushered his company, who followed, with little attention to order or ceremony, into the eating-room, where a substantial supper was provided.

In this manner, Peveril, although entitled according to ordinary ceremonial, to some degree of precedence—a matter at that time considered of much importance, although now little regarded—was left among the last of those who quitted the parlour; and might indeed have brought up the rear of all, had not one of the company, who was himself late in the retreat, bowed and resigned to Julian the rank in the company which had been usurped by others.

This act of politeness naturally induced Julian to examine the features of the person who had offered him this civility; and he started to observe, under the pinched velvet cap, and above the short band-strings, the countenance of Ganlesse, as he called himself—his companion on the preceding evening. He looked again and again, especially when all were placed at the supper board, and when, consequently, he had frequent opportunities of observing this person fixedly without any breach of good manners. At first he wavered in his belief, and was much inclined to doubt the reality of his recollection; for the difference of dress was such as to effect a considerable change of appearance; and the countenance itself, far from exhibiting anything marked or memorable, was one of those ordinary visages which we see almost without remarking them, and which leave our memory so soon as the object is withdrawn from our eyes. But the impression upon his mind returned, and became stronger, until it induced him to watch with peculiar attention the manners of the individual who had thus attracted his notice.

During the time of a very prolonged grace before meat, which was delivered by one of the company—who, from his Geneva band and serge doublet, presided, as Julian supposed, over some dissenting congregation—he noticed that this man kept the same demure and severe cast of countenance usually affected by the Puritans, and which rather caricatured the reverence unquestionably due upon such occasions. His eyes were turned upward, and his huge penthouse hat, with a high crown and broad brim, held in both hands before him, rose and fell with the cadences of the speaker's voice; thus marking time, as it were, to the periods of the benediction. Yet when the slight bustle took place which attends the adjusting of chairs, &c., as men sit down to table, Julian's eye encountered that of the stranger; and as their looks met, there glanced from those of the latter an expression of satirical humour and scorn, which seemed to intimate internal ridicule of the gravity of his present demeanour.

Julian again sought to fix his eye, in order to ascertain that he had not mistaken the tendency of this transient expression, but the stranger did not allow him another opportunity. He might have been discovered by the tone of his voice; but the individual in question spoke little, and in whispers, which was indeed the fashion of the whole company, whose demeanour at table resembled that of mourners at a funeral feast.

The entertainment itself was coarse, though plentiful; and must, according to Julian's opinion, be distasteful to one so exquisitely skilled in good cheer, and so capable of enjoying, critically and scientifically, the genial preparations of his companion Smith, as Ganlesse had shown himself on the preceding evening. Accordingly, upon close observation, he remarked that the food which he took upon his plate remained there unconsumed; and that his actual supper consisted only of a crust of bread, with a glass of wine.

The repast was hurried over with the haste of those who think it shame, if not sin, to make mere animal enjoyments the means of consuming time, or of receiving pleasure; and when men wiped their mouths and moustaches, Julian remarked that the object of his curiosity used a handkerchief of the finest cambric—an article rather inconsistent with the exterior plainness, not to say coarseness, of his appearance. He used also several of the more minute refinements, then only observed at tables of the higher rank; and Julian thought he could discern, at every turn, something of courtly manners and gestures, under the precise and rustic simplicity of the character which he had assumed.*

But if this were indeed that same Ganlesse with whom Julian had met on the preceding evening, and who had boasted the facility with which he could assume any character which he pleased to represent for the time, what could be the purpose of his present disguise? He was, if his own words could be credited, a person of some importance, who dared to defy the danger of those officers and informers, before whom all ranks at that time trembled; nor was he likely, as Julian conceived, without some strong purpose, to subject himself to such a

---

* A Scottish gentleman *in hiding*, as it was emphatically termed, for some concern in a Jacobite insurrection or plot, was discovered among a number of ordinary persons, by the use of his toothpick.

masquerade as the present, which could not be otherwise than irksome to one whose conversation proclaimed him of light life and free opinions. Was his appearance here for good or for evil? Did it respect his father's house, or his own person, or the family of Bridgenorth? Was the real character of Ganlesse known to the master of the house, inflexible as he was in all which concerned morals as well as religion? If not, might not the machinations of a brain so subtile affect the peace and happiness of Alice Bridgenorth?

These were questions which no reflection could enable Peveril to answer. His eyes glanced from Alice to the stranger; and new fears, and undefined suspicions, in which the safety of that beloved and lovely girl was implicated, mingled with the deep anxiety which already occupied his mind, on account of his father and his father's house.

He was in this tumult of mind, when, after a thanksgiving as long as the grace, the company arose from table, and were instantly summoned to the exercise of family worship. A train of domestics, grave, sad, and melancholy as their superiors, glided in to assist at this act of devotion, and ranged themselves at the lower end of the apartment. Most of these men were armed with long tucks, as the straight stabbing swords, much used by Cromwell's soldiery, were then called. Several had large pistols also; and the corselets or cuirasses of some were heard to clank, as they seated themselves to partake in this act of devotion. The ministry of him whom Julian had supposed a preacher was not used on this occasion. Major Bridgenorth himself read and expounded a chapter of Scripture, with much strength and manliness of expression, although so as not to escape the charge of fanaticism. The nineteenth chapter of Jeremiah was the portion of Scripture which he selected; in which, under the type of breaking a potter's vessel, the prophet presages the desolation of the Jews. The lecturer was not naturally eloquent; but a strong, deep, and sincere conviction of the truth of what he said supplied him with language of energy and fire, as he drew a parallel between the abominations of the worship of Baal, and the corruptions of the Church of Rome— so favourite a topic with the Puritans of that period; and denounced against the Catholics, and those who favoured them, that hissing and desolation which the prophet directed against the city of Jerusalem. His hearers made a yet closer application than the lecturer himself suggested; and many a dark proud eye intimated, by a glance on Julian, that on his father's house were already, in some part, realised those dreadful maledictions.

The lecture finished, Bridgenorth summoned them to unite with him in prayer; and on a slight change of arrangements amongst the company, which took place as they were about to kneel down, Julian found his place next to the single-minded and beautiful object of his affection, as she knelt, in her loveliness, to adore her Creator. A short time was permitted for mental devotion; during which Peveril could hear her half-breathed petition for the promised blessings of peace on earth, and good-will towards the children of men.

The prayer which ensued was in a different tone. It was poured forth by the same person who had officiated as chaplain at the table; and was in the tone of a Boanerges, or Son of Thunder—a denouncer of crimes—an invoker of judgments— almost a prophet of evil and of destruction. The testimonies and the sins of the day were not forgotten—the mysterious murder of Sir Edmondsbury Godfrey was insisted upon—and thanks and praise were offered, that the very night on which they were assembled, had not seen another offering of a Protestant magistrate, to the bloodthirsty fury of the revengful Catholics.

Never had Julian found it more difficult, during an act of devotion, to maintain his mind in a frame befitting the posture and the occasion; and when he heard the speaker return thanks for the downfall and devastation of his family, he was strongly tempted to have started upon his feet, and charged him with offering a tribute, stained with falsehood and calumny, at the throne of truth itself. He resisted, however, an impulse which it would have been insanity to have yielded to, and his patience was not without its reward; for when his fair neighbour arose from her knees, the lengthened and prolonged prayer being at last concluded, he observed that her eyes were streaming with tears; and one glance with which she looked at him in that moment, showed more of affectionate interest for him in his fallen fortunes and precarious condition, than he had been able to obtain from her when his worldly estate seemed so much the more exalted of the two.

Cheered and fortified with the conviction that one bosom in the company, and that in which he most eagerly longed to secure an interest, sympathised with his distress, he felt strong to endure whatever was to follow, and shrunk not from the stern still smile with which, one by one, the meeting regarded him, as, gliding to their several places of repose, they indulged themselves at parting with a look of triumph on one whom they considered as their captive enemy.

Alice also passed by her lover, her eyes fixed on the ground, and answered his low obeisance without raising them. The room was now empty, but for Bridgenorth and his guest, or prisoner; for it is difficult to say in which capacity Peveril ought to regard himself. He took an old brazen lamp from the table, and, leading the way, said at the same time, "I must be the uncourtly chamberlain, who am to usher you to a place of repose, more rude, perhaps, than you have been accustomed to occupy."

Julian followed him, in silence, up an old-fashioned winding staircase, within a turret. At the landing-place on the top was a small apartment, where an ordinary pallet bed, two chairs, and a small stone table, were the only furniture. "Your bed," continued Bridgenorth, as if desirous to prolong their interview, "is not of the softest; but innocence sleeps as sound upon straw as on down."

"Sorrow, Major Bridgenorth, finds little rest on either," replied Julian. "Tell me, for you seem to await some question from me, what is to be the fate of my parents, and why you separate me from them?"

Bridgenorth, for answer, indicated with his finger the mark which his countenance still showed from the explosion of Julian's pistol.

"That," replied Julian, "is not the real cause of your proceedings against me. It cannot be, that you, who have been a soldier, and are a man, can be surprised or displeased by my interference in the defence of my father. Above all, you cannot, and I must needs say you do not, believe that I would have raised my hand against you personally, had there been a moment's time for recognition."

"I may grant all this," said Bridgenorth; "but what the better are you for my good opinion, or for the ease with which I can forgive you the injury which you aimed at me? You are in my custody as a magistrate, accused of abetting the foul, bloody, and heathenish plot, for the establishment of Popery, the murder of the King, and the general massacre of all true Protestants."

"And on what grounds, either of fact or suspicion, dare any one accuse me of such a crime?" said Julian. "I have hardly heard of the plot, save by the mouth of common rumour, which, while it speaks of nothing else, takes care to say nothing distinctly even on that subject."

"It may be enough for me to tell you," replied Bridgenorth, "and perhaps it is a word too much—that you are a discovered intriguer—a spied spy—who carries tokens and messages betwixt the Popish Countess of Derby and the Catholic party in London. You have not conducted your matters with such discretion, but that this is well known, and can be sufficiently proved. To this charge, which you are well aware you cannot deny, these men, Everett and Dangerfield, are not unwilling to add, from the recollection of your face, other passages, which will certainly cost you your life when you come before a Protestant jury."

"They lie like villains," said Peveril, "who hold me accessory to any plot either against the King, the nation, or the state of religion; and for the Countess, her loyalty has been too long, and too highly proved, to permit her being implicated in such injurious suspicions."

"What she has already done," said Bridgenorth, his face darkening as he spoke, "against the faithful champions of pure religion, hath sufficiently shown of what she is capable. She hath betaken herself to her rock, and sits, as she thinks, in security, like the eagle reposing after his bloody banquet. But the arrow of the fowler may yet reach her—the shaft is whetted —the bow is bended—and it will be soon seen whether Amalek or Israel shall prevail. But for thee, Julian Peveril—why should I conceal it from thee?—my heart yearns for thee as a woman's for her first-born. To thee I will give, at the expense of my own reputation—perhaps at the risk of personal suspicion —for who, in these days of doubt, shall be exempted from it— to thee, I say, I will give means of escape, which else were impossible to thee. The staircase of this turret descends to the gardens — the postern-gate is unlatched — on the right hand lie the stables, where you will find your own horse— take it, and make for Liverpool—I will give you credit with a friend under the name of Simon Simonson, one persecuted by the prelates; and he will expedite your passage from the kingdom."

"Major Bridgenorth," said Julian, "I will not deceive you. Were I to accept your offer of freedom, it would be to attend to a higher call than that of mere self-preservation. My father is in danger—my mother in sorrow—the voices of religion and nature call me to their side. I am their only child—their only hope—I will aid them, or perish with them!"

"Thou art mad," said Bridgenorth—"aid them thou canst not—perish with them thou well mayst, and even accelerate their ruin; for, in addition to the charges with which thy unhappy father is loaded, it would be no slight aggravation, that while he meditated arming and calling together the Catholics and High Churchmen of Cheshire and Derbyshire, his son should prove to be the confidential agent of the Countess of Derby, who aided her in making good her stronghold against the Protestant commissioners, and was despatched by her to open secret communication with the Popish interest in London."

"You have twice stated me as such an agent," said Peveril, resolved that his silence should not be construed into an admission of the charge, though he felt that it was in some degree well founded — "What reason have you for such an allegation?"

"Will it suffice for a proof of my intimate acquaintance with your mystery," replied Bridgenorth, "if I should repeat to you the last words which the Countess used to you when you left the Castle of that Amalekitish woman? Thus she spoke : 'I am now a forlorn widow,' she said, 'whom sorrow has made selfish.'"

Peveril started, for these were the very words the Countess had used; but he instantly recovered himself, and replied, "Be your information of what nature it will, I deny, and I defy it, so far as it attaches aught like guilt to me. There lives not a man more innocent of a disloyal thought, or of a traitorous purpose. What I say for myself, I will, to the best of my knowledge, say and maintain on account of the noble Countess, to whom I am indebted for nurture."

"Perish, then, in thy obstinacy!" said Bridgenorth; and turning hastily from him, he left the room, and Julian heard him hasten down the narrow staircase, as if distrusting his own resolution.

With a heavy heart, yet with that confidence in an overruling Providence which never forsakes a good and brave man, Peveril betook himself to his lowly place of repose.

CHAPTER XXV

The course of human life is changeful still,
As is the fickle wind and wandering rill ;
Or, like the light dance which the wild-breeze weaves
Amidst the fated race of fallen leaves ;
Which now its breath bears down, now tosses high,
Beats to the earth, or wafts to middle sky.
Such, and so varied, the precarious play
Of fate with man, frail tenant of a day !

—ANONYMOUS.

WHILST, overcome with fatigue, and worn out by anxiety, Julian Peveril slumbered as a prisoner in the house of his hereditary enemy, Fortune was preparing his release by one of those sudden frolics with which she loves to confound the calculations and expectancies of humanity ; and as she fixes on strange agents for such purposes, she condescended to employ, on the present occasion, no less a personage than Mistress Deborah Debbitch.

Instigated, doubtless, by the pristine reminiscences of former times, no sooner had that most prudent and considerate dame found herself in the vicinity of the scenes of her earlier days, than she bethought herself of a visit to the ancient house-keeper of Martindale Castle, Dame Ellesmere by name, who, long retired from active service, resided at the keeper's lodge, in the west thicket, with her nephew, Lance Outram, subsisting upon the savings of her better days, and on a small pension allowed by Sir Geoffrey to her age and faithful services.

Now Dame Ellesmere and Mistress Deborah had not by any means been formerly on so friendly a footing, as this haste to visit her might be supposed to intimate. But years had taught Deborah to forget and forgive; or perhaps she had no special objection, under cover of a visit to Dame Ellesmere, to take the chance of seeing what changes time had made on her old admirer the keeper. Both inhabitants were in the cottage, when, after having seen her master set forth on his expedition to the Castle, Mistress Debbitch, dressed in her very best gown, footed it through gutter, and over stile, and by pathway green, to knock at their door, and to lift the latch at the hospitable invitation which bade her come in.

Dame Ellesmere's eyes were so often dim, that, even with the aid of spectacles, she failed to recognise, in the portly and mature personage who entered their cottage, the tight well-made lass, who, presuming on her good looks and flippant tongue, had so often provoked her by insubordination; and her former lover, the redoubted Lance, not being conscious that ale had given rotundity to his own figure, which was formerly so slight and active, and that brandy had transferred to his nose the colour which had once occupied his cheeks, was unable to discover that Deborah's French cap, composed of sarsenet and Brussels lace, shaded the features which had so often procured him a rebuke from Dr. Dummerar, for suffering his eyes, during the time of prayers, to wander to the maid-servants' bench.

In brief, the blushing visitor was compelled to make herself known; and when known, was received by aunt and nephew with the most sincere cordiality.

The home-brewed was produced; and, in lieu of more vulgar food, a few slices of venison presently hissed in the frying-pan, giving strong room for inference that Lance Outram, in his capacity of keeper, neglected not his own cottage when he supplied the larder at the Castle. A modest sip of the excellent Derbyshire ale, and a taste of the highly-seasoned hash, soon placed Deborah entirely at home with her old acquaintance.

Having put all necessary questions, and received all suitable answers, respecting the state of the neighbourhood, and such of her own friends as continued to reside there, the conversation began rather to flag, until Deborah found the art of again renewing its interest, by communicating to her friends the dismal intelligence that they must soon look for deadly bad news from the Castle; for that her present master, Major Bridgenorth, had been summoned, by some great people from London, to assist in taking her old master, Sir Geoffrey; and that all Master

Bridgenorth's servants, and several other persons whom she named, friends and adherents of the same interest, had assembled a force to surprise the Castle; and that as Sir Geoffrey was now so old, and gouty withal, it could not be expected he should make the defence he was wont; and then he was known to be so stout-hearted, that it was not to be supposed that he would yield up without stroke of sword; and then if he was killed, as he was like to be, amongst them that liked never a bone of his body, and now had him at their mercy, why, in that case, she, Dame Deborah, would look upon Lady Peveril as little better than a dead woman; and undoubtedly there would be a general mourning through all that country, where they had such great kin; and silks were likely to rise on it, as Master Lutestring, the mercer of Chesterfield, was like to feel in his purse bottom. But for her part, let matters wag how they would, an if Master Julian Peveril was to come to his own, she could give as near a guess as e'er another who was likely to be Lady at Martindale.

The text of this lecture, or, in other words, the fact that Bridgenorth was gone with a party to attack Sir Geoffrey Peveril in his own Castle of Martindale, sounded so stunningly strange in the ears of those old retainers of his family, that they had no power either to attend to Mistress Deborah's inferences, or to interrupt the velocity of speech with which she poured them forth. And when at length she made a breathless pause, all that poor Dame Ellesmere could reply, was the emphatic question, "Bridgenorth brave Peveril of the Peak!—Is the woman mad?"

"Come, come, dame," said Deborah, "woman me no more than I woman you. I have not been called Mistress at the head of the table for so many years, to be woman'd here by you. And for the news, it is as true as that you are sitting there in a white hood, who will wear a black one ere long."

"Lance Outram," said the old woman, "make out, if thou be'st a man, and listen about if aught stirs up at the Castle."

"If there should," said Outram, "I am even too long here;" and he caught up his crossbow, and one or two arrows, and rushed out of the cottage.

"Well-a-day!" said Mistress Deborah, "see if my news have not frightened away Lance Outram too, whom they used to say nothing could start. But do not take on so, dame; for I dare say if the Castle and the lands pass to my new master, Major Bridgenorth, as it is like they will—for I have heard that he has powerful debts over the estate—you shall have my good word with him, and I promise you he is no bad man; something precise about preaching and praying, and about the dress which one should wear, which, I must own, beseems not a gentleman, as, to be sure, every woman knows best what becomes her. But for you, dame, that wear a prayer-book at your girdle, with your housewife-case, and never change the fashion of your white hood, I dare say he will not grudge you the little matter you need, and are not able to win."

"Out, sordid jade!" exclaimed Dame Ellesmere, her very flesh quivering betwixt apprehension and anger, "and hold your peace this instant, or I will find those that shall flay the very hide from thee with dog-whips. Hast thou ate thy noble master's bread, not only to betray his trust, and fly from his service, but wouldst thou come here, like an ill-omened bird as thou art, to triumph over his downfall?"

"Nay, dame," said Deborah, over whom the violence of the old woman had obtained a certain predominance; "it is not I that say it—only the warrant of the Parliament folks."

"I thought we had done with their warrants ever since the blessed twenty-ninth of May," said the old housekeeper of Martindale Castle; "but this I tell thee, sweetheart, that I have seen such warrants crammed, at the sword's point, down the throats of them that brought them; and so shall this be, if there is one true man left to drink of the Dove."

As she spoke, Lance Outram re-entered the cottage. "Naunt," he said in dismay, "I doubt it is true what she says. The beacon tower is as black as my belt. No Pole-star of Peveril. What does that betoken?"

"Death, ruin, and captivity," exclaimed old Ellesmere. "Make for the Castle, thou knave. Thrust in thy great body. Strike for the house that bred thee and fed thee; and if thou art buried under the ruins, thou diest a man's death."

"Nay, naunt, I shall not be slack," answered Outram. "But here come folks that I warrant can tell us more on't."

One or two of the female servants, who had fled from the Castle during the alarm, now rushed in with various reports of the case; but all agreeing that a body of armed men were in possession of the Castle, and that Major Bridgenorth had taken young Master Julian prisoner, and conveyed him down to Moultrassie Hall, with his feet tied under the belly of the nag —a shameful sight to be seen—and he so well born and so handsome.

Lance scratched his head; and though feeling the duty incumbent upon him as a faithful servant, which was indeed specially dinned into him by the cries and exclamations of his aunt, he seemed not a little dubious how to conduct himself. "I would to God, naunt," he said at last, "that old Whitaker were alive now, with his long stories about Marston Moor and Edge Hill, that made us all yawn our jaws off their hinges, in spite of broiled rashers and double beer! When a man is missed, he is moaned, as they say; and I would rather than a broad piece he had been here to have sorted this matter, for it is clean out of my way as a woodsman, that have no skill of war. But dang it, if old Sir Geoffrey go to the wall without a knock for it!—Here you, Nell"—(speaking to one of the fugitive maidens from the Castle)—"but, no—you have not the heart of a cat, and are afraid of your own shadow by moon-light—But, Cis, you are a stout-hearted wench, and know a buck from a bullfinch. Hark thee, Cis, as you would wish to be married, get up to the Castle again, and get thee in—thou best knowest where—for thou hast oft gotten out of postern to a dance or junketing, to my knowledge—Get thee back to the Castle, as ye hope to be married—See my lady—they cannot hinder thee of that—my lady has a head worth twenty of ours—If I am to gather force, light up the beacon for a signal; and spare not a tar barrel on't. Thou mayst do it safe enough. I warrant the Roundheads busy with drink and plunder.—And, hark thee, say to my lady I am gone down to the miners' houses at Bonadventure. The rogues were mutinying for their wages but yesterday; they will be all ready for good or bad. Let her send orders down to me; or do you come yourself, your legs are long enough."

"Whether they are or not, Master Lance (and you know nothing of the matter), they shall do your errand to-night, for love of the old knight and his lady."

So Cisly Sellok, a kind of Derbyshire Camilla, who had won the smock at the foot-race at Ashbourne, sprung forward towards the Castle with a speed which few could have equalled.

"There goes a mettled wench," said Lance; "and now, naunt, give me the old broadsword—it is above the bed-head—and my wood-knife; and I shall do well enough."

"And what is to become of me?" bleated the unfortunate Mistress Deborah Debbitch.

"You must remain here with my aunt, Mistress Deb; and, for old acquaintance' sake, she will take care no harm befalls you; but take heed how you attempt to break bounds."

So saying, and pondering in his own mind the task which he had undertaken, the hardy forester strode down the moonlight glade, scarcely hearing the blessings and cautions which Dame Ellesmere kept showering after him. His thoughts were not altogether warlike. "What a tight ankle the jade hath!—she trips it like a doe in summer over the dew. Well, but here are the huts—Let us to this gear.—Are ye all asleep, ye dammers, sinkers, and drift-drivers? turn out, ye subterranean badgers. Here is your master, Sir Geoffrey, dead, for aught ye know or care. Do not you see the beacon is unlit, and you sit there like so many asses?"

"Why," answered one of the miners, who now began to come out of their huts—

> "An he be dead,
> He will eat no more bread."

"And you are like to eat none neither," said Lance; "for the works will be presently stopped, and all of you turned off."

"Well, and what of it, Master Lance? As good play for nought as work for nought. Here is four weeks we have scarce seen the colour of Sir Geoffrey's coin; and you ask us to care whether he be dead or in life? For you, that goes about, trotting upon your horse, and doing for work what all men do for pleasure, it may be well enough; but it is another matter to be leaving God's light, and burrowing all day and night in darkness, like a toad in a hole—that's not to be done for nought, I trow; and if Sir Geoffrey is dead, his soul will suffer for't; and if he's alive, we'll have him in the Barmoot Court."

"Hark ye, gaffer," said Lance, "and take notice, my mates, all of you," for a considerable number of these rude and subterranean people had now assembled to hear the discussion— "Has Sir Geoffrey, think you, ever put a penny in his pouch out of this same Bonadventure mine?"

"I cannot say as I think he has," answered old Ditchley, the party who maintained the controversy.

"Answer on your conscience, though it be but a leaden one. Do not you know that he hath lost a good penny?"

"Why, I believe he may," said Gaffer Ditchley. "What then!—lose to-day, win to-morrow—the miner must eat in the meantime."

"True; but what will you eat when Master Bridgenorth gets the land, that will not hear of a mine being wrought on his own ground? Will he work on at dead loss, think ye?" demanded trusty Lance.

"Bridgenorth?—he of Moultrassie Hall, that stopped the great Felicity Work, on which his father laid out, some say, ten thousand pounds, and never got in a penny? Why, what has he to do with Sir Geoffrey's property down here at Bonadventure? It was never his, I trow."

"Nay, what do I know?" answered Lance, who saw the impression he had made. "Law and debt will give him half Derbyshire, I think, unless you stand by old Sir Geoffrey."

"But if Sir Geoffrey be dead," said Ditchley cautiously, "what good will our standing by do to him?"

"I did not say he was dead, but only as bad as dead; in the hands of the Roundheads—a prisoner up yonder, at his own Castle," said Lance; "and will have his head cut off, like the good Earl of Derby's at Bolton-le-Moors."

"Nay, then, comrades," said Gaffer Ditchley, " an it be as Master Lance says, I think we should bear a hand for stout old Sir Geoffrey, against a low-born mean-spirited fellow like Bridgenorth, who shut up a shaft had cost thousands, without getting a penny profit on't. So hurra for Sir Geoffrey, and down with the Rump! But hold ye a blink—hold "—(and the waving of his hand stopped the commencing cheer)—" Hark ye, Master Lance, it must be all over, for the beacon is as black as night; and you know yourself that marks the Lord's death."

"It will kindle again in an instant," said Lance; internally adding, " I pray to God it may !—It will kindle in an instant— lack of fuel, and the confusion of the family."

"Ay, like enow, like enow," said Ditchley; "but I winna budge till I see it blazing."

"Why then, there a-goes !" said Lance. "Thank thee, Cis —thank thee, my good wench.—Believe your own eyes, my lads, if you will not believe me; and now hurra for Peveril of the Peak—the King and his friends—and down with Rumps and Roundheads !"

The sudden rekindling of the beacon had all the effect which Lance could have desired upon the minds of his rude and ignorant hearers, who, in their superstitious humour, had strongly associated the Polar-star of Peveril with the fortunes of the family. Once moved, according to the national character of their countrymen, they soon became enthusiastic; and Lance found himself at the head of thirty stout fellows and upwards, armed with their pick-axes, and ready to execute whatever task he should impose on them.

Trusting to enter the Castle by the postern, which had served to accommodate himself and other domestics upon an emergency, his only anxiety was to keep his march silent; and he earnestly recommended to his followers to reserve their shouts for the moment of the attack. They had not advanced far on their road to the Castle, when Cisly Sellok met them, so breathless with haste, that the poor girl was obliged to throw herself into Master Lance's arms.

"Stand up, my mettled wench," said he, giving her a sly kiss at the same time, " and let us know what is going on up at the Castle."

" My lady bids you, as you would serve God and your master, not to come up to the Castle, which can but make bloodshed; for she says Sir Geoffrey is lawfully in hand, and that he must bide the issue ; and that he is innocent of what he is charged with, and is going up to speak for himself before King and Council, and she goes up with him. And besides, they have found out the postern, the Roundhead rogues ; for two of them saw me when I went out of door, and chased me ; but I showed them a fair pair of heels."

"As ever dashed dew from the cowslip," said Lance. "But what the foul fiend is to be done ? for if they have secured the postern, I know not how the dickens we can get in."

"All is fastened with bolt and staple, and guarded with gun and pistol, at the Castle," quoth Cisly ; "and so sharp are they, that they nigh caught me coming with my lady's message, as I told you. But my lady says, if you could deliver her son, Master Julian, from Bridgenorth, that she would hold it good service."

"What !" said Lance, "is young master at the Castle ? I taught him to shoot his first shaft. But how to get in !"

"He was at the Castle in the midst of the ruffle, but old Bridgenorth has carried him down prisoner to the hall," answered Cisly. "There was never faith nor courtesy in an old Puritan who never had pipe and tabor in his house since it was built."

"Or who stopped a promising mine," said Ditchley, "to save a few thousand pounds, when he might have made himself as rich as the Lord of Chatsworth, and fed a hundred good fellows all the whilst."

"Why, then," said Lance, "since you are all of a mind, we will go draw the cover for the old badger ; and I promise you that the Hall is not like one of your real houses of quality, where the walls are as thick as whinstone-dikes, but foolish brick-work, that your pick-axes will work through as if it were cheese. Huzza once more for Peveril of the Peak ! down with Bridgenorth, and all upstart cuckoldy Roundheads !"

Having indulged the throats of his followers with one buxom huzza, Lance commanded them to cease their clamours, and proceeded to conduct them, by such paths as seemed the least likely to be watched, to the courtyard of Moultrassie Hall. On the road they were joined by several stout yeoman farmers, either followers of the Peveril family, or friends to the High Church and Cavalier party ; most of whom, alarmed by the news which began to fly fast through the neighbourhood, were armed with sword and pistol.

Lance Outram halted his party, at the distance, as he himself described it, of a flight-shot from the house, and advanced alone, and in silence, to reconnoitre ; and having previously commanded Ditchley and his subterranean allies to come to his assistance whenever he should whistle, he crept cautiously forward, and soon found that those whom he came to surprise, true to the discipline which had gained their party such decided superiority during the Civil War, had posted a sentinel, who paced through the courtyard, piously chanting a psalm-tune, while his arms, crossed on his bosom, supported a gun of formidable length.

"Now, a true soldier," said Lance Outram to himself, "would put a stop to thy snivelling ditty, by making a broad arrow quiver in your heart, and no great alarm given. But, dang it, I have not the right spirit for a soldier—I cannot fight a man till my blood's up; and for shooting him from behind a wall, it is cruelly like to stalking a deer. I'll e'en face him, and try what to make of him."

With this doughty resolution, and taking no farther care to conceal himself, he entered the courtyard boldly, and was making forward to the front door of the hall, as a matter of course. But the old Cromwellian, who was on guard, had not so learned his duty. "Who goes there?—Stand, friend—stand; or, verily, I will shoot thee to death!" were challenges which followed each other quick, the last being enforced by the levelling and presenting the said long-barrelled gun with which he was armed.

"Why, what a murrain!" answered Lance. "Is it your fashion to go a-shooting at this time o' night? Why, this is but a time for bat-fowling."

"Nay, but hark thee, friend," said the experienced sentinel, "I am none of those who do this work negligently. Thou canst not snare me with thy crafty speech, though thou wouldst make it to sound simple in mine ear. Of a verity I will shoot, unless thou tell thy name and business."

"Name!" said Lance; "why, what a dickens should it be but Robin Round—honest Robin of Redham; and for business, an you must needs know, I come on a message from some Parliament man, up yonder at the Castle, with letters for worshipful Master Bridgenorth of Moultrassie Hall; and this be the place, as I think; though why ye be marching up and down at his door, like the sign of a Red Man, with your old firelock there, I cannot so well guess."

"Give me the letters, my friend," said the sentinel, to whom this explanation seemed very natural and probable, "and I will cause them forthwith to be delivered into his worship's own hand."

Rummaging in his pockets, as if to pull out the letters which never existed, Master Lance approached within the sentinel's piece, and, before he was aware, suddenly seized him by the collar, whistled sharp and shrill, and exerting his skill as a wrestler, for which he had been distinguished in his youth, he stretched his antagonist on his back—the musket for which they struggled going off in the fall.

The miners rushed into the courtyard at Lance's signal; and, hopeless any longer of prosecuting his design in silence, Lance commanded two of them to secure the prisoner, and the rest to cheer loudly, and attack the door of the house.

Instantly the courtyard of the mansion rang with the cry of "Peveril of the Peak for ever!" with all the abuse which the Royalists had invented to cast upon the Roundheads, during so many years of contention; and at the same time, while some assailed the door with their mining implements, others directed their attack against the angle, where a kind of porch joined to the main front of the building; and there, in some degree protected by the projection of the wall, and of a balcony which overhung the porch, wrought in more security, as well as with more effect, than the others; for the doors being of oak, thickly studded with nails, offered a more effectual resistance to violence than the brick-work.

The noise of this hubbub on the outside, soon excited wild alarm and tumult within. Lights flew from window to window, and voices were heard demanding the cause of the attack; to which the party cries of those who were in the courtyard afforded a sufficient, or at least the only answer, which was vouchsafed. At length the window of a projecting staircase opened, and the voice of Bridgenorth himself demanded authoritatively what the tumult meant, and commanded the rioters to desist, upon their own proper and immediate peril.

"We want our young master, you canting old thief," was the reply; "and if we have him not instantly, the topmost stone of your house shall lie as low as the foundation."

"We will try that presently," said Bridgenorth; "for if there is another blow struck against the walls of my peaceful house, I will fire my carabine among you, and your blood be upon your own head. I have a score of friends, well armed with musket and pistol, to defend my house; and we have both the means and heart, with Heaven's assistance, to repay any violence you can offer."

"Master Bridgenorth," replied Lance, who, though no soldier, was sportsman enough to comprehend the advantage which those under cover, and using firearms, must necessarily have over his party, exposed to their aim, in a great measure, and without means of answering their fire,—"Master Bridgenorth, let us crave parley with you, and fair conditions. We desire to do you no evil, but will have back our young master; it is enough that you have got our old one and his lady. It is foul chasing to kill hart, hind, and fawn; and we will give you some light on the subject in an instant."

This speech was followed by a great crash amongst the lower windows of the house, according to a new species of attack which had been suggested by some of the assailants.

"I would take the honest fellow's word, and let young Peveril go," said one of the garrison, who, carelessly yawning, approached on the inside the post at which Bridgenorth had stationed himself.

"Are you mad?" said Bridgenorth; "or do you think me poor enough in spirit to give up the advantages I now possess over the family of Peveril, for the awe of a parcel of boors, whom the first discharge will scatter like chaff before the whirlwind?"

"Nay," answered the speaker, who was the same individual that had struck Julian by his resemblance to the man who called himself Ganlesse, "I love a dire revenge, but we shall buy it somewhat too dear if these rascals set the house on fire, as they are like to do, while you are parleying from the window. They have thrown torches or firebrands into the hall; and it is all our friends can do to keep the flame from catching the wainscoting, which is old and dry."

"Now, may Heaven judge thee for thy lightness of spirit," answered Bridgenorth; "one would think mischief was so properly thy element, that to thee it was indifferent whether friend or foe was the sufferer."

So saying, he ran hastily downstairs towards the hall, into which, through broken casements, and betwixt the iron bars, which prevented human entrance, the assailants had thrust lighted straw, sufficient to excite much smoke and some fire, and to throw the defenders of the house into great confusion; insomuch, that of several shots fired hastily from the windows, little or no damage followed to the besiegers, who, getting warm in the onset, answered the hostile charges with loud shouts of "Peveril for ever!" and had already made a practicable breach through the brick-wall of the tenement, through which Lance, Ditchley, and several of the most adventurous among their followers, made their way into the hall.

The complete capture of the house remained, however, as far off as ever. The defenders mixed with much coolness and skill that solemn and deep spirit of enthusiasm which sets life at less than nothing, in comparison to real or supposed duty. From the half-open doors which led into the hall, they maintained a fire which began to grow fatal. One miner was shot dead; three or four were wounded; and Lance scarce knew whether he should draw his forces from the house, and leave it a prey to the flames, or, making a desperate attack on the posts occupied by the defenders, try to obtain unmolested possession of the place. At this moment, his course of conduct was determined by an unexpected occurrence, of which it is necessary to trace the cause.

Julian Peveril had been, like other inhabitants of Moultrassie Hall on that momentous night, awakened by the report of the sentinel's musket, followed by the shouts of his father's vassals and followers; of which he collected enough to guess that Bridgenorth's house was attacked with a view to his liberation.

Very doubtful of the issue of such an attempt, dizzy with the slumber from which he had been so suddenly awakened, and confounded with the rapid succession of events to which he had been lately a witness, he speedily put on a part of his clothes, and hastened to the window of his apartment. From this he could see nothing to relieve his anxiety, for it looked towards a quarter different from that on which the attack was made. He attempted his door; it was locked on the outside; and his perplexity and anxiety became extreme, when suddenly the lock was turned, and in an undress, hastily assumed in the moment of alarm, her hair streaming on her shoulders, her eyes gleaming betwixt fear and resolution, Alice Bridgenorth rushed into his apartment, and seized his hand with the fervent exclamation, "Julian, save my father!"

The light which she bore in her hand served to show those features which could rarely have been viewed by any one without emotion, but which bore an expression irresistible to a lover.

"Alice," he said, "what means this? What is the danger? Where is your father?"

"Do not stay to question," she answered; "but if you would save him, follow me!"

At the same time she led the way, with great speed, half-way down the turret staircase which led to his room, thence turning through a side door, along a long gallery, to a larger and wider stair, at the bottom of which stood her father, surrounded by four or five of his friends, scarce discernible through the smoke of the fire which began to take hold in the hall, as well as that which arose from the repeated discharge of their own firearms.

Julian saw there was not a moment to be lost, if he meant to be a successful mediator. He rushed through Bridgenorth's party ere they were aware of his approach, and throwing himself amongst the assailants who occupied the hall in considerable numbers, he assured them of his personal safety, and conjured them to depart.

"Not without a few more slices at the Rump, master," answered Lance. "I am principally glad to see you safe and well; but here is Joe Rimegap shot as dead as a buck in season, and more of us are hurt; and we'll have revenge, and roast the Puritans like apples for lambswool!"

"Then you shall roast me along with them," said Julian; "for I vow to God, I will not leave the hall, being bound by parole of honour to abide with Major Bridgenorth till lawfully dismissed."

"Now out on you, an you were ten times a Peveril!" said Ditchley; "to give so many honest fellows loss and labour on your behalf, and to show them no kinder countenance.—I say, beat up the fire, and burn all together!"

"Nay, nay; but peace, my masters, and hearken to reason," said Julian; "we are all here in evil condition, and you will only make it worse by contention. Do you help to put out this same fire, which will else cost us all dear. Keep yourselves under arms. Let Master Bridgenorth and me settle some grounds of accommodation, and I trust all will be favourably made up on both sides; and if not, you shall have my consent and countenance to fight it out; and come on it what will, I will never forget this night's good service."

He then drew Ditchley and Lance Outram aside, while the rest stood suspended at his appearance and words, and expressing the utmost thanks and gratitude for what they had already done, urged them, as the greatest favour which they could do towards him and his father's house, to permit him to negotiate the terms of his emancipation from thraldom; at the same time forcing on Ditchley five or six gold pieces, that the brave lads of Bonadventure might drink his health; whilst to Lance he expressed the warmest sense of his active kindness, but protested he could only consider it as good service to his house, if he was allowed to manage the matter after his own fashion.

"Why," answered Lance, "I am well out on it, Master Julian; for it is matter beyond my mastery. All that I stand to is, that I will see you safe out of this same Moultrassie Hall; for our old Naunt Ellesmere will else give me but cold comfort when I come home. Truth is, I began unwillingly; but when I saw the poor fellow Joe shot beside me, why, I thought we should have some amends. But I put it all in your Honour's hands."

During this colloquy both parties had been amicably employed in extinguishing the fire, which might otherwise have been fatal to all. It required a general effort to get it under; and both parties agreed on the necessary labour, with as much unanimity, as if the water they brought in leathern buckets from the well to throw upon the fire, had some effect in slaking their mutual hostility.

CHAPTER XXVI

Necessity—thou best of peacemakers,
As well as surest prompter of invention—
Help us to composition!
—ANONYMOUS.

WHILE the fire continued, the two parties laboured in active union, like the jarring factions of the Jews during the siege of Jerusalem, when compelled to unite in resisting an assault of the besiegers. But when the last bucket of water had hissed on the few embers that continued to glimmer—when the sense of mutual hostility, hitherto suspended by a feeling of common danger, was in its turn rekindled—the parties, mingled as they had hitherto been in one common exertion, drew off from each other, and began to arrange themselves at opposite sides of the hall, and handle their weapons, as if for a renewal of the fight.

Bridgenorth interrupted any farther progress of this menaced hostility. "Julian Peveril," he said, "thou art free to walk thine own path, since thou wilt not walk with me that road which is more safe, as well as more honourable. But if you do by my counsel, you will get soon beyond the British seas."

"Ralph Bridgenorth," said one of his friends, "this is but evil and feeble conduct on thine own part. Wilt thou withhold thy hand from the battle, to defend, from these sons of Belial, the captive of thy bow and of thy spear? Surely we are enow to deal with them in the security of our good old cause; nor should we part with this spawn of the old serpent, until we essay whether the Lord will not give us victory therein."

A hum of stern assent followed; and had not Ganlesse now interfered, the combat would probably have been renewed. He took the advocate for war apart into one of the window recesses, and apparently satisfied his objections; for as he returned to his companions, he said to them, "Our friend hath so well argued this matter, that, verily, since he is of the same mind with the worthy Major Bridgenorth, I think the youth may be set at liberty."

As no farther objection was offered, it only remained with Julian to thank and reward those who had been active in his assistance. Having first obtained from Bridgenorth a promise of indemnity to them for the riot they had committed, a few kind words conveyed his sense of their services; and some broad pieces, thrust into the hand of Lance Outram, furnished the means for affording them a holiday. They would have remained to protect him, but, fearful of farther disorder, and relying entirely on the good faith of Major Bridgenorth, he dismissed them all excepting Lance, whom he detained to attend upon him for a few minutes, till he should depart from Moultrassie. But ere leaving the Hall, he could not repress his desire to speak with Bridgenorth in secret; and advancing towards him, he expressed such a desire.

Tacitly granting what was asked of him, Bridgenorth led the way to a small summer saloon adjoining to the Hall, where, with his usual gravity and indifference of manner, he seemed to await in silence what Peveril had to communicate.

Julian found it difficult, where so little opening was afforded him, to find a tone in which to open the subjects he had at heart, that should be at once dignified and conciliating. "Major Bridgenorth," he said at length, "you have been a son, and an affectionate one—You may conceive my present anxiety—My father!—What has been designed for him?"

"What the law will," answered Bridgenorth. "Had he walked by the counsels which I procured to be given to him, he might have dwelt safely in the house of his ancestors. His fate is now beyond my control—far beyond yours. It must be with him as his country shall decide."

"And my mother?" said Peveril.

"Will consult, as she has ever done, her own duty; and create her own happiness by doing so," replied Bridgenorth. "Believe, my designs towards your family are better than they may seem through the mist which adversity has spread around your house. I may triumph as a man; but as a man I must also remember, in my hour, that mine enemies have had theirs.—Have you aught else to say?" he added, after a momentary pause. "You have rejected once, yea, and again, the hand I stretched out to you. Methinks little more remains between us."

These words, which seemed to cut short farther discussion, were calmly spoken; so that though they appeared to discourage farther question, they could not interrupt that which still trembled on Julian's tongue. He made a step or two towards the door; then suddenly returned. "Your daughter?" he said—"Major Bridgenorth—I should ask—I *do* ask forgiveness for mentioning her name—but may I not inquire after her?—May I not express my wishes for her future happiness?"

"Your interest in her is but too flattering," said Bridgenorth; "but you have already chosen your part; and you must be, in future, strangers to each other. I may have wished it otherwise, but the hour of grace is passed, during which your compliance with my advice might—I will speak it plainly—have led to your union. For her happiness—if such a word belongs to mortal pilgrimage—I shall care for it sufficiently. She leaves this place to-day, under the guardianship of a sure friend."

"Not of ——?" exclaimed Peveril, and stopped short; for he felt he had no right to pronounce the name which came to his lips.

"Why do you pause?" said Bridgenorth; "a sudden thought is often a wise, almost always an honest one. With whom did you suppose I meant to entrust my child, that the idea called forth so anxious an expression?"

"Again I should ask your forgiveness," said Julian, "for meddling where I have little right to interfere. But I saw a face here that is known to me—the person calls himself Ganlesse—Is it with him that you mean to entrust your daughter?"

"Even to the person who calls himself Ganlesse," said Bridgenorth, without expressing either anger or surprise.

"And do you know to whom you commit a charge so precious to all who know her, and so dear to yourself?" said Julian.

"Do *you* know, who ask me the question?" answered Bridgenorth.

"I own I do not," answered Julian; "but I have seen him in a character so different from that he now wears, that I feel it my duty to warn syou, how you entrust the charge of your child to one who can alternately play the profligate or the hypocrite, as it suits his own interest or humour."

Bridgenorth smiled contemptuously. "I might be angry," he said, "with the officious zeal which supposes that its green conceptions can instruct my grey hairs; but, good Julian, I do but only ask from you the liberal construction, that I, who have had much converse with mankind, know with whom I trust what is dearest to me. He of whom thou speakest hath one visage to his friends, though he may have others to the world, living amongst those before whom honest features should be concealed under a grotesque vizard; even as in the sinful sports of the day, called maskings and mummeries, where the wise, if he show himself at all, must be contented to play the apish and fantastic fool."

"I would only pray your wisdom to beware," said Julian, "of one, who, as he has a vizard for others, may also have one which can disguise his real features from you yourself."

"This is being over careful, young man," replied Bridgenorth, more shortly than he had hitherto spoken; "if you would walk by my counsel, you will attend to your own affairs, which, credit me, deserve all your care, and leave others to the management of theirs."

This was too plain to be misunderstood; and Peveril was compelled to take his leave of Bridgenorth, and of Moultrassie Hall, without farther parley or explanation. The reader may imagine how oft he looked back, and tried to guess, amongst the lights which continued to twinkle in various parts of the building, which sparkle it was that gleamed from the bower of Alice. When the road turned into another direction, he sunk into a deep reverie, from which he was at length roused by the voice of Lance, who demanded where he intended to quarter for the night. He was unprepared to answer the question, but the honest keeper himself prompted a solution of the problem, by requesting that he would occupy a spare bed in the Lodge; to which Julian willingly agreed. The rest of the inhabitants had retired to rest when they entered; but Dame Ellesmere, apprised by a messenger of her nephew's hospitable intent, had everything in the best readiness she could, for the son of her

ancient patron. Peveril betook himself to rest; and, notwithstanding so many subjects of anxiety, slept soundly till the
morning was far advanced.

His slumbers were first broken by Lance, who had been long
up, and already active in his service. He informed him, that
his horse, arms, and small cloak-bag had been sent from the
Castle by one of Major Bridgenorth's servants, who brought a
letter, discharging from the Major's service the unfortunate
Deborah Debbitch, and prohibiting her return to the Hall.
The officer of the House of Commons, escorted by a strong
guard, had left Martindale Castle that morning early, travelling
in Sir Geoffrey's carriage—his lady being also permitted to attend
on him. To this he had to add, that the property at the Castle
was taken possession of by Master Win-the-fight, the attorney,
from Chesterfield, with other officers of law, in name of Major
Bridgenorth, a large creditor of the unfortunate knight.

Having told these Job's tidings, Lance paused; and, after a
moment's hesitation, declared he was resolved to quit the
country, and go up to London along with his young master.
Julian argued the point with him; and insisted he had better
stay to take charge of his aunt, in case she should be disturbed
by these strangers. Lance replied, "She would have one with
her, who would protect her well enough; for there was where-
withal to buy protection amongst them. But for himself, he
was resolved to follow Master Julian to the death."

Julian heartily thanked him for his love.

"Nay, it is not altogether out of love neither," said Lance,
"though I am as loving as another; but it is, as it were, partly
out of fear, lest I be called over the coals for last night's
matter; for as for the miners, they will never trouble them, as
the creatures only act after their kind."

"I will write in your behalf to Major Bridgenorth, who is
bound to afford you protection, if you have such fear," said
Julian.

"Nay, for that matter, it is not altogether fear, more than
altogether love," answered the enigmatical keeper, "although
it hath a tasting of both in it. And, to speak plain truth, thus
it is—Dame Debbitch and Naunt Ellesmere have resolved to set
up their horses together, and have made up all their quarrels.
And of all ghosts in the world, the worst is, when an old true-
love comes back to haunt a poor fellow like me. Mistress
Deborah, though distressed enow for the loss of her place, has
been already speaking of a broken sixpence, or some such
token, as if a man could remember such things for so many
years, even if she had not gone over seas, like a woodcock, in
the meanwhile."

Julian could scarce forbear laughing. "I thought you too

much of a man, Lance, to fear a woman marrying you whether you would or no."

"It has been many an honest man's luck, for all that," said Lance; "and a woman in the very house has so many deuced opportunities. And then there would be two upon one; for Naunt, though high enough when any of *your* folks are concerned, hath some look to the main chance; and it seems Mistress Deb is as rich as a Jew."

"And you, Lance," said Julian, "have no mind to marry for cake and pudding."

"No, truly, master," answered Lance, "unless I knew of what dough they were baked. How the devil do I know how the jade came by so much? And then if she speaks of tokens and love-passages, let her be the same tight lass I broke the sixpence with, and I will be the same true lad to her. But I never heard of true love lasting ten years; and hers, if it lives at all, must be nearer twenty."

"Well, then, Lance," said Julian, "since you are resolved on the thing, we will go to London together; where, if I cannot retain you in my service, and if my father recovers not these misfortunes, I will endeavour to promote you elsewhere."

"Nay, nay," said Lance, "I trust to be back to bonny Martindale before it is long, and to keep the greenwood, as I have been wont to do; for, as to Dame Debbitch, when they have not me for their common butt, Naunt and she will soon bend bows on each other. So here comes old Dame Ellesmere with your breakfast. I will but give some directions about the deer to Rough Ralph, my helper, and saddle my forest pony, and your honour's horse, which is no prime one, and we will be ready to trot."

Julian was not sorry for this addition to his establishment; for Lance had shown himself, on the preceding evening, a shrewd and bold fellow, and attached to his master. He therefore set himself to reconcile his aunt to parting with her nephew for some time. Her unlimited devotion for " the family," readily induced the old lady to acquiesce in his proposal, though not without a gentle sigh over the ruins of a castle in the air, which was founded on the well-saved purse of Mistress Deborah Debbitch. " At any rate," she thought, " it was as well that Lance should be out of the way of that bold, long-legged, beggarly trollop, Cis Sellok." But to poor Deb herself, the expatriation of Lance, whom she had looked to as a sailor to a port under his lee, for which he can run, if weather becomes foul, was a second severe blow, following close on her dismissal from the profitable service of Major Bridgenorth.

Julian visited the disconsolate damsel, in hopes of gaining some light upon Bridgenorth's projects regarding his daughter

—the character of this Ganlesse—and other matters, with which her residence in the family might have made her acquainted; but he found her by far too much troubled in mind to afford him the least information. The name of Ganlesse she did not seem to recollect—that of Alice rendered her hysterical—that of Bridgenorth, furious. She numbered up the various services she had rendered in the family—and denounced the plague of swartness to the linen—of leanness to the poultry—of dearth and dishonour to the housekeeping—and of lingering sickness and early death to Alice;—all which evils, she averred, had only been kept off by her continued, watchful, and incessant cares.—Then again turning to the subject of the fugitive Lance, she expressed such a total contempt of that mean-spirited fellow, in a tone between laughing and crying, as satisfied Julian it was not a topic likely to act as a sedative; and that, therefore, unless he made a longer stay than the urgent state of his affairs permitted, he was not likely to find Mistress Deborah in such a state of composure as might enable him to obtain from her any rational or useful information.

Lance, who good-naturedly took upon himself the whole burden of Dame Debbitch's mental alienation, or "taking on," as such fits of *passio hysterica* are usually termed in the country, had too much feeling to present himself before the victim of her own sensibility, and of his obduracy. He therefore intimated to Julian, by his assistant Ralph, that the horses stood saddled behind the Lodge, and that all was ready for their departure.

Julian took the hint, and they were soon mounted, and clearing the road, at a rapid trot, in the direction of London; but not by the most usual route. Julian calculated that the carriage in which his father was transported would travel slowly; and it was his purpose, if possible, to get to London before it should arrive there, in order to have time to consult, with the friends of his family, what measures should be taken in his father's behalf.

In this manner they advanced a day's journey towards London; at the conclusion of which, Julian found his resting-place in a small inn upon the road. No one came, at the first call, to attend upon the guests and their horses, although the house was well lighted up; and there was a prodigious chattering in the kitchen, such as can only be produced by a French cook when his mystery is in the very moment of projection. It instantly occurred to Julian—so rare was the ministry of these Gallic artists at that time—that the clamour he heard must necessarily be produced by the Sieur Chaubert, on whose *plats* he had lately feasted, along with Smith and Ganlesse. One, or both of these, were therefore probably in the little inn; and if so, he might have some opportunity to discover their real purpose and character. How to avail himself of such a meeting he knew not; but chance favoured him more than he could have expected.

"I can scarce receive you, gentlefolks," said the landlord, who at length appeared at the door; "here be a sort of quality in my house to-night, whom less than all will not satisfy; nor all neither, for that matter."

"We are but plain fellows, landlord," said Julian; "we are bound for Moseley-market, and can get no farther to-night. Any hole will serve us, no matter what."

"Why," said the honest host, "if that be the case, I must e'en put one of you behind the bar, though the gentlemen have desired to be private; the other must take heart of grace and help me at the tap."

"The tap for me," said Lance, without waiting his master's decision. "It is an element which I could live and die in."

"The bar, then, for me," said Peveril; and stepping back, whispered to Lance to exchange cloaks with him, desirous, if possible, to avoid being recognised.

The exchange was made in an instant; and presently afterwards the landlord brought a light; and as he guided Julian into his hostelry, cautioned him to sit quiet in the place where he should stow him; and if he was discovered, to say that he was one of the house, and leave him to make it good. "You will hear what the gallants say," he added; "but I think thou wilt carry away but little on it; for when it is not French, it is Court gibberish; and that is as hard to construe."

The bar, into which our hero was inducted on these conditions, seemed formed, with respect to the public room, upon the principle of a citadel, intended to observe and bridle a rebellious capital. Here sat the host on the Saturday evenings, screened from the observation of his guests, yet with the power of observing both their wants and their behaviour, and also that of overhearing their conversation—a practice which he was much addicted to, being one of that numerous class of philanthropists, to whom their neighbours' business is of as much consequence, or rather more, than their own.

Here he planted his new guest, with a repeated caution not to disturb the gentlemen by speech or motion; and a promise that he should be speedily accommodated with a cold buttock of beef, and a tankard of home-brewed. And here he left him with no other light than that which glimmered from the well-illuminated apartment within, through a sort of shuttle which accommodated the landlord with a view into it.

This situation, inconvenient enough in itself, was, on the present occasion, precisely what Julian would have selected.

He wrapped himself in the weather-beaten cloak of Lance Outram, which had been stained, by age and weather, into a thousand variations from its original Lincoln green; and with as little noise as he could, set himself to observe the two inmates, who had engrossed to themselves the whole of the apartment, which was usually open to the public. They sat by a table well covered with such costly rarities, as could only have been procured by much forecast, and prepared by the exquisite Mons. Chaubert; to which both seemed to do much justice.

Julian had little difficulty in ascertaining, that one of the travellers was, as he had anticipated, the master of the said Chaubert, or, as he was called by Ganlesse, Smith; the other, who faced him, he had never seen before. This last was dressed like a gallant of the first order. His periwig, indeed, as he travelled on horseback, did not much exceed in size the bar-wig of a modern lawyer; but then the essence which he shook from it with every motion, impregnated a whole apartment, which was usually only perfumed by that vulgar herb, tobacco. His riding-coat was laced in the newest and most courtly style; and Grammont himself might have envied the embroidery of his waistcoat, and the peculiar cut of his breeches, which buttoned above the knee, permitting the shape of a very handsome leg to be completely seen. This, by the proprietor thereof, had been stretched out upon a stool, and he contemplated its proportions, from time to time, with infinite satisfaction.

The conversation between these worthies was so interesting, that we propose to assign to it another chapter.

CHAPTER XXVII

―― This is some creature of the elements,
Most like your sea-gull. He can wheel and whistle
His screaming song, e'en when the storm is loudest―
Take for his sheeted couch the restless foam
Of the wild wave-crest―slumber in the calm,
And dally with the storm. Yet 'tis a gull,
An arrant gull, with all this.
—THE CHIEFTAIN.

"AND here is to thee," said the fashionable gallant whom we have described, "honest Tom; and a cup of welcome to thee out of Looby-land. Why, thou hast been so long in the country, that thou hast got a bumpkinly clod-compelling sort of look thyself. That greasy doublet fits thee as if it were thy reserved Sunday's apparel; and the points seem as if they were stay-laces bought for thy true-love Marjory. I marvel thou canst still relish a ragout. Methinks now, to a stomach bound in such a jacket, eggs and bacon were a diet more conforming."

"Rally away, my good lord, while wit lasts," answered his companion; "yours is not the sort of ammunition which will bear much expenditure. Or rather, tell me news from Court, since we have met so opportunely."

"You would have asked me these an hour ago," said the lord, "had not your very soul been under Chaubert's covered dishes. You remembered King's affairs will keep cool, and *entre-mets* must be eaten hot."

"Not so, my lord; I only kept common talk whilst that eavesdropping rascal of a landlord was in the room; so that, now the coast is clear once more, I pray you for news from Court."

"The Plot is nonsuited," answered the courtier—"Sir George Wakeman acquitted—the witnesses discredited by the jury —Scroggs, who ranted on one side, is now ranting on t'other."

"Rat the Plot, Wakeman, witnesses, Papists, and Protestants, all together! Do you think I care for such trash as that?—Till the Plot comes up the Palace backstair, and gets possession of old Rowley's own imagination, I care not a farthing who believes or disbelieves. I hang by him will bear me out."

"Well, then," said my lord, "the next news is Rochester's disgrace."

"Disgraced!—How, and for what? The morning I came off he stood as fair as any one."

"That's over—the epitaph * has broken his neck—and now he may write one for his own Court favour, for it is dead and buried."

"The epitaph!" exclaimed Tom; "why, I was by when it was made; and it passed for an excellent good jest with him whom it was made upon."

"Ay, so it did amongst ourselves," answered his companion; "but it got abroad, and had a run like a mill-race. It was in every coffee-house, and in half the diurnals. Grammont translated it into French too; and there is no laughing at so sharp a jest, when it is dinned into your ears on all sides. So disgraced

---

* The epitaph alluded to is the celebrated epigram made by Rochester on Charles II. It was composed at the King's request, who nevertheless resented its poignancy.

The lines are well known:—

"Here lies our sovereign lord the King,
  Whose word no man relies on,
Who never said a foolish thing,
  And never did a wise one."

is the author; and but for his Grace of Buckingham, the Court would be as dull as my Lord Chancellor's wig."

"Or as the head it covers.—Well, my lord, the fewer at Court, there is the more room for those that can bustle there. But there are two mainstrings of Shaftesbury's fiddle broken—the Popish Plot fallen into discredit—and Rochester disgraced. Changeful times—but here is to the little man who shall mend them."

"I apprehend you," replied his lordship; "and meet your health with my love. Trust me, my lord loves you, and longs for you.—Nay, I have done you reason.—By your leave, the cup is with me. Here is to his buxom Grace of Bucks."

"As blithe a peer," said Smith, "as ever turned night to day. Nay, it shall be an overflowing bumper, an you will; and I will drink it *super naculum*.—And how stands the great Madam?" *

"Stoutly against all change," answered my lord—"Little Anthony † can make nought of her."

"Then he shall bring her influence to nought. Hark in thine ear. Thou knowest——" (Here he whispered so low that Julian could not catch the sound.)

"Know him?" answered the other—"Know Ned of the Island?—To be sure I do."

"He is the man that shall knot the great fiddle-strings that have snapped. Say I told you so; and thereupon I give thee his health."

"And thereupon I pledge thee," said the young nobleman, "which on any other argument I were loath to do—thinking of Ned as somewhat the cut of a villain."

"Granted, man—granted," said the other,—"a very thorough-paced rascal; but able, my lord, able and necessary; and, in this plan, indispensable.—Pshaw!—This champagne turns stronger as it gets older, I think."

"Hark, mine honest fellow," said the courtier; "I would thou wouldst give me some item of all this mystery. Thou hast it, I know; for whom do men entrust but trusty Chiffinch?"

"It is your pleasure to say so, my lord," answered Smith (whom we shall hereafter call by his real name of Chiffinch) with much drunken gravity, for his speech had become a little altered by his copious libations in the course of the evening,—"few men know more, or say less, than I do; and it well becomes my station. *Conticuere omnes*, as the grammar hath it—all men should learn to hold their tongue."

---

* The Duchess of Portsmouth, Charles II.'s favourite mistress; very unpopular at the time of the Popish Plot, as well from her religion as her country, being a Frenchwoman and a Catholic.

† Anthony Ashley Cooper, Earl of Shaftesbury, the politician and intriguer of the period.

"Except with a friend, Tom—except with a friend. Thou wilt never be such a dogbolt as to refuse a hint to a friend? Come, you get too wise and statesman-like for your office.—The ligatures of thy most peasantly jacket there are like to burst with thy secret. Come, undo a button, man; it is for the health of thy constitution—Let out a reef; and let thy chosen friend know what is meditating. Thou knowest I am as true as thyself to little Anthony, if he can but get uppermost."

"*If*, thou lordly infidel!" said Chiffinch—"talk'st thou to me of *ifs*?—There is neither *if* nor *and* in the matter. The great Madam shall be pulled a peg down—the great Plot screwed a peg or two up. Thou knowest Ned?—Honest Ned had a brother's death to revenge."

"I have heard so," said the nobleman; "and that his persevering resentment of that injury was one of the few points which seemed to be a sort of heathenish virtue in him."

"Well," continued Chiffinch, "in manœuvring to bring about this revenge, which he hath laboured at many a day, he hath discovered a treasure."

"What!—In the Isle of Man?" said his companion.

"Assure yourself of it.—She is a creature so lovely, that she needs but be seen to put down every one of the favourites, from Portsmouth and Cleveland down to that threepenny baggage, Mistress Nelly."

"By my word, Chiffinch," said my lord, "that is a reinforcement after the fashion of thine own best tactics. But bethink thee, man! To make such a conquest, there wants more than a cherry-cheek and a bright eye—there must be wit—wit, man, and manners, and a little sense besides, to keep influence when it is gotten."

"Pshaw! will you tell me what goes to this vocation?" said Chiffinch. "Here, pledge me her health in a brimmer.—Nay, you shall do it on knees, too.—Never such a triumphant beauty was seen—I went to church on purpose, for the first time these ten years—Yet I lie, it was not to church neither—it was to chapel."

"To chapel!—What the devil, is she a Puritan?" exclaimed the other courtier.

"To be sure she is. Do you think I would be accessory to bringing a Papist into favour in these times, when, as my good Lord said in the House, there should not be a Popish man-servant, nor a Popish maid-servant, not so much as dog or cat, left to bark or mew about the King!" *

"But consider, Chiffie, the dislikelihood of her pleasing," said the noble courtier.—"What! old Rowley, with his wit, and love of wit—his wildness, and love of wildness—he form a

* Such was the extravagance of Shaftesbury's eloquence.

league with a silly, scrupulous, unidea'd Puritan!—Not if she were Venus."

"Thou knowest nought of the matter," answered Chiffinch. "I tell thee, the fine contrast between the seeming saint and falling sinner will give zest to the old gentleman's inclinations. If I do not know him, who does?—Her health, my lord, on your bare knee, as you would live to be of the bedchamber."

"I pledge you most devoutly," answered his friend. "But you have not told me how the acquaintance is to be made; for you cannot, I think, carry her to Whitehall."

"Aha, my dear lord, you would have the whole secret! but that I cannot afford—I can spare a friend a peep at my ends, but no one must look on the means by which they are achieved." —So saying, he shook his drunken head most wisely.

The villainous design which this discourse implied, and which his heart told him was designed against Alice Bridgenorth, stirred Julian so extremely, that he involuntarily shifted his posture, and laid his hand on his sword hilt.

Chiffinch heard a rustling, and broke off, exclaiming, "Hark! —Zounds, something moved—I trust I have told the tale to no ears but thine."

"I will cut off any which have drunk in but a syllable of thy words," said the nobleman; and raising a candle, he took a hasty survey of the apartment. Seeing nothing that could incur his menaced resentment, he replaced the light and continued: —"Well, suppose the Belle Louise de Querouaille * shoots from her high station in the firmament, how will you rear up the downfallen Plot again—for without that same Plot, think of it as thou wilt, we have no change of hands—and matters remain as they were, with a Protestant courtezan instead of a Papist— Little Anthony can but little speed without that Plot of his—I believe, in my conscience, he begot it himself." †

"Whoever begot it," said Chiffinch, "he hath adopted it; and a thriving babe it has been to him. Well, then, though it lies out of my way, I will play Saint Peter again—up with t'other key, and unlock t'other mystery."

"Now thou speakest like a good fellow; and I will, with my own hands, unwire this fresh flask, to begin a brimmer to the success of thy achievement."

"Well, then," continued the communicative Chiffinch, "thou knowest that they have long had a nibbling at the old Countess of Derby.—So Ned was sent down—he owes her an old accompt,

* Charles's principal mistress *en titre*. She was created Duchess of Portsmouth.

† Shaftesbury himself is supposed to have said that he knew not who was the inventor of the Plot, but that he himself had all the advantage of the discovery.

thou knowest—with private instructions to possess himself of
the island, if he could, by help of some of his old friends. He
hath ever kept up spies upon her; and happy man was he, to
think his hour of vengeance was come so nigh. But he missed
his blow; and the old girl being placed on her guard, was soon
in a condition to make Ned smoke for it. Out of the island
he came with little advantage for having entered it; when, by
some means—for the devil, I think, stands ever his friend—he
obtained information concerning a messenger, whom her old
Majesty of Man had sent to London to make party in her
behalf. Ned stuck himself to this fellow—a raw, half-bred lad,
son of an old blundering Cavalier of the old stamp, down in
Derbyshire—and so managed the swain, that he brought him
to the place where I was waiting, in anxious expectation of the
pretty one I told you of. By Saint Anthony, for I will swear
by no meaner oath, I stared when I saw this great lout—not
that the fellow is so ill-looked neither—I stared like—like—
good now, help me to a simile."

"Like Saint Anthony's pig, an it were sleek," said the young
lord; "your eyes, Chiffie, have the very blink of one. But
what hath all this to do with the Plot? Hold, I have had wine
enough."

"You shall not balk me," said Chiffinch; and a jingling was
heard, as if he were filling his comrade's glass with a very
unsteady hand. "Hey—What the devil is the matter?—I used
to carry my glass steady—very steady."

"Well, but this stranger?"

"Why, he swept at game and ragout as he would at spring
beef or summer mutton. Never saw so unnurtured a cub—
Knew no more what he ate than an infidel—I cursed him by
my gods when I saw Chaubert's *chef-d'œuvres* glutted down so
indifferent a throat. We took the freedom to spice his goblet
a little, and ease him of his packet of letters; and the fool
went on his way the next morning with a budget artificially
filled with grey paper. Ned would have kept him, in hopes
to have made a witness of him, but the boy was not of that
mettle."

"How will you prove your letters?" said the courtier.

"La you there, my lord," said Chiffinch; "one may see with
half an eye, for all your laced doublet, that you have been of
the family of Furnival's, before your brother's death sent you
to Court. How prove the letters?—Why, we have but let the
sparrow fly with a string round his foot.—We have him again
so soon as we list."

"Why, thou art turned a very Machiavel, Chiffinch," said his
friend. "But how if the youth proved restive?—I have heard
these Peak men have hot heads and hard hands."

"Trouble not yourself—that was cared for, my lord," said Chiffinch—"his pistols might bark, but they could not bite."

"Most exquisite Chiffinch, thou art turned micher as well as padder—Canst both rob a man and kidnap him!"

"Micher and padder—what terms be these?" said Chiffinch. "Methinks these are sounds to lug out upon. You will have me angry to the degree of falling foul—robber and kidnapper!"

"You mistake verb for noun-substantive," replied his lordship; "I said *rob* and *kidnap*—a man may do either once and away without being professional."

"But not without spilling a little foolish noble blood, or some such red-coloured gear," said Chiffinch, starting up.

"Oh yes," said his lordship; "all this may be without these direful consequences, and as you will find to-morrow, when you return to England; for at present you are in the land of Champagne, Chiffie; and that you may continue so, I drink thee this parting cup to line thy nightcap."

"I do not refuse your pledge," said Chiffinch; "but I drink to thee in dudgeon and in hostility—It is a cup of wrath, and a gage of battle. To-morrow, by dawn, I will have thee at point of fox, wert thou the last of the Savilles.—What the devil! think you I fear you because you are a lord?"

"Not so, Chiffinch," answered his companion. "I know thou fearest nothing but beans and bacon, washed down with bumpkin-like beer.—Adieu, sweet Chiffinch—to bed—Chiffinch —to bed."

So saying, he lifted a candle, and left the apartment. And Chiffinch, whom the last draught had nearly overpowered, had just strength enough left to do the same, muttering, as he staggered out, "Yes, he shall answer it.—Dawn of day? D—n me—It is come already—Yonder's the dawn—No, d—n me, 'tis the fire glancing on the cursed red lattice—I am whistled drunk, I think—This comes of a country inn—It is the smell of the brandy in this cursed room—It could not be the wine— Well, old Rowley shall send me no more errands to the country again—Steady, steady."

So saying, he reeled out of the apartment, leaving Peveril to think over the extraordinary conversation he had just heard.

The name of Chiffinch, the well-known minister of Charles's pleasures, was nearly allied to the part which he seemed about to play in the present intrigue; but that Christian, whom he had always supposed a Puritan as strict as his brother-in-law, Bridgenorth, should be associated with him in a plot so infamous, seemed alike unnatural and monstrous. The near relationship might blind Bridgenorth, and warrant him in confiding his daughter to such a man's charge; but what a wretch he must be, that could coolly meditate such an igno-

minious abuse of his trust! In doubt whether he could credit
for a moment the tale which Chiffinch had revealed, he hastily
examined his packet, and found that the sealskin case in which
it had been wrapt up, now only contained an equal quantity
of waste paper. If he had wanted farther confirmation, the
failure of the shot which he had fired at Bridgenorth, and of
which the wadding only struck him, showed that his arms had
been tampered with. He examined the pistol which still remained charged, and found that the ball had been drawn.
"May I perish," said he to himself, "amid these villainous
intrigues, but thou shalt be more surely loaded, and to better
purpose! The contents of these papers may undo my benefactress—their having been found on me, may ruin my father
—that I have been the bearer of them, may cost, in these fiery
times, my own life—that I care least for—they form a branch
of the scheme laid against the honour and happiness of a
creature so innocent, that it is almost sin to think of her within
the neighbourhood of such infamous knaves. I will recover the
letters at all risks—But how?—that is to be thought on.—Lance
is stout and trusty; and when a bold deed is once resolved upon,
there never yet lacked the means of executing it."

His host now entered, with an apology for his long absence;
and after providing Peveril with some refreshments, invited
him to accept, for his night-quarters, the accommodation of a
remote hayloft, which he was to share with his comrade; professing, at the same time, he could hardly have afforded them
this courtesy, but out of deference to the exquisite talents of
Lance Outram, as assistant at the tap; where, indeed, it seems
probable that he, as well as the admiring landlord, did that
evening contrive to drink nearly as much liquor as they drew.

But Lance was a seasoned vessel, on whom liquor made no
lasting impression; so that when Peveril awaked that trusty
follower at dawn, he found him cool enough to comprehend
and enter into the design which he expressed, of recovering the
letters which had been abstracted from his person.

Having considered the whole matter with much attention,
Lance shrugged, grinned, and scratched his head; and at
length manfully expressed his resolution. "Well, my naunt
speaks truth in her old saw—

> ' He that serves Peveril maunna be slack,
> Neither for weather, nor yet for wrack.'

And then again, my good dame was wont to say, that whenever Peveril was in a broil, Outram was in a stew; so I will
never bear a base mind, but even hold a part with you as my
fathers have done with yours, for four generations, whatever
more."

"Spoken like a most gallant Outram," said Julian; "and were we but rid of that puppy lord and his retinue, we two could easily deal with the other three."

"Two Londoners and a Frenchman?" said Lance,—"I would take them in mine own hand. And as for my Lord Saville, as they call him, I heard word last night that he and all his men of gilded gingerbread—that looked at an honest fellow like me, as if they were the ore and I the dross—are all to be off this morning to some races, or such-like junketings, about Tutbury. It was that brought him down here, where he met this other civet-cat by accident."

In truth, even as Lance spoke, a trampling was heard of horses in the yard; and from the hatch of their hayloft they beheld Lord Saville's attendants mustered, and ready to set out as soon as he should make his appearance.

"So ho, Master Jeremy," said one of the fellows, to a sort of principal attendant, who just came out of the house, "methinks the wine has proved a sleeping cup to my lord this morning."

"No," answered Jeremy, "he hath been up before light writing letters for London; and to punish thy irreverence, thou, Jonathan, shalt be the man to ride back with them."

"And so to miss the race?" said Jonathan sulkily; "I thank you for this good turn, good Master Jeremy; and hang me if I forget it."

Farther discussion was cut short by the appearance of the young nobleman, who, as he came out of the inn, said to Jeremy, "These be the letters. Let one of the knaves ride to London for life and death, and deliver them as directed; and the rest of them get to horse and follow me."

Jeremy gave Jonathan the packet with a malicious smile; and the disappointed groom turned his horse's head sullenly towards London, while Lord Saville, and the rest of his retinue, rode briskly off in an opposite direction, pursued by the benedictions of the host and his family, who stood bowing and courtesying at the door, in gratitude, doubtless, for the receipt of an unconscionable reckoning.

It was not full three hours after their departure, that Chiffinch lounged into the room in which they had supped, in a brocade nightgown, and green velvet cap, turned up with the most costly Brussels lace. He seemed but half awake; and it was with drowsy voice that he called for a cup of cold small beer. His manner and appearance were those of a man who had wrestled hard with Bacchus on the preceding evening, and had scarce recovered the effects of his contest with the joly god. Lance, instructed by his master to watch the motions of the courtier, officiously attended with the cooling beverage he called for, pleading, as an excuse to the landlord, his wish to see a Londoner in his morning-gown and cap.

No sooner had Chiffinch taken his morning draught, than he inquired after Lord Saville.

"His lordship was mounted and away by peep of dawn," was Lance's reply.

"What, the devil!" exclaimed Chiffinch; "why, this is scarce civil.—What! off for the races with his whole retinue?"

"All but one," replied Lance, "whom his lordship sent back to London with letters."

"To London with letters!" said Chiffinch. "Why, I am for London, and could have saved his express a labour.—But stop—hold—I begin to recollect—d——n, can I have blabbed?—I have—I have—I remember it all now—I have blabbed; and to the very weasel of the Court, who sucks the yelk out of every man's secret. Furies and fire—that my afternoons should ruin my mornings thus!—I must turn boon companion and good fellow in my cups—and have my confidences and my quarrels—my friends and my enemies, with a plague to me, as if any one could do a man much good or harm but his own self. His messenger must be stopped, though—I will put a spoke in his wheel. —Hark ye, drawer-fellow—call my groom hither—call Tom Beacon."

Lance obeyed; but failed not, when he had introduced the domestic, to remain in the apartment, in order to hear what should pass betwixt him and his master.

"Hark ye, Tom," said Chiffinch, "here are five pieces for you."

"What's to be done now, I trow?" said Tom, without even the ceremony of returning thanks, which he was probably well aware would not be received even in part payment of the debt he was incurring.

"Mount your fleet nag, Tom—ride like the devil—overtake the groom whom Lord Saville despatched to London this morning—lame his horse—break his bones—fill him as drunk as the Baltic sea; or do whatever may best and most effectually stop his journey.—Why does the lout stand there without answering me? Dost understand me?"

"Why, ay, Master Chiffinch," said Tom; "and so I am thinking doth this honest man here, who need not have heard quite so much of your counsel, an it had been your will."

"I am bewitched this morning," said Chiffinch to himself, "or else the champagne runs in my head still. My brain has become the very lowlands of Holland—a gill-cup would inundate it—Hark thee, fellow," he added, addressing Lance, "keep my counsel—there is a wager betwixt Lord Saville and me, which of us shall first have a letter in London. Here is to drink my health, and bring luck on my side. Say nothing of it; but

PEVERIL AND CHIFFINCH

Etching by Cruikshank

help Tom to his nag.—Tom, ere thou startest come for thy credentials—I will give thee a letter to the Duke of Bucks, that may be evidence thou wert first in town."

Tom Beacon ducked and exit; and Lance, after having made some show of helping him to horse, ran back to tell his master the joyful intelligence, that a lucky accident had abated Chiffinch's party to their own number.

Peveril immediately ordered his horses to be got ready; and, so soon as Tom Beacon was despatched towards London, on a rapid trot, had the satisfaction to observe Chiffinch, with his favourite Chaubert, mount to pursue the same journey, though at a more moderate rate. He permitted them to attain such a distance, that they might be dogged without suspicion; then paid his reckoning, mounted his horse, and followed, keeping his men carefully in view, until he should come to a place proper for the enterprise which he meditated.

It had been Peveril's intention, that when they came to some solitary part of the road, they should gradually mend their pace, until they overtook Chaubert—that Lance Outram should then drop behind, in order to assail the man of spits and stoves, while he himself, spurring onwards, should grapple with Chiffinch. But this scheme presupposed that the master and servant should travel in the usual manner—the latter riding a few yards behind the former. Whereas, such and so interesting were the subjects of discussion betwixt Chiffinch and the French cook, that, without heeding the rules of etiquette, they rode on together, amicably abreast, carrying on a conversation on the mysteries of the table, which the ancient Comus, or a modern gastronome, might have listened to with pleasure. It was therefore necessary to venture on them both at once.

For this purpose, when they saw a long tract of road before them, unvaried by the least appearance of man, beast, or human habitation, they began to mend their pace, that they might come up to Chiffinch, without giving him any alarm, by a sudden and suspicious increase of haste. In this manner they lessened the distance which separated them till they were within about twenty yards, when Peveril, afraid that Chiffinch might recognise him at a nearer approach, and so trust to his horse's heels, made Lance the signal to charge.

At the sudden increase of their speed, and the noise with which it was necessarily attended, Chiffinch looked around, but had time to do no more, for Lance, who had pricked his pony (which was much more speedy than Julian's horse) into full gallop, pushed, without ceremony, betwixt the courtier and his attendant; and ere Chaubert had time for more than one exclamation, he upset both horse and Frenchman,—*mortbleu!* thrilling from his tongue as he rolled on the ground amongst the various articles of his occupation, which, escaping from the budget in which he bore them, lay tumbled upon the highway in strange disorder; while Lance, springing from his palfrey, commanded his foeman to be still, under no less a penalty than that of death, if he attempted to rise.

Before Chiffinch could avenge his trusty follower's downfall, his own bridle was seized by Julian, who presented a pistol with the other hand, and commanded him to stand or die.

Chiffinch, though effeminate, was no coward. He stood still as commanded, and said, with firmness, "Rogue, you have taken me at surprise. If you are highwaymen, there is my purse. Do us no bodily harm, and spare the budget of spices and sauces."

"Look you, Master Chiffinch," said Peveril, "this is no time for dallying. I am no highwayman, but a man of honour. Give me back that packet which you stole from me the other night; or, by all that is good, I will send a brace of balls through you, and search for it at leisure."

"What night?—What packet?" answered Chiffinch, confused; yet willing to protract the time for the chance of assistance, or to put Peveril off his guard. "I know nothing of what you mean. If you are a man of honour, let me draw my sword, and I will do you right, as a gentleman should do to another."

"Dishonourable rascal!" said Peveril, "you escape not in this manner. You plundered me when you had me at odds; and I am not the fool to let my advantage escape, now that my turn is come. Yield up the packet; and then, if you will, I will fight you on equal terms. But first," he reiterated, "yield up the packet, or I will instantly send you where the tenor of your life will be hard to answer for."

The tone of Peveril's voice, the fierceness of his eye, and the manner in which he held the loaded weapon, within a hand's-breadth of Chiffinch's head, convinced the last there was neither room for compromise, nor time for trifling. He thrust his hand into a side pocket of his cloak, and with visible reluctance, produced those papers and despatches with which Julian had been entrusted by the Countess of Derby.

"They are five in number," said Julian; "and you have given me only four. Your life depends on full restitution."

"It escaped from my hand," said Chiffinch, producing the missing document—"There it is. Now, sir, your pleasure is fulfilled, unless," he added sulkily, "you design either murder or farther robbery."

"Base wretch!" said Peveril, withdrawing his pistol, yet keeping a watchful eye on Chiffinch's motions, "thou art unworthy any honest man's sword; and yet, if you dare draw your

wn, as you proposed but now, I am willing to give you a chance
pon fair equality of terms."

"Equality!" said Chiffinch sneeringly; "yes, a proper
quality—sword and pistol against single rapier, and two men
pon one, for Chaubert is no fighter. No, sir; I shall seek
mends upon some more fitting occasion, and with more equal
eapons."

"By backbiting, or by poison, base pander!" said Julian;
these are thy means of vengeance. But mark me—I know
our vile purpose respecting a lady who is too worthy that her
ame should be uttered in such a worthless ear. Thou hast
one me one injury, and thou see'st I have repaid it. But
rosecute this farther villainy, and be assured I will put thee
 death like a foul reptile, whose very slaver is fatal to
umanity. Rely upon this, as if Machiavel had sworn it; for
 surely as you keep your purpose, so surely will I prosecute
ly revenge.—Follow me, Lance, and leave him to think on
vhat I have told him."

Lance had, after the first shock, sustained a very easy part in
his rencontre; for all he had to do, was to point the butt of his
vhip, in the manner of a gun, at the intimidated Frenchman,
vho, lying on his back, and gazing at random on the skies, had
s little the power or purpose of resistance, as any pig which had
ver come under his own slaughter-knife.

Summoned by his master from the easy duty of guarding
uch an unresisting prisoner, Lance remounted his horse, and
hey both rode off, leaving their discomfited antagonists to con-
ole themselves for their misadventure as they best could. But
onsolation was hard to come by in the circumstances. The
'rench artist had to lament the dispersion of his spices, and
he destruction of his magazine of sauces—an enchanter de-
poiled of his magic wand and talisman, could scarce have been
n more desperate extremity. Chiffinch had to mourn the
lownfall of his intrigue, and its premature discovery. "To
his fellow, at least," he thought, "I can have bragged none—
ere my evil genius alone has betrayed me. With this infernal
liscovery, which may cost me so dear on all hands, champagne
ad nought to do. If there be a flask left unbroken, I will
lrink it after dinner, and try if it may not even yet suggest
ome scheme of redemption and of revenge."

With this manly resolution, he prosecuted his journey to
London.

CHAPTER XXVIII

A man so various, that he seem'd to be
Not one, but all mankind's epitome ;
Stiff in opinions—always in the wrong—
Was everything by starts, but nothing long ;
Who, in the course of one revolving moon,
Was chemist, fiddler, statesman, and buffoon ;
Then, all for women, painting, fiddling, drinking ;
Besides a thousand freaks that died in thinking.

—DRYDEN.

WE must now transport the reader to the magnificent hote in —— Street, inhabited at this time by the celebrated Georg Villiers, Duke of Buckingham, whom Dryden has doomed to painful immortality by the few lines which we have prefixed t this chapter. Amid the gay and the licentious of the laughin, Court of Charles, the Duke was the most licentious and mos gay ; yet, while expending a princely fortune, a strong consti tution, and excellent talents, in pursuit of frivolous pleasure he nevertheless nourished deeper and more extensive designs in which he only failed from want of that fixed purpose an regulated perseverance essential to all important enterprises but particularly in politics.

It was long past noon ; and the usual hour of the Duke' levee—if anything could be termed usual where all was irre gular—had been long past. His hall was filled with lackey and footmen, in the most splendid liveries ; the interior apart ments, with the gentlemen and pages of his household, arrayec as persons of the first quality, and, in that respect, rather ex ceeding than falling short of the Duke in personal splendour But his antechamber, in particular, might be compared to ; gathering of eagles to the slaughter, were not the simile too dignified to express that vile race, who, by a hundred device: all tending to one common end, live upon the wants of needy greatness, or administer to the pleasures of summer-teeming luxury, or stimulate the wild wishes of lavish and wastefu1 extravagance, by devising new modes and fresh motives o profusion. There stood the projector, with his mysterious brow, promising unbounded wealth to whomsoever might choose to furnish the small preliminary sum necessary to change egg-shells into the great *arcanum.* There was Captain Seagull, undertaker for a foreign settlement, with the map under his arm of Indian or American kingdoms, beautiful as the primitive Eden, waiting the bold occupants, for whom a generous patron should equip two brigantines and a fly-boat. Thither came, fast and frequent, the gamesters, in their different forms and alling. This, light, young, gay in appearance, the thoughtless outh of wit and pleasure—the pigeon rather than the rook— ut at heart the same sly, shrewd, cold-blooded calculator, as onder old hard-featured professor of the same science, whose yes are grown dim with watching the dice at midnight; and whose fingers are even now assisting his mental computation f chances and of odds. The fine arts, too—I would it were therwise—have their professors amongst this sordid train. The oor poet, half ashamed, in spite of habit, of the part which he s about to perform, and abashed by consciousness at once of is base motive and his shabby black coat, lurks in yonder orner for the favourable moment to offer his dedication. Much etter attired, the architect presents his splendid vision of front nd wings, and designs a palace, the expense of which may ransfer his employer to a jail. But uppermost of all, the avourite musician, or singer, who waits on my lord to receive, n solid gold, the value of the dulcet sounds which solaced the anquet of the preceding evening.

Such, and many such like, were the morning attendants of he Duke of Buckingham — all genuine descendants of the aughter of the horse-leech, whose cry is "Give, give."

But the levee of his Grace contained other and very different haracters; and was indeed as various as his own opinions and ursuits. Besides many of the young nobility and wealthy entry of England, who made his Grace the glass at which hey dressed themselves for the day, and who learned from him ow to travel, with the newest and best grace, the general Road o Ruin; there were others of a graver character—discarded tatesmen, political spies, opposition orators, servile tools of dministration, men who met not elsewhere, but who regarded he Duke's mansion as a sort of neutral ground; sure, that if e was not of their opinion to-day, this very circumstance endered it most likely he should think with them to-morrow. The Puritans themselves did not shun intercourse with a man whose talents must have rendered him formidable, even if they ad not been united with high rank and an immense fortune. Several grave personages, with black suits, short cloaks, and and-strings of a formal cut, were mingled, as we see their ortraits in a gallery of paintings, among the gallants who uffled in silk and embroidery. It is true, they escaped the candal of being thought intimates of the Duke, by their busi- ess being supposed to refer to money matters. Whether these rave and professing citizens mixed politics with money lend- ng, was not known; but it had been long observed, that the Jews, who in general confine themselves to the latter depart- ment, had become for some time faithful attendants at the Duke's levee.

It was high-tide in the antechamber, and had been so fo
more than an hour, ere the Duke's gentleman-in-ordinar
ventured into his bedchamber, carefully darkened, so as t
make midnight at noonday, to know his Grace's pleasure
His soft and serene whisper, in which he asked whether i
were his Grace's pleasure to rise, was briefly and sharpl
answered by the counter questions, " Who waits ?—What
o'clock ? "

" It is Jerningham, your Grace," said the attendant. " It i
one, afternoon ; and your Grace appointed some of the peopl
without at eleven."

" Who are they ?—What do they want ? "

" A message from Whitehall, your Grace."

" Pshaw ! it will keep cold. Those who make all other
wait, will be the better of waiting in their turn. Were I t
be guilty of ill-breeding, it should rather be to a king than i
beggar."

" The gentlemen from the city."

" I am tired of them—tired of their all cant, and no religio
—all Protestantism, and no charity. Tell them to go to Shaftes
bury—to Aldersgate Street with them—that's the best marke
for their wares."

" Jockey, my lord, from Newmarket."

" Let him ride to the devil—he has horse of mine, and spur
of his own. Any more ? "

" The whole antechamber is full, my lord—knights anc
squires, doctors and dicers."

" The dicers, with their doctors * in their pockets, I presume.
" Counts, captains, and clergymen."

" You are alliterative, Jerningham," said the Duke ; " anc
that is a proof you are poetical. Hand me my writing things."

Getting half out of bed—thrusting one arm into a brocade
nightgown, deeply furred with sables, and one foot into i
velvet slipper, while the other pressed in primitive nudity the
rich carpet—his Grace, without thinking farther on the assembly
without, began to pen a few lines of a satirical poem ; then
suddenly stopped—threw the pen into the chimney—exclaimec
that the humour was past—and asked his attendant if there
were any letters. Jerningham produced a huge packet.

" What the devil ! " said his Grace, " do you think I will read
all these ? I am like Clarence, who asked a cup of wine, and
was soused into a butt of sack. I mean, is there anything
which presses ? "

" This letter, your Grace," said Jerningham, " concerning
the Yorkshire mortgage."

" Did I not bid thee carry it to old Gatheral, my steward ? "

* Doctor, a cant name for false dice.

"I did, my lord," answered the other; "but Gatheral says there are difficulties."

"Let the usurers foreclose, then—there is no difficulty in that; and out of a hundred manors I shall scarce miss one," answered the Duke. "And hark ye, bring me my chocolate."

"Nay, my lord, Gatheral does not say it is impossible—only difficult."

"And what is the use of him, if he cannot make it easy? But you are all born to make difficulties," replied the Duke.

"Nay, if your Grace approves the terms in this schedule, and pleases to sign it, Gatheral will undertake for the matter," answered Jerningham.

"And could you not have said so at first, you blockhead?" said the Duke, signing the paper without looking at the contents—"What other letters? And remember, I must be plagued with no more business."

"Billets-doux, my lord—five or six of them. This left at the porter's lodge by a vizard mask."

"Pshaw!" answered the Duke, tossing them over, while his attendant assisted in dressing him—"an acquaintance of a quarter's standing."

"This given to one of the pages by my Lady ——'s waiting-woman."

"Plague on it—a Jeremiade on the subject of perjury and treachery, and not a single new line to the old tune," said the Duke, glancing over the billet. "Here is the old cant—*cruel man—broken vows—Heaven's just revenge.* Why, the woman is thinking of murder—not of love. No one should pretend to write upon so threadbare a topic without having at least some novelty of expression. *The despairing Araminta*—Lie there, fair desperate. And this—how comes it?"

"Flung into the window of the hall, by a fellow who ran off at full speed," answered Jerningham.

"This is a better text," said the Duke; "and yet it is an old one too—three weeks old at least—The little Countess with the jealous lord—I should not care a farthing for her, save for that same jealous lord—Plague on't, and he's gone down to the country—*this evening—in silence and safety—written with a quill pulled from the wing of Cupid*—Your ladyship has left him pen-feathers enough to fly away with—better clipped his wings when you had caught him, my lady—And *so confident of her Buckingham's faith,*—I hate confidence in a young person. She must be taught better—I will not go."

"Your Grace will not be so cruel!" said Jerningham.

"Thou art a compassionate fellow, Jerningham; but conceit must be punished."

"But if your lordship should resume your fancy for her?"

"Why, then, you must swear the billet-doux miscarried," answered the Duke. "And stay, a thought strikes me—it shall miscarry in great style. Hark ye—Is—what is the fellow's name—the poet—is he yonder?"

"There are six gentlemen, sir, who, from the reams of paper in their pocket, and the threadbare seams at their elbows, appear to wear the livery of the Muses."

"Poetical once more, Jerningham. He, I mean, who wrote the last lampoon," said the Duke.

"To whom your Grace said you owed five pieces and a beating!" replied Jerningham.

"The money for his satire, and the cudgel for his praise—Good—find him—give him the five pieces, and thrust the Countess's billet-doux—Hold—take Araminta's and the rest of them—thrust them all into his portfolio—All will come out at the Wit's Coffee-house; and if the promulgator be not cudgelled into all the colours of the rainbow, there is no spite in woman, no faith in crabtree, or pith in heart of oak—Araminta's wrath alone would overburden one pair of mortal shoulders."

"But, my Lord Duke," said his attendant, "this Settle * is so dull a rascal, that nothing he can write will take."

"Then as we have given him steel to head the arrow," said the Duke, "we will give him wings to waft it with—wood, he has enough of his own to make a shaft or bolt of. Hand me my own unfinished lampoon—give it to him with the letters—let him make what he can of them all."

"My Lord Duke—I crave pardon—but your Grace's style will be discovered; and though the ladies' names are not at the letters, yet they will be traced."

"I would have it so, you blockhead. Have you lived with me so long, and cannot discover that the éclat of an intrigue is, with me, worth all the rest of it?"

"But the danger, my Lord Duke?" replied Jerningham. "There are husbands, brothers, friends, whose revenge may be awakened."

"And beaten to sleep again," said Buckingham haughtily. "I have Black Will and his cudgel for plebeian grumblers; and those of quality I can deal with myself. I lack breathing and exercise of late."

"But yet your Grace——"

"Hold your peace, fool! I tell you that your poor dwarfish spirit cannot measure the scope of mine. I tell thee I would have the course of my life a torrent—I am weary of easy

* Elkana Settle, the unworthy scribbler whom the envy of Rochester and others tried to raise to public estimation, as a rival to Dryden ; a circumstance which has been the means of elevating him to a very painful species of immortality.

achievements, and wish for obstacles, that I can sweep before my irresistible course."

Another gentleman now entered the apartment. "I humbly crave your Grace's pardon," he said; "but Master Christian is so importunate for admission instantly, that I am obliged to take your Grace's pleasure."

"Tell him to call three hours hence. Damn his politic pate, that would make all men dance after his pipe!"

"I thank thee for the compliment, my Lord Duke," said Christian, entering the apartment in somewhat a more courtly garb, but with the same unpretending and undistinguished mien, and in the same placid and indifferent manner with which he had accosted Julian Peveril upon different occasions during his journey to London. "It is precisely my present object to pipe to you; and you may dance to your own profit, if you will."

"On my word, Master Christian," said the Duke haughtily, "the affair should be weighty, that removes ceremony so entirely from betwixt us. If it relates to the subject of our last conversation, I must request our interview be postponed to some farther opportunity. I am engaged in an affair of some weight." Then turning his back on Christian, he went on with his conversation with Jerningham. "Find the person you wot of, and give him the papers; and hark ye, give him this gold to pay for the shaft of his arrow—the steel-head and peacock's wing we have already provided."

"This is all well, my lord," said Christian calmly, and taking his seat at the same time in an easy-chair at some distance; "but your Grace's levity is no match for my equanimity. It is necessary I should speak with you; and I will await your Grace's leisure in the apartment."

"*Very well*, sir," said the Duke peevishly; "if an evil is to be undergone, the sooner it is over the better—I can take measures to prevent its being renewed. So let me hear your errand without farther delay."

"I will wait till your Grace's toilette is completed," said Christian, with the indifferent tone which was natural to him. "What I have to say must be between ourselves."

"Begone, Jerningham; and remain without till I call. Leave my doublet on the couch.—How now, I have worn this cloth of silver a hundred times."

"Only twice, if it please your Grace," replied Jerningham.

"As well twenty times—keep it for yourself, or give it to my valet, if you are too proud of your gentility."

"Your Grace has made better men than me wear your cast clothes," said Jerningham submissively.

"Thou art sharp, Jerningham," said the Duke—"in one sense I have, and I may again. So now, that pearl-coloured

т

thing will do with the ribbon and George. Get away with thee.
—And now that he is gone, Master Christian, may I once more
crave your pleasure?"

"My Lord Duke," said Christian, "you are a worshipper of
difficulties in state affairs, as in love matters."

"I trust you have been no eavesdropper, Master Christian,"
replied the Duke; "it scarce argues the respect due to me, or
to my roof."

"I know not what you mean, my lord," replied Christian.

"Nay, I care not if the whole world heard what I said but
now to Jerningham. But to the matter," replied the Duke of
Buckingham.

"Your Grace is so much occupied with conquests over the
fair and over the witty, that you have perhaps forgotten what
a stake you have in the little Island of Man."

"Not a whit, Master Christian. I remember well enough
that my roundheaded father-in-law, Fairfax, had the island
from the Long Parliament; and was ass enough to quit hold
of it at the Restoration, when, if he had closed his clutches,
and held fast, like a true bird of prey, as he should have done,
he might have kept it for him and his. It had been a rare
thing to have had a little kingdom—made laws of my own—
had my Chamberlain with his white staff—I would have taught
Jerningham, in half a day, to look as wise, walk as stiffly, and
speak as sillily, as Harry Bennet."

"You might have done this, and more, if it had pleased
your Grace."

"Ay, and if it had pleased my Grace, thou, Ned Christian,
shouldst have been the Jack Ketch of my dominions."

"*I* your Jack Ketch, my lord?" said Christian, more in a
tone of surprise than of displeasure.

"Why, ay; thou hast been perpetually intriguing against the
life of yonder poor old woman. It were a kingdom to thee to
gratify thy spleen with thy own hands."

"I only seek justice against the Countess," said Christian.

"And the end of justice is always a gibbet," said the
Duke.

"Be it so," answered Christian. "Well, the Countess is in
the Plot."

"The devil confound the Plot, as I believe he first invented
it!" said the Duke of Buckingham; "I have heard of nothing
else for months. If one must go to hell, I would it were by
some new road, and in gentlemen's company. I should not
like to travel with Oates, Bedlow, and the rest of that famous
cloud of witnesses."

"Your Grace is then resolved to forego all the advantages
which may arise? If the House of Derby fall under forfeiture,

the grant to Fairfax, now worthily represented by your Duchess, revives, and you become the Lord and Sovereign of Man."

"In right of a woman," said the Duke; "but, in troth, my godly dame owes me some advantage for having lived the first year of our marriage with her and old Black Tom, her grim, fighting, puritanic father. A man might as well have married the Devil's daughter, and set up housekeeping with his father-in-law." *

"I understand you are willing, then, to join your interest for a heave at the House of Derby, my Lord Duke?"

"As they are unlawfully possessed of my wife's kingdom, they certainly can expect no favour at my hand. But thou knowest there is an interest at Whitehall predominant over mine."

"That is only by your Grace's sufferance," said Christian.

"No, no; I tell thee a hundred times, no," said the Duke, rousing himself to anger at the recollection. "I tell thee that base courtezan, the Duchess of Portsmouth, hath impudently set herself to thwart and contradict me; and Charles has given me both cloudy looks and hard words before the Court. I would he could but guess what is the offence between her and me! I would he knew but that! But I will have her plumes picked, or my name is not Villiers. A worthless French fille-de-joie to brave me thus!—Christian, thou art right; there is no passion so spirit-stirring as revenge. I will patronise the Plot, if it be but to spite her, and make it impossible for the King to uphold her."

As the Duke spoke, he gradually wrought himself into a passion, and traversed the apartment with as much vehemence as if the only object he had on earth was to deprive the Duchess of her power and favour with the King. Christian smiled internally to see him approach the state of mind in which he was most easily worked upon, and judiciously kept silence, until the Duke called out to him, in a pet, "Well, Sir Oracle, you that have laid so many schemes to supplant this she-wolf of Gaul, where are all your contrivances now?—Where is the exquisite beauty who was to catch the Sovereign's eye at the first glance?—Chiffinch, hath he seen her?—and what does he say, that exquisite critic in beauty and blanc-mange, women and wine?"

"He has *seen* and approves, but has not yet heard her; and her speech answers to all the rest. We came here yesterday; and to-day I intend to introduce Chiffinch to her, the instant

* Mary, daughter of Thomas, Lord Fairfax, was wedded to the Duke of Buckingham, whose versatility made him capable of rendering himself for a time as agreeable to his father-in-law, though a rigid Presbyterian, as to the gay Charles II.

he arrives from the country; and I expect him every hour. I am but afraid of the damsel's peevish virtue, for she hath been brought up after the fashion of our grandmothers—our mothers had better sense."

"What! so fair, so young, so quick-witted, and so difficult?" said the Duke. "By your leave, you shall introduce me as well as Chiffinch."

"That your Grace may cure her of her intractable modesty?" said Christian.

"Why," replied the Duke, "it will but teach her to stand in her own light. Kings do not love to court and sue; they should have their game run down for them."

"Under your Grace's favour," said Christian, "this cannot be —*Non omnibus dormio*—Your Grace knows the classic allusion. If this maiden become a Prince's favourite, rank gilds the shame and the sin. But to any under Majesty, she must not vail topsail."

"Why, thou suspicious fool, I was but in jest," said the Duke. "Do you think I would interfere to spoil a plan so much to my own advantage as that which you have laid before me?"

Christian smiled and shook his head. "My lord," he said, "I know your Grace as well, or better, perhaps, than you know yourself. To spoil a well-concerted intrigue by some cross stroke of your own, would give you more pleasure, than to bring it to a successful termination according to the plans of others. But Shaftesbury, and all concerned, have determined that our scheme shall at least have fair play. We reckon, therefore, on your help; and—forgive me when I say so—we will not permit ourselves to be impeded by your levity and fickleness of purpose."

"Who?—I light and fickle of purpose?" said the Duke. "You see me here as resolved as any of you, to dispossess the mistress, and to carry on the plot; these are the only two things I live for in this world. No one can play the man of business like me, when I please, to the very filing and labelling of my letters. I am regular as a scrivener."

"You have Chiffinch's letter from the country; he told me he had written to you about some passages betwixt him and the young Lord Saville."

"He did so—he did so," said the Duke, looking among his letters; "but I see not his letter just now—I scarcely noted the contents—I was busy when it came—but I have it safely."

"You should have acted on it," answered Christian. "The fool suffered himself to be choused out of his secret, and prayed you to see that my lord's messenger got not to the Duchess with some despatches which he sent up from Derbyshire, betraying our mystery."

The Duke was now alarmed, and rang the bell hastily. Jerningham appeared. "Where is the letter I had from Master Chiffinch some hours since?"

"If it be not amongst those your Grace has before you, I know nothing of it," said Jerningham. "I saw none such arrive."

"You lie, you rascal," said Buckingham; "have you a right to remember better than I do?"

"If your Grace will forgive me reminding you, you have scarce opened a letter this week," said his gentleman.

"Did you ever hear such a provoking rascal?" said the Duke. "He might be a witness in the Plot. He has knocked my character for regularity entirely on the head with his damned counter-evidence."

"Your Grace's talent and capacity will at least remain unimpeached," said Christian; "and it is those that must serve yourself and your friends. If I might advise, you will hasten to Court, and lay some foundation for the impression we wish to make. If your Grace can take the first word, and throw out a hint to crossbite Saville, it will be well. But above all, keep the King's ear employed, which no one can do so well as you. Leave Chiffinch to fill his heart with a proper object. Another thing is, there is a blockhead of an old Cavalier, who must needs be a bustler in the Countess of Derby's behalf—he is fast in hold, with the whole tribe of witnesses at his haunches."

"Nay, then, take him, Topham."

"Topham has taken him already, my lord," said Christian; "and there is, besides, a young gallant, a son of the said Knight, who was bred in the household of the Countess of Derby, and who has brought letters from her to the Provincial of the Jesuits, and others in London."

"What are their names?" said the Duke dryly.

"Sir Geoffrey Peveril of Martindale Castle, in Derbyshire, and his son Julian."

"What! Peveril of the Peak?" said the Duke,—"a stout old Cavalier as ever swore an oath.—A Worcester-man, too—and, in truth, a man of all work, when blows were going. I will not consent to his ruin, Christian. These fellows must be flogged off such false scents—flogged in every sense, they must, and will be, when the nation comes to its eyesight again."

"It is of more than the last importance, in the meantime, to the furtherance of our plan," said Christian, "that your Grace should stand for a space between them and the King's favour. The youth hath influence with the maiden, which we should find scarce favourable to our views; besides, her father holds him as high as he can any one who is no such puritanic fool as himself."

"Well, most Christian Christian," said the Duke, "I have heard your commands at length. I will endeavour to stop the earths under the throne, that neither the lord, knight, nor squire in question, shall find it possible to burrow there. For the fair one, I must leave Chiffinch and you to manage her introduction to her high destinies, since I am not to be trusted. Adieu, most Christian Christian."

He fixed his eyes on him, and then exclaimed, as he shut the door of the apartment,—"Most profligate and damnable villain! And what provokes me most of all, is the knave's composed insolence. Your Grace will do this—and your Grace will condescend to do that—A pretty puppet I should be, to play the second part, or rather the third, in such a scheme! No, they shall all walk according to my purpose, or I will cross them. I will find this girl out in spite of them, and judge if their scheme is likely to be successful. If so, she shall be mine—mine entirely, before she becomes the King's; and I will command her who is to guide Charles.—Jerningham" (his gentleman entered), "cause Christian to be dogged wherever he goes, for the next four-and-twenty hours, and find out where he visits a female newly come to town.—You smile, you knave?"

"I did but suspect a fresh rival to Araminta and the little Countess," said Jerningham.

"Away to your business, knave," said the Duke, "and let me think of mine.—To subdue a Puritan in Esse—a King's favourite in Posse—the very muster of western beauties—that is point first. The impudence of this Manx mongrel to be corrected—the pride of Madame la Duchesse to be pulled down —an important state intrigue to be farthered, or baffled, as circumstances render most to my own honour and glory—I wished for business but now, and I have got enough of it. But Buckingham will keep his own steerage-way through shoal and through weather."

CHAPTER XXIX

——Mark you this, Bassanio—
The devil can quote Scripture for his purpose.
—MERCHANT OF VENICE.

AFTER leaving the proud mansion of the Duke of Buckingham, Christian, full of the deep and treacherous schemes which he meditated, hastened to the city, where, in a decent inn, kept by a person of his own persuasion, he had been unexpectedly summoned to meet with Ralph Bridgenorth of Moultrassie.

He was not disappointed—the Major had arrived that morning, and anxiously expected him. The usual gloom of his countenance was darkened into a yet deeper shade of anxiety, which was scarcely relieved, even while, in answer to his inquiry after his daughter, Christian gave the most favourable account of her health and spirits, naturally and unaffectedly intermingled with such praises of her beauty and her disposition, as were likely to be most grateful to a father's ear.

But Christian had too much cunning to expatiate on this theme, however soothing. He stopped short exactly at the point where, as an affectionate relative, he might be supposed to have said enough. "The lady," he said, "with whom he had placed Alice, was delighted with her aspect and manners, and undertook to be responsible for her health and happiness. He had not, he said, deserved so little confidence at the hand of his brother, Bridgenorth, as that the Major should, contrary to his purpose, and to the plan which they had adjusted together, have hurried up from the country, as if his own presence were necessary for Alice's protection."

"Brother Christian," said Bridgenorth in reply, "I must see my child—I must see this person with whom she is entrusted."

"To what purpose?" answered Christian. "Have you not often confessed that the over excess of the carnal affection which you have entertained for your daughter, hath been a snare to you?—Have you not, more than once, been on the point of resigning those great designs which should place righteousness as a counsellor beside the throne, because you desired to gratify your daughter's girlish passion for this descendant of your old persecutor—this Julian Peveril?"

"I own it," said Bridgenorth; "and worlds would I have given, and would yet give, to clasp that youth to my bosom, and call him my son. The spirit of his mother looks from his eye, and his stately step is as that of his father, when he daily spoke comfort to me in my distress, and said, 'The child liveth.'"

"But the youth walks," said Christian, "after his own lights, and mistakes the meteor of the marsh for the Polar star. Ralph Bridgenorth, I will speak to thee in friendly sincerity. Thou must not think to serve both the good cause and Baal. Obey, if thou wilt, thine own carnal affections, summon this Julian Peveril to thy house, and let him wed thy daughter— But mark the reception she will meet with from the proud old knight, whose spirit is now, even now, as little broken with his chains, as after the sword of the Saints had prevailed at Worcester. Thou wilt see thy daughter spurned from his feet like an outcast."

"Christian," said Bridgenorth, interrupting him, "thou dost

urge me hard; but thou dost it in love, my brother, and I forgive thee—Alice shall never be spurned.—But this friend of thine—this lady—thou art my child's uncle; and after me, thou art next to her in love and affection—Still, thou art not her father—hast not her father's fears. Art thou sure of the character of this woman to whom my child is entrusted?"

"Am I sure of my own?—Am I sure that my name is Christian—yours Bridgenorth?—Is it a thing I am likely to be insecure in?—Have I not dwelt for many years in this city?—Do I not know this Court?—And am I likely to be imposed upon? For I will not think you can fear my imposing upon you."

"Thou art my brother," said Bridgenorth—"the blood and bone of my departed Saint—and I am determined that I will trust thee in this matter."

"Thou dost well," said Christian; "and who knows what reward may be in store for thee?—I cannot look upon Alice, but it is strongly borne in on my mind, that there will be work for a creature so excellent beyond ordinary women. Courageous Judith freed Bethulia by her valour, and the comely features of Esther made her a safeguard and a defence to her people in the land of captivity, when she found favour in the sight of King Ahasuerus."

"Be it with her as Heaven wills," said Bridgenorth; "and now tell me what progress there is in the great work."

"The people are weary of the iniquity of this Court," said Christian; "and if this man will continue to reign, it must be by calling to his councils men of another stamp. The alarm excited by the damnable practices of the Papists has called up men's souls, and awakened their eyes to the dangers of their state.—He himself—for he will give up brother and wife to save himself— is not averse to a change of measures; and though we cannot at first see the Court purged as with a winnowing fan, yet there will be enough of the good to control the bad—enough of the sober party to compel the grant of that universal toleration, for which we have sighed so long, as a maiden for her beloved. Time and opportunity will lead the way to more thorough reformation; and that will be done without stroke of sword, which our friends failed to establish on a sure foundation, even when their victorious blades were in their hands."

"May God grant it!" said Bridgenorth; "for I fear me I should scruple to do aught which should once more unsheath the civil sword; but welcome all that comes in a peaceful and parliamentary way."

"Ay," said Christian, "and which will bring with it the bitter amends, which our enemies have so long merited at our hands. How long hath our brother's blood cried for vengeance from the altar !—Now shall that cruel Frenchwoman find that neither lapse of years, nor her powerful friends, nor the name of Stanley, nor the Sovereignty of Man, shall stop the stern course of the pursuer of blood. Her name shall be struck from the noble, and her heritage shall another take."

"Nay, but, brother Christian," said Bridgenorth, "art thou not over eager in pursuing this thing?—It is thy duty as a Christian to forgive thine enemies."

"Ay, but not the enemies of Heaven—not those who shed the blood of the saints," said Christian, his eyes kindling with that vehement and fiery expression which at times gave to his uninteresting countenance the only character of passion which it ever exhibited. "No, Bridgenorth," he continued, "I esteem this purpose of revenge holy—I account it a propitiatory sacrifice for what may have been evil in my life. I have submitted to be spurned by the haughty—I have humbled myself to be as a servant; but in my breast was the proud thought, I who do this—do it that I may avenge my brother's blood."

"Still, my brother," said Bridgenorth, "although I participate thy purpose, and have aided thee against this Moabitish woman, I cannot but think thy revenge is more after the law of Moses than after the law of love."

"This comes well from thee, Ralph Bridgenorth," answered Christian; "from thee, who hast just smiled over the downfall of thine own enemy."

"If you mean Sir Geoffrey Peveril," said Bridgenorth, "I smile not on his ruin. It is well he is abased; but if it lies with me, I may humble his pride, but will never ruin his house."

"You know your purpose best," said Christian; "and I do justice, brother Bridgenorth, to the purity of your principles; but men who see with but worldly eyes, would discern little purpose of mercy in the strict magistrate and severe creditor—and such have you been to Peveril."

"And, brother Christian," said Bridgenorth, his colour rising as he spoke, "neither do I doubt your purpose, nor deny the surprising address with which you have procured such perfect information concerning the purposes of yonder woman of Ammon. But it is free to me to think, that in your intercourse with the Court, and with courtiers, you may, in your carnal and worldly policy, sink the value of those spiritual gifts, for which you were once so much celebrated among the brethren."

"Do not apprehend it," said Christian, recovering his temper, which had been a little ruffled by the previous discussion. "Let us but work together as heretofore; and I trust each of us shall be found doing the work of a faithful servant to that good old cause for which we have heretofore drawn the sword."

So saying, he took his hat, and bidding Bridgenorth farewell, declared his intention of returning in the evening.

"Fare thee well!" said Bridgenorth; "to that cause wilt thou find me ever a true and devoted adherent. I will act by that counsel of thine, and will not even ask thee—though it may grieve my heart as a parent—with whom, or where, thou hast entrusted my child. I will try to cut off, and cast from me, even my right hand, and my right eye; but for thee, Christian, if thou dost deal otherwise than prudently and honestly in this matter, it is what God and man will require at thy hand."

"Fear not me," said Christian hastily, and left the place, agitated by reflections of no pleasant kind.

"I ought to have persuaded him to return," he said, as he stepped out into the street. "Even his hovering in this neighbourhood may spoil the plan on which depends the rise of my fortunes—ay, and of his child's. Will men say I have ruined her, when I shall have raised her to the dazzling height of the Duchess of Portsmouth, and perhaps made her a mother to a long line of princes? Chiffinch hath vouched for opportunity; and the voluptuary's fortune depends upon his gratifying the taste of his master for variety. If she makes an impression, it must be a deep one; and once seated in his affections, I fear not her being supplanted.—What will her father say? Will he, like a prudent man, put his shame in his pocket, because it is well gilded? or will he think it fitting to make a display of moral wrath and parental frenzy? I fear the latter—He has ever kept too strict a course to admit his conniving at such licence. But what will his anger avail?—I need not be seen in the matter—those who are will care little for the resentment of a country Puritan. And after all, what I am labouring to bring about is best for himself, the wench, and above all, for me, Edward Christian."

With such base opiates did this unhappy wretch stifle his own conscience, while anticipating the disgrace of his friend's family, and the ruin of a near relative, committed in confidence to his charge. The character of this man was of no common description; nor was it by an ordinary road that he had arrived at the present climax of unfeeling and infamous selfishness.

Edward Christian, as the reader is aware, was the brother of that William Christian, who was the principal instrument in delivering up the Isle of Man to the Republic, and who became the victim of the Countess of Derby's revenge on that account. Both had been educated as Puritans, but William was a soldier, which somewhat modified the strictness of his religious opinions; Edward, a civilian, seemed to entertain these principles in the utmost rigour. But it was only seeming. The exactness of deportment, which procured him great honour and influence among the *sober party*, as they were wont to term themselves, covered a voluptuous disposition, the gratification of which was sweet to him as stolen waters, and pleasant as bread eaten in secret. While, therefore, his seeming godliness brought him worldly gain, his secret pleasures compensated for his outward austerity; until the Restoration, and the Countess's violent proceedings against his brother interrupted the course of both. He then fled from his native island, burning with the desire of revenging his brother's death—the only passion foreign to his own gratification which he was ever known to cherish, and which was also, at least, partly selfish, since it concerned the restoration of his own fortunes.

He found easy access to Villiers, Duke of Buckingham, who, in right of his Duchess, claimed such of the Derby estate as had been bestowed by the Parliament on his celebrated father-in-law, Lord Fairfax. His influence at the Court of Charles, where a jest was a better plea than a long claim of faithful service, was so successfully exerted, as to contribute greatly to the depression of that loyal and ill-rewarded family. But Buckingham was incapable, even for his own interest, of pursuing the steady course which Christian suggested to him; and his vacillation probably saved the remnant of the large estates of the Earl of Derby.

Meantime, Christian was too useful a follower to be dismissed. From Buckingham, and others of that stamp, he did not affect to conceal the laxity of his morals; but towards the numerous and powerful party to which he belonged, he was able to disguise them by a seeming gravity of exterior, which he never laid aside. Indeed, so wide and absolute was then the distinction betwixt the Court and the city, that a man might have for some time played two several parts, as in two different spheres, without its being discovered in the one that he exhibited himself in a different light in the other. Besides, when a man of talent shows himself an able and useful partisan, his party will continue to protect and accredit him, in spite of conduct the most contradictory to their own principles. Some facts are, in such cases, denied—some are glossed over—and party zeal is permitted to cover at least as many defects as ever doth charity.

Edward Christian had often need of the partial indulgence of his friends; but he experienced it, for he was eminently useful. Buckingham, and other courtiers of the same class, however dissolute in their lives, were desirous of keeping some connection with the Dissenting or Puritanic party, as it was termed; thereby to strengthen themselves against their opponents at Court. In such intrigues, Christian was a notable agent; and at one time had nearly procured an absolute union between a class which professed the most rigid principles of religion and morality, and the latitudinarian courtiers, who set all principle at defiance.

Amidst the vicissitudes of a life of intrigue, during which Buckingham's ambitious schemes, and his own, repeatedly sent him across the Atlantic, it was Edward Christian's boast that he never lost sight of his principal object,—revenge on the Countess of Derby. He maintained a close and intimate correspondence with his native island, so as to be perfectly informed of whatever took place there; and he stimulated, on every favourable opportunity, the cupidity of Buckingham to possess himself of this petty kingdom, by procuring the forfeiture of its present Lord. It was not difficult to keep his patron's wild wishes alive on this topic, for his own mercurial imagination attached particular charms to the idea of becoming a sort of sovereign even in this little island; and he was, like Catiline, as covetous of the property of others, as he was profuse of his own.

But it was not until the pretended discovery of the Papist Plot that the schemes of Christian could be brought to ripen; and then, so odious were the Catholics in the eyes of the credulous people of England, that, upon the accusation of the most infamous of mankind, common informers, the scourings of jails, and the refuse of the whipping-post, the most atrocious charges against persons of the highest rank and fairest character were readily received and credited.

This was a period which Christian did not fail to improve. He drew close his intimacy with Bridgenorth, which had indeed never been interrupted, and readily engaged him in his schemes, which, in the eyes of his brother-in-law, were alike honourable and patriotic. But, while he flattered Bridgenorth with the achieving a complete reformation in the state— checking the profligacy of the Court—relieving the consciences of the Dissenters from the pressures of the penal laws—amending, in fine, the crying grievances of the time—while he showed him also, in prospect, revenge upon the Countess of Derby, and a humbling dispensation on the house of Peveril, from whom Bridgenorth had suffered such indignity, Christian did not neglect, in the meanwhile, to consider how he could best benefit himself by the confidence reposed in him by his unsuspicious relation.

The extreme beauty of Alice Bridgenorth—the great wealth which time and economy had accumulated on her father— pointed her out as a most desirable match to repair the wasted fortunes of some of the followers of the Court; and he flattered himself that he could conduct such a negotiation so as to be in a high degree conducive to his own advantage. He found there would be little difficulty in prevailing on Major Bridgenorth to entrust him with the guardianship of his daughter. That unfortunate gentleman had accustomed himself, from the very period of her birth, to regard the presence of his child as a worldly indulgence too great to be allowed to him; and Christian had little trouble in convincing him that the strong inclination which he felt to bestow her on Julian Peveril, provided he could be brought over to his own political opinions, was a blameable compromise with his more severe principles. Late circumstances had taught him the incapacity and unfitness of Dame Debbitch for the sole charge of so dear a pledge; and he readily and thankfully embraced the kind offer of her maternal uncle, Christian, to place Alice under the protection of a lady of rank in London, whilst he himself was to be engaged in the scenes of bustle and blood, which, in common with all good Protestants, he expected was speedily to take place on a general rising of the Papists, unless prevented by the active and energetic measures of the good people of England. He even confessed his fears, that his partial regard for Alice's happiness might enervate his efforts in behalf of his country; and Christian had little trouble in eliciting from him a promise, that he would forbear to inquire after her for some time.

Thus certain of being the temporary guardian of his niece for a space long enough, he flattered himself, for the execution of his purpose, Christian endeavoured to pave the way by consulting Chiffinch, whose known skill in Court policy qualified him best as an adviser on this occasion. But this worthy person, being, in fact, a purveyor for his Majesty's pleasures, and on that account high in his good graces, thought it fell within the line of his duty to suggest another scheme than that on which Christian consulted him. A woman of such exquisite beauty as Alice was described, he deemed more worthy to be a partaker of the affections of the merry Monarch, whose taste in female beauty was so exquisite, than to be made the wife of some worn-out prodigal of quality. And then, doing perfect justice to his own character, he felt it would not be one whit impaired, while his fortune would be, in every respect, greatly amended, if, after sharing the short reign of the Gwyns, the Davises, the Robertses, and so forth, Alice Bridgenorth should retire from the state of a royal favourite, into the humble condition of Mrs. Chiffinch.

After cautiously sounding Christian, and finding that the near prospect of interest to himself effectually prevented his starting at this iniquitous scheme, Chiffinch detailed it to him fully, carefully keeping the final termination out of sight, and talking of the favour to be acquired by the fair Alice as no passing caprice, but the commencement of a reign as long and absolute as that of the Duchess of Portsmouth, of whose avarice and domineering temper Charles was now understood to be much tired, though the force of habit rendered him unequal to free himself of her yoke.

Thus chalked out, the scene prepared was no longer the intrigue of a Court pander, and a villainous resolution for the ruin of an innocent girl, but became a state intrigue, for the removal of an obnoxious favourite, and the subsequent change of the King's sentiments upon various material points, in which he was at present influenced by the Duchess of Portsmouth. In this light it was exhibited to the Duke of Buckingham, who, either to sustain his character for daring gallantry, or in order to gratify some capricious fancy, had at one time made love to the reigning favourite, and experienced a repulse which he had never forgiven.

But one scheme was too little to occupy the active and enterprising spirit of the Duke. An appendix of the Popish Plot was easily so contrived as to involve the Countess of Derby, who, from character and religion, was precisely the person whom the credulous part of the public were inclined to suppose the likely accomplice of such a conspiracy. Christian and Bridgenorth undertook the perilous commission of attacking her even in her own little kingdom of Man, and had commissions for this purpose, which were only to be produced in case of their scheme taking effect.

It miscarried, as the reader is aware, from the Countess's alert preparations for defence ; and neither Christian nor Bridgenorth held it sound policy to practise openly, even under parliamentary authority, against a lady so little liable to hesitate upon the measures most likely to secure her feudal sovereignty ; wisely considering that even the omnipotence, as it has been somewhat too largely styled, of Parliament, might fail to relieve them from the personal consequences of a failure.

On the continent of Britain, however, no opposition was to be feared ; and so well was Christian acquainted with all the motions in the interior of the Countess's little court, or household, that Peveril would have been arrested the instant he set foot on shore, but for the gale of wind which obliged the vessel, in which he was a passenger, to run for Liverpool. Here Christian, under the name of Ganlesse, unexpectedly met with him, and preserved him from the fangs of the well-breathed witnesses of the Plot, with the purpose of securing his despatches, or, if necessary, his person also, in such a manner as to place him at his own discretion—a narrow and perilous game, which he thought it better, however. to undertake, than to permit these subordinate agents, who were always ready to mutiny against all in league with them, to obtain the credit which they must have done by the seizure of the Countess of Derby's despatches. It was, besides, essential to Buckingham's schemes that these should not pass into the hands of a public officer like Topham, who, however pompous and stupid, was upright and well-intentioned, until they had undergone the revisal of a private committee, where something might have probably been suppressed, even supposing that nothing had been added. In short, Christian, in carrying on his own separate and peculiar intrigue, by the agency of the Great Popish Plot, as it was called, acted just like an engineer, who derives the principle of motion which turns his machinery, by means of a steam-engine, or large water-wheel, constructed to drive a separate and larger engine. Accordingly, he was determined that, while he took all the advantage he could from their supposed discoveries, no one should be admitted to tamper or interfere with his own plans of profit and revenge.

Chiffinch, who, desirous of satisfying himself with his own eyes of that excellent beauty which had been so highly extolled, had gone down to Derbyshire on purpose, was infinitely delighted, when, during the course of a two hours' sermon at the dissenting chapel in Liverpool, which afforded him ample leisure for a deliberate survey, he arrived at the conclusion that he had never seen a form or face more captivating. His eyes having confirmed what was told him, he hurried back to the little inn which formed their place of rendezvous, and there awaited Christian and his niece, with a degree of confidence in the success of their project which he had not before entertained; and with an apparatus of luxury, calculated, as he thought, to make a favourable impression on the mind of a rustic girl. He was somewhat surprised, when, instead of Alice Bridgenorth, to whom he expected that night to have been introduced, he found that Christian was accompanied by Julian Peveril. It was indeed a severe disappointment, for he had prevailed on his own indolence to venture thus far from the Court, in order that he might judge, with his own paramount taste, whether Alice was really the prodigy which her uncle's praises had bespoken her, and, as such, a victim worthy of the fate to which she was destined.

A few words betwixt the worthy confederates determined them on the plan of stripping Peveril of the Countess's despatches; Chiffinch absolutely refusing to take any share in arresting him, as a matter of which his Master's approbation might be very uncertain.

Christian had also his own reasons for abstaining from so decisive a step. It was by no means likely to be agreeable to

Bridgenorth, whom it was necessary to keep in good humour;
—it was not necessary, for the Countess's despatches were of
far more importance than the person of Julian. Lastly, it was
superfluous in this respect also, that Julian was on the road to
his father's castle, where it was likely he would be seized, as
a matter of course, along with the other suspicious persons
who fell under Topham's warrant, and the denunciations of
his infamous companions. He, therefore, far from using any
violence to Peveril, assumed towards him such a friendly tone,
as might seem to warn him against receiving damage from
others, and vindicate himself from having any share in depriving
him of his charge. This last manœuvre was achieved by an
infusion of a strong narcotic into Julian's wine; under the
influence of which he slumbered so soundly, that the confederates were easily able to accomplish their inhospitable
purpose.

The events of the succeeding days are already known to the
reader. Chiffinch set forward to return to London, with the
packet, which it was desirable should be in Buckingham's
hands as soon as possible; while Christian went to Moultrassie,
to receive Alice from her father, and convey her safely to
London—his accomplice agreeing to defer his curiosity to see
more of her until they should have arrived in that city.

Before parting with Bridgenorth, Christian had exerted his
utmost address to prevail on him to remain at Moultrassie;
he had even overstepped the bounds of prudence, and, by his
urgency, awakened some suspicions of an indefinite nature,
which he found it difficult to allay. Bridgenorth, therefore,
followed his brother-in-law to London; and the reader has
already been made acquainted with the arts which Christian
used to prevent his farther interference with the destinies of
his daughter, or the unhallowed schemes of her ill-chosen
guardian. Still Christian, as he strode along the street in
profound reflection, saw that his undertaking was attended with
a thousand perils; and the drops stood like beads on his brow
when he thought of the presumptuous levity and fickle temper of
Buckingham—the frivolity and intemperance of Chiffinch—the
suspicions of the melancholy and bigoted, yet sagacious and
honest Bridgenorth. "Had I," he thought, "but tools fitted,
each to their portion of the work, how easily could I heave
asunder and disjoint the strength that opposes me! But with
these frail and insufficient implements, I am in daily, hourly,
momentary danger, that one lever or other gives way, and that
the whole ruin recoils on my own head. And yet, were it not
for those failings I complain of, how were it possible for me to
have acquired that power over them all which constitutes them
my passive tools, even when they seem most to exert their own

free will? Yes, the bigots have some right when they affirm that all is for the best."

It may seem strange, that, amidst the various subjects of Christian's apprehension, he was never visited by any long or permanent doubt that the virtue of his niece might prove the shoal on which his voyage should be wrecked. But he was an arrant rogue, as well as a hardened libertine; and, in both characters, a professed disbeliever in the virtue of the fair sex.

CHAPTER XXX

As for John Dryden's Charles, I own that King
Was never any very mighty thing;
And yet he was a devilish honest fellow—
Enjoy'd his friend and bottle, and got mellow.
                                        —DR. WOLCOT.

LONDON, the grand central point of intrigues of every description, had now attracted within its dark and shadowy region the greater number of the personages whom we have had occasion to mention.

Julian Peveril, amongst others of the *dramatis personæ*, had arrived, and taken up his abode in a remote inn in the suburbs. His business, he conceived, was to remain incognito until he should have communicated in private with the friends who were most likely to lend assistance to his parents, as well as to his patroness, in their present situation of doubt and danger. Amongst these, the most powerful was the Duke of Ormond, whose faithful services, high rank, and acknowledged worth and virtue, still preserved an ascendency in that very Court, where, in general, he was regarded as out of favour. Indeed, so much consciousness did Charles display in his demeanour towards that celebrated noble, and servant of his father, that Buckingham once took the freedom to ask the King whether the Duke of Ormond had lost his Majesty's favour, or his Majesty the Duke's? since, whenever they chanced to meet, the King appeared the more embarrassed of the two. But it was not Peveril's good fortune to obtain the advice or countenance of this distinguished person. His Grace of Ormond was not at that time in London.

The letter, about the delivery of which the Countess had seemed most anxious after that to the Duke of Ormond, was addressed to Captain Barstow (a Jesuit, whose real name was Fenwicke), to be found, or at least to be heard of, in the house of one Martin Christal in the Savoy. To this place hastened

Peveril, upon learning the absence of the Duke of Ormond. He was not ignorant of the danger which he personally incurred, by thus becoming a medium of communication betwixt a Popish priest and a suspected Catholic. But when he undertook the perilous commission of his patroness, he had done so frankly, and with the unreserved resolution of serving her in the manner in which she most desired her affairs to be conducted. Yet he could not forbear some secret apprehension, when he felt himself engaged in the labyrinth of passages and galleries, which led to different obscure sets of apartments in the ancient building termed the Savoy.

This antiquated and almost ruinous pile occupied a part of the site of the public offices in the Strand, commonly called Somerset House. The Savoy had been formerly a palace, and took its name from an Earl of Savoy, by whom it was founded. It had been the habitation of John of Gaunt, and various persons of distinction—had become a convent, an hospital, and finally, in Charles II.'s time, a waste of dilapidated buildings and ruinous apartments, inhabited chiefly by those who had some connection with, or dependence upon, the neighbouring palace of Somerset House, which, more fortunate than the Savoy, had still retained its royal title, and was the abode of a part of the Court, and occasionally of the King himself, who had apartments there.

It was not without several inquiries, and more than one mistake, that, at the end of a long and dusky passage, composed of boards so wasted by time that they threatened to give way under his feet, Julian at length found the name of Martin Christal, broker and appraiser, upon a shattered door. He was about to knock, when some one pulled his cloak; and looking round, to his great astonishment, which indeed almost amounted to fear, he saw the little mute damsel, who had accompanied him for a part of the way on his voyage from the Isle of Man. "Fenella!" he exclaimed, forgetting that she could neither hear nor reply,—"Fenella! Can this be you?"

Fenella, assuming the air of warning and authority, which she had heretofore endeavoured to adopt towards him, interposed betwixt Julian and the door at which he was about to knock—pointed with her finger towards it in a prohibiting manner, and at the same time bent her brows, and shook her head sternly.

After a moment's consideration, Julian could place but one interpretation upon Fenella's appearance and conduct, and that was, by supposing her lady had come up to London, and had despatched this mute attendant, as a confidential person, to apprise him of some change of her intended operations, which might render the delivery of her letters to Barstow, *alias*

Fenwicke, superfluous, or perhaps dangerous. He made signs to Fenella, demanding to know whether she had any commission from the Countess. She nodded. " Had she any letter ?" he continued, by the same mode of inquiry. She shook her head impatiently, and, walking hastily along the passage, made a signal to him to follow. He did so, having little doubt that he was about to be conducted into the Countess's presence ; but his surprise, at first excited by Fenella's appearance, was increased by the rapidity and ease with which she seemed to track the dusky and decayed mazes of the dilapidated Savoy, equal to that with which he had seen her formerly lead the way through the gloomy vaults of Castle Rushin, in the Isle of Man.

When he recollected, however, that Fenella had accompanied the Countess on a long visit to London, it appeared not improbable that she might then have acquired this local knowledge which seemed so accurate. Many foreigners, dependent on the Queen or Queen Dowager, had apartments in the Savoy. Many Catholic priests also found refuge in its recesses, under various disguises, and in defiance of the severity of the laws against Popery. What was more likely than that the Countess of Derby, a Catholic and a Frenchwoman, should have had secret commissions amongst such people ; and that the execution of such should be entrusted, at least occasionally, to Fenella ?

Thus reflecting, Julian continued to follow her light and active footsteps as she glided from the Strand to Spring-Garden, and thence into the Park.

It was still early in the morning, and the Mall was untenanted, save by a few walkers, who frequented these shades for the wholesome purposes of air and exercise. Splendour, gaiety, and display, did not come forth, at that period, until noon was approaching. All readers have heard that the whole space where the Horse Guards are now built, made, in the time of Charles II., a part of St. James's Park ; and that the old building, now called the Treasury, was a part of the ancient Palace of Whitehall, which was thus immediately connected with the Park. The canal had been constructed, by the celebrated Le Notre, for the purpose of draining the Park ; and it communicated with the Thames by a decoy, stocked with a quantity of the rarer waterfowl. It was towards this decoy that Fenella bent her way with unabated speed ; and they were approaching a group of two or three gentlemen, who sauntered by its banks, when, on looking closely at him who appeared to be the chief of the party, Julian felt his heart beat uncommonly thick, as if conscious of approaching some one of the highest consequence.

The person whom he looked upon was past the middle age of life, of a dark complexion, corresponding with the long, black,

full-bottomed periwig, which he wore instead of his own hair.
His dress was plain black velvet, with a diamond star, however,
on his cloak, which hung carelessly over one shoulder. His
features, strongly lined, even to harshness, had yet an expression
of dignified good-humour; he was well and strongly built,
walked upright and yet easily, and had upon the whole the air
of a person of the highest consideration. He kept rather in
advance of his companions, but turned and spoke to them, from
time to time, with much affability, and probably with some
liveliness, judging by the smiles, and sometimes the scarce
restrained laughter, by which some of his sallies were received
by his attendants. They also wore only morning dresses; but
their looks and manner were those of men of rank, in presence
of one in station still more elevated. They shared the attention
of their principal in common with seven or eight little black
curly-haired spaniels, or rather, as they are now called, cockers,
which attended their master as closely, and perhaps with as
deep sentiments of attachment, as the bipeds of the group;
and whose gambols, which seemed to afford him much amusement, he sometimes checked, and sometimes encouraged. In
addition to this pastime, a lackey, or groom, was also in attendance, with one or two little baskets and bags, from which the
gentleman we have described took, from time to time, a handful
of seeds, and amused himself with throwing them to the
waterfowl.

This the King's favourite occupation, together with his
remarkable countenance, and the deportment of the rest of the
company towards him, satisfied Julian Peveril that he was approaching, perhaps indecorously, near to the person of Charles
Stewart, the second of that unhappy name.

While he hesitated to follow his dumb guide any nearer,
and felt the embarrassment of being unable to communicate to
her his repugnance to further intrusion, a person in the royal
retinue touched a light and lively air on the flageolet, at a
signal from the King, who desired to have some tune repeated
which had struck him in the theatre on the preceding evening.
While the good-natured monarch marked time with his foot,
and with the motion of his hand, Fenella continued to approach
him, and threw into her manner the appearance of one who was
attracted, as it were in spite of herself, by the sounds of the
instrument.

Anxious to know how this was to end, and astonished to see
the dumb girl imitate so accurately the manner of one who
actually heard the musical notes, Peveril also drew near, though
at somewhat greater distance.

The King looked good-humouredly at both, as if he admitted
their musical enthusiasm as an excuse for their intrusion; but

his eyes became riveted on Fenella, whose face and appearance, although rather singular than beautiful, had something in them wild, fantastic, and, as being so, even captivating, to an eye which had been gratified perhaps to satiety with the ordinary forms of female beauty. She did not appear to notice how closely she was observed; but, as if acting under an irresistible impulse, derived from the sounds to which she seemed to listen, she undid the bodkin round which her long tresses were winded, and flinging them suddenly over her slender person, as if using them as a natural veil, she began to dance, with infinite grace and agility, to the tune which the flageolet played.

Peveril lost almost his sense of the King's presence, when he observed with what wonderful grace and agility Fenella kept time to notes, which could only be known to her by the motions of the musician's fingers. He had heard, indeed, among other prodigies, of a person in Fenella's unhappy situation acquiring, by some unaccountable and mysterious tact, the power of acting as an instrumental musician, nay, becoming so accurate a performer as to be capable of leading a musical band; and he had also heard of deaf and dumb persons dancing with sufficient accuracy, by observing the motions of their partner. But Fenella's performance seemed more wonderful than either, since the musician was guided by his written notes, and the dancer by the motions of the others; whereas Fenella had no intimation, save what she seemed to gather, with infinite accuracy, by observing the motion of the artist's fingers on his small instrument.

As for the King, who was ignorant of the particular circumstances which rendered Fenella's performance almost marvellous, he was contented, at her first commencement, to authorise what seemed to him the frolic of this singular-looking damsel, by a good-honoured smile, but when he perceived the exquisite truth and justice, as well as the wonderful combination of grace and agility, with which she executed to his favourite air a dance which was perfectly new to him, Charles turned his mere acquiescence into something like enthusiastic applause. He bore time to her motions with the movement of his foot— applauded with head and with hand—and seemed, like herself, carried away by the enthusiasm of the gestic art.

After a rapid yet graceful succession of *entrechats*, Fenella introduced a slow movement, which terminated the dance; then dropping a profound courtesy, she continued to stand motionless before the King, her arms folded on her bosom, her head stooped, and her eyes cast down, after the manner of an Oriental slave; while through the misty veil of her shadowy locks, it might be observed, that the colour which exercise had called to her cheeks was dying fast away, and resigning them to their native dusky hue.

"By my honour," exclaimed the King, "she is like a fairy who trips it in moonlight. There must be more of air and fire than of earth in her composition. It is well poor Nelly Gwyn saw her not, or she would have died of grief and envy. Come, gentlemen, which of you contrived this pretty piece of morning pastime?"

The courtiers looked at each other, but none of them felt authorised to claim the merit of a service so agreeable.

"We must ask the quick-eyed nymph herself then," said the King; and, looking at Fenella, he added, "Tell us, my pretty one, to whom we owe the pleasure of seeing you?—I suspect the Duke of Buckingham; for this is exactly a *tour de son métier*."

Fenella, on observing that the King addressed her, bowed low, and shook her head, in signal that she did not understand what he said. "Oddsfish, that is true," said the King; "she must perforce be a foreigner—her complexion and agility speak it. France or Italy has had the moulding of these elastic limbs, dark cheek, and eye of fire." He then put to her in French, and again in Italian, the question, "By whom she had been sent hither?"

At the second repetition, Fenella threw back her veiling tresses, so as to show the melancholy which sat on her brow; while she sadly shook her head, and intimated by imperfect muttering, but of the softest and most plaintive kind, her organic deficiency.

"Is it possible Nature can have made such a fault?" said Charles. "Can she have left so curious a piece as thou art without the melody of voice, whilst she has made thee so exquisitely sensible to the beauty of sound?—Stay: what means this? and what young fellow are you bringing up there? Oh, the master of the show, I suppose.—Friend," he added, addressing himself to Peveril, who, on the signal of Fenella, stepped forward almost instinctively, and kneeled down, "we thank thee for the pleasure of this morning.—My Lord Marquis, you rooked me at piquet last night; for which disloyal deed thou shalt now atone, by giving a couple of pieces to this honest youth, and five to the girl."

As the nobleman drew out his purse and came forward to perform the King's generous commission, Julian felt some embarrassment ere he was able to explain, that he had no title to be benefited by the young person's performance, and that his Majesty had mistaken his character.

"And who art thou, then, my friend?" said Charles; "but, above all, and particularly, who is this dancing nymph, whom thou standest waiting on like an attendant fawn?"

"The young person is a retainer of the Countess-Dowager of

Derby, so please your Majesty," said Peveril, in a low tone of voice; "and I am——"

"Hold, hold," said the King; "this is a dance to another tune, and not fit for a place so public. Hark thee, friend; do thou and the young woman follow Empson where he will conduct thee.—Empson, carry them—hark in thy ear."

"May it please your Majesty, I ought to say," said Peveril, "that I am guiltless of any purpose of intrusion ——"

"Now a plague on him who can take no hint," said the King, cutting short his apology. "Oddsfish, man, there are times when civility is the greatest impertinence in the world. Do thou follow Empson, and amuse thyself for a half-hour's space with the fairy's company, till we shall send for you."

Charles spoke this not without casting an anxious eye around, and in a tone which intimated apprehension of being overheard. Julian could only bow obedience, and follow Empson, who was the same person that played so rarely on the flageolet.

When they were out of sight of the King and his party, the musician wished to enter into conversation with his companions, and addressed himself first to Fenella with a broad compliment of, "By the mass, ye dance rarely—ne'er a slut on the boards shows such a shank! I would be content to play to you till my throat were as dry as my whistle. Come, be a little free— old Rowley will not quit the Park till nine. I will carry you to Spring Gardens, and bestow sweet-cakes and a quart of Rhenish on both of you; and we'll be cameradoes,—What the devil? no answer?—How's this, brother?—Is this neat wench of yours deaf or dumb, or both? I should laugh at that, and she trip it so well to the flageolet."

To rid himself of this fellow's discourse, Peveril answered him in French, that he was a foreigner, and spoke no English; glad to escape, though at the expense of a fiction, from the additional embarrassment of a fool, who was likely to ask more questions than his own wisdom might have enabled him to answer.

"*Étranger* — that means stranger," muttered their guide; "more French dogs and jades come to lick the good English butter off our bread, or perhaps an Italian puppet-show. Well, if it were not that they have a mortal enmity to the whole *gamut,* this were enough to make any honest fellow turn Puritan. But if I am to play to her at the Duchess's, I'll be d—d but I put her out in the tune, just to teach her to have the impudence to come to England, and to speak no English."

Having muttered to himself this truly British resolution, the musician walked briskly on towards a large house near the bottom of St. James's Street, and entered the court, by a grated door, from the Park, of which the mansion commanded an extensive prospect.

Peveril finding himself in front of a handsome portico, under which opened a stately pair of folding-doors, was about to ascend the steps that led to the main entrance, when his guide seized him by the arm, exclaiming, "Hold, Mounseer! What! you'll lose nothing, I see, for want of courage; but you must keep the back way, for all your fine doublet. Here it is not, knock and it shall be opened; but may be instead, knock and you shall be knocked."

Suffering himself to be guided by Empson, Julian deviated from the principal door, to one which opened, with less ostentation, in an angle of the courtyard. On a modest tap from the flute-player, admittance was afforded him and his companions by a footman, who conducted them through a variety of stone passages, to a very handsome summer parlour, where a lady, or something resembling one, dressed in a style of extra elegance, was trifling with a play-book while she finished her chocolate. It would not be easy to describe her, but by weighing her natural good qualities against the affectations which counterbalanced them. She would have been handsome, but for rouge and *minauderie*—would have been civil, but for overstrained airs of patronage and condescension—would have had an agreeable voice, had she spoken in her natural tone—and fine eyes, had she not made such desperate hard use of them. She could only spoil a pretty ankle by too liberal display; but her shape, though she could not yet be thirty years old, had the embonpoint which might have suited better with ten years more advanced. She pointed Empson to a seat with the air of a Duchess, and asked him, languidly, how he did this age, that she had not seen him? and what folks these were he had brought with him?

"Foreigners, madam; d—d foreigners," answered Empson; "starving beggars, that our old friend has picked up in the Park this morning—the wench dances, and the fellow plays on the Jew's trump, I believe. On my life, madam, I begin to be ashamed of old Rowley; I must discard him, unless he keeps better company in future."

"Fie, Empson," said the lady; "consider it is our duty to countenance him, and keep him afloat; and indeed I always make a principle of it. Hark ye, he comes not hither this morning?"

"He will be here," answered Empson, "in the walking of a minuet."

"My God!" exclaimed the lady, with unaffected alarm; and starting up with utter neglect of her usual and graceful languor, she tripped as swiftly as a milk-maid into an adjoining apartment, where they heard presently a few words of eager and animated discussion.

"Something to be put out of the way, I suppose," said Empson. "Well for madam I gave her the hint. There he goes, the happy swain."

Julian was so situated, that he could, from the same casement through which Empson was peeping, observe a man in a laced roquelaure, and carrying his rapier under his arm, glide from the door by which he had himself entered, and out of the court, keeping as much as possible under the shade of the buildings.

The lady re-entered at this moment, and observing how Empson's eyes were directed, said with a slight appearance of hurry, "A gentleman of the Duchess of Portsmouth's with a billet; and so tiresomely pressing for an answer, that I was obliged to write without my diamond pen. I have daubed my fingers, I dare say," she added, looking at a very pretty hand, and presently after dipping her fingers in a little silver vase of rose-water. "But that little exotic monster of yours, Empson, I hope she really understands no English?—On my life she coloured.—Is she such a rare dancer?—I must see her dance, and hear him play on the Jew's harp."

"Dance!" replied Empson; "she danced well enough when *I* played to her. I can make anything dance. Old Counsellor Clubfoot danced when he had a fit of the gout; you have seen no such *pas seul* in the theatre. I would engage to make the Archbishop of Canterbury dance the hays like a Frenchman. There is nothing in dancing; it all lies in the music. Rowley does not know that now. He saw this poor wench dance; and thought so much on't, when it was all along of me. I would have defied her to sit still. And Rowley gives her the credit of it, and five pieces to boot; and I have only two for my morning's work!"

"True, Master Empson," said the lady; "but you are of the family, though in a lower station; and you ought to con-sider——" "By G—, madam," answered Empson, "all I consider is, that I play the best flageolet in England; and that they can no more supply my place, if they were to discard me, than they could fill Thames from Fleet-Ditch."

"Well, Master Empson, I do not dispute but you are a man of talents," replied the lady; "still, I say, mind the main chance—you please the ear to-day—another has the advantage of you to-morrow."

"Never, mistress, while ears have the heavenly power of distinguishing one note from another."

"Heavenly power, say you, Master Empson?" said the lady.

"Ay, madam, heavenly; for some very neat verses which we had at our festival say,

> 'What know we of the blest above,
> But that they sing and that they love?'

It is Master Waller wrote them, as I think; who, upon my word, ought to be encouraged."

"And so should you, my dear Empson," said the dame, yawning, "were it only for the honour you do to your own profession. But in the meantime, will you ask these people to have some refreshment?—and will you take some yourself?—the chocolate is that which the Ambassador Portuguese fellow brought over to the Queen."

"If it be genuine," said the musician.

"How, sir?" said the fair one, half rising from her pile of cushions—"Not genuine, and in this house!—Let me understand you, Master Empson—I think, when I first saw you, you scarce knew chocolate from coffee."

"By G—, madam," answered the flageolet-player, "you are perfectly right. And how can I show better how much I have profited by your ladyship's excellent cheer, except by being critical?"

"You stand excused, Master Empson," said the *petite maitresse,* sinking gently back on the downy couch, from which a momentary irritation had startled her—"I think the chocolate will please you, though scarce equal to what we had from the Spanish resident Mendoza.—But we must offer these strange people something. Will you ask them if they would have coffee and chocolate, or cold wild-fowl, fruit, and wine? They must be treated, so as to show them where they are, since here they are."

"Unquestionably, madam," said Empson; "but I have just at this instant forgot the French for chocolate, hot bread, coffee, game, and drinkables."

"It is odd," said the lady; "and I have forgot my French and Italian at the same moment. But it signifies little—I will order the things to be brought, and they will remember the names of them themselves."

Empson laughed loudly at this jest, and pawned his soul that the cold sirloin which entered immediately after, was the best emblem of roast-beef all the world over. Plentiful refreshments were offered to all the party, of which both Fenella and Peveril partook.

In the meanwhile, the flageolet-player drew closer to the side of the lady of the mansion—their intimacy was cemented, and their spirits set afloat, by a glass of liqueur, which gave them additional confidence in discussing the characters, as well of the superior attendants of the Court, as of the inferior rank, to which they themselves might be supposed to belong.

The lady, indeed, during this conversation, frequently exerted her complete and absolute superiority over Master Empson; in which that musical gentleman humbly acquiesced whenever the circumstance was recalled to his attention, whether in the way of blunt contradiction, sarcastic insinuation, downright assumption of higher importance, or in any of the other various modes by which such superiority is usually asserted and maintained. But the lady's obvious love of scandal was the lure which very soon brought her again down from the dignified part which for a moment she assumed, and placed her once more on a gossiping level with her companion.

Their conversation was too trivial, and too much allied to petty Court intrigues, with which he was totally unacquainted, to be in the least interesting to Julian. As it continued for more than an hour, he soon ceased to pay the least attention to a discourse consisting of nicknames, patchwork, and innuendo; and employed himself in reflecting on his own complicated affairs, and the probable issue of his approaching audience with the King, which had been brought about by so singular an agent, and by means so unexpected. He often looked to his guide, Fenella; and observed that she was, for the greater part of the time, drowned in deep and abstracted meditation. But three or four times—and it was when the assumed airs and affected importance of the musician and their hostess rose to the most extravagant excess—he observed that Fenella dealt askance on them some of those bitter and almost blighting elfin looks, which in the Isle of Man were held to imply contemptuous execration. There was something in all her manner so extraordinary, joined to her sudden appearance, and her demeanour in the King's presence, so oddly, yet so well contrived to procure him a private audience—which he might, by graver means, have sought in vain—that it almost justified the idea, though he smiled at it internally, that the little mute agent was aided in her machinations by the kindred imps, to whom, according to Manx superstition, her genealogy was to be traced.

Another idea sometimes occurred to Julian, though he rejected the question, as being equally wild with those doubts which referred Fenella to a race different from that of mortals —" Was she really afflicted with those organical imperfections which had always seemed to sever her from humanity?—If not, what could be the motives of so young a creature practising so dreadful a penance for such an unremitted term of years? And how formidable must be the strength of mind which could condemn itself to so terrific a sacrifice—How deep and strong the purpose for which it was undertaken!"

But a brief recollection of past events enabled him to dismiss this conjecture as altogether wild and visionary. He had but to call to memory the various stratagems practised by his light-hearted companion, the young Earl of Derby, upon this forlorn girl—the conversations held in her presence, in which the character of a creature so irritable and sensitive upon all occasions, was freely, and sometimes satirically discussed, without her expressing the least acquaintance with what was going forward, to convince him that so deep a deception could never have been practised for so many years, by a being of a turn of mind so peculiarly jealous and irascible.

He renounced, therefore, the idea, and turned his thoughts to his own affairs, and his approaching interview with his Sovereign; in which meditation we propose to leave him, until we briefly review the changes which had taken place in the situation of Alice Bridgenorth.

CHAPTER XXXI

I fear the devil worst when gown and cassock,
Or, in the lack of them, old Calvin's cloak,
Conceals his cloven hoof.
—ANONYMOUS.

JULIAN PEVERIL had scarce set sail for Whitehaven, when Alice Bridgenorth and her governante, at the hasty command of her father, were embarked with equal speed and secrecy on board of a bark bound for Liverpool. Christian accompanied them on their voyage, as the friend to whose guardianship Alice was to be consigned during any future separation from her father, and whose amusing conversation, joined to his pleasing though cold manners, as well as his near relationship, induced Alice, in her forlorn situation, to consider her fate as fortunate in having such a guardian.

At Liverpool, as the reader already knows, Christian took the first overt step in the villainy which he had contrived against the innocent girl, by exposing her at a meeting-house to the unhallowed gaze of Chiffinch, in order to convince him she was possessed of such uncommon beauty as might well deserve the infamous promotion to which they meditated to raise her.

Highly satisfied with her personal appearance, Chiffinch was no less so with the sense and delicacy of her conversation, when he met her in company with her uncle afterwards in London. The simplicity, and at the same time the spirit of her remarks, made him regard her as his scientific attendant the cook might have done a newly invented sauce, sufficiently *piquante* in its qualities to awaken the jaded appetite of a cloyed and gorged epicure. She was, he said and swore, the very corner-stone on which, with proper management, and with his instructions, a few honest fellows might build a Court fortune.

That the necessary introduction might take place, the confederates judged fit she should be put under the charge of an experienced lady, whom some called Mistress Chiffinch, and others Chiffinch's mistress—one of those obliging creatures who are willing to discharge all the duties of a wife, without the inconvenient and indissoluble ceremony.

It was one, and not perhaps the least prejudicial consequence of the licence of that ill-governed time, that the bounds betwixt virtue and vice were so far smoothed down and levelled, that the frail wife, or the tender friend who was no wife, did not necessarily lose their place in society; but, on the contrary, if they moved in the higher circles, were permitted and encouraged to mingle with women whose rank was certain, and whose reputation was untainted.

A regular *liaison*, like that of Chiffinch and his fair one, inferred little scandal; and such was his influence, as prime minister of his master's pleasures, that, as Charles himself expressed it, the lady whom we introduced to our readers in the last chapter, had obtained a brevet commission to rank as a married woman. And to do the gentle dame justice, no wife could have been more attentive to forward his plans, or more liberal in disposing of his income.

She inhabited a set of apartments called Chiffinch's—the scene of many an intrigue, both of love and politics; and where Charles often held his private parties for the evening, when, as frequently happened, the ill-humour of the Duchess of Portsmouth, his reigning Sultana, prevented his supping with her. The hold which such an arrangement gave a man like Chiffinch, used as he well knew how to use it, made him of too much consequence to be slighted even by the first persons in the state, unless they stood aloof from all manner of politics and Court intrigue.

In the charge of Mistress Chiffinch, and of him whose name she bore, Edward Christian placed the daughter of his sister, and of his confiding friend, calmly contemplating her ruin as an event certain to follow; and hoping to ground upon it his own chance of a more assured fortune, than a life spent in intrigue had hitherto been able to procure for him.

The innocent Alice, without being able to discover what was wrong either in the scenes of unusual luxury with which she was surrounded, or in the manners of her hostess, which, both from nature and policy, were kind and caressing—felt nevertheless an instinctive apprehension that all was not right—a feeling in the human mind, allied, perhaps, to that sense of danger which animals exhibit when placed in the vicinity of the natural enemies of their race, and which makes birds cower when the hawk is in the air, and beasts tremble when the tiger is abroad in the desert. There was a heaviness at her heart which she could not dispel; and the few hours which she had already spent at Chiffinch's were like those passed in prison by one unconscious of the cause or event of his captivity. It was the third morning after her arrival in London, that the scene took place which we now recur to.

The impertinence and vulgarity of Empson, which was permitted to him as an unrivalled performer upon his instrument, were exhausting themselves at the expense of all other musical professors, and Mrs. Chiffinch was listening with careless indifference, when some one was heard speaking loudly, and with animation, in the inner apartment.

"Oh, gemini and gilliflower water!" exclaimed the damsel, startled out of her fine airs into her natural vulgarity of exclamation, and running to the door of communication—"if he has not come back again after all!—and if old Rowley——"

A tap at the farther and opposite door here arrested her attention—she quitted the handle of that which she was about to open as speedily as if it had burnt her fingers, and, moving back towards her couch, asked, "Who is there?"

"Old Rowley himself, madam," said the King, entering the apartment with his usual air of easy composure.

"O crimini!—your Majesty!—I thought——"

"That I was out of hearing, doubtless," said the King; "and spoke of me as folk speak of absent friends. Make no apology. I think I have heard ladies say of their lace, that a rent is better than a darn.—Nay, be seated.—Where is Chiffinch?"

"He is down at York House, your Majesty," said the dame, recovering, though with no small difficulty, the calm affectation of her usual demeanour. "Shall I send your Majesty's commands?"

"I will wait his return," said the King.—"Permit me to taste your chocolate."

"There is some fresh frothed in the office," said the lady; and using a little silver call, or whistle, a black boy, superbly dressed, like an Oriental page, with gold bracelets on his naked arms, and a gold collar around his equally bare neck, attended with the favourite beverage of the morning, in an apparatus of the richest china.

While he sipped his cup of chocolate, the King looked round the apartment, and observing Fenella, Peveril, and the musician, who remained standing beside a large Indian screen, he con-

tinued, addressing Mistress Chiffinch, though with polite indifference, "I sent you the fiddles this morning—or rather the
flute—Empson, and a fairy elf whom I met in the Park, who
dances divinely. She has brought us the very newest saraband
from the Court of Queen Mab, and I sent her here, that you
may see it at leisure."

"Your Majesty does me by far too much honour," said Chiffinch, her eyes properly cast down, and her accents minced into
becoming humility.

"Nay, little Chiffinch," answered the King, in a tone of as
contemptuous familiarity as was consistent with his good-breed-
ing, "it was not altogether for thine own private ear, though
quite deserving of all sweet sounds; but I thought Nelly had
been with thee this morning."

"I can send Bajazet for her, your Majesty," answered the lady.

"Nay, I will not trouble your little heathen sultan to go so
far. Still it strikes me that Chiffinch said you had company—
some country cousin, or such a matter—Is there not such a
person?"

"There is a young person from the country," said Mistress
Chiffinch, striving to conceal a considerable portion of embarrassment; "but she is unprepared for such an honour as to be
admitted into your Majesty's presence, and——"

"And therefore the fitter to receive it, Chiffinch. There is
nothing in nature so beautiful as the first blush of a little rustic
between joy and fear, and wonder and curiosity. It is the
down on the peach—pity it decays so soon!—the fruit remains,
but the first high colouring and exquisite flavour are gone.—
Never put up thy lip for the matter, Chiffinch, for it is as I tell
you; so pray let us have *la belle cousine.*"

Mistress Chiffinch, more embarrassed than ever, again advanced towards the door of communication, which she had been
in the act of opening when his Majesty entered. But just as
she coughed pretty loudly, perhaps as a signal to some one
within, voices were again heard in a raised tone of altercation
—the door was flung open, and Alice rushed out of the inner
apartment, followed to the door of it by the enterprising Duke
of Buckingham, who stood fixed with astonishment on finding
his pursuit of the flying fair one had hurried him into the
presence of the King.

Alice Bridgenorth appeared too much transported with anger
to permit her to pay attention to the rank or character of the
company into which she had thus suddenly entered. "I remain
no longer here, madam," she said to Mrs. Chiffinch, in a tone
of uncontrollable resolution; "I leave instantly a house where
I am exposed to company which I detest, and to solicitations
which I despise."

The dismayed Mrs. Chiffinch could only implore her, in broken whispers, to be silent; adding, while she pointed to Charles, who stood with his eyes fixed rather on his audacious courtier than on the game which he pursued, "The King— the King!"

"If I am in the King's presence," said Alice aloud, and in the same torrent of passionate feeling, while her eye sparkled through tears of resentment and insulted modesty, "it is the better—it is his Majesty's duty to protect me; and on his protection I throw myself."

These words, which were spoken aloud, and boldly, at once recalled Julian to himself, who had hitherto stood, as it were, bewildered. He approached Alice, and, whispering in her ear that she had beside her one who would defend her with his life, implored her to trust to his guardianship in this emergency.

Clinging to his arm in all the ecstasy of gratitude and joy, the spirit which had so lately invigorated Alice in her own defence, gave way in a flood of tears, when she saw herself supported by him whom perhaps she most wished to recognise as her protector. She permitted Peveril gently to draw her back towards the screen before which he had been standing; where, holding by his arm, but at the same time endeavouring to conceal herself behind him, they waited the conclusion of a scene so singular.

The King seemed at first so much surprised at the unexpected apparition of the Duke of Buckingham, as to pay little or no attention to Alice, who had been the means of thus unceremoniously introducing his Grace into the presence at a most unsuitable moment. In that intriguing Court, it had not been the first time that the Duke had ventured to enter the lists of gallantry in rivalry of his Sovereign, which made the present insult the more intolerable. His purpose of lying concealed in those private apartments was explained by the exclamations of Alice; and Charles, notwithstanding the placidity of his disposition, and his habitual guard over his passions, resented the attempt to seduce his destined mistress, as an Eastern Sultan would have done the insolence of a vizier, who anticipated his intended purchases of captive beauty in the slave-market. The swarthy features of Charles reddened, and the strong lines on his dark visage seemed to become inflated, as he said, in a voice which faltered with passion, "Buckingham, you dared not have thus insulted your equal! To your master you may securely offer any affront, since his rank glues his sword to the scabbard."

The haughty Duke did not brook this taunt unanswered. "My sword," he said, with emphasis, "was never in the scabbard, when your Majesty's service required it should be unsheathed."

"Your Grace means, when its service was required for its master's interest," said the King; "for you could only gain the coronet of a Duke by fighting for the royal crown. But it is over—I have treated you as a friend—a companion—almost an equal—you have repaid me with insolence and ingratitude."

"Sire," answered the Duke firmly, but respectfully, "I am unhappy in your displeasure; yet thus far fortunate, that while your words can confer honour, they cannot impair or take it away.—It is hard," he added, lowering his voice, so as only to be heard by the King,—"It is hard that the squall of a peevish wench should cancel the services of so many years!"

"It is harder," said the King, in the same subdued tone, which both preserved through the rest of the conversation, "that a wench's bright eyes can make a nobleman forget the decencies due to his Sovereign's privacy."

"May I presume to ask your Majesty what decencies are those?" said the Duke.

Charles bit his lip to keep himself from smiling. "Bucking-ham," he said, "this is a foolish business; and we must not forget (as we have nearly done), that we have an audience to witness this scene, and should walk the stage with dignity. I will show you your fault in private."

"It is enough that your Majesty has been displeased, and that I have unhappily been the occasion," said the Duke, kneeling; "although quite ignorant of any purpose beyond a few words of gallantry; and I sue thus low for your Majesty's pardon."

So saying, he kneeled gracefully down. "Thou hast it, George," said the placable Prince. "I believe thou wilt be sooner tired of offending than I of forgiving."

"Long may your Majesty live to give the offence, with which it is your royal pleasure at present to charge my innocence," said the Duke.

"What mean you by that, my lord?" said Charles, the angry shade returning to his brow for a moment.

"My Liege," replied the Duke, "you are too honourable to deny your custom of shooting with Cupid's bird-bolts in other men's warrens. You have ta'en the royal right of free-forestry over every man's park. It is hard that you should be so much displeased at hearing a chance arrow whizz near your own pales."

"No more on't," said the King; "but let us see where the dove has harboured."

"The Helen has found a Paris while we were quarrelling," replied the Duke.

x

"Rather an Orpheus," said the King; "and what is worse, one that is already provided with a Eurydice—She is clinging to the fiddler."

"It is mere fright," said Buckingham, "like Rochester's, when he crept into the bass-viol to hide himself from Sir Dermot O'Cleaver."

"We must make the people show their talents," said the King, "and stop their mouths with money and civility, or we shall have this foolish encounter over half the town."

The King then approached Julian, and desired him to take his instrument, and cause his female companion to perform a saraband.

"I had already the honour to inform your Majesty," said Julian, "that I cannot contribute to your pleasure in the way you command me; and that this young person is——"

"A retainer of the Lady Powis," said the King, upon whose mind things not connected with his pleasures made a very slight impression. "Poor lady, she is in trouble about the lords in the Tower."

"Pardon me, sir," said Julian, "she is a dependant of the Countess of Derby."

"True, true," answered Charles; "it is indeed of Lady Derby, who hath also her own distresses in these times. Do you know who taught the young person to dance? Some of her steps mightily resemble Le Jeune's of Paris."

"I presume she was taught abroad, sir," said Julian; "for myself, I am charged with some weighty business by the Countess, which I would willingly communicate to your Majesty."

"We will send you to our Secretary of State," said the King. "But this dancing envoy will oblige us once more, will she not?—Empson, now that I remember, it was to your pipe that she danced—Strike up, man, and put mettle into her feet."

Empson began to play a well-known measure; and, as he had threatened, made more than one false note, until the King, whose ear was very accurate, rebuked him with, "Sirrah, art thou drunk at this early hour, or must thou too be playing thy slippery tricks with me? Thou thinkest thou art born to beat time, but I will have time beat into thee."

The hint was sufficient, and Empson took good care so to perform his air as to merit his high and deserved reputation. But on Fenella it made not the slightest impression. She rather leant than stood against the wall of the apartment; her countenance as pale as death, her arms and hands hanging down as if stiffened, and her existence only testified by the sobs which agitated her bosom, and the tears which flowed from her half-closed eyes.

"A plague on it," said the King, "some evil spirit is abroad

this morning; and the wenches are all bewitched, I think.
Cheer up, my girl. What, in the devil's name, has changed
thee at once from a Nymph to a Niobe? If thou standest
there longer thou wilt grow to the very marble wall—Or—
oddsfish, George, have you been bird-bolting in this quarter
also?"

Ere Buckingham could answer to this charge, Julian again
kneeled down to the King, and prayed to be heard, were it only
for five minutes. "The young woman," he said, "had been long
in attendance on the Countess of Derby. She was bereaved
of the faculties of speech and hearing."

"Oddsfish, man, and dances so well?" said the King. "Nay,
all Gresham College shall never make me believe that."

"I would have thought it equally impossible, but for what I
to-day witnessed," said Julian; "but only permit me, sir, to
deliver the petition of my lady the Countess."

"And who art thou thyself, man?" said the Sovereign;
"for though everything which wears bodice and breast-knot
has a right to speak to a King, and be answered, I know
not that they have a title to audience through an envoy
extraordinary."

"I am Julian Peveril of Derbyshire," answered the suppli-
cant, "the son of Sir Geoffrey Peveril of Martindale Castle,
who——"

"Body of me—the old Worcester man?" said the King.
"Oddsfish, I remember him well—some harm has happened to
him, I think—Is he not dead, or very sick at least?"

"Ill at ease, and it please your Majesty, but not ill in health.
He has been imprisoned on account of an alleged accession to
this Plot."

"Look you there," said the King; "I knew he was in
trouble; and yet how to help the stout old Knight, I can hardly
tell. I can scarce escape suspicion of the Plot myself, though
the principal object of it is to take away my own life. Were I
to stir to save a plotter, I should certainly be brought in as an
accessary.—Buckingham, thou hast some interest with those
who built this fine state engine, or at least who have driven it
on—be good-natured for once, though it is scarcely thy wont,
and interfere to shelter our old Worcester friend, Sir Godfrey.
You have not forgot him?"

"No, sir," answered the Duke; "for I never heard the
name."

"It is Sir Geoffrey his Majesty would say," said Julian.

"And if his Majesty did say Sir Geoffrey, Master Peveril, I
cannot see of what use I can be to your father," replied the
Duke coldly. "He is accused of a heavy crime; and a British
subject so accused, can have no shelter either from prince or

peer, but must stand to the award and deliverance of God and his country."

"Now, Heaven forgive thee thy hypocrisy, George," said the King hastily. "I would rather hear the devil preach religion than thee teach patriotism. Thou knowest as well as I, that the nation is in a scarlet fever for fear of the poor Catholics, who are not two men to five hundred; and that the public mind is so harassed with new narrations of conspiracy, and fresh horrors every day, that people have as little real sense of what is just or unjust as men who talk in their sleep of what is sense or nonsense. I have borne, and borne with it—I have seen blood flow on the scaffold, fearing to thwart the nation in its fury—and I pray to God that I or mine be not called on to answer for it. I will no longer swim with the torrent, which honour and conscience call upon me to stem—I will act the part of a Sovereign, and save my people from doing injustice, even in their own despite."

Charles walked hastily up and down the room as he expressed these unwonted sentiments, with energy equally unwonted. After a momentary pause, the Duke answered him gravely, "Spoken like a Royal King, sir, but—pardon me—not like a King of England."

Charles paused, as the Duke spoke, beside a window which looked full on Whitehall, and his eye was involuntarily attracted by the fatal window of the Banqueting House out of which his unhappy father was conducted to execution. Charles was naturally, or, more properly, constitutionally brave; but a life of pleasure, together with the habit of governing his course rather by what was expedient than by what was right, rendered him unapt to dare the same scene of danger or of martyrdom, which had closed his father's life and reign; and the thought came over his half-formed resolution, like the rain upon a kindling beacon. In another man, his perplexity would have seemed almost ludicrous; but Charles would not lose, even under these circumstances, the dignity and grace, which were as natural to him as his indifference and good humour. "Our Council must decide in this matter," he said, looking to the Duke; "and be assured, young man," he added, addressing Julian, "your father shall not want an intercessor in his King, so far as the laws will permit my interference in his behalf."

Julian was about to retire, when Fenella, with a marked look, put into his hand a slip of paper, on which she had hastily written, "The packet—give him the packet."

After a moment's hesitation, during which he reflected that Fenella was the organ of the Countess's pleasure, Julian resolved to obey. "Permit me, then, Sire," he said, "to place in your royal hands this packet, entrusted to me by the Countess of Derby. The letters have already been once taken from me; and I have little hope that I can now deliver them as they are addressed. I place them, therefore, in your royal hands, certain that they will evince the innocence of the writer."

The King shook his head as he took the packet reluctantly. "It is no safe office you have undertaken, young man. A messenger has sometimes his throat cut for the sake of his despatches—But give them to me; and, Chiffinch, give me wax and a taper." He employed himself in folding the Countess's packet in another envelope. "Buckingham," he said, "you are evidence that I do not read them till the Council shall see them."

"Buckingham approached, and offered his services in folding the parcel, but Charles rejected his assistance; and having finished his task, he sealed the packet with his own signet-ring. The Duke bit his lip and retired.

"And now, young man," said the King, "your errand is sped, so far as it can at present be forwarded."

Julian bowed deeply, as to take leave at these words, which he rightly interpreted as a signal for his departure. Alice Bridgenorth still clung to his arm, and motioned to withdraw along with him. The King and Buckingham looked at each other in conscious astonishment, and yet not without a desire to smile, so strange did it seem to them that a prize, for which, an instant before, they had been mutually contending, should thus glide out of their grasp, or rather be borne off by a third and very inferior competitor.

"Mistress Chiffinch," said the King, with a hesitation which he could not disguise, "I hope your fair charge is not about to leave you?"

"Certainly not, your Majesty," answered Chiffinch. "Alice, my love—you mistake—that opposite door leads to your apartments."

"Pardon me, madam," answered Alice; "I have indeed mistaken my road, but it was when I came hither."

"The errant damosel," said Buckingham, looking at Charles with as much intelligence as etiquette permitted him to throw into his eye, and then turning it towards Alice, as she still held by Julian's arm, "is resolved not to mistake her road a second time. She has chosen a sufficient guide."

"And yet stories tell that such guides have led maidens astray," said the King.

Alice blushed deeply, but instantly recovered her composure so soon as she saw that her liberty was likely to depend upon the immediate exercise of resolution. She quitted, from a sense of insulted delicacy, the arm of Julian, to which she had hitherto clung; but as she spoke, she continued to retain a slight grasp of his cloak. "I have indeed mistaken my way," she repeated, still addressing Mrs. Chiffinch, "but it was when I crossed this threshold. The usage to which I have been exposed in your house has determined me to quit it instantly."

"I will not permit that, my young mistress," answered Mrs. Chiffinch, "until your uncle, who placed you under my care, shall relieve me of the charge of you."

"I will answer for my conduct, both to my uncle, and, what is of more importance, to my father," said Alice. "You must permit me to depart, madam; I am free-born, and you have no right to detain me."

"Pardon me, my young madam," said Mistress Chiffinch, "I have a right, and I will maintain it too."

"I will know that before quitting this presence," said Alice firmly; and, advancing a step or two, she dropped on her knee before the King. "Your Majesty," said she, "if indeed I kneel before King Charles, is the father of your subjects."

"Of a good many of them," said the Duke of Buckingham, apart.

"I demand protection of you, in the name of God, and of the oath your Majesty swore when you placed on your head the crown of this kingdom!"

"You have my protection," said the King, a little confused by an appeal so unexpected and so solemn. "Do but remain quiet with this lady, with whom your parents have placed you; neither Buckingham nor any one else shall intrude on you."

"His Majesty," added Buckingham, in the same tone, and speaking from the restless and mischief-making spirit of contra-diction, which he never could restrain, even when indulging it was most contrary, not only to propriety, but to his own interest,—"His Majesty will protect you, fair lady, from all intrusion save what must not be termed such."

Alice darted a keen look on the Duke, as if to read his mean-ing; another on Charles, to know whether she had guessed it rightly. There was a guilty confession on the King's brow, which confirmed Alice's determination to depart. "Your Majesty will forgive me," she said; "it is not here that I can enjoy the advantage of your royal protection. I am resolved to leave this house. If I am detained, it must be by violence, which I trust no one dare offer to me in your Majesty's presence. This gentleman, whom I have long known, will conduct me to my friends."

"We make but an indifferent figure in this scene, methinks," said the King, addressing the Duke of Buckingham, and speaking in a whisper; "but she must go—I neither will, nor dare, stop her from returning to her father."

"And if she does," swore the Duke internally, "I would, as Sir Andrew Smith saith, I might never touch fair lady's hand." And stepping back, he spoke a few words with Empson the musician, who left the apartment, for a few minutes, and presently returned.

The King seemed irresolute concerning the part he should act under circumstances so peculiar. To be foiled in a gallant intrigue, was to subject himself to the ridicule of his gay court; to persist in it by any means which approached to constraint, would have been tyrannical; and, what perhaps he might judge as severe an imputation, it would have been unbecoming a gentleman. "Upon my honour, young lady," he said, with an emphasis, "you have nothing to fear in this house. But it is improper, for your own sake, that you should leave it in this abrupt manner. If you will have the goodness to wait but a quarter of an hour, Mistress Chiffinch's coach will be placed at your command, to transport you where you will. Spare yourself the ridicule, and me the pain of seeing you leave the house of one of my servants, as if you were escaping from a prison."

The King spoke in good-natured sincerity, and Alice was inclined for an instant to listen to his advice; but recollecting that she had to search for her father and uncle, or, failing them, for some suitable place of secure residence, it rushed on her mind that the attendants of Mistress Chiffinch were not likely to prove trusty guides or assistants in such a purpose. Firmly and respectfully she announced her purpose of instant departure. She needed no other escort, she said, than what this gentleman, Master Julian Peveril, who was well known to her father, would willingly afford her; nor did she need that farther than until she had reached her father's residence.

"Farewell, then, lady, a God's name!" said the King; "I am sorry so much beauty should be wedded to so many shrewish suspicions.—For you, Master Peveril, I should have thought you had enough to do with your own affairs without interfering with the humours of the fair sex. The duty of conducting all strayed damsels into the right path is, as matters go in this good city, rather too weighty an undertaking for your youth and inexperience."

Julian, eager to conduct Alice from a place of which he began fully to appreciate the perils, answered nothing to this taunt, but bowing reverently, led her from the apartment. Her sudden appearance, and the animated scene which followed, had entirely absorbed, for the moment, the recollection of his father, and of the Countess of Derby; and while the dumb attendant of the latter remained in the room, a silent, and, as it were, stunned spectator of all that had happened, Peveril had become, in the predominating interest of Alice's critical situation, totally forgetful of her presence. But no sooner had he left the room, without noticing or attending to her, than Fenella, starting, as from a trance, drew herself up, and looked wildly around, like one waking from a dream, as if to assure herself that her companion was gone, and gone without paying the slightest attention to her. She folded her hands together, and cast her eyes upwards, with an expression of such agony as explained to Charles (as he thought) what painful ideas were passing in her mind. "This Peveril is a perfect pattern of successful perfidy," said the King; "he has not only succeeded at first sight in carrying off this Queen of the Amazons, but he has left us, I think, a disconsolate Ariadne in her place.—But weep not, my princess of pretty movements," he said, addressing himself to Fenella; "if we cannot call in Bacchus to console you, we will commit you to the care of Empson, who shall drink with *Liber Pater* for a thousand pounds, and I will say done first."

As the King spoke these words, Fenella rushed past him with her wonted rapidity of step, and, with much less courtesy than was due to the royal presence, hurried downstairs, and out of the house, without attempting to open any communication with the Monarch. He saw her abrupt departure with more surprise than displeasure; and presently afterwards, bursting into a fit of laughter, he said to the Duke, "Oddsfish, George, this young spark might teach the best of us how to manage the wenches. I have had my own experience, but I could never yet contrive either to win or lose them with so little ceremony."

"Experience, sir," replied the Duke, "cannot be acquired without years."

"True, George; and you would, I suppose, insinuate," said Charles, "that the gallant who acquires it, loses as much in youth as he gains in art? I defy your insinuation, George. You cannot overreach your master, old as you think him, either in love or politics. You have not the secret *plumer la poule sans la faire crier,* witness this morning's work. I will give you odds at all games—ay, and at the Mall too, if thou darest accept my challenge.—Chiffinch, what for dost thou convulse thy pretty throat and face with sobbing and hatching tears, which seem rather unwilling to make their appearance!"

"It is for fear," whined Chiffinch, "that your Majesty should think—that you should expect——"

"That I should expect gratitude from a courtier, or faith from a woman?" answered the King, patting her at the same time under the chin, to make her raise her face—"Tush! chicken, I am not so superfluous."

"There it is now," said Chiffinch, continuing to sob the more bitterly, as she felt herself unable to produce any tears; "I see your Majesty is determined to lay all the blame on me, when I am innocent as an unborn babe—I will be judged by his Grace."

"No doubt, no doubt, Chiffie," said the King. "His Grace and you will be excellent judges in each other's cause, and as good witnesses in each other's favour. But to investigate the matter impartially, we must examine our evidence apart.—My Lord Duke, we meet at the Mall at noon, if your Grace dare accept my challenge."

His Grace of Buckingham bowed, and retired.

CHAPTER XXXII

> But when the bully with assuming pace,
> Cocks his broad hat, edged round with tarnish'd lace,
> Yield not the way—defy his strutting pride,
> And thrust him to the muddy kennel's side,
> Yet rather bear the shower and toils of mud,
> Than in the doubtful quarrel risk thy blood.
>
> —Gay's Trivia.

JULIAN PEVERIL, half-leading, half-supporting, Alice Bridge-north, had reached the middle of Saint James's Street ere the doubt occurred to him which way they should bend their course. He then asked Alice whither he should conduct her, and learned, to his surprise and embarrassment, that, far from knowing where her father was to be found, she had no certain knowledge that he was in London, and only hoped that he had arrived, from the expressions which he had used at parting. She mentioned her uncle Christian's address, but it was with doubt and hesitation, arising from the hands in which he had already placed her; and her reluctance to go again under his protection was strongly confirmed by her youthful guide, when a few words had established to his conviction the identity of Ganlesse and Christian.—What then was to be done?

"Alice," said Julian, after a moment's reflection, "you must seek your earliest and best friend—I mean my mother. She has now no castle in which to receive you—she has but a miserable lodging, so near the jail in which my father is confined, that it seems almost a cell of the same prison. I have not seen her since my coming hither; but thus much have I learned by inquiry. We will now go to her apartment; such as it is, I know she will share it with one so innocent and so unprotected as you are."

"Gracious Heaven!" said the poor girl, "am I then so totally deserted, that I must throw myself on the mercy of her who, of all the world, has most reason to spurn me from her?—Julian, can you advise me to this?—Is there none else who will afford me a few hours' refuge, till I can hear from my father?—No other protectress but her whose ruin has, I fear, been accelerated by——Julian, I dare not appear before your mother! she must hate me for my family, and despise me for my meanness. To be a second time cast on her protection, when the first has been so evil repaid—Julian, I dare not go with you."

"She has never ceased to love you, Alice," said her conductor, whose steps she continued to attend, even while declaring her resolution not to go with him, "she never felt anything but kindness towards you, nay, towards your father; for though his dealings with us have been harsh, she can allow much for the provocation which he has received. Believe me, with her you will be safe as with a mother—perhaps it may be the means of reconciling the divisions by which we have suffered so much."

"Might God grant it!" said Alice. "Yet how shall I face your mother? And will she be able to protect me against these powerful men—against my uncle Christian? Alas, that I must call him my worst enemy!"

"She has the ascendency which honour hath over infamy, and virtue over vice," said Julian; "and to no human power but your father's will she resign you, if you consent to choose her for your protectress. Come, then, with me, Alice; and——"

Julian was interrupted by some one, who, laying an unceremonious hold of his cloak, pulled it with so much force as compelled him to stop and lay his hand on his sword. He turned at the same time, and, when he turned, beheld Fenella. The cheek of the mute glowed like fire; her eyes sparkled, and her lips were forcibly drawn together, as if she had difficulty to repress those wild screams which usually attended her agonies of passion, and which, uttered in the open street, must instantly have collected a crowd. As it was, her appearance was so singular, and her emotion so evident, that men gazed as they came on, and looked back after they had passed, at the singular vivacity of her gestures; while, holding Peveril's cloak with one hand, she made with the other the most eager and imperious signs that he should leave Alice Bridgenorth and follow her. She touched the plume in her bonnet to remind him of the Earl—pointed to her heart, to imitate the Countess—raised her closed hand, as if to command him in their name—and next moment folded both, as if to supplicate him in her own; while pointing to Alice with an expression at once of angry and scornful derision, she waved her hand repeatedly and

disdainfully, to intimate that Peveril ought to cast her off, as
something undeserving his protection.

Frightened, she knew not why, at these wild gestures, Alice
clung closer to Julian's arm than she had at first dared to do:
and this mark of confidence in his protection seemed to increase
the passion of Fenella.

Julian was dreadfully embarrassed; his situation was sufficiently precarious, even before Fenella's ungovernable passions
threatened to ruin the only plan which he had been able to
suggest. What she wanted with him—how far the fate of the
Earl and Countess might depend on his following her, he could
not even conjecture; but be the call how peremptory soever,
he resolved not to comply with it until he had seen Alice
placed in safety. In the meantime, he determined not to lose
sight of Fenella; and disregarding her repeated, disdainful,
and impetuous rejection of the hand which he offered her, he
at length seemed so far to have soothed her, that she seized
upon his right arm, and, as if despairing of his following *her*
path, appeared reconciled to attend him on that which he himself should choose.

Thus, with a youthful female clinging to each arm, and both
remarkably calculated to attract the public eye, though from
very different reasons, Julian resolved to make the shortest
road to the water-side, and there to take boat for Blackfriars,
as the nearest point of landing to Newgate, where he concluded
that Lance had already announced his arrival in London to Sir
Geoffrey, then inhabiting that dismal region, and to his lady,
who, so far as the jailer's rigour permitted, shared and softened
his imprisonment.

Julian's embarrassment in passing Charing Cross and North-
umberland House was so great as to excite the attention of the
passengers; for he had to compose his steps so as to moderate
the unequal and rapid pace of Fenella to the timid and faint
progress of his left-hand companion; and while it would have
been needless to address himself to the former, who could not
comprehend him, he dared not speak himself to Alice, for
fear of awakening into frenzy the jealousy, or at least the
impatience of Fenella.

Many passengers looked at them with wonder, and some
with smiles; but Julian remarked that there were two who
never lost sight of them, and to whom his situation, and the
demeanour of his companions, seemed to afford matter of undisguised merriment. These were young men, such as may be
seen in the same precincts in the present day, allowing for the
difference in the fashion of their apparel. They abounded in
periwig, and fluttered with many hundred yards of ribbon, disposed in bow-knots upon their sleeves, their breeches, and their

waistcoats, in the very extremity of the existing mode. A quantity of lace and embroidery made their habits rather fine than tasteful. In a word, they were dressed in that caricature of the fashion, which sometimes denotes a harebrained man of quality who has a mind to be distinguished as a fop of the first order, but is much more frequently the disguise of those who desire to be esteemed men of rank on account of their dress, having no other pretension to the distinction.

These two gallants passed Peveril more than once, linked arm in arm, then sauntered, so as to oblige him to pass them in turn, laughing and whispering during these manœuvres—staring broadly at Peveril and his female companions—and affording them, as they came into contact, none of those facilities of giving place which are required on such occasions by the ordinary rules of the pavé.

Peveril did not immediately observe their impertinence; but when it was too gross to escape his notice, his gall began to arise; and, in addition to all the other embarrassments of his situation, he had to combat the longing desire which he felt to cudgel handsomely the two coxcombs who seemed thus determined on insulting him. Patience and sufferance were indeed strongly imposed on him by circumstances; but at length it became scarcely possible to observe their dictates any longer.

When, for the third time, Julian found himself obliged, with his companions, to pass this troublesome brace of fops, they kept walking close behind him, speaking so loud as to be heard, and in a tone of perfect indifference whether he listened to them or not.

"This is bumpkin's best luck," said the taller of the two (who was indeed a man of remarkable size, alluding to the plainness of Peveril's dress, which was scarce fit for the streets of London)—"Two such fine wenches, and under guard of a grey frock and an oaken riding-rod!"

"Nay, Puritan's luck rather, and more than enough of it," said his companion. "You may read Puritan in his pace and in his patience."

"Right as a pint bumper, Tom," said his friend—"Issachar is an ass that stoopeth between two burdens."

"I have a mind to ease long-eared Laurence of one of his encumbrances," said the shorter fellow. "That black-eyed sparkler looks as if she had a mind to run away from him."

"Ay," answered the taller, "and the blue-eyed trembler looks as if she would fall behind into my loving arms."

At these words, Alice, holding still closer by Peveril's arm than formerly, mended her pace almost to running, in order to escape from men whose language was so alarming; and

Fenella walked hastily forward in the same manner, having perhaps caught, from the men's gestures and demeanour, that apprehension which Alice had taken from their language.

Fearful of the consequences of a fray in the streets, which must necessarily separate him from these unprotected females, Peveril endeavoured to compound betwixt the prudence necessary for their protection and his own rising resentment; and as this troublesome pair of attendants endeavoured again to pass them close to Hungerford Stairs, he said to them with constrained calmness, "Gentlemen, I owe you something for the attention you have bestowed on the affairs of a stranger. If you have any pretension to the name I have given you, you will tell me where you are to be found."

"And with what purpose," said the taller of the two sneeringly, "does your most rustic gravity, or your most grave rusticity, require of us such information?"

So saying, they both faced about, in such a manner as to make it impossible for Julian to advance any farther.

"Make for the stairs, Alice," he said; "I will be with you in an instant." Then freeing himself with difficulty from the grasp of his companions, he cast his cloak hastily round his left arm, and said, sternly, to his opponents, "Will you give me your names, sirs; or will you be pleased to make way?"

"Not till we know for whom we are to give place," said one of them.

"For one who will else teach you what you want—good manners," said Peveril, and advanced as if to push between them.

They separated, but one of them stretched forth his foot before Peveril, as if he meant to trip him. The blood of his ancestors was already boiling within him; he struck the man on the face with the oaken rod which he had just sneered at, and throwing it from him, instantly unsheathed his sword. Both the others drew, and pushed at once; but he caught the point of the one rapier in his cloak, and parried the other thrust with his own weapon. He might have been less lucky in the second close, but a cry arose among the watermen, of "Shame, shame! two upon one!"

"They are men of the Duke of Buckingham's," said one fellow—"there's no safe meddling with them."

"They may be the devil's men, if they will," said an ancient Triton, flourishing his stretcher; "but I say fair play, and old England for ever; and, I say, knock the gold-laced puppies down, unless they will fight turn about with grey jerkin, like honest fellows. One down—t'other come on."

The lower orders of London have in all times been remarkable for the delight which they have taken in club-law, or fist-

law ; and for the equity and impartiality with which they see
it administered. The noble science of defence was then so
generally known, that a bout at single rapier excited at that
time as much interest and as little wonder as a boxing-match
in our own days. The bystanders, experienced in such affrays,
presently formed a ring, within which Peveril and the taller
and more forward of his antagonists were soon engaged in close
combat with their swords, whilst the other, overawed by the
spectators, was prevented from interfering.

"Well done the tall fellow!"—"Well thrust, long-legs!"—
"Huzza for two ells and a quarter!" were the sounds with which
the fray was at first cheered ; for Peveril's opponent not only
showed great activity and skill in fence, but had also a decided
advantage, from the anxiety with which Julian looked out for
Alice Bridgenorth ; the care for whose safety diverted him in
the beginning of the onset from that which he ought to have
exclusively bestowed on the defence of his own life. A slight
flesh-wound in the side at once punished, and warned him of
his inadvertence ; when, turning his whole thoughts on the
business in which he was engaged, and animated with anger
against his impertinent intruder, the rencontre speedily began
to assume another face, amidst cries of "Well done, grey
jerkin!"—"Try the metal of his gold doublet!"—"Finely
thrust!"—"Curiously parried!"—"There went another eyelet
hole to his broidered jerkin!"—"Fairly pinked, by G—d!" In
fact, the last exclamation was uttered amid a general roar of
applause, accompanying a successful and conclusive lounge
by which Peveril ran his gigantic antagonist through the
body. He looked at his prostrate foe for a moment ; then
recovering himself, called loudly to know what had become of
the lady.

"Never mind the lady, if you be wise," said one of the
watermen ; "the constable will be here in an instant. I'll
give your honour a cast across the water in a moment. It
may be as much as your neck's worth. Shall only charge a
Jacobus."

"You be d—d!" said one of his rivals in profession, "as
your father was before you ; for a Jacobus, I'll set the gentleman into Alsatia, where neither bailiff nor constable dare
trespass."

"The lady, you scoundrels, the lady!" exclaimed Peveril—
"Where is the lady?"

"I'll carry your honour where you shall have enough of
ladies, if that be your want," said the old Triton ; and as he
spoke, the clamour amongst the watermen was renewed, each
hoping to cut his own profit out of the emergency of Julian's
situation.

"A sculler will be least suspected, your honour," said one fellow.

"A pair of oars will carry you through the water like a wild-duck," said another.

"But you have got never a tilt, brother," said a third. "Now I can put the gentleman as snug as if he were under hatches."

In the midst of the oaths and clamour attending this aquatic controversy for his custom, Peveril at length made them understand that he would bestow a Jacobus, not on him whose boat was first oars, but on whomsoever should inform him of the fate of the lady.

"Of which lady?" said a sharp fellow; "for, to my thought, there was a pair on them."

"Of both, of both," answered Peveril; "but first, of the fair-haired lady?"

"Ay, ay, that was she that shrieked so when gold-jacket's companion handed her into No. 20."

"Who—what—who dared to hand her?" exclaimed Peveril.

"Nay, master, you have heard enough of my tale without a fee," said the waterman.

"Sordid rascal!" said Peveril, giving him a gold piece, "speak out, or I'll run my sword through you!"

"For the matter of that, master," answered the fellow, "not while I can handle this trunnion—but a bargain's a bargain; and so I'll tell you, for your gold piece, that the comrade of the fellow forced one of your wenches, her with the fair hair, will she, nill she, into Tickling Tom's wherry; and they are far enough up Thames by this time, with wind and tide."

"Sacred Heaven, and I stand here!" exclaimed Julian.

"Why, that is because your honour will not take a boat."

"You are right, my friend—a boat—a boat instantly!"

"Follow me, then, squire.—Here, Tom, bear a hand—the gentleman is our fare."

A volley of water language was exchanged betwixt the successful candidate for Peveril's custom and his disappointed brethren, which concluded by the ancient Triton's bellowing out, in a tone above them all, "that the gentleman was in a fair way to make a voyage to the isle of gulls, for that sly Jack was only bantering him—No. 20 had rowed for York Buildings."

"To the isle of gallows," cried another; "for here comes one who will mar his trip up Thames, and carry him down to Execution Dock."

In fact, as he spoke the word, a constable, with three or four of his assistants, armed with the old-fashioned brown bills, which were still used for arming those guardians of the peace,

cut off our hero's farther progress to the water's edge, by arrest
ing him in the King's name. To attempt resistance would have
been madness, as he was surrounded on all sides; so Peveril
was disarmed, and carried before the nearest Justice of the
Peace, for examination and committal.

The legal sage before whom Julian was taken was a man
very honest in his intentions, very bounded in his talents, and
rather timid in his disposition. Before the general alarm given
to England, and to the city of London in particular, by the
notable discovery of the Popish Plot, Master Maulstatute had
taken serene and undisturbed pride and pleasure in the discharge of his duties as a Justice of the Peace, with the exercise
of all its honorary privileges and awful authority. But the
murder of Sir Edmondsbury Godfrey had made a strong, nay
an indelible impression on his mind; and he walked the Courts
of Themis with fear and trembling after that memorable and
melancholy event.

Having a high idea of his official importance, and rather an
exalted notion of his personal consequence, his honour saw
nothing from that time but cords and daggers before his eyes,
and never stepped out of his own house, which he fortified, and
in some measure garrisoned, with half-a-dozen tall watchmen
and constables, without seeing himself watched by a Papist in
disguise, with a drawn sword under his cloak. It was even
whispered, that, in the agonies of his fears, the worshipful
Master Maulstatute mistook the kitchen-wench with a tinder-
box, for a Jesuit with a pistol; but if any one dared to laugh
at such an error, he would have done well to conceal his mirth,
lest he fell under the heavy inculpation of being a banterer
and stifler of the Plot—a crime almost as deep as that of being
himself a plotter. In fact, the fears of the honest Justice, however ridiculously exorbitant, were kept so much in countenance
by the outcry of the day, and the general nervous fever, which
afflicted every good Protestant, that Master Maulstatute was
accounted the bolder man and the better magistrate, while,
under the terror of the air-drawn dagger which fancy placed
continually before his eyes, he continued to dole forth justice
in the recesses of his private chamber, nay, occasionally to
attend Quarter-Sessions, when the hall was guarded by a sufficient body of the militia. Such was the wight, at whose door,
well chained and doubly bolted, the constable who had Julian
in custody now gave his important and well-known knock.

Notwithstanding this official signal, the party was not admitted until the clerk, who acted the part of high-warder, had
reconnoitred them through a grated wicket; for who could say
whether the Papists might not have made themselves master of
Master Constable's sign, and have prepared a pseudo watch to

burst in and murder the Justice, under pretence of bringing a
criminal before him?—Less hopeful projects had figured in the
Narrative of the Popish Plot.

All being found right, the key was turned, the bolts were
drawn, and the chain unhooked, so as to permit entrance to the
constable, the prisoner, and the assistants; and the door was
then as suddenly shut against the witnesses, who, as less trust-
worthy persons, were requested (through the wicket) to remain
in the yard, until they should be called in their respective
turns.

Had Julian been inclined for mirth, as was far from being
the case, he must have smiled at the incongruity of the clerk's
apparel, who had belted over his black buckram suit a buff
baldric, sustaining a broadsword, and a pair of huge horse-pistols;
and, instead of the low flat hat, which, coming in place of the
city cap, completed the dress of a scrivener, had placed on his
greasy locks a rusted steel-cap, which had seen Marston-Moor;
across which projected his well-used quill, in the guise of a
plume—the shape of the morion not admitting of its being
stuck, as usual, behind his ear.

This whimsical figure conducted the constable, his assistants,
and the prisoner, into the low hall, where his principal dealt
forth justice; who presented an appearance still more singular
than that of his dependant.

Sundry good Protestants, who thought so highly of themselves as to suppose they were worthy to be distinguished as
objects of Catholic cruelty, had taken to defensive arms on the
occasion. But it was quickly found that a breast-plate and
back-plate of proof, fastened together with iron clasps, was no
convenient enclosure for a man who meant to eat venison and
custard; and that a buff-coat or shirt of mail was scarcely
more accommodating to the exertions necessary on such active
occasions. Besides, there were other objections, as the alarming
and menacing aspects which such warlike habiliments gave to
the Exchange, and other places, where merchants most do con-
gregate; and excoriations were bitterly complained of by many,
who, not belonging to the artillery company, or trained bands,
had no experience in bearing defensive armour.

To obviate these objections, and, at the same time, to secure
the persons of all true Protestant citizens against open force or
privy assassinations on the part of the Papists, some ingenious
artist, belonging, we may presume, to the worshipful Mercers'
Company, had contrived a species of armour, of which neither
the horse-armory in the Tower, nor Gwynnap's Gothic Hall,
no, nor Dr. Meyrick's invaluable collection of ancient arms, has
preserved any specimen. It was called silk-armour, being
composed of a doublet and breeches of quilted silk, so closely

Y

stitched, and of such thickness, as to be proof against either bullet or steel; while a thick bonnet of the same materials, with ear-flaps attached to it, and on the whole, much resembling a nightcap, completed the equipment and ascertained the security of the wearer from the head to the knee.

Master Maulstatute, among other worthy citizens, had adopted this singular panoply, which had the advantage of being soft, and warm, and flexible, as well as safe. And he now sat in his judicial elbow-chair—a short, rotund figure, hung round, as it were, with cushions, for such was the appearance of the quilted garments; and with a nose protruded from under the silken casque, the size of which, together with the unwieldiness of the whole figure, gave his worship no indifferent resemblance to the sign of the Hog in Armour, which was considerably improved by the defensive garment being of a dusty orange colour, not altogether unlike the hue of those half-wild swine which are to be found in the forest of Hampshire.

Secure in these invulnerable envelopments, his worship had rested content, although severed from his own death-doing weapons, of rapier, poniard, and pistols, which were placed, nevertheless, at no great distance from his chair. One offensive implement, indeed, he thought it prudent to keep on the table beside his huge Coke upon Lyttleton. This was a sort of pocket flail, consisting of a piece of strong ash, about eighteen inches long, to which was attached a swinging club of *lignum-vitæ*, nearly twice as long as the handle, but jointed so as to be easily folded up. This instrument, which bore at that time the singular name of the Protestant flail, might be concealed under the coat, until circumstances demanded its public appearance. A better precaution against surprise than his arms, whether offensive or defensive, was a strong iron grating, which, crossing the room in front of the justice's table, and communicating by a grated door, which was usually kept locked, effectually separated the accused party from his judge.

Justice Maulstatute, such as we have described him, chose to hear the accusation of the witnesses before calling on Peveril for his defence. The detail of the affray was briefly given by the bystanders, and seemed deeply to touch the spirit of the examinator. He shook his silken casque emphatically, when he understood that, after some language betwixt the parties, which the witnesses did not quite understand, the young man in custody struck the first blow, and drew his sword before the wounded party had unsheathed his weapon. Again he shook his crested head yet more solemnly, when the result of the conflict was known; and yet again, when one of the witnesses declared, that, to the best of his knowledge, the sufferer in the fray was a gentleman belonging to the household of his Grace the Duke of Buckingham.

"A worthy peer," quoth the armed magistrate—"a true Protestant, and a friend to his country. Mercy on us, to what a height of audacity hath this age arisen! We see well, and could, were we as blind as a mole, out of what quiver this shaft hath been drawn."

He then put on his spectacles, and having desired Julian to be brought forward, he glared upon him awfully with those glazen eyes, from under the shade of his quilted turban.

"So young," he said, "and so hardened—lack-a-day!—and a Papist, I'll warrant."

Peveril had time enough to recollect the necessity of his being at large, if he could possibly obtain his freedom, and interposed here a civil contradiction of his worship's gracious supposition. "He was no Catholic," he said, "but an unworthy member of the Church of England."

"Perhaps but a lukewarm Protestant, notwithstanding," said the sage Justice; "there are those amongst us who ride tantivy to Rome, and have already made out half the journey —ahem!"

Peveril disowned his being any such.

"And who art thou, then?" said the Justice; "for, friend, to tell you plainly, I like not your visage—ahem!"

These short and emphatic coughs were accompanied each by a succinct nod, intimating the perfect conviction of the speaker that he had made the best, the wisest, and the most acute observation, of which the premises admitted.

Julian, irritated by the whole circumstances of his detention, answered the Justice's interrogation in rather a lofty tone. "My name is Julian Peveril!"

"Now, Heaven be around us!" said the terrified Justice— "the son of that black-hearted Papist and traitor, Sir Geoffrey Peveril, now in hands, and on the verge of trial!"

"How, sir!" exclaimed Julian, forgetting his situation, and, stepping forward to the grating, with a violence which made the bars clatter, he so startled the appalled Justice, that, snatching his Protestant flail, Master Maulstatute aimed a blow at his prisoner, to repel what he apprehended was a premeditated attack. But whether it was owing to the Justice's hurry of mind, or inexperience in managing the weapon, he not only missed his aim, but brought the swinging part of the machine round his own skull, with such a severe counter-buff, as completely to try the efficacy of his cushioned helmet, and, in spite of its defence, to convey a stunning sensation, which he rather hastily imputed to the consequence of a blow received from Peveril.

His assistants did not directly confirm the opinion which the Justice had so unwarrantably adopted; but all with one voice agreed that, but for their own active and instantaneous interference, there was no knowing what mischief might have been done by a person so dangerous as the prisoner. The general opinion that he meant to proceed in the matter of his own rescue, *par voie du fait,* was indeed so deeply impressed on all present, that Julian saw it would be in vain to offer any defence, especially being but too conscious that the alarming and probably the fatal consequences of his rencontre with the bully, rendered his commitment inevitable. He contented himself with asking into what prison he was to be thrown; and when the formidable word Newgate was returned as full answer, he had at least the satisfaction to reflect, that, stern and dangerous as was the shelter of that roof, he should at least enjoy it in company with his father; and that, by some means or other, they might perhaps obtain the satisfaction of a melancholy meeting, under the circumstances of mutual calamity, which seemed impending over their house.

Assuming the virtue of more patience than he actually possessed, Julian gave the magistrate (to whom all the mildness of his demeanour could not, however, reconcile him), the direction to the house where he lodged, together with a request that his servant, Lance Outram, might be permitted to send him his money and wearing apparel; adding, that all which might be in his possession, either of arms or writings,—the former amounting to a pair of travelling pistols, and the last to a few memoranda of little consequence, he willingly consented to place at the disposal of the magistrate. It was in that moment that he entertained, with sincere satisfaction, the comforting reflection, that the important papers of Lady Derby were already in the possession of the sovereign.

The Justice promised attention to his requests; but reminded him, with great dignity, that his present complacent and submissive behaviour ought, for his own sake, to have been adopted from the beginning, instead of disturbing the presence of magistracy with such atrocious marks of the malignant, rebellious, and murderous spirit of Popery, as he had at first exhibited. "Yet," he said, "as he was a goodly young man, and of honourable quality, he would not suffer him to be dragged through the streets as a felon, but had ordered a coach for his accommodation."

His honour, Master Maulstatute, uttered the word "coach" with the importance of one who, as Dr. Johnson saith of later date, is conscious of the dignity of putting horses to his chariot. The worshipful Master Maulstatute did not, however, on this occasion, do Julian the honour of yoking to his huge family caroche the two "frampal jades" (to use the term of the period), which were wont to drag that ark to the meeting-house of pure and precious Master Howlaglass, on a Thursday's evening for lecture, and on a Sunday for a four-hours' sermon. He had recourse to a leathern convenience, then more rare, but just introduced, with every prospect of the great facility which has since been afforded by hackney coaches, to all manner of communication, honest and dishonest, legal and illegal. Our friend Julian, hitherto much more accustomed to the saddle than to any other conveyance, soon found himself in a hackney carriage, with the constable and two assistants for his companions, armed up to the teeth—the port of destination being, as they had already intimated, the ancient fortress of Newgate.

CHAPTER XXXIII

'Tis the black ban-dog of our jail—Pray look on him,
But at a wary distance—rouse him not—
He bays not till he worries.
—THE BLACK DOG OF NEWGATE.

THE coach stopped before those tremendous gates, which resemble those of Tartarus, save only that they rather more frequently permit safe and honourable egress; although at the price of the same anxiety and labour with which Hercules, and one or two of the demi-gods, extricated themselves from the Hell of the ancient mythology, and sometimes, it is said, by the assistance of the golden boughs.

Julian stepped out of the vehicle, carefully supported on either side by his companions, and also by one or two turnkeys, whom the first summons of the deep bell at the gate had called to their assistance. That attention, it may be guessed, was not bestowed lest he should make a false step, so much as for fear of his attempting an escape, of which he had no intentions. A few prentices and straggling boys of the neighbouring market, which derived considerable advantage from increase of custom, in consequence of the numerous committals on account of the Popish Plot, and who therefore were zealous Protestants, saluted him on his descent with jubilee shouts of "Whoop, Papist! whoop, Papist! D——n to the Pope, and all his adherents!"

Under such auspices, Peveril was ushered in beneath that gloomy gateway, where so many bid adieu on their entrance at once to honour and to life. The dark and dismal arch under which he soon found himself opened upon a large courtyard, where a number of debtors were employed in playing at hand-ball, pitch-and-toss, hustle-cap, and other games, for which relaxations the rigour of their creditors afforded them full leisure, while it debarred them the means of pursuing the honest labour by which they might have redeemed their affairs, and maintained their starving and beggared families.

But with this careless and desperate group Julian was not to be numbered, being led, or rather forced, by his conductors, into a low arched door, which, carefully secured by bolts and bars, opened for his reception on one side of the archway, and closed, with all its fastenings, the moment after his hasty entrance. He was then conducted along two or three gloomy passages, which, where they intersected each other, were guarded by as many strong wickets, one of iron gates, and the others of stout oak, clinched with plates, and studded with nails of the same metal. He was not allowed to pause until he found himself hurried into a little round vaulted room, which several of these passages opened into, and which seemed, with respect to the labyrinth through part of which he had passed, to resemble the central point of a spider's web, in which the main lines of that reptile's curious maze are always found to terminate.

The resemblance did not end here; for in this small vaulted apartment, the walls of which were hung round with musketoons, pistols, cutlasses, and other weapons, as well as with many sets of fetters and irons of different construction, all disposed in great order, and ready for employment, a person sat, who might not unaptly be compared to a huge bloated and bottled spider, placed there to secure the prey which had fallen into his toils.

This official had originally been a very strong and square-built man, of large size, but was now so overgrown, from over-feeding, perhaps, and want of exercise, as to bear the same resemblance to his former self which a stall-fed ox still retains to a wild bull. The look of no man is so inauspicious as a fat man, upon whose features ill-nature has marked an habitual stamp. He seems to have reversed the old proverb of "laugh and be fat," and to have thriven under the influence of the worst affections of the mind. Passionate we can allow a jolly mortal to be; but it seems unnatural to his goodly case to be sulky and brutal. Now this man's features, surly and tallow-coloured; his limbs, swelled and disproportioned; his huge paunch and unwieldy carcass, suggested the idea, that, having once found his way into this central recess, he had there fattened, like the weasel in the fable, and fed largely and foully, until he had become incapable of retreating through any of the narrow paths that terminated at his cell; and was thus compelled to remain, like a toad under the cold stone, fattening amid the squalid airs of the dungeons by which he was surrounded, which would have proved pestiferous to any other than such a congenial inhabitant. Huge iron-clasped books lay before this ominous specimen of pinguitude—the records of the realm of misery, in which office he officiated as prime minister; and had Peveril come thither as an unconcerned visitor, his heart would have sunk within him at considering the mass of human wretchedness which must needs be registered in these fatal volumes. But his own distresses sat too heavy on his mind to permit any general reflections of this nature.

The constable and this bulky official whispered together, after the former had delivered to the latter the warrant of Julian's commitment. The word *whispered* is not quite accurate, for their communication was carried on less by words than by looks and expressive signs; by which, in all such situations, men learn to supply the use of language, and to add mystery to what is in itself sufficiently terrible to the captive. The only words which could be heard were those of the Warden, or, as he was called then, the Captain of the Jail, "Another bird to the cage——?"

"Who will whistle ' Pretty Pope of Rome,' with any starling in your Knight's ward," answered the constable, with a facetious air, checked, however, by the due respect to the superior presence in which he stood.

The Grim Feature relaxed into something like a smile as he heard the officer's observation; but instantly composing himself into the stern solemnity which for an instant had been disturbed, he looked fiercely at his new guest, and pronounced with an awful and emphatic, yet rather an under-voice, the single and impressive word, " *Garnish !* "

Julian Peveril replied with assumed composure; for he had heard of the customs of such places, and was resolved to comply with them, so as if possible to obtain the favour of seeing his father, which he shrewdly guessed must depend on his gratifying the avarice of the keeper. " I am quite ready," he said, " to accede to the customs of the place in which I unhappily find myself. You have but to name your demands, and I will satisfy them."

So saying, he drew out his purse, thinking himself at the same time fortunate that he had retained about him a considerable sum of gold. The Captain remarked its width, depth, its extension, and depression, with an involuntary smile, which had scarce contorted his hanging under-lip, and the wiry and greasy moustache which thatched the upper, when it was checked by the recollection that there were regulations which set bounds to his rapacity, and prevented him from pouncing on his prey like a kite, and swooping it all off at once.

This chilling reflection produced the following sullen reply to Peveril: — "There were sundry rates. Gentlemen must choose for themselves. He asked nothing but his fees. But civility," he muttered, "must be paid for."

"And shall, if I can have it for payment," said Peveril; "but the price, my good sir, the price?"

He spoke with some degree of scorn, which he was the less anxious to repress, that he saw, even in this jail, his purse gave him an indirect but powerful influence over his jailer.

The Captain seemed to feel the same; for, as he spoke, he plucked from his head, almost involuntarily, a sort of scalded fur-cap, which served it for covering. But his fingers revolting from so unusual an act of complaisance, began to indemnify themselves by scratching his grizzly shock-head, as he muttered, in a tone resembling the softened growling of a mastiff when he has ceased to bay the intruder who shows no fear of him,— "There are different rates. There is the Little Ease, for common fees of the crown—rather dark, and the common sewer runs below it; and some gentlemen object to the company, who are chiefly padders and michers. Then the Master's side—the garnish came to one piece—and none lay stowed there but who were in for murder at the least."

"Name your highest price, sir, and take it," was Julian's concise reply.

"Three pieces for the Knight's ward," answered the governor of this terrestrial Tartarus.

"Take five, and place me with Sir Geoffrey," was again Julian's answer, throwing down the money upon the desk before him.

"Sir Geoffrey?—Hum!—ay, Sir Geoffrey," said the jailer, as if meditating what he ought to do. "Well, many a man has paid money to see Sir Geoffrey—Scarce so much as you have, though. But then you are like to see the last of him.— Ha, ha, ha!"

These broken muttered exclamations, which terminated some-what like the joyous growl of a tiger over his meal, Julian could not comprehend; and only replied to by repeating his request to be placed in the same cell with Sir Geoffrey.

"Ay, master," said the jailer, "never fear; I'll keep word with you, as you seem to know something of what belongs to your station and mine. And hark ye, Jem Clink will fetch you the darbies."

"Derby!" interrupted Julian,— "Has the Earl or Coun-tess——"

"Earl or Countess!—Ha, ha, ha!" again laughed, or rather growled, the warden. "What is your head running on? You are a high fellow belike! but all is one here. The darbies are the fetlocks—the fast-keepers, my boy—the bail for good behaviour, my darling; and if you are not the more conforming, I can add you a steel nightcap, and a curious bosom-friend, to keep you warm of a winter night. But don't be disheartened; you have behaved genteel; and you shall not be put upon. And as for this here matter, ten to one it will turn out chance-medley, or manslaughter, at the worst on it; and then it is but a singed thumb instead of a twisted neck—always if there be no Papistry about it, for then I warrant nothing.—Take the gentleman's worship away, Clink."

A turnkey, who was one of the party that had ushered Peveril into the presence of this Cerberus, now conveyed him out in silence; and, under his guidance, the prisoner was carried through a second labyrinth of passages with cells opening on each side, to that which was destined for his reception.

On the road through this sad region, the turnkey more than once ejaculated, "Why, the gentleman must be stark-mad! Could have had the best crown cell to himself for less than half the garnish, and must pay double to pig in with Sir Geoffrey! Ha, ha!—Is Sir Geoffrey akin to you, if any one may make free to ask?"

"I am his son," answered Peveril sternly, in hopes to impose some curb on the fellow's impertinence; but the man only laughed louder than before.

"His son!—Why, that's best of all—Why, you are a strapping youth—five feet ten, if you be an inch—and Sir Geoffrey's son!—Ha, ha, ha!"

"Truce with your impertinence," said Julian. "My situation gives you no title to insult me!'"

"No more I do," said the turnkey, smothering his mirth at the recollection, perhaps, that the prisoner's purse was not exhausted. "I only laughed because you said you were Sir Geoffrey's son. But no matter—'tis a wise child that knows his own father. And here is Sir Geoffrey's cell; so you and he may settle the fatherhood between you."

So saying, he ushered his prisoner into a cell, or rather a strong room of the better order, in which there were four chairs, a truckle-bed, and one or two other articles of furniture.

Julian looked eagerly around for his father; but to his surprise the room appeared totally empty. He turned with anger on the turnkey, and charged him with misleading him; but the fellow answered, "No, no, master; I have kept faith with you. Your father, if you call him so, is only tappiced in some corner. A small hole will hide him; but I'll rouse him out presently for you.—Here, hoicks!—Turn out, Sir Geoffrey! —Here is—Ha, ha, ha!—your son—or your wife's son—for I think you can have but little share in him—come to wait on you."

Peveril knew not how to resent the man's insolence; and indeed his anxiety, and apprehension of some strange mistake, mingled with, and in some degree neutralised his anger. He looked again and again, around and around the room; until at length he became aware of something rolled up in a dark corner, which rather resembled a small bundle of crimson cloth than any living creature. At the vociferation of the turnkey, however, the object seemed to acquire life and motion, uncoiled itself in some degree, and, after an effort or two, gained an erect posture; still covered from top to toe with the crimson drapery in which it was at first wrapped. Julian, at the first glance, imagined from the size that he saw a child of five years old; but a shrill and peculiar tone of voice soon assured him of his mistake.

"Warder," said this unearthly sound, "what is the meaning of this disturbance? Have you more insults to heap on the head of one who hath ever been the butt of fortune's malice? But I have a soul that can wrestle with all my misfortunes; it is as large as any of your bodies."

"Nay, Sir Geoffrey, if this be the way you welcome your own son!" said the turnkey; "but you quality folks know your own ways best."

"My son!" exclaimed the little figure. "Audacious——"

"Here is some strange mistake," said Peveril, in the same breath. "I sought Sir Geoffrey——"

"And you have him before you, young man," said the pigmy tenant of the cell, with an air of dignity; at the same time casting on the floor his crimson cloak, and standing before them in his full dignity of three feet six inches of height. "I who was the favoured servant of three successive Sovereigns of the Crown of England, am now the tenant of this dungeon, and the sport of its brutal keepers. I am Sir Geoffrey Hudson."

Julian, though he had never before seen this important personage, had no difficulty in recognising, from description, the celebrated dwarf of Henrietta Maria, who had survived the dangers of civil war and private quarrel—the murder of his royal master, Charles I., and the exile of his widow—to fall upon evil tongues and evil days, amidst the unsparing accusations connected with the Popish Plot. He bowed to the unhappy old man, and hastened to explain to him, and to the turnkey, that it was Sir Geoffrey Peveril, of Martindale Castle in Derbyshire, whose prison he had desired to share.

"You should have said that before you parted with the gold-dust, my master," answered the turnkey; "for t'other Sir Geoffrey, that is the big, tall, grey-haired man, was sent to the

Tower last night; and the Captain will think he has kept his word well enow with you, by lodging you with this here Sir Geoffrey Hudson, who is the better show of the two."

"I pray you go to your master," said Peveril; "explain the mistake; and say to him I beg to be sent to the Tower."

"The Tower!—Ha, ha, ha!" exclaimed the fellow. "The Tower is for lords and knights, and not for squires of low degree —for high treason, and not for ruffling on the streets with rapier and dagger; and there must go a secretary's warrant to send you there."

"At least, let me not be a burden on this gentleman," said Julian. "There can be no use in quartering us together, since we are not even acquainted. Go tell your master of the mistake."

"Why, so I should," said Clink, still grinning, "if I were not sure that he knew it already. You paid to be sent to Sir Geoffrey, and he sent you to Sir Geoffrey. You are so put down in the register, and he will blot it for no man. Come, come, be conformable, and you shall have light and easy irons— that's all I can do for you."

Resistance and expostulation being out of the question, Peveril submitted to have a light pair of fetters secured on his ankles, which allowed him, nevertheless, the power of traversing the apartment.

During this operation, he reflected that the jailer, who had taken the advantage of the equivoque betwixt the two Sir Geoffreys, must have acted as his assistant had hinted, and cheated him from malice prepense, since the warrant of committal described him as the son of Sir Geoffrey Peveril. It was therefore in vain, as well as degrading, to make farther application to such a man on the subject. Julian determined to submit to his fate, as what could not be averted by any effort of his own.

Even the turnkey was moved in some degree by his youth, good mien, and the patience with which, after the first effervescence of disappointment, the new prisoner resigned himself to his situation. "You seem a brave young gentleman," he said; "and shall at least have a good dinner, and as good a pallet to sleep on, as is within the walls of Newgate. —And, Master Sir Geoffrey, you ought to make much of him, since you do not like tall fellows; for I can tell you that Master Peveril is in for pinking long Jack Jenkins, that was the Master of Defence—as tall a man as is in London, always excepting the King's Porter, Master Evans, that carried you about in his pocket, Sir Geoffrey, as all the world has heard tell."

"Begone, fellow!" answered the dwarf. "Fellow, I scorn you!"

The turnkey sneered, withdrew, and locked the door behind him.

CHAPTER XXXIV

Degenerate youth, and not of Tydeus' kind,
Whose little body lodged a mighty mind.
                                        —ILIAD.

LEFT quiet at least, if not alone, for the first time after the events of this troubled and varied day, Julian threw himself on an old oaken seat, beside the embers of a sea-coal fire, and began to muse on the miserable situation of anxiety and danger in which he was placed; where, whether he contemplated the interests of his love, his family affections, or his friendships, all seemed such a prospect as that of a sailor who looks upon breakers on every hand, from the deck of a vessel which no longer obeys the helm.

As Peveril sat sunk in despondency, his companion in misfortune drew a chair to the opposite side of the chimney-corner, and began to gaze at him with a sort of solemn earnestness, which at length compelled him, though almost in spite of himself, to pay some attention to the singular figure who seemed so much engrossed with contemplating him.

Geoffrey Hudson (we drop occasionally the title of knighthood, which the King had bestowed on him in a frolic, but which might introduce some confusion into our history), although a dwarf of the least possible size, had nothing positively ugly in his countenance, or actually distorted in his limbs. His head, hands, and feet were indeed large, and disproportioned to the height of his body, and his body itself much thicker than was consistent with symmetry, but in a degree which was rather ludicrous than disagreeable to look upon. His countenance, in particular, had he been a little taller, would have been accounted, in youth, handsome, and now, in age, striking and expressive; it was but the uncommon disproportion betwixt the head and the trunk which made the features seem whimsical and bizarre—an effect which was considerably increased by the dwarf's moustaches, which it was his pleasure to wear so large, that they almost twisted back amongst, and mingled with, his grizzled hair.

The dress of this singular wight announced that he was not entirely free from the unhappy taste which frequently induces those whom nature has marked by personal deformity, to distinguish, and at the same time to render themselves ridiculous, by the use of showy colours, and garments fantastically and extraordinarily fashioned. But poor Geoffrey Hudson's laces, embroideries, and the rest of his finery, were sorely worn and tarnished by the time which he had spent in jail, under the vague and malicious accusation that he was somehow or other an accomplice in this all-involving, all-devouring whirlpool of a Popish conspiracy—an impeachment which, if pronounced by a mouth the foulest and most malicious, was at that time sufficiently predominant to sully the fairest reputation. It will presently appear, that in the poor man's manner of thinking, and tone of conversation, there was something analogous to his absurd fashion of apparel; for, as in the latter, good stuff and valuable decorations were rendered ludicrous by the fantastic fashion in which they were made up; so, such glimmerings of good sense and honourable feeling as the little man often evinced, were made ridiculous by a restless desire to assume certain airs of importance, and a great jealousy of being despised, on account of the peculiarity of his outward form.

After the fellow-prisoners had looked at each other for some time in silence, the dwarf, conscious of his dignity as first owner of their joint apartment, thought it necessary to do the honours of it to the new-comer. "Sir," he said, modifying the alternate harsh and squeaking tones of his voice into accents as harmonious as they could attain, "I understand you to be the son of my worthy namesake, and ancient acquaintance, the stout Sir Geoffrey Peveril of the Peak. I promise you, I have seen your father where blows have been going more plenty than gold pieces; and for a tall heavy man, who lacked, as we martialists thought, some of the lightness and activity of our more slightly made Cavaliers, he performed his duty as a man might desire. I am happy to see you, his son; and, though by a mistake, I am glad we are to share this comfortless cabin together."

Julian bowed, and thanked his courtesy; and Geoffrey Hudson, having broken the ice, proceeded to question him without further ceremony. "You are no courtier, I presume, young gentleman?"

Julian replied in the negative.

"I thought so," continued the dwarf; "for although I have now no official duty at Court, the region in which my early years were spent, and where I once held a considerable office, yet I still, when I had my liberty, visited the Presence from time to time, as in duty bound for former service; and am wont, from old habit, to take some note of the courtly gallants, those choice spirits of the age, among whom I was once enrolled. You are, not to compliment you, a marked figure, Master Peveril—though something of the tallest, as was your father's case; I think, I could scarce have seen you anywhere without remembering you."

Peveril thought he might, with great justice, have returned the compliment, but contented himself with saying, "he had scarce seen the British Court."

"'Tis pity," said Hudson; "a gallant can hardly be formed without frequenting it. But you have been perhaps in a rougher school; you have served, doubtless?"

"My Maker, I hope," said Julian.

"Fie on it, you mistake. I meant," said Hudson, "*à la Françoise,*—you have served in the army?"

"No. I have not yet had that honour," said Julian.

"What! neither courtier nor soldier, Master Peveril?" said the important little man: "your father is to blame. By cock and pie he is, Master Peveril! How shall a man be known, or distinguished, unless by his bearing in peace and war? I tell you, sir, that at Newberry, where I charged with my troop abreast with Prince Rupert, and when, as you may have heard, we were both beaten off by those cuckoldly hinds the Trained Bands of London,—we did what men could; and I think it was a matter of three or four minutes after most of our gentlemen had been driven off, that his Highness and I continued to cut at their long pikes with our swords; and I think might have broken in, but that I had a tall, long-legged brute of a horse, and my sword was somewhat short,—in fine, at last we were obliged to make volte-face, and then, as I was going to say, the fellows were so glad to get rid of us, that they set up a great jubilee cry of ' There goes Prince Robin and Cock Robin!'—Ay, ay, every scoundrel among them knew me well. But those days are over.—And where were you educated, young gentleman?"

Peveril named the household of the Countess of Derby.

"A most honourable lady, upon my word as a gentleman," said Hudson.—"I knew the noble Countess well when I was about the person of my royal mistress, Henrietta Maria. She was then the very muster of all that was noble, loyal, and lovely. She was, indeed, one of the fifteen fair ones of the Court, whom I permitted to call me Piccoluomini—a foolish jest on my somewhat diminutive figure, which always distinguished me from ordinary beings, even when I was young— have now lost much stature by stooping; but, always the ladies had their jest at me.—Perhaps, young man, I had my own amends of some of them somewhere, and somehow or other—I *say* nothing if I had or no; far less do I insinuate disrespect to the noble Countess. She was daughter of the Duc de la Tremouille, or, more correctly, des Thouars. But certainly to serve the ladies, and condescend to their humours, even when somewhat too free, or too fantastic, is the true decorum of gentle blood."

Depressed as his spirits were, Peveril could scarce forbear smiling when he looked at the pigmy creature, who told these stories with infinite complacency, and appeared disposed to proclaim, as his own herald, that he had been a very model of valour and gallantry, though love and arms seemed to be pursuits totally irreconcilable to his shrivelled, weather-beaten countenance, and wasted limbs. Julian was, however, so careful to avoid giving his companion pain, that he endeavoured to humour him, by saying, that, "unquestionably, one bred up like Sir Geoffrey Hudson, in courts and camps, knew exactly when to suffer personal freedoms, and when to control them."

The little Knight, with great vivacity, though with some difficulty, began to drag his seat from the side of the fire opposite to that where Julian was seated, and at length succeeded in bringing it near him, in token of increasing cordiality.

"You say well, Master Peveril," said the dwarf; "and I have given proofs both of bearing and forbearing. Yes, sir, there was not that thing which my most royal mistress, Henrietta Maria, could have required of me, that I would not have complied with, sir; I was her sworn servant, both in war and in festival, in battle and pageant, sir. At her Majesty's particular request, I once condescended to become—ladies, you know, have strange fancies—to become the tenant, for a time, of the interior of a pie."

"Of a pie?" said Julian, somewhat amazed.

"Yes, sir, of a pie. I hope you find nothing risible in my complaisance?" replied his companion, something jealously.

"Not I, sir," said Peveril; "I have other matters than laughter in my head at present."

"So had I," said the dwarfish champion, "when I found myself imprisoned in a huge platter, of no ordinary dimensions you may be assured, since I could lie at length in it, and when I was entombed, as it were, in walls of standing crust, and a huge cover of pastry, the whole constituting a sort of sarcophagus, of size enough to have recorded the epitaph of a general officer or an archbishop on the lid. Sir, notwithstanding the conveniences which were made to give me air, it was more like being buried alive than aught else which I could think of."

"I conceive it, sir," said Julian.

"Moreover, sir," continued the dwarf, "there were few in the secret, which was contrived for the Queen's divertisement; for advancing of which I would have crept into a filbert nut, had it been possible; and few, as I said, being private in the scheme, there was a risk of accidents. I doubted, while in my darksome abode, whether some awkward attendant might not have let me fall, as I have seen happen to a venison pasty; or whether some hungry guest might not anticipate the moment of my resurrection, by sticking his knife into my upper crust. And though I had my weapons about me, young man, as has been my custom in every case of peril, yet, if such a rash person had plunged deep into the bowels of the supposed pasty, my sword and dagger could barely have served me to avenge, assuredly not to prevent, either of these catastrophes."

"Certainly I do so understand it," said Julian, who began, however, to feel that the company of little Hudson, talkative as he showed himself, was likely rather to aggravate than to alleviate the inconveniences of a prison.

"Nay," continued the little man, enlarging on his former topic, "I had other subjects of apprehension; for it pleased my Lord of Buckingham, his Grace's father who now bears the title, in his plenitude of Court favour, to command the pasty to be carried down to the office, and committed anew to the oven, alleging preposterously that it was better to be eaten warm than cold."

"And did this, sir, not disturb your equanimity?" said Julian.

"My young friend," said Geoffrey Hudson, "I cannot deny it.—Nature will claim her rights from the best and boldest of us.—I thought of Nebuchadnezzar and his fiery furnace; and I waxed warm with apprehension.—But, I thank Heaven, I also thought of my sworn duty to my royal mistress; and was thereby obliged and enabled to resist all temptations to make myself prematurely known. Nevertheless, the Duke—if of malice, may Heaven forgive him—followed down into the office himself, and urged the master-cook very hard that the pasty should be heated, were it but for five minutes. But the master-cook, being privy to the very different intentions of my royal mistress, did most manfully resist the order; and I was again reconveyed in safety to the royal table."

"And in due time liberated from your confinement, I doubt not?" said Peveril.

"Yes, sir; that happy, and I may say, glorious moment, at length arrived," continued the dwarf. "The upper crust was removed—I started up to the sound of trumpet and clarion, like the soul of a warrior when the last summons shall sound— or rather (if that simile be over audacious), like a spell-bound champion relieved from his enchanted state. It was then that, with my buckler on my arm, and my trusty Bilboa in my hand, I executed a sort of warlike dance, in which my skill and agility then rendered me pre-eminent, displaying, at the same time, my postures, both of defence and offence, in a manner so totally inimitable, that I was almost deafened with the applause of all around me, and half-drowned by the scented waters with which the ladies of the Court deluged me from their casting bottles. I had amends of his Grace of Buckingham also; for as I tripped a hasty morris hither and thither upon the dining-table, now offering my blade, now recovering it, I made a blow at his nose—a sort of estramaçon—the dexterity of which consists in coming mighty near to the object you seem to aim at, yet not attaining it. You may have seen a barber make such a flourish with his razor. I promise you his Grace sprung back a half-yard at least. He was pleased to threaten to brain me with a chicken-bone, as he disdainfully expressed it; but the King said, 'George, you have but a Rowland for an Oliver.' And so I tripped on, showing a bold heedlessness of his displeasure, which few dared to have done at that time, albeit countenanced to the utmost like me by the smiles of the brave and the fair. But, well-a-day! sir, youth, its fashions, its follies, its frolics, and all its pomp and pride, are as idle and transitory as the crackling of thorns under a pot."

"The flower that is cast into the oven were a better simile," thought Peveril. "Good God, that a man should live to regret not being young enough to be still treated as baked meat, and served up in a pie!"

His companion, whose tongue had for many days been as closely imprisoned as his person, seemed resolved to indemnify his loquacity, by continuing to indulge it on the present occasion at his companion's expense. He proceeded, therefore, in a solemn tone, to moralise on the adventure which he had narrated.

"Young men will no doubt think one to be envied," he said, "who was thus enabled to be the darling and admiration of the Court"—(Julian internally stood self-exculpated from the suspicion)—"and yet it is better to possess fewer means of distinction, and remain free from the backbiting, the slander, and the odium, which are always the share of Court favour. Men who had no other cause, cast reflections upon me because my size varied somewhat from the common proportion; and jests were sometimes unthinkingly passed upon me by those I was bound to, who did not in that case, peradventure, sufficiently consider that the wren is made by the same hand which formed the bustard, and that the diamond, though small in size, outvalues ten thousand-fold the rude granite. Nevertheless, they proceeded in the vein of humour; and as I could not in duty or gratitude retort upon nobles and princes, I was compelled to cast about in my mind how to vindicate my honour towards those, who, being in the same rank with myself, as servants and courtiers, nevertheless bore themselves towards me as if they were of a superior class in the rank of honour, as well as in the accidental circumstance of stature. And as a lesson to my own pride, and that of others, it so happened, that the pageant which I have but just narrated—which I justly reckon the most honourable moment of my life, excepting perhaps my distinguished share in the battle of Round-way-down—became the cause of a most tragic event, in which I acknowledge the greatest misfortune of my existence."

z

The dwarf here paused, fetched a sigh, big at once with regret, and with the importance becoming the subject of a tragic history; then proceeded as follows:—

"You would have thought in your simplicity, young gentleman, that the pretty pageant I have mentioned could only have been quoted to my advantage, as a rare masking frolic, prettily devised, and not less deftly executed; and yet the malice of the courtiers, who maligned and envied me, made them strain their wit, and exhaust their ingenuity, in putting false and ridiculous constructions upon it. In short, my ears were so much offended with allusions to pies, puff-paste, ovens, and the like, that I was compelled to prohibit such subject of mirth, under penalty of my instant and severe displeasure. But it happ'd there was then a gallant about the Court, a man of good quality, son to a knight baronet, and in high esteem with the best in that sphere, also a familiar friend of mine own, from whom, therefore, I had no reason to expect any of that species of gibing which I had intimated my purpose to treat as offensive. Howbeit, it pleased the Honourable Mr. Crofts, so was this youth called and designed, one night, at the Groom Porter's being full of wine and waggery, to introduce this threadbare subject, and to say something concerning a goose-pie, which I could not but consider as levelled at me. Nevertheless, I did but calmly and solidly pray him to choose a different subject; failing which, I let him know I should be sudden in my resentment. Notwithstanding, he continued in the same tone, and even aggravated the offence, by speaking of a tomtit, and other unnecessary and obnoxious comparisons; whereupon I was compelled to send him a cartel, and we met accordingly. Now, as I really loved the youth, it was my intention only to correct him by a flesh wound or two; and I would willingly that he had named the sword for his weapon. Nevertheless, he made pistols his election; and being on horseback, he produced by way of his own weapon, a foolish engine, which children are wont, in their roguery, to use for spouting water; a—a—in short, I forget the name."

"A squirt, doubtless," said Peveril, who began to recollect having heard something of this adventure.

"You are right," said the dwarf; "you have indeed the name of the little engine, of which I have had experience in passing the yards at Westminster.—Well, sir, this token of slight regard compelled me to give the gentleman such language, as soon rendered it necessary for him to take more serious arms. We fought on horseback — breaking ground, and advancing by signal; and, as I never miss aim, I had the misadventure to kill the Honourable Master Crofts at the first shot. I would not wish my worst foe the pain which I felt, when I saw him reel on his saddle, and so fall down to the earth!—and, when I perceived that the life-blood was pouring fast, I could not but wish to Heaven that it had been my own instead of his. Thus fell youth, hopes, and bravery, a sacrifice to a silly and thoughtless jest; yet, alas! wherein had I choice, seeing that honour is, as it were, the very breath in our nostrils; and that in no sense can we be said to live, if we permit ourselves to be deprived of it?"

The tone of feeling in which the dwarfish hero concluded his story, gave Julian a better opinion of his heart, and even of his understanding, than he had been able to form of one who gloried in having, upon a grand occasion, formed the contents of a pasty. He was indeed enabled to conjecture that the little champion was seduced into such exhibitions, by the necessity attached to his condition, by his own vanity, and by the flattery bestowed on him by those who sought pleasure in practical jokes. The fate of the unlucky Master Crofts, however, as well as various exploits of this diminutive person during the Civil Wars, in which he actually, and with great gallantry, commanded a troop of horse, rendered most men cautious of openly rallying him; which was indeed the less necessary, as, when left alone, he seldom failed voluntarily to show himself on the ludicrous side.

At one hour after noon, the turnkey, true to his word, supplied the prisoners with a very tolerable dinner and a flask of well-flavoured, though light claret; which the old man, who was something of a bon-vivant, regretted to observe, was nearly as diminutive as himself. The evening also passed away, but not without continued symptoms of garrulity on the part of Geoffrey Hudson.

It is true these were of a graver character than he had hitherto exhibited, for when the flask was empty, he repeated a long Latin prayer. But the religious act in which he had been engaged, only gave his discourse a more serious turn than belonged to his former themes, of war, lady's love, and courtly splendour.

The little Knight harangued, at first on polemical points of divinity, and diverged from this thorny path, into the neighbouring and twilight walk of mysticism. He talked of secret warnings—of the predictions of sad-eyed prophets—of the visits of monitory spirits, and the Rosicrucian secrets of the Cabala; all which topics he treated of with such apparent conviction, nay, with so many appeals to personal experience, that one would have supposed him a member of the fraternity of gnomes, or fairies, whom he resembled so much in point of size.

In short, he persevered for a stricken hour in such a torrent of unnecessary tattle, as determined Peveril, at all events, to

endeavour to procure a separate lodging. Having repeated his
evening prayers in Latin, as formerly (for the old gentleman
was a Catholic, which was the sole cause of his falling under
suspicion), he set off on a new score, as they were undressing,
and continued to prattle until he had fairly talked both himself
and his companion to sleep.

CHAPTER XXXV

Of airy tongues that syllable men's names.
—Comus.

JULIAN had fallen asleep, with his brain rather filled with his
own sad reflections, than with the mystical lore of the little
Knight; and yet it seemed as if in his visions the latter had
been more present to his mind than the former.

He dreamed of gliding spirits, gibbering phantoms, bloody
hands, which, dimly seen by twilight, seemed to beckon him
forward like errant-knight on sad adventure bound. More
than once he started from his sleep, so lively was the influence
of these visions on his imagination; and he always awaked
under the impression that some one stood by his bedside. The
chillness of his ankles, the weight and clatter of the fetters,
as he turned himself on his pallet, reminded him on these
occasions where he was, and under what circumstances. The
extremity to which he saw all that was dear to him at present
reduced, struck a deeper cold on his heart than the iron upon
his limbs; nor could he compose himself again to rest without
a mental prayer to Heaven for protection. But when he had
been for a third time awakened from repose by these thick-
stirring fancies, his distress of mind vented itself in speech, and
he was unable to suppress the almost despairing ejaculation,
"God have mercy upon us!"

"Amen!" answered a voice as sweet and "soft as honey
dew," which sounded as if the words were spoken close by his
bedside.

The natural inference was, that Geoffrey Hudson, his companion in calamity, had echoed the prayer which was so proper
to the situation of both. But the tone of voice was so different
from the harsh and dissonant sounds of the dwarf's enunciation,
that Peveril was impressed with the certainty it could not
proceed from Hudson. He was struck with involuntary terror,
for which he could give no sufficient reason; and it was not
without an effort that he was able to utter the question, "Sir
Geoffrey, did you speak?"

No answer was returned. He repeated the question louder; and the same silver-toned voice, which had formerly said "*Amen*" to his prayers, answered to his interrogatory, "Your companion will not awake while I am here."

"And who are you?—What seek you?—How came you into this place?" said Peveril, huddling, eagerly, question upon question.

"I am a wretched being, but one who loves you well.—I come for your good.—Concern yourself no farther."

It now rushed on Julian's mind that he had heard of persons possessed of the wonderful talent of counterfeiting sounds to such accuracy, that they could impose on their hearers the belief, that they proceeded from a point of the apartment entirely opposite to that which the real speaker occupied. Persuaded that he had now gained the depth of the mystery, he replied, "This trifling, Sir Geoffrey, is unseasonable. Say what you have to say in your own voice and manner. These apish pleasantries do not become midnight in a Newgate dungeon."

"But the being who speaks with you," answered the voice, "is fitted for the darkest hour, and the most melancholy haunts."

Impatient of suspense, and determined to satisfy his curiosity, Julian jumped at once from his pallet, hoping to secure the speaker, whose voice indicated he was so near. But he altogether failed in his attempt, and grasped nothing save thin air.

For a turn or two, Peveril shuffled at random about the room, with his arms extended; and then at last recollected, that with the impediment of his shackles, and the noise which necessarily accompanied his motions, and announced where he was, it would be impossible for him to lay hands on any one who might be disposed to keep out of his reach. He therefore endeavoured to return to his bed; but, in groping for his way, lighted first on that of his fellow-prisoner. The little captive slept deep and heavy, as was evinced from his breathing; and upon listening a moment, Julian became again certain, either that his companion was the most artful of ventriloquists and of dissemblers, or that there was actually within the precincts of that guarded chamber, some third being, whose very presence there seemed to intimate that it belonged not to the ordinary line of humanity.

Julian was no ready believer in the supernatural; but that age was very far from being so incredulous concerning ghostly occurrences as our own; and it was no way derogatory to his good sense, that he shared the prejudices of his time. His hair began to bristle, and the moisture to stand on his brow, as he called on his companion to awake, for Heaven's sake.

The dwarf answered—but he spoke without awaking.—" The day may dawn and be d—d. Tell the master of the horse I will not go to the hunting, unless I have the little black jennet."

" I tell you," said Julian, " there is some one in the apartment. Have you not a tinder-box to strike a light ?"

" I care not how slight my horse be," replied the slumberer, pursuing his own train of ideas, which, doubtless, carried him back to the green woods of Windsor, and the royal deer-hunts which he had witnessed there. " I am not overweight.—I will not ride that great Holstein brute, that I must climb up to by a ladder, and then sit on his back like a pin-cushion on an elephant."

Julian at length put his hand to the sleeper's shoulder, and shook him, so as to awake him from his dream ; when, after two or three snorts and groans, the dwarf asked peevishly, what the devil ailed him ?

" The devil himself, for what I know," said Peveril, " is at this very moment in the room here beside us."

The dwarf on this information started up, crossed himself, and began to hammer a flint and steel with all despatch, until he had lighted a little piece of candle, which he said was consecrated to Saint Bridget, and as powerful as the herb called *fuga dæmonum,* or the liver of the fish burnt by Tobit in the house of Raguel, for chasing all goblins, and evil or dubious spirits, from the place of its radiance ; "if, indeed," as the dwarf carefully guarded his proposition, " they existed anywhere, save in the imagination of his fellow-prisoner."

Accordingly, the apartment was no sooner enlightened by this holy candle's end, than Julian began to doubt the evidence of his own ears ; for not only was there no one in the room save Sir Geoffrey Hudson and himself, but all the fastenings of the door were so secure, that it seemed impossible that they could have been opened and again fixed, without a great deal of noise, which, on the last occasion at least, could not possibly have escaped his ears, seeing that he must have been on his feet, and employed in searching the chamber, when the unknown, if an earthly being, was in the act of retreating from it.

Julian gazed for a moment with great earnestness, and no little perplexity, first on the bolted door, then on the grated window ; and began to accuse his own imagination of having played him an unpleasant trick. He answered little to the questions of Hudson, and, returning to his bed, heard, in silence, a long studied oration on the merits of Saint Bridget, which comprehended the greater part of her long-winded legend, and concluded with the assurance, that, from all accounts preserved of her, that holy saint was the least of all possible women, except those of the pigmy kind.

By the time the dwarf had ceased to speak, Julian's desire of sleep had returned; and after a few glances around the apartment, which was still illuminated by the expiring beams of the holy taper, his eyes were again closed in forgetfulness, and his repose was not again disturbed in the course of that night.

Morning dawns on Newgate, as well as on the freest mountain-turf which Welshman or wild-goat ever trode; but in so different a fashion, that the very beams of heaven's precious sun, when they penetrate into the recesses of the prison-house, have the air of being committed to jail. Still, with the light of day around him, Peveril easily persuaded himself of the vanity of his preceding night's visions; and smiled when he reflected that fancies, similar to those to which his ear was often exposed in the Isle of Man, had been able to arrange themselves in a manner so impressive, when he heard them from the mouth of so singular a character as Hudson, and in the solitude of a prison.

Before Julian had awaked, the dwarf had already quitted his bed, and was seated in the chimney-corner of the apartment, where, with his own hands, he had arranged a morsel of fire, partly attending to the simmering of a small pot, which he had placed on the flame, partly occupied with a huge folio volume which lay on the table before him, and seemed well-nigh as tall and bulky as himself. He was wrapped up in the dusky crimson cloak already mentioned, which served him for a morning-gown, as well as a mantle against the cold, and which corresponded with a large montero-cap, that enveloped his head. The singularity of his features, and of the eyes, armed with spectacles, which were now cast on the subject of his studies, now directed towards his little cauldron, would have tempted Rembrandt to exhibit him on canvas, either in the character of an alchymist, or of a necromancer, engaged in some strange experiment, under the direction of one of the huge manuals which treat of the theory of these mystic arts.

The attention of the dwarf was bent, however, upon a more domestic object. He was only preparing soup, of no unsavoury quality, for breakfast, which he invited Peveril to partake with him. "I am an old soldier," he said, "and, I must add, an old prisoner; and understand how to shift for myself better than you can do, young man.—Confusion to the scoundrel Clink, he has put the spice-box out of my reach!—Will you hand it me from the mantelpiece?—I will teach you, as the French have it, *faire la cuisine;* and then, if you please, we will divide, like brethren, the labours of our prison house."

Julian readily assented to the little man's friendly proposal, without interposing any doubt as to his continuing an inmate of the same cell. Truth is, that although, upon the whole, he was inclined to regard the whispering voice of the preceding evening as the impression of his own excited fancy, he felt, nevertheless, curiosity to see how a second night was to pass over in the same cell; and the tone of the invisible intruder, which at midnight had been heard by him with terror, now excited, on recollection, a gentle and not unpleasing species of agitation—the combined effect of awe, and of awakened curiosity.

Days of captivity have little to mark them as they glide away. That which followed the night which we have described, afforded no circumstance of note. The dwarf imparted to his youthful companion a volume similar to that which formed his own studies, and which proved to be a tome of one of Scuderi's now forgotten romances, of which Geoffrey Hudson was a great admirer, and which were then very fashionable both at the French and English Courts; although they contrive to unite in their immense folios all the improbabilities and absurdities of the old romances of chivalry, without that tone of imagination which pervades them, and all the metaphysical absurdities which Cowley and the poets of the age had heaped upon the passion of love, like so many load of small coal upon a slender fire, which it smothers instead of aiding.

But Julian had no alternative, saving only to muse over the sorrows of Artamenes and Mandane, or on the complicated distresses of his own situation; and in these disagreeable divertisements, the morning crept through as it could.

Noon first, and thereafter nightfall, were successively marked by a brief visit from their stern turnkey, who, with noiseless step and sullen demeanour, did in silence the necessary offices about the meals of the prisoners, exchanging with them as few words as an official in the Spanish Inquisition might have permitted himself upon a similar occasion. With the same taciturn gravity, very different from the laughing humour into which he had been surprised on a former occasion, he struck their fetters with a small hammer, to ascertain, by the sound thus produced, whether they had been tampered with by file or otherwise. He next mounted on a table, to make the same experiment on the window-grating.

Julian's heart throbbed; for might not one of those grates have been so tampered with as to give entrance to the nocturnal visitant? But they returned to the experienced ear of Master Clink, when he struck them in turn with the hammer, a clear and ringing sound, which assured him of their security."

"It would be difficult for any one to get in through these defences," said Julian, giving vent in words to his own feelings.

"Few wish that," answered the surly groom, misconstruing what was passing in Peveril's mind; "and let me tell you, master, folks will find it quite as difficult to get out." He retired, and night came on.

The dwarf, who took upon himself for the day the whole duties of the apartment, trundled about the room, making a most important clatter as he extinguished their fire, and put aside various matters which had been in use in the course of the day, talking to himself all the while in a tone of no little consequence, occasionally grounded on the dexterity with which an old soldier could turn his hand to everything; and at other times, on the wonder that a courtier of the first rank should condescend to turn his hand to anything. Then came the repetition of his accustomed prayers; but his disposition to converse did not, as on the former occasion, revive after his devotions. On the contrary, long before Julian had closed an eye, the heavy breathing from Sir Geoffrey Hudson's pallet declared that the dwarf was already in the arms of Morpheus.

Amid the total darkness of the apartment, and with a longing desire, and at the same time no small fear, for the recurrence of the mysterious address of the preceding evening, Julian lay long awake without his thoughts receiving any interruption save when the clock told the passing hour from the neighbouring steeple of St. Sepulchre. At length he sunk into slumber; but had not slept to his judgment, above an hour, when he was roused by the sound which his waking ear had so long expected in vain.

"Can you sleep?—Will you sleep?—Dare you sleep?" were the questions impressed on his ear, in the same clear, soft, and melodious voice, which had addressed him on the preceding night.

"Who is it asks me the question?" answered Julian. "But be the questioner good or evil, I reply that I am a guiltless prisoner; and that innocence may wish and dare to sleep soundly."

"Ask no questions of me," said the voice; "neither attempt to discover who speaks to you; and be assured that folly alone can sleep, with fraud around and danger before him."

"Can you, who tell me of dangers, counsel me how to combat or how to avoid them?" said Julian.

"My power is limited," said the voice; "yet something I can do, as the glow-worm can show a precipice. But you must confide in me."

"Confidence must beget confidence," answered Julian. "I cannot repose trust in I know not what or whom."

"Speak not so loud," replied the voice, sinking almost into a whisper.

"Last night you said my companion would not awake," said Julian.

"To-night I warrant not that he shall sleep," said the voice. And as it spoke, the hoarse, snatching, discordant tones of the dwarf were heard, demanding of Julian why he talked in his sleep—wherefore he did not rest himself, and let other people rest—and, finally, whether his visions of last night were returned upon him again?

"Say yes," said the voice in a whisper, so low, yet so distinct, that Julian almost doubted whether it was not an echo of his own thought.—"Say but yes—and I part to return no more!"

In desperate circumstances men look to strange and unusual remedies; and although unable to calculate the chances of advantage which this singular communication opened to him, Julian did not feel inclined to let them at once escape from him. He answered the dwarf, that he had been troubled by an alarming dream.

"I could have sworn it, from the sound of your voice," said Hudson. "It is strange, now, that you overgrown men never possess the extreme firmness of nerves proper to us who are cast in a more compact mould. My own voice retains its masculine sounds on all occasions. Dr. Cockerel was of opinion, that there was the same allowance of nerve and sinew to men of every size, and that nature spun the stock out thinner or stronger, according to the extent of surface which they were to cover. Hence, the least creatures are oftentimes the strongest. Place a beetle under a tall candlestick, and the insect will move it by its efforts to get out; which is, in point of comparative strength, as if one of us should shake his Majesty's prison of Newgate by similar struggles. Cats also, and weasels, are creatures of greater exertion or endurance than dogs or sheep. And in general, you may remark, that little men dance better, and are more unwearied under exertion of every kind, than those to whom their own weight must necessarily be burdensome. I respect you, Master Peveril, because I am told you have killed one of those gigantic fellows, who go about swaggering as if their souls were taller than ours, because their noses are nearer to the clouds by a cubit or two. But do not value yourself on this as anything very unusual. I would have you to know it hath been always thus; and that, in the history of all ages, the clean, tight, dapper little fellow, hath proved an overmatch for his bulky antagonist. I need only instance out of Holy Writ, the celebrated downfall of Goliah, and of another lubbard, who had more fingers to his hand, and more inches to his stature, than ought to belong to an honest man, and who was slain by a nephew of good King David; and of many others whom I do not remember; nevertheless they were all Philistines of gigantic stature. In the classics, also, you have Tydeus, and other tight, compact heroes, whose diminutive bodies were the abode of large minds. And indeed you may observe, in sacred as well as profane history, that your giants are ever heretics and blasphemers, robbers and oppressors, outragers of the female sex, and scoffers at regular authority. Such were Gog and Magog, whom our authentic chronicles vouch to have been slain near to Plymouth, by the good little Knight Corineus, who gave name to Cornwall. Ascaparte also was subdued by Bevis, and Colbrand by Guy, as Southampton and Warwick can testify. Like unto these was the giant Hoel, slain in Bretagne by King Arthur. And if Ryence, King of North Wales, who was done to death by the same worthy champion of Christendom, be not actually termed a giant, it is plain he was little better, since he required twenty-four kings' beards, which were then worn full and long, to fur his gown; whereby computing each beard at eighteen inches (and you cannot allow less for a beard-royal), and supposing only the front of the gown trimmed therewith, as we use ermine; and that the back was mounted and lined, instead of cat-skins and squirrels' fur, with the beards of earls and dukes, and other inferior dignitaries—may amount to—But I will work the question to-morrow."

Nothing is more soporific to any (save a philosopher or moneyed man) than the operation of figures; and when in bed, the effect is irresistible. Sir Geoffrey fell asleep in the act of calculating King Ryence's height, from the supposed length of his mantle. Indeed, had he not stumbled on this abstruse subject of calculation, there is no guessing how long he might have held forth upon the superiority of men of little stature, which was so great a favourite with him, that, numerous as such narratives are, the dwarf had collected almost all the instances of their victories over giants, which history or romance afforded.

No sooner had unequivocal signs of the dwarf's sound slumbers reached Julian's ears, than he began again to listen eagerly for the renewal of that mysterious communication which was at once interesting and awful. Even whilst Hudson was speaking, he had, instead of bestowing his attention upon his eulogy on persons of low stature, kept his ears on watchful guard to mark, if possible, the lightest sounds of any sort which might occur in the apartment; so that he thought it scarce possible that even a fly should have left it without its motion being overheard. If, therefore, his invisible monitor was indeed a creature of this world—an opinion which Julian's sound sense rendered him unwilling to renounce—that being could not have left the apartment; and he waited impatiently for a renewal of their communication. He was disappointed; not the slightest sound reached his ear; and the nocturnal visitor, if still in the room, appeared determined on silence.

It was in vain that Peveril coughed, hemmed, and gave other symptoms of being awake; at length, such became his impatience, that he resolved, at any risk, to speak first, in hopes of renewing the communication betwixt them. "Whoever thou art," he said, in a voice loud enough to be heard by a waking person, but not so high as to disturb his sleeping companion —"Whoever, or whatever thou art, thou hast shown some interest in the fate of such a castaway as Julian Peveril, speak once more, I conjure thee; and be your communication for good or evil, believe me, I am equally prepared to abide the issue."

No answer of any kind was returned to this invocation; nor did the least sound intimate the presence of the being to whom it was so solemnly addressed.

"I speak in vain," said Julian; "and perhaps I am but invoking that which is insensible of human feeling, or which takes a malign pleasure in human suffering."

There was a gentle and half-broken sigh from a corner of the apartment, which, answering to this exclamation, seemed to contradict the imputation which it conveyed.

Julian, naturally courageous, and familiarised by this time to his situation, raised himself in bed, and stretched out his arm, to repeat his adjuration, when the voice, as if alarmed at his action and energy, whispered, in a tone more hurried than that which it had hitherto used, "Be still—move not—or I am mute for ever!"

"It is then a mortal being who is present with me," was the natural inference of Julian, "and one who is probably afraid of being detected; I have then some power over my visitor, though I must be cautious how I use it.—If your intents are friendly," he proceeded, "there was never a time in which I lacked friends more, or would be more grateful for kindness. The fate of all who are dear to me is weighed in the balance, and with worlds would I buy the tidings of their safety."

"I have said my power is limited," replied the voice. "*You* I may be able to preserve—the fate of your friends is beyond my control."

"Let me at least know it," said Julian; "and, be it as it may, I will not shun to share it."

"For whom would you inquire?" said the soft, sweet voice,

not without a tremulousness of accent, as if the question was put with diffident reluctance.

"My parents," said Julian, after a moment's hesitation; "how fare they?—What will be their fate?"

"They fare as the fort under which the enemy has dug a deadly mine. The work may have cost the labour of years, such were the impediments to the engineers; but Time brings opportunity upon its wings."

"And what will be the event?" said Peveril.

"Can I read the future," answered the voice, "save by comparison with the past?—Who has been hunted on these stern and unmitigable accusations, but has been at last brought to bay? Did high and noble birth, honoured age, and approved benevolence, save the unfortunate Lord Stafford? Did learning, capacity of intrigue, or high Court favour, redeem Coleman, although the confidential servant of the heir presumptive of the Crown of England?—Did subtilty and genius, and the exertions of a numerous sect, save Fenwicke, or Whitbread, or any other of the accused priests?—Were Groves, Pickering, or the other humble wretches who have suffered, safe in their obscurity? There is no condition in life, no degree of talent, no form of principle, which affords protection against an accusation, which levels conditions, confounds characters, renders men's virtues their sins, and rates them as dangerous in proportion as they have influence, though attained in the noblest manner, and used for the best purposes. Call such a one but an accessory to the Plot—let him be mouthed in the evidence of Oates or Dugdale—and the blindest shall foresee the issue of their trial."

"Prophet of Evil!" said Julian, "my father has a shield invulnerable to protect him. He is innocent."

"Let him plead his innocence at the bar of Heaven," said the voice; "it will serve him little where Scroggs presides."

"Still I fear not," said Julian, counterfeiting more confidence than he really possessed; "my father's cause will be pleaded before twelve Englishmen."

"Better before twelve wild beasts," answered the Invisible, "than before Englishmen, influenced with party prejudice, passion, and the epidemic terror of an imaginary danger. They are bold in guilt in proportion to the number amongst whom the crime is divided."

"Ill-omened speaker," said Julian, "thine is indeed a voice fitted only to sound with the midnight bell, and the screech-owl. Yet speak again. Tell me, if thou canst"—(he would have said of Alice Bridgenorth, but the word would not leave his tongue)—"Tell me," he said, "if the noble house of Derby——"

"Let them keep their rock like the sea-fowl in the tempest; and it may so fall out," answered the voice, "that their rock may be a safe refuge. But there is blood on their ermine; and revenge has dogged them for many a year, like a blood-hound that hath been distanced in the morning chase, but may yet grapple the quarry ere the sun shall set. At present, however, they are safe.—Am I now to speak farther on your own affairs, which involve little short of your life and honour? or are there yet any whose interests you prefer to your own?"

"There is," said Julian, "one, from whom I was violently parted yesterday; if I knew but of her safety, I were little anxious for my own."

"One!" returned the voice, "only *one* from whom you were parted yesterday?"

"But in parting from whom," said Julian, "I felt separated from all happiness which the world can give me."

"You mean Alice Bridgenorth," said the Invisible, with some bitterness of accent; "but her you will never see more. Your own life and hers depend on your forgetting each other."

"I cannot purchase my own life at that price," replied Julian.

"Then DIE in your obstinacy," returned the Invisible; nor to all the entreaties which he used was he able to obtain another word in the course of that remarkable night.

CHAPTER XXXVI

A short hough'd man, but full of pride.
—ALLAN RAMSAY.

THE blood of Julian Peveril was so much fevered by the state in which his invisible visitor left him, that he was unable, for a length of time, to find repose. He swore to himself, that he would discover and expose the nocturnal demon which stole on his hours of rest, only to add gall to bitterness, and to pour poison into those wounds which already smarted so severely. There was nothing which his power extended to, that, in his rage, he did not threaten. He proposed a closer and a more rigorous survey of his cell, so that he might discover the mode by which his tormentor entered, were it as unnoticeable as an auger-hole. If his diligence should prove unavailing, he determined to inform the jailers, to whom it could not be indifferent to know, that their prison was open to such intrusions. He proposed to himself, to discover from their looks whether they were already privy to these visits; and if so, to denounce them to the magistrates, to the judges, to the House of Commons, was the least that his resentment proposed. Sleep surprised his worn-out frame in the midst of his projects of discovery and vengeance, and, as frequently happens, the light of the ensuing day proved favourable to calmer resolutions.

He now reflected that he had no ground to consider the motives of his visitor as positively malevolent, although he had afforded him little encouragement to hope for assistance on the points he had most at heart. Towards himself, there had been expressed a decided feeling, both of sympathy and interest; if through means of these he could acquire his liberty, he might, when possessed of freedom, turn it to the benefit of those for whom he was more interested than for his own welfare. "I have behaved like a fool," he said; "I ought to have temporised with this singular being, learned the motives of its interference, and availed myself of its succour, provided I could do so without any dishonourable conditions. It would have been always time enough to reject such when they should have been proposed to me."

So saying, he was forming projects for regulating his intercourse with the stranger more prudently, in case their communication should be renewed, when his meditations were interrupted by the peremptory summons of Sir Geoffrey Hudson, that he would, in his turn, be pleased to perform those domestic duties of their common habitation, which the dwarf had yesterday taken upon himself.

There was no resisting a request so reasonable, and Peveril accordingly rose and betook himself to the arrangement of their prison, while Sir Hudson, perched upon a stool from which his legs did not by half-way reach the ground, sat in a posture of elegant languor, twangling upon an old broken-winded guitar, and singing songs in Spanish, Moorish, and Lingua Franca, most detestably out of tune. He failed not, at the conclusion of each ditty, to favour Julian with some account of what he had sung, either in the way of translation, or historical anecdote, or as the lay was connected with some peculiar part of his own eventful history, in the course of which the poor little man had chanced to have been taken by a Sallee rover, and carried captive into Morocco.

This part of his life Hudson used to make the era of many strange adventures; and, if he could himself be believed, he had made wild work among the affections of the Emperor's seraglio. But, although few were in a situation to cross-examine him on gallantries and intrigues of which the scene was so remote, the officers of the garrison of Tangier had a report current amongst them, that the only use to which the tyrannical Moors could convert a slave of such slender corporeal strength, was to employ him to lie a-bed all day and hatch turkey's eggs. The least allusion to this rumour used to drive him well-nigh frantic, and the fatal termination of his duel with young Crofts, which began in wanton mirth, and ended in bloodshed, made men more coy than they had formerly been, of making the fiery little hero the subject of their raillery.

While Peveril did the drudgery of the apartment, the dwarf remained much at his ease, carolling in the manner we have described; but when he beheld Julian attempting the task of the cook, Sir Geoffrey Hudson sprang from the stool on which he sat *en Signor*, at the risk of breaking both his guitar and his neck, exclaiming, " That he would rather prepare breakfast every morning betwixt this and the day of judgment, than commit a task of such consequence to an inexperienced bungler like his companion."

The young man gladly resigned his task to the splenetic little Knight, and only smiled at his resentment when he added, that, to be but a mortal of middle stature, Julian was as stupid as a giant. Leaving the dwarf to prepare the meal after his own pleasure, Peveril employed himself in measuring the room with his eyes on every side, and in endeavouring to discover some private entrance, such as might admit his midnight visitant, and perhaps could be employed in case of need for effecting his own escape. The floor next engaged a scrutiny equally minute, but more successful.

Close by his own pallet, and dropped in such a manner that he must have seen it sooner but for the hurry with which he obeyed the summons of the impatient dwarf, lay a slip of paper, sealed, and directed with the initial letters, J. P., which seemed to ascertain that it was addressed to himself. He took the opportunity of opening it while the soup was in the very moment of projection, and the full attention of his companion was occupied by what he, in common with wiser and taller men, considered as one of the principal occupations of life ; so that, without incurring his observation or awaking his curiosity, Julian had the opportunity to read as follows :—

" Rash and infatuated as you are, there is one who would forfeit much to stand betwixt you and your fate. You are to-morrow to be removed to the Tower, where your life cannot be assured for a single day ; for, during the few hours you have been in London, you have provoked a resentment which is not easily slaked. There is but one chance for you,—renounce A. B.—think no more of her. If that be impossible, think of her but as one whom you can never see again. If your heart can resolve to give up an attachment which it should never have entertained, and which it would be madness to cherish

THE TOWER OF LONDON IN 1670

DRAWING BY D. ROBERTS

longer, make your acquiescence in this condition known by putting on your hat a white band, or white feather, or knot of ribbon of the same colour, whichever you may most easily come by. A boat will, in that case, run, as if by accident, on board of that which is to convey you to the Tower. Do you in the confusion jump overboard, and swim to the Southwark side of the Thames. Friends will attend there to secure your escape, and you will find yourself with one who will rather lose character and life, than that a hair of your head should fall to the ground; but who, if you reject the warning, can only think of you as of the fool who perishes in his folly. May Heaven guide you to a sound judgment of your condition! So prays one who would be your friend, if you pleased,

"UNKNOWN."

The Tower!—it was a word of terror, even more so than a civil prison; for how many passages to death did that dark structure present! The severe executions which it had witnessed in preceding reigns, were not perhaps more numerous than the secret murders which had taken place within its walls; yet Peveril did not a moment hesitate on the part which he had to perform. "I will share my father's fate," he said; "I thought but of him when they brought me hither; I will think of nothing else when they convey me to yonder still more dreadful place of confinement; it is his, and it is but meet that it should be his son's.—And thou, Alice Bridgenorth, the day that I renounce thee, may I be held alike a traitor and a dastard! —Go, false adviser, and share the fate of seducers and heretical teachers!"

He could not help uttering this last expression aloud, as he threw the billet into the fire, with a vehemence which made the dwarf start with surprise. "What say you of burning heretics, young man?" he exclaimed; "by my faith, your zeal must be warmer than mine, if you talk on such a subject when the heretics are the prevailing number. May I measure six feet without my shoes, but the heretics would have the best of it if we came to that work. Beware of such words."

"Too late to beware of words spoken and heard," said the turnkey, who, opening the door with unusual precautions to avoid noise, had stolen unperceived into the room; "however, Master Peveril has behaved like a gentleman, and I am no tale-bearer, on condition he will consider I have had trouble in his matters."

Julian had no alternative but to take the fellow's hint and administer a bribe, with which Master Clink was so well satisfied, that he exclaimed, "It went to his heart to take leave of such a kind-natured gentleman, and that he could have turned the key on him for twenty years with pleasure. But the best friends must part."

"I am to be removed, then?" said Julian.

"Ay, truly, master, the warrant is come from the Council."

"To convey me to the Tower."

"Whew!" exclaimed the officer of the law—"who the devil told you that? But since you do know it, there is no harm to say ay. So make yourself ready to move immediately; and first, hold out your dew-beaters till I take off the darbies."

"Is that usual?" said Peveril, stretching out his feet as the fellow directed, while his fetters were unlocked.

"Why, ay, master, these fetters belong to the keeper; they are not a-going to send them to the Lieutenant, I trow. No, no, the warders must bring their own gear with them; they get none here, I promise them. Nevertheless, if your honour hath a fancy to go in fetters, as thinking it may move compassion of your case——"

"I have no intention to make my case seem worse than it is," said Julian; whilst at the same time it crossed his mind that his anonymous correspondent must be well acquainted both with his own personal habits, since the letter proposed a plan of escape which could only be executed by a bold swimmer, and with the fashions of the prison, since it was foreseen that he would not be ironed on his passage to the Tower. The turnkey's next speech made him carry conjecture still farther.

"There is nothing in life I would not do for so brave a guest," said Clink; "I would nab one of my wife's ribbons for you, if your honour had the fancy to mount the white flag in your beaver."

"To what good purpose?" said Julian, shortly connecting, as was natural, the man's proposed civility with the advice given and the signal prescribed in the letter.

"Nay, to no good purpose I know of," said the turnkey; "only it is the fashion to seem white and harmless—a sort of token of not-guiltiness, as I may say, which folks desire to show the world, whether they be truly guilty or not; but I cannot say that guiltiness or not-guiltiness argufies much, saving they be words in the verdict."

"Strange," thought Peveril, although the man seemed to speak quite naturally, and without any double meaning, "strange that all should apparently combine to realise the plan of escape, could I but give my consent to it! And had I not better consent? Whoever does so much for me must wish me well, and a well-wisher would never enforce the unjust conditions on which I am required to consent to my liberation."

But this misgiving of his resolution was but for a moment. He speedily recollected, that whoever aided him in escaping, must be necessarily exposed to great risk, and had a right to name the stipulation on which he was willing to incur it. He also recollected that falsehood is equally base, whether expressed in words or in dumb show; and that he should lie as flatly by using the signal agreed upon in evidence of his renouncing Alice Bridgenorth, as he would in direct terms if he made such renunciation without the purpose of abiding by it.

"If you would oblige me," he said to the turnkey, "let me have a piece of black silk or crape for the purpose you mention."

"Of crape!" said the fellow; "what should that signify? Why, the bien morts, who bing out to tour at you,* will think you a chimney-sweeper on Mayday."

"It will show my settled sorrow," said Julian, "as well as my determined resolution."

"As you will, sir," answered the fellow; "I'll provide you with a black rag of some kind or other. So, now; let us be moving."

Julian intimated his readiness to attend him, and proceeded to bid farewell to his late companion, the stout Geoffrey Hudson. The parting was not without emotion on both sides, more particularly on that of the poor little man, who had taken a particular liking to the companion of whom he was now about to be deprived. "Fare ye well," he said, "my young friend," taking Julian's hand in both his own uplifted palms, in which action he somewhat resembled the attitude of a sailor pulling a rope overhead,—"Many in my situation would think himself wronged, as a soldier and servant of the king's chamber, in seeing you removed to a more honourable prison than that which I am limited unto. But, I thank God, I grudge you not the Tower, nor the rocks of Scilly, nor even Carisbrooke Castle, though the latter was graced with the captivity of my blessed and martyred master. Go where you will, I wish you all the distinction of an honourable prison-house, and a safe and speedy deliverance in God's own time. For myself, my race is near a close, and that because I fall a martyr to the over-tenderness of my own heart. There is a circumstance, good Master Julian Peveril, which should have been yours, had Providence permitted our farther intimacy, but it fits not the present hour. Go, then, my friend, and bear witness in life and death, that Geoffrey Hudson scorns the insults and persecutions of fortune, as he would despise, and has often despised, the mischievous pranks of an overgrown schoolboy."

So saying, he turned away, and hid his face with his little handkerchief, while Julian felt towards him that tragi-comic sensation which makes us pity the object which excites it, not the less that we are somewhat inclined to laugh amid our

* The smart girls, who turn out to look at you.

sympathy. The jailer made him a signal, which Peveril obeyed, leaving the dwarf to disconsolate solitude.

As Julian followed the keeper through the various windings of his penal labyrinth, the man observed, that "he was a rum fellow, that little Sir Geoffrey, and, for gallantry, a perfect Cock of Bantam, for as old as he was. There was a certain gay wench," he said, "that had hooked him; but what she could make of him, save she carried him to Smithfield, and took money for him, as for a motion of puppets, it was," he said, "hard to gather."

Encouraged by this opening, Julian asked if his attendant knew why his prison was changed. "To teach you to become a King's post without commission," answered the fellow.

He stopped in his tattle as they approached that formidable central point, in which lay couched on his leathern elbow-chair the fat commander of the fortress, stationed apparently for ever in the midst of his citadel, as the huge Boa is sometimes said to lie stretched as a guard upon the subterranean treasures of Eastern Rajahs. This overgrown man of authority eyed Julian wistfully and sullenly, as the miser the guinea which he must part with, or the hungry mastiff the food which is carried to another kennel. He growled to himself as he turned the leaves of his ominous register, in order to make the necessary entry respecting the removal of his prisoner. "To the Tower—to the Tower—ay, ay, all must to the Tower—that's the fashion of it—free Britons to a military prison, as if we had neither bolts nor chains here!—I hope Parliament will have it up, this Towering work, that's all.—Well, the youngster will take no good by the change, and that is one comfort."

Having finished at once his official act of registration, and his soliloquy, he made a signal to his assistants to remove Julian, who was led along the same stern passages which he had traversed upon his entrance, to the gate of the prison, whence a coach, escorted by two officers of justice, conveyed him to the water-side.

A boat here waited him, with four warders of the Tower, to whose custody he was formally resigned by his late attendants. Clink, however, the turnkey, with whom he was more especially acquainted, did not take leave of him without furnishing him with the piece of black crape which he requested. Peveril fixed it on his hat amid the whispers of his new guardians. "The gentleman is in a hurry to go into mourning," said one; "mayhap he had better wait till he has cause."

"Perhaps others may wear mourning for him, ere he can mourn for any one," answered another of these functionaries.

Yet, notwithstanding the tenor of these whispers, their behaviour to their prisoner was more respectful than he had experienced from his former keepers, and might be termed a sullen civility. The ordinary officers of the law were in general rude, as having to do with felons of every description; whereas these men were only employed with persons accused of state crimes—men who were from birth and circumstances usually entitled to expect, and able to reward, decent usage.

The change of keepers passed unnoticed by Julian, as did the gay and busy scene presented by the broad and beautiful river on which he was now launched. A hundred boats shot past them, bearing parties intent on business, or on pleasure. Julian only viewed them with the stern hope, that whoever had endeavoured to bribe him from his fidelity by the hope of freedom, might see, from the colour of the badge which he had assumed, how determined he was to resist the temptation presented to him.

It was about high-water, and a stout wherry came up the river, with sail and oar, so directly upon that in which Julian was embarked, that it seemed as if likely to run her aboard. "Get your carabines ready," cried the principal warder to his assistants. "What the devil can these scoundrels mean?"

But the crew in the other boat seemed to have perceived their error, for they suddenly altered their course, and struck off into the middle stream, while a torrent of mutual abuse was exchanged betwixt them and the boat whose course they had threatened to impede.

"The Unknown has kept his faith," said Julian to himself; "I too have kept mine."

It even seemed to him, as the boats neared each other, that he heard, from the other wherry, something like a stifled scream or groan; and when the momentary bustle was over, he asked the warder who sat next him, what boat that was.

"Men-of-war's-men, on a frolic, I suppose," answered the warder. "I know no one else would be so impudent as run foul of the King's boat; for I am sure the fellow put the helm up on purpose. But mayhap you, sir, know more of the matter than I do."

This insinuation effectually prevented Julian from putting farther questions, and he remained silent until the boat came under the dusky bastions of the Tower. The tide carried them up under a dark and lowering arch, closed at the upper end by the well-known Traitor's gate,* formed like a wicket of huge intersecting bars of wood, through which might be seen a dim and imperfect view of soldiers and warders upon duty, and of the steep ascending causeway which leads up from the river into the interior of the fortress. By this gate,—and it is the well-known circumstance which assigned its name,—those

* See note, "Fortunes of Nigel."

accused of state crimes were usually committed to the Tower. The Thames afforded a secret and silent mode of conveyance for transporting thither such whose fallen fortunes might move the commiseration, or whose popular qualities might excite the sympathy, of the public ; and even where no cause for especial secrecy existed, the peace of the city was undisturbed by the tumult attending the passage of the prisoner and his guards through the most frequented streets.

Yet this custom, however recommended by state policy, must have often struck chill upon the heart of the criminal, who thus, stolen, as it were, out of society, reached the place of his confinement, without encountering even one glance of compassion on the road ; and as, from under the dusky arch, he landed on those flinty steps, worn by many a footstep anxious as his own, against which the tide lapped fitfully with small successive waves, and hence looked forward to the steep ascent into a Gothic state prison, and backward to such part of the river as the low-brow'd vault suffered to become visible, he must often have felt that he was leaving daylight, hope, and life itself, behind him.

While the warder's challenge was made and answered, Peveril endeavoured to obtain information from his conductors where he was likely to be confined; but the answer was brief and general—" Where the Lieutenant should direct."

" Could he not be permitted to share the imprisonment of his father, Sir Geoffrey Peveril ?" He forgot not, on this occasion, to add the surname of his house.

The warder, an old man of respectable appearance, stared, as if at the extravagance of the demand, and said bluntly, " It is impossible."

" At least," said Peveril, " show me where my father is confined, that I may look upon the walls which separate us."

" Young gentleman," said the senior warder, shaking his grey head, " I am sorry for you; but asking questions will do you no service. In this place we know nothing of fathers and sons."

Yet chance seemed, in a few minutes afterwards, to offer Peveril that satisfaction which the rigour of his keepers was disposed to deny to him. As he was conveyed up the steep passage which leads under what is called the Wakefield Tower, a female voice, in a tone wherein grief and joy were indescribably mixed, exclaimed, " My son !—My dear son ! "

Even those who guarded Julian seemed softened by a tone of such acute feeling. They slackened their pace. They almost paused to permit him to look up towards the casement from which the sounds of maternal agony proceeded ; but the aperture was so narrow, and so closely grated, that nothing was visible save a white female hand, which grasped one of those rusty barricadoes, as if for supporting the person within, while another streamed a white handkerchief, and then let it fall. The casement was instantly deserted.

"Give it me," said Julian to the officer who lifted the handkerchief; "it is perhaps a mother's last gift."

The old warder lifted the napkin, and looked at it with the jealous minuteness of one who is accustomed to detect secret correspondence in the most trifling acts of intercourse.

"There may be writing on it with invisible ink," said one of his comrades.

"It is wetted, but I think it is only with tears, answered the senior. "I cannot keep it from the poor young gentleman."

"Ah, Master Coleby," said his comrade, in a gentle tone of reproach, "you would have been wearing a better coat than a yeoman's to-day, had it not been for your tender heart."

"It signifies little," said old Coleby, "while my heart is true to my King, what I feel in discharging my duty, or what coat keeps my old bosom from the cold weather."

Peveril, meanwhile, folded in his breast the token of his mother's affection which chance had favoured him with; and when placed in the small and solitary chamber which he was told to consider as his own during his residence in the Tower, he was soothed even to weeping by this trifling circumstance, which he could not help considering as an omen, that his unfortunate house was not entirely deserted by Providence.

But the thoughts and occurrences of a prison are too uniform for a narrative, and we must now convey our readers into a more bustling scene.

CHAPTER XXXVII

Henceforth 'tis done—Fortune and I are friends;
And I must live, for Buckingham commends.
—POPE.

THE spacious mansion of the Duke of Buckingham, with the demesne belonging to it, originally bore the name of York House, and occupied a large portion of the ground adjacent to the Savoy.

This had been laid out by the munificence of his father, the favourite of Charles the First, in a most splendid manner, so as almost to rival Whitehall itself. But during the increasing rage for building new streets, and the creating of almost an additional town, in order to connect London and Westminster, this ground had become of very great value; and the second Duke of Buckingham, who was at once fond of scheming, and needy of money, had agreed to a plan laid before him by some adventurous architect, for converting the extensive grounds around his palace into those streets, lanes, and courts, which still perpetuate his name and titles; though those who live in Buckingham Street, Duke Street, Villiers Street, or in Of-alley (for even that connecting particle is locally commemorated), probably think seldom of the memory of the witty, eccentric, and licentious George Villiers, Duke of Buckingham, whose titles are preserved in the names of their residence and its neighbourhood.

This building-plan the Duke had entered upon with all the eagerness which he usually attached to novelty. His gardens were destroyed—his pavilions levelled—his splendid stables demolished—the whole pomp of his suburban demesne laid waste, cumbered with ruins, and intersected with the foundations of new buildings and cellars, and the process of levelling different lines for the intended streets. But the undertaking, although it proved afterwards both lucrative and successful, met with a check at the outset, partly from want of the necessary funds, partly from the impatient and mercurial temper of the Duke, which soon carried him off in pursuit of some more new object. So that, though much was demolished, very little, in comparison, was reared up in the stead, and nothing was completed. The principal part of the ducal mansion still remained uninjured; but the demesne in which it stood bore a strange analogy to the irregular mind of its noble owner. Here stood a beautiful group of exotic trees and shrubs, the remnant of the garden, amid yawning common-sewers, and heaps of rubbish. In one place an old tower threatened to fall upon the spectator; and in another he ran the risk of being swallowed up by a modern vault. Grandeur of conception could be discovered in the undertaking, but was almost everywhere marred by poverty or negligence of execution. In short, the whole place was the true emblem of an understanding and talents run to waste, and become more dangerous than advantageous to society, by the want of steady principle, and the improvidence of the possessor.

There were men who took a different view of the Duke's purpose in permitting his mansion to be thus surrounded, and his demesne occupied by modern buildings which were incomplete, and ancient which were but half demolished. They alleged, that, engaged as he was in so many mysteries of love and of politics, and having the character of the most daring and dangerous intriguer of his time, his Grace found it convenient to surround himself with this ruinous arena, into which officers of justice could not penetrate without some difficulty and hazard; and which might afford, upon occasion, a safe and secret shelter for such tools as were fit for desperate enterprises, and a private and unobserved mode of access to those whom he might have any special reason for receiving in secret.

Leaving Peveril in the Tower, we must once more convey our readers to the Levee of the Duke, who, on the morning of Julian's transference to that fortress, thus addressed his minister-in-chief, and principal attendant: "I have been so pleased with your conduct in this matter, Jerningham, that if Old Nick were to arise in our presence, and offer me his best imp as a familiar in thy room, I would hold it but a poor compliment."

"A legion of imps," said Jerningham, bowing, "could not have been more busy than I in your Grace's service; but if your Grace will permit me to say so, your whole plan was well-nigh marred by your not returning home till last night, or rather this morning."

"And why, I pray you, sage Master Jerningham," said his Grace, "should I have returned home an instant sooner than my pleasure and convenience served?"

"Nay, my Lord Duke," replied the attendant, "I know not; only, when you sent us word by Empson, in Chiffinch's apartment, to command us to make sure of the girl at any rate, and at all risks, you said you would be here so soon as you could get freed of the King."

"Freed of the King, you rascal! What sort of phrase is that?" demanded the Duke.

"It was Empson who used it, my lord, as coming from your Grace."

"There is much very fit for my Grace to say, that misbecomes such mouths as Empson's or yours to repeat," answered the Duke haughtily, but instantly resumed his tone of familiarity, for his humour was as capricious as his pursuits. "But I know what thou wouldst have; first, your wisdom would know what became of me since thou hadst my commands at Chiffinch's; and next, your valour would fain sound another flourish of trumpets on thine own most artificial retreat, leaving thy comrade in the hands of the Philistines."

"May it please your Grace," said Jerningham, "I did but retreat for the preservation of the baggage."

"What! do you play at crambo with me?" said the Duke. "I would have you to know that the common parish fool should be whipt, were he to attempt to pass pun or quodlibet as a genuine jest, even amongst ticket-porters and hackney chairmen."

"And yet I have heard your Grace indulge in the *jeu de mots*," answered the attendant.

"Sirrah Jerningham," answered the patron, "discard thy memory, or keep it under correction, else it will hamper thy rise in the world. Thou mayst perchance have seen me also have a fancy to play at trap-ball, or to kiss a serving wench, or to guzzle ale and eat toasted cheese in a porterly whimsy; but is it fitting thou shouldst remember such follies? No more on't.—Hark you; how came the long lubberly fool, Jenkins, being a master of the noble science of defence, to suffer himself to be run through the body so simply by a rustic swain like this same Peveril?"

"Please your Grace, this same Corydon is no such novice. I saw the onset; and, except in one hand, I never saw a sword managed with such life, grace, and facility."

"Ay, indeed?" said the Duke, taking his own sheathed rapier in his hand, "I could not have thought that. I am somewhat rusted, and have need of breathing. Peveril is a name of note. As well go to the Barns-elms, or behind Montagu House, with him as with another. His father a rumoured plotter, too. The public would have noted it in me as becoming a zealous Protestant. Needful I do something to maintain my good name in the city, to atone for non-attendance on prayer and preaching. But your Laertes is fast in the Fleet; and I suppose his blundering blockhead of an antagonist is dead or dying."

"Recovering, my lord, on the contrary," replied Jerningham; "the blade fortunately avoided his vitals."

"D—n his vitals!" answered the Duke. "Tell him to postpone his recovery, or I will put him to death in earnest."

"I will caution his surgeon," said Jerningham, "which will answer equally well."

"Do so; and tell him he had better be on his own deathbed as cure his patient till I send him notice.—That young fellow must be let loose again at no rate."

"There is little danger," said the attendant. "I hear some of the witnesses have got their net flung over him on account of some matters down in the north; and that he is to be translated to the Tower for that, and for some letters of the Countess of Derby, as rumour goes."

"To the Tower let him go, and get out as he can," replied the Duke; "and when you hear he is fast there, let the fencing fellow recover as fast as the surgeon and he can mutually settle it."

The Duke, having said this, took two or three turns in the apartment, and appeared to be in deep thought. His attendant waited the issue of his meditations with patience, being well aware that such moods, during which his mind was strongly directed in one point, were never of so long duration with his patron as to prove a severe burden to his own patience.

Accordingly, after the silence of seven or eight minutes, the Duke broke through it, taking from the toilette a large silk purse, which seemed full of gold. "Jerningham," he said, "thou art a faithful fellow, and it would be sin not to cherish thee. I beat the King at Mall on his bold defiance. The honour is enough for me ; and thou, my boy, shalt have the winnings."

Jerningham pocketed the purse with due acknowledgments.

"Jerningham," his Grace continued, " I know you blame me for changing my plans too often ; and on my soul I have heard you so learned on the subject, that I have become of your opinion, and have been vexed at myself for two or three hours together, for not sticking as constantly to one object, as doubtless I shall, when age (touching his forehead) shall make this same weathercock too rusty to turn with the changing breeze. But as yet, while I have spirit and action, let it whirl like the vane at the mast-head, which teaches the pilot how to steer his course ; and when I shift mine, think I am bound to follow Fortune, and not to control her."

"I can understand nothing from all this, please your Grace," replied Jerningham, " save that you have been pleased to change some purposed measures, and think that you have profited by doing so."

"You shall judge yourself," replied the Duke. " I have seen the Duchess of Portsmouth.—You start. It is true, by Heaven ! I have seen her, and from sworn enemies we have become sworn friends. The treaty between such high and mighty powers had some weighty articles; besides, I had a French negotiator to deal with; so that you will allow a few hours' absence was but a necessary interval to make up our matters of diplomacy."

"Your Grace astonishes me," said Jerningham. " Christian's plan of supplanting the great lady is then entirely abandoned ? I thought you had but desired to have the fair successor here, in order to carry it on under your own management."

"I forget what I meant at the time," said the Duke; "unless that I was resolved she should not jilt me as she did the good-natured man of royalty ; and so I am still determined, since you put me in mind of the fair Dowsabelle. But I had a contrite note from the Duchess while we were at the Mall. I went to see her, and found her a perfect Niobe.—On my soul, in spite of red eyes and swelled features, and dishevelled hair, there are, after all, Jerningham, some women who do, as the poets say, look lovely in affliction. Out came the cause ; and with such humility, such penitence, such throwing herself on my mercy (she the proudest devil, too, in the whole Court), that I must have had heart of steel to resist it all. In short, Chiffinch in a drunken fit had played the babbler, and let young Saville into our intrigue. Saville plays the rogue, and informs the Duchess by a messenger, who luckily came a little late into the market. She learned, too, being a very devil for intelligence, that there had been some jarring between the master and me about this new Phillis; and that I was most likely to catch the bird,—as any one may see who looks on us both. It must have been Empson who fluted all this into her Grace's ear; and thinking she saw how her ladyship and I could hunt in couples, she entreats me to break Christian's scheme, and keep the wench out of the King's sight, especially if she were such a rare piece of perfection as fame has reported her."

"And your Grace has promised her your hand to uphold the influence which you have so often threatened to ruin?" said Jerningham.

"Ay, Jerningham; my turn was as much served when she seemed to own herself in my power, and cry me mercy.—And observe, it is all one to me by which ladder I climb into the King's cabinet. That of Portsmouth is ready fixed—better ascend by it than fling it down to put up another—I hate all unnecessary trouble."

"And Christian?" said Jerningham.

"May go to the devil for a self-conceited ass. One pleasure of this twist of intrigue, is, to revenge me of that villain, who thought himself so essential, that, by Heaven! he forced himself on my privacy, and lectured me like a schoolboy. Hang the cold-blooded hypocritical vermin! If he mutters, I will have his nose slit as wide as Coventry's.*—Hark ye, is the Colonel come?"

"I expect him every moment, your Grace."

"Send him up when he arrives," said the Duke.——"Why do you stand looking at me? What would you have?"

"Your Grace's direction respecting the young lady," said Jerningham.

"Odd zooks," said the Duke, "I had totally forgotten her.— Is she very tearful?—Exceedingly afflicted?"

"She does not take on so violently as I have seen some do," said Jerningham; "but for a strong, firm, concentrated indignation, I have seen none to match her."

"Well, we will permit her to cool. I will not face the

* The ill-usage of Sir John Coventry by some of the Life Guardsmen, in revenge of something said in Parliament concerning the King's theatrical amours, gave rise to what was called Coventry's Act, against cutting and maiming the person.

affliction of a second fair one immediately. I am tired of snivelling, and swelled eyes, and blubbered cheeks for some time; and, moreover, must husband my powers of consolation. Begone, and send the Colonel."

"Will your Grace permit me one other question?" demanded his confidant.

"Ask what thou wilt, Jerningham, and then begone."

"Your Grace has determined to give up Christian," said the attendant. "May I ask what becomes of the kingdom of Man?"

"Forgotten, as I have a Christian soul!" said the Duke; "as much forgotten as if I had never nourished that scheme of royal ambition.—D—n it, we must knit up the ravelled skein of that intrigue.—Yet it is but a miserable rock, not worth the trouble I have been bestowing on it; and for a kingdom—it has a sound indeed; but, in reality, I might as well stick a cock-chicken's feather into my hat, and call it a plume. Besides, now I think upon it, it would scarce be honourable to sweep that petty royalty out of Derby's possession. I won a thousand pieces of the young Earl when he was last here, and suffered him to hang about me at Court. I question if the whole revenue of his kingdom is worth twice as much. Easily I could win it of him, were he here, with less trouble than it would cost me to carry on these troublesome intrigues of Christian's."

"If I may be permitted to say so, please your Grace," answered Jerningham, "although your Grace is perhaps somewhat liable to change your mind, no man in England can afford better reasons for doing so."

"I think so myself, Jerningham," said the Duke; "and it may be it is one reason for my changing. One likes to vindicate his own conduct, and to find out fine reasons for doing what one has a mind to.—And now, once again, begone. Or, hark ye—hark ye—I shall need some loose gold. You may leave the purse I gave you; and I will give you an order for as much, and two years' interest, on old Jacob Doublefee."

"As your Grace pleases," said Jerningham, his whole stock of complaisance scarcely able to conceal his mortification at exchanging for a distant order, of a kind which of late had not been very regularly honoured, the sunny contents of the purse which had actually been in his pocket. Secretly, but solemnly did he make a vow, that two years' interest alone should not be the compensation for this involuntary exchange in the form of his remuneration.

As the discontented dependant left the apartment, he met, at the head of the grand staircase, Christian himself, who, exercising the freedom of an ancient friend of the house, was making his way, unannounced, to the Duke's dressing apartment. Jerningham, conjecturing that his visit at this crisis would be anything but well timed, or well taken, endeavoured to avert his purpose, by asserting that the Duke was indisposed, and in his bedchamber; and this he said so loud that his master might hear him, and, if he pleased, realise the apology which he offered in his name, by retreating into the bedroom as his last sanctuary, and drawing the bolt against intrusion.

But, far from adopting a stratagem to which he had had recourse on former occasions, in order to avoid those who came upon him, though at an appointed hour, and upon business of importance, Buckingham called, in a loud voice, from his dressing apartment, commanding his chamberlain instantly to introduce his good friend Master Christian, and censuring him for hesitating for an instant to do so.

"Now," thought Jerningham within himself, "if Christian knew the Duke as well as I do, he would sooner stand the leap of a lion, like the London 'prentice bold, than venture on my master at this moment, who is even now in a humour nearly as dangerous as the animal."

He then ushered Christian into his master's presence, taking care to post himself within earshot of the door.

CHAPTER XXXVIII

"Speak not of niceness, when there's chance of wreck,"
The captain said, as ladies writhed their neck
To see the dying dolphin flap the deck:
"If we go down, on us these gentry sup;
We dine upon them, if we haul them up.
Wise men applaud us when we eat the eaters,
As the devil laughs when keen folks cheat the cheaters."
—THE SEA VOYAGE.

THERE was nothing in the Duke's manner towards Christian which could have conveyed to that latter personage, experienced as he was in the worst possible ways of the world, that Buckingham would, at that particular moment, rather have seen the devil then himself; unless it was that Buckingham's reception of him, being rather extraordinarily courteous towards so old an acquaintance, might have excited some degree of suspicion.

Having escaped with some difficulty from the vague region of general compliments, which bears the same relation to that of business that Milton informs us the *Limbo Patrum* has to the sensible and material earth, Christian asked his Grace of

Buckingham, with the same blunt plainness with which he usually veiled a very deep and artificial character, whether he had lately seen Chiffinch or his helpmate?

"Neither of them lately," answered Buckingham. "Have not you waited on them yourself?—I thought you would have been more anxious about the great scheme."

"I have called once and again," said Christian, "but I can gain no access to the sight of that important couple. I begin to be afraid they are paltering with me."

"Which, by the welkin and its stars, you would not be slow in avenging, Master Christian. I know your puritanical principles on that point well," said the Duke. "Revenge may be well said to be sweet, when so many grave and wise men are ready to exchange for it all the sugar-plums which pleasures offer to the poor sinful people of the world, besides the reversion of those which they talk of expecting in the way of *post obit.*"

"You may jest, my lord," said Christian, "but still——"

"But still you will be revenged on Chiffinch, and his little commodious companion. And yet the task may be difficult—Chiffinch has so many ways of obliging his master—his little woman is such a convenient pretty sort of a screen, and has such winning little ways of her own, that, in faith, in your case, I would not meddle with them. What is this refusing their door, man? We all do it to our best friends now and then, as well as to duns and dull company."

"If your Grace is in a humour of rambling thus wildly in your talk," said Christian, "you know my old faculty of patience—I can wait till it be your pleasure to talk more seriously."

"Seriously!" said his Grace—"Wherefore not?—I only wait to know what your serious business may be."

"In a word, my lord, from Chiffinch's refusal to see me, and some vain calls which I have made at your Grace's mansion, I am afraid either that our plan has miscarried, or that there is some intention to exclude me from the farther conduct of the matter." Christian pronounced these words with considerable emphasis.

"That were folly as well as treachery," returned the Duke, "to exclude from the spoil the very engineer who conducted the attack. But hark ye, Christian—I am sorry to tell bad news without preparation; but as you insist on knowing the worst, and are not ashamed to suspect your best friends, out it must come—Your niece left Chiffinch's house the morning before yesterday."

Christian staggered, as if he had received a severe blow; and the blood ran to his face in such a current of passion, that the Duke concluded he was struck with an apoplexy. But, exerting the extraordinary command which he could maintain under the most trying circumstances, he said, with a voice, the composure of which had an unnatural contrast with the alteration of his countenance, "Am I to conclude, that in leaving the protection of the roof in which I placed her, the girl has found shelter under that of your Grace?"

"Sir," replied Buckingham gravely, "the supposition does my gallantry more credit than it deserves."

"Oh, my Lord Duke," answered Christian, "I am not one whom you can impose on by this species of courtly jargon. I know of what your Grace is capable; and that to gratify the caprice of a moment you would not hesitate to disappoint even the schemes at which you yourself have laboured most busily. —Suppose this jest played off. Take your laugh at those simple precautions by which I intended to protect your Grace's interest, as well as that of others. Let us know the extent of your frolic, and consider how far its consequences can be repaired."

"On my word, Christian," said the Duke, laughing, "you are the most obliging of uncles and of guardians. Let your niece pass through as many adventures as Boccaccio's bride of the King of Garba, you care not. Pure or soiled, she will still make the footstool of your fortune."

An Indian proverb says, that the dart of contempt will even pierce through the shell of the tortoise; but this is more peculiarly the case when conscience tells the subject of the sarcasm that it is justly merited. Christian, stung with Buckingham's reproach, at once assumed a haughty and threatening mien, totally inconsistent with that in which sufferance seemed to be as much his badge as that of Shylock. "You are a foul-mouthed and most unworthy lord," he said; "and as such I will proclaim you, unless you make reparation for the injury you have done me."

"And what," said the Duke of Buckingham, "shall I proclaim *you*, that can give you the least title to notice from such as I am? What name shall I bestow on the little transaction which has given rise to such unexpected misunderstanding?"

Christian was silent, either from rage or from mental conviction.

"Come, come, Christian," said the Duke, smiling, "we know too much of each other to make a quarrel safe. Hate each other we may—circumvent each other—it is the way of Courts —but proclaim!—a fico for the phrase."

"I used it not," said Christian, "till your Grace drove me to extremity. You know, my lord, I have fought both at home and abroad; and you should not rashly think that I will endure any indignity which blood can wipe away."

"On the contrary," said the Duke, with the same civil and sneering manner, "I can confidently assert, that the life of half a score of your friends would seem very light to you, Christian, if their existence interfered, I do not say with your character, as being a thing of much less consequence, but with any advantage which their existence might intercept. Fie upon it, man, we have known each other long. I never thought you a coward; and am only glad to see I could strike a few sparkles of heat out of your cold and constant disposition. I will now, if you please, tell you at once the fate of the young lady, in which I pray you to believe that I am truly interested."

"I hear you, my Lord Duke," said Christian. "The curl of your upper lip, and your eyebrow, does not escape me. Your Grace knows the French proverb, 'He laughs best who laughs last.' But I hear you."

"Thank Heaven you do," said Buckingham; "for your case requires haste, I promise you, and involves no laughing matter. Well then, hear a simple truth, on which (if it became me to offer any pledge for what I assert to be such) I could pledge life, fortune, and honour. It was the morning before last, when meeting with the King at Chiffinch's unexpectedly—in fact I had looked in to fool an hour away, and to learn how your scheme advanced—I saw a singular scene. Your niece terrified little Chiffinch—(the hen Chiffinch, I mean)—bid the King defiance to his teeth, and walked out of the presence triumphantly, under the guardianship of a young fellow of little mark or likelihood, excepting a tolerable personal presence, and the advantage of a most unconquerable impudence. Egad, I can hardly help laughing to think how the King and I were both baffled; for I will not deny, that I had tried to trifle for a moment with the fair Indamora. But, egad, the young fellow swooped her off from under our noses, like my own Drawcansir clearing off the banquet from the two Kings of Brentford. There was a dignity in the gallant's swaggering retreat which I must try to teach Mohun;* it will suit his part admirably."

"This is incomprehensible, my Lord Duke," said Christian, who by this time had recovered all his usual coolness; "you cannot expect me to believe this. Who dared be so bold as to carry off my niece in such a manner, and from so august a presence? And with whom, a stranger as he must have been, would she, wise and cautious as I know her, have consented to depart in such a manner?—My lord, I cannot believe this."

"One of your priests, my most devout Christian," replied the Duke, "would only answer, Die, infidel, in thine unbelief; but I am only a poor worldling sinner, and I will add what

* Then a noted actor.

mite of information I can. The young fellow's name, as I am given to understand, is Julian, son of Sir Geoffrey, whom men call Peveril of the Peak."

"Peveril of the Devil, who hath his cavern there!" said Christian warmly; "for I know that gallant, and believe him capable of anything bold and desperate. But how could he intrude himself into the royal presence? Either Hell aids him, or Heaven looks nearer into mortal dealings than I have yet believed. If so, may God forgive us, who deemed he thought not on us at all!"

"Amen, most Christian Christian," replied the Duke. "I am glad to see thou hast yet some touch of grace that leads thee to augur so. But Empson, the hen Chiffinch, and half-a-dozen more, saw the swain's entrance and departure. Please examine these witnesses with your own wisdom, if you think your time may not be better employed in tracing the fugitives. I believe he gained entrance as one of some dancing or masking party. Rowley, you know, is accessible to all who will come forth to make him sport. So in stole this termagant tearing gallant, like Samson among the Philistines, to pull down our fine scheme about our ears."

"I believe you, my lord," said Christian; "I cannot but believe you; and I forgive you, since it is your nature, for making sport of what is ruin and destruction. But which way did they take?"

"To Derbyshire, I should presume, to seek her father," said the Duke. "She spoke of going into the paternal protection, instead of yours, Master Christian. Something had chanced at Chiffinch's, to give her cause to suspect that you had not altogether provided for his daughter in the manner which her father was likely to approve of."

"Now, Heaven be praised," said Christian, "she knows not her father is come to London! and they must be gone down either to Martindale Castle, or to Moultrassie Hall; in either case they are in my power—I must follow them close. I will return instantly to Derbyshire—I am undone if she meet her father until these errors are amended. Adieu, my lord. I forgive the part which I fear your Grace must have had in baulking our enterprise—it is no time for mutual reproaches."

"You speak truth, Master Christian," said the Duke, "and I wish you all success. Can I help you with men, or horses, or money?"

"I thank your Grace," said Christian, and hastily left the apartment.

The Duke watched his descending footsteps on the staircase, until they could be heard no longer, and then exclaimed to Jerningham, who entered, "*Victoria! victoria! magna est veritas*

et prævalebit!—Had I told the villain a word of a lie, he is so
familiar with all the regions of falsehood—his whole life has
been such an absolute imposture, that I had stood detected
in an instant; but I told him truth, and that was the only
means of deceiving him. Victoria! my dear Jerningham, I
am prouder of cheating Christian, than I should have been of
circumventing a minister of state."

"Your Grace holds his wisdom very high," said the attendant.

"His cunning, at least, I do, which, in Court affairs, often
takes the weather-gage of wisdom,—as in Yarmouth Roads a
herring-buss will baffle a frigate. He shall not return to London
if I can help it, until all these intrigues are over."

As his Grace spoke, the Colonel, after whom he had repeatedly
made inquiry, was announced by a gentleman of his household.
"He met not Christian, did he?" said the Duke hastily.

"No, my lord," returned the domestic, "the Colonel came
by the old garden staircase."

"I judged as much," replied the Duke; "'tis an owl that will
not take wing in daylight, when there is a thicket left to skulk
under. Here he comes from threading lane, vault, and ruinous
alley, very near as ominous a creature as the fowl of ill augury
which he resembles."

The Colonel, to whom no other appellation seemed to be
given, than that which belonged to his military station, now
entered the apartment. He was tall, strongly built, and past
the middle period of life, and his countenance, but for the heavy
cloud which dwelt upon it, might have been pronounced a
handsome one. While the Duke spoke to him, either from
humility or some other cause, his large serious eye was cast
down upon the ground; but he raised it when he answered,
with a keen look of earnest observation. His dress was very
plain, and more allied to that of the Puritans than of the
Cavaliers of the time; a shadowy black hat, like the Spanish
sombrero; a large black mantle or cloak, and a long rapier,
gave him something the air of a Castilione, to which his gravity
and stiffness of demeanour added considerable strength.

"Well, Colonel," said the Duke, "we have been long strangers
—how have matters gone with you?"

"As with other men of action in quiet times," answered the
Colonel, "or as a good war-caper * that lies high and dry in a
muddy creek, till seams and planks are rent and riven."

"Well, Colonel," said the Duke, "I have used your valour
before now, and I may again; so that I shall speedily see that
the vessel is careened, and undergoes a thorough repair."

"I conjecture, then," said the Colonel, "that your Grace has
some voyage in hand?"

* A privateer.

"No, but there is one which I want to interrupt," replied the Duke.

"'Tis but another stave of the same tune.—Well, my lord, I listen," answered the stranger.

"Nay," said the Duke, "it is but a trifling matter after all. —You know Ned Christian?"

"Ay, surely, my lord," replied the Colonel, "we have been long known to each other."

"He is about to go down to Derbyshire to seek a certain niece of his, whom he will scarcely find there. Now, I trust to your tried friendship to interrupt his return to London. Go with him, or meet him, cajole him, or assail him, or do what thou wilt with him—only keep him from London for a fort-night at least, and then I care little how soon he comes."

"For by that time, I suppose," replied the Colonel, "any one may find the wench that thinks her worth the looking for."

"Thou mayst think her worth the looking for thyself, Colonel," rejoined the Duke; "I promise you she hath many a thousand stitched to her petticoat; such a wife would save thee from skeldering on the public."

"My lord, I sell my blood and my sword, but not my honour," answered the man sullenly; "if I marry, my bed may be a poor, but it shall be an honest one."

"Then thy wife will be the only honest matter in thy possession, Colonel—at least since I have known you," replied the Duke.

"Why, truly, your Grace may speak your pleasure on that point. It is chiefly your business which I have done of late; and if it were less strictly honest than I could have wished, the employer was to blame as well as the agent. But for marrying a cast-off mistress, the man (saving your Grace, to whom I am bound) lives not who dares propose it to me."

The Duke laughed loudly. "Why, this is mine Ancient Pistol's vein," he replied.

—— "Shall I Sir Pandarus of Troy become,
And by my side wear steel?—then Lucifer take all!"

"My breeding is too plain to understand ends of playhouse verse, my lord," said the Colonel suddenly. "Has your Grace no other service to command me?"

"None—only I am told you have published a Narrative concerning the Plot."

"What should ail me, my lord?" said the Colonel; "I hope I am a witness as competent as any that has yet appeared?"

"Truly, I think so to the full," said the Duke; "and it

would have been hard, when so much profitable mischief was going, if so excellent a Protestant as yourself had not come in for a share."

"I came to take your Grace's commands, not to be the object of your wit," said the Colonel.

"Gallantly spoken, most resolute and most immaculate Colonel! As you are to be on full pay in my service for a month to come, I pray your acceptance of this purse, for contingents and equipments, and you shall have my instructions from time to time."

"They shall be punctually obeyed, my lord," said the Colonel; "I know the duty of a subaltern officer. I wish your Grace a good morning."

So saying, he pocketed the purse, without either affecting hesitation, or expressing gratitude, but merely as a part of a transaction in the regular way of business, and stalked from the apartment with the same sullen gravity which marked his entrance. "Now, there goes a scoundrel after my own heart," said the Duke; "a robber from his cradle, a murderer since he could hold a knife, a profound hypocrite in religion, and a worse and deeper hypocrite in honour,—would sell his soul to the devil to accomplish any villainy, and would cut the throat of his brother, did he dare to give the villainy he had so acted its right name.—Now, why stand you amazed, good Master Jerningham, and look on me as you would on some monster of Ind, when you had paid your shilling to see it, and were staring out your pennyworth with your eyes as round as a pair of spectacles? Wink, man, and save them, and then let thy tongue untie the mystery."

"On my word, my Lord Duke," answered Jerningham, "since I am compelled to speak, I can only say, that the longer I live with your Grace, I am the more at a loss to fathom your motives of action. Others lay plans, either to attain profit or pleasure by their execution; but your Grace's delight is to counteract your own schemes, when in the very act of performance; like a child—forgive me—that breaks its favourite toy, or a man who should set fire to the house he has half built."

"And why not, if he wanted to warm his hands at the blaze?" said the Duke.

"Ay, my lord," replied his dependent; "but what if, in doing so, he should burn his fingers?—My lord, it is one of your noblest qualities, that you will sometimes listen to the truth without taking offence; but were it otherwise, I could not, at this moment, help speaking out at every risk."

"Well, say on, I can bear it," said the Duke, throwing himself into an easy-chair, and using his toothpick with graceful indifference and equanimity; "I love to hear what such potsherds as thou art, think of the proceedings of us who are of the pure porcelain clay of the earth."

"In the name of Heaven, my lord, let me then ask you," said Jerningham, "what merit you claim, or what advantage you expect, from having embroiled everything in which you are concerned to a degree which equals the chaos of the blind old Roundhead's poem which your Grace is so fond of? To begin with the King. In spite of good-humour, he will be incensed at your repeated rivalry."

"His Majesty defied me to it."

"You have lost all hopes of the Isle, by quarrelling with Christian."

"I have ceased to care a farthing about it," replied the Duke.

"In Christian himself, whom you have insulted, and to whose family you intend dishonour, you have lost a sagacious, artful, and cool-headed instrument and adherent," said the monitor.

"Poor Jerningham!" answered the Duke; "Christian would say as much for thee, I doubt not, wert thou discarded to-morrow. It is the common error of such tools as you and he to think themselves indispensable. As to his family, what was never honourable cannot be dishonoured by any connection with my house."

"I say nothing of Chiffinch," said Jerningham, "offended as he will be when he learns why, and by whom, his scheme has been ruined, and the lady spirited away—He and his wife, I say nothing of them."

"You need not," said the Duke; "for were they even fit persons to speak to me about, the Duchess of Portsmouth has bargained for their disgrace."

"Then this bloodhound of a Colonel, as he calls himself, your Grace cannot even lay *him* on a quest which is to do you service, but you must do him such indignity at the same time, as he will not fail to remember, and be sure to fly at your throat should he ever have an opportunity of turning on you."

"I will take care he has none," said the Duke; "and yours, Jerningham, is a low-lived apprehension. Beat your spaniel heartily if you would have him under command. Ever let your agents see you know what they are, and prize them accordingly. A rogue, who must needs be treated as a man of honour, is apt to get above his work. Enough, therefore, of your advice and censure, Jerningham; we differ in every particular. Were we both engineers, you would spend your life in watching some old woman's wheel, which spins flax by the ounce; I must be in the midst of the most varied and coun-teracting machinery, regulating checks and counter - checks, balancing weights, proving springs and wheels, directing and controlling a hundred combined powers."

"And your fortune, in the meanwhile?" said Jerningham; "pardon this last hint, my lord."

"My fortune," said the Duke, "is too vast to be hurt by a petty wound; and I have, as thou knowest, a thousand salves in store for the scratches and scars which it sometimes receives in greasing my machinery."

"Your Grace does not mean Dr. Wilderhead's powder of projection?"

'Pshaw! he is a quacksalver, and mountebank, and beggar."

"Or Solicitor Drowndland's plan for draining the fens?"

"He is a cheat,—*videlicet*, an attorney."

"Or the Laird of Lackpelf's sale of Highland woods?"

"He is a Scotsman," said the Duke,—"*videlicet*, both cheat and beggar."

"These streets here, upon the site of your noble mansion-house?" said Jerningham.

"The architect's a bite, and the plan's a bubble. I am sick of the sight of this rubbish, and I will soon replace our old alcoves, alleys, and flower-pots by an Italian garden and a new palace."

"That, my lord, would be to waste, not to improve your fortune," said his domestic.

"Clodpate, and muddy spirit that thou art, thou hast forgot the most hopeful scheme of all—the South Sea Fisheries—their stock is up 50 per cent. already. Post down to the Alley, and tell old Manasses to buy £20,000 for me.—Forgive me, Plutus, I forgot to lay my sacrifice on thy shrine, and yet expected thy favours!—Fly post-haste, Jerningham—for thy life, for thy life, for thy life!" *

With hands and eyes uplifted, Jerningham left the apartment; and the Duke, without thinking a moment farther on old or new intrigues—on the friendship he had formed, or the enmity he had provoked—on the beauty whom he had carried off from her natural protectors, as well as from her lover—or on the monarch against whom he had placed himself in rivalship,— sat down to calculate chances with all the zeal of Demoivre, tired of the drudgery in half-an-hour, and refused to see the zealous agent whom he had employed in the city, because he was busily engaged in writing a new lampoon.

---

* Stock-jobbing, as it is called, that is, dealing in shares of monopolies, patent, and joint-stock companies of every description, was at least as common in Charles II.'s time as our own; and as the exercise of ingenuity in this way promised a road to wealth without the necessity of industry, it was then much pursued by dissolute courtiers.

CHAPTER XXXIX

Ah ! changeful head, and fickle heart !
—PROGRESS OF DISCONTENT.

No event is more ordinary in narratives of this nature, than the abduction of the female on whose fate the interest is supposed to turn ; but that of Alice Bridgenorth was thus far particular, that she was spirited away by the Duke of Buckingham, more in contradiction than in the rivalry of passion ; and that, as he made his first addresses to her at Chiffinch's, rather in the spirit of rivalry to his Sovereign, than from any strong impression which her beauty had made on his affections, so he had formed the sudden plan of spiriting her away by means of his dependents, rather to perplex Christian, the King, Chiffinch, and all concerned, than because he had any particular desire for her society at his own mansion. Indeed, so far was this from being the case, that his Grace was rather surprised than delighted with the success of the enterprise which had made her an inmate there, although it is probable he might have thrown himself into an uncontrollable passion, had he learned its miscarriage instead of its success.

Twenty-four hours had passed over since he had returned to his own roof, before, notwithstanding sundry hints from Jerningham, he could even determine on the exertion necessary to pay his fair captive a visit ; and then it was with the internal reluctance of one who can only be stirred from indolence by novelty.

"I wonder what made me plague myself about this wench," said he, "and doom myself to encounter all the hysterical rhapsodies of a country Phillis, with her head stuffed with her grandmother's lessons about virtue and the Bible-book, when the finest and best-bred women in town may be had upon more easy terms. It is a pity one cannot mount the victor's car of triumph without having a victory to boast of, yet, faith, it is what most of our modern gallants do, though it would not become Buckingham.—Well, I must see her," he concluded, "though it were but to rid the house of her. The Portsmouth will not hear of her being set at liberty near Charles, so much is she afraid of a new fair seducing the old sinner from his allegiance. So how the girl is to be disposed of—for I shall have little fancy to keep her here, and she is too wealthy to be sent down to Cliefden as a housekeeper—is a matter to be thought on."

He then called for such a dress as might set off his natural good mien—a compliment which he considered as due to his own merit; for as to anything farther, he went to pay his respects to his fair prisoner with almost as little zeal in the cause, as a gallant to fight a duel in which he has no warmer interest than the maintenance of his reputation as a man of honour.

The set of apartments consecrated to the use of those favourites who occasionally made Buckingham's mansion their place of abode, and who were, so far as liberty was concerned, often required to observe the regulations of a convent, were separated from the rest of the Duke's extensive mansion. He lived in the age when what was called gallantry warranted the most atrocious actions of deceit and violence; as may be best illustrated by the catastrophe of an unfortunate actress, whose beauty attracted the attention of the last De Vere, Earl of Oxford. While her virtue defied his seductions, he ruined her under colour of a mock marriage, and was rewarded for a success which occasioned the death of his victim, by the general applause of the men of wit and gallantry who filled the drawing-room of Charles.

Buckingham had made provision in the interior of his ducal mansion for exploits of a similar nature; and the set of apartments which he now visited were alternately used to confine the reluctant, and to accommodate the willing.

Being now destined for the former purpose, the key was delivered to the Duke by a hooded and spectacled old lady, who sat reading a devout book in the outer hall which divided these apartments (usually called the Nunnery) from the rest of the house. This experienced dowager acted as mistress of the ceremonies on such occasions, and was the trusty depositary of more intrigues than were known to any dozen of her worshipful calling besides.

" As sweet a linnet," she said, as she undid the outward door, " as ever sung in a cage."

" I was afraid she might have been more for moping than for singing, Dowlas," said the Duke.

" Till yesterday she was so, please your Grace," answered Dowlas; " or, to speak sooth, till early this morning, we heard of nothing but Lachrymæ. But the air of your noble Grace's house is favourable to singing-birds; and to-day matters have been a-much mended."

" 'Tis sudden, dame," said the Duke; " and 'tis something strange, considering that I have never visited her, that the pretty trembler should have been so soon reconciled to her fate."

" Ah, your Grace has such magic, that it communicates itself to your very walls; as wholesome Scripture says, Exodus, first and seventh, 'It cleaveth to the walls and the door-posts.'"

"You are too partial, Dame Dowlas," said the Duke of Buckingham.

"Not a word but truth," said the dame; "and I wish I may be an outcast from the fold of the lambs, but I think this damsel's very frame has changed since she was under your Grace's roof. Methinks she hath a lighter form, a finer step, a more displayed ankle—I cannot tell, but I think there is a change. But, lack-a-day, your Grace knows I am as old as I am trusty, and that my eyes wax something uncertain."

"Especially when you wash them with a cup of canary, Dame Dowlas," answered the Duke, who was aware that temperance was not amongst the cardinal virtues which were most familiar to the old lady's practice.

"Was it canary, your Grace said?—Was it indeed with canary, that your Grace should have supposed me to have washed my eyes?" said the offended matron. "I am sorry that your Grace should know me no better."

"I crave your pardon, dame," said the Duke, shaking aside, fastidiously, the grasp which, in the earnestness of her excul-pation, Madam Dowlas had clutched upon his sleeve. "I crave your pardon. Your nearer approach has convinced me of my erroneous imputation—I should have said nantz—not canary."

So saying, he walked forward into the inner apartments, which were fitted up with an air of voluptuous magnificence.

"The dame said true, however," said the proud deviser and proprietor of the splendid mansion—"A country Phillis might well reconcile herself to such a prison as this, even without a skilful bird-fancier to touch a bird-call. But I wonder where she can be, this rural Phidele. Is it possible she can have retreated, like a despairing commandant, into her bedchamber, the very citadel of the place, without even an attempt to defend the outworks?"

As he made this reflection, he passed through an antechamber and little eating parlour, exquisitely furnished, and hung with excellent paintings of the Venetian school.

Beyond these lay a withdrawing-room, fitted up in a style of still more studied elegance. The windows were darkened with painted glass, of such a deep and rich colour, as made the mid-day beams, which found their way into the apartment, imitate the rich colours of sunset; and, in the celebrated expression of the poet, "taught light to counterfeit a gloom."

Buckingham's feelings and taste had been too much, and too often, and too readily gratified, to permit him, in the general case, to be easily accessible, even to those pleasures which it had been the business of his life to pursue. The hackneyed voluptuary is like the jaded epicure, the mere listlessness of whose appetite becomes at length a sufficient penalty for having made it the principal object of his enjoyment and cultivation. Yet novelty has always some charms, and uncertainty has more.

The doubt how he was to be received—the change of mood which his prisoner was said to have evinced—the curiosity to know how such a creature as Alice Bridgenorth had been described, was likely to bear herself under the circumstances in which she was so unexpectedly placed, had upon Buckingham the effect of exciting unusual interest. On his own part, he had none of those feelings of anxiety with which a man, even of the most vulgar mind, comes to the presence of the female whom he wishes to please, far less the more refined sentiments of love, respect, desire, and awe, with which the more refined lover approaches the beloved object. He had been, to use an expressive French phrase, too completely *blasé* even from his earliest youth, to permit him now to experience the animal eagerness of the one, far less the more sentimental pleasure of the other. It is no small aggravation of this jaded and uncomfortable state of mind, that the voluptuary cannot renounce the pursuits with which he is satiated, but must continue, for his character's sake, or from the mere force of habit, to take all the toil, fatigue, and danger of the chase, while he has so little real interest in the termination.

Buckingham, therefore, felt it due to his reputation as a successful hero of intrigue, to pay his addresses to Alice Bridgenorth with dissembled eagerness; and, as he opened the door of the inner apartment, he paused to consider, whether the tone of gallantry, or that of passion, was fittest to use on the occasion. This delay enabled him to hear a few notes of a lute touched with exquisite skill, and accompanied by the still sweeter strains of a female voice, which, without executing any complete melody, seemed to sport itself in rivalship of the silver sound of the instrument.

"A creature so well educated," said the Duke, "with the sense she is said to possess, would, rustic as she is, laugh at the assumed rants of Oroondates. It is the vein of Dorimont— once, Buckingham, thine own—that must here do the feat, besides that the part is easier."

So thinking, he entered the room with that easy grace which characterised the gay courtiers among whom he flourished, and approached the fair tenant, whom he found seated near a table covered with books and music, and having on her left hand the large half-open casement, dim with stained glass, admitting only a doubtful light into this lordly retiring-room, which, hung with the richest tapestry of the Gobelines, and ornamented with piles of china and splendid mirrors, seemed like a bower built for a prince to receive his bride.

The splendid dress of the inmate corresponded with the taste of the apartment which she occupied, and partook of the Oriental costume which the much-admired Roxalana had then brought into fashion. A slender foot and ankle, which escaped from the wide trowser of richly ornamented and embroidered blue satin, was the only part of her person distinctly seen; the rest was enveloped, from head to foot, in a long veil of silver gauze, which, like a feathery and light mist on a beautiful landscape, suffered you to perceive that what it concealed was rarely lovely, yet induced the imagination even to enhance the charms it shaded. Such part of the dress as could be discovered was, like the veil and the trowsers, in the Oriental taste; a rich turban, and splendid caftan, were rather indicated than distinguished through the folds of the former. The whole attire argued at least coquetry on the part of a fair one, who must have expected, from her situation, a visitor of some pretension; and induced Buckingham to smile internally at Christian's account of the extreme simplicity and purity of his niece.

He approached the lady *en cavalier*, and addressed her with the air of being conscious, while he acknowledged his offences, that his condescending to do so formed a sufficient apology for them. "Fair Mistress Alice," he said, "I am sensible how deeply I ought to sue for pardon for the mistaken zeal of my servants, who, seeing you deserted and exposed without protection during an unlucky affray, took it upon them to bring you under the roof of one who would expose his life rather than suffer you to sustain a moment's anxiety. Was it my fault that those around me should have judged it necessary to interfere for your preservation; or that, aware of the interest I must take in you, they have detained you till I could myself, in personal attendance, receive your commands?"

"That attendance has not been speedily rendered, my lord," answered the lady. "I have been a prisoner for two days—neglected, and left to the charge of menials."

"How say you, lady?—Neglected!" exclaimed the Duke. "By Heaven, if the best in my household has failed in his duty, I will discard him on the instant!"

"I complain of no lack of courtesy from your servants, my lord," she replied; "but methinks it had been but complaisant in the Duke himself to explain to me earlier wherefore he has had the boldness to detain me as a state prisoner."

"And can the divine Alice doubt," said Buckingham, "that, had time and space, those cruel enemies to the flight of passion, given permission, the instant in which you crossed your vassal's

threshold had seen its devoted master at your feet, who hath
thought, since he saw you, of nothing but the charms which
that fatal morning placed before him at Chiffinch's?"

"I understand, then, my lord," said the lady, "that you have
been absent, and have had no part in the restraint which has
been exercised upon me?"

"Absent on the King's command, lady, and employed in the
discharge of his duty," answered Buckingham without hesitation. "What could I do?—The moment you left Chiffinch's,
his Majesty commanded me to the saddle in such haste, that
I had no time to change my satin buskins for riding-boots.*
If my absence has occasioned you a moment of inconvenience,
blame the inconsiderate zeal of those who, seeing me depart
from London, half distracted at my separation from you, were
willing to contribute their unmannered, though well-meant
exertions, to preserve their master from despair, by retaining
the fair Alice within his reach. To whom, indeed, could they
have restored you? He whom you selected as your champion
is in prison, or fled—your father absent from town—your uncle
in the north. To Chiffinch's house you had expressed your well-
founded aversion; and what fitter asylum remained than that of
your devoted slave, where you must ever reign a queen?"

"An imprisoned one," said the lady. "I desire not such
royalty."

"Alas! how wilfully you misconstrue me!" said the Duke,
kneeling on one knee; "and what right can you have to complain of a few hours' gentle restraint—you, who destine so many
to hopeless captivity? Be merciful for once, and withdraw that
envious veil; for the divinities are ever most cruel when they
deliver their oracles from such clouded recesses. Suffer at least
my rash hand——"

"I will save your Grace that unworthy trouble," said the lady
haughtily; and rising up, she flung back over her shoulders the
veil which shrouded her, saying, at the same time, "Look on
me, my Lord Duke, and see if these be indeed the charms
which have made on your Grace an impression so powerful."

Buckingham did look; and the effect produced on him by
surprise was so strong, that he rose hastily from his knee, and
remained for a few seconds as if he had been petrified. The
figure that stood before him had neither the height nor the rich
shape of Alice Bridgenorth; and, though perfectly well made,
was so slightly formed, as to seem almost infantine. Her dress

---

* This case is not without precedent. Among the jealousies and fears
expressed by the Long Parliament, they insisted much upon an agent
for the King departing for the continent so abruptly, that he had not
time to change his court dress—white buskins, to wit, and black silk
pantaloons—for an equipment more suitable to travel with.

was three or four short vests of embroidered satin, disposed one over the other, of different colours, or rather different shades of similar colours; for strong contrast was carefully avoided. These opened in front, so as to show part of the throat and neck, partially obscured by an inner covering of the finest lace; over the uppermost vest was worn a sort of mantle, or coat of rich fur. A small but magnificent turban was carelessly placed on her head, from under which flowed a profusion of coal-black tresses, which Cleopatra might have envied. The taste and splendour of the Eastern dress corresponded with the complexion of the lady's face, which was brunette, of a shade so dark as might almost have served an Indian.

Amidst a set of features, in which rapid and keen expression made amends for the want of regular beauty, the essential points of eyes as bright as diamonds, and teeth as white as pearls, did not escape the Duke of Buckingham, a professed connoisseur in female charms. In a word, the fanciful and singular female who thus unexpectedly produced herself before him, had one of those faces which are never seen without making an impression; which, when removed, are long after remembered; and for which, in our idleness, we are tempted to invent a hundred histories, that we may please our fancy by supposing the features under the influence of different kinds of emotion. Every one must have in recollection countenances of this kind, which, from a captivating and stimulating originality of expression, abide longer in the memory, and are more seductive to the imagination, than even regular beauty.

"My Lord Duke," said the lady, "it seems the lifting of my veil has done the work of magic upon your Grace. Alas, for the captive princess, whose nod was to command a vassal so costly as your Grace! She runs, methinks, no slight chance of being turned out of doors, like a second Cinderella, to seek her fortune among lackeys and lightermen."

"I am astonished!" said the Duke. "That villain, Jerningham—I will have the scoundrel's blood!"

"Nay, never abuse Jerningham for the matter," said the Unknown; "but lament your own unhappy engagements. While you, my Lord Duke, were posting northward, in white satin buskins, to toil in the King's affairs, the right and lawful princess sat weeping in sables in the uncheered solitude to which your absence condemned her. Two days she was disconsolate in vain; on the third came an African enchantress to change the scene for her, and the person for your Grace. Methinks, my lord, this adventure will tell but ill, when some faithful squire shall recount or record the gallant adventures of the second Duke of Buckingham."

"Fairly bit and bantered to boot," said the Duke—"the

monkey has a turn for satire, too, by all that is *piquante*.— Hark ye, fair Princess, how dared you adventure on such a trick as you have been accomplice to?"

"Dare, my lord," answered the stranger; "put the question to others, not to one who fears nothing."

"By my faith, I believe so; for thy front is bronzed by nature.—Hark ye, once more, mistress—What is your name and condition?"

"My condition I have told you—I am a Mauritanian sorceress by profession, and my name is Zarah," replied the Eastern maiden.

"But methinks that face, shape, and eyes"—said the Duke —"when didst thou pass for a dancing fairy?—Some such imp thou wert not many days since."

"My sister you may have seen—my twin sister; but not me, my lord," answered Zarah.

"Indeed," said the Duke, "that duplicate of thine, if it was not thy very self, was possessed with a dumb spirit, as thou with a talking one. I am still in the mind that you are the same; and that Satan, always so powerful with your sex, had art enough on our former meeting, to make thee hold thy tongue."

"Believe what you will of it, my lord," replied Zarah, "it cannot change the truth.—And now, my lord, I bid you farewell. Have you any commands to Mauritania?"

"Tarry a little, my Princess," said the Duke; "and remember, that you have voluntarily entered yourself as pledge for another; and are justly subjected to any penalty which it is my pleasure to exact. None must brave Buckingham with impunity."

"I am in no hurry to depart, if your Grace hath any commands for me."

"What! are you neither afraid of my resentment, nor of my love, fair Zarah?" said the Duke.

"Of neither, by this glove," answered the lady. "Your resentment must be a pretty passion indeed, if it could stoop to such a helpless object as I am; and for your love—good lack! good lack!"

"And why good lack with such a tone of contempt, lady?" said the Duke, piqued in spite of himself. "Think you Buckingham cannot love, or has never been beloved in return?"

"He may have thought himself beloved," said the maiden; "but by what slight creatures!—things whose heads could be rendered giddy by a playhouse rant—whose brains were only filled with red-heeled shoes and satin buskins—and who run altogether mad on the argument of a George and a star."

"And are there no such frail fair ones in your climate, most scornful Princess?" said the Duke.

" There are," said the lady; " but men rate them as parrots and monkeys—things without either sense or soul, head or heart. The nearness we bear to the sun has purified, while it strengthens, our passions. The icicles of your frozen climate shall as soon hammer hot bars into ploughshares, as shall the foppery and folly of your pretended gallantry make an instant's impression on a breast like mine."

" You speak like one who knows what passion is," said the Duke. " Sit down, fair lady, and grieve not that I detain you. Who can consent to part with a tongue of so much melody, or an eye of such expressive eloquence !—You have known then what it is to love ? "

" I know—no matter if by experience, or through the report of others—but I do know, that to love, as I would love, would be to yield not an iota to avarice, not one inch to vanity, not to sacrifice the slightest feeling to interest or to ambition; but to give up all to fidelity of heart and reciprocal affection."

" And how many women, think you, are capable of feeling such disinterested passion ? "

" More, by thousands, than there are men who merit it," answered Zarah. " Alas ! how often do you see the female, pale, and wretched, and degraded, still following with patient constancy the footsteps of some predominating tyrant, and submitting to all his injustice with the endurance of a faithful and misused spaniel, which prizes a look from his master, though the surliest groom that ever disgraced humanity, more than all the pleasure which the world besides can furnish him ? Think what such would be to one who merited and repaid her devotion."

" Perhaps the very reverse," said the Duke ; " and for your simile, I can see little resemblance. I cannot charge my spaniel with any perfidy; but for my mistresses—to confess truth, I must always be in a cursed hurry if I would have the credit of changing them before they leave me."

" And they serve you but rightly, my lord," answered the lady ; " for what are you ?—Nay, frown not; for you must hear the truth for once. Nature has done its part, and made a fair outside, and courtly education hath added its share. You are noble, it is the accident of birth—handsome, it is the caprice of Nature—generous, because to give is more easy than to refuse —well-apparelled, it is to the credit of your tailor—well-natured in the main, because you have youth and health— brave, because to be otherwise were to be degraded—and witty, because you cannot help it."

The Duke darted a glance on one of the large mirrors. " Noble, and handsome, and court-like, generous, well-attired, good-humoured, brave, and witty !—You allow me more, madam, than I have the slightest pretension to, and surely enough to make my way, at some point at least, to female favour."

"I have neither allowed you a heart nor a head," said Zarah calmly.—"Nay, never redden as if you would fly at me. I say not but nature may have given you both; but folly has confounded the one, and selfishness perverted the other. The man whom I call deserving the name is one whose thoughts and exertions are for others, rather than himself,—whose high purpose is adopted on just principles, and never abandoned while heaven or earth affords means of accomplishing it. He is one who will neither seek an indirect advantage by a specious road, nor take an evil path to gain a real good purpose. Such a man were one for whom a woman's heart should beat constant while he breathes, and break when he dies."

She spoke with so much energy that the water sparkled in her eyes, and her cheek coloured with the vehemence of her feelings.

"You speak," said the Duke, "as if you had yourself a heart which could pay the full tribute to the merit which you describe so warmly."

"And have I not?" said she, laying her hand on her bosom. "Here beats one that would bear me out in what I have said, whether in life or in death."

"Were it in my power," said the Duke, who began to get farther interested in his visitor than he could at first have thought possible—"Were it in my power to deserve such faithful attachment, methinks it should be my care to requite it."

"Your wealth, your titles, your reputation as a gallant—all you possess, were too little to merit such sincere affection."

"Come, fair lady," said the Duke, a good deal piqued, "do not be quite so disdainful. Bethink you, that if your love be as pure as coined gold, still a poor fellow like myself may offer you an equivalent in silver—The quantity of my affection must make up for its quality."

"But I am not carrying my affection to market, my lord; and therefore I need none of the base coin you offer in change for it."

"How do I know that, my fairest?" said the Duke. "This is the realm of Paphos—You have invaded it, with what purpose you best know; but I think with none consistent with your present assumption of cruelty. Come, come—eyes that are so intelligent can laugh with delight, as well as gleam with scorn and anger. You are here a waif on Cupid's manor, and I must seize on you in name of the deity."

"Do not think of touching me, my lord," said the lady. "Approach me not, if you would hope to learn the purpose of my being here. Your Grace may suppose yourself a Solomon if you please; but I am no travelling princess, come from distant climes, either to flatter your pride, or wonder at your glory."

2 c

"A defiance, by Jupiter!" said the Duke.

"You mistake the signal," said the 'dark ladye'; "I came not here without taking sufficient precautions for my retreat."

"You mouth it bravely," said the Duke; "but never fortress so boasted its resources but the garrison had some thoughts of surrender. Thus I open the first parallel."

They had been hitherto divided from each other by a long narrow table, which, placed in the recess of the large casement we have mentioned, had formed a sort of barrier on the lady's side, against the adventurous gallant. The Duke went hastily to remove it as he spoke; but, attentive to all his motions, his visitor instantly darted through the half-open window. Buckingham uttered a cry of horror and surprise, having no doubt, at first, that she had precipitated herself from a height of at least fourteen feet; for so far the window was distant from the ground. But when he sprung to the spot, he perceived, to his astonishment, that she had effected her descent with equal agility and safety.

The outside of this stately mansion was decorated with a quantity of carving, in the mixed state, betwixt the Gothic and Grecian styles, which marks the age of Elizabeth and her successor; and though the feat seemed a surprising one, the projections of these ornaments were sufficient to afford footing to a creature so light and active, even in her hasty descent.

Inflamed alike by mortification and curiosity, Buckingham at first entertained some thought of following her by the same dangerous route, and had actually got upon the sill of the window for that purpose; and was contemplating what might be his next safe movement, when, from a neighbouring thicket of shrubs, amongst which his visitor had disappeared, he heard her chant a verse of a comic song, then much in fashion, concerning a despairing lover who had recourse to a precipice—

> " But when he came near,
>   Beholding how steep
> The sides did appear,
>   And the bottom how deep;
> Though his suit was rejected,
>   He sadly reflected,
> That a lover forsaken
>   A new love may get;
> But a neck that's once broken
>   Can never be set."

The Duke could not help laughing, though much against his will, at the resemblance which the verses bore to his own absurd situation, and, stepping back into the apartment, desisted from an attempt which might have proved dangerous as well as ridiculous. He called his attendants, and contented himself with watching the little thicket, unwilling to think that a female, who had thrown herself in a great measure into his way, meant absolutely to mortify him by a retreat.

That question was determined in an instant. A form, wrapped in a mantle, with a slouched hat and shadowy plume, issued from the bushes, and was lost in a moment amongst the ruins of ancient and of modern buildings, with which, as we have already stated, the demesne formerly termed York House, was now encumbered in all directions.

The Duke's servants, who had obeyed his impatient summons, were hastily directed to search for this tantalising siren in every direction. Their master, in the meantime, eager and vehement in every new pursuit, but especially when his vanity was piqued, encouraged their diligence by bribes, and threats, and commands. All was in vain. They found nothing of the Mauritanian Princess, as she called herself, but the turban and the veil; both of which she had left in the thicket, together with her satin slippers; which articles, doubtless, she had thrown aside as she exchanged them for others less remarkable.

Finding all his search in vain, the Duke of Buckingham, after the example of spoiled children of all ages and stations, gave a loose to the frantic vehemence of passion; and fiercely he swore vengeance on his late visitor, whom he termed by a thousand opprobrious epithets, of which the elegant phrase " Jilt " was most frequently repeated.

Even Jerningham, who knew the depths and shallows of his master's mood, and was bold to fathom them at almost every state of his passions, kept out of his way on the present occasion ; and, cabineted with the pious old housekeeper, declared to her, over a bottle of ratafia, that, in his apprehension, if his Grace did not learn to put some control on his temper, chains, darkness, straw, and Bedlam, would be the final doom of the gifted and admired Duke of Buckingham.

CHAPTER XL

——Contentions fierce,
Ardent, and dire, spring from no petty cause.
—ALBION.

THE quarrels between man and wife are proverbial ; but let not these honest folks think that connections of a less permanent nature are free from similar jars. The frolic of the Duke of Buckingham, and the subsequent escape of Alice Bridgenorth, had kindled fierce dissension in Chiffinch's family, when, on his arrival in town, he learned these two stunning events: "I tell you," he said to his obliging helpmate, who seemed but little moved by all that he could say on the subject, "that your d—d carelessness has ruined the work of years."

"I think it is the twentieth time you have said so," replied the dame; "and without such frequent assurance, I was quite ready to believe that a very trifling matter would overset any scheme of yours, however long thought of."

"How on earth could you have the folly to let the Duke into the house when you expected the King?" said the irritated courtier.

"Lord, Chiffinch," answered the lady, "ought not you to ask the porter rather than me, that sort of question?—I was putting on my cap to receive his Majesty."

"With the address of a madge-howlet," said Chiffinch, "and in the meanwhile you gave the cat the cream to keep."

"Indeed, Chiffinch," said the lady, "these jaunts to the country do render you excessively vulgar! there is a brutality about your very boots! nay, your muslin ruffles, being somewhat soiled, give to your knuckles a sort of rural rusticity, as I may call it."

"It were a good deed," muttered Chiffinch, "to make both boots and knuckles bang the folly and affectation out of thee." Then speaking aloud, he added, like a man who would fain break off an argument, by extorting from his adversary a confession that he has reason on his side, "I am sure, Kate, you must be sensible that our all depends on his Majesty's pleasure."

"Leave that to me," said she; "I know how to pleasure his Majesty better than you can teach me. Do you think his Majesty is booby enough to cry like a schoolboy because his sparrow has flown away? His Majesty has better taste. I am surprised at you, Chiffinch," she added, drawing herself up, "who were once thought to know the points of a fine woman, that you should have made such a roaring about this country wench. Why, she has not even the country quality of being plump as a barn-door fowl, but is more like a Dunstable lark, that one must crack bones and all if you would make a mouthful of it. What signifies whence she came, or where she goes? There will be those behind that are much more worthy of his Majesty's condescending attention, even when the Duchess of Portsmouth takes the frumps."

"You mean your neighbour, Mistress Nelly," said her worthy helpmate; "but Kate, her date is out. Wit she has, let her keep herself warm with it in worse company, for the cant of a gang of strollers is not language for a prince's chamber." *

"It is no matter what I mean, or whom I mean," said Mrs. Chiffinch; "but I tell you, Tom Chiffinch, that you will find your master quite consoled for loss of the piece of prudish puritanism that you would needs saddle him with; as if the good man were not plagued enough with them in Parliament, but you must, forsooth, bring them into his very bed-chamber."

"Well, Kate," said Chiffinch, "if a man were to speak all the sense of the seven wise masters, a woman would find non-sense enough to overwhelm him with; so I shall say no more, but that I would to Heaven I may find the King in no worse humour than you describe him. I am commanded to attend him down the river to the Tower to-day, where he is to make some survey of arms and stores. They are clever fellows who contrive to keep Rowley from engaging in business, for, by my word, he has a turn for it."

"I warrant you," said Chiffinch the female, nodding, but rather to her own figure, reflected from a mirror, than to her politic husband,—"I warrant you we will find means of occupy-ing him that will sufficiently fill up his time."

"On my honour, Kate," said the male Chiffinch, "I find you strangely altered, and, to speak truth, grown most extremely opinionative. I shall be happy if you have good reason for your confidence."

The dame smiled superciliously, but deigned no other answer, unless this were one,—"I shall order a boat to go upon the Thames to-day with the royal party."

"Take care what you do, Kate; there are none dare pre-sume so far but women of the first rank. Duchess of Bolton— of Buckingham—of——"

"Who cares for a list of names? why may not I be as forward as the greatest B. amongst your string of them?"

"Nay, faith, thou mayest match the greatest B. in Court already," answered Chiffinch; "so e'en take thy own course of it. But do not let Chaubert forget to get some collation ready, and a *souper au petit couvert*, in case it should be commanded for the evening."

"Ay, there your boasted knowledge of Court matters begins

* In Evelyn's Memoirs is the following curious passage respecting Nell Gwyn, who is hinted at in the text:—"I walked with him [King Charles II.] through Saint James Park to the garden, where I both saw and heard a very familiar discourse between . . . [*the King*] and Mrs. Nelly, as they called her, an intimate comedian, she looking out of her garden on a terrace at the top of the wall, and [*the King*] standing on the green walk under it. I was heartily sorry at this scene."—EVELYN'S *Memoirs*, vol. i. p. 413.

and ends.—Chiffinch, Chaubert, and Company;—dissolve that partnership, and you break Tom Chiffinch for a courtier."

"Amen, Kate," replied Chiffinch; "and let me tell you it is as safe to rely on another person's fingers as on our own wit. But I must give orders for the water.—If you will take the pinnace, there are the cloth-of-gold cushions in the chapel may serve to cover the benches for the day. They are never wanted where they lie, so you may make free with them too."

Madam Chiffinch accordingly mingled with the flotilla which attended the King on his voyage down the Thames, amongst whom was the Queen, attended by some of the principal ladies of the Court. The little plump Cleopatra, dressed to as much advantage as her taste could devise, and seated upon her embroidered cushions like Venus in her shell, neglected nothing that effrontery and minauderie could perform to draw upon herself some portion of the King's observation; but Charles was not in the vein, and did not even pay her the slightest passing attention of any kind, until her boatmen having ventured to approach nearer to the Queen's barge than etiquette permitted, received a peremptory order to back their oars, and fall out of the royal procession. Madam Chiffinch cried for spite, and transgressed Solomon's warning, by cursing the King in her heart; but had no better course than to return to Westminster, and direct Chaubert's preparations for the evening.

In the meantime the royal barge paused at the Tower; and, accompanied by a laughing train of ladies and of courtiers, the gay Monarch made the echoes of the old prison-towers ring with the unwonted sounds of mirth and revelry. As they ascended from the rivers-ide to the centre of the building, where the fine old keep of William the Conqueror, called the White Tower, predominates over the exterior defences, Heaven only knows how many gallant jests, good or bad, were run on the comparison of his Majesty's state-prison to that of Cupid, and what killing similes were drawn between the ladies' eyes and the guns of the fortress, which, spoken with a fashionable congée, and listened to with a smile from a fair lady, formed the fine conversation of the day.

This gay swarm of flutterers did not, however, attend close on the King's person, though they had accompanied him upon his party on the river. Charles, who often formed manly and sensible resolutions, though he was too easily diverted from them by indolence or pleasure, had some desire to make himself personally acquainted with the state of the military stores, arms, &c. of which the Tower was then, as now, the magazine; and, although he had brought with him the usual number of his courtiers, only three or four attended him ou the scrutiny which he intended. Whilst, therefore, the rest of the train amused themselves as they might in other parts of the Tower, the King, accompanied by the Dukes of Buckingham, Ormond, and one or two others, walked through the well-known hall, in which is preserved the most splendid magazine of arms in the world, and which, though far from exhibiting its present extraordinary state of perfection, was even then an arsenal worthy of the great nation to which it belonged.

The Duke of Ormond, well known for his services during the Great Civil War, was, as we have elsewhere noticed, at present rather on cold terms with his Sovereign, who nevertheless asked his advice on many occasions, and who required it on the present amongst others, when it was not a little feared that the Parliament, in their zeal for the Protestant religion, might desire to take the magazines of arms and ammunition under their own exclusive orders. While Charles sadly hinted at such a termination of the popular jealousies of the period, and discussed with Ormond the means of resisting, or evading it, Buckingham, falling a little behind, amused himself with ridiculing the antiquated appearance and embarrassed demeanour of the old warder who attended on the occasion, and who chanced to be the very same that escorted Julian Peveril to his present place of confinement. The Duke prosecuted his raillery with the greater activity, that he found the old man, though restrained by the place and presence, was rather upon the whole testy, and disposed to afford what sportsmen call *play* to his persecutor. The various pieces of ancient armour, with which the wall was covered, afforded the principal source of the Duke's wit, as he insisted upon knowing from the old man, who, he said, could best remember matters from the days of King Arthur downwards at the least, the history of the different warlike weapons, and anecdotes of the battles in which they had been wielded. The old man obviously suffered, when he was obliged, by repeated questions, to tell the legends (often sufficiently absurd) which the tradition of the place had assigned to particular relics. Far from flourishing his partisan, and augmenting the emphasis of his voice, as was and is the prevailing fashion of these warlike Ciceroni, it was scarcely possible to extort from him a single word concerning those topics on which their information is usually overflowing.

"Do you know, my friend," said the Duke to him at last, "I begin to change my mind respecting you. I supposed you must have served as a Yeoman of the Guard since bluff King Henry's time, and expected to hear something from you about the Field of the Cloth of Gold,—and I thought of asking you the colour of Anne Bullen's breastknot, which cost the Pope three kingdoms; but I am afraid you are but a novice in such recollections of love and chivalry. Art sure thou didst not creep into thy warlike office from some dark shop in the Tower-Hamlets, and that thou hast not converted an unlawful measuring-yard into that glorious halberd?—I warrant thou canst not even tell one whom this piece of antique panoply pertained to?"

The Duke pointed at random to a cuirass which hung amongst others, but was rather remarkable from being better cleansed.

"I should know that piece of iron," said the warder bluntly, yet with some change in his voice; "for I have known a man within side of it who would not have endured half the impertinence I have heard spoken to-day."

The tone of the old man, as well as the words, attracted the attention of Charles and the Duke of Ormond, who were only two steps before the speaker. They both stopped, and turned round; the former saying at the same time,—"How now, sirrah! —what answers are these?—What man do you speak of?"

"Of one who is none now," said the warder, "whatever he may have been."

"The old man surely speaks of himself," said the Duke of Ormond, closely examining the countenance of the warder, which he in vain endeavoured to turn away. "I am sure I remember these features—Are not you my old friend, Major Coleby?"

"I wish your Grace's memory had been less accurate," said the old man, colouring deeply, and fixing his eyes on the ground.

The King was greatly shocked.—"Good God!" he said, "the gallant Major Coleby, who joined us with his four sons and a hundred and fifty men at Warrington!—And is this all we could do for an old Worcester friend?"

The tears rushed thick into the old man's eyes as he said in broken accents, "Never mind me, sire; I am well enough here —a worn-out soldier rusting among old armour. Where one old Cavalier is better, there are twenty worse.—I am sorry your Majesty should know anything of it, since it grieves you."

With that kindness, which was a redeeming point of his character, Charles, while the old man was speaking, took the partisan from him with his own hand, and put it into that of Buckingham, saying, "What Coleby's hand has borne, can disgrace neither yours nor mine,—and you owe him this atonement. Time has been with him, that, for less provocation, he would have laid it about your ears."

The Duke bowed deeply, but coloured with resentment, and took an immediate opportunity to place the weapon carelessly against a pile of arms. The King did not observe a contemptuous motion, which, perhaps, would not have pleased him, being at the moment occupied with the veteran, whom he exhorted to lean upon him, as he conveyed him to a seat, permitting no other person to assist him. "Rest there," he said, "my brave old friend; and Charles Stewart must be poor indeed, if you wear that dress an hour longer.—You look very pale, my good Coleby, to have had so much colour a few minutes since. Be not vexed at what Buckingham says; no one minds his folly.—You look worse and worse. Come, come, you are too much hurried by this meeting. Sit still—do not rise—do not attempt to kneel. I command you to repose yourself till I have made the round of these apartments."

The old Cavalier stooped his head in token of acquiescence in the command of his Sovereign, but he raised it not again. The tumultuous agitation of the moment had been too much for spirits which had been long in a state of depression, and health which was much decayed. When the King and his attendants, after half-an-hour's absence, returned to the spot where they had left the veteran, they found him dead, and already cold, in the attitude of one who has fallen easily asleep. The King was dreadfully shocked; and it was with a low and faltering voice that he directed the body, in due time, to be honourably buried in the chapel of the Tower.* He was then silent, until he attained the steps in front of the arsenal, where the party in attendance upon his person began to assemble at his approach, along with some other persons of respectable appearance, whom curiosity had attracted.

"This is dreadful," said the King. "We must find some means of relieving the distresses, and rewarding the fidelity of our suffering followers, or posterity will cry fie upon our memory."

"Your Majesty has had often such plans agitated in your Council," said Buckingham.

"True, George," said the King. "I can safely say it is not my fault. I have thought of it for years."

"It cannot be too well considered," said Buckingham; "besides, every year makes the task of relief easier."

"True," said the Duke of Ormond, "by diminishing the number of sufferers. Here is poor old Coleby will no longer be a burden to the Crown."

"You are too severe, my Lord of Ormond," said the King, "and should respect the feelings you trespass on. You cannot suppose that we would have permitted this poor man to hold such a situation, had we known of the circumstance?"

"For God's sake, then, sire," said the Duke of Ormond,

---

* A story of this nature is current in the legends of the Tower. The affecting circumstances are, I believe, recorded in one of the little manuals which are put into the hands of visitors, but are not to be found in the later editions.

"turn your eyes, which have just rested on the corpse of one old friend, upon the distresses of others. Here is the valiant old Sir Geoffrey Peveril of the Peak, who fought through the whole war, wherever blows were going, and was the last man, I believe, in England, who laid down his arms—Here is his son, of whom I have the highest accounts, as a gallant of spirit, accomplishments, and courage—Here is the unfortunate House of Derby—for pity's sake, interfere in behalf of these victims, whom the folds of this hydra-plot have entangled, in order to crush them to death—rebuke the fiends that are seeking to devour their lives, and disappoint the harpies that are gaping for their property. This very day seven-night the unfortunate family, father and son, are to be brought upon trial for crimes of which they are as guiltless, I boldly pronounce, as any who stand in this presence. For God's sake, sire, let us hope that, should the prejudices of the people condemn them, as it has done others, you will at last step in between the blood-hunters and their prey."

The King looked, as he really was, exceedingly perplexed.

Buckingham, between whom and Ormond there existed a constant and almost mortal quarrel, interfered to effect a diversion in Charles's favour. "Your Majesty's royal benevolence," he said, "needs never want exercise, while the Duke of Ormond is near your person. He has his sleeve cut in the old and ample fashion, that he may always have store of ruined cavaliers stowed in it to produce at demand, rare old raw-boned boys, with Malmsey noses, bald heads, spindle shanks, and merciless histories of Edgehill and Naseby."

"My sleeve is, I dare say, of an antique cut," said Ormond, looking full at the Duke; "but I pin neither bravoes nor ruffians upon it, my Lord of Buckingham, as I see fastened to coats of the new mode."

"That is a little too sharp for our presence, my lord," said the King.

"Not if I make my words good," said Ormond.—"My Lord of Buckingham, will you name the man you spoke to as you left the boat?"

"I spoke to no one," said the Duke hastily—"nay, I mistake, I remember a fellow whispered in my ear, that one, who I thought had left London, was still lingering in town. A person whom I had business with."

"Was yon the messenger?" said Ormond, singling out from the crowd who stood in the court-yard a tall dark-looking man, muffled in a large cloak, wearing a broad shadowy black beaver hat, with a long sword of the Spanish fashion—the very Colonel, in short, whom Buckingham had despatched in quest of Christian, with the intention of detaining him in the country.

When Buckingham's eyes had followed the direction of Ormond's finger, he could not help blushing so deeply as to attract the King's attention.

"What new frolic is this, George?" he said. "Gentlemen, bring that fellow forward. On my life, a truculent-looking caitiff—Hark ye, friend, who are you? If an honest man, Nature has forgot to label it upon your countenance.—Does none here know him?

> ' With every symptom of a knave complete,
> If he be honest, he's a devilish cheat.' "

"He is well known to many, sire," replied Ormond; "and that he walks in this area with his neck safe, and his limbs unshackled, is an instance, amongst many, that we live under the sway of the most merciful Prince of Europe."

"Oddsfish! who is the man, my Lord Duke?" said the King. "Your Grace talks mysteries—Buckingham blushes—and the rogue himself is dumb."

"That honest gentleman, please your Majesty," replied the Duke of Ormond, "whose modesty makes him mute, though it cannot make him blush, is the notorious Colonel Blood, as he calls himself, whose attempt to possess himself of your Majesty's royal crown took place at no very distant date, in this very Tower of London."

"That exploit is not easily forgotten," said the King; "but that the fellow lives, shows your Grace's clemency as well as mine."

"I cannot deny that I was in his hands, sire," said Ormond, "and had certainly been murdered by him, had he chosen to take my life on the spot, instead of destining me—I thank him for the honour—to be hanged at Tyburn. I had certainly been sped, if he had thought me worth knife or pistol, or anything short of the cord.—Look at him, sire! If the rascal dared, he would say at this moment, like Caliban in the play, 'Ho, ho, I would I had done it!' "

"Why, oddsfish!" answered the King, "he hath a villainous sneer, my lord, which seems to say as much; but, my Lord Duke, we have pardoned him, and so has your Grace."

"It would ill have become me," said the Duke of Ormond, "to have been severe in prosecuting an attempt on my poor life, when your Majesty was pleased to remit his more outrageous and insolent attempt upon your royal crown. But I must conceive it as a piece of supreme insolence on the part of this bloodthirsty bully, by whomsoever he may be now backed, to appear in the Tower, which was the theatre of one of his villainies, or before me, who was well-nigh the victim of another."

"It shall be amended in future," said the King.—"Hark ye, sirrah Blood, if you again presume to thrust yourself in the way you have done but now, I will have the hangman's knife and your knavish ears made acquainted."

Blood bowed, and with a coolness of impudence which did his nerves great honour, he said he had only come to the Tower accidentally, to communicate with a particular friend on business of importance. "My Lord Duke of Buckingham," he said, "knew he had no other intentions."

"Get you gone, you scoundrelly cut-throat," said the Duke, as much impatient of Colonel Blood's claim of acquaintance, as a town-rake of the low and blackguard companions of his midnight rambles, when they accost him in daylight amidst better company; "if you dare to quote my name again, I will have you thrown into the Thames."

Blood, thus repulsed, turned round with the most insolent composure, and walked away down from the parade, all men looking at him, as at some strange and monstrous prodigy, so much was he renowned for daring and desperate villainy. Some even followed him, to have a better survey of the notorious Colonel Blood, like the smaller tribe of birds which keep fluttering round an owl when he appears in the light of the sun. But as, in the latter case, these thoughtless flutterers are careful to keep out of reach of the beak and claws of the bird of Minerva, so none of those who followed and gazed on Blood as something ominous, cared to bandy looks with him, or to endure and return the lowering and deadly glances, which he shot from time to time on those who pressed nearest to him. He stalked on in this manner, like a daunted, yet sullen wolf, afraid to stop, yet unwilling to fly, until he reached the Traitor's Gate, and getting on board a sculler which waited for him, he disappeared from their eyes.

Charles would fain have obliterated all recollection of his appearance, by the observation, "It were shame that such a reprobate scoundrel should be the subject of discord between two noblemen of distinction;" and he recommended to the Dukes of Buckingham and Ormond to join hands, and forget a misunderstanding which rose on so unworthy a subject.

Buckingham answered carelessly, "That the Duke of Ormond's honoured white hairs were a sufficient apology for his making the first overtures to a reconciliation," and he held out his hand accordingly. But Ormond only bowed in return, and said, "The King had no cause to expect that the Court would be disturbed by his personal resentments, since time would not yield him back twenty years, nor the grave restore his gallant son Ossory.

As to the ruffian who had intruded himself there, he was obliged to him, since, by showing that his Majesty's clemency extended even to the very worst of criminals, he strengthened his hopes of obtaining the King's favour for such of his innocent friends as were now in prison, and in danger, from the odious charges brought against them on the score of the Popish Plot."

The King made no other answer to this insinuation, than by directing that the company should embark for their return to Whitehall; and thus took leave of the officers of the Tower who were in attendance, with one of those well-turned compliments to their discharge of duty, which no man knew better how to express; and issued at the same time strict and anxious orders for protection and defence of the important fortress confided to them, and all which it contained.

Before he parted with Ormond on their arrival at Whitehall, he turned round to him, as one who has made up his resolution, and said, " Be satisfied, my Lord Duke—our friends' case shall be looked to."

In the same evening the Attorney-General, and North, Lord Chief Justice of the Common Pleas, had orders with all secrecy, to meet his Majesty that evening on especial matters of state, at the apartments of Chiffinch, the centre of all affairs, whether of gallantry or business.

CHAPTER XLI

Yet, Corah, thou shalt from oblivion pass ;
Erect thyself, thou monumental brass,
High as the serpent of thy metal made,
While nations stand secure beneath thy shade.
—ABSALOM AND ACHITOPHEL.

THE morning which Charles had spent in visiting the Tower, had been very differently employed by those unhappy individuals, whom their bad fate, and the singular temper of the times, had made the innocent tenants of that state prison, and who had received official notice that they were to stand their trial in the Court of Queen's Bench at Westminster, on the seventh succeeding day. The stout old Cavalier at first only railed at the officer for spoiling his breakfast with the news, but evinced great feeling when he was told that Julian was to be put under the same indictment.

We intend to dwell only very generally on the nature of their trial, which corresponded, in the outline, with almost all those which took place during the prevalence of the Popish Plot. That is, one or two infamous and perjured evidences, whose profession of common informers had become frightfully lucrative, made oath to the prisoners having expressed themselves interested in the great confederacy of the Catholics. A number of others brought forward facts or suspicions, affecting the character of the parties as honest Protestants and good subjects; and betwixt the direct and presumptive evidence, enough was usually extracted for justifying, to a corrupted court and perjured jury, the fatal verdict of Guilty.

The fury of the people had, however, now begun to pass away, exhausted even by its own violence. The English nation differ from all others, indeed even from those of the sister kingdoms, in being very easily sated with punishment, even when they suppose it most merited. Other nations are like the tamed tiger, which, when once its native appetite for slaughter is indulged in one instance, rushes on in promiscuous ravages. But the English public have always rather resembled what is told of the sleuth-dog, which, eager, fierce, and clamorous in pursuit of his prey, desists from it so soon as blood is sprinkled upon his path.

Men's minds were now beginning to cool—the character of the witnesses was more closely sifted—their testimonies did not in all cases tally—and a wholesome suspicion began to be entertained of men, who would never say they had made a full discovery of all they knew, but avowedly reserved some points of evidence to bear on future trials.

The King also, who had lain passive during the first burst of popular fury, was now beginning to bestir himself, which produced a marked effect on the conduct of the Crown Counsel, and even the Judges. Sir George Wakeman had been acquitted in spite of Oates's direct testimony; and public attention was strongly excited concerning the event of the next trial; which chanced to be that of the Peverils, father and son, with whom, I know not from what concatenation, little Hudson the dwarf was placed at the bar of the Court of King's Bench.

It was a piteous sight to behold a father and son, who had been so long separated, meet under circumstances so melancholy; and many tears were shed, when the majestic old man —for such he was, though now broken with years—folded his son to his bosom, with a mixture of joy, affection, and a bitter anticipation of the event of the impending trial. There was a feeling in the Court that for a moment overcame every prejudice and party feeling. Many spectators shed tears; and there was even a low moaning, as of those who weep aloud.

Such as felt themselves sufficiently at ease to remark the conduct of poor little Geoffrey Hudson, who was scarcely observed amid the preponderating interest created by his companions in misfortune, could not but notice a strong degree of mortification on the part of that diminutive gentleman. He had soothed his great mind by the thoughts of playing the character which he was called on to sustain, in a manner which should be long remembered in that place; and on his entrance, had saluted the numerous spectators, as well as the Court, with a cavalier air, which he meant should express grace, high-breeding, perfect coolness, with a noble disregard to the issue of their proceedings. But his little person was so obscured and jostled aside, on the meeting of the father and son, who had been brought in different boats from the Tower, and placed at the bar at the same moment, that his distress and his dignity were alike thrown into the background, and attracted neither sympathy nor admiration.

The dwarf's wisest way to attract attention would have been to remain quiet, when so remarkable an exterior would certainly have received in its turn the share of public notice which he so eagerly coveted. But when did personal vanity listen to the suggestions of prudence ?—Our impatient friend scrambled, with some difficulty, on the top of the bench intended for his seat; and there, "paining himself to stand a-tiptoe," like Chaucer's gallant Sir Chaunticlere, he challenged the notice of the audience as he stood bowing and claiming acquaintance of his namesake Sir Geoffrey the larger, with whose shoulders, notwithstanding his elevated situation, he was scarcely yet upon a level.

The taller Knight, whose mind was occupied in a very different manner, took no notice of these advances upon the dwarf's part, but sat down with the determination rather to die on the spot than evince any symptoms of weakness before Roundheads and Presbyterians; under which obnoxious epithets, being too old-fashioned to find out party designations of newer date, he comprehended all persons concerned in his present trouble.

By Sir Geoffrey the larger's change of position, his face was thus brought on a level with that of Sir Geoffrey the less, who had an opportunity of pulling him by the cloak. He of Mar-tindale Castle, rather mechanically than consciously, turned his head towards the large wrinkled visage, which, struggling between an assumed air of easy importance, and an anxious desire to be noticed, was grimacing within a yard of him. But neither the singular physiognomy, the nods and smiles of greeting and recognition into which it was wreathed, nor the strange little form by which it was supported, had at that moment the power of exciting any recollections in the old Knight's mind; and having stared for a moment at the poor little man, his bulky namesake turned away his head without farther notice.

Julian Peveril, the dwarf's more recent acquaintance, had,

even amid his own anxious feelings, room for sympathy with those of his little fellow-sufferer. As soon as he discovered that he was at the same terrible bar with himself, although he could not conceive how their causes came to be conjoined, he acknowledged him by a hearty shake of the hand, which the old man returned with affected dignity and real gratitude. "Worthy youth," he said, "thy presence is restorative, like the nepenthe of Homer even in this syncopé of our mutual fate. I am concerned to see that your father hath not the same alacrity of soul as that of ours, which are lodged within smaller compass ; and that he hath forgotten an ancient comrade and fellow-soldier, who now stands beside him to perform, perhaps, their last campaign."

Julian briefly replied, that his father had much to occupy him. But the little man—who, to do him justice, cared no more (in his own phrase) for imminent danger or death, than he did for the puncture of a flea's proboscis—did not so easily renounce the secret object of his ambition, which was to acquire the notice of the large and lofty Sir Geoffrey Peveril, who, being at least three inches taller than his son, was in so far possessed of that superior excellence, which the poor dwarf, in his secret soul, valued before all other distinctions, although, in his conversation, he was constantly depreciating it. "Good comrade and namesake," he proceeded, stretching out his hand, so as again to reach the elder Peveril's cloak, "I forgive your want of reminiscence, seeing it is long since I saw you at Naseby, fighting as if you had as many arms as the fabled Briareus."

The Knight of Martindale, who had again turned his head towards the little man, and had listened, as if endeavouring to make something out of his discourse, here interrupted him with a peevish "Pshaw !"

"Pshaw !" repeated Sir Geoffrey the less ; "*Pshaw* is an expression of slight esteem,—nay, of contempt,—in all languages ; and were this a befitting place——"

But the Judges had now taken their places, the criers called silence, and the stern voice of the Lord Chief Justice (the notorious Scroggs) demanded what the officers meant by permitting the accused to communicate together in open court.

It may here be observed, that this celebrated personage was, upon the present occasion, at a great loss how to proceed. A calm, dignified, judicial demeanour, was at no time the characteristic of his official conduct. He always ranted and roared either on the one side or the other ; and of late, he had been much unsettled which side to take, being totally incapable of anything resembling impartiality. At the first trials for the Plot, when the whole stream of popularity ran against the accused, no one had been so loud as Scroggs ; to attempt to

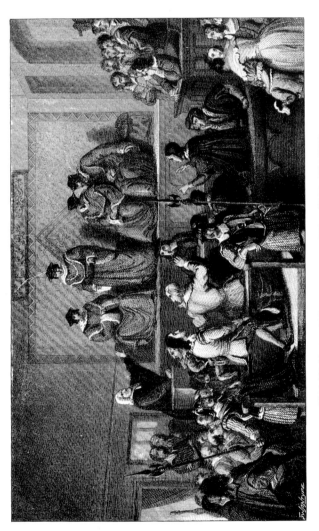

THE TRIAL OF THE PEVERILS—OATES GIVING EVIDENCE

PAINTING BY S. A. HART

impeach the character of Oates or Bedlowe, or any other leading witnesses, he treated as a crime more heinous than it would have been to blaspheme the Gospel on which they had been sworn—it was a stifling of the Plot, or discrediting of the King's witnesses—a crime not greatly, if at all, short of high treason against the King himself.

But, of late, a new light had begun to glimmer upon the understanding of this interpreter of the laws. Sagacious in the signs of the times, he began to see that the tide was turning; and that Court favour at least, and probably popular opinion also, were likely, in a short time, to declare against the witnesses, and in favour of the accused.

The opinion which Scroggs had hitherto entertained of the high respect in which Shaftesbury, the patron of the Plot, was held by Charles, had been definitely shaken by a whisper from his brother North to the following effect: "His Lordship has no more interest at Court than your footman."

This notice, from a sure hand, and received but that morning, had put the Judge to a sore dilemma; for, however indifferent to actual consistency, he was most anxious to save appearances. He could not but recollect how violent he had been on former occasions in favour of these prosecutions; and being sensible at the same time that the credit of the witnesses, though shaken in the opinion of the more judicious, was, amongst the bulk of the people out of doors, as strong as ever, he had a difficult part to play. His conduct, therefore, during the whole trial, resembled the appearance of a vessel about to go upon another tack, when her sails are shivering in the wind, ere they have yet caught the impulse which is to send her forth in a new direction. In a word, he was so uncertain which side it was his interest to favour, that he might be said on that occasion to have come nearer a state of total impartiality than he was ever capable of attaining, whether before or afterwards. This was shown by his bullying now the accused, and now the witnesses, like a mastiff too much irritated to lie still without baying, but uncertain whom he shall first bite.

The indictment was then read; and Sir Geoffrey Peveril heard, with some composure, the first part of it, which stated him to have placed his son in the household of the Countess of Derby, a recusant Papist, for the purpose of aiding the horrible and bloodthirsty Popish Plot — with having had arms and ammunition concealed in his house—and with receiving a blank commission from the Lord Stafford, who had suffered death on account of the Plot. But when the charge went on to state that he had communicated for the same purpose with Geoffrey Hudson, sometimes called Sir Geoffrey Hudson, now, or formerly in the domestic service of the Queen Dowager, he looked at his companion as if he suddenly recalled him to remembrance, and broke out impatiently, "These lies are too gross to require a moment's consideration. I might have had enough of intercourse, though in nothing but what was loyal and innocent, with my noble kinsman, the late Lord Stafford—I will call him so in spite of his misfortunes—and with my wife's relation, the Honourable Countess of Derby. But what likelihood can there be that I should have colleagued with a decrepit buffoon, with whom I never had an instant's communication, save once at an Easter feast, when I whistled a hornpipe, as he danced on a trencher to amuse the company?"

The rage of the poor dwarf brought tears in his eyes, while, with an affected laugh, he said, that instead of those juvenile and festive passages, Sir Geoffrey Peveril might have remembered his charging along with him at Wiggan Lane.

"On my word," said Sir Geoffrey, after a moment's recollection, "I will do you justice, Master Hudson—I believe you were there—I think I heard you did good service. But you will allow you might have been near one without his seeing you."

A sort of titter ran through the Court at the simplicity of the larger Sir Geoffrey's testimony, which the dwarf endeavoured to control, by standing on his tiptoes, and looking fiercely around, as if to admonish the laughers that they indulged their mirth at their own peril. But perceiving that this only excited farther scorn, he composed himself into a semblance of careless contempt, observing, with a smile, that no one feared the glance of a chained lion; a magnificent simile, which rather increased than diminished the mirth of those who heard it.

Against Julian Peveril there failed not to be charged the aggravated fact, that he had been bearer of letters between the Countess of Derby and other Papists and priests, engaged in the universal treasonable conspiracy of the Catholics; and the attack of the house at Moultrassie Hall,—with his skirmish with Chiffinch, and his assault, as it was termed, on the person of John Jenkins, servant to the Duke of Buckingham, were all narrated at length, as so many open and overt acts of treasonable import. To this charge Peveril contented himself with pleading—Not Guilty.

His little companion was not satisfied with so simple a plea; for when he heard it read, as a part of the charge applying to him, that he had received from an agent of the Plot a blank commission as Colonel of a regiment of grenadiers, he replied, in wrath and scorn, that if Goliath of Gath had come to him with such a proposal, and proffered him the command of the whole sons of Anak in a body, he should never have had

occasion or opportunity to repeat the temptation to another.
" I would have slain him," said the little man of loyalty, " even
where he stood."

The charge was stated anew by the Counsel for the Crown;
and forth came the notorious Doctor Oates, rustling in the
full silken canonicals of priesthood, for it was a time when he
affected no small dignity of exterior decoration and deportment.

This singular man, who, aided by the obscure intrigues of
the Catholics themselves, and the fortuitous circumstance of
Godfrey's murder, had been able to cram down the public
throat such a mass of absurdity as his evidence amounts to,
had no other talent for imposture than an impudence which
set conviction and shame alike at defiance.   A man of sense
or reflection, by trying to give his plot an appearance of more
probability, would most likely have failed, as wise men often
do in addressing the multitude, from not daring to calculate
upon the prodigious extent of their credulity, especially where
the figments presented to them involve the fearful and the
terrible.

Oates was by nature choleric; and the credit he had acquired
made him insolent and conceited.   Even his exterior was portentous.   A fleece of white periwig showed a most uncouth
visage, of great length, having the mouth, as the organ by use
of which he was to rise to eminence, placed in the very centre
of the countenance, and exhibiting to the astonished spectator
as much chin below as there was nose and brow above the aperture.   His pronunciation, too, was after a conceited fashion of
his own, in which he accented the vowels in a manner altogether
peculiar to himself.

This notorious personage, such as we have described him,
stood forth on the present trial, and delivered his astonishing
testimony concerning the existence of a Catholic Plot for the
subversion of the government and murder of the King, in the
same general outline in which it may be found in every English
history.   But as the doctor always had in reserve some special
piece of evidence affecting those immediately on trial, he was
pleased, on the present occasion, deeply to inculpate the Countess
of Derby.   " He had seen," as he said, " that honourable lady
when he was at the Jesuits' College at Saint Omer's.   She had
sent for him to an inn, or *auberge*, as it was there termed—the
sign of the Golden Lamb; and had ordered him to breakfast in
the same room with her ladyship; and afterwards told him, that,
knowing he was trusted by the Fathers of the Society, she was
determined that he should have a share of her secrets also; and
therewithal, that she drew from her bosom a broad sharp-pointed
knife, such as butchers kill sheep with, and demanded of him
what he thought of it for *the purpose;* and when he, the witness,

said for what purpose, she rapt him on the fingers with her fan, called him a dull fellow, and said it was designed to kill the King with."

Here Sir Geoffrey Peveril could no longer refrain his indignation and surprise. "Mercy of Heaven!" he said, "did ever one hear of ladies of quality carrying butchering knives about them, and telling every scurvy companion she meant to kill the King with them?—Gentlemen of the Jury, do but think if this is reasonable—though, if the villain could prove by any honest evidence, that my Lady of Derby ever let such a scum as himself come to speech of her, I would believe all he can say."

"Sir Geoffrey," said the Judge, "rest you quiet—You must not fly out—passion helps you not here—the Doctor must be suffered to proceed."

Doctor Oates went on to state how the lady complained of the wrongs the House of Derby had sustained from the King, and the oppression of her religion, and boasted of the schemes of the Jesuits and seminary priests; and how they would be farthered by her noble kinsman of the House of Stanley. He finally averred that both the Countess and the Fathers of the seminary abroad, founded much upon the talents and courage of Sir Geoffrey Peveril and his son—the latter of whom was a member of her family. Of Hudson, he only recollected of having heard one of the Fathers say, that although but a dwarf in stature, he would prove a giant in the cause of the Church."

When he had ended his evidence, there was a pause, until the Judge, as if the thought had suddenly occurred to him, demanded of Dr. Oates, whether he had ever mentioned the names of the Countess of Derby in any of the previous informations which he had lodged before the Privy Council, and elsewhere, upon this affair.

Oates seemed rather surprised at the question, and coloured with anger, as he answered, in his peculiar mode of pronunciation, "Whoy, no, maay laard."

"And pray, Doctor," said the Judge, "how came so great a revealer of mysteries as you have lately proved, to have suffered so material a circumstance as the accession of this powerful family to the Plot to have remained undiscovered?"

"Maay laard," said Oates, with much effrontery, "aye do not come here to have my evidence questioned as touching the Plaat."

"I do not question your evidence, Doctor," said Scroggs, for the time was not arrived that he dared treat him roughly; "nor do I doubt the existence of the *Plaat*, since it is your pleasure to swear to it. I would only have you, for your own sake, and the satisfaction of all good Protestants, to explain why you have kept back such a weighty point of information from the King and country."

"Maay laard," said Oates, "I will tell you a pretty fable."

"I hope," answered the Judge, "it may be the first and last which you shall tell in this place."

"Maay laard," continued Oates, "there was once a faux, who having to carry a goose over a frazen river, and being afraid the aice would not bear him and his booty, did caarry aaver a staane, my laard, in the first instance, to prove the strength of the aice."

"So your former evidence was but the stone, and now, for the first time, you have brought us the goose?" said Sir William Scroggs; "to tell us this, Doctor, is to make geese of the Court and Jury."

"I desoire your laardship's honest construction," said Oates, who saw the current changing against him, but was determined to pay the score with effrontery. "All men knaw at what coast and praice I have given my evidence, which has been always, under Gaad, the means of awakening this poor naation to the dangerous state in which it staunds. Many here knaw that I have been obliged to faartify my ladging at Whitehall against the bloody Papists. It was not to be thought that I should have brought all the story out at aance. I think your wisdom would have advised me otherwise."*

"Nay, Doctor," said the Judge, "it is not for me to direct you in this affair; and it is for the Jury to believe you or not; and as for myself, I sit here to do justice to both—the Jury have heard your answer to my question."

Doctor Oates retired from the witness-box reddening like a turkey-cock, as one totally unused to have such accounts questioned as he chose to lay before the courts of justice; and there was, perhaps, for the first time, amongst the counsel and solicitors, as well as the templars and students of law there present, a murmur, distinct and audible, unfavourable to the character of the great father of the Popish Plot.

Everett and Dangerfield, with whom the reader is already acquainted, were then called in succession to sustain the accusation. They were subordinate informers—a sort of under-spur-leathers, as the cant term went—who followed the path of Oates, with all deference to his superior genius and invention, and made their own fictions chime in and harmonise with his, as

---

* It was on such terms that Dr. Oates was pleased to claim the extraordinary privilege of dealing out the information which he chose to communicate to a court of justice. The only sense in which his story of the fox, stone, and goose could be applicable, is by supposing that he was determined to ascertain the extent of his countrymen's credulity before supplying it with a full meal.

well as their talents could devise. But as their evidence had at no time received the full credence into which the impudence of Oates had cajoled the public, so they now began to fall into discredit rather more hastily than their prototype, as the super-added turrets of an ill-constructed building are naturally the first to give way.

It was in vain that Everett, with the precision of a hypocrite, and Dangerfield, with the audacity of a bully, narrated, with added circumstances of suspicion and criminality, their meeting with Julian Peveril in Liverpool, and again at Martindale Castle. It was in vain they described the arms and accoutrements which they pretended to have discovered in old Sir Geoffrey's possession; and that they gave a most dreadful account of the escape of the younger Peveril from Moultrassie Hall, by means of an armed force.

The Jury listened coldly, and it was visible that they were but little moved by the accusation; especially as the Judge, always professing his belief in the Plot, and his zeal for the Protestant religion, was ever and anon reminding them that presumptions were no proofs—that hearsay was no evidence— that those who made a trade of discovery were likely to aid their researches by invention—and that without doubting the guilt of the unfortunate persons at the bar, he would gladly hear some evidence brought against them of a different nature. "Here we are told of a riot, and an escape achieved by the younger Peveril, at the house of a grave and worthy magistrate, known, I think, to most of us. Why, Master Attorney, bring ye not Master Bridgenorth himself to prove the fact, or all his household, if it be necessary?—A rising in arms is an affair over public to be left on the hearsay tale of these two men— though Heaven forbid that I should suppose they speak one word more than they believe! They are the witnesses for the King—and, what is equally dear to us, the Protestant religion —and witnesses against a most foul and heathenish Plot. On the other hand, here is a worshipful old knight, for such I must suppose him to be, since he has bled often in battle for the King,—such, I must say, I suppose him to be, until he is proved otherwise. And here is his son, a hopeful young gentle-man—we must see that they have right, Master Attorney."

"Unquestionably, my lord," answered the Attorney. "God forbid else! But we will make out these matters against these unhappy gentlemen in a manner more close, if your lordship will permit us to bring in our evidence."

"Go on, Master Attorney," said the Judge, throwing himself back in his seat. "Heaven forbid I hinder proving the King's accusation! I only say, what you know as well as I, that *de non apparentibus et non existentibus eadem est ratio.*"

"We shall then call Master Bridgenorth, as your lordship advises, who I think is in waiting."

"No!" answered a voice from the crowd, apparently that of a female; "he is too wise and too honest to be here."

The voice was distinct as that of Lady Fairfax, when she expressed herself to a similar effect on the trial of Charles the First; but the researches which were made on the present occasion to discover the speaker were unsuccessful.

After the slight confusion occasioned by this circumstance was abated, the Attorney, who had been talking aside with the conductors of the prosecution, said, "Whoever favoured us with that information, my lord, had good reason for what they said. Master Bridgenorth has become, I am told, suddenly invisible since this morning."

"Look you there now, Master Attorney," said the Judge— "This comes of not keeping the crown witnesses together and in readiness—I am sure I cannot help the consequences."

"Nor I either, my lord," said the Attorney pettishly. "I could have proved by this worshipful gentleman, Master Justice Bridgenorth, the ancient friendship betwixt this party, Sir Geoffrey Peveril, and the Countess of Derby, of whose doings and intentions Dr. Oates has given such a deliberate evidence. I could have proved his having sheltered her in his Castle against a process of law, and rescued her, by force of arms, from this very Justice Bridgenorth, not without actual violence. Moreover, I could have proved against young Peveril the whole affray charged upon him by the same worshipful evidence."

Here the Judge stuck his thumbs into his girdle, which was a favourite attitude of his on such occasions, and exclaimed, "Pshaw, pshaw, Master Attorney!—Tell me not that you *could* have proved this, and you *could* have proved that, or that, or this—Prove what you will, but let it be through the mouths of your evidence. Men are not to be licked out of their lives by the rough side of a lawyer's tongue."

"Nor is a foul Plot to be smothered," said the Attorney, "for all the haste your lordship is in. I cannot call Master Chiffinch neither, as he is employed on the King's especial affairs, as I am this instant certiorated from the Court at Whitehall."

"Produce the papers, then, Master Attorney, of which this young man is said to be the bearer," said the Judge.

"They are before the Privy Council, my lord."

"Then why do you found on them here?" said the Judge— "This is something like trifling with the Court."

"Since your lordship gives it that name," said the Attorney, sitting down in a huff, "you may manage the cause as you will."

"If you do not bring more evidence, I pray you to charge the Jury," said the Judge.

"I shall not take the trouble to do so," said the Crown Counsel. "I see plainly how the matter is to go."

"Nay, but be better advised," said Scroggs. "Consider, your case is but half proved respecting the two Peverils, and doth not pinch on the little man at all, saving that Doctor Oates said that he was in a certain case to prove a giant, which seems no very probable Popish miracle."

This sally occasioned a laugh in the Court, which the Attorney-General seemed to take in great dudgeon.

"Master Attorney," said Oates, who always interfered in the management of these law-suits, "this is a plain and absolute giving away of the cause—I must needs say it, a mere stoifling of the Plaat."

"Then the devil who bred it may blow wind into it again, if he lists," answered the Attorney-General; and, flinging down his brief, he left the Court, as if in a huff with all who were concerned in the affair.

The Judge having obtained silence,—for a murmur arose in the Court when the Counsel for the prosecution threw up his brief,—began to charge the Jury, balancing, as he had done throughout the whole day, the different opinions by which he seemed alternately swayed. He protested on his salvation that he had no more doubt of the existence of the horrid and damnable conspiracy called the Popish Plot, than he had of the treachery of Judas Iscariot; and that he considered Oates as the instrument under Providence of preserving the nation from all the miseries of his Majesty's assassination, and of a second Saint Bartholomew, acted in the streets of London. But then he stated it was the candid construction of the law of England, that the worse the crime, the more strong should be the evidence. Here was the case of accessories tried, whilst their principal—for such he should call the Countess of Derby —was unconvicted and at large; and for Doctor Oates, he had but spoke of matters which personally applied to that noble lady, whose words, if she used such in passion, touching aid which she expected in some treasonable matters from these Peverils, and from her kinsmen, or her son's kinsmen, of the House of Stanley, may have been but a burst of female resentment—*dulcis Amaryllidis ira*, as the poet hath it. Who knoweth but Doctor Oates did mistake—he being a gentleman of a comely countenance and easy demeanour—this same rap with the fan as a chastisement for lack of courage in the Catholic cause, when, peradventure, it was otherwise meant, as Popish ladies will put, it is said, such neophytes and youthful candidates for orders, to many severe trials. "I speak these things jocularly," said the Judge, "having no wish to stain the reputation either of the Honourable Countess or the Reverend Doctor; only I think the bearing between them may have related to something short of high treason. As for what the Attorney-General hath set forth of rescues and force, and I wot not what, sure I am, that in a civil country, when such things happen, such things may be proved; and that you and I, gentlemen, are not to take them for granted gratuitously. Touching this other prisoner, this *Galfridus minimus,* he must needs say," he continued, " he could not discover even a shadow of suspicion against him. Was it to be thought so abortive a creature would thrust himself into depths of policy, far less into stratagems of war? They had but to look at him to conclude the contrary —the creature was, from his age, fitter for the grave than a conspiracy—and by his size and appearance, for the inside of a raree-show, than the mysteries of a plot."

The dwarf here broke in upon the Judge by force of screaming, to assure him that he had been, simple as he sat there, engaged in seven plots in Cromwell's time; and, as he proudly added, with some of the tallest men of England. The matchless look and air with which Sir Geoffrey made this vaunt, set all a-laughing, and increased the ridicule with which the whole trial began to be received; so that it was amidst shaking sides and watery eyes that a general verdict of Not Guilty was pronounced, and the prisoners dismissed from the bar.

But a warmer sentiment awakened among those who saw the father and son throw themselves into each other's arms, and, after a hearty embrace, extend their hands to their poor little companion in peril, who, like a dog, when present at a similar scene, had at last succeeded, by stretching himself up to them and whimpering at the same time, to secure to himself a portion of their sympathy and gratulation.

Such was the singular termination of this trial. Charles himself was desirous to have taken considerable credit with the Duke of Ormond for the evasion of the law, which had been thus effected by his private connivance; and was both surprised and mortified at the coldness with which his Grace replied, that he was rejoiced at the poor gentlemen's safety, but would rather have had the King redeem them like a prince, by his royal prerogative of mercy, than that his Judge should convey them out of the power of the law, like a juggler with his cups and balls.

CHAPTER XLII

—— On fair ground
I could beat forty of them !
—CORIOLANUS.

It doubtless occurred to many that were present at the trial
we have described, that it was managed in a singular manner,
and that the quarrel, which had the appearance of having
taken place between the Court and the Crown Counsel, might
proceed from some private understanding betwixt them, the
object of which was the miscarriage of the accusation. Yet
though such underhand dealing was much suspected, the greater
part of the audience, being well educated and intelligent, had
already suspected the bubble of the Popish Plot, and were glad
to see that accusations, founded on what had already cost so
much blood, could be evaded in any way. But the crowd, who
waited in the Court of Requests, and in the hall, and without
doors, viewed in a very different light the combination, as they
interpreted it, between the Judge and the Attorney-General,
for the escape of the prisoners.

Oates, whom less provocation than he had that day received
often induced to behave like one frantic with passion, threw
himself amongst the crowd, and repeated till he was hoarse,
"Theay are stoifling the Plaat!—theay are straangling the
Plaat!—My Laard Justice and Maaster Attarney are in league
to secure the escape of the plaaters and Paapists!"

"It is the device of the Papist whore of Portsmouth," said one.

"Of old Rowley himself," said another.

"If he could be murdered by himself, why hang those that
would hinder it!" exclaimed a third.

"He should be tried," said a fourth, "for conspiring his own
death, and hanged *in terrorem.*"

In the meanwhile, Sir Geoffrey, his son, and their little companion, left the hall, intending to go to Lady Peveril's lodgings,
which had been removed to Fleet Street. She had been relieved
from considerable inconvenience, as Sir Geoffrey gave Julian
hastily to understand, by an angel, in the shape of a young
friend, and she now expected them doubtless with impatience.
Humanity, and some indistinct idea of having unintentionally
hurt the feelings of the poor dwarf, induced the honest Cavalier
to ask this unprotected being to go with them. "He knew
Lady Peveril's lodgings were but small," he said; "but it would
be strange, if there was not some cupboard large enough to
accommodate the little gentleman."

The dwarf registered this well-meant remark in his mind, to be the subject of a proper explanation, along with the unhappy reminiscence of the trencher-hornpipe, whenever time should permit an argument of such nicety.

And thus they sallied from the hall, attracting general observation, both from the circumstances in which they had stood so lately, and from their resemblance, as a wag of the Inner Temple expressed it, to the three degrees of comparison, Large, Lesser, Least. But they had not passed far along the street, when Julian perceived that more malevolent passions than mere curiosity began to actuate the crowd which followed, and, as it were, dogged their motions.

"There go the Papist cut-throats, tantivy for Rome!" said one fellow.

"Tantivy to Whitehall, you mean!" said another.

"Ah! the bloodthirsty villains!" cried a woman: "Shame, one of them should be suffered to live, after poor Sir Edmondsbury's cruel murder."

"Out upon the mealy-mouthed Jury, that turned out the bloodhounds on an innocent town!" cried a fourth.

In short, the tumult thickened, and the word began to pass among the more desperate, "Lambe them, lads; lambe them!"—a cant phrase of the time, derived from the fate of Dr. Lambe, an astrologer and quack, who was knocked on the head by the rabble in Charles the First's time.

Julian began to be much alarmed at these symptoms of violence, and regretted that they had not gone down to the city by water. It was now too late to think of that mode of retreating, and he therefore requested his father in a whisper, to walk steadily forward towards Charing Cross, taking no notice of the insults which might be cast upon them, while the steadiness of their pace and appearance might prevent the rabble from resorting to actual violence. The execution of this prudent resolution was prevented after they had passed the palace, by the hasty disposition of the elder Sir Geoffrey, and the no less choleric temper of Galfridus Minimus, who had a soul which spurned all odds, as well of numbers as of size.

"Now a murrain take the knaves, with their hollowing and whooping," said the larger knight; "by this day, if I could but light on a weapon, I would cudgel reason and loyalty into some of their carcasses!"

"And I also," said the dwarf, who was toiling to keep up with the longer strides of his companions, and therefore spoke in a very phthisical tone.—"I also will cudgel the plebeian knaves beyond measure—he!—hem!"

Among the crowd who thronged around them, impeded, and did all but assault them, was a mischievous shoemaker's apprentice, who, hearing this unlucky vaunt of the valorous dwarf, repaid it by flapping him on the head with a boot which he was carrying home to the owner, so as to knock the little gentleman's hat over his eyes. The dwarf, thus rendered unable to discover the urchin that had given him the offence, flew with instinctive ambition against the biggest fellow in the crowd, who received the onset with a kick on the stomach, which made the poor little champion reel back to his companions. They were now assaulted on all sides; but fortune complying with the wish of Sir Geoffrey the larger, ordained that the scuffle should happen near the booth of a cutler, from amongst whose wares, as they stood exposed to the public, Sir Geoffrey Peveril snatched a broadsword, which he brandished with the formidable address of one who had for many a day been in the familiar practice of using such a weapon. Julian, while at the same time he called loudly for a peace-officer, and reminded the assailants that they were attacking inoffensive passengers, saw nothing better for it than to imitate his father's example, and seized also one of the weapons thus opportunely offered.

When they displayed these demonstrations of defence, the rush which the rabble at first made towards them was so great as to throw down the unfortunate dwarf, who would have been trampled to death in the scuffle, had not his stout old namesake cleared the rascal crowd from about him with a few flourishes of his weapon, and seizing on the fallen champion, put him out of danger (except from missiles), by suddenly placing him on the bulk-head, that is to say, the flat wooden roof of the cutler's projecting booth. From the rusty ironware, which was displayed there, the dwarf instantly snatched an old rapier and target, and covering himself with the one, stood making passes with the other, at the faces and eyes of the people in the street; so much delighted with his post of vantage, that he called loudly to his friends who were skirmishing with the riotous on more equal terms as to position, to lose no time in putting themselves under his protection. But far from being in a situation to need his assistance, the father and son might easily have extricated themselves from the rabble by their own exertions, could they have thought of leaving the mannikin in the forlorn situation, in which, to every eye but his own, he stood like a diminutive puppet, tricked out with sword and target as a fencing-master's sign.

Stones and sticks began now to fly very thick, and the crowd, notwithstanding the exertions of the Peverils to disperse them with as little harm as possible, seemed determined on mischief, when some gentlemen who had been at the trial, understanding that the prisoners who had been just acquitted were in danger of being murdered by the populace, drew their swords, and

made forward to effect their rescue, which was completed by a
small party of the King's Life Guards, who had been despatched
from their ordinary post of alarm, upon intelligence of what was
passing. When this unexpected reinforcement arrived, the old
jolly Knight at once recognised, amidst the cries of those who
then entered upon action, some of the sounds which had animated his more active years.

"Where be these cuckoldly Roundheads," cried some.—
"Down with the sneaking knaves!" cried others.—"The King
and his friends, and the devil a one else!" exclaimed a third
set, with more oaths and d——n me's, than, in the present more
correct age, it is necessary to commit to paper.

The old soldier, pricking up his ears like an ancient hunter
at the cry of the hounds, would gladly have scoured the Strand,
with the charitable purpose, now he saw himself so well supported, of knocking the London knaves, who had insulted him,
into twiggen bottles; but he was withheld by the prudence of
Julian, who, though himself extremely irritated by the unpro-
voked ill-usage which they had received, saw himself in a
situation in which it was necessary to exercise more caution
than vengeance. He prayed and pressed his father to seek
some temporary place of retreat from the fury of the populace,
while that prudent measure was yet in their power. The subaltern officer, who commanded the party of the Life Guards,
exhorted the old Cavalier eagerly to the same sage counsel,
using, as a spice of compulsion, the name of the King; while
Julian strongly urged that of his mother. The old Knight
looked at his blade, crimsoned with cross-cuts and slashes which
he had given to the most forward of the assailants, with the eye
of one not half sufficed.

"I would I had pinked one of the knaves at least—but I
know not how it was, when I looked on their broad round
English faces, I shunned to use my point, and only sliced the
rogues a little."

"But the King's pleasure," said the officer, "is, that no
tumult be prosecuted."

"My mother," said Julian, "will die with fright, if the
rumour of this scuffle reaches her ere we see her."

"Ay, ay," said the Knight, "the King's Majesty and my
good dame—well, their pleasure be done, that's all I can say
—Kings and ladies must be obeyed. But which way to retreat,
since retreat we needs must?"

Julian would have been at some loss to advise what course
to take, for everybody in the vicinity had shut up their shops,
and chained their doors, upon observing the confusion become
so formidable. The poor cutler, however, with whose goods
they made so free, offered them an asylum on the part of his

landlord, whose house served as a rest for his shop, and only intimated gently, he hoped the gentlemen would consider him for the use of his weapons.

Julian was hastily revolving whether they ought, in prudence, to accept this man's invitation, aware, by experience, how many trepans, as they were then termed, were used betwixt two contending factions, each too inveterate to be very scrupulous of the character of fair play to an enemy, when the dwarf, exerting his cracked voice to the uttermost, and shrieking like an exhausted herald, from the exalted station which he still occupied on the bulk-head, exhorted them to accept the offer of the worthy man of the mansion. "He himself," he said, as he reposed himself after the glorious conquest in which he had some share, "had been favoured with a beatific vision, too splendid to be described to common and mere mortal ears, but which had commanded him, in a voice to which his heart had bounded as to a trumpet sound, to take refuge with the worthy person of the house, and cause his friends to do so."

"Vision!" said the Knight of the Peak, — "sound of a trumpet!—the little man is stark mad."

But the cutler, in great haste, intimated to them that their little friend had received an intimation from a gentlewoman of his acquaintance, who spoke to him from the window, while he stood on the bulk-head, that they would find a safe retreat in his landlord's; and desiring them to attend to two or three deep though distant huzzas, made them aware that the rabble were up still, and would soon be upon them with renewed violence, and increased numbers.

The father and son, therefore, hastily thanked the officer and his party, as well as the other gentlemen who had volunteered in their assistance, lifted little Sir Geoffrey Hudson from the conspicuous post which he had so creditably occupied during the skirmish, and followed the footsteps of the tenant of the booth, who conducted them down a blind alley and through one or two courts, in case, as he said, any one might have watched where they burrowed, and so into a back-door. This entrance admitted them to a staircase carefully hung with straw mats to exclude damp, from the upper step of which they entered upon a tolerably large withdrawing-room, hung with coarse green serge edged with gilded leather, which the poorer or more economical citizens at that time used instead of tapestry or wainscoting.

Here the poor cutler received from Julian such a gratuity for the loan of the swords, that he generously abandoned the property to the gentlemen who had used them so well; "the rather," he said, "that he saw, by the way they handled their weapons, that they were men of mettle, and tall fellows."

Here the dwarf smiled on him courteously, and bowed, thrusting, at the same time, his hand into his pocket, which however, he withdrew carelessly, probably because he found he had not the means of making the small donation which he had meditated.

The cutler proceeded to say, as he bowed and was about to withdraw, that he saw there would be merry days yet in Old England, and that Bilboa blades would fetch as good a price as ever. "I remember," he said, "gentlemen, though I was then but a 'prentice, the demand for weapons in the years forty-one and forty-two; sword blades were more in request than tooth-picks, and Old Ironsides, my master, took more for rascally Provant rapiers, than I dare ask nowadays for a Toledo. But, to be sure, a man's life then rested on the blade he carried; the Cavaliers and Roundheads fought every day at the gates of Whitehall, as it is like, gentlemen, by your good example, they may do again, when I shall be enabled to leave my pitiful booth, and open a shop of better quality. I hope you will recommend me, gentlemen, to your friends. I am always provided with ware which a gentleman may risk his life on."

"Thank you, good friend," said Julian, "I prithee begone. I trust we shall need thy ware no more for some time at least."

The cutler retired, while the dwarf hollowed after him downstairs, that he would call on him soon, and equip himself with a longer blade, and one more proper for action; although, he said, the little weapon he had did well enough for a walking-sword, or in a skirmish with such *canaille* as they had been engaged with.

The cutler returned at this summons, and agreed to pleasure the little man with a weapon more suitable to his magnanimity; then, as if the thought had suddenly occurred to him, he said, "But, gentlemen, it will be wild work to walk with your naked swords through the Strand, and it can scarce fail to raise the rabble again. If you please, while you repose yourselves here, I can fit the blades with sheaths."

The proposal seemed so reasonable, that Julian and his father gave up their weapons to the friendly cutler, an example which the dwarf followed, after a moment's hesitation, not caring, as he magnificently expressed it, to part so soon with the trusty friend which fortune had but the moment before restored to his hand. The man retired with the weapons under his arm; and, in shutting the door behind him, they heard him turn the key.

"Did you hear that?" said Sir Geoffrey to his son—"and we are disarmed!"

Julian, without reply, examined the door, which was fast secured; and then looked at the casements, which were at a storey's height from the ground, and grated besides with iron. "I cannot think," he said, after a moment's pause, "that the fellow means to trepan us ; and, in any event, I trust we should have no difficulty in forcing the door, or otherwise making an escape. But, before resorting to such violent measures, I think it is better to give the rabble leisure to disperse, by waiting this man's return with our weapons within a reasonable time, when, if he does not appear, I trust we shall find little difficulty in extricating ourselves." As he spoke thus, the hangings were pulled aside, and from a small door which was concealed behind them, Major Bridgenorth entered the room.

CHAPTER XLIII

He came amongst them like a new raised spirit
To speak of dreadful judgments that impend,
And of the wrath to come.
—THE REFORMER.

THE astonishment of Julian at the unexpected apparition of Bridgenorth, was instantly succeeded by apprehension of his father's violence, which he had every reason to believe would break forth against one, whom he himself could not but reverence on account of his own merits, as well as because he was the father of Alice. The appearance of Bridgenorth was not however, such as to awaken resentment. His countenance was calm, his step slow and composed, his eye not without the indication of some deep-seated anxiety, but without any expression either of anger or of triumph. "You are welcome," he said, "Sir Geoffrey Peveril, to the shelter and hospitality of this house ; as welcome as you would have been in other days, when we called each other neighbours and friends."

"Odzooks," said the old Cavalier ; "and had I known it was thy house, man, I would sooner had my heart's blood run down the kennel, than my foot should have crossed your threshold— in the way of seeking safety, that is."

"I forgive your inveteracy," said Major Bridgenorth, "on account of your prejudices."

"Keep your forgiveness," answered the Cavalier, "until you are pardoned yourself. By Saint George I have sworn, if ever I got my heels out of yon rascally prison, whither I was sent much through your means, Master Bridgenorth,—that you should pay the reckoning for my bad lodging.—I will strike no man in his own house ; but if you will cause the fellow to bring back my weapon, and take a turn in that blind court there below, along with me, you shall soon see what chance a traitor hath with a true man, and a kennel-blooded Puritan with Peveril of the Peak."

Bridgenorth smiled with much composure. "When I was younger and more warm-blooded," he replied, "I refused your challenge, Sir Geoffrey; it is not likely I should now accept it, when each is within a stride of the grave. I have not spared, and will not spare, my blood, when my country wants it."

"That is when there is any chance of treason against the King," said Sir Geoffrey.

"Nay, my father," said Julian, "let us hear Master Bridgenorth! We have been sheltered in his house; and although we now see him in London, we should remember that he did not appear against us this day, when perhaps his evidence might have given a fatal turn to our situation."

"You are right, young man," said Bridgenorth; "and it should be some pledge of my sincere goodwill, that I was this day absent from Westminster, when a few words from my mouth had ended the long line of Peveril of the Peak: it needed but ten minutes to walk to Westminster Hall, to have ensured your condemnation. But could I have done this, knowing, as I now know, that to thee, Julian Peveril, I owe the extrication of my daughter—of my dearest Alice—the memory of her departed mother—from the snares which hell and profligacy had opened around her?"

"She is, I trust, safe," said Peveril eagerly, and almost forgetting his father's presence; "she is, I trust, safe, and in your own wardship?"

"Not in mine," said the dejected father; "but in that of one in whose protection, next to that of Heaven, I can most fully confide."

"Are you sure—are you very sure of that?" repeated Julian eagerly. "I found her under the charge of one to whom she had been trusted, and who yet——"

"And who yet was the basest of women," answered Bridgenorth; "but he who selected her for the charge was deceived in her character."

"Say rather you were deceived in his; remember that when we parted at Moultrassie, I warned you of that Ganlesse —that——"

"I know your meaning," said Bridgenorth; "nor did you err in describing him as a worldly-wise man. But he has atoned for his error by recovering Alice from the dangers into which she was plunged when separated from you; and besides, I have not thought meet again to entrust him with the charge that is dearest to me."

"I thank God your eyes are thus far opened!" said Julian.

2 E

"This day will open them wide, or close them for ever," answered Bridgenorth.

During this dialogue, which the speakers hurried through without attending to the others who were present, Sir Geoffrey listened with surprise and eagerness, endeavouring to catch something which should render their conversation intelligible; but as he totally failed in gaining any such key to their meaning, he broke in with,—"'Sblood and thunder, Julian, what unprofitable gossip is this? What hast thou to do with this fellow, more than to bastinado him, if you should think it worth while to beat so old a rogue?"

"My dearest father," said Julian, "you know not this gentleman—I am certain you do him injustice. My own obligations to him are many; and I am sure when you come to know them——"

"I hope I shall die ere that moment come," said Sir Geoffrey; and continued with increasing violence, "I hope in the mercy of Heaven, that I shall be in the grave of my ancestors, ere I learn that my son—my only son—the last hope of my ancient house—the last remnant of the name of Peveril—hath consented to receive obligations from the man on earth I am most bound to hate, were I not still more bound to contemn him!— Degenerate dog-whelp!" he repeated with great vehemence, "you colour without replying! Speak, and disown such disgrace; or, by the God of my fathers——"

The dwarf suddenly stepped forward, and called out, "Forbear!" with a voice at once so discordant and commanding, that it sounded supernatural. "Man of sin and pride," he said, "forbear; and call not the name of a holy God to witness thine unhallowed resentments."

The rebuke so boldly and decidedly given, and the moral enthusiasm with which he spoke, gave the despised dwarf an ascendency for the moment over the fiery spirit of his gigantic namesake. Sir Geoffrey Peveril eyed him for an instant askance and shyly, as he might have done a supernatural apparition, and then muttered, "What knowest thou of my cause of wrath?"

"Nothing," said the dwarf;—"nothing but this—that no cause can warrant the oath thou wert about to swear. Ungrateful man! thou wert to-day rescued from the devouring wrath of the wicked, by a marvellous conjunction of circumstances—Is this a day, thinkest thou, on which to indulge thine own hasty resentments?"

"I stand rebuked," said Sir Geoffrey, "and by a singular monitor—the grasshopper, as the prayer-book saith, hath become a burden to me.—Julian, I will speak to thee of these matters hereafter;—and for you, Master Bridgenorth, I desire to have no farther communication with you, either in peace or in anger. Our time passes fast, and I would fain return to my family. Cause our weapons to be restored; unbar the doors, and let us part without farther altercation, which can but disturb and aggravate our spirits."

"Sir Geoffrey Peveril," said Bridgenorth, "I have no desire to vex your spirit or my own; but, for thus soon dismissing you, that may hardly be, it being a course inconsistent with the work which I have on hand."

"How, sir! Do you mean that we should abide here, whether with or against our inclinations?" said the dwarf. "Were it not that I am laid under charge to remain here, by one who hath the best right to command this poor microcosm, I would show thee that bolts and bars are unavailing restraints on such as I am."

"Truly," said Sir Geoffrey, "I think, upon an emergency, the little man might make his escape through the keyhole."

Bridgenorth's face was moved into something like a smile at the swaggering speech of the pigmy hero, and the contemptuous commentary of Sir Geoffrey Peveril; but such an expression never dwelt on his features for two seconds together, and he replied in these words:—"Gentlemen, each and all of you must be fain to content yourselves. Believe me, no hurt is intended towards you; on the contrary, your remaining here will be a means of securing your safety, which would be otherwise deeply endangered. It will be your own fault if a hair of your head is hurt. But the stronger force is on my side; and, whatever harm you may meet with should you attempt to break forth by violence, the blame must rest with yourselves. If you will not believe me, I will permit Master Julian Peveril to accompany me, where he shall see that I am provided fully with the means of repressing violence."

"Treason!—treason!" exclaimed the old Knight—"Treason against God and King Charles!—Oh, for one half-hour of the broadsword which I parted with like an ass!"

"Hold, my father, I conjure you!" said Julian. "I will go with Master Bridgenorth, since he requests it. I will satisfy myself whether there be danger, and of what nature. It is possible I may prevail on him to desist from some desperate measure, if such be indeed in agitation. Should it be necessary, fear not that your son will behave as he ought to do."

"Do your pleasure, Julian," said his father; "I will confide in thee. But if you betray my confidence, a father's curse shall cleave to you."

Bridgenorth now motioned to Peveril to follow him, and they passed through the small door by which he had entered.

The passage led to a vestibule or anteroom, in which several other doors and passages seemed to centre. Through one of these Julian was conducted by Bridgenorth, walking with silence and precaution, in obedience to a signal made by his guide to that effect. As they advanced, he heard sounds, like those of the human voice, engaged in urgent and emphatic declamation. With slow and light steps Bridgenorth conducted him through a door which terminated this passage; and as he entered a little gallery, having a curtain in front, the sound of the preacher's voice—for such it now seemed—became distinct and audible.

Julian now doubted not that he was in one of those conventicles, which, though contrary to the existing laws, still continued to be regularly held in different parts of London and the suburbs. Many of these, as frequented by persons of moderate political principles, though dissenters from the Church for conscience' sake, were connived at by the prudence or timidity of the government. But some of them, in which assembled the fiercer and more exalted sects of Independents, Anabaptists, Fifth-Monarchy men, and other sectaries, whose stern enthusiasm had contributed so greatly to effect the overthrow of the late King's throne, were sought after, suppressed, and dispersed, whenever they could be discovered.

Julian was soon satisfied that the meeting into which he was thus secretly introduced was one of the latter class; and, to judge by the violence of the preacher, of the most desperate character. He was still more effectually convinced of this, when, at a sign from Bridgenorth, he cautiously unclosed a part of the curtain which hung before the gallery, and thus, unseen himself, looked down on the audience, and obtained a view of the preacher.

About two hundred persons were assembled beneath, in an area filled up with benches, as if for the exercise of worship; and they were all of the male sex, and well armed with pikes and muskets, as well as swords and pistols. Most of them had the appearance of veteran soldiers, now past the middle of life, yet retaining such an appearance of strength as might well supply the loss of youthful agility. They stood, or sat, in various attitudes of stern attention; and, resting on their spears and muskets, kept their eyes firmly fixed on the preacher, who ended the violence of his declamation by displaying from the pulpit a banner, on which was represented a lion, with the motto, "*Vicit Leo ex tribu Judæ.*"

The torrent of mystical yet animating eloquence of the preacher—an old grey-haired man, whom zeal seemed to supply with the powers of voice and action, of which years had deprived him—was suited to the taste of his audience, but could not be transferred to these pages without scandal and impro-

priety. He menaced the rulers of England with all the judgments denounced on those of Moab and Assyria—he called
upon the saints to be strong, to be up and doing; and promised
those miracles which, in the campaigns of Joshua, and his suc-
cessors, the valiant Judges of Israel, supplied all odds against
the Amorites, Midianites, and Philistines. He sounded trumpets,
opened vials, broke seals, and denounced approaching judgments
under all the mystical signs of the Apocalypse. The end of
the world was announced, accompanied with all its preliminary
terrors.

Julian, with deep anxiety, soon heard enough to make him
aware that the meeting was likely to terminate in open insurrection, like that of the Fifth-Monarchy men, under Venner, at
an earlier period of Charles's reign; and he was not a little
concerned at the probability of Bridgenorth being implicated
in so criminal and desperate an undertaking. If he had retained any doubts of the issue of the meeting, they must have
been removed when the preacher called on his hearers to renounce all expectation which had hitherto been entertained
of safety to the nation, from the execution of the ordinary laws
of the land. This, he said, was at best but a carnal seeking
after earthly aid—a going down to Egypt for help, which the
jealousy of their Divine Leader would resent as a fleeing to
another rock, and a different banner, from that which was this
day displayed over them.—And here he solemnly swung the
bannered lion over their heads, as the only sign under which
they ought to seek for life and safety. He then proceeded
to insist, that recourse to ordinary justice was vain as well as
sinful.

"The event of that day at Westminster," he said, "might
teach them that the man at Whitehall was even as the man
his father;" and closed a long tirade against the vices of the
Court, with assurance "that Tophet was ordained of old—for
the King it was made hot."

As the preacher entered on a description of the approaching
theocracy, which he dared to prophesy, Bridgenorth, who appeared for a time to have forgotten the presence of Julian,
whilst with stern and fixed attention he drunk in the words of
the preacher, seemed suddenly to collect himself, and, taking
Julian by the hand, led him out of the gallery, of which he
carefully closed the door, into an apartment at no great
distance.

When they arrived there, he anticipated the expostulations
of Julian, by asking him, in a tone of severe triumph, whether
these men he had seen were likely to do their work negligently,
or whether it would not be perilous to attempt to force their
way from a house, when all the avenues were guarded by

such as he had now seen—men of war from their childhood upwards.

"In the name of Heaven," said Julian, without replying to Bridgenorth's question, "for what desperate purpose have you assembled so many desperate men? I am well aware that your sentiments of religion are peculiar; but beware how you deceive yourself—No views of religion can sanction rebellion and murder; and such are the natural and necessary consequences of the doctrine we have just heard poured into the ears of fanatical and violent enthusiasts."

"My son," said Bridgenorth calmly, "in the days of my non-age, I thought as you do. I deemed it sufficient to pay my tithes of cummin and aniseed—my poor petty moral observances of the old law; and I thought I was heaping up precious things, when they were in value no more than the husks of the swine-trough. Praised be Heaven, the scales are fallen from mine eyes; and after forty years' wandering in the desert of Sinai, I am at length arrived in the Land of Promise —My corrupt human nature has left me—I have cast my slough, and can now with some conscience put my hand to the plough, certain that there is no weakness left in me where-through I may look back. The furrows," he added, bending his brows, while a gloomy fire filled his large eyes, "must be drawn long and deep, and watered by the blood of the mighty."

There was a change in Bridgenorth's tone and manner, when he used these singular expressions, which convinced Julian that his mind, which had wavered for so many years between his natural good sense and the insane enthusiasm of the time, had finally given way to the latter; and, sensible of the danger in which the unhappy man himself, the innocent and beautiful Alice, and his own father, were likely to be placed—to say nothing of the general risk of the community by a sudden insurrection, he at the same time felt that there was no chance of reasoning effectually with one, who would oppose spiritual conviction to all arguments which reason could urge against his wild schemes. To touch his feelings seemed a more probable resource; and Julian therefore conjured Bridgenorth to think how much his daughter's honour and safety were concerned in his abstaining from the dangerous course which he meditated. "If you fall," he said, "must she not pass under the power and guardianship of her uncle, whom you allow to have shown himself capable of the grossest mistake in the choice of her female protectress; and whom I believe, upon good grounds, to have made that infamous choice with his eyes open?"

"Young man," answered Bridgenorth, "you make me feel like the poor bird, around whose wing some wanton boy has fixed a line, to pull the struggling wretch to earth at his pleasure. Know, since thou wilt play this cruel part, and drag me down from higher contemplations, that she with whom Alice is placed, and who hath in future full power to guide her motions, and decide her fate, despite of Christian and every one else, is—I will not tell thee who she is—Enough—no one —thou least of all, needs to fear for her safety."

At this moment a side-door opened, and Christian himself came into the apartment. He started and coloured when he saw Julian Peveril; then turning to Bridgenorth with an assumed air of indifference, asked, "Is Saul among the prophets? —Is a Peveril among the saints?"

"No, brother," replied Bridgenorth, "his time is not come more than thine own—thou art too deep in the ambitious intrigues of manhood, and he in the giddy passions of youth, to hear the still calm voice—You will both hear it, as I trust and pray."

"Master Ganlesse, or Christian, or by whatever name you are called," said Julian, "by whatever reasons you guide yourself in this most perilous matter, *you* at least are not influenced by any idea of an immediate divine command for commencing hostilities against the state. Leaving, therefore, for the present, whatever subjects of discussion may be between us, I implore you, as a man of shrewdness and sense, to join with me in dissuading Master Bridgenorth from the fatal enterprise which he now meditates."

"Young gentleman," said Christian, with great composure, "when we met in the west, I was willing to have made a friend of you, but you rejected the overture. You might, however, even then have seen enough of me to be assured, that I am not likely to rush too rashly on any desperate undertaking. As to this which lies before us, my brother Bridgenorth brings to it the simplicity, though not the harmlessness of the dove, and I the subtilty of the serpent. He hath the leading of saints who are moved by the spirit; and I can add to their efforts a powerful body, who have for their instigators the world, the devil, and the flesh."

"And can you," said Julian, looking at Bridgenorth, "accede to such an unworthy union?"

"I unite not with them," said Bridgenorth; "but I may not, without guilt, reject the aid which Providence sends to assist His servants. We are ourselves few, though determined —Those whose swords come to help the cutting down of the harvest, must be welcome—When their work is wrought, they will be converted or scattered.—Have you been at York Place, brother, with that unstable epicure? We must have his last resolution, and that within an hour."

Christian looked at Julian, as if his presence prevented him from returning an answer; upon which Bridgenorth arose, and taking the young man by the arm, led him out of the apartment, into that in which they had left his father; assuring him by the way, that determined and vigilant guards were placed in every different quarter by which escape could be effected, and that he would do well to persuade his father to remain a quiet prisoner for a few hours.

Julian returned him no answer, and Bridgenorth presently retired, leaving him alone with his father and Hudson. To their questions he could only briefly reply, that he feared they were trepanned, since they were in the house with at least two hundred fanatics, completely armed, and apparently prepared for some desperate enterprise. Their own want of arms precluded the possibility of open violence; and however unpleasant it might be to remain in such a condition, it seemed difficult, from the strength of the fastenings at doors and windows, to attempt any secret escape without instantaneous detection.

The valiant dwarf alone nursed hopes, with which he in vain endeavoured to inspire his companions in affliction. "The fair one, whose eyes," he said, "were like the twin stars of Leda"—for the little man was a great admirer of lofty language—"had not invited him, the most devoted, and, it might be, not the least favoured of her servants, into this place as a harbour, in order that he might therein suffer shipwreck; and he generously assured his friends, that in his safety they also should be safe."

Sir Geoffrey, little cheered by this intimation, expressed his despair at not being able to get the length of Whitehall, where he trusted to find as many jolly Cavaliers as would help him to stifle the whole nest of wasps in their hive; while Julian was of opinion that the best service he could now render Bridgenorth, would be timeously to disclose his plot, and, if possible, to send him at the same time warning to save his person.

But we must leave them to meditate over their plans at leisure; no one of which, as they all depended on their previous escape from confinement, seemed in any great chance of being executed.

CHAPTER XLIV

And some for safety took the dreadful leap ;
Some for the voice of Heaven seem'd calling on them ;
Some for advancement, or for lucre's sake—
I leap'd in frolic.
—THE DREAM.

AFTER a private conversation with Bridgenorth, Christian hastened to the Duke of Buckingham's hotel, taking at the same time such a route as to avoid meeting with any acquaintance. He was ushered into the apartment of the Duke, whom he found cracking and eating filberts, with a flask of excellent white wine at his elbow. "Christian," said his Grace, "come help me to laugh—I have bit Sir Charles Sedley—flung him for a thousand, by the gods !"

"I am glad at your luck, my Lord Duke," replied Christian ; "but I am come here on serious business."

"Serious ?—why, I shall hardly be serious in my life again —ha, ha, ha !—and for luck, it was no such thing—sheer wit, and excellent contrivance ; and but that I don't care to affront Fortune, like the old Greek general, I might tell her to her face—In this thou hadst no share. You have heard, Ned Christian, that Mother Cresswell is dead ?"

"Yes, I did hear that the devil hath got his due," answered Christian.

"Well," said the Duke, "you are ungrateful ; for I know you have been obliged to her, as well as others. Before George, a most benevolent and helpful old lady ; and that she might not sleep in an unblest grave, I betted—do you mark me— with Sedley, that I would write her funeral sermon ; that it should be every word in praise of her life and conversation, that it should be all true, and yet that the diocesan should be unable to lay his thumb on Quodling, my little chaplain, who should preach it."

"I perfectly see the difficulty, my lord," said Christian, who well knew that if he wished to secure attention from this volatile nobleman, he must first suffer, nay, encourage him, to exhaust the topic, whatever it might be, that had got temporary possession of his pineal gland.

"Why," said the Duke, "I had caused my little Quodling to go through his oration thus—'That whatever evil reports had passed current during the lifetime of the worthy matron whom they had restored to dust that day, malice herself could not deny that she was born well, married well, lived well, and died well ; since she was born in Shadwell, married to Cresswell, lived in Camberwell, and died in Bridewell.' Here ended the oration, and with it Sedley's ambitious hopes of overreaching Buckingham—ha, ha, ha!—And now, Master Christian, what are your commands for me to-day?"

"First, to thank your Grace for being so attentive as to send so formidable a person as Colonel Blood, to wait upon your poor friend and servant. Faith, he took such an interest in my leaving town, that he wanted to compel me to do it at point of fox, so I was obliged to spill a little of his malapert blood. Your Grace's swordsmen have had ill luck of late; and it is hard, since you always choose the best hands, and such scrupleless knaves too."

"Come now, Christian," said the Duke, "do not thus exult over me; a great man, if I may so call myself, is never greater than amid miscarriage. I only played this little trick on you, Christian, to impress on you a wholesome idea of the interest I take in your motions. The scoundrel's having dared to draw upon you, is a thing not to be forgiven.—What! injure my old friend Christian?"

"And why not," said Christian coolly, "if your old friend was so stubborn as not to go out of town, like a good boy, when your Grace required him to do so, for the civil purpose of entertaining his niece in his absence?"

"How—what!—how do you mean by *my* entertaining your niece, Master Christian?" said the Duke. "She was a personage far beyond my poor attentions, being destined, if I recollect aright, to something like royal favour."

"It was her fate, however, to be the guest of your Grace's convent for a brace of days, or so. Marry, my lord, the father confessor was not at home, and—for convents have been scaled of late—returned not till the bird was flown."

"Christian, thou art an old reynard—I see there is no doubling with thee. It was thou, then, that stole away my pretty prize, but left me something so much prettier in my mind, that, had it not made itself wings to fly away with, I would have placed it in a cage of gold. Never be downcast, man; I forgive thee—I forgive thee."

"Your Grace is of a most merciful disposition, especially considering it is I who have had the wrong; and sages have said, that he who doth the injury is less apt to forgive than he who only sustains it."

"True, true, Christian," said the Duke, "which, as you say, is something quite new, and places my clemency in a striking point of view. Well, then, thou forgiven man, when shall I see my Mauritanian Princess again?"

"Whenever I am certain that a quibble, and a carwhichit, for a play or a sermon, will not banish her from your Grace's memory."

"Not all the wit of South, or of Etherege," said Buckingham hastily, "to say nothing of my own, shall in future make me oblivious of what I owe the Morisco Princess."

"Yet, to leave the fair lady out of thought for a little while —a very little while," said Christian, "since I swear that in due time your Grace shall see her, and know in her the most extraordinary woman that the age has produced—to leave her, I say, out of sight for a little while, has your Grace had late notice of your Duchess's health?"

"Health," said the Duke. "Umph—no—nothing particular. She has been ill—but——"

"She is no longer so," subjoined Christian; "she died in Yorkshire forty-eight hours since."

"Thou must deal with the devil," said the Duke.

"It would ill become one of my name to do so," replied Christian. "But in the brief interval, since your Grace hath known of an event which hath not yet reached the public ear, you have, I believe, made proposals to the King for the hand of the Lady Anne, second daughter of the Duke of York, and your Grace's proposals have been rejected."

"Fiends and firebrands, villain!" said the Duke, starting up and seizing Christian by the collar; "who hath told thee that?"

"Take your hand from my cloak, my Lord Duke, and I may answer you," said Christian. "I have a scurvy touch of old puritanical humour about me. I abide not the imposition of hands—take off your grasp from my cloak, or I will find means to make you unloose it."

The Duke, who had kept his right hand on his dagger-hilt while he held Christian's collar with his left, unloosed it as he spoke, but slowly, and as one who rather suspends than abandons the execution of some hasty impulse; while Christian, adjusting his cloak with perfect composure, said, "Soh—my cloak being at liberty, we speak on equal terms. I come not to insult your Grace, but to offer you vengeance for the insult you have received."

"Vengeance!" said the Duke—"It is the dearest proffer man can present to me in my present mood. I hunger for vengeance—thirst for vengeance—could die to ensure vengeance! —'Sdeath!" he continued, walking up and down the large apartment with the most unrestrained and violent agitation; "I have chased this repulse out of my brain with ten thousand trifles, because I thought no one knew it. But it is known, and to thee, the very common-sewer of Court-secrets—the honour of Villiers is in thy keeping, Ned Christian! Speak, thou man of wiles and of intrigue—on whom dost thou promise the vengeance? Speak! and if thy answers meet my desires,

I will make a bargain with thee as willingly as with thy master, Satan himself."

" I will not be," said Christian, " so unreasonable in my terms as stories tell of the old apostate; I will offer your Grace, as he might do, temporal prosperity and revenge, which is his frequent recruiting money, but I leave it to yourself to provide, as you may be pleased, for your future salvation."

The Duke, gazing upon him fixedly and sadly, replied, " I would to God, Christian, that I could read what purpose of damnable villainy thou hast to propose to me in thy countenance, without the necessity of thy using words ! "

" Your Grace can but try a guess," said Christian, calmly smiling.

" No," replied the Duke, after gazing at him again for the space of a minute; " thou art so deeply dyed a hypocrite, that thy mean features, and clear grey eye, are as likely to conceal treason, as any petty scheme of theft or larceny more corresponding to your degree."

" Treason, my lord ! " echoed Christian ; " you may have guessed more nearly than you were aware of. I honour your Grace's penetration."

" Treason ! " echoed the Duke. " Who dare name such a crime to me ? "

" If a name startles your Grace, you may call it vengeance —vengeance on the cabal of councillors, who have ever countermined you, in spite of your wit and your interest with the King.—Vengeance on Arlington, Ormond—on Charles himself."

" No, by Heaven," said the Duke, resuming his disordered walk through the apartment—" Vengeance on these rats of the Privy Council,—come at it as you will. But the King !—never —never. I have provoked him a hundred times, where he has stirred me once. I have crossed his path in state intrigue— rivalled him in love—had the advantage in both,—and, d—n it, he has forgiven me ! If treason would put me in his throne, I have no apology for it—it were worse than bestial ingratitude."

" Nobly spoken, my lord," said Christian ; " and consistent alike with the obligations under which your Grace lies to Charles Stewart, and the sense you have ever shown of them.—But it signifies not. If your Grace patronise not our enterprise, there is Shaftesbury—there is Monmouth——"

" Scoundrel ! " exclaimed the Duke, even more vehemently agitated than before, " think you that you shall carry on with others an enterprise which I have refused ?—No, by every heathen and every Christian god !—Hark ye, Christian, I will arrest you on the spot—I will, by gods and devils, and carry you to unravel your plot at Whitehall."

"Where the first words I speak," answered the imperturbable Christian, "will be to inform the Privy Council in what place they may find certain letters, wherewith your Grace has honoured your poor vassal, containing, as I think, particulars which his Majesty will read with more surprise than pleasure."

"'Sdeath, villain!" said the Duke, once more laying his hand on his poniard-hilt, "thou hast me again at advantage. I know not why I forbear to poniard you where you stand!"

"I might fall, my Lord Duke," said Christian, slightly colouring, and putting his right hand into his bosom, "though not, I think, unavenged—for I have not put my person into this peril altogether without means of defence. I might fall, but, alas! your Grace's correspondence is in hands, which, by that very act, would be rendered sufficiently active in handing them to the King and the Privy Council. What say you to the Moorish Princess, my Lord Duke? What if I have left her executrix of my will, with certain instructions how to proceed if I return not unharmed from York Place? Oh, my lord, though my head is in the wolf's mouth, I was not goose enough to place it there without settling how many carabines should be fired on the wolf, so soon as my dying cackle was heard.—Pshaw, my Lord Duke! you deal with a man of sense and courage, yet you speak to him as a child and a coward."

The Duke threw himself into a chair, fixed his eyes on the ground, and spoke without raising them. "I am about to call Jerningham," he said; "but fear nothing—it is only for a draught of wine—That stuff on the table may be a vehicle for filberts, and walnuts, but not for such communications as yours.—Bring me champagne," he said to the attendant who answered on his summons.

The domestic returned, and brought a flask of champagne, with two large silver cups. One of them he filled for Buckingham, who, contrary to the usual etiquette, was always served first at home, and then offered the other to Christian, who declined to receive it.

The Duke drank off the large goblet which was presented to him, and for a moment covered his forehead with the palm of his hand; then instantly withdrew it, and said, "Christian, speak your errand plainly. We know each other. If my reputation be in some degree in your hands, you are well aware that your life is in mine. Sit down," he said, taking a pistol from his bosom and laying it on the table—"Sit down, and let me hear your proposal."

"My lord," said Christian, smiling, "I shall produce no

such ultimate argument on my part, though possibly, in time of need, I may not be found destitute of them. But my defence is in the situation of things, and in the composed view which, doubtless, your Majesty will take of them."

"Majesty!" repeated the Duke—"My good friend Christian, you have kept company with the Puritans so long, that you confuse the ordinary titles of the Court."

"I know not how to apologise," said Christian, "unless your Grace will suppose that I spoke by prophecy."

"Such as the devil delivered to Macbeth," said the Duke—again paced the chamber, and again seated himself, and said, "Be plain, Christian—speak out at once, and manfully, what is it you intend?"

"I," said Christian—"What should I do?—I can do nothing in such a matter; but I thought it right that your Grace should know that the godly of this city"—(he spoke the word with a kind of ironical grin)—"are impatient of inactivity, and must needs be up and doing. My brother Bridgenorth is at the head of all old Weiver's congregation; for you must know, that, after floundering from one faith to another, he hath now got beyond ordinances, and is become a Fifth-Monarchy man. He has nigh two hundred of Weiver's people, fully equipped, and ready to fall on; and, with slight aid from your Grace's people, they must carry Whitehall, and make prisoners of all within it."

"Rascal!" said the Duke, "and is it to a Peer of England you make this communication?"

"Nay," answered Christian, "I admit it would be extreme folly in your Grace to appear until all is over. But let me give Blood and the others a hint on your part. There are the four Germans also—right Knipperdolings and Anabaptists—will be specially useful. You are wise, my lord, and know the value of a corps of domestic gladiators, as well as did Octavius, Lepidus, and Anthony, when, by such family forces, they divided the world by indenture tripartite."

"Stay, stay," said the Duke. "Even if these bloodhounds were to join with you—not that I would permit it without the most positive assurances for the King's personal safety—but say the villains were to join, what hope have you of carrying the Court?"

"Bully Tom Armstrong,* my lord, hath promised his interest with the Life Guards. Then there are my Lord Shaftesbury's

---

* Thomas, or Sir Thomas Armstrong, a person who had distinguished himself in youth by duels and drunken exploits. He was particularly connected with the Duke of Monmouth, and was said to be concerned in the Rye-House Plot, for which he suffered capital punishment, 20th June 1684.

brisk boys in the city—thirty thousand on the holding up a finger."

"Let him hold up both hands, and if he count a hundred for each finger," said the Duke, "it will be more than I expect. You have not spoken to him?"

"Surely not till your Grace's pleasure was known. But, if he is not applied to, there is the Dutch train, Hans Snorehout's congregation, in the Strand—there are the French Protestants in Piccadilly—there are the family of Levi in Lewkenor's Lane —the Muggletonians in Thames Street——"

"Ah, faugh!—Out upon them—out upon them!—How the knaves will stink of cheese and tobacco when they come upon action!—they will drown all the perfumes in Whitehall. Spare me the detail; and let me know, my dearest Ned, the sum total of thy most odoriferous forces."

"Fifteen hundred men, well armed," said Christian, "besides the rabble that will rise to a certainty—they have already nearly torn to pieces the prisoners who were this day acquitted on account of the Plot."

"All, then, I understand.—And now, hark ye, most Christian Christian," said he, wheeling his chair full in front of that on which his agent was seated, "you have told me many things to-day—Shall I be equally communicative? Shall I show you that my accuracy of information matches yours? Shall I tell you, in a word, why you have at once resolved to push every one, from the Puritan to the free-thinker, upon a general attack of the Palace at Whitehall, without allowing me, a peer of the realm, time either to pause upon or to prepare for a step so desperate? Shall I tell you why you would lead or drive, seduce or compel me, into countenancing your measures?"

"My lord, if you please to form a guess," said Christian, "I will answer with all sincerity, if you have assigned the right cause."

"The Countess of Derby is this day arrived, and attends the Court this evening, with hopes of the kindest reception. She may be surprised amid the mêlée?—Ha! said I not right, Master Christian? You, who pretend to offer me revenge, know yourself its exquisite sweetness."

"I would not presume," said Christian, half smiling, "to offer your Grace a dish without acting as your taster as well as purveyor."

"That's honestly said," said the Duke. "Away then, my friend. Give Blood this ring—he knows it, and knows how to obey him who bears it. Let him assemble my gladiators, as thou dost most wittily term my *coup jarrets*. The old scheme of the German music may be resorted to, for I think thou hast the instruments ready. But take notice, I know nothing on't;

and Rowley's person must be safe—I will hang and burn on all hands if a hair of his black periwig * be but singed.—Then what is to follow—a Lord Protector of the realm—or stay—Cromwell has made the word somewhat slovenly and unpopular—a Lord Lieutenant of the Kingdom?—The patriots who take it on themselves to avenge the injustice done to the country, and to remove evil counsellors from before the King's throne, that it may be henceforward established in righteousness—so I think the rubric runs—cannot fail to make a fitting choice."

"They cannot, my Lord Duke," said Christian, "since there is but one man in the three kingdoms on whom that choice can possibly fall."

"I thank you, Christian," said his Grace; "and I trust you. Away, and make all ready. Be assured your services shall not be forgot. We will have you near to us."

"My Lord Duke," said Christian, "you bind me doubly to you. But remember that as your Grace is spared any obnoxious proceedings which may befall in the way of military execution, or otherwise, so it will be advisable that you hold yourself in preparation, upon a moment's notice, to put yourself at the head of a band of honourable friends and allies, and come presently to the palace, where you will be received by the victors as a commander, and by the vanquished as a preserver."

"I conceive you—I conceive you. I will be in prompt readiness," said the Duke.

"Ay, my lord," continued Christian; "and for Heaven's sake, let none of those toys, which are the very Delilahs of your imagination, come across your Grace this evening, and interfere with the execution of this sublime scheme."

"Why, Christian, dost think me mad?" was his Grace's emphatic reply. "It is you who linger, when all should be ordered for a deed so daring. Go then.—But hark ye, Ned; ere you go, tell me when I shall again see yonder thing of fire and air—yon Eastern Peri, that glides into apartments by the keyhole, and leaves them through the casement—yon black-eyed houri of the Mahometan paradise—when, I say, shall I see her once more?"

"When your Grace has the truncheon of Lord Lieutenant of the Kingdom," said Christian, and left the apartment.

Buckingham stood fixed in contemplation for a moment after he was gone. "Should I have done this?" he said, arguing the matter with himself; "or had I the choice rather of doing

* Charles, to suit his dark complexion, always wore a black peruke. He used to say of the players, that if they wished to represent a villain on the stage, "Oddsfish, they always clapp'd on him a black periwig, whereas the greatest rogue in England [meaning, probably, Dr. Oates] wears a white one."—*See* CIBBER'S *Apology*.

aught else? Should I not hasten to the Court, and make Charles aware of the treason which besets him? I will, by Heaven?—Here, Jerningham, my coach, with the despatch of light!—I will throw myself at his feet, and tell him of all the follies which I have dreamed of with this Christian.—And then he will laugh at me, and spurn me.—No, I have kneeled to him to-day already, and my repulse was nothing gentle. To be spurned once in the sun's daily round is enough for Buckingham."

Having made this reflection, he seated himself, and began hastily to mark down the young nobles and gentlemen of quality, and others, their very ignoble companions, who he supposed might be likely to assume him for their leader in any popular disturbance. He had nearly completed it, when Jerningham entered, to say the coach would be ready in an instant, and to bring his master's sword, hat, and cloak.

"Let the coachman draw off," said the Duke, "but be in readiness. And send to the gentlemen thou wilt find named in this list; say I am but ill at ease, and wish their company to a slight collation. Let instant expedition be made, and care not for expense; you will find most of them at the Club House in Fuller's Rents." *

The preparations for festivity were speedily made, and the intended guests, most of them persons who were at leisure for any call that promised pleasure, though sometimes more deaf to those of duty, began speedily to assemble. There were many youths of the highest rank, and with them, as is usual in those circles, many of a different class, whom talents, or impudence, or wit, or a turn for gambling, had reared up into companions for the great and the gay. The Duke of Buckingham was a general patron of persons of this description; and a numerous attendance took place on the present occasion.

The festivity was pursued with the usual appliances of wine, music, and games of hazard; with which, however, there mingled in that period much more wit, and a good deal more gross profligacy of conversation, than the talents of the present generation can supply, or their taste would permit.

The Duke himself proved the complete command which he possessed over his versatile character, by maintaining the frolic,

---

* The place of meeting of the Green Ribbon Club. " Their place of meeting," says Roger North, "was in a sort of Carrefour at Chancery Lane, in a centre of business and company most proper for such anglers of fools. The house was double balconied in front, as may yet be seen, for the clubbers to issue forth *in fresco*, with hats and no perukes, pipes in their mouths, merry faces, and dilated throats for vocal encouragement of the canaglia below on usual and unusual occasions."

the laugh, and the jest, while his ear caught up, and with eagerness, the most distant sounds, as intimating the commencement of Christian's revolutionary project. Such sounds were heard from time to time, and from time to time they died away, without any of those consequences which Buckingham expected.

At length, and when it was late in the evening, Jerningham announced Master Chiffinch from the Court; and that worthy personage followed the annunciation.

"Strange things have happened, my Lord Duke," he said; "your presence at Court is instantly required by his Majesty."

"You alarm me," said Buckingham, standing up. "I hope nothing has happened—I hope there is nothing wrong—I hope his Majesty is well?"

"Perfectly well," said Chiffinch; "and desirous to see your Grace without a moment's delay."

"This is sudden," said the Duke. "You see I have had merry fellows about me, and am scarce in case to appear, Chiffinch."

"Your Grace seems to be in very handsome plight," said Chiffinch; "and you know his Majesty is gracious enough to make allowances."

"True," said the Duke, not a little anxious in his mind, touching the cause of this unexpected summons—"True—his Majesty is most gracious—I will order my coach."

"Mine is below," replied the royal messenger; "it will save time, if your Grace will condescend to use it."

Forced from every evasion, Buckingham took a goblet from the table, and requested his friends to remain at his palace so long as they could find the means of amusement there. He expected, he said, to return almost immediately; if not, he would take farewell of them with his usual toast, "May all of us that are not hanged in the interval, meet together again here on the first Monday of next month."

This standing toast of the Duke bore reference to the character of several of his guests; but he did not drink it on the present occasion without some anticipation concerning his own fate, in case Christian had betrayed him. He hastily made some addition to his dress, and attended Chiffinch in the chariot to Whitehall.

CHAPTER XLV

High feasting was there there—the gilded roofs
Rung to the wassail-health—the dancer's step
Sprung to the chord responsive—the gay gamester
To fate's disposal flung his heap of gold,
And laugh'd alike when it increased or lessen'd :
Such virtue hath court-air to teach us patience
Which schoolmen preach in vain.
        —WHY COME YE NOT TO COURT?

UPON the afternoon of this eventful day, Charles held his
Court in the Queen's apartments, which were opened at a
particular hour to invited guests of a certain lower degree,
but accessible without restriction to the higher classes of
nobility who had from birth, and to the courtiers who held by
office the privilege of the *entrée*.

It was one part of Charles's character, which unquestionably
rendered him personally popular, and postponed to a subsequent
reign the precipitation of his family from the throne, that he
banished from his Court many of the formal restrictions with
which it was in other reigns surrounded. He was conscious of
the good-natured grace of his manners, and trusted to it, often
not in vain, to remove evil impressions arising from actions,
which he was sensible could not be justified on the grounds of
liberal or national policy.

In the daytime the King was commonly seen in the public
walks alone, or only attended by one or two persons ; and his
answer to the remonstrance of his brother, on the risk of thus
exposing his person, is well known :—" Believe me, James," he
said, "no one will murder *me*, to make *you* King."

In the same manner, Charles's evenings, unless such as were
destined to more secret pleasures, were frequently spent amongst
all who had any pretence to approach a courtly circle ; and
thus it was upon the night which we are treating of. Queen
Catherine, reconciled or humbled to her fate, had long ceased
to express any feelings of jealousy, nay, seemed so absolutely
dead to such a passion, that she received at her drawing-room,
without scruple, and even with encouragement, the Duchesses
of Portsmouth and Cleveland, and others, who enjoyed, though
in a less avowed character, the credit of having been royal
favourites. Constraint of every kind was banished from a circle
so composed, and which was frequented at the same time, if
not by the wisest, at least by the wittiest courtiers, who ever
assembled round a monarch, and who, as many of them had
shared the wants, and shifts, and frolics of his exile, had then
acquired a sort of prescriptive licence, which the good-natured

prince, when he attained his period of prosperity, could hardly have restrained had it suited his temper to do so. This, however, was the least of Charles's thoughts. His manners were such as secured him from indelicate obtrusion; and he sought no other protection from over-familiarity, than what these and his ready wit afforded him.

On the present occasion, he was peculiarly disposed to enjoy the scene of pleasure which had been prepared. The singular death of Major Coleby, which, taking place in his own presence, had proclaimed, with the voice of a passing bell, the ungrateful neglect of the Prince for whom he had sacrificed everything, had given Charles much pain. But, in his own opinion at least, he had completely atoned for this negligence by the trouble which he had taken for Sir Geoffrey Peveril and his son, whose liberation he looked upon not only as an excellent good deed in itself, but, in spite of the grave rebuke of Ormond, as achieved in a very pardonable manner, considering the difficulties with which he was surrounded. He even felt a degree of satisfaction on receiving intelligence from the city that there had been disturbances in the streets, and that some of the more violent fanatics had betaken themselves to their meeting-houses, upon sudden summons, to inquire, as their preachers phrased it, into the causes of Heaven's wrath, and into the backsliding of the Court, lawyers, and jury, by whom the false and bloody favourers of the Popish Plot were screened and cloaked from deserved punishment.

The King, we repeat, seemed to hear these accounts with pleasure, even when he was reminded of the dangerous and susceptible character of those with whom such suspicions originated. "Will any one now assert," he said, with self-complacence, "that I am so utterly negligent of the interest of friends?—You see the peril in which I place myself, and even the risk to which I have exposed the public peace, to rescue a man whom I have scarce seen for twenty years, and then only in his buff-coat and bandoleers, with other Train-Band officers who kissed hands upon the Restoration. They say Kings have long hands—I think they have as much occasion for long memories, since they are expected to watch over and reward every man in England, who hath but shown his goodwill by crying 'God save the King!'"

"Nay, the rogues are even more unreasonable still," said Sedley; "for every knave of them thinks himself entitled to your Majesty's protection in a good cause, whether he has cried God save the King or no."

The King smiled, and turned to another part of the stately hall, where everything was assembled which could, according to the taste of the age, make the time glide pleasantly away.

In one place, a group of the young nobility, and of the ladies of the Court, listened to the reader's acquaintance Empson, who was accompanying with his unrivalled breathings on the flute, a young siren, who, while her bosom palpitated with pride and with fear, warbled to the courtly and august presence the beautiful air beginning—

> " Young I am, and yet unskill'd,
> How to make a lover yield," &c.

She performed her task in a manner so corresponding with the strains of the amatory poet, and the voluptuous air with which the words had been invested by the celebrated Purcel, that the men crowded around in ecstasies, while most of the ladies thought it proper either to look extremely indifferent to the words she sung, or to withdraw from the circle as quietly as possible. To the song succeeded a concerto, performed by a select band of most admirable musicians, which the King, whose taste was indisputable, had himself selected.

At other tables in the apartment, the elder courtiers worshipped Fortune, at the various fashionable games of ombre, quadrille, hazard, and the like; while heaps of gold which lay before the players, augmented or dwindled with every turn of a card or cast of a die. Many a year's rent of fair estates was ventured upon the main or the odds; which, spent in the old deserted manor-house, had repaired the ravages of Cromwell upon its walls, and replaced the sources of good housekeeping and hospitality, that, exhausted in the last age by fine and sequestration, were now in a fair way of being annihilated by careless prodigality. Elsewhere, under cover of observing the gamester, or listening to the music, the gallantries of that all-licensed age were practised among the gay and fair, closely watched the whilst by the ugly or the old, who promised themselves at least the pleasure of observing, and it may be that of proclaiming, intrigues in which they could not be sharers.

From one table to another glided the merry Monarch, exchanging now a glance with a Court beauty, now a jest with a Court wit, now beating time to the music, and anon losing or winning a few pieces of gold on the chance of the game to which he stood nearest;—the most amiable of voluptuaries— the gayest and best-natured of companions—the man that would, of all others, have best sustained his character, had life been a continued banquet, and its only end to enjoy the passing hour, and send it away as pleasantly as might be.

But Kings are least of all exempted from the ordinary lot of humanity; and Seged of Ethiopia is, amongst monarchs, no solitary example of the vanity of reckoning on a day or an hour of undisturbed serenity. An attendant on the Court announced suddenly to their Majesties that a lady, who would only announce herself as a Peeress of England, desired to be admitted into the presence.

The Queen said, hastily, it was *impossible*. No peeress, without announcing her title, was entitled to the privilege of her rank.

"I could be sworn," said a nobleman in attendance, "that it is some whim of the Duchess of Newcastle."

The attendant who brought the message, said that he did indeed believe it to be the Duchess, both from the singularity of the message, and that the lady spoke with somewhat a foreign accent.

"In the name of madness, then," said the King, "let us admit her. Her Grace is an entire raree-show in her own person—a universal masquerade—indeed a sort of private Bedlam-hospital, her whole ideas being like so many patients crazed upon the subjects of love and literature, who act nothing in their vagaries, save Minerva, Venus, and the nine Muses."

"Your Majesty's pleasure must always supersede mine," said the Queen. "I only hope I shall not be expected to entertain so fantastic a personage. The last time she came to Court, Isabella"—(she spoke to one of her Portuguese ladies of honour)—"you had not returned from our lovely Lisbon!—her Grace had the assurance to assume a right to bring a train-bearer into my apartment; and when this was not allowed, what then, think you, she did?—even caused her train to be made so long, that three mortal yards of satin and silver remained in the antechamber, supported by four wenches, while the other end was attached to her Grace's person, as she paid her duty at the upper end of the presence-room. Full thirty yards of the most beautiful silk did her Grace's madness employ in this manner."

"And most beautiful damsels they were who bore this portentous train," said the King—"a train never equalled save by that of the great comet in sixty-six. Sedley and Etherege told us wonders of them; for it is one advantage of this new fashion brought up by the Duchess, that a matron may be totally unconscious of the coquetry of her train and its attendants."

"Am I to understand, then, your Majesty's pleasure is, that the lady is to be admitted?" said the usher.

"Certainly," said the King; "that is, if the incognita be really entitled to the honour.—It may be as well to inquire her title—there are more madwomen abroad than the Duchess of Newcastle. I will walk into the anteroom myself, and receive your answer."

But ere Charles had reached the lower end of the apartment in his progress to the anteroom, the usher surprised the assembly by announcing a name which had not for many a year been heard in these courtly halls—" the Countess of Derby!"

Stately and tall, and still, at an advanced period of life, having a person unbroken by years, the noble lady advanced towards her Sovereign, with a step resembling that with which she might have met an equal. There was indeed nothing in her manner that indicated either haughtiness or assumption unbecoming that presence; but her consciousness of wrongs, sustained from the administration of Charles, and of the superiority of the injured party over those from whom, or in whose name, the injury had been offered, gave her look dignity, and her step firmness. She was dressed in widow's weeds, of the same fashion which were worn at the time her husband was brought to the scaffold; and which, in the thirty years subsequent to that event, she had never permitted her tirewoman to alter.

The surprise was no pleasing one to the King; and cursing in his heart the rashness which had allowed the lady entrance on the gay scene in which they were engaged, he saw at the same time the necessity of receiving her in a manner suitable to his own character, and her rank in the British Court. He approached her with an air of welcome, into which he threw all his natural grace, while he began, " *Chère Comtesse de Derby, puissante Reine de Man, notre très auguste sœur——*"

"Speak English, sire, if I may presume to ask such a favour," said the Countess. "I am a Peeress of this nation—mother to one English Earl, and widow, alas, to another! In England I have spent my brief days of happiness, my long years of widowhood and sorrow. France and its language are but to me the dreams of an uninteresting childhood. I know no tongue save that of my husband and my son. Permit me, as the widow and mother of Derby, thus to render my homage."

She would have kneeled, but the King gracefully prevented her, and, saluting her cheek, according to the form, led her towards the Queen, and himself performed the ceremony of introduction. "Your Majesty," he said, "must be informed that the Countess has imposed a restriction on French—the language of gallantry and compliment. I trust your Majesty will, though a foreigner, like herself, find enough of honest English to assure the Countess of Derby with what pleasure we see her at Court, after the absence of so many years."

"I will endeavour to do so, at least," said the Queen, on whom the appearance of the Countess of Derby made a more favourable impression than that of many strangers, whom, at the King's request, she was in the habit of receiving with courtesy.

Charles himself again spoke. "To any other lady of the same rank I might put the question, why she was so long absent from the circle? I fear I can only ask the Countess of Derby, what fortunate cause produces the pleasure of seeing her here?"

"No fortunate cause, my liege, though one most strong and urgent."

The King augured nothing agreeable from this commencement; and in truth, from the Countess's first entrance, he had anticipated some unpleasant explanation, which he therefore hastened to parry, having first composed his features into an expression of sympathy and interest.

"If," said he, "the cause is of a nature in which we can render assistance, we cannot expect your ladyship should enter upon it at the present time; but a memorial addressed to our secretary, or, if it is more satisfactory, to ourselves directly, will receive our immediate, and I trust I need not add, our favourable construction."

The Countess bowed with some state, and answered, "My business, sire, is indeed important; but so brief, that it need not for more than a few minutes withdraw your ear from what is more pleasing;—yet it is so urgent, that I am afraid to postpone it even for a moment."

"This is unusual," said Charles. "But you, Countess of Derby, are an unwonted guest, and must command my time. Does the matter require my private ear?"

"For my part," said the Countess, "the whole Court might listen; but your Majesty may prefer hearing me in the presence of one or two of your counsellors."

"Ormond," said the King, looking around, "attend us for an instant—and do you, Arlington, do the same."

The King led the way into an adjoining cabinet, and, seating himself, requested the Countess would also take a chair. "It needs not, sire," she replied; then pausing for a moment, as if to collect her spirits, she proceeded with firmness.

"Your Majesty well said that no light cause had drawn me from my lonely habitation. I came not hither when the property of my son—that property which descended to him from a father who died for your Majesty's rights—was conjured away from him under pretext of justice, that it might first feed the avarice of the rebel Fairfax, and then supply the prodigality of his son-in-law, Buckingham."

"These are over harsh terms, lady," said the King. "A legal penalty was, as we remember, incurred by an act of irregular violence—so our courts and our laws term it, though personally I have no objection to call it, with you, an honourable revenge. But admit it were such, in prosecution of the laws of honour, bitter legal consequences are often necessarily incurred."

"I come not to argue for my son's wasted and forfeited inheritance, sire," said the Countess; "I only take credit for my patience, under that afflicting dispensation. I now come to redeem the honour of the House of Derby, more dear to me than all the treasures and lands which ever belonged to it."

"And by whom is the honour of the House of Derby impeached?" said the King; "for on my word you bring me the first news of it."

"Has there one Narrative, as these wild fictions are termed, been printed with regard to the Popish Plot—this pretended Plot as I will call it—in which the honour of our house has not been touched and tainted? And are there not two noble gentlemen, father and son, allies of the House of Stanley, about to be placed in jeopardy of their lives, on account of matters in which we are the parties first impeached?"

The King looked around, and smiled to Arlington and Ormond. "The Countess's courage, methinks, shames ours. What lips dared have called the immaculate Plot *pretended*, or the Narrative of the witnesses, our preservers from Popish knives, a wild fiction?—But, madam," he said, "though I admire the generosity of your interference in behalf of the two Peverils, I must acquaint you, that your interference is unnecessary—they are this morning acquitted."

"Now may God be praised!" said the Countess, folding her hands. "I have scarce slept since I heard the news of their impeachment; and have arrived here to surrender myself to your Majesty's justice, or to the prejudices of the nation, in hopes, by so doing, I might at least save the lives of my noble and generous friends, enveloped in suspicion only, or chiefly, by their connection with us.—Are they indeed acquitted?"

"They are, by my honour," said the King. "I marvel you heard it not."

"I arrived but last night, and remained in the strictest seclusion," said the Countess, "afraid to make any inquiries that might occasion discovery ere I saw your Majesty."

"And now that we *have* met," said the King, taking her hand kindly—"a meeting which gives me the greatest pleasure—may I recommend to you speedily to return to your royal island with as little *éclat* as you came thither? The world, my dear Countess, has changed since we were young. Men fought in the Civil War with good swords and muskets; but now we fight with indictments and oaths, and such like legal weapons. You are no adept in such warfare; and though I am well aware you know how to hold out a castle, I doubt much if you have the art to parry off an impeachment. This Plot has come upon us like a land storm—there is no steering the vessel in the teeth of the tempest—we must run for the nearest haven, and happy if we can reach one."

"This is cowardice, my liege," said the Countess—"Forgive the word!—it is but a woman who speaks it. Call your noble friends around you, and make a stand like your royal father. There is but one right and one wrong—one honourable and forward course; and all others which deviate are oblique and unworthy."

"Your language, my venerated friend," said Ormond, who saw the necessity of interfering betwixt the dignity of the actual Sovereign and the freedom of the Countess, who was generally accustomed to receive, not to pay observance,—"your language is strong and decided, but it applies not to the times. It might occasion a renewal of the Civil War, and of all its miseries, but could hardly be attended with the effects you sanguinely anticipate."

"You are too rash, my Lady Countess," said Arlington, "not only to rush upon this danger yourself, but to desire to involve his Majesty. Let me say plainly, that, in this jealous time, you have done but ill to exchange the security of Castle Rushin for the chance of a lodging in the Tower of London."

"And were I to kiss the block there," said the Countess, "as did my husband at Bolton-on-the-Moors, I would do so willingly, rather than forsake a friend!—and one, too, whom, as in the case of the younger Peveril, I have thrust upon danger."

"But have I not assured you that both of the Peverils, elder and younger, are freed from peril?" said the King; "and, my dear Countess, what can else tempt you to thrust *yourself* on danger, from which, doubtless, you expect to be relieved by my intervention? Methinks a lady of your judgment should not voluntarily throw herself into a river, merely that her friends might have the risk and merit of dragging her out."

The Countess reiterated her intention to claim a fair trial. —The two counsellors again pressed their advice that she should withdraw, though under the charge of absconding from justice, and remain in her own feudal kingdom.

The King, seeing no termination to the debate, gently reminded the Countess that her Majesty would be jealous if he detained her ladyship longer, and offered her his hand to conduct her back to the company. This she was under the necessity of accepting, and returned accordingly to the apartments of state, where an event occurred immediately afterwards, which must be transferred to the next chapter.

CHAPTER XLVI

Here stand I tight and trim,
Quick of eye, though little of limb;
He who denieth the word I have spoken,
Betwixt him and me shall lances be broken.
—LAY OF THE LITTLE JOHN DE SAINTRE.

WHEN Charles had reconducted the Countess of Derby into the presence-chamber, before he parted with her, he entreated her, in a whisper, to be governed by good counsel, and to regard her own safety; and then turned easily from her, as if to distribute his attentions equally among the other guests.

These were a good deal circumscribed at the instant, by the arrival of a party of five or six musicians; one of whom, a German, under the patronage of the Duke of Buckingham, was particularly renowned for his performance on the violoncello, but had been detained in inactivity in the antechamber by the non-arrival of his instrument, which had now at length made its appearance.

The domestic who placed it before the owner, shrouded as it was within its wooden case, seemed heartily glad to be rid of his load, and lingered for a moment, as if interested in discovering what sort of instrument was to be produced that could weigh so heavily. His curiosity was satisfied, and in a most extraordinary manner; for, while the musician was fumbling with the key, the case being for his greater convenience placed upright against the wall, the case and instrument itself at once flew open, and out started the dwarf, Geoffrey Hudson,—at sight of whose unearthly appearance, thus suddenly introduced, the ladies shrieked, and ran backwards; the gentlemen started, and the poor German, on seeing the portentous delivery of his fiddle-case, tumbled on the floor in an agony, supposing, it might be, that his instrument was metamorphosed into the strange figure which supplied its place. So soon, however, as he recovered, he glided out of the apartment, and was followed by most of his companions.

"Hudson!" said the King—"My little old friend, I am not sorry to see you; though Buckingham, who I suppose is the purveyor of this jest, hath served us up but a stale one."

"Will your Majesty honour me with one moment's attention?" said Hudson.

"Assuredly, my good friend," said the King. "Old acquaintances are springing up in every quarter to-night; and our leisure can hardly be better employed than in listening to them.—It was an idle trick of Buckingham," he added, in a whisper to Ormond, "to send the poor thing hither, especially as he was to-day tried for the affair of the Plot. At any rate he comes not to ask protection from us, having had the rare fortune to come off *Plot-free*. He is but fishing, I suppose, for some little present or pension."

The little man, precise in Court etiquette, yet impatient of the King's delaying to attend to him, stood in the midst of the floor, most valorously pawing and prancing, like a Scots pony assuming the airs of a war-horse, waving meanwhile his little hat with the tarnished feather, and bowing from time to time, as if impatient to be heard.

"Speak on, then, my friend," said Charles; "if thou hast some poetical address penned for thee, out with it, that thou mayst have time to repose these flourishing little limbs of thine."

"No poetical speech have I, most mighty Sovereign," answered the dwarf; "but, in plain and most loyal prose, I do accuse, before this company, the once noble Duke of Buckingham of high treason!"

"Well spoken, and manfully—Get on, man," said the King, who never doubted that this was the introduction to something burlesque or witty, not conceiving that the charge was made in solemn earnest.

A great laugh took place among such courtiers as heard, and among many who did not hear, what was uttered by the dwarf; the former entertained by the extravagant emphasis and gesticulation of the little champion, and the others laughing not the less loud that they laughed for example's sake, and upon trust.

"What matter is there for all this mirth?" said he, very indignantly—"Is it fit subject for laughing, that I, Geoffrey Hudson, Knight, do, before King and nobles, impeach George Villiers, Duke of Buckingham, of high treason?"

"No subject of mirth, certainly," said Charles, composing his features; "but great matter of wonder.—Come, cease this mouthing, and prancing, and mummery.—If there be a jest, come out with it, man; and if not, even get thee to the beauffet, and drink a cup of wine to refresh thee after thy close lodging."

"I tell you, my liege," said Hudson impatiently, yet in a whisper, intended only to be audible by the King, "that if you spend overmuch time in trifling, you will be convinced by dire experience of Buckingham's treason. I tell you,—I asseverate to your Majesty,—two hundred armed fanatics will be here within the hour, to surprise the guards."

"Stand back, ladies," said the King, "or you may hear more than you will care to listen to. My Lord of Buckingham's jests are not always, you know, quite fitted for female ears; besides, we want a few words in private with our little friend. You, my Lord of Ormond—you, Arlington" (and he named one or two others), "may remain with us."

The gay crowd bore back, and dispersed through the apartment—the men to conjecture what the end of this mummery, as they supposed it, was likely to prove; and what jest, as Sedley said, the bass-fiddle had been brought to bed of—and the ladies to admire and criticise the antique dress, and richly embroidered ruff and hood of the Countess of Derby, to whom the Queen was showing particular attention.

"And now, in the name of Heaven, and amongst friends," said the King to the dwarf, "what means all this?"

"Treason, my lord the King!—Treason to his Majesty of England!—When I was chambered in yonder instrument, my lord, the High-Dutch fellows who bore me, carried me into a certain chapel, to see, as they said to each other, that all was ready. Sire, I went where bass-fiddle never went before, even into a conventicle of Fifth-Monarchists; and when they brought me away, the preacher was concluding his sermon, and was within a 'Now to apply' of setting off like the bell-wether at the head of his flock, to surprise your Majesty in your royal Court! I heard him through the sound-holes of my instrument, when the fellow set me down for a moment to profit by this precious doctrine."

"It would be singular," said Lord Arlington, "were there some reality at the bottom of this buffoonery; for we know these wild men have been consulting together to-day, and five conventicles have held a solemn fast."

"Nay," said the King, "if that be the case, they are certainly determined on some villainy."

"Might I advise," said the Duke of Ormond, "I would summon the Duke of Buckingham to this presence. His connections with the fanatics are well known, though he affects to conceal them."

"You would not, my lord, do his Grace the injustice to treat him as a criminal on such a charge as this?" said the King. "However," he added, after a moment's consideration, "Buckingham is accessible to every sort of temptation, from the flightiness of his genius. I should not be surprised if he nourished hopes of an aspiring kind—I think we had some proof of it but lately.—Hark ye, Chiffinch; go to him instantly, and bring him here on any fair pretext thou canst devise. I would fain save him from what lawyers call an overt act. The Court would be dull as a dead horse were Buckingham to miscarry."

"Will not your Majesty order the Horse Guards to turn out?" said young Selby, who was present, and an officer.

"No, Selby," said the King, "I like not horse-play. But let them be prepared; and let the High Bailiff collect his civil officers, and command the Sheriffs to summon their worshipful attendants from javelin-men to hangmen, and have them in readiness, in case of any sudden tumult—double the sentinels on the doors of the palace—and see no strangers get in."

"Or *out*," said the Duke of Ormond. "Where are the foreign fellows who brought in the dwarf?"

They were sought for, but they were not to be found. They had retreated, leaving their instruments—a circumstance which seemed to bear hard on the Duke of Buckingham, their patron.

Hasty preparations were made to provide resistance to any effort of despair which the supposed conspirators might be driven to; and in the meanwhile, the King, withdrawing with Arlington, Ormond, and a few other counsellors, into the cabinet where the Countess of Derby had had her audience, resumed the examination of the little discoverer. His declaration, though singular, was quite coherent; the strain of romance intermingled with it, being in fact a part of his character, which often gained him the fate of being laughed at, when he would otherwise have been pitied, or even esteemed.

He commenced with a flourish about his sufferings for the Plot, which the impatience of Ormond would have cut short, had not the King reminded his Grace, that a top, when it is not flogged, must needs go down of itself at the end of a definite time, while the application of the whip may keep it up for hours.

Geoffrey Hudson was, therefore, allowed to exhaust himself on the subject of his prison-house, which he informed the King was not without a beam of light—an emanation of loveliness— a mortal angel—quick of step and beautiful of eye, who had more than once visited his confinement with words of cheering and comfort.

"By my faith," said the King, "they fare better in Newgate than I was aware of. Who would have thought of the little gentleman being solaced with female society in such a place?"

"I pray your Majesty," said the dwarf, after the manner of a solemn protest, "to understand nothing amiss. My devotion to this fair creature is rather like what we poor Catholics pay to the blessed saints, than mixed with any grosser quality. Indeed, she seems rather a sylphid of the Rosicrucian system, than aught more carnal; being slighter, lighter, and less than the females of common life, who have something of that coarseness of make which is doubtless derived from the sinful and gigantic race of the antediluvians."

"Well, say on, man," quoth Charles. "Didst thou not discover this sylph to be a mere mortal wench after all?"

" Who ?—I, my liege ?—Oh, fie ! "

" Nay, little gentleman, do not be so particularly scandalised," said the King ; " I promise you I suspect you of no audacity of gallantry."

"Time wears fast," said the Duke of Ormond impatiently, and looking at his watch. " Chiffinch hath been gone ten minutes, and ten minutes will bring him back."

" True," said Charles gravely. " Come to the point, Hudson ; and tell us what this female has to do with your coming hither in this extraordinary manner."

"Everything, my lord," said little Hudson. " I saw her twice during my confinement in Newgate, and, in my thought, she is the very angel who guards my life and welfare ; for, after my acquittal, as I walked towards the city with two tall gentlemen, who had been in trouble along with me, and just while we stood to our defence against a rascally mob, and just as I had taken possession of an elevated situation, to have some vantage against the great odds of numbers, I heard a heavenly voice sound, as it were, from a window behind me, counselling me to take refuge in a certain house ; to which measure I readily persuaded my gallant friends the Peverils, who have always shown themselves willing to be counselled by me."

" Showing therein their wisdom at once and modesty," said the King. " But what chanced next ? Be brief—be like thyself, man."

" For a time, sire," said the dwarf, " it seemed as if I were not the principal object of attention. First, the younger Peveril was withdrawn from us by a gentleman of venerable appearance, though something smacking of a Puritan, having boots of neat's leather, and wearing his weapon without a sword-knot. When Master Julian returned, he informed us, for the first time, that we were in the power of a body of armed fanatics who were, as the poet says, prompt for direful act. And your Majesty will remark, that both father and son were in some measure desperate, and disregardful from that moment of the assurances which I gave them, that the star which I was bound to worship, would, in her own time, shine forth in signal of our safety. May it please your Majesty, in answer to my hilarious exhortations to confidence, the father did but say *tush*, and the son *pshaw*, which showed how men's prudence and manners are disturbed by affliction. Nevertheless, these two gentlemen, the Peverils, forming a strong opinion of the necessity there was to break forth, were it only to convey a knowledge of these dangerous passages to your Majesty, commenced an assault on the door of the apartment, I also assisting with the strength which Heaven hath given, and some three-score years have left me. We could not, as it unhappily proved, manage our attempt so silently, but that our guards overheard us, and, entering in numbers, separated us from each other, and compelled my companions, at point of pike and poniard, to go to some other and more distant apartment, thus separating our fair society. I was again enclosed in the now solitary chamber, and I will own that I felt a certain depression of soul. But when bale is at highest, as the poet singeth, boot is at nighest, for a door of hope was suddenly opened——"

"In the name of God, my liege," said the Duke of Ormond, "let this poor creature's story be translated into the language of common sense by some of the scribblers of romances about Court, and we may be able to make meaning of it."

Geoffrey Hudson looked with a frowning countenance of reproof upon the impatient old Irish nobleman, and said, with a very dignified air, "That one Duke upon a poor gentleman's hand was enough at a time, and that, but for his present engagement and dependency with the Duke of Buckingham, he would have endured no such terms from the Duke of Ormond."

"Abate your valour, and diminish your choler, at our request, most puissant Sir Geoffrey Hudson," said the King; "and forgive the Duke of Ormond for my sake; but at all events go on with your story."

Geoffrey Hudson laid his hand on his bosom, and bowed in proud and dignified submission to his Sovereign; then waved his forgiveness gracefully to Ormond, accompanied with a horrible grin, which he designed for a smile of gracious forgiveness and conciliation. "Under the Duke's favour, then," he proceeded, "when I said a door of hope was opened to me, I meant a door behind the tapestry, from whence issued that fair vision—yet not so fair as lustrously dark, like the beauty of a continental night, where the cloudless azure sky shrouds us in a veil more lovely than that of day!—but I note your Majesty's impatience;—enough. I followed my beautiful guide into an apartment, where there lay, strangely intermingled, warlike arms and musical instruments. Amongst these I saw my own late place of temporary obscurity—a violoncello. To my astonishment, she turned around the instrument, and opening it behind by pressure of a spring, showed that it was filled with pistols, daggers, and ammunition made up in bandoleers. 'These,' she said, 'are this night destined to surprise the Court of the unwary Charles'—your Majesty must pardon my using her own words; 'but if thou darest go in their stead, thou mayst be the saviour of king and kingdoms; if thou art afraid, keep secret, I will myself try the adventure.' Now may Heaven forbid, that Geoffrey Hudson were craven enough, said I, to let thee run such a risk! You know not—you cannot know, what belongs to such ambuscades and concealments—I am accustomed to them—havel urked in the pocket of a giant, and have formed the contents of a pasty. 'Get in then,' she said, 'and lose no time.' Nevertheless, while I prepared to obey, I will not deny that some cold apprehensions came over my hot valour, and I confessed to her, if it might be so, I would rather find my way to the palace on my own feet. But she would not listen to me, saying hastily, ' I would be intercepted, or refused admittance, and that I must embrace the means she offered me of introduction into the presence, and when there, tell the King to be on his guard—little more is necessary ; for once the scheme is known, it becomes desperate.' Rashly and boldly, I bid adieu to the daylight which was then fading away. She withdrew the contents of the instrument destined for my con-cealment, and having put them behind the chimney-board, introduced me in their room. As she clasped me in, I implored her to warn the men who were to be entrusted with me, to take heed and keep the neck of the violoncello uppermost; but ere I had completed my request, I found I was left alone, and in darkness. Presently, two or three fellows entered, whom, by their language, which I in some sort understood, I perceived to be Germans, and under the influence of the Duke of Buck-ingham. I heard them receive from the leader a charge how they were to deport themselves, when they should assume the concealed arms—and—for I will do the Duke no wrong—I understood their orders were precise, not only to spare the person of the King, but also those of the courtiers, and to pro-tect all who might be in the presence against an irruption of the fanatics. In other respects, they had charge to disarm the Gentlemen-pensioners in the guard-room, and, in fine, to obtain the command of the Court."

The King looked disconcerted and thoughtful at this com-munication, and bade Lord Arlington see that Selby quietly made search into the contents of the other cases which had been brought as containing musical instruments. He then signed to the dwarf to proceed in his story, asking him again and again, and very solemnly, whether he was sure that he heard the Duke's name mentioned, as commanding or approving this action.

The dwarf answered in the affirmative.

"This," said the King, "is carrying the frolic somewhat far."

The dwarf proceeded to state, that he was carried after his metamorphosis into the chapel, where he heard the preacher seemingly about the close of his harangue, the tenor of which he also mentioned. Words, he said, could not express the agony which he felt when he found that his bearer, in placing the instrument in a corner, was about to invert its position, in which case, he said, human frailty might have proved too great for love, for loyalty, for true obedience, nay, for the fear of death, which was like to ensue on discovery; and he concluded, that he greatly doubted he could not have stood on his head for many minutes without screaming aloud.

"I could not have blamed you," said the King; "placed in such a posture in the royal oak, I must needs have roared myself.—Is this all you have to tell us of this strange conspiracy?" Sir Geoffrey Hudson replied in the affirmative, and the King presently subjoined—"Go, my little friend, your services shall not be forgotten. Since thou hast crept into the bowels of a fiddle for our service, we are bound, in duty and conscience, to find you a more roomy dwelling in future."

"It was a violoncello, if your Majesty is pleased to remember," said the little jealous man, "not a common fiddle; though, for your Majesty's service, I would have crept even into a kit."

"Whatever of that nature could have been performed by any subject of ours, thou wouldst have enacted in our behalf—of that we hold ourselves certain. Withdraw for a little; and hark ye, for the present, beware what you say about this matter. Let your appearance be considered—do you mark me —as a frolic of the Duke of Buckingham; and not a word of conspiracy."

"Were it not better to put him under some restraint, sire?" said the Duke of Ormond, when Hudson had left the room.

"It is unnecessary," said the King. "I remember the little wretch of old. Fortune, to make him the model of absurdity, has closed a most lofty soul within that little miserable carcass. For wielding his sword and keeping his word, he is a perfect Don Quixote in decimo-octavo. He shall be taken care of.— But, oddsfish, my lords, is not this freak of Buckingham too villainous and ungrateful?"

"He had not had the means of being so, had your Majesty," said the Duke of Ormond, "been less lenient on other occasions."

"My lord, my lord," said Charles hastily—"your lordship is Buckingham's known enemy—we will take other and more impartial counsel—Arlington, what think you of all this?"

"May it please your Majesty," said Arlington, "I think the thing is absolutely impossible, unless the Duke has had some quarrel with your Majesty, of which we know nothing. His Grace is very flighty, doubtless, but this seems actual insanity."

"Why, faith," said the King, "some words passed betwixt us this morning—his Duchess it seems is dead—and to lose no time, his Grace had cast his eyes about for means of repairing the loss, and had the assurance to ask our consent to woo my niece Lady Anne."

"Which your Majesty of course rejected?" said the statesman.

"And not without rebuking his assurance," added the King.

"In private, sire, or before any witnesses?" said the Duke of Ormond.

"Before no one," said the King,—"excepting, indeed, little Chiffinch; and he, you know, is no one."

"*Hinc illæ lachrymæ*," said Ormond. "I know his Grace well. While the rebuke of his aspiring petulance was a matter betwixt your Majesty and him, he might have let it pass by; but a check before a fellow from whom it was likely enough to travel through the Court, was a matter to be revenged."

Here Selby came hastily from the other room, to say, that his Grace of Buckingham had just entered the presence-chamber.

The King rose. "Let a boat be in readiness, with a party of the yeomen," said he. "It may be necessary to attach him of treason, and send him to the Tower."

"Should not a Secretary of State's warrant be prepared?" said Ormond.

"No, my Lord Duke," said the King sharply. "I still hope that the necessity may be avoided."

CHAPTER XLVII

High-reaching Buckingham grows circumspect.
—RICHARD III.

BEFORE giving the reader an account of the meeting betwixt Buckingham and his injured Sovereign, we may mention a trifling circumstance or two which took place betwixt his Grace and Chiffinch, in the short drive betwixt York Place and Whitehall.

In the outset, the Duke endeavoured to learn from the courtier the special cause of his being summoned so hastily to the Court. Chiffinch answered, cautiously, that he believed there were some gambols going forward, at which the King desired the Duke's presence.

This did not quite satisfy Buckingham, for, conscious of his own rash purpose, he could not but apprehend discovery. After a moment's silence, "Chiffinch," he said abruptly, "did you mention to any one what the King said to me this morning touching the Lady Anne?"

"My Lord Duke," said Chiffinch, hesitating, "surely my duty to the King—my respect to your Grace——"

"You mentioned it to no one, then?" said the Duke sternly.

"To no one," replied Chiffinch faintly, for he was intimidated by the Duke's increasing severity of manner.

"Ye lie, like a scoundrel!" said the Duke—"You told Christian!"

"Your Grace," said Chiffinch—"your Grace—your Grace ought to remember that I told you Christian's secret; that the Countess of Derby was come up."

"And you think the one point of treachery may balance for the other? But no. I must have a better atonement. Be assured I will blow your brains out, ere you leave this carriage, unless you tell me the truth of this message from Court."

As Chiffinch hesitated what reply to make, a man, who, by the blaze of the torches, then always borne, as well by the lackeys who hung behind the carriage, as by the footmen who ran by the side, might easily see who sat in the coach, approached, and sung in a deep manly voice, the burden of an old French song on the battle of Marignan, in which is imitated the German French of the defeated Swiss.

> " Tout est verlore
> La tintelore,
> Tout est verlore
> Bei Got."

"I am betrayed," said the Duke, who instantly conceived that this chorus, expressing "all is lost," was sung by one of his faithful agents, as a hint to him that their machinations were discovered.

He attempted to throw himself from the carriage, but Chiffinch held him with a firm, though respectful grasp. "Do not destroy yourself, my lord," he said, in a tone of deep humility—"there are soldiers and officers of the peace around the carriage, to enforce your Grace's coming to Whitehall, and to prevent your escape. To attempt it would be to confess guilt; and I advise you strongly against that—the King is your friend —be your own."

The Duke, after a moment's consideration, said sullenly, "I believe you are right. Why should I fly, when I am guilty of nothing but sending some fireworks to entertain the Court, instead of a concert of music?"

"And the dwarf, who came so unexpectedly out of the bass-viol——"

"Was a masking device of my own, Chiffinch," said the Duke, though the circumstance was then first known to him. "Chiffinch, you will bind me for ever, if you will permit me to have a minute's conversation with Christian."

"With Christian, my lord?—Where could you find him?— You are aware we must go straight on to the Court."

"True," said the Duke, "but I think I cannot miss finding him; and you, Master Chiffinch, are no officer, and have no warrant either to detain me prisoner, or prevent my speaking to whom I please."

Chiffinch replied, "My Lord Duke, your genius is so great, and your escapes so numerous, that it will be from no wish of my own if I am forced to hurt a man so skilful and so popular."

"Nay, then, there is life in it yet," said the Duke, and whistled; when, from beside the little cutler's booth, with which the reader is acquainted, appeared, suddenly, Master Christian, and was in a moment at the side of the coach. "*Ganz ist verloren*," said the Duke.

"I know it," said Christian; "and all our godly friends are dispersed upon the news. Lucky the Colonel and these German rascals gave a hint. All is safe—You go to Court—Hark ye, I will follow."

"You, Christian? that would be more friendly than wise."

"Why, what is there against me?" said Christian. "I am innocent as the child unborn—so is your Grace. There is but one creature who can bear witness to our guilt; but I trust to bring her on the stage in our favour—besides, if I went not, I should presently be sent for."

"The familiar of whom I have heard you speak, I warrant?"

"Hark in your ear again."

"I understand," said the Duke, "and will delay Master Chiffinch,—for he, you must know, is my conductor,—no longer. —Well, Chiffinch, let them drive on.—*Vogue la Galère!*" he exclaimed, as the carriage went onward; "I have sailed through worse perils than this yet."

"It is not for me to judge," said Chiffinch; "your Grace is a bold commander; and Christian hath the cunning of the devil for a pilot; but——However, I remain your Grace's poor friend, and will heartily rejoice in your extrication."

"Give me a proof of your friendship," said the Duke. "Tell me what you know of Christian's familiar, as he calls her."

"I believe it to be the same dancing wench who came with Empson to my house on the morning that Mistress Alice made her escape from us. But you have seen her, my lord?"

"I?" said the Duke; "when did I see her?"

"She was employed by Christian, I believe, to set his niece at liberty, when he found himself obliged to gratify his fanatical brother-in-law, by restoring his child; besides being prompted by a private desire, as I think, of bantering your Grace."

"Umph! I suspected so much. I will repay it," said the Duke. "But first to get out of this dilemma.—That little Numidian witch, then, was his familiar; and she joined in the plot to tantalise me?—But here we reach Whitehall.—Now,

Chiffinch, be no worse than thy word, and—now, Buckingham, be thyself!"

But ere we follow Buckingham into the presence, where he had so difficult a part to sustain, it may not be amiss to follow Christian after his brief conversation with him. On re-entering the house, which he did by a circuitous passage, leading from a distant alley, and through several courts, Christian hastened to a low matted apartment, in which Bridgenorth sat alone, reading the Bible by the light of a small brazen lamp, with the utmost serenity of countenance.

" Have you dismissed the Peverils ? " said Christian hastily.

" I have," said the Major.

" And upon what pledge—that they will not carry information against you to Whitehall ? "

" They gave me their promise voluntarily, when I showed them our armed friends were dismissed. To-morrow, I believe, it is their purpose to lodge informations."

" And why not to-night, I pray you ? " said Christian.

" Because they allow us that time for escape."

" Why, then, do you not avail yourself of it ? Wherefore are you here ? " said Christian.

" Nay, rather, why do *you* not fly ? " said Bridgenorth. " Of a surety, you are as deeply engaged as I."

" Brother Bridgenorth, I am the fox, who knows a hundred modes of deceiving the hounds ; you are the deer, whose sole resource is in hasty flight. Therefore lose no time—begone to the country—or rather, Zedekiah Fish's vessel, the *Good Hope*, lies in the river, bound for Massachusetts—take the wings of the morning, and begone—she can fall down to Gravesend with the tide."

" And leave to thee, brother Christian," said Bridgenorth, " the charge of my fortune and my daughter ? No, brother ; my opinion of your good faith must be re-established ere I again trust thee."

" Go thy ways, then, for a suspicious fool," said Christian, suppressing his strong desire to use language more offensive ; " or rather stay where thou art, and take thy chance of the gallows ! "

" It is appointed to all men to die once," said Bridgenorth ; " my life hath been a living death. My fairest boughs have been stripped by the axe of the forester—that which survives must, if it shall blossom, be grafted elsewhere, and at a distance from my aged trunk. The sooner, then, the root feels the axe, the stroke is more welcome. I had been pleased, indeed, had I been called to bringing yonder licentious Court to a purer character, and relieving the yoke of the suffering people of God. That youth too—son to that precious woman, to whom I

owe the last tie that feebly links my wearied spirit to humanity
—could I have travailed with *him* in the good cause !—But that,
with all my other hopes is broken for ever ; and since I am not
worthy to be an instrument in so great a work, I have little
desire to abide longer in this vale of sorrow."

"Farewell, then, desponding fool !" said Christian, unable,
with all his calmness, any longer to suppress his contempt for
the resigned and hopeless predestinarian. "That fate should
have clogged me with such confederates !" he muttered, as he
left the apartment—"this bigoted fool is now nearly irreclaim-
able—I must to Zarah ; for she, or no one, must carry us through
these straits. If I can but soothe her sullen temper, and excite
her vanity to action,—betwixt her address, the King's partiality
for the Duke, Buckingham's matchless effrontery, and my own
hand upon the helm, we may yet weather the tempest that
darkens around us. But what we do must be hastily done."

In another apartment he found the person he sought—the
same who visited the Duke of Buckingham's harem, and,
having relieved Alice Bridgenorth from her confinement there,
had occupied her place as has been already narrated, or rather
intimated. She was now much more plainly attired than when
she had tantalised the Duke with her presence ; but her dress
had still something of the Oriental character, which corresponded with the dark complexion and quick eye of the wearer.
She had the kerchief at her eyes as Christian entered the
apartment, but suddenly withdrew it, and, flashing on him
a glance of scorn and indignation, asked him what he meant
by intruding where his company was alike unsought for and
undesired.

"A proper question," said Christian, "from a slave to her
master !"

"Rather say, a proper question, and of all questions the most
proper, from a mistress to her slave ! Know you not, that from
the hour in which you discovered your ineffable baseness, you
have made me mistress of your lot ? While you seemed but a
demon of vengeance, you commanded terror, and to good
purpose ; but such a foul fiend as thou hast of late shown thyself—such a very worthless, base trickster of the devil—such a
sordid grovelling imp of perdition, can gain nothing but scorn
from a soul like mine."

"Gallantly mouthed," said Christian, "and with good emphasis."

"Yes," answered Zarah, "I can speak—sometimes—I can
also be mute ; and that no one knows better than thou."

"Thou art a spoiled child, Zarah, and dost but abuse the
indulgence I entertain for your freakish humour," replied
Christian ; "thy wits have been disturbed since ever you landed
in England, and all for the sake of one who cares for thee no

more than for the most worthless object who walks the streets, amongst whom he left you to engage in a brawl for one he loved better."

"It is no matter," said Zarah, obviously repressing very bitter emotion; "it signifies not that he loves another better; there is none—no, none—that ever did, or can, love him so well."

"I pity you, Zarah!" said Christian, with some scorn.

"I deserve your pity," she replied, "were your pity worth my accepting. Whom have I to thank for my wretchedness but you?—You bred me up in thirst of vengeance, ere I knew that good and evil were anything better than names;—to gain your applause, and to gratify the vanity you had excited, I have for years undergone a penance, from which a thousand would have shrunk."

"A thousand, Zarah!" answered Christian; "ay, a hundred thousand, and a million to boot; the creature is not on earth, being mere mortal woman, that would have undergone the thirtieth part of thy self-denial."

"I believe it," said Zarah, drawing up her slight but elegant figure; "I believe it—I have gone through a trial that few indeed could have sustained. I have renounced the dear intercourse of my kind; compelled my tongue only to utter, like that of a spy, the knowledge which my ear had only collected as a base eavesdropper. This I have done for years—for years —and all for the sake of your private applause—and the hope of vengeance on a woman, who, if she did ill in murdering my father, has been bitterly repaid by nourishing a serpent in her bosom, that had the tooth, but not the deafened ear, of the adder."

"Well—well—well," reiterated Christian; "and had you not your reward in my approbation—in the consciousness of your own unequalled dexterity—by which, superior to anything of thy sex that history has ever known, you endured what woman never before endured, insolence without notice, admiration without answer, and sarcasm without reply?"

"Not without reply!" said Zarah fiercely. "Gave not Nature to my feelings a course of expression more impressive than words? and did not those tremble at my shrieks, who would have little minded my entreaties or my complaints? And my proud lady, who sauced her charities with the taunts she thought I heard not—she was justly paid by the passing of her dearest and most secret concerns into the hands of her mortal enemy; and the vain Earl—yet he was a thing as insignificant as the plume that nodded in his cap;—and the maidens and ladies who taunted me—I had, or can easily have, my revenge upon them. But there is *one*," she added, looking upward, "who never taunted me; one whose generous feelings could treat the poor dumb girl even as his sister; who never spoke word of her but it was to excuse or defend—and you tell me I must not love him, and that it is madness to love him!—I *will* be mad then, for I will love him till the latest breath of my life!"

"Think but an instant, silly girl—silly but in one respect, since in all others thou mayest brave the world of women. Think what I have proposed to thee, for the loss of this hopeless affection, a career so brilliant!—Think only that it rests with thyself to be the wife—the wedded wife—of the princely Buckingham! With my talents—with thy wit and beauty—with his passionate love of these attributes — a short space might rank you among England's princesses.—Be but guided by me—he is now at deadly pass—needs every assistance to retrieve his fortunes—above all, that which we alone can render him. Put yourself under my conduct, and not fate itself shall prevent your wearing a Duchess's coronet."

"A coronet of thistle-down, entwined with thistle-leaves," said Zarah.—"I know not a slighter thing than your Buckingham! I saw him at your request—saw him when, as a man, he should have shown himself generous and noble—I stood the proof at your desire, for I laugh at those dangers from which the poor blushing wailers of my sex shrink and withdraw themselves. What did I find him?—a poor wavering voluptuary—his nearest attempt to passion like the fire on a wretched stubble-field, that may singe, indeed, or smoke, but can neither warm nor devour. Christian! were his coronet at my feet this moment, I would sooner take up a crown of gilded gingerbread, than extend my hand to raise it."

"You are mad, Zarah—with all your taste and talent, you are utterly mad! But let Buckingham pass—Do you owe *me* nothing on this emergency?—Nothing to one who rescued you from the cruelty of your owner, the posture-master, to place you in ease and affluence?"

"Christian," she replied, "I owe you much. Had I not felt I did so, I would, as I have been often tempted to do, have denounced thee to the fierce Countess, who would have gibbeted you on her feudal walls of Castle Rushin, and bid your family seek redress from the eagles, that would long since have thatched their nest with your hair, and fed their young ospreys with your flesh."

"I am truly glad you have had so much forbearance for me," answered Christian.

"I have it, in truth and in sincerity," replied Zarah—"Not for your benefits to me—such as they were, they were every one interested, and conferred from the most selfish considerations. I have overpaid them a thousand times by the devotion to your will, which I have displayed at the greatest personal risk. But till of late I respected your powers of mind—your inimitable command of passion—the force of intellect which I have ever seen you exercise over all others, from the bigot Bridgenorth to the debauched Buckingham—in that, indeed, I have recognised my master."

"And those powers," said Christian, "are unlimited as ever; and with thy assistance, thou shalt see the strongest meshes that the laws of civil society ever wove to limit the natural dignity of man, broke asunder like a spider's web."

She paused and answered, "While a noble motive fired thee—ay, a noble motive, though irregular—for I was born to gaze on the sun which the pale daughters of Europe shrink from—I could serve thee—I could have followed, while revenge or ambition had guided thee—but love of *wealth*, and by what means acquired !—What sympathy can I hold with that ?—Wouldst thou not have pandered to the lust of the King, though the object was thine own orphan niece ?—You smile ? —Smile again when I ask you whether you meant not my own prostitution, when you charged me to remain in the house of that wretched Buckingham ?—Smile at that question, and by Heaven, I stab you to the heart !" And she thrust her hand into her bosom, and partly showed the hilt of a small poniard.

"And if I smile," said Christian, "it is but in scorn of so odious an accusation. Girl, I will not tell thee the reason, but there exists not on earth the living thing over whose safety and honour I would keep watch as over thine. Buckingham's wife, indeed, I wished thee ; and through thy own beauty and thy wit, I doubted not to bring the match to pass."

"Vain flatterer," said Zarah, yet seeming soothed even by the flattery which she scoffed at, "you would persuade me that it was honourable love which you expected the Duke was to have offered me. How durst you urge so gross a deception, to which time, place, and circumstance gave the lie ?—How dare you now again mention it, when you well know, that at the time you mention, the Duchess was still in life ?"

"In life, but on her deathbed," said Christian; "and for time, place, and circumstance, had your virtue, my Zarah, depended on these, how couldst thou have been the creature thou art ? I knew thee all-sufficient to bid him defiance—else —for thou art dearer to me than thou thinkest—I had not risked thee to win the Duke of Buckingham ; ay, and the kingdom of England to boot. So now, wilt thou be ruled and go on with me ?"

Zarah, or Fenella, for our readers must have been long aware of the identity of these two personages, cast down her eyes, and was silent for a long time. "Christian," she said at last, in a solemn voice, "if my ideas of right and of wrong be wild and incoherent, I owe it, first, to the wild fever which my native sun communicated to my veins; next, to my child-hood, trained amidst the shifts, tricks, and feats of jugglers and mountebanks; and then, to a youth of fraud and decep-tion, through the course thou didst prescribe me, in which I might, indeed, hear everything, but communicate with no one. The last cause of my wild errors, if such they are, originates, O Christian, with you alone; by whose intrigues I was placed with yonder lady, and who taught me, that to revenge my father's death, was my first great duty on earth, and that I was bound by nature to hate and injure her by whom I was fed and fostered, though as she would have fed and caressed a dog, or any other mute animal. I also think—for I will deal fairly with you—that you had not so easily detected your niece, in the child whose surprising agility was making yonder brutal mountebank's fortune; nor so readily induced him to part with his bond-slave, had you not, for your own purposes, placed me under his charge, and reserved the privilege of claiming me when you pleased. I could not, under any other tuition, have identified myself with the personage of a mute, which it has been your desire that I should perform through life."

"You do me injustice, Zarah," said Christian—"I found you capable of discharging, to an uncommon degree, a task necessary to the avenging of your father's death—I consecrated you to it, as I consecrated my own life and hopes; and you held the duty sacred, till these mad feelings towards a youth who loves your cousin——"

"Who—loves—my—cousin," repeated Zarah (for we will continue to call her by her real name) slowly, and as if the words dropped unconsciously from her lips. "Well—be it so! —Man of many wiles, I will follow thy course for a little, a very little farther; but take heed—tease me not with remonstrances against the treasure of my secret thoughts—I mean my most hopeless affection to Julian Peveril—and bring me not as an assistant to any snare which you may design to cast around him. You and your Duke shall rue the hour most bitterly, in which you provoke me. You may suppose you have me in your power; but remember, the snakes of my burning climate are never so fatal as when you grasp them."

"I care not for these Peverils," said Christian—"I care not for their fate a poor straw, unless where it bears on that of the destined woman, whose hands are red in your father's blood. Believe me, I can divide her fate and theirs. I will explain to you how. And for the Duke, he may pass among men of the town for wit, and among soldiers for valour, among courtiers for manners and for form; and why, with his high rank and immense fortune, you should throw away an opportunity, which, as I could now improve it——"

"Speak not of it," said Zarah, "if thou wouldst have our truce—remember it is no peace—if, I say, thou wouldst have our truce grow to be an hour old!"

"This, then," said Christian, with a last effort to work upon the vanity of this singular being, "is she who pretended such superiority to human passion, that she could walk indifferently and unmoved through the halls of the prosperous, and the prison cells of the captive, unknowing and unknown, sympathising neither with the pleasures of the one, nor the woes of the other, but advancing with sure, though silent steps, her own plans, in despite and regardless of either!"

"My own plans!" said Zarah—"*Thy* plans, Christian—thy plans of extorting from the surprised prisoners, means whereby to convict them—thine own plans, formed with those more powerful than thyself, to sound men's secrets, and, by using them as a matter of accusation, to keep up the great delusion of the nation."

"Such access was indeed given you as my agent," said Christian, "and for advancing a great national change. But how did you use it?—to advance your insane passion."

"Insane!" said Zarah—"Had he been less than insane whom I addressed, he and I had ere now been far from the toils which you have pitched for us both. I had means prepared for everything; and ere this, the shores of Britain had been lost to our sight for ever."

"The dwarf, too," said Christian—"Was it worthy of you to delude that poor creature with flattering visions—lull him asleep with drugs! Was *that* my doing?"

"He was my destined tool," said Zarah haughtily. "I remembered your lessons too well not to use him as such. Yet scorn him not too much. I tell you, that yon very miserable dwarf, whom I made my sport in the prison—yon wretched abortion of nature, I would select for a husband, ere I would marry your Buckingham;—the vain and imbecile pigmy has yet the warm heart and noble feelings, that a man should hold his highest honour."

"In God's name, then, take your own way," said Christian; "and, for my sake, let never man hereafter limit a woman in the use of her tongue, since he must make it amply up to her, in allowing her the privilege of her own will. Who would have thought it? But the colt has slipped the bridle, and I must needs follow, since I cannot guide her."

Our narrative returns to the Court of King Charles at Whitehall.

CHAPTER XLVIII

———But oh!
What shall I say to thee, Lord Scroop; thou cruel,
Ingrateful, savage, and inhuman creature!
Thou that didst bear the key of all my counsels,
That knew'st the very bottom of my soul,
That almost mightst have coined me into gold,
Wouldst thou have practised on me for thy use?

—HENRY V.

AT no period of his life, not even when that life was in imminent danger, did the constitutional gaiety of Charles seem more overclouded, than when waiting for the return of Chiffinch with the Duke of Buckingham. His mind revolted at the idea, that the person to whom he had been so particularly indulgent, and whom he had selected as the friend of his lighter hours and amusements, should prove capable of having tampered with a plot apparently directed against his liberty and life. He more than once examined the dwarf anew, but could extract nothing more than his first narrative contained. The apparition of the female to him in the cell of Newgate, he described in such fanciful and romantic colours, that the King could not help thinking the poor man's head a little turned; and, as nothing was found in the kettledrum, and other musical instruments brought for the use of the Duke's band of foreigners, he nourished some slight hope that the whole plan might be either a mere jest, or that the idea of an actual conspiracy was founded in mistake.

The persons who had been despatched to watch the motions of Mr. Weiver's congregation, brought back word that they had quietly dispersed. It was known, at the same time, that they had met in arms, but this augured no particular design of aggression, at a time when all true Protestants conceived themselves in danger of immediate massacre; when the fathers of the city had repeatedly called out the Train-Bands, and alarmed the citizens of London, under the idea of an instant insurrection of the Catholics; and when, to sum the whole up, in the emphatic words of an alderman of the day, there was a general belief that they would all waken some unhappy morning with their throats cut. Who was to do these dire deeds, it was more difficult to suppose; but all admitted the possibility that they might be achieved, since one Justice of the Peace was already murdered. There was, therefore, no inference of hostile intentions against the State, to be decidedly derived from a congregation of Protestants *par excellence*, military from old associations, bringing their arms with them to a place of worship, in the midst of a panic so universal.

Neither did the violent language of the minister, supposing that to be proved, absolutely infer meditated violence. The favourite parables of the preachers, and the metaphors and ornaments which they selected, were at all times of a military cast; and the taking the kingdom of heaven by storm, a strong and beautiful metaphor, when used generally as in Scripture, was detailed in their sermons in all the technical language of the attack and defence of a fortified place. The danger, in short, whatever might have been its actual degree, had disappeared as suddenly as a bubble upon the water, when broken by a casual touch, and had left as little trace behind it. It became, therefore, matter of much doubt, whether it had ever actually existed.

While various reports were making from without, and while their tenor was discussed by the King, and such nobles and statesmen as he thought proper to consult on the occasion, a gradual sadness and anxiety mingled with, and finally silenced, the mirth of the evening. All became sensible that something unusual was going forward; and the unwonted distance which Charles maintained from his guests, while it added greatly to the dulness that began to predominate in the presence-chamber, gave intimation that something unusual was labouring in the King's mind.

Thus play was neglected—the music was silent, or played without being heard—gallants ceased to make compliments, and ladies to expect them; and a sort of apprehensive curiosity pervaded the circle. Each asked the others why they were grave; and no answer was returned, any more than could have been rendered by a herd of cattle instinctively disturbed by the approach of a thunderstorm.

To add to the general apprehension, it began to be whispered, that one or two of the guests, who were desirous of leaving the palace, had been informed no one could be permitted to retire until the general hour of dismissal. And these, gliding back into the hall, communicated in whispers that the sentinels at the gates were doubled, and that there was a troop of the Horse Guards drawn up in the court—circumstances so unusual, as to excite the most anxious curiosity.

Such was the state of the Court, when wheels were heard without, and the bustle which took place denoted the arrival of some person of consequence.

"Here comes Chiffinch," said the King, "with his prey in his clutch."

It was indeed the Duke of Buckingham; nor did he approach the royal presence without emotion. On entering the court, the flambeaux which were borne around the carriage gleamed on the scarlet coats, laced hats, and drawn broadswords of the Horse Guards—a sight unusual, and calculated to strike terror into a conscience which was none of the clearest.

The Duke alighted from the carriage, and only said to the officer, whom he saw upon duty, "You are late under arms to-night, Captain Carleton."

"Such are our orders, sir," answered Carleton, with military brevity; and then commanded the four dismounted sentinels at the under gate to make way for the Duke of Buckingham. His Grace had no sooner entered, than he heard behind him the command, "Move close up, sentinels—closer yet to the gate." And he felt as if all chance of rescue were excluded by the sound.

As he advanced up the grand staircase, there were other symptoms of alarm and precaution. The Yeomen of the Guard were mustered in unusual numbers, and carried carabines instead of their halberds; and the Gentlemen-pensioners, with their partisans, appeared also in proportional force. In short, all that sort of defence which the royal household possesses within itself, seemed, for some hasty and urgent reason, to have been placed under arms, and upon duty.

Buckingham ascended the royal staircase with an eye attentive to these preparations, and a step steady and slow, as if he counted each step on which he trode. "Who," he asked himself, "shall ensure Christian's fidelity? Let him but stand fast, and we are secure. Otherwise——"

As he shaped the alternative, he entered the presence-chamber.

The King stood in the midst of the apartment, surrounded by the personages with whom he had been consulting. The rest of the brilliant assembly, scattered into groups, looked on at some distance. All were silent when Buckingham entered, in hopes of receiving some explanation of the mysteries of the evening. All bent forward, though etiquette forbade them to advance, to catch, if possible, something of what was about to pass betwixt the King and his intriguing statesman. At the same time, those counsellors who stood around Charles, drew back on either side, so as to permit the Duke to pay his respects to his Majesty in the usual form. He went through the ceremonial with his accustomed grace, but was received by Charles with much unwonted gravity.

"We have waited for you for some time, my Lord Duke. It is long since Chiffinch left us, to request your attendance here. I see you are elaborately dressed. Your toilette was needless on the present occasion."

"Needless to the splendour of your Majesty's Court," said

the Duke, "but not needless on my part. This chanced to be
Black Monday at York Place, and my club of *Pendables* were
in full glee when your Majesty's summons arrived. I could not
be in the company of Ogle, Maniduc, Dawson, and so forth, but
what I must needs make some preparation, and some ablution,
ere entering the circle here."

"I trust the purification will be complete," said the King,
without any tendency to the smile which always softened
features, that, ungilded by its influence, were dark, harsh, and
even severe. "We wished to ask your Grace concerning the
import of a sort of musical mask which you designed us here,
but which miscarried, as we are given to understand."

"It must have been a great miscarriage indeed," said the
Duke, "since your Majesty looks so serious on it. I thought
to have done your Majesty a pleasure (as I have seen you condescend to be pleased with such passages), by sending the
contents of that bass-viol; but I fear the jest has been unac-
ceptable—I fear the fireworks may have done mischief."

"Not the mischief they were designed for, perhaps," said
the King gravely; "you see, my lord, we are all alive, and
unsinged."

"Long may your Majesty remain so," said the Duke; "yet
I see there is something misconstrued on my part—it must be
a matter unpardonable, however little intended, since it hath
displeased so indulgent a master."

"Too indulgent a master, indeed, Buckingham," replied the
King; "and the fruit of my indulgence has been to change
loyal men into traitors."

"May it please your Majesty, I cannot understand this,"
said the Duke.

"Follow us, my lord," answered Charles, "and we will
endeavour to explain our meaning."

Attended by the same lords who stood around him, and
followed by the Duke of Buckingham, on whom all eyes were
fixed, Charles retired into the same cabinet which had been
the scene of repeated consultations in the course of the evening. There, leaning with his arms crossed on the back of an
easy-chair, Charles proceeded to interrogate the suspected
nobleman.

"Let us be plain with each other. Speak out, Buckingham.
What, in one word, was to have been the regale intended for
us this evening?"

"A petty mask, my lord. I had destined a little dancing-
girl to come out of that instrument, who, I thought, would have
performed to your Majesty's liking—a few Chinese fireworks
there were, which, thinking the entertainment was to have
taken place in the marble hall, might, I hoped, have been

discharged with good effect, and without the slightest alarm, at the first appearance of my little sorceress, and were designed to have masked, as it were, her entrance upon the stage. I hope there have been no perukes singed—no ladies frightened—no hopes of noble descent interrupted by my ill-fancied jest."

"We have seen no such fireworks, my lord; and your female dancer, of whom we now hear for the first time, came forth in the form of our old acquaintance Geoffrey Hudson, whose dancing days are surely ended."

"Your Majesty surprises me! I beseech you, let Christian be sent for—Edward Christian—he will be found lodging in a large old house near Sharper the cutler's, in the Strand. As I live by bread, sire, I trusted him with the arrangement of this matter, as indeed the dancing-girl was his property. If he has done aught to dishonour my concert, or disparage my character, he shall die under the baton."

"It is singular," said the King, "and I have often observed it, that this fellow Christian bears the blame of all men's enormities—he performs the part which, in a great family, is usually assigned to that mischief-doing personage, Nobody. When Chiffinch blunders, he always quotes Christian. When Sheffield writes a lampoon, I am sure to hear of Christian having corrected, or copied, or dispersed it—he is the *ame damnée* of every one about my Court—the scapegoat, who is to carry away all their iniquities; and he will have a cruel load to bear into the wilderness. But for Buckingham's sins, in particular, he is the regular and uniform sponsor; and I am convinced his Grace expects Christian should suffer every penalty he has incurred, in this world or the next."

"Not so," with the deepest reverence replied the Duke. "I have no hope of being either hanged or damned by proxy; but it is clear some one hath tampered with and altered my device. If I am accused of aught, let me at least hear the charge, and see my accuser."

"That is but fair," said the King. "Bring our little friend from behind the chimney-board. [Hudson being accordingly produced, he continued.] There stands the Duke of Buckingham. Repeat before him the tale you told us. Let him hear what were those contents of the bass-viol which were removed that you might enter it. Be not afraid of any one, but speak the truth boldly."

"May it please your Majesty," said Hudson, "fear is a thing unknown to me."

"His body has no room to hold such a passion; or there is too little of it to be worth fearing for," said Buckingham.— "But let him speak."

Ere Hudson had completed his tale, Buckingham interrupted him by exclaiming, "Is it possible that I can be suspected by your Majesty on the word of this pitiful variety of the baboon tribe?"

"Villain-Lord, I appeal thee to the combat!" said the little man, highly offended at the appellation thus bestowed on him.

"La you there now!" said the Duke—"The little animal is quite crazed, and defies a man who need ask no other weapon than a corking-pin to run him through the lungs, and whose single kick could hoist him from Dover to Calais without yacht or wherry. And what can you expect from an idiot, who is *engoué* of a common rope-dancing girl, that capered on a pack-thread at Ghent in Flanders, unless they were to club their talents to set up a booth at Bartholomew Fair?—Is it not plain, that supposing the little animal is not malicious, as indeed his whole kind bear a general and most cankered malice against those who have the ordinary proportions of humanity— Grant, I say, that this were not a malicious falsehood of his, why, what does it amount to?—That he has mistaken squibs and Chinese crackers for arms! He says not he himself touched or handled them; and judging by the sight alone, I question if the infirm old creature, when any whim or preconception hath possession of his noddle, can distinguish betwixt a blunderbuss and a black-pudding."

The horrible clamour which the dwarf made so soon as he heard this disparagement of his military skill—the haste with which he blundered out a detail of his warlike experiences— and the absurd grimaces which he made in order to enforce his story, provoked not only the risibility of Charles, but even of the statesmen around him, and added absurdity to the motley complexion of the scene. The King terminated this dispute, by commanding the dwarf to withdraw.

A more regular discussion of his evidence was then resumed, and Ormond was the first who pointed out, that it went farther than had been noticed, since the little man had mentioned a certain extraordinary and treasonable conversation held by the Duke's dependents, by whom he had been conveyed to the palace.

"I am sure not to lack my lord of Ormond's good word," said the Duke scornfully; "but I defy him alike, and all my other enemies, and shall find it easy to show that this alleged conspiracy, if any grounds for it at all exist, in a mere sham-plot, got up to turn the odium justly attached to the Papists upon the Protestants. Here is a half-hanged creature, who, on the very day he escapes from the gallows, which many believe was his most deserved destiny, comes to take away the reputation of a Protestant Peer—and on what?—on the treasonable conversation of three or four German fiddlers, heard through the sound-holes of a violoncello, and that, too, when the creature was incased in it, and mounted on a man's shoulders! The urchin, too, in repeating their language, shows he understands German as little as my horse does; and if he did rightly hear, truly comprehend, and accurately report what they said, still, is my honour to be touched by the language held by such persons as these are, with whom I have never communicated, otherwise than men of my rank do with those of their calling and capacity?—Pardon me, sire, if I presume to say, that the profound statesmen who endeavoured to stifle the Popish conspiracy by the pretended Meal-tub Plot, will take little more credit by their figments about fiddles and concertos."

The assistant counsellors looked at each other; and Charles turned on his heel, and walked through the room with long steps.

At this period the Peverils, father and son, were announced to have reached the palace, and were ordered into the royal presence.

These gentlemen had received the royal mandate at a moment of great interest. After being dismissed from their confinement by the elder Bridgenorth, in the manner and upon the terms which the reader must have gathered from the conversation of the latter with Christian, they reached the lodgings of Lady Peveril, who awaited them with joy, mingled with terror and uncertainty. The news of the acquittal had reached her by the exertions of the faithful Lance Outram, but her mind had been since harassed by the long delay of their appearance, and rumours of disturbances which had taken place in Fleet Street and in the Strand.

When the first rapturous meeting was over, Lady Peveril, with an anxious look towards her son, as if recommending caution, said she was now about to present to him the daughter of an old friend, whom he had *never* (there was an emphasis on the word) seen before. "This young lady," she continued, "was the only child of Colonel Mitford, in North Wales, who had sent her to remain under her guardianship for an interval, finding himself unequal to attempt the task of her education."

"Ay, ay," said Sir Geoffrey, "Dick Mitford must be old now —beyond the threescore and ten, I think. He was no chicken, though a cock of the game, when he joined the Marquis of Hertford at Namptwich with two hundred wild Welshmen.— Before George, Julian, I love that girl as if she was my own flesh and blood! Lady Peveril would never have got through this work without her; and Dick Mitford sent me a thousand pieces, too, in excellent time, when there was scarce a cross to keep the devil from dancing in our pockets, much more for these law-doings. I used it without scruple, for there is wood ready to be cut at Martindale when we get down there, and Dick Mitford knows I would have done the like for him. Strange that he should have been the only one of my friends to reflect I might want a few pieces."

Whilst Sir Geoffrey thus run on, the meeting betwixt Alice and Julian Peveril was accomplished, without any particular notice on his side, except to say, " Kiss her, Julian—kiss her. What the devil! is that the way you learned to accost a lady at the Isle of Man, as if her lips were a red-hot horseshoe?—And do not you be offended, my pretty one; Julian is naturally bash-ful, and has been bred by an old lady, but you will find him, by-and-by, as gallant as thou hast found me, my princess.—And now, Dame Peveril, to dinner, to dinner! the old fox must have his belly-timber, though the hounds have been after him the whole day."

Lance, whose joyous congratulations were next to be under-gone, had the consideration to cut them short, in order to provide a plain but hearty meal from the next cook's shop, at which Julian sat, like one enchanted, betwixt his mistress and his mother. He easily conceived that the last was the confidential friend to whom Bridgenorth had finally committed the charge of his daughter, and his only anxiety now was, to anticipate the confusion that was likely to arise when her real parentage was made known to his father. Wisely, however, he suffered not these anticipations to interfere with the delight of his present situation, in the course of which many slight but delightful tokens of recognition were exchanged, without censure, under the eye of Lady Peveril, under cover of the boisterous mirth of the old Baronet, who spoke for two, ate for four, and drank wine for half-a-dozen. His progress in the latter exercise might have proceeded rather too far, had he not been interrupted by a gentleman bearing the King's orders, that he should instantly attend upon the presence at Whitehall, and bring his son along with him.

Lady Peveril was alarmed, and Alice grew pale with sympa-thetic anxiety; but the old Knight, who never saw more than what lay straight before him, set it down to the King's hasty anxiety to congratulate him on his escape; an interest on his Majesty's part which he considered by no means extravagant, conscious that it was reciprocal on his own side. It came upon him, indeed, with the more joyful surprise that he had received a previous hint, ere he left the court of justice, that it would be prudent in him to go down to Martindale before presenting himself at Court—a restriction which he supposed as repugnant to his Majesty's feelings as it was to his own.

While he consulted with Lance Outram about cleaning his buff-belt and sword-hilt, as well as time admitted, Lady Peveril had the means to give Julian more distinct information, that Alice was under her protection by her father's authority, and with his consent to their union, if it could be accomplished. She added that it was her determination to employ the mediation of the Countess of Derby, to overcome the obstacles which might be foreseen on the part of Sir Geoffrey.

CHAPTER XLIX

In the King's name,
Let fall your swords and daggers !
—CRITIC.

WHEN the father and son entered the cabinet of audience, it was easily visible that Sir Geoffrey had obeyed the summons as he would have done the trumpet's call to horse ; and his dishevelled grey locks and half-arranged dress, though they showed zeal and haste, such as he would have used when Charles I. called him to attend a council of war, seemed rather indecorous in a pacific drawing-room. He paused at the door of the cabinet, but when the King called on him to advance, came hastily forward, with every feeling of his earlier and later life afloat, and contending in his memory, threw himself on his knees before the King, seized his hand, and, without even an effort to speak, wept aloud. Charles, who generally felt deeply so long as an impressive object was before his eyes, indulged for a moment the old man's rapture.—"My good Sir Geoffrey," he said, "you have had some hard measure ; we owe you amends, and will find time to pay our debt."

"No suffering—no debt," said the old man ; "I cared not what the rogues said of me—I knew they could never get twelve honest fellows to believe a word of their most damnable lies. I did long to beat them when they called me traitor to your Majesty—that I confess—But to have such an early opportunity of paying my duty to your Majesty, overpays it all. The villains would have persuaded me I ought not to come to Court —aha !"

The Duke of Ormond perceived that the King coloured much ; for in truth it was from the Court that the private intimation had been given to Sir Geoffrey to go down to the country, without appearing at Whitehall ; and he, moreover, suspected that the jolly old Knight had not risen from his dinner altogether dry-lipped, after the fatigues of a day so agitating.—" My old friend," he whispered, " you forget that your son is to be presented—permit me to have that honour."

" I crave your Grace's pardon humbly," said Sir Geoffrey, " but it is an honour I design for myself, as I apprehend no one can so utterly surrender and deliver him up to his Majesty's service as the father that begot him is entitled to do.—Julian, come forward, and kneel.—Here he is, please your Majesty— Julian Peveril—a chip of the old block—as stout, though scarce so tall a tree, as the old trunk, when at the freshest. Take him to you, sir, for a faithful servant, *à vendre et à pendre*, as the French say; if he fears fire or steel, axe or gallows, in your Majesty's service, I renounce him—he is no son of mine—I disown him, and he may go to the Isle of Man, the Isle of Dogs, or the Isle of Devils, for what I care."

Charles winked to Ormond, and having, with his wonted courtesy, expressed his thorough conviction that Julian would imitate the loyalty of his ancestors, and especially of his father, added, that he believed his Grace of Ormond had something to communicate which was of consequence to his service. Sir Geoffrey made his military reverence at this hint, and marched off in the rear of the Duke, who proceeded to inquire of him concerning the events of the day. Charles, in the meanwhile, having in the first place, ascertained that the son was not in the same genial condition with the father, demanded and received from him a precise account of all the proceedings subsequent to the trial.

Julian, with the plainness and precision which such a subject demanded, when treated in such a presence, narrated all that had happened down to the entrance of Bridgenorth; and his Majesty was so much pleased with his manner, that he congratulated Arlington on their having gained the evidence of at least one man of sense to these dark and mysterious events. But when Bridgenorth was brought upon the scene, Julian hesitated to bestow a name upon him; and although he mentioned the chapel which he had seen filled with men in arms, and the violent language of the preacher, he added, with earnestness, that notwithstanding all this, the men departed without coming to any extremity, and had all left the place before his father and he were set at liberty.

" And you retired quietly to your dinner in Fleet Street, young man," said the King severely, " without giving a magistrate notice of the dangerous meeting which was held in the vicinity of our palace, and who did not conceal their intention of proceeding to extremities ? "

Peveril blushed, and was silent. The King frowned, and

stepped aside to communicate with Ormond, who reported that the father seemed to have known nothing of the matter.

"And the son, I am sorry to say," said the King, "seems more unwilling to speak the truth than I should have expected. We have all variety of evidence in this singular investigation—a mad witness like the dwarf, a drunken witness like the father, and now a dumb witness.—Young man," he continued, addressing Julian, "your behaviour is less frank than I expected from your father's son. I must know who this person is with whom you held such familiar intercourse—you know him, I presume?"

Julian acknowledged that he did, but, kneeling on one knee, entreated his Majesty's forgiveness for concealing his name; "he had been freed," he said, "from his confinement, on promising to that effect."

"That was a promise made, by your own account, under compulsion," answered the King, "and I cannot authorise your keeping it; it is your duty to speak the truth—if you are afraid of Buckingham, the Duke shall withdraw."

"I have no reason to fear the Duke of Buckingham," said Peveril; "that I had an affair with one of his household, was the man's own fault and not mine."

"Oddsfish!" said the King, "the light begins to break in on me—I thought I remembered thy physiognomy. Wert thou not the very fellow whom I met at Chiffinch's yonder morning?—The matter escaped me since; but now I recollect thou saidst then, that thou wert the son of that jolly old three-bottle Baronet yonder."

"It is true," said Julian, "that I met your Majesty at Master Chiffinch's, and I am afraid had the misfortune to displease you; but——"

"No more of that, young man—no more of that—But I recollect you had with you that beautiful dancing siren.—Buckingham, I will hold you gold to silver, that she was the intended tenant of that bass-fiddle?"

"Your Majesty has rightly guessed it," said the Duke; "and I suspect she has put a trick upon me, by substituting the dwarf in her place; for Christian thinks——"

"Damn Christian!" said the King hastily—"I wish they would bring him hither, that universal referee."—And as the wish was uttered, Christian's arrival was announced. "Let him attend," said the King: "But hark—a thought strikes me.—Here, Master Peveril—yonder dancing maiden that introduced you to us by the singular agility of her performance, is she not, by your account, a dependent on the Countess of Derby?"

"I have known her such for years," answered Julian.

"Then will we call the Countess hither," said the King: "It is fit we should learn who this little fairy really is; and if she be now so absolutely at the beck of Buckingham, and this Master Christian of his—why I think it would be but charity to let her ladyship know so much, since I question if she will wish, in that case, to retain her in her service. Besides," he continued, speaking apart, "this Julian, to whom suspicion attaches in these matters from his obstinate silence, is also of the Countess's household. We will sift this matter to the bottom, and do justice to all."

The Countess of Derby, hastily summoned, entered the royal closet at one door, just as Christian and Zarah, or Fenella, were ushered in by the other. The old Knight of Martindale, who had ere this returned to the presence, was scarce controlled, even by the signs which she made, so much was he desirous of greeting his old friend; but as Ormond laid a kind restraining hand upon his arm, he was prevailed on to sit still.

The Countess, after a deep reverence to the King, acknowledged the rest of the nobility present by a slighter reverence, smiled to Julian Peveril, and looked with surprise at the unexpected apparition of Fenella. Buckingham bit his lip, for he saw the introduction of Lady Derby was likely to confuse and embroil every preparation which he had arranged for his defence; and he stole a glance at Christian, whose eye, when fixed on the Countess, assumed the deadly sharpness which sparkles in the adder's, while his cheek grew almost black under the influence of strong emotion.

"Is there any one in this presence whom your ladyship recognises," said the King graciously, "besides your old friends of Ormond and Arlington?"

"I see, my liege, two worthy friends of my husband's house," replied the Countess; "Sir Geoffrey Peveril and his son—the latter a distinguished member of my son's household."

"Any one else?" continued the King.

"An unfortunate female of my family, who disappeared from the Island of Man at the same time when Julian Peveril left it upon business of importance. She was thought to have fallen from the cliff into the sea."

"Had your ladyship any reason to suspect—pardon me," said the King, "for putting such a question—any improper intimacy between Master Peveril and this same female attendant?"

"My liege," said the Countess, colouring indignantly, "my household is of reputation."

"Nay, my lady, be not angry," said the King; "I did but ask—such things will befall in the best regulated families."

"Not in mine, sire," said the Countess. "Besides that, in common pride and in common honesty, Julian Peveril is incapable of intriguing with an unhappy creature, removed by her misfortune almost beyond the limits of humanity."

Zarah looked at her, and compressed her lips, as if to keep in the words that would fain break from them.

"I know not how it is," said the King—"What your ladyship says may be true in the main, yet men's tastes have strange vagaries. This girl is lost in Man as soon as the youth leaves it, and is found in Saint James's Park, bouncing and dancing like a fairy, so soon as he appears in London."

"Impossible!" said the Countess; "she cannot dance."

"I believe," said the King, "she can do more feats than your ladyship either suspects or would approve of."

The Countess drew up, and was indignantly silent.

The King proceeded—"No sooner is Peveril in Newgate, than, by the account of the venerable little gentleman, this merry maiden is even there also for company. Now, without inquiring how she got in, I think charitably that she had better taste than to come there on the dwarf's account.—Ah ha! I think Master Julian is touched in conscience!"

Julian did indeed start as the King spoke, for it reminded him of the midnight visit in his cell.

The King looked fixedly at him, and then proceeded—"Well, gentlemen, Peveril is carried to his trial, and is no sooner at liberty, than we find him in the house where the Duke of Buckingham was arranging what he calls a musical mask.—Egad, I hold it next to certain, that this wench put the change on his Grace, and popt the poor dwarf into the bass-viol, reserving her own more precious hours to be spent with Master Julian Peveril.—Think you not so, Sir Christian, you, the universal referee? Is there any truth in this conjecture?"

Christian stole a glance at Zarah, and read that in her eye which embarrassed him. "He did not know," he said; "he had indeed engaged this unrivalled performer to take the proposed part in the mask; and she was to have come forth in the midst of a shower of lambent fire, very artificially prepared with perfumes, to overcome the smell of the powder; but he knew not why—excepting that she was wilful and capricious, like all great geniuses—she had certainly spoiled the concert by cramming in that more bulky dwarf."

"I should like," said the King, "to see this little maiden stand forth, and bear witness, in such manner as she can express herself, on this mysterious matter. Can any one here understand her mode of communication?"

Christian said, he knew something of it since he had become

acquainted with her in London. The Countess spoke not till the King asked her, and then owned dryly, that she had necessarily some habitual means of intercourse with one who had been immediately about her person for so many years.

"I should think," said Charles, "that this same Master Peveril has the more direct key to her language, after all we have heard."

The King looked first at Peveril, who blushed like a maiden at the inference which the King's remark implied, and then suddenly turned his eyes on the supposed mute, on whose cheek a faint colour was dying away. A moment afterwards, at a signal from the Countess, Fenella, or Zarah, stepped forward, and having kissed her lady's hand, stood with her arms folded on her breast, with a humble air, as different from that which she wore in the harem of the Duke of Buckingham, as that of a Magdalene from a Judith. Yet this was the least show of her talent of versatility, for so well did she play the part of the dumb girl, that Buckingham, sharp as his discernment was, remained undecided whether the creature which stood before him could possibly be the same with her, who had, in a different dress, made such an impression on his imagination, or indeed was the imperfect creature she now represented. She had at once all that could mark the imperfection of hearing, and all that could show the wonderful address by which nature so often makes up for the deficiency. There was the lip that trembled not at any sound—the seeming insensibility to the conversation that passed around; while, on the other hand, was the quick and vivid glance; that seemed anxious to devour the meaning of those sounds, which she could gather no otherwise than by the motion of the lips.

Examined after her own fashion, Zarah confirmed the tale of Christian in all its points, and admitted that she had deranged the project laid for a mask, by placing the dwarf in her own stead; the cause of her doing so she declined to assign, and the Countess pressed her no farther.

"Everything tells to exculpate my Lord of Buckingham," said Charles, "from so absurd an accusation: the dwarf's testimony is too fantastic, that of the two Peverils does not in the least affect the Duke; that of the dumb damsel completely contradicts the possibility of his guilt. Methinks, my lords, we should acquaint him that he stands acquitted of a complaint, too ridiculous to have been subjected to a more serious scrutiny than we have hastily made upon this occasion."

Arlington bowed in acquiescence, but Ormond spoke plainly. —"I should suffer, sire, in the opinion of the Duke of Buckingham, brilliant as his talents are known to be, should I say that I am satisfied in my own mind on this occasion. But I subscribe to the spirit of the times; and I agree it would be highly dangerous, on such accusations as we have been able to collect, to impeach the character of a zealous Protestant like his Grace—Had he been a Catholic, under such circumstances of suspicion, the Tower had been too good a prison for him."

Buckingham bowed to the Duke of Ormond, with a meaning which even his triumph could not disguise.—"*Tu me la pagherai!*" he muttered, in a tone of deep and abiding resentment; but the stout old Irishman, who had long since braved his utmost wrath, cared little for this expression of his displeasure.

The King then, signing to the other nobles to pass into the public apartments, stopped Buckingham as he was about to follow them; and when they were alone, asked, with a significant tone, which brought all the blood in the Duke's veins into his countenance, " When was it, George, that your useful friend Colonel Blood became a musician?—You are silent," he said ; "do not deny the charge, for yonder villain, once seen, is remembered for ever. Down, down on your knees, George, and acknowledge that you have abused my easy temper.—Seek for no apology—none will serve your turn. I saw the man myself, among your Germans as you call them ; and you know what I must needs believe from such a circumstance."

" Believe that I have been guilty—most guilty, my liege and King," said the Duke, conscience-stricken, and kneeling down ; —"believe that I was misguided—that I was mad—Believe anything but that I was capable of harming, or being accessory to harm, your person."

" I do not believe it," said the King; "I think of you, Villiers, as the companion of my dangers and my exile, and am so far from supposing you mean worse than you say, that I am convinced you acknowledge more than ever you meant to attempt."

" By all that is sacred," said the Duke, still kneeling, " had I not been involved to the extent of life and fortune with the villain Christian——"

" Nay, if you bring Christian on the stage again," said the King, smiling, " it is time for me to withdraw. Come, Villiers, rise—I forgive thee, and only recommend one act of penance— the curse you yourself bestowed on the dog who bit you—marriage, and retirement to your country-seat."

The Duke rose abashed, and followed the King into the circle, which Charles entered, leaning on the shoulder of his repentant peer ; to whom he showed so much countenance, as led the most acute observers present, to doubt the possibility of there existing any real cause for the surmises to the Duke's prejudice.

The Countess of Derby had in the meanwhile consulted with the Duke of Ormond, with the Peverils, and with her other friends ; and, by their unanimous advice, though with considerable difficulty, became satisfied, that to have thus shown herself at Court, was sufficient to vindicate the honour of her house ; and that it was her wisest course, after having done so, to retire to her insular dominions, without farther provoking the resentment of a powerful faction.   She took farewell of the King in form, and demanded his permission to carry back with her the helpless creature who had so strangely escaped from her protection, into a world where her condition rendered her so subject to every species of misfortune.

"Will your ladyship forgive me ?" said Charles.   "I have studied your sex long—I am mistaken if your little maiden is not as capable of caring for herself as any of us."

"Impossible !" said the Countess.

"Possible, and most true," whispered the King.   "I will instantly convince you of the fact, though the experiment is too delicate to be made by any but your ladyship.   Yonder she stands, looking as if she heard no more than the marble pillar against which she leans.   Now, if Lady Derby will contrive either to place her hand near the region of the damsel's heart, or at least on her arm, so that she can feel the sensation of the blood when the pulse increases, then do you, my Lord of Ormond, beckon Julian Peveril out of sight—I will show you in a moment that it can stir at sounds spoken."

The Countess, much surprised, afraid of some embarrassing pleasantry on the part of Charles, yet unable to repress her curiosity, placed herself near Fenella, as she called her little mute ; and, while making signs to her, contrived to place her hand on her wrist.

At this moment the King, passing near them, said, "This is a horrid deed—the villain Christian has stabbed young Peveril !"

The mute evidence of the pulse, which bounded as if a cannon had been discharged close by the poor girl's ear, was accompanied by such a loud scream of agony, as distressed, while it startled, the good-natured monarch himself.   "I did but jest," he said ; "Julian is well, my pretty maiden.   I only used the wand of a certain blind deity, called Cupid, to bring a deaf and dumb vassal of his to the exercise of her faculties."

"I am betrayed !" she said, with her eyes fixed on the ground —"I am betrayed !—and it is fit that she, whose life has been spent in practising treason on others, should be caught in her own snare. But where is my tutor in iniquity?—where is Christian, who taught me to play the part of spy on this unsuspicious lady, until I had well-nigh delivered her into his bloody hands?"

"This," said the King, "craves more secret examination. Let all leave the apartment who are not immediately connected with these proceedings, and let this Christian be again brought before us.—Wretched man," he continued, addressing Christian, "what wiles are these you have practised, and by what extraordinary means?"

"She has betrayed me, then!" said Christian—"Betrayed me to bonds and death, merely for an idle passion, which can never be successful!—But know, Zarah," he added, addressing her sternly, "when my life is forfeited through thy evidence, the daughter has murdered the father!"

The unfortunate girl stared on him in astonishment. "You said," at length she stammered forth, "that I was the daughter of your slaughtered brother?"

"That was partly to reconcile thee to the part thou wert to play in my destined drama of vengeance—partly to hide what men call the infamy of thy birth. But *my* daughter thou art! and from the eastern clime, in which thy mother was born, you derive that fierce torrent of passion which I laboured to train to my purposes, but which, turned into another channel, has become the cause of your father's destruction.—My destiny is the Tower, I suppose?"

He spoke these words with great composure, and scarce seemed to regard the agonies of his daughter, who, throwing herself at his feet, sobbed and wept most bitterly.

"This must not be," said the King, moved with compassion at this scene of misery. "If you consent, Christian, to leave this country, there is a vessel in the river bound for New England—Go, carry your dark intrigues to other lands."

"I might dispute the sentence," said Christian boldly; "and if I submit to it, it is a matter of my own choice.—One half-hour had made me even with that proud woman, but fortune hath cast the balance against me.—Rise, Zarah, Fenella no more! Tell the Lady of Derby, that, if the daughter of Edward Christian, the niece of her murdered victim, served her as a menial, it was but for the purpose of vengeance—miserably, miserably frustrated!—Thou seest thy folly now—thou wouldst follow yonder ungrateful stripling—thou wouldst forsake all other thoughts to gain his slightest notice; and now thou art a forlorn outcast, ridiculed and insulted by those on whose necks you might have trod, had you governed yourself with more wisdom!—But come, thou art still my daughter—there are other skies than that which canopies Britain."

"Stop him," said the King; "we must know by what means this maiden found access to those confined in our prisons."

"I refer your Majesty to your most Protestant jailer, and to the most Protestant Peers, who, in order to obtain perfect knowledge of the depth of the Popish Plot, have contrived these ingenious apertures for visiting them in their cells by night or day. His Grace of Buckingham can assist your Majesty, if you are inclined to make the inquiry." *

"Christian," said the Duke, "thou art the most barefaced villain who ever breathed."

"Of a commoner, I may," answered Christian, and led his daughter out of the presence.

"See after him, Selby," said the King; "lose not sight of him till the ship sail; if he dare return to Britain, it shall be at his peril. Would to God we had as good riddance of others as dangerous! And I would also," he added, after a moment's pause, "that all our political intrigues and feverish alarms could terminate as harmlessly as now. Here is a plot without a drop of blood; and all the elements of a romance, without its conclusion. Here we have a wandering island princess (I pray my Lady of Derby's pardon), a dwarf, a Moorish sorceress, an impenitent rogue, and a repentant man of rank, and yet all ends without either hanging or marriage."

"Not altogether without the latter," said the Countess, who had an opportunity, during the evening, of much private conversation with Julian Peveril. "There is a certain Major Bridgenorth, who, since your Majesty relinquishes farther inquiry into these proceedings, which he had otherwise intended to abide, designs, as we are informed, to leave England for ever. Now, this Bridgenorth, by dint of the law, hath acquired strong possession over the domains of Peveril, which he is desirous to restore to the ancient owners, with much fair land besides, conditionally, that our young Julian will receive them as the dowry of his only child and heir."

"By my faith," said the King, "she must be a foul-favoured wench, indeed, if Julian requires to be pressed to accept her on such fair conditions."

"They love each other like lovers of the last age," said the Countess; "but the stout old Knight likes not the round-headed alliance."

"Our royal recommendation shall put that to rights," said the King; "Sir Geoffrey Peveril has not suffered hardship so often at our command, that he will refuse our recommendation when it comes to make him amends for all his losses."

---

* It was said that very unfair means were used to compel the prisoners, committed on account of the Popish Plot, to make disclosures, and that several of them were privately put to the torture.

It may be supposed the King did not speak without being fully aware of the unlimited ascendency which he possessed over the old Tory; for within four weeks afterwards, the bells of Martindale-Moultrassie were ringing for the union of the families, from whose estates it takes its compound name, and the beacon-light of the Castle blazed high over hill and dale, and summoned all to rejoice who were within twenty miles of its gleam.

THE END

Printed by BALLANTYNE, HANSON & CO.
Edinburgh & London

a